WRITE ME OFF

USW SERIES : BOOK 1

BRANDY DAVIS

To the little girl who always dreamed of writing a book—this one's for you. You did it.

WRITE
ME OFF

ONE

I've been rejected again.

I don't need to read through the rest of the letter to get the gist, it's always the same no matter which school sends it—*Thanks for applying to our graduate program, but you're not good enough to come here; feel free to apply again soon, though, we appreciate all the application fees.*

Of course they do. I've been draining my bank account to apply to graduate schools in the hope that they won't just accept me, but offer me some kind of financial aid. The irony of the situation doesn't escape me; the fact that I have to spend money and pray that a school will realize how desperately I need it is more frustrating than getting rejected from the actual school itself.

What's the point of getting accepted into a school if I can't afford to actually go to it?

"Another no?"

Jenny, one of my two roommates, is leaning against the door frame of my bedroom. She has a steaming mug cupped in her hands and a sympathetic frown pulling at her lips. This is the second rejection letter I've gotten this month and each time it's felt like a slap to the face.

"Columbia." I nod, dropping the letter back onto my desk.

"I'm sorry, Abs."

"It's fine." I shake my head and try to pull on a convincing smile as I look back up at her. "It was kind of a reach anyway."

I'll admit, some of the other rejections were a little surprising, but I really wasn't expecting to actually get into Columbia. I have a 3.9 GPA, and my GRE scores are pretty good, but to get into Columbia you can't just be *pretty good*, you have to be perfect. The only reason I even applied in the first place was because my mother lectured me on the phone for half an hour about how I *"don't fully apply myself"* and how I'll *"never get anywhere if I keep dragging my feet."*

Honestly, it was one of her nicer lectures.

"You'll get into the next one, Abs. I promise. Plus, none of these other schools even matter because you're going to get into NYU. I can feel it in my bones."

She drops down onto my bed, crossing her legs under her, and when she beams up at me with an encouraging smile, her energizer-bunny energy practically ripples through the room. By the excited smile pulling at her lips, I can already tell she's not planning on letting me throw myself a pity party over this.

"You know what you need? A night out. One with enough alcohol to forget about grad schools and rejection letters, and whatever else is worrying that pretty little head of yours."

I raise a brow as I consider that. "I'll take the alcohol, but if it requires me putting on anything other than pajama pants, count me out."

Getting wine drunk on the couch while watching *The Bachelor* sounds pretty great right about now, but knowing Jenny, she's not interested in staying in tonight.

"Okay, I was hoping that would work, but since it didn't . . . I have a favor to ask." She gives me a *please don't kill me* look before hurrying on. "And I know you're probably going to say no, so I feel like I should remind you that you love me very much, and I also just watched that entire Ted Bundy docuseries with you the other day, which I think earned me some brownie points that I'd like to cash in right now." She sits up a little straighter, flashing a pleading smile.

"First of all, I know you were just as invested in that docuseries as I was," I counter as I drop down onto my bed, watching her cheek twitch while she shrugs in begrudging agreement. Jenny and Nia used to think I was crazy for watching shows like *Snapped* and *Forensic Files*, but now, three years later, they're both just as hooked as I am. "And second, I have too much left on my to-do list to go anywhere tonight."

"*Please*, Abby. It's the Spring Formal tonight." She juts out her lips in her signature pout, and my heart sinks in my chest because I already know that no matter how much I don't want to, I'm going to end up at this formal tonight.

If there's one thing Jenny McPherson is good at, it's knowing how to guilt me into doing things with her. Namely things like attending her sorority's philanthropy events or going to O'Malley's—the University of Southern Washington's favorite sports bar—on nights when I definitely should be studying. I'd say it's twenty percent her amazing guilting skills and eighty percent my innate need to please people, but either way, the result is always the same: Jenny asks, and I end up sitting at a bar until three in the morning, drinking more vodka cranberry than I really should while playing *Words With Friends* with my early-bird Nana who's on East Coast time.

"That's tonight?" I groan.

"Come on, Abs. We've been back in Washington for two days and haven't left the apartment—hell, we've barely even left the couch. We both need this. Some fresh air, a little social interaction, and a few shots of Fireball will be good for us."

She's not wrong. Instead of getting a head start on printing my new semester syllabi or proofreading the article I wrote for the university's newspaper over break, I've spent the majority of my time wrapped up like a burrito in my favorite knit blanket on the living room couch with her and Nia. We managed to watch almost an entire season of *The Bachelor* on Hulu, not even bothering to get up for dinner, because with a few taps of Nia's perfectly lacquered fingernails, she managed to place a delivery order for sushi, pizza, and wine, all while barely taking her eyes off the rose ceremony. She truly is one of a kind.

"Can't you take Nia?"

"She's still sick from that sushi."

My last-ditch effort is weak, but I try anyway.

"What about Steffy?"

Steffy Soranto is my favorite of all Jenny and Nia's sorority sisters, mostly because she doesn't eye me like expired food every time I get dragged along as a plus-one to whatever Greek life event they're hosting.

"She always ditches me." Jenny shakes her head before taking a sip of her tea.

"Anna?"

"She's running the event. She's going to be so busy I won't even be able to talk to her."

"Jenny," I whine, pulling the duvet over my head. I'm already mentally skimming our catalog of liquor in the cabinet above the refrigerator. If I'm going to waste the last night of winter break at a sorority formal, I deserve to be buzzed, at the very least.

"Please, please, please, Abby. I'll make you breakfast for a week."

I let the offer marinate.

"A veggie omelet?" I clarify, glad that the blanket is blocking my smile. I would have eventually caved and gone without any incentive, but if she's offering to make me breakfast, I'm not one to look a gift horse in the mouth.

"A veggie omelet," she agrees quickly.

Sitting up against my gray, pleated headboard, I try to tame the flyaway hairs that have gone haywire from the static under the blanket.

"Fine." I sigh, watching her eyes brighten as she beams at me. "But I'm pre-gaming."

———

The University of Southern Washington's Greek life hosts two formals a semester, and tonight is the first of the spring term. I've been to a few of these events in the three-and-a-half years that Jenny, Nia, and I have been roommates.

The first time they invited me with them freshman year I tried to get out of it, but I think Nia felt bad leaving me home alone because she insisted that she couldn't go without me. I tried to argue, but an hour later all three of us were waiting at the campus shuttle station just outside of our dorm, dressed in floor-length gowns and heels tall enough to snap an ankle.

While I would have much rather been in bed watching TV on the night of that first formal, I'm glad I went. We were sitting on the shuttle, halfway to the convention center, when Nia found out that her date, Shawn Oliver, told his entire fraternity he was planning on *"shagging and bagging"* her afterwards. So, when she showed up in an impossibly tight dress that gave her legs for days, unbelievable cleavage, and a *fuck-you* attitude, he practically followed us around all night begging Nia to speak to him, promising that he didn't actually mean anything by it.

Jenny and I stayed by her side the entire time, fueling her confidence—as any good best friends would have—while simultaneously drinking way too much, especially considering that we were underage freshmen. The night ended in a blur of Nia rushing the stage, stealing the microphone, and declaring in front of the entire formal that Shawn

Oliver was, in fact, a *"fuck boy"* before dropping the mic and running off stage. I don't remember much after that, aside from being corralled into a taxi by one of the house moms and sent back to our dorm.

All in all, it was a pretty eventful night. Neither Jenny nor Nia have brought a date to a formal since, which means that, twice a semester, I get the puppy dog eyes and cheesy grins from my best friends as they beg me to come along with them again. Sometimes I have a good enough excuse to get out of it, but most times, like tonight, I find myself standing in the middle of the Carson Hall convention center feeling trapped in a sea of sorority sisters.

"—We hooked up in his car a few times, but it was nothing serious. He was kind of a bad lay, to be honest, but there's not much to pick from in Wyoming," Steffy mumbles, shrugging her bare shoulders as she downs the rest of the water from her glass. I grin at her nonchalance at spilling the details of her winter break hookups; it's a welcome distraction from being completely ignored by the rest of Jenny's sorority.

"What about you, Abby? Did you get to see that Florida boyfriend of yours over break? What's his name? Taylor?" She winks as she pulls out a flask from her bra.

"Tyler," I correct, clearing my throat. "And no, we broke up."

"What?" Her eyes widen as she nearly chokes on the liquor in her mouth, but she recovers quickly and reaches out for my hand, squeezing it reassuringly.

"It's not a big deal." I shrug. "It just wasn't working."

"But weren't you guys together for like *years*?"

I think I've spoken to her about Tyler once or twice in the three years that I've known her, and apparently, it wasn't even memorable enough for her to remember his name.

"Three." I nod.

It didn't really feel like three years, though; not when the majority of those years were spent with an entire country separating us. Tyler and I met the summer before I left for USW, and after he asked me out on our third date down on the pier, we decided to try long distance. I came back for winter, spring, and summer breaks, but most of our relationship was spent texting, calling, and tagging each other in funny online posts.

I guess I became attached to him as a friend more than anything else, but after three years, the thought of not having him there to call every night, or text every morning, terrified me. It wasn't until I realized that I was purposely missing his calls, and putting off texting him back, that I knew I needed to end it. There's really no good way to break up with someone thousands of miles away, but by the time I got home for summer break a few weeks later, he had a pretty good idea of what was coming. The whole thing was kind of anticlimactic, though, because if we were really honest with ourselves, we had broken up long before then, at least emotionally.

"Long-distance can be hard." She nods solemnly, rubbing my arm.

"Mhm," I hum, trying not to be too obvious as I scan the crowd above her head for Jenny. I'm barely five-five, but with my heels, I'm almost an entire head taller than her.

"How was the sex though?" she asks loudly, taking a sip from her flask.

I look back down at her with an open mouth as a few gazes sweep over us. They look away quickly, disinterest apparent on their faces when they realize it's just me, a lowly outsider to their Greek members-only club, being interrogated.

"He lived in Florida," I remind her awkwardly, taking a sip from the cup of water in my hands. I had a few shots of Fireball with Jenny before we left, but it definitely wasn't enough to prepare me for this conversation.

"Right, so you had a lot of phone sex then. Do you have a good webcam? Video sex is even better." She grins, and my face flames as she eyes me expectantly, as if I'm going to give her a play-by-play or highlight reel of my sex life with my ex-boyfriend.

"I—" I don't want to talk about my sex life—or non-existent sex life—with Steffy Soranto, and I definitely don't want to talk about it in the middle of Carson Hall where anyone can hear.

"Wait, this means you're single now. I'm totally going to find you a boyfriend." She taps the edge of her empty cup against her lips, scanning the crowd around us. "Or at least a fuck buddy. How do you feel about Nick Myers? Or Brett Barnett? Football players are my favorite, but I could totally see you with a basketball player. Oh, what about Micah Costa? He's kind of an asshole, but he's *amazing* in bed. Or, wait, even better, Beck."

My eyes grow wide and I nearly choke on the sip of water I had just taken when Jenny's arm intertwines with my own. She pulls me away quickly, calling over her shoulder to Steffy that we'll be right back.

"Why was Steffy Soranto talking about finding you a fuck buddy?" Her voice is low—a much more appropriate volume for this mortifying conversation—as she navigates us to an empty table on the other side of the room.

I relax a little as I settle into a chair and watch Jenny readjust her straps uncomfortably. The black dress fits her perfectly, and while the front of it is conservative with a high neckline and long hem, the sun-kissed skin on her back is almost entirely exposed. It's a beautiful contrast against the white-blonde hair falling around her shoulders in shiny curls. Hopefully, her desire to get out of the gown will inspire her to sneak us home early.

"The usual with Steffy." I shrug.

A busty girl in a white mini dress walks by, and I glance down at my own dress to make sure the bodice of the gown hasn't shifted. In the three years that I've been dragged to these events, I've never worn my own gown, namely because I don't own a gown, and I sure as hell am not planning on spending five shifts worth of tips from the diner on one dress. This leaves me with two options: either wear one of Jenny's dresses or one of Nia's. I usually opt for the latter since we have similar figures.

Jenny is the kind of slender that could walk runways and look perfect in candid pictures, no matter what angle it's taken from. Which is frustrating as hell, because she eats just as much as Nia and I, but never seems to show the evidence of our late-night pizza binges like I do.

Nia's satin gold dress fits for the most part, except for the slightly too small bust, but it was either deal with the excessive cleavage, or go out and buy a dress. I went with the cleavage. Plus, as Nia pointed out, it accessorizes well with the stripper heels.

"I can't believe I missed out on that conversation," Jenny snorts.

"She was telling me about the guy she hooked up with over winter break and then she asked about Tyler. When she found out we broke up, she decided she needed to find me a new boyfriend."

Jenny groans and pulls a face that's clearly meant to say, *I'm sorry I dragged you here to be borderline sexually harassed by Steffy Soranto.* She's been a victim of Steffy's matchmaking obsession before and it never ends well.

"Oh, and apparently, in the meantime, I need to find a fuck buddy,"

I say, laughing at how serious Steffy sounded when she said it, as if the idea of not having a fuck buddy between boyfriends was ludicrous.

Jenny's mouth pops open as her eyes scan up above my head, and I suddenly realize that I've abandoned my conversation appropriate volume, meaning that whoever is standing behind me, has definitely heard at least the tail end of my comment.

The rough echo of a man clearing his throat sounds behind me. I turn to catch a pair of emerald eyes staring down into my own as Jenny's words wash over me, sending a shock wave of white-hot embarrassment straight through my veins.

"Hey, Beck."

TWO

ABBY

When I look over my shoulder and see Tristan Beck standing with his hands tucked into his pockets, I have to concentrate on not letting my face fall into the *what the hell* expression that I know it wants to settle in.

He smiles politely at me and takes his right hand out of his pocket, extending it to me. I stare at his tanned, calloused fingers before raising my gaze back up to his.

"I was hoping I might be able to steal you away for a dance," he says, his voice smooth and calm, as if this isn't the most bizarre thing happening in the room at the moment.

Tristan Beck, star basketball player, playboy extraordinaire, is asking me to dance.

I stare up at him in shock, distrust quickly coursing through me as I glance back down at his outstretched hand. Jenny makes a soft coughing noise, and when I look back at her, she's lit up with equal parts excitement and confusion as she nods at me.

I look back to Beck, who's still standing with his hand extended, his calm demeanor unfazed.

What the hell is going on?

My initial reaction is to decline, to come up with some excuse and make a beeline for the door, because this obviously can't be real. It's a setup for a punchline I'm clearly not privy to, or a bet that the rest of his basketball team gave him. I can practically see the conversation playing out as I stare at him—*Find the last girl you'd ever talk to and ask her to dance.*

But the small voice in the back of my mind coaxing me to live a little is growing louder as Jenny's excited nod helps to shove the thoughts of bets and jokes to the back of my mind.

I stand, placing my hand in Beck's, and follow him out on the dance floor. His hand swallows my own and I can feel the rough edges of his fingertips against my knuckles. His hands are warm despite the chill coming from the entrance doors, which keep swiveling open and closed with each couple who goes out *"for fresh air"* and comes back in with swollen lips and spotty lipstick.

My hands find his shoulders when he turns around, and I keep my eyes trained on a spot on the far wall over his shoulder as his hands slide into place on my waist. His touch warms the satin fabric and heats right through to my skin.

The music has slowed, from the high-tempo and booming bass that vibrated right through the floor and up my legs, to a slow melody that I would have made a note to look up later, if I could get my brain to function correctly.

I don't know how to slow dance. I've never actually done it before, aside from with my dad at the few weddings we went to growing up; but he didn't know how to, either, so we usually just pulled out our go-to, old-school moves and made a joke out of it. I don't think doing the robot is going to help me out much in this situation, though.

I think he can sense my hesitation, because his grip on my waist tightens as he leads me into a slow swaying motion, perfectly timed with the tempo of the song.

What is proper slow dance etiquette?

Am I supposed to make conversation, or is this more of a silent experience?

Jenny's giving me a thumbs up from the table, like a proud mother watching her child make their first friend on the playground, and the sight makes me want to melt on the spot. If that wasn't bad enough, the surrounding crowd is now catching onto our odd pairing, and a few of the girls have started to stare. Apparently, I'm not the only one shocked that Beck asked me to dance.

I want to quiet the rampant thoughts, to just enjoy this experience of being asked to dance by a guy who isn't my dad, but the thoughts racing through my mind, paired with the half a dozen eyes staring at me incredulously, make the moment kind of hard to appreciate.

The words are out of my mouth before I even register what I'm asking, and when I finally catch up with my question, my face ignites in a slow, torturous burn.

"Was it a bet?"

"Hmm?" He looks down at me, his expression bored. The top of my head doesn't even reach his shoulder, and I have to look up to catch his expression, even with the added height of my heels.

"Was it a bet?" I repeat. "Or a dare, maybe?"

"Was what a bet?" His brows furrow, but I can tell he knows exactly what I'm talking about.

Besides the fact that Beck and I have been in a few classes together over the past three years, and even crossed paths at some of the parties that Jenny and Nia have dragged me to, we've never actually acknowledged each other, let alone had a conversation.

"This. You asking me to dance," I say, watching his eyes flash with hooded amusement. I guess most of the girls he asks to dance don't interrogate him mid-song.

"Why would you assume—"

I cut him off with a glare.

"Alright, alright." He laughs and shakes his head. "I'm just fulfilling my duties as wingman, that's all," he admits with a noncommittal shrug.

"Wingman duties?" My brows knit together as I consider that.

He nods over my head, and when I follow his gaze to see his best friend, James Parsons, dancing with Jenny, everything starts to click.

"I see." I nod and tense slightly when I realize that my arms currently wrapped around his shoulders now feel incredibly awkward. "You could have just told me that from the beginning. Honesty is the best policy."

Realizing how childlike I sound, I glance back up at him, relieved to see him looking over my head again, not paying attention to me ramble as he watches James and Jenny across the room. I start to pull away, but his hold around my waist tightens and he leads us toward the middle of the dance floor in a few smooth glides.

"Two more minutes," he murmurs, leaning down a bit. His warm breath hits my cheek in a cloud of hot air, and the scent of spearmint and cinnamon liquor mixes pleasantly. I guess we weren't the only ones who pre-gamed for this notoriously dry event.

The haughty set of his jaw and amusement in his eyes is attractive, to say the least, but it also makes me want to stomp on his foot with my weapon of a heel.

"Excuse me?"

"Just give them a few more minutes. At least until the end of this song. James has been trying to get Jenny's attention since junior year. He deserves a chance, don't you think?"

I stare up at him shocked, but hesitantly move my arms back into place on his shoulders. We're on the same team here, ironically enough, because I happen to know that Jenny has had a thing for James Parsons for a while. He grins and looks back up at them.

"I wasn't going to steal Jenny away from him. I was just going to get a drink," I mumble, suddenly feeling like I need to defend myself from whatever he thought I was planning on doing.

He shrugs, keeping his curious gaze on his friend, who has successfully managed to get the most beautiful girl in the room to laugh. I follow his stare, and I can't help but laugh at the dazed look on James's face as he watches Jenny. Her movements are in sync with the beat, while his are just a few seconds behind. She seems to be whispering words of encouragement as he follows her lead, and I bite back a smile as I watch him try his hardest to match her movements.

"It's not that simple, Ryan. If you walk away, Jenny will follow you. She's not one to let her friends sit alone in the corner."

It takes me a moment to register his words as I absently watch our two friends swaying to the beat. When his words finally register, I look up at him, shocked. I'm stunned that he actually knows my last name, impressed that he has the foresight to know that Jenny would do exactly that, and mildly offended that he thinks I would sit in the corner of the room without her.

My smile fades and my cheeks burn again as I look away, realizing that I would most definitely be sitting alone in the corner if I wasn't here with him right now. The realization stings more than I'm willing to admit.

"Why are you here anyway?" he muses softly, tightening his grip on my waist as he sways us perfectly on tempo with the slow music.

My eyes shoot up to meet his, and the burning in my face ignites further. Burn after burn, this guy really knows how to stomp out my dwindling self-esteem.

"I didn't mean it like that—I just meant, where's Nia? She's my usual target to distract at these sorority things so James can talk to Jenny." His voice is softer, sympathetic even, as he watches my face flush.

"She has food poisoning."

"I have to admit, it's kind of nice to get a break from her," he says dryly, looking back up at James, who's now twirling Jenny around, her dress fanning out around her legs slowly as her pretty smile flashes.

"She'd be so flattered to hear that." I laugh, but selfishly, I revel in the idea of someone, even someone like Tristan Beck, enjoying my company over someone like Nia, who hasn't sat alone in a corner since the day I met her.

He just shrugs, a grin growing on his lips. The shallow dimple on his right cheek indents slightly as his gaze lingers on me. "Hey, honesty is the best policy, right?"

"Well, yes, but—" His grin turns into a full-blown smile, and I almost forget what I was going to say. Seeing him like this—his emerald eyes bright and crinkled, his lips pulled back into a tooth-baring grin, revealing the full dimple in his cheek—I can see why so many girls find him attractive.

"But what?" he goads. His smile molds into something a little smugger as my brief pause lets on to my momentary daze.

"Honesty without tact is cruelty," I say.

His eyes widen slightly, and he nods his head a few times as he considers my comment. "That's quite a profound statement, Ryan. Who said that?"

I open my mouth, but then shut it quickly. I have no idea. It's one of the quotes I pinned earlier today, but I can't exactly tell him I have an entire Pinterest board dedicated to inspirational life quotes. I've embarrassed myself enough tonight.

"Can I steal Abby away?" Jenny asks.

I jump slightly and look away from Beck. Jenny's standing next to us as a dazed-looking James walks up behind her. The music seems to have ended, and there's a short interlude between songs that neither of us noticed, because we're still swaying in silence.

"Oh—yeah, sure." Beck steps back, and I drop my arms to my sides. The loss of warmth is instantaneous as his hands slip from my waist, but I don't have time to even think about saying goodbye before Jenny intertwines her arm in mine and pulls me away toward the drinks.

I glance back at him and James before they disappear behind a throng of people moving in the crowd as the next song begins, this one a much livelier beat that sends perfectly timed vibrations through the soles of my heels.

"I'm so sorry about that. Nia usually hangs out with Beck whenever James comes to talk to me. I didn't even think about it when he asked you to dance," she apologizes, finding us a straight path toward the doors.

"It's fine." I shrug, searching over my shoulder until James's familiar black hair catches my eye on the opposite end of the room. Beck's standing beside him while a red-headed girl clings drunkenly to his shoulders. He bends down slightly so she can pop up onto her tiptoes and bring her lips up to his ear, and he nods absently at whatever she's saying to him while he takes a long sip from the cup in his hand. He nods again, snaking his arm around her waist as she tips her head back in a laugh that gets lost in the loud music around us, her vibrant red lipstick shining in the strobing lights.

"Are you ready to go?" Jenny sighs, checking the time on her phone. "We should probably check on Nia." She tosses her cup into the trash by the door and hands the freshman working the coat closet our tickets.

"Mhm." I hum absently as I look back over my shoulder again.

The bombshell with cherry lips wraps her arms low around Beck's waist, grazing her hand down his chest as her lips brush against his exposed neck, and when his emerald eyes flick up, they search the crowded room until they finally lock on mine.

THREE

I'm late again.

Well, late for me. I'm on time according to my class schedule, but since Coach Kennley has beaten the idea of *if you're not ten minutes early, then you're ten minutes late* into my head for the past three years, it's bled over into my everyday life. It only took one time of Coach screaming at me about the importance of punctuality while he had me running suicides for me to never show up late to practice again.

Coach might be an old man, but he sure as hell knows how to get a point across.

I down the last of my protein shake and toss the empty carton into a trashcan just outside of the general science building. I'm more than a little shocked that I don't have a hangover after last night. After ditching the formal, the team went to one of the frat's notorious after-parties. Six games of beer pong and four shots of Fireball later, I was lucky that I found a bed to stumble into. Not my bed, though. No, last night I was riding the glorious wave of drunken bliss with Tori Hanson, or rather, she was riding me.

The memory of her perky body grinding on top of me is hazy at best, but the trail of fresh hickeys on my stomach is more evidence of what I can't remember. I could have easily banked another round this morning when she woke me up with her hand down my boxers, but I couldn't show up late to class on the first day, Coach would kill me.

Two guys standing by the entrance of the building stare at me as I walk up, and I watch their eyes widen as the recognition sets in. I have to stop myself from groaning outwardly as the familiar scene begins to play out.

If I passed up a good morning fuck from Tori Hanson so I wouldn't be late, I sure as hell won't be late to talk to these guys about shooting percentages and NBA Draft picks. I keep my gaze straight and pick up my pace, trying to look like I'm in a rush, but the shorter one with a *USW Warriors* sweatshirt extends his hand for a handshake.

Random people interacting with me like they know me was kind of a shock at first, but after three years, the oddity of it has worn off and I just kind of go with it. I nod to them and slap the guy's outstretched hand, keeping my stride so I don't get pulled into a conversation with two strangers.

"Nice game against Utah, Beck. You've been fucking killing it, dude," he calls after me as I pull open the door. "You keep that hand hot and we'll crush Stanford on Friday."

"Thanks, man." I nod over my shoulder noncommittally before turning to scan the classroom numbers for the one listed on my new semester schedule.

The building's heat hits me instantly, and my cheeks and ears prickle as they start to defrost. Early mornings in January are always freezing, but the fact that it's not snowing, or spewing down fat raindrops cold enough to feel like an assault, is enough for me to be thankful for this weather.

I haven't stepped into the general science building since freshman year, but the same smell of old-furniture and cleaning supplies hasn't changed since I was here last. A few message boards line the walls, overflowing with flyers, most of them old enough to be archived in some kind of USW time capsule. The familiar crimson paper listing out the basketball game schedule is stapled on top of the rest.

I've played basketball for as long as I can remember, and I've played with the intention of going to the NBA since my high school coach called me up to varsity as a freshman. It wasn't until he benched the starting senior to give me his spot that I realized I might actually have a chance at something more.

Benching Joey definitely didn't earn me many friends on the team at first, but when the guys finally started to trust me, we were able to turn our twelve-year losing streak into a near championship win. The next three years we went all the way, and the result was multiple offers all across the country for full-ride scholarships. I could have been a Blue Devil, or a Jayhawk, or even a Wildcat, but instead of packing up and moving away, I chose to stay close to home and play for the team I grew up watching with my dad.

Being the starting point guard has made me a focus of conversation since I started here at the University of Southern Washington. The eyes following me as I walk across campus, the whispers when I walk into a classroom, hell, even the guys who try to make small talk while I'm trying to piss in the urinal, it's all amplified now that we're mid-season and projected to win it all again.

Walking toward the back of the building, I scan the empty hall. Most students don't elect to take classes at eight in the morning, and neither would I, if Coach wouldn't have vetoed the gym class I signed up for to fill my last elective slot. Unfortunately, by the time I logged in to sign up for another elective, the only thing left open was a sad mixture of humanities classes, History of Classical Music, Interpretative Dance 101, and Water Aerobics.

I would have happily sat my ass in a water aerobics class if it meant that I didn't have to attend any of those other classes, but I knew better than to run that option by Coach. So, here I am, walking into the only class that was still open that wouldn't require me to write a ten-page essay at the end of the semester.

The Fundamentals of Chemistry room is more of a laboratory than a classroom. The chilly air hits me immediately, along with the distinct smell of sterilizer, which almost makes my eyes water. The fluorescent lights are not doing any favors in helping me stave off a hangover, and I have to blink a few times to adjust to the harsh lighting.

I do a double-take when I see a hot blonde sitting at the professor's desk. Her hair is pulled back into a loose bun, and her dark-rimmed glasses inspire a few choice images that I'll definitely remember later. She doesn't look up at the class as she types, but occasionally glances at the open notebook on her desk.

There are a few rows of large, black lab tables spaced out across the room, with two stools placed under each one. I want to shoot myself at the sight of everyone blatantly gawking at me from their seats. I quickly scan the tables, looking for an empty seat somewhere in the back, hopefully alone, to save myself from having to make awkward small talk for the rest of the semester.

Fundamentals of Chemistry is typically a freshman class since it's an introductory course, a fact that honestly made me reconsider whether or not I should take the interpretive dancing class, but when my eyes scan over the tables near the back, my interest immediately piques.

Abby Ryan's wide eyes meet mine, and her mouth drops open slightly as she watches me walk straight toward her. I ignore the blatant stares and whispers of the surrounding freshmen as I pass by, and when I stop in front of her table, the skinny kid sitting next to her stares up at me wide-eyed.

"One dance and you're stalking me now, Ryan?" I tease, leaning back against the table in front of her.

Her eyes narrow at me as an amused grin pulls at her lips. "I don't know, Beck, are you here to distract me some more so James can hit on Jenny? Because she's not in this class."

"Well, James didn't send me this time. But I'd be happy to distract you, if that what you'd like." I raise a brow and smirk at the way her eyes widen a little.

"Yo, Beck, do you want to sit next to your girl? I can move." The kid next to her packs up his bag, and I thank him by slapping his outstretched hand as Abby tries to correct him.

"I'm not—"

"Yeah, thanks, man."

He stands up and drops his stuff onto the next table over.

"No problem. Hey, good game against Utah. You've got one of the sickest shots I've ever seen."

"Thanks, I appreciate it," I say, settling down onto the steel stool.

I glance over at Abby, my gaze taking a slow descent down her body. She's wearing a heavy, cream-colored knit sweater and black yoga pants that hug her ass and thighs. The dress she was in last night gave me a newfound appreciation for her tits, but damn, these leggings are a close second.

Abby Ryan isn't someone I've paid much attention to over the past three years. Not until last night when James asked for a wingman. She's not my typical type, but I sure as hell wouldn't mind spending a drunken night in her bed. I glance down to appreciate her lips again, and when her dark blue eyes meet mine, she raises an amused brow.

"What are you doing in Fundamentals of Chemistry? This is supposed to be a freshman class," she asks, watching as I pull out my spiral notebook and pen. Compared to her already set up station, complete with the textbook, a binder, her planner, and three pens aligned perfectly next to her coffee, my side of the table looks comically bare.

"Needed an elective credit and Coach wouldn't let me take a gym class. He said if I tore a muscle before the tournament, he'd kick my ass," I laugh.

He's not lying, he *would* kick my ass, and I'd have to let him because I respect the old man too much.

"So you picked chemistry? Why would you voluntarily put yourself through the torture of chemistry?" She looks back down to her planner with knotted brows, as if she genuinely can't fathom someone choosing to take chemistry for any reason other than it being a requirement.

I follow her gaze down to the open planner in front of her. The ridiculous array of multi-colored highlighters and notes written out for each day of the week is on full display. I can barely read the small handwriting, aside from a few notes reminding her of certain deadlines and what looks like a work-shift schedule.

"It was this or Interpretive Dance 101." I shrug.

"Interpretive dance, huh?" she hums, amused.

"Well, you already know how great of a dancer I am. I figured I might as well leave the spot open for someone who needs the help."

"Ah, how considerate of you." She places her hand over her heart in mock appreciation as I bow my head dramatically back. She laughs and tucks a strand of hair behind her ear. The sweet aroma of apples and vanilla drifts across the space between us and I recognize it as the same sweet scent she wore last night.

"I'm guessing you didn't take this class for fun then?" I ask, leaning my forearms on the table. The position stretches my triceps, and the sore muscle aches before easing slightly. Our first practice back from break was yesterday morning and Coach took no mercy on us. I went on a run every day of the break, but I sure as hell wasn't prepared for that ass-kicking.

"I found out I was missing a science credit, and all the easy classes were already taken."

I raise a brow at that. What exactly is her idea of an easy class? Fundamentals of Chemistry is about as basic as it gets. It's literally an introduction to chemistry. That's why I took it—I could sleep through this class and still walk out with an A.

"You know, classes like Earth Science, Environmental Science,

Human Sexuality," she rattles them off quickly, ticking them off on each one of her fingers.

Ah, those classes. They're notorious for being easy A's. Mostly because they don't require anything other than the memorization of key terms and knowing how to apply a few easy theories. You don't have to actually understand any concepts to pass the classes, which is exactly why they fill up so quickly.

They're also the classes that are off-limits for all engineering majors. About ninety percent of our required classes are science-based, save for the English and history requirements for graduation. If I ever tried to talk my advisor into letting me take Earth Science for one of my science credits, he would have laughed my ass out of his office.

"Ah, see, there's a class I'd actually like to take." I smirk at her, and she rolls her eyes, but her tight grin gives her away.

"From what I've heard, you've got more than enough experience in that area." She takes a sip of her coffee and raises a single brow, as if to say, *Am I wrong?*

"I don't know what you mean." I feign innocence, drawing my brows together in confusion.

Except, I do. I made a rule freshman year that I wouldn't let a girl distract me. *Priorities, priorities, priorities* as Coach would say. So, instead of dating girls, I just hookup with them. And only once. It helps to keep the line from blurring. Which is another reason why I had to drag myself away from Tori this morning. One and done, that's the rule. A rule that all of my hookups know going into it.

"I think you do," she counters, drawing out the last word playfully.

I raise a brow and hold back a smile as I try to look shocked. To be fair, I've never been called out on it. Especially not by a girl whose cheeks flame at the mere insinuation of sex. Abby Ryan radiates innocence. Even last night when her too-tight dress put her tits on display, she looked like a deer in headlights.

Her cheeks are still pink when I ask, "Are you slut-shaming me, Abby Ryan?"

A few heads turn in our direction, but I ignore the audience, reveling in the way her cheeks go from pink to red and her eyes dart around the room quickly, visibly uncomfortable with the attention.

"And if I remember correctly, *you* were the one talking about finding a fuck buddy last night when I asked you to dance." I lean in close enough so no one around us can hear, and when she tucks her fallen hair behind her ear, I appreciate the sweet aroma and watch as she balks.

"I—I was joking."

"Hmm." I nod in mock disbelief.

Of course, I believe her. Abby Ryan is the last person I would expect to have a fuck buddy. She practically has a neon sign on her forehead flashing *relationship*. Which is great for a guy who wants one, but it's an obvious sign to steer clear of her if you're not looking for something serious.

"Are you going to distract me like this all semester?" she whispers harshly, trying to keep the conversation private.

"Are you going to be this easily distracted all semester?" I whisper back.

She tries not to smile. "I need to focus. I need this class to graduate."

"It's Fundamentals of Chemistry," I counter. "It doesn't get much easier."

"It could be *Chemistry for Dummies*, it's still chemistry," she argues. Clicking open her pen to expose the nib, she writes the date and class name on the top of her blank notebook paper. Her handwriting is clear and looks so precise that it could be a printed font.

"I get the feeling you're not going to be much help to me in here," I tease, watching to see if her lips will pull back into that attractive smile.

"Yeah, you'll probably want to find a different study buddy." She shrugs, but the tightening of her cheek tells me she's holding back a smile. "I'm sure you won't have trouble finding one." She looks around the room pointedly, and I follow her gaze. Heads turn away quickly when I look around.

I glance back at the girl next to me, her smug smile has broken the surface, and her eyes are trained on the professor, who's just stood up from her seat and is now rummaging through a pile of papers on her desk. I take the moment to let my eyes coast over her again, before I nod and look forward, trying to keep a straight face.

"Probably for the best, Ryan," I agree. "I don't think we'd get much studying done, anyway."

I don't have to look over at her to see her mouth drop open.

FOUR

TRISTAN

Practice was brutal tonight.

We're two months away from the start of March Madness and Coach isn't fucking around. With three straight championship wins under his belt, this win is just as important to him as it is to us. Which is why nearly two-and-a-half hours into practice, he has us lined up on the court about to run keep up's—a sprinting drill where the entire team has to keep up with the person designated by Coach. If they look like they're slowing down on purpose to let the rest catch up, they get chewed out and sent for a mile run around the track. If the team doesn't keep up, we redo the drill until we get it right. The goal is for everyone to reach the same speed. It's fucking grueling, but it's Coach's favorite drill to run for conditioning.

We've already run it six times, bouncing around between different lead sprinters. Now, as he motions for us to step back onto the starting line, all I can hear down the row of my teammates beside me are desperate breaths trying to rake in ask much air as possible.

"Alright, if you can keep up on your first try, I'll end practice right now. If you don't, we're going to go down the line until every one of you has led the sprint." He glances at his wristwatch. "It's eight-thirty now. I'll need to call Mary and tell her to wrap up my dinner for me, but I can stay here all night if I need to, ladies."

My chest is heaving, and I cross my arms above my head in a desperate attempt to get more air into my lungs.

"Emery sets the pace," he yells, sticking his whistle between his teeth and moving his arm above his head in a circular motion, signaling for us to get on the starting line.

I glance down the line at my teammates, whose faces are drenched in sweat and red from exertion. Some of them are bent over, their hands braced on their thighs for support, while others are mirroring my position with their arms above their head, trying to regulate their breathing.

Scanning their faces, I can tell they're fading quickly, and to make matters worse, Nathan Emery is now getting death glares because he's our fastest sprinter and this round is high stakes.

"We're fucked, T," Micah says under his breath.

I push the drenched hair pasted to my forehead away from my face and groan as the very real possibility of us being stuck here for another hour starts to set in.

"Listen up," I yell, shaking out my arms to get some energy back. One last burst of adrenaline is all I need to catch up to Emery's pace. The collective eyes of the fourteen men down the line all turn to me, and I can feel the weight of their exhaustion weighing down on top of my own.

"When we're dead tired at the end of the fourth, do we quit?" I yell louder, and my voice echoes through the empty practice arena.

"No!" The team answers in unison, their rough voices sounding more alive than they look.

"When we're down with seconds left on the clock, do we quit?" I yell back.

"No!" I can see the energy in their faces building.

"No! We fight until the buzzer," I yell, bending my knee and getting into position to sprint.

The rest of the bodies down the line follow suit, and I grit my teeth as I eye the line at the opposite end of the court, beads of sweat dripping off my face and onto the floor.

"We've got seconds left now, so let's fight!"

A second passes, and the arena is dead silent apart from the labored breathing. When the whistle sounds, I launch forward, keeping my eyes trained on Emery, who's only one step ahead. The rush of adrenaline spikes my blood just in time, propelling me forward.

My heart is a deafening drum in my ears and my lungs are on fire, but just as my feet are about the cross the line at the other end of the court, I look over to my teammates and watch as we pass over the line together, perfectly in sync.

Coach's whistle blows, and he's standing mid-court with a smirk on his face as he tucks his clipboard under his arm and waves us over.

"Huddle up. Come on now, hurry. I've got dinner waiting for me at home." He eyes the drenched faces in front of him with a satisfied nod of his head. "I won't hold you up for much longer; I know it's the first day back, and you've all got to go home and get studying." He eyes us pointedly, knowing damn well that we'll be doing something after practice but it sure as hell won't involve textbooks.

"But before I end this practice, I have one matter of business to discuss with you all." He pulls the clipboard from under his arm and scans it stoically. "According to this letter, we seem to have an official NBA Draft candidate in our presence." He holds up the clipboard, and all I can make out is the NBA logo on the very top center of the page.

Before I can fully process his words, I'm being attacked by my teammates, their near-deafening cheers ringing in my ears as Micah and McConnell sweep their shoulders under me and lift me into the air.

"Hey now, put him down," Coach snaps. "Do you want to risk injuring my very first NBA alum?" He slaps McConnell with the clipboard, and I'm back on my feet as the freshman rubs his chest.

"You heard him, hands off the precious goods, guys," McConnell calls, dodging a second hit from Coach's clipboard with a wicked grin.

"Okay, get to the showers, all of you," Coach gruffs, waving his hands around, ushering them toward the locker room. He turns to me, extending the large packet of papers from his clipboard.

"This is all the draft information. We can go over it in more detail tomorrow after practice." He smiles, a real genuine smile that I swear I've only seen once after we won our first championship my freshman year.

"I'm—well, damn it, I'm proud of you, son." He clears his throat and pats me hard on the shoulder.

"Thank you, Coach," I say, unable to look away from the papers in my hands.

We look forward to seeing you at this year's official NBA Draft is printed boldly on the top of the page, and I read it over and over until it's burned into my memory.

He grunts, and I glance up to see his entire face starting to turn red. I look back down quickly when I realize that he's trying not to cry.

"You, uh, should probably go and keep an eye on the rest of those boys." He clears his throat again. "Keep them from celebrating too hard, don't want any drunken mishaps taking out any of my players."

I nod quickly and turn toward the door but hesitate and look back over my shoulder.

"Thank you again, Coach. I couldn't have done this without you." I hold up the stack of papers in my hand, and when his eyes meet mine, he nods noncommittally as his lips pull down into a fine line to keep from showing that he's more affected by this than he's willing to admit.

I shake his outstretched hand before turning and jogging out of the practice arena with the ticket to my lifelong dream clutched in my hands.

———

By the time I showered and stepped back into the locker room, Micah and McConnell had already planned our team's trip to O'Malley's for *"celebratory pints and pussy."*

James, who always seems to run the logistics for these outings, divvied up the designated driver duties between the freshmen, excluding McConnell, since he already served his time when he waited up to drive everyone home from the frat party last night.

Most of us ended up catching rides with the girls we were going home with, so he rode home alone with a very drunk James, who was stuck playing the long game with Jenny McPherson.

After following the team out of the locker room, and promising Coach we wouldn't make asses of ourselves tonight, I piled into the back of Aaron Penn's Toyota Corolla. That same shitty old Corolla is now blasting the workout playlist Micah has on his phone while I scroll through my contacts. I keep nodding as I absently listen to James grumble about how Jenny McPherson still hasn't accepted his request on Instagram, and since her account is private, he's shit out of luck.

"What about her friend, Abby? The one she was with last night," he says, typing her name into the search bar.

I glance over at his phone to see Abby's face smiling up at me as she holds up a fruity looking drink in her profile picture. She's wearing a sundress that shows a lot more skin than I saw this morning, but still covers her more than last night's impossibly tight-fitting dress that made it hard for me to keep my eyes from locking in on her chest. Her hair is a little lighter, as if it was bleached by the sun, which she definitely saw a lot of based on the tan and the beach in the background. Her account is private, too, so James really *is* shit out of luck.

"Add her." I shrug, glancing back down at my phone to find Olivia's number.

"I can't add her, I don't even know her. It would look like I'm trying to stalk Jenny."

"You *are* trying to stalk Jenny," I snort.

"Can you just add her for me?" he asks.

The defeated sound of his voice keeps me from messing with him further as I open my own Instagram. I find her account easily since her username is literally *abbyryan*, and hold my phone up so James can watch as I click the follow request button and click out of the app.

"Still stuck on that McPherson chick?" McConnell laughs from the other side of me.

"Still fucking every jersey chaser that looks your way?" James counters.

"You say that like it's a bad thing." McConnell grins.

After Brody graduated last year, and Coach found out we had an open room in the house James, Micah, and I rent every year, he practically signed McConnell's name on the lease himself.

Luke McConnell has been scouted since his freshman year of high school. He's got an insane shot, it's almost unbelievable to watch, but he's young and he still has a lot to learn, on and off the court, which is why we got stuck rooming with him.

We're essentially babysitting him to make sure he doesn't do anything stupid enough to get himself kicked off the team, but what Coach didn't take into account is the fact that Luke McConnell and Micah Costa are two peas in a very fucking stupid pod. So far, they haven't gotten into too much trouble together, which is a fucking miracle since Micah's got the connections and Luke's got the money to fund whatever ridiculous plan they've conceived together—like hosting a wet t-shirt contest in our backyard and Instagram-living it to all of their followers. Practice the next day was killer. The dumbasses didn't think about the fact that our assistant coach follows both of them.

I glance back down at my phone and finally find the name that I've been scrolling through my contacts for.

"Can you turn that down? I've got to call my parents and tell them the news," I ask as I click the FaceTime button on my sister's contact and nod a thanks to Micah in the passenger seat who turns the radio down to a barely audible hum.

I would call my mom directly, but I'd be willing to bet that she doesn't even know what FaceTime is, let alone know how to answer it, and I really want to see their faces when I tell them the news. The call only rings twice before Olivia's face pops onto the screen. She's sitting on her bed, and I can hear the British dating show that she's obsessed with in the background.

"Hey, bruv." She smiles as she tosses a popcorn kernel into her mouth.

"Damn, *that's* your sister?" McConnell leans into the shot and gives a toothy grin to the camera. I elbow him so hard in the ribs, he drops his phone and falls out of shot with a loud groan.

"Fuck off." I glare at him.

"Who was that?" Olivia asks curiously, sitting up in bed, as if that would somehow help her to see the freshman who's now bent over next to me holding his ribs.

"Don't worry about it. Can you go grab Mom and Dad?"

"I'm eighteen, Tristan, you don't get to police who I can and can't talk to." She rolls her eyes.

"You can talk to whoever you want to, Liv, just not him."

She narrows her eyes at me, and I can tell she's deciding whether or not to be difficult. She rolls her eyes again and pops another kernel into her mouth before sliding off her bed and walking into the living room. I glare at McConnell, because now that he's sitting up straight again, he's not even being discreet about the fact that he's checking her out.

"Tristan's on FaceTime," she says, handing over the phone. Mom's face pops onto the screen, and her eyes light up as she waves into the camera.

"Hi, sweetie," she says too loudly.

"You can talk normally, Mom," Olivia instructs, repositioning the phone in her hands for a better angle.

"Oh, sorry. How are you, honey?"

"Great, just got out of practice. How are you?"

"I'm exhausted. I've been baking all day for Olivia's volleyball bake sale." She turns the camera around to show off the trays of cookies lining the kitchen counters. McConnell makes an approving sound next to me, and I have to tell myself it's because the cookies look damn good and not because he's now picturing my baby sister in her volleyball uniform.

"Those look amazing, Mrs. B." James pops his head into the shot and gives my mom the most brown-nosing smile I've ever seen. It works, though, because now she's fawning over him, asking how his mom is doing and what they did for the holidays. After James summarizes his vacation to the mountains with his family, I try to steal back the conversation.

"Can you grab Dad?" I ask quickly before she can ask James any more questions. He must have been walking into the kitchen because my dad pops onto the screen, his eyes squinting as he considers the camera.

"Is this that Skype thing?" he asks.

"Kind of." Olivia's voice echoes through the phone again, and she takes it from him, holding it out like a selfie to get all three of them into the shot.

"Ah, there you go," Dad says, putting his arm around Olivia's shoulders and pulling her close, smiling up at the phone as if he were posing for a picture.

"I have some exciting news," I say, and suddenly, I can't stop myself from grinning like an idiot. "I'm officially declared for the NBA Draft."

It takes a moment for my words to register, but when they do, I watch with a shit-eating grin as my family explodes on the screen.

FIVE

The first night of the spring semester isn't spent in its typical fashion.

Nia, who would usually drag me out to a bar to get drunk off tequila shots and vodka cranberry to celebrate our last semester, is currently lounging right next to me on the couch. She's three episodes deep into the serial killer documentary series she's been binging, all the while stealing more than her fair share of the knit blanket we're sharing.

She has a water bottle the size of my forearm cradled in her arms, and her short black hair is pulled back into a haphazard bun on top of her head while a red headband attempts to keep the mane of flyaways at bay. Somehow, she still looks more attractive than anyone recovering from a nasty bout of food poisoning should ever be allowed to look.

Sliding down further into the couch, she opts to use my shoulder as a pillow rather than one of the fifteen different decorative pillows we have piled around us.

Nia is a touchy person. She's always pulling us in for hugs, or playing with our hair, or smacking our butts when we walk by. It's something I've grown used to in the three years of living together, but sick Nia is a whole new level of cuddly. I don't mind, though, aside from the fact that Nia is one of my favorite people on the planet, she's also like a little heater who generates more body heat than anyone else I've ever met, which is something that comes in handy in the early months here in Washington.

"Find anything new?" Her voice is still a little hoarse, and she takes a long sip of her water bottle to soothe her throat. She's watching me scroll through the scholarship website, and I groan in response, clicking from one link to another, rereading the same posts I've already looked at a hundred times.

As much as I'd like to toss my laptop aside and just relax into the couch, the voice in the back of my head telling me I'm running out of time to find a scholarship just keeps getting louder.

"It's all the same," I sigh.

The site hasn't been updated for a few days and I'm starting to worry this is all I'm going to have to choose from.

Finding a scholarship is Plan A. Taking a few years off to work and save up enough money to pay for classes is Plan B. Throwing my inhibitions to the wind and becoming a stripper is Plan C. And taking out even more student loans is Plan D.

At this point, Plan C is looking mighty fine.

I'm not against student loans, and if I wasn't already nearly forty-thousand deep in them, I wouldn't have a problem taking out more. But at this point, I'm already going to struggle to pay them back, and I don't even want to know how much more it's going to cost to finish my entire graduate degree.

The logical question to ask myself is whether or not grad school is even a realistic option at this point. If I have to take out more loans to pay for it, is it even worth it? Sure, going to grad school is the only chance I'll have of securing a good job in the journalism field, but if I'm being honest here, I don't even know what kind of journalism I want to specialize in. Political? Entertainment? Investigative? Freelance? Column? Feature? Hell, even travel journalism is on the table at this point.

I've stuck to the typical articles since joining the university's newspaper freshman year, writing about the school's new additions, the different student-run concerts and plays, and even a few feature articles on certain students who were being recognized for their academic achievements. While they were all fun to write, none of them really caught my attention enough for me to think, *hey, I should keep writing stuff like this.*

That's what I've been hoping grad school would help me with— finding my niche.

I refresh the website to keep myself from falling too far into the should-I-go or shouldn't-I-go rabbit hole, and sigh in frustration when the only scholarship designated for journalism students stares back at me on my screen. I bite the inside of my cheek as I click it for the hundredth time and read through the description.

USA Sports Network offers competitive sports journalism scholarships in hopes of finding and fueling the next generation of sports enthusiasts with a passion for writing and broadcasting. Here at USASN, we strive to foster the same passion and enthusiasm for journalism in our employees as we see in the players we interview.

The rules for the scholarship competition are simple. Show us who you are as a journalist: write a piece that speaks to us and to the millions of fans who read USASN every day.

The possibilities are endless, and we encourage you to leave it all on the court— or the page—in this case.

Submit your article to scholarships@USASN.com by February 22nd at midnight to be considered.

The reward for the scholarship winner is more money than all the other scholarships I've seen so far. It would be enough to pay for my entire first semester, no matter which school I choose—room and board, textbooks, and classes. I reread the description again.

"Has it covered Bundy yet?" Jenny pads across the living room from the hallway with her hair wrapped up in a towel and a charcoal mask painted onto her face. Her plaid pajama shorts and matching short sleeve button-up top are comical compared to my hoodie and sweatpants, but then again, she grew up in the Northeast and I grew up in Florida, where it barely ever drops below the seventies. She falls onto the cushion beside Nia and pulls her legs under her, her eyes instantly glued to the TV mounted above the fireplace.

"Not yet, I think he's next," I say, readjusting the blanket so all three of us can fit under it.

I close my laptop and toss it onto the cushion beside me and give in to the lure of the docuseries until the small ding of my phone pulls my attention away. I glance down at the screen for a second and then focus back to the TV before my mind fully registers the notification. My eyes dart back down, and I stare at my phone in disbelief as I reread the notification.

Tristan Beck's follow request is staring back at me, and I have to blink a few times before I'm convinced that I'm not seeing things.

What the hell?

I click on his page and the blue verified checkmark takes me by surprise.

A verified check and almost two million followers.

I click off his page and click back to make sure I'm seeing this correctly.

I scroll through his feed quickly to see a few selfies, some pictures of him and his teammates on an airplane as they travel to away games, and a bunch of action shots of him playing in different games—which I can differentiate by the changing jerseys of his opponents in each picture.

"Earth to Abby." Nia's voice registers, but I look up a second too late to dodge the couch pillow that makes contact with the side of my face. I look over to see both of them staring at me expectantly.

"What?"

"What are you looking at? Your eyes are practically popping out of your head," Jenny says as she sits up straighter. They have the TV paused, and my cheeks flood as I click the top button on my phone. When the locking sound echoes through the room, both of them narrow their eyes at me.

"Just on Instagram." I shrug, turning back to the TV, hoping they won't pry.

I don't know why I feel like I just got caught looking at porn, but my face burns as they both eye me skeptically.

Nia purses her lips and raises a perfectly sculpted brow. I can feel her stare boring into my soul as if she's trying to read my mind, and I sigh, knowing there's no use in trying to hide anything from them. When I toss my phone to Nia, she quickly types in my passcode. Her eyes go wide and mouth drops open as her thumb scrolls through the feed, and when Jenny leans over to get a look, her eyes dart up to meet mine as an excited smile pulls at her lips.

"Tristan Beck followed you?" she squeals, trying to take the phone out of Nia's hand, but Nia dodges her and holds it out of her reach as she scrolls through his feed, clicking on one of his more impressive photos. He's in a gym, and the way he's holding the camera gives a great view of his abs in that, *I'm not trying to show off my body, but I kind of am* way.

"Don't like anything," I yell frantically, lunging for the phone, but as Nia leans away from me, Jenny grabs the phone and pops up, walking back until her legs hit the other side of the couch. She's scrolling through his feed now as Nia and I watch her expectantly.

"He's only following like a hundred people; that means something, Abs."

"I don't think it does," I counter, standing up and detangling myself from the blanket. "We have a class together this semester; we're lab partners in chem," I say, trying to make sense of it, but the rush of excitement is pulsing through my veins and part of me wants to take my phone and run into my room to stare at his shirtless pictures all night.

"Yeah, I'm sure Beck follows all of his lab partners." Nia snorts as she rolls her eyes.

"Oh, look at this." Jenny grins, walking back and leaning over so we can both see as she points to a picture of Beck with two girls at a beach. His abs and arms are on full display as he grins at the person taking the picture. Jenny clicks on the post and the two tagged girls' usernames pop up. I try to ignore the immediate rush of relief when their handles come up *LivBeck* and *MelodyBeck*. Looking back at the girls, I can easily see the family resemblance—the same deeply tanned olive skin, brown curly hair, and all-around gorgeous genetics.

She clicks out of the picture and scrolls back up to the top and onto his following tab. As she flicks through the short list, I realize it's pretty much entirely made up of his teammates, a few people who share his last name, and the rest are all verified, which leads me to believe that they're NBA players or fellow draftees. Not a single girl who doesn't share his last name is on there.

"How does he have almost two million followers?" Nia gapes.

"How is he *verified?*" Jenny adds.

"He's a projected first-round pick," I say, suddenly making sense of it. "All the players projected to be drafted are verified."

I've edited a few articles for the university's newspaper recently about his projected draft pick, and I've watched more than enough NBA Drafts with my dad and brothers when I was younger to know what it takes to be drafted in the top five of the first round. He's got it.

"He's going to the NBA?" Jenny balks.

"I mean, it's not set in stone or anything, he still has to be drafted," I explain.

"Okay, you're accepting it," Nia decides, grabbing the phone from Jenny. I watch in horror as she clicks out of his following tab and presses the accept button on his request.

"Nia," I scream, lunging for my phone, but Jenny grabs for it before I can and she backs away again.

"You were just saying the other night how you need a fuck buddy—who better to fuck around with than Beck?" Jenny grins as my face instantly turns a deep red.

I glance at Nia, whose jaw drops as she stares at me like I just grew three heads.

Why is everyone bringing this up?

"Abby?" She looks at Jenny for confirmation as she points at me. "Abby Ryan, my sweet, innocent best friend who blushes at the mere thought of sex said she wanted a *fuck buddy*?" she asks incredulously.

"No," I correct. "Well, yes, I said that, but I was joking." I stop when I fully digest her comment. "And I'm not that innocent. You know I'm not a virgin; I slept with Tyler."

"You had PG-13 vanilla sex with Tyler." Nia rolls her eyes.

"Sex is sex." I cross my arms across my chest, but even as I say it, I know that I'm lying.

Sex with Tyler was . . . well . . . it was sex.

It hurt the first couple of times, and then it didn't, and then it felt kind of good. We were both virgins, so neither of us really knew what we were doing, and I was always across the country so we didn't have a ton of opportunity to actually do it, but when we did it was . . . nice. But it wasn't like anything that I've seen on TV or read in the smutty books I always brought home from the library and hid from my parents and brothers under my bed.

"Sex is not sex, my naïve little grasshopper." Nia smirks, motioning for me to sit down. I put my hand out for my phone, and Jenny begrudgingly gives it back as she falls beside Nia on the couch. I follow suit and look down at Tristan's page again, scrolling through to make sure they haven't liked anything on accident—or on purpose.

"How would you rate your sex with Tyler?" Nia asks seriously, watching me curiously as I pull the blanket around me again, like it could somehow shield me from this conversation. My face flames again as my eyes flick between hers and Jenny's.

"I don't know." I shrug.

How do you translate *nice* into a number?

"Well, there are factors to consider." Nia sits back on the couch and pulls her legs under her, grabbing for her water bottle again. "You have to take into account foreplay—oral always gives bonus points," she explains, ticking them off on her finger.

"If he knows how to actually to find your G-spot." Jenny snorts.

"True." Nia laughs. "And how often he actually made you orgasm."

I feel like I'm on fire, sitting here burning to a crisp in front of my two best friends who are staring at me expectantly, waiting for me to explain the details of my sex life, which I now realize was extremely PG-13.

I was always so particular about our times together. The lights were always off, we were under the covers, and the one time he tried to go down on me, I ended up chickening out. Most of our sexual experiences together were spent silently in the missionary position and lasted all of two minutes, and if I'm being completely honest, I don't know if I've ever had an orgasm. The sex felt good, but he was always finished before I really got into the rhythm of it, and I wasn't exactly going to ask him to keep going after he already came.

"I don't know if I've ever actually . . ."

Nia raises her brows, and as the realization starts to dawn on her, her eyes grow wide and her mouth pops open.

I look down and click out of Tristan's Instagram page, as if having it open might somehow give him access to this mortifying conversation. He's the last person on the planet that I would want to know that I've probably never had an orgasm, especially since his level of *expertise* is well known around campus.

"Wait . . . *never?*" Jenny asks, looking absolutely appalled.

"I don't know." I shrug, looking back down at my phone, willing myself to evaporate into thin air.

"You'd know," they say in unison.

I can't take much longer of this conversation or I'll actually combust from embarrassment. I stand up and grab my laptop from the cushion next to me.

"If you'll excuse me, I'm going to go die of embarrassment now," I say, skirting past them toward the hallway leading to our bedrooms.

"Don't be embarrassed, Abs," Jenny calls after me.

"Yeah, it's not your fault Tyler was a bad lay," Nia agrees.

I wave my hand over my head dismissively as I round the corner and slip out of view, desperate for a hot shower to help ease away the embarrassment and the newfound realization that maybe I should be looking for something more than just a grad school scholarship before graduating from college.

SIX

ABBY

I take a long sip of my coffee and readjust myself on the ice-cold stool in the chemistry classroom.

I was one of the last students to file into the lab this morning, and not having the full fifteen minutes I always give myself before class to get settled and go over the lecture notes from the previous class is really starting to stress me out. That, and the fact that, thanks to the mortifying conversation with my roommates, I could barely sleep last night.

The stool beside me is still empty, and I glance up to the classroom entrance between sips of coffee and reading my notes, praying that Beck isn't planning on skipping class today, because the small stack of papers sitting on each table labeled *LAB 001* will be almost impossible to complete on my own. I've already flipped through the lab packet and spotted most of the keywords and concepts from the reading listed throughout, but the execution is the part I'm worried about.

I push the lab papers back to the center of the table and grab my planner out of my bag. Scanning the monthly layout for today's date, I read over the to-do list I made yesterday. My day is planned out by the hour today since I have more than usual on my list. I'll be in classes from eight to two, then I need to go to the newspaper room to get everything organized for our first staff meeting of the semester, then find time to call my mom back before she has a heart attack since I've missed the last two times she's tried to call. And somehow, I have to get all of this done before five, when my first shift back at the diner starts.

I pencil in my mom's phone call for four-thirty. It's enough time to catch her up while also giving me the perfect excuse to get off the phone when my shift starts. If gone unchecked, my mother could lecture me on pretty much anything for hours.

I stare down at the bolded letters highlighted at the bottom of the page, reminding me that I'm running out of time to start my scholarship article. The one good thing that came from my inability to sleep last night was the embarrassing amount of time I spent scrolling through Beck's Instagram. Admittedly, at first, it was simply for the shirtless pictures, though, after stopping to look at some of his basketball action shots, the realization of how good of a basketball player he actually is had started to dawn on me. It didn't take long before I was typing away on my computer, drafting up different article ideas, keeping in mind the USASN audience and which kind of article would be the most interesting to read.

Growing up with a stay-at-home dad and two older brothers, most of my evenings were spent sitting with my dad in the bleachers at basketball practices. He even tried to get me to sign up for my own team, but after throwing a big enough tantrum, he agreed to let me skip that humiliation.

My hand-eye coordination is less than stellar, a fact that's been proven time and time again when my brothers coerced me into playing with them on the half-court we have in the backyard. After getting nailed in the face one too many times because I wasn't fast enough to catch the ball, it became very apparent that I didn't inherit the same athletic gene they did.

While I wasn't meant to be on the court, I couldn't deny the interest that I had in it. I always seemed to end up on USASN whenever I would watch TV, knowing it wouldn't take long for my dad to find his way onto the couch next to me so we could debate about the latest game or player to get traded.

After he passed away my junior year of high school, I haven't been able to watch USASN or any sports network without inevitably spiraling into a full-blown meltdown. I've avoided it as much as possible since.

I look down at my planner and try to read over my to-do list again, focusing on something other than the memory of my dad so I don't end up crying in the middle of this class.

My eyes dart up at the sound of the stool being dragged back as Tristan's lengthy body settles down next to me. A small wave of relief washes over me, mostly because now I won't have to complete this lab by myself, but also because if I'm going to apply for the USASN scholarship, I'll need to get started on the article as soon as possible, and the first thing I need to do is ask Tristan if he's okay with me interviewing him.

He doesn't look up until after he's pulled his books from his bag, but when he does, the unmistakable haze of a hangover is clear in his eyes. Suddenly, the random Instagram follow request makes a lot more sense.

"Rough night?" I laugh, trying to keep my excitement for the article at bay. I don't want to freak him out, but I do honestly think this is my best shot at winning the scholarship.

"You could say that." He smirks as he uncaps the water bottle he pulls from his bag and downs half of the contents. I dig through my bag and pull out two ibuprofen from the travel-size bottle I always keep on me. He thanks me as I drop them into his palm, and I watch him throw them back and wash them down quickly.

"We've got a big lab today," Hannigan calls as she walks to the back of the classroom and wheels a cart laden with beakers to the front of the room, placing them onto each of the tables down the row as she goes. "The lab is outlined in the packet on each of your tables. You should recognize these concepts from your assigned reading last night. These are your materials here." She holds up one of the beakers. "The utensils are in the cabinet in the back. If you need assistance, let me know." She stops at our table to set four beakers of liquid in front of us.

I don't know why, but I hadn't expected to be working with actual chemicals in here.

"Do not forget your protective eye-wear, aprons, and gloves. I don't want another safety incident this year," she calls over her shoulder as she continues down the row of tables.

I glance around the room to the rest of the students who are sliding aprons over their heads and putting on their safety goggles. No one else seems to be as freaked out as I am at the thought that we even *need* safety wear.

What kind of class requires safety wear?

Certainly not one I want to be in.

Beck laughs as my eyes scan the room, finally landing on his outstretched hands which are holding my own set of safety wear.

"*Another* safety incident?" I blanch, pulling on the goggles quickly before I tug on the elbow-length rubber gloves. The apron is much heavier than I was expecting, as it's made from a similar rubber as the gloves, and wearing the gloves makes it hard to tie the strings of the apron. If I'm having trouble just getting dressed for this lab experiment, how am I going to actually complete it?

Beck, who seems to be amused by my struggles, reaches over and pulls softly on the string of the goggles hanging by my ear, tightening it so that the goggles fit snug on my nose rather than sitting low on my cheeks. The woody spice of his cologne lingers in the air between us.

"Thanks," I say, nudging them into place with the back of my glove-clad hand.

He nods and turns back to the lab paper on our desk. "Okay, let's get started."

As Beck works through the lab, I watch and assist whenever necessary while making sure to keep a distance when he handles the chemicals. He seems to understand pretty quickly that I'm wary of being around the chemicals, but still finds easy things for me to do when Hannigan walks past our table so I can still get my full participation grade.

"Mix this with this," he says quietly, putting two small beakers down in front of me just as Hannigan reaches the table behind us. Hesitantly, I begin to mix the two and watch in awe as the two clear liquids mix and turn a light purple color before my eyes.

"Excellent work over here." She beams and compliments my stirring skills before continuing to the next table. Beck nudges me with his elbow.

"Look at you, at this rate you be the next Marie Curie." He grins.

"I'm a natural, I guess." I smirk, making a show of stirring the liquid as if it's an impressive feat.

We continue in this same fashion for most of the class—Beck does most of the leg work while I assist him with stirring, recording numbers and observations on our lab report, and grabbing utensils from the counter in the back of the room whenever he asks for them.

As I place a freshly cleaned stirring utensil on the table, Beck looks down at me. His goggles magnify his eyes in a comical way, but there's still an undeniable attractiveness to him as his curls fall onto his forehead and his dimple indents as he reads the directions on the lab report.

The thought makes me realize how ridiculous I must look in the goggles, and I groan inwardly at the realization that I'm going to have to put on these god-awful goggles and heavy apron and gloves for the rest of the semester and wear them in front of, arguably, the most attractive man I've ever seen in real life.

"I'm guessing you're not a chemistry major, Ryan," he says, picking up the stirring utensil and whirling around the now magenta liquid.

He doesn't seem to struggle like I do when handling the small utensils in the rubber gloves. Probably because the gloves actually fit him, while mine dwarf my hands, making it difficult to even pick up my pencil.

"Is it that obvious?" I ask, making a crab-like clawing motion with my gloves as I attempt to get them to slide back into place.

He grins and shakes his head. "No, not at all, you look right at home here with the chemicals."

I shoot him a pointed look but can't keep a straight face when his magnified eyes meet mine.

"I'm a journalism major, actually," I say, realizing this is as good a time as ever to bring up the fact that I want to write an article on him.

"Journalism." His eyes grow slightly, as if he wasn't expecting that answer.

He recovers his casual expression fast as he sets the three beakers full of chemicals in the middle of the table, each one sitting on a paper labeling their contents. After placing the final beaker into place, he pulls off his gloves and places his goggles onto the table. I follow suit, thankful that these torture contraptions are finally coming off.

"Sounds like a lot of English classes." He grimaces.

"It is." I nod, laughing at the look of utter distaste on his face. "But I'd rather write an essay than do something like this." I motion toward the lab report in front of him and he cocks a brow, as if the thought of someone choosing to write an essay is absurd.

"So what kind of journalism are you interested in? Are you planning on writing a how-to column in a magazine or something? *How-to Obsessively Plan Out Your Day by the Hour Like a Psychopath* could be your first article." His eyes are bright and hooded with amusement as I swat at him. He dodges my arm easily and grins at me as if to say, *Am I wrong?*

I glance over at the open planner next to me and roll my eyes as I flick it closed and push it as far away from him as I can.

"I'm not much of a how-to writer," I counter.

"So, what then?" he asks, the humor fading from his voice as he sits back in the stool and considers me.

"I don't really know yet," I admit, biting the inside of my cheek. "I guess I'm kind of counting on grad school to help me figure that out."

"Grad school, huh? That's impressive, Ryan." His eyes widen slightly as he nods, leaning forward to rest his forearms on the table. He doesn't seem to be joking, and I appreciate the compliment.

It's nice to have someone acknowledge that going to grad school is actually kind of impressive. That it's not something that should just be expected of someone. But when your mother runs her own law firm, grad school is the least of her expectations.

"Thanks." I smile down at my hands.

I might as well do it now. I've barely spoken to Beck, aside from the past two days, but even in that short amount of time, I can tell he appreciates that I don't focus on the fact that he's our star basketball player.

Last night, after I decided to ask him for the interview, I began to research as much as I could. Although, when I read through some of his interviews, I realized pretty quickly how short he is with reporters.

The student-reporters on the university's newspaper were given the same answers that the more notable professional reporters were: *"I'm lucky to have such a good team to play with"; "It's always a team effort"; "We had a great game, but we couldn't have done it without Coach Kennley's support and direction."* It's the telltale response of players who are uncomfortable speaking to the media, which makes asking this question that much harder.

"If you haven't finished your lab yet, I advise you finish up quickly; our class ends in a few minutes." Hannigan's voice pulls me from my daze, and I watch Tristan collect the empty beakers and utensils on our table.

"I've been trying to get a scholarship for grad school," I say, attempting to sound as casual as possible.

He glances over at me as I continue.

"There's one for USASN, specifically for journalism students. I would need to write an article and submit it for the scholarship contest," I say, allowing the comment to hang in the air between us for a moment before plucking up the courage to finally ask. "And I was hoping to interview you for it."

He blinks, obviously surprised.

"You're into sports journalism?" His brows knit together.

"No, not really, it's mostly for the scholarship money," I admit, praying that he's not going to shut me down.

He considers that for a moment. "Okay. Yeah, sure."

"Really?" I gape for a second before trying to wipe the shock off my face.

"Yeah. I've done a ton of pre and post-game interviews before. They aren't too bad." He shrugs and stands up, piling the used utensils in his hands before turning on his heel to bring them to the designated bin on the back counter.

I nod absently as the instant rush of guilt starts to build in my chest. I know I should tell him that the interview I'm planning on doing with him will require a lot more than a few pre-rehearsed answers. If I want a chance at actually winning this scholarship, I need to write something with more substance. Something more impactful. Something like a feature article.

The thought sparks a charge of inspiration and I have to fight off the urge to pull out my laptop and start drafting my interview questions right here. Features on players are always a fan favorite. Before every game, USASN shows a feature on a player. It helps the fans get to know the players better, and in a field where sports players are looked at as entertainers as much as they are athletes, the demand for features is incredibly high.

"Alright, times up." Hannigan's voice pulls me back, and when Tristan walks back to our table, he rips off a piece of paper and scribbles a phone number across it in his messy scrawl.

"Let me know when you want to do the interview," he says, sliding the paper over to me before pulling his bag onto his shoulder.

"I will. Thank you, again."

He flashes a lazy grin before walking to the front of the classroom.

I know I should tell him my intentions for the article—to give him a fair warning for how in-depth I'm planning on going—but if this is my only shot at a scholarship, I can't mess it up, and I can't chance him pulling out before it's even begun.

I pick up the small scrap of paper, allowing the wave of guilt to hit me full force as I look back up and watch Tristan walk out of the room, completely unaware of just how deep this article is going to get.

SEVEN

I glance down at the dash on my truck as I pull into the neighborhood.

It's five minutes past eleven and I'm running late. Ryan didn't waste any time setting up a date for us to do the interview. After comparing our schedules, we decided on meeting at my place since one of her roommates was hosting a study group at her apartment this morning.

Glancing into the rearview mirror, I spot my mom's red Honda Civic following behind me and I can just barely make out her and Olivia's silhouettes.

I hadn't planned to go out to breakfast with them this morning, especially since I usually crash after my morning workout if I don't have class, but when I woke up to a FaceTime call from Liv, who was walking into Over Easy, my favorite diner just down the road, it didn't take much persuading to get me to join them.

I would have made it back in time if it wasn't for my mom's un-canny ability to make friends with everyone she meets. After picking up the bill, I was seconds away from sliding out of the booth and heading back to the house to meet Abby before my mom delved into a full con-versation with the waitress about her daughter who also attends USW.

Abby texted me while they were mid-conversation to tell me she was here for the interview, and I quickly apologized that I wasn't back yet and told her to feel free to wait inside for me.

That was ten minutes ago.

I tried to politely excuse myself, but my mom insisted that she needed to get her Tupperware back from when I took leftovers home on Thanksgiving. And after I'd forgotten to bring it home to her for the past two months, she figured she might as well get it now while she's near campus.

As I pull into the driveway, I spot the black Jetta parked right out front. Glancing around the driveway, all three of my roommates' cars are also here—well, two cars and one motorcycle.

Mom and Olivia are out of the car and walking up the driveway by the time I lock my car, and I remind them again that I have a school project to work on so they can't stay too long.

My mom waves me off and Olivia ignores me as she blanches at the matte black Audi R8 sitting in the driveway.

"Whose car is that?"

I had a similar reaction when I saw it for the first time when McConnell pulled up on move-in day. It's probably worth more than my parents' house, but since his dad owns a multimillion-dollar finance company, McConnell was gifted the sports car on his sixteenth birthday.

"McConnell's," I say as I push open the front door and stand back so they can walk in before me. I glance absently at the couch where all three of my roommates are sitting, their eyes glued to the flat screen TV as the sound of an automatic gun being fired in quick succession fills the room.

"Behind you." Micah's voice bellows through the room, and a new round of gunshots fires. I glance into the kitchen, but frown at the empty room.

If she's not in here, or in the living room, where would she be? Down the hall, a flush sounds from the bathroom, and I relax a little. So they didn't scare her away then.

My mom and sister follow me into the kitchen, and I groan at the three boxes of beer sitting on the kitchen island and the handle of Captain Morgan propped on the empty pizza box next to the refrigerator.

I quickly search through the cabinets until I find the matching lid for the Tupperware and hand it to my mom, who sighs and smiles as she looks at the glass container.

"This is my favorite one," she says, examining it.

"I can't believe you have a favorite Tupperware set." Olivia snorts, picking up the nearly empty Captain Morgan bottle to inspect it.

She's about to graduate from high school in a few months and she's already gotten her acceptance letter to USW—a full ride scholarship for volleyball—but it still feels wrong to see her in this setting. Somehow, no matter how old she gets, she always seems like the same little girl I used to cart around on my back and play airplane with as a kid.

"She beat the level—she beat the fucking level." Micah's voice echoes loudly through the house and when I walk out of the kitchen, I realize that one of the three bodies on the couch is Abby. She's sitting in between Micah and James who are high fiving over her head as she laughs, holding up the Xbox controller like it's a trophy. It's almost comical to see her sandwiched between the two, who look like giants next to her small frame.

Micah catches sight of me and grins.

"Ryan's got some serious COD skills." He nods toward her, and I smirk at the girl who's now blowing on the controller like it's a smoking gun.

Her eyes are crinkled in a laugh as she smiles at me over her shoulder, and when her eyes slide away from mine, they widen slightly as my mom and sister step up beside me.

James and Micah are on their feet instantly, rounding the couch to come say hello. They haven't seen my mom since our last game before winter break, and since a lot of my teammates are from other states, my mom decided my freshman year to appoint herself the unofficial *Team Mom*. I think it was her way to make up for some of my teammates missing their own.

She hosts team dinners a few times a month just to make sure that the guys get a good home cooked meal instead of eating take out every night. Conveniently, Olivia is usually at volleyball practice while we're there, so I haven't had to worry about the freshmen getting any ideas.

Abby walks over behind them, tucking her hair behind her ear as she smiles up at me.

"Sorry I'm late," I say, taking in her dark jeans and off-white knit sweater. Her hair is down and falls to her chest, curling at the ends where the strands all soften into a lighter hue.

"It's okay." She shakes her head quickly, and her bright eyes flick to my mom and sister as a polite smile pulls at her lips.

"Oh, um—Abby, this is my mom, Dorothy, and my sister, Olivia," I say motioning toward each of them.

My mom's eyes light up at the introduction, and instead of taking Abby's outstretched hand, she pulls her into a hug. Abby's shoulders tense for a moment, but she relaxes quickly and squeezes my mom back. When she finally pulls away from my mom's embrace, she looks over her shoulder at me, and her toothy smile makes me grin.

"It's a pleasure to meet you, Mrs. Beck," she says, tucking the hair that escaped back behind her ear.

"Oh, honey, you can call me Dorothy," she corrects with a wave of her hand. My mom's eyes flick from Abby to me and back, and I can already see the gears in her head turning. I can tell that she's going to take this and run with it if I don't stomp it out immediately.

"Abby's my *lab partner*; she's going to write an article about me for a scholarship," I say flatly so they get the hint as Olivia pulls Abby in for a hug. My sister ignores my comment as she asks Abby where she got her sweater.

"An article?" Mom asks as her eyes grow wide again, as if it's the most impressive thing she's ever heard.

To be fair, it is pretty fucking impressive. I couldn't write an article to save my life—not a good one, at least.

She nods, and her eyes light up at my mom's obvious interest. "Yes, it's for USASN. I'm going to submit it for a scholarship contest."

"That's amazing, Abby," she gasps.

When she looks back at me with bright eyes, I already know she's planning on laminating the article and adding it to her collection that she started when my high school newspaper wrote an article on me for the first time. She nearly cried when I brought it home for her, and ever since, she's collected every single article written about me. She has them all safely tucked away in photo books in my old bedroom closet.

"If you need anything—baby pictures, old videos, old team rosters—anything at all, you let me know."

"This isn't that kind of article, Mom." I shake my head, looking at Abby for backup. I'm expecting her to agree with me and tell my mom that she just needs a few quotes for the article, but when she gives me a sheepish smile, my heart sinks in my chest.

"Well, actually—" She coughs and looks up at me nervously. "—I was thinking that maybe, if you're okay with it, I would write a feature article."

I stare at her as her words sink in.

A feature article. That's a hell of a lot more intense than a few quick quotes.

"What a great idea, Abby." My mom gasps, grabbing Abby's hands to pull her attention back to her. "I have bins full of pictures that you could use for it. I could probably try to find pictures of him from when he was a toddler on his first little league team. Oh, he was so precious; he had the cutest little cheeks and that dimple."

Micah and James take the baby picture talk as their cue to slip away, and I'm left watching as my mom delves into the story about how I peed myself during my first basketball game when I was three. Apparently, I got so nervous that I pissed myself, which is a story that seems to come up more than it really should.

Abby's laugh echoes through the room, and the throaty sound piques my attention. When she smiles at me over her shoulder, her cheeks glowing with that pretty, rosy color, the resolve in my body starts to reluctantly wither away.

It couldn't be that bad, could it?

"I can't wait to read the article. When will it be ready?" my mom asks.

"Well, we still need to do the interview," Abby says, looking over at me with a shameless smirk. "And I still need to convince him to let me *write* the feature article."

I raise a brow at her and watch as her plan perfectly unfolds right in front of my eyes.

"Oh, honey, you should let her write this article," my mom chirps. "It's for a scholarship."

Abby's smiling up at me, trying to look innocent, as if she didn't just purposely use my own mother against me.

"I don't know," I say, rubbing a rough hand through my hair.

"You can approve it before I submit it, and I'll take out anything you're not comfortable with," she offers quickly, looking up at me with pleading eyes.

"That seems fair." Olivia smiles at Abby.

I glance at my sister, raising my brows. *Et Tu, Brute?*

When I look back to Abby, she's watching me with furrowed brows, as if she's already preparing for me to say no.

Honestly, I would usually say no. I fucking hate interviews. The only reason I even agreed to this was because I figured she'd just need a few easy quotes to add in, but when I look back up at my mom, she nods at me with a look that I know is meant to say, *It's for a scholarship, Tristan, you shouldn't say no.*

I take a deep breath and shrug. "Yeah, that's fine, I guess."

Abby bites back a smile, and I watch the way her teeth sink into her bottom lip, pulling it into her mouth as her eyes brighten.

"Well, we should probably let you two get started then," Mom says, grabbing her keys out of her purse. She pulls me into a hug and presses a kiss to my cheek before turning to Abby.

"I look forward to reading your article, Abby." She pulls her into a hug, rubbing her back a few times before squeezing her tightly and letting her go. "And please reach out if you need anything at all."

"I will," she agrees as her lips pull back into a bright smile. "Thank you so much—for everything."

Abby looks over at me quickly and then back at my mom, and I know she knows that I only agreed to this feature because my mom was here. My mom seems to sense that, too, because nods back at her with a satisfied smile.

"You let me know if he's being difficult. I'll sort him right out for you."

"Alright, Mom. Thanks for that." I groan, opening the door for them. Liv grins up at me as she walks through, but it's my mom's pointed smile as she looks between Abby and I one last time before turning and walking out of the house that catches my attention. It's a smile that means she's going to ask about Abby and this damn article every time she calls me to check in.

I close the door behind them, inwardly groaning at the fact that I just committed myself to a full fucking feature article, and when I look down at Abby standing in the middle of the hall with an excited smile tugging at her lips, I run a hand through my hair quickly.

"So . . ." I sigh, watching her cheeks fill with that rosy color again. "Where we doing this, Ryan?"

———

I drop into my desk chair and watch as Abby settles onto the very edge of my bed. She looks around my room as she pulls her bag onto her lap and riffles through it, pulling out a notebook, a pen, and a voice recorder.

"Do you mind if I record this interview?" she asks, setting her bag onto the floor by her feet.

I shake my head and lean back into the chair, trying not to smirk.

I never would've imagined Abby Ryan in my bed, but I'm really starting to like the sight.

Pulling the notebook onto her lap, she flips it open to a page filled entirely with bullet points, which I can only assume are her questions listed out. She looks up at me and takes a deep breath, clicking the recorder on before setting it down between us on my nightstand.

"What has your experience been like playing for USW?" She reads off the first bullet point on her paper as she uncaps her pen.

"It's been great. I'm so grateful to be out on the court with players like Micah Costa, James Parsons, Nathan Emery, and Luke McConnell."

She doesn't look up at me as she writes on her notepad.

"How has your relationship with Coach Kennley changed since you met him?"

I relax into the chair a bit more.

"When I first met Coach, he was the most intimidating person I'd ever seen. I remember the first time I was late to practice he ran me until I thought I was going to puke. He didn't fuck around—" I look up at her, a little wide-eyed when I realize that I cursed. For some reason, it feels wrong when she's sitting there so professionally, as if we're in a media room interview rather than my bedroom. "—Sorry, he didn't mess around."

Her eyes raise up to mine and she smiles encouragingly, nodding her head for me to continue.

"Well, at first I was terrified of him." I laugh at the memory of Coach when I met him freshman year. He was more of a hard ass then, or he seemed it, at least. Maybe I've just gotten used to it. "But over the years, I've learned that he's hard on us because he really cares. He wants us to succeed, and the harder he pushes us, the more he gets out of us. He's a role model, a mentor, and a damn good coach."

She smiles down at her paper as she writes. A few strands of her hair have fallen from behind her ear, and the loose waves sway in front of her face as her hand slides easily across the page.

"What is the hardest part of playing a college sport?"

The answer spills out of my mouth quickly since this is one of the questions that every reporter seems to ask.

"Time management; you've got to be organized or you'll fall behind. Going from weight room workouts with the team at six in the morning to classes and then practice in the evening; there's always something that needs to be done. And if you fall behind, it's almost impossible to catch back up."

She smirks at the paper, and when her eyes flick up to mine, the playful set of her brow catches my attention. She slides the cap of her pen across her lips slowly before pointing it at me.

"Sounds to me like you plan out your day by the hour, Beck." She looks smug, and our conversation from the other day flashes in my mind. "Some might say that sounds like something a psychopath might do."

"Only if you write it down with sixteen different colored highlighters," I counter, watching her eyes narrow as her cheek twitches. When her eyes roll playfully, she looks back down to the paper.

"How do you handle the pressure of being one of college basketball's best players at the moment?"

I pause, and her eyes flick up to meet mine.

"I don't think I am," I admit. "I think I was lucky to be recruited onto a team with incredible talent. I think Micah Costa is one of the best defensemen I've ever played with—hell, the best defenseman in the entire league. I think Luke McConnell, while only a freshman, has better knowledge of the game and shooting skills than anyone else in the league right now. He's the person that I can look to, no matter what position we're in on that court, and trust that he'll be able to make that shot if I get him the ball. I think I have a lot of players helping me to be the best that I can be, so I can't take credit for something my entire team helps me to achieve."

She watches me as I talk, considering my words as her hands still on the paper.

"Are you nervous about the draft?" she asks. Her voice loses the professional emphasis and falls into a more conversational tone as she pulls her legs under her, settling into a more comfortable position on my bed.

I grab the tennis-ball-sized basketball from my desk and toss it between my hands. "Yeah," I admit, running my finger over the pebbled surface.

"Why?" She places the notebook onto the bed beside her.

"It's the NBA Draft." I laugh, keeping my eyes on the small basketball in my hands. "There's a lot to be nervous about."

"Not for you." She laughs as if my comment is ridiculous. "You're a top-three pick—top two, honestly. What could you possibly have to be worried about?"

"That." I motion toward her. "People assuming that I'm worth a top pick."

She stays quiet for a beat, and I glance up from the ball in my hands to see her studying me.

"You don't think you are?"

I hesitate as I consider that, but before I can answer, we both jump at the soft knock on my door. When it cracks open slightly, Jackie's head peers around the door into my room. She opens it a little more when she catches sight of Abby on my bed.

Fuck.

Jackie messaged me last night on Instagram asking if I was free to hang out today. I thought I'd be done with the interview in time, but glancing down at my phone, I now realize that my timing was way off.

"Hey, Jackie—uh, this is Abby." I motion toward the girl sitting on my bed, who now looks uncomfortable as she meets the curious gaze of the girl standing by my door.

"I'm sorry, I didn't mean to interrupt you . . ." she trails off as her eyes rake down Abby's body, inconspicuously checking for any signs that her clothes were just off.

"Oh, it's okay," Abby supplies quickly, grabbing for the tape recorder and her bag. "I was just interviewing him for an article, but I can finish up another time if you have plans."

"Are you sure?" I ask, standing up as I run an awkward hand through my hair. "I can reschedule our—" I don't know exactly what to call whatever it is that Jackie is here for without coming off as a complete asshole, so I just gesture to Jackie.

"Yeah, it's not a problem. If you have a date, I could just—"

"It's not a date," I correct. More like a pre-planned fuck.

Jackie's cheeks turn a deep red and her eyes find the textbook on the dresser by the door. I can already tell where her mind is taking her, but I can't stop her before she speaks.

"We have a big chemistry test coming up, so I came over to study," she says quickly.

Abby looks at the textbook, and then back up to the girl. When her eyes widen slightly, I can tell that she's starting to figure out what's happening.

"You're in Fundamentals of Chemistry?" she asks, confirming Jackie's lie.

"Yeah, we've got it together. Right, Beck?" She smiles up at me, completely unaware that her lie is blowing up in her face.

"Mhm." I try to hold back the laugh, but it comes out as a sort of strangled cough.

Abby nods and bites the inside of her cheek, holding back her own laugh.

"Okay. Well, have fun studying." She slips past Jackie toward the door.

"Should we reschedule to finish the interview?" I ask, trying to stay focused, but the flash of lace that I see under Jackie's buttoned-up jacket has my mind pulling me into another direction.

"Sure," she says, smirking at me. "I'll text you to figure out a new time."

Turning to Jackie, she smiles. "It was nice to meet you, Jackie. I'm sure I'll see you on Monday in class." She taps the chemistry textbook as she turns on her heel and walks out of the room, leaving me to watch the color drain from Jackie's face as she looks up at me with wide eyes.

I see the exact moment it clicks in her head.

"She's in your chemistry class, isn't she?"

EIGHT

ABBY

"Take your fifteen now, Abby, before the game starts and we get slammed."

I look up from the stack of receipts to see Nancy, the diner's owner, shooing me away as she takes my place in front of the register, plucking the receipts out of my hand.

I glance over my shoulder at the large display clock centered below the sign flashing *Over Easy* in neon red lights. I've been here for five hours already, waiting tables, ringing in orders, mopping up spilled milkshakes, and even hopping in to do dishes since Melvin, our usual dishwasher and busboy, called in sick five minutes before his shift.

I usually don't mind picking up the extra work, but Fridays are always our busiest day, and paired with the basketball game tonight, we're about to get absolutely slammed when the remaining part of the student population who isn't at the game inevitably floods into the diner. Especially because O'Malley's bar is already overflowing with people just down the street and there aren't many other options around here unless they're willing to drive to get to the nearest city. By the look of the snowfall outside, I can't imagine many people are going to opt to drive farther than necessary when we're going to have the game broadcasted on all five of our huge flat screens.

I pull my phone from the back pocket of my jeans as I walk into the empty ladies room, swiping through the junk emails and social media notifications until I finally click on the text Nia sent to our roommate group chat. A picture of basketball players scattered across the court quickly loads and I immediately recognize Tristan mid-shot, his arms on full display in his jersey. I click out of the picture, and her message pulls a breathy laugh out of me.

NIA: *Yesss, this is what I came for, hot, sweaty boys.*

I bite the inside of my lip as my fingers tap out my response.

ME: *Don't drool too much, babe. Have fun!*

NIA: *If anyone's drooling, it's Jenny, she's been eye-fucking James Parsons since we sat down.*

JENNY: *I HAVE NOT.*

NIA: *I'm sitting right here, sis, do you think I'm blind?*

I slip my phone back into my pocket and slide into a stall, reveling in the first bathroom break I've been able to take since getting here. The sound of the toilet flushing echoes around the quiet room as I button my pants back up, but before I can open the door of the stall, the bathroom door swings open and the two girls who walk in don't break conversation as they stop in front of the mirror.

I freeze when I recognize the voice.

Jackie, Beck's study date from earlier, is standing on the other side of the stall.

"I don't know, he just said he needed to get ready for the game." I can practically feel the pissed-off energy radiating through the bathroom.

"Was this pre or post hookup?" The second girl asks as she turns on the faucet.

"There was no hookup," Jackie snaps.

"Nothing?" The second girl sounds confused as the sound of the soap dispenser being pressed a few times echoes around us. I try to peek through the small crack in the stall but abort mission at the thought of Jackie somehow seeing me.

"We made out for like two minutes. I mean, he was feeling me up at first, but then I took off my jacket, and I was wearing that new Victoria Secret lingerie set I bought over break, you know, the hot pink one I showed you? Well, I was wearing that, and I could tell he liked it, but when we were making out, he wasn't even trying to undress me, so I started to do it myself."

"Guys love that." The second girl nods as she pulls out way more paper towels than necessary from the dispenser on the wall.

"Yeah, but when I reached back to unclip my bra, he shot me down instantly. He said something about *"needing to get ready for the game"* and then walked over to the door and waited for me to get dressed."

Ouch.

There's a bitterness in her voice, and a part of me feels bad for the girl, but another much larger part of me feels a little smug that the girl who cut my interview short at least didn't get the hook up she so desperately wanted.

"Do you think it was because of that girl? The one that was there when you got there?" The second girl gasps conspiratorially and I stop breathing, as if the sound alone will give away my identity.

Jackie's silent for a moment as she considers that possibility and then snorts loudly. "No, definitely not." The laugh that echoes through the bathroom is like a knife to my self-confidence. "She wasn't that cute. She was wearing this god-awful sweater and just seemed so . . ." She trails off, and I suddenly feel like melting on the spot as the white-hot flood of embarrassment washes over me. ". . . So prudish. Definitely not Beck's type. It's a shame, too. The poor girl looked so uptight; she could probably use a good fuck." She turns around and starts toward the door, her friend following close behind her, but even after the restroom door clicks shut, I stay frozen in place as I consider her words.

Is that really how I look to people? Like *an uptight prude who could probably use a good fuck?* The look on Nia and Jenny's faces when they realized I've never actually had an orgasm flashes in my mind again and my stomach turns.

Maybe that is what I look like.

I step out of the stall and examine my face as I lather my hands in soap and run them under the faucet, searching for something about me that stands out as prudish. My sweater is a crew neck, but it's snowing outside, so I don't know exactly how much skin she expects me to be showing off right now.

I turn off the water and pull out an appropriate amount of paper towels to dry my hands, biting down on the inside of my lip as I toss the crumpled ball into the trash, trying not to focus on the part that hurt the most.

Definitely not Beck's type.

By the time I shake off the bathroom incident and step out of the ladies room, my break is over, which I don't mind, because if anything, I need the distraction to keep me from simmering over Jackie's comments.

Glancing around, I spot her sitting in a booth with her back turned to me, and I relax at the realization that she's not in my section.

"You've got a new twelve top in your section," Nancy says as I walk behind the bar top and tie my apron around my waist, fingering through the front pocket to double check that my order pad, pens, and straws all are in place.

"The game's about to start. Godspeed." She winks and pats me on the shoulder as I walk past, saluting her as I head toward my section of tables.

The diner's overflowing with students by half-time.

All the tables, booths, and bar top seating are taken, and crowds of students looking to escape the snow outside have congregated in all the open spots around the diner, which makes carrying out trays of food a lot more difficult.

After checking in on all of my tables and booths, I head back to the bar top where at least six new people are sitting in my section. I go down the line of people quickly, grabbing drink orders and explaining any questions about the menu until I'm fully caught up.

"I just had two new twelve tops walk in, could you help me with my bar top section?" Josie asks, readjusting her apron as she fills the two pitchers in her hands with ice water. I glance down the bar top to her section to see three people examining menus and two more down the bar with empty cups.

"Yeah, of course, Jo," I nod, stepping back against the wall so she can pass by.

"Tips are yours. Thank you so much, Abs," she calls over her shoulder as she just nearly misses getting toppled over by a drunk guy looking for the bathroom. When she looks over her shoulder at me with wide eyes and a dropped jaw that I know is meant to say, *Oh, my God, I almost just died*, I can't help the laugh that slips out of my mouth. She turns back around and slowly edges her way past a group of guys standing by the TV. None of them seem to notice her pass by since their heads are all tilted back, fully focused on the sports reporters discussing the first half.

I can hear the reporters arguing back and forth as I grab six glasses from the shelf and start pouring the drink orders from the soda fountain, taking more time than necessary when Tristan's name catches my attention.

"He's secured a double-double before the second half's even started. This is one of the best performances we've seen from Tristan Beck this year." The deep voice of the analyst is barely audible over the roar of conversation in the diner. "He's got a real hot hand tonight, and if he keeps making those kinds of shots, he's well on his way to breaking the record for most threes in a game."

I glance over my shoulder to the TV to see a play from the first half on the screen. The clip is slowed down, and the camera is zoomed in on Tristan as he fakes out his defender and steps back, well past the three-point line, and releases the ball. It falls into the basket without touching the rim and the crowd in the stadium jumps to their feet before the clip is cut and the reporters are back in shot.

I turn back to the soda fountain and scoop ice into another cup before filling it with Diet Coke.

"He's having a hell of a game, Greg, and I'd be willing to bet there are at least five scouts here tonight," a much lighter voice says. "If the rest of his season continues like this, he's going to secure that first draft pick."

I look over my shoulder and watch another slow-motion clip of Tristan shooting the ball on the screen, but when someone clears their throat across the bar top, I look over to see a guy eyeing his newly re-filled cup sitting in front of me pointedly. I give him a sheepish smile as I place his drink in front of him before I stack the rest of the cups on a tray and deliver them down the line of the bar, taking food orders, grabbing more refills, and checking on customers as I go.

The game is a blow-out.

USW was up by almost thirty for most of the second half, and by the end of the game, most of the customers had already cleared out, leaving a mess of dishes, spilled food, and trash littering the floor.

Only a few stragglers are left, opting to not join the rest of the students on their way to whatever frat houses are hosting the after-parties tonight.

"That was insane." Josie sighs, sweeping under the table closest to me as I input the tips into the register. She's so short the industrial sized broom is almost as tall as her.

Lacie sprays down the table next to her and shakes her head, push-ing back the few red curls that escaped from her bun as she groans. "We need a *no drunks* rule. Everyone gets sloshed at O'Malley's and then comes here for food after half-time. Two different guys almost puked on me while ordering."

The other two waitresses on staff tonight, Maria and Chloe, are bus-sing the tables on the other end of the diner. I catch Chloe tossing a napkin at Maria's head, her laugh echoing through the now nearly empty diner as Maria picks up a fry from the booth and throws it back. At least we can have fun after getting wrecked like that, otherwise, we'd all go crazy.

"On the bright side, we made good tips," I say, grinning as I wave the thick stack of receipts in my hand. I've only input a third of them so far and it's already totaled more than a hundred and fifty dollars—*each*.

We usually don't make that much unless there's a big game like this, so as terrible as it is to have to work in the madness, it's worth it to walk out with two hundred dollars cash stashed in your pocket.

Josie and Lacie both turn when the bell on the front door echoes through the mostly empty diner, but they both look relieved when only one guy walks in. He's taking off his beanie and scarf as he walks straight towards the bar top and drops onto a stool a few down from the register.

When I place the menu in front of him, he looks up and grins. His dark blue eyes consider me for a moment, and my cheeks burn slightly when he smiles. "Did I miss something?" He laughs, nodding toward the piles of mess on the floor that Josie's trying to sweep into the dustpan.

"I take it you're not a basketball fan?" I laugh, pulling my order pad out of my apron. He shakes his head, eyes coasting down my body and then back up to meet my gaze again.

"Not really, I'm more of a football fan." He smirks and looks down at the menu. There's a faint southern accent in his voice, the kind that only comes out with certain words.

"Can I get you a drink?" I ask, grabbing for a glass under the counter.

"Coke, please."

I fill his cup and place it in front of him.

His short blond hair is damp from the snow and is matted in the back from his beanie, which is now sitting on the stool next to him on top of his coat and backpack.

"You look familiar," he says, looking down to the name tag on my chest.

"I go to USW," I say, tucking my hair behind my ear.

"Abby," he reads aloud, and after a moment of silence, his eyes flick back to mine, widening, as if he's suddenly remembered something. "You're Nia's friend, right?"

"Yeah." I look down at my order pad, trying to recall where he might know me from.

"We met at that sorority thing last year, remember? When Nia threw up on my friend, Steve. I'm Dean."

The comment sparks the blurry memory of that night. Nia and Jenny brought me to a sorority party with them and Nia introduced us to her friend, Steve, and his roommate, Dean, before she ditched us to go take shots. We talked to Dean for a few minutes before Nia reappeared and dragged us out of the house. Apparently, she accidentally threw up all over Steve and needed to make a quick getaway. To be honest, I had completely forgotten all about Dean, until now.

"Yeah, that was really gross." I wince and shake my head at the memory of Nia drunkenly pulling us down the street to the next frat house. "I'm sorry about that," I add.

He shrugs and smiles. "Hey, it wasn't me."

"Abs, you're good to go, babe. I'll cover your tables." I look over my shoulder to see Lacie wiping her hands on her apron as she walks behind the bar top.

Glancing at the clock, I'm shocked to see it read five after ten. My shift ended five minutes ago.

"My shift is over, but it was nice to see you again, Dean." I smile before bending down to grab my purse from the locked cabinet under the register.

"Abby," he calls quickly, just as I'm about to turn.

He looks down at his menu for a moment, blinking a few times before looking back up. "Could I get your number?"

My eyes widen and I glance over at Lacie and Josie who are both grinning at each other as they continue to work around us, pretending like they're not listening to our conversation.

I look back to Dean, whose cheeks are a little pinker than before. A wave of excitement rushes through me and I bite down on my lip as I nod, hoping that my cheeks aren't burning too bright as I grab for a napkin and pen and write out my number.

When I hand it to him, he grins and tucks it into his pocket. "Thank you."

"You're welcome." I grin back.

Turning back toward the door again, I catch the smirks on Josie and Lacie's faces as I wave goodnight. I try to keep a casual pace as I hurry out of the diner and into the snowy parking lot, but by the time I close my car door and crank up the heating in my Jetta, I'm already three rings deep into calling Nia.

NINE

The next week flashes by in a blur of snow and coursework.

A snowstorm hit this weekend, which I took full advantage of by bundling up in my favorite pajamas while camping out on the living room couch next to the fireplace to stay warm. With a hot chocolate in my hands and my planner laid out in front of me, I systematically checked off everything on my to-do list, starting with all of my assigned reading, then my homework, and then finally, both essays for my Writing for Publication class.

After Nia, Jenny, and I cleaned the entire apartment while blasting our favorite early 2000s hits playlist—shout out to Britney and Christina for turning mopping into a full-on concert—I started the outline for my USASN article.

I've had a pretty good idea of where I wanted the article to go since Beck agreed to let me write it. I want to break it down into three sections—past, present, and future. I'm hoping that structure will allow me to introduce him to the reader, and get them to care about him and his journey as an athlete, so that when I end on the future section, they'll not only want to know where he's going from here, but hopefully, they'll also want to keep up with him afterwards.

That's the effect of a good feature—turning curious readers into new fans. And since I know this whole interview process is the last thing Tristan Beck wants to be doing, I want to make sure it's worth his while. I want to make sure I do it justice. Which is exactly why I spent the entire rest of the weekend typing away on my laptop, drafting up as many questions as I could for the article, making sure to touch on subjects that I knew would help personalize the player behind the jersey.

The snow didn't ease when classes resumed again on Monday,

and while Tristan still kept me entertained—and to be honest, completely distracted—during chemistry, I tried my hardest to ignore his jokes and the ridiculous notes he would always pass me. They were usually terrible drawings of the molecules we were learning about, personified to have arms and legs and faces, and almost always had a speech bubble with a corny chemistry joke.

I'd gotten so used to his antics, that when I went to class this morning and he wasn't there, I could actually feel his absence. While it wasn't great for my entertainment, it did wonders for my attention span. I was actually able to get through the entire lecture without missing huge chunks of information. For once, I wasn't too busy drawing my own personified molecules on his notebook paper or elbowing him in the side when he would make a soft, barely audible snoring noises in my ear as he pretended to fall asleep.

After my final class ended, I spent a few hours in the newspaper room making the final touches on the article I wrote on the two freshmen pre-med students who created a fundraiser to offer free women's health screenings at the student health center on campus. After picking through it with a fine-tooth comb—or rather, a red ballpoint pen in this case—I turned the final draft into the submission box on the editor-in-chief's desk and headed home to study for the Writing for Publication test I have on Monday.

I somehow have to memorize all the listed articles, publishers, and authors, along with the publication dates for extra credit. Now, two hours later, I'm sitting on my bedroom floor surrounded by different colored flashcards as I try to organize them into *definitely know*, *kind of know*, and *don't know at all* piles.

When the knock on my bedroom door sounds, I don't look up from the cards as I call for them to come in. The door opens and a quick glance at the fuzzy black slippers tells me it's Nia who's standing in the doorway.

"What the hell is going on in here? Are you studying or performing a seance?" She blanches, taking in the flashcards surrounding me on the floor as she leans against my door frame. I finally look up at her, amused by her dramatics.

"I've got a test on Monday." I shrug and pick up the green card closest to my toe and sort it into the *kind of know* pile.

"Okay, let's put all of this—" She motions to the explosion of flashcards surrounding me, "—on hold for tonight, because you're coming out to O'Malley's with me and Jen."

"Nia," I groan, shaking my head. "I have to study. This test is worth a quarter of my grade. Plus, I have another essay to write, and I really should do some laundry because I've been putting it off since last weekend." I motion toward the explosion of cards around me and then to the overflowing laundry basket near my closet.

"You have until Monday to do all of that, Abs. You need to go out and have some fun. You've been staring at your phone all week like a sad puppy."

She's not wrong, but I still glare at her for saying it out loud.

Dean never texted me. And it sucks. It's not that I care that *Dean* hasn't texted me, I've barely spoken to the guy, it's more about the fact that an attractive guy even showed interest in me at all, got my hopes up, and then completely forgot about me. It also doesn't help that Jackie's comments keep replaying in my head.

"Come on, Abs, please don't make me beg," she pleads, jutting her lower lip out and scrunching her brows in a dramatic pout. "I need a night out after the calculus test I took today, and you need to relax because this . . ." she motions towards the flashcards with a serious look on her face, "is not normal. Not for a Friday night, at least."

I look down at the cards surrounding me on the floor and bite the inside of my cheek, trying to rationalize whether or not I have time to go sit out at the sports bar until three in the morning. When I realize that I'm trying to see if I have enough time to schedule *fun* into my calendar, I nod, pushing all thoughts of schedules and to-do lists from my head.

"Alright." I sigh, taking extra care not to jostle the piles of cards as I get up. "I'll go, but I'm not taking straight shots. The last time I drank tequila, I could barely get out of bed the next day."

Nia's right. I need to get out, and have fun, and take a step back from my planner. And really, what's the worst that could happen? It's one night.

Nia eyes my polka dotted pajama pants with a smile.

"Great, I have the perfect outfit for you."

———

O'Malley's is packed, as always.

It's the only sports bar near campus, and thanks to their three-dollar beer specials and free chips and salsa, it's been our go-to bar since freshman year. Nia has my hand clutched in hers as she weaves us through the crowd, making a beeline for the bar. I keep my eyes down as we pass through the crowd, making sure not to step on anyone's feet with the insane heels that she talked me into wearing.

They're cute, and they go perfectly with the short, leather, high-waisted skirt and lacy top that looks more like lingerie to me than a blouse, but apparently, according to Nia, it counts. I wanted to hand it back to her and look for something a little less revealing, but the rush of satisfaction that flooded my veins when I put it on and looked in the mirror was too much to deny. Because I knew, looking at my reflection in the mirror, that this was definitely not a shirt an uptight prude would wear.

Now, as the eyes of all the guys around me all zero in on my chest as I walk by, I'm starting to regret that stubborn streak.

"Do you want a vodka cranberry?" Nia asks us when we finally reach the bar. I nod, pulling out my phone from my purse. The last fledgling of hope that Dean would text me expires when my empty screen shines back at me.

"Stop checking your phone, Abby," Nia chides, slapping my wrist. "We're here to have fun, get drunk, and not think about the asshole guys who don't text us." She grabs the drinks from the bartender with a bright smile and slides over her card.

I want to roll my eyes at that. I'd be willing to bet Nia has never been forgotten by a guy before.

"We'll start a tab. Their drinks are on me," she says to the bartender who nods and walks toward the register with her card in hand.

I've always been a little envious of her little black card. Nia's family has money—the kind of money that spends holidays in the south of France and has credit cards with no limits—which is why I usually don't object to her picking up my tab whenever she pulls me along for a night out.

When the bartender brings her card back, she motions for Jenny and me to follow her toward the end of the bar where three seats are open and away from the crowd of people waiting to order.

"I can't believe you actually came with us," she yells over the music. "You look fantastic tonight."

"You really do," Jenny adds with an encouraging smile.

"Thanks." I laugh, adjusting my skirt as I cross my leg over the other on my stool. I glance down at my outfit as I take another long sip of my drink. My boobs are honestly on another level right now. I've never looked so . . . uncovered before. But somehow, sitting here in the middle of O'Malley's, with the curious gazes of the male passersby, I feel kind of free because of it.

It's a far jump from my usual sweater and jeans, but after Nia gave me the "*It doesn't matter that it's snowing, we're going to look good tonight*" speech, I rallied up the determination to step outside of my comfort zone and try something new. I feel good, comfortable from the combination of the bar heating and the buzz that's starting to warm me from the inside, but I still have to will myself not to think about the fact that if I went outside right now, there's a good possibility I'd freeze to death.

"You look better in that outfit than I do. I never had the boobs to fill it out." She smirks as I down my drink, and I nod when the bartender asks if I want another. Hell, if I'm already at a bar half naked, I might as well commit and get drunk.

"Nia?" We both turn to see an incredibly tall guy walking toward us. He looks vaguely familiar, but I can't place where I might have seen him. Nia reaches out and pulls him into a hug, and I don't miss the way his hands linger around her waist when she pulls back, as if she's familiar to him.

"You know Abby Ryan, right?" She gestures toward me. "Abby, this is Nathan Emery, he's on the basketball team with Beck."

His red hair is so dark it fades into brown at the roots and the dark stubble along his jaw is a stark contrast against his piercing blue eyes. He raises his brows as his eyes flick down my body before meeting mine again.

"You know Beck?" he asks, leaning forward to be heard over the music.

"She's writing an article on him," Nia says, nodding excitedly at Nate's impressed expression. "She's amazing, I know." She grins, squeezing my hand.

"It's not that impressive." I shake my head and take another long sip of my drink when I realize neither of them are paying attention to me anymore.

"Do you want to dance?" He leans in to yell over the music that's pulsating through the bar.

Nia's eyes flick from mine to Jenny's in question. Jenny just shrugs noncommittally with a smile as she brings her drink up to her lips, happy just to be here, and when Nia's eyes meet mine again, she raises a brow, making sure I don't mind her leaving the group for a little while.

"Go ahead." I nod encouragingly, practically shooing her away. "Jen and I will be here getting drunk on your tab." I smirk, taking another sip of the new drink the bartender brought me as Jenny leans over the bar to grab a stack of napkins. She's already spilled on herself.

Nia grins and kisses my cheek before hopping off the stool and following Nathan through the crowd toward the dance floor.

"James is here," Jenny gasps, craning her head to look over the crowd of people in the middle of the dance floor. "I should go tell him how good he was in the game last week, right?" She sticks her straw into her mouth and downs the liquid until the harsh sucking sound makes her crinkle her nose.

"Yes, you definitely should." I grin.

"Are you sure? I don't want to leave you here alone. Do you want to come with me?"

"No, I'm fine here. I'll just eat some chips and hang out." I pick up a chip from the basket in front of me and take a bite, but when she raises an unconvinced brow and settles back into the chair, I know she doesn't want to leave me by myself.

I would usually appreciate that, but when her eyes flick back over to the back of the bar where I assume James is, I shake my head and motion for her to go ahead. Ever since the formal, I've found myself rooting for the Jenny and James train to finally take off. He likes her, she likes him, only she's too stubborn to actually admit it to him. She's been playing hard to get for a while, probably because up until recently, James was as notorious of a playboy as his best friend.

"I promise I'll be fine here. Go have fun, Jenny."

She considers me for a second, as if trying to figure out if I'm going to be okay by myself, and when she smiles and pushes the newly filled salsa bowl across the bar to me, along with a little stack of napkins, she grins at me as she slides off of her stool. Weaving past the small group standing behind us, she disappears into the crowd.

I turn back to the bar and take another sip of my drink, and then another, until my second drink is done and I'm motioning for a third.

Sitting alone at the bar isn't as bad as it sounds, especially because as a people watcher, it gives me the perfect vantage point to scan the crowd. Just as I find a short guy with a man bun doing some kind of robot dance in the middle of the dance floor, my drink spills onto my bare legs as someone knocks into my back.

"Oh, shit—sorry."

I turn quickly to see familiar emerald eyes staring back into mine, and I watch them widen as his gaze rakes down my body. By the look of complete shock on his face, you'd think I was sitting here completely naked.

"Abby?" he asks incredulously. I can smell the beer practically aerating off of him, and when his eyes finally flick up from my chest to meet mine again, they're glossy. He's definitely a little drunk right now.

"Hey, Beck." I laugh, reaching for a napkin to wipe off the vodka that's now trailing down my bare legs. He watches as I blot up the liquid before bunching up the napkin and placing it on the bar. "I thought you were sick," I say.

He scrunches his brows and leans in close, and I repeat myself louder this time.

"Sick? No." He nods toward the bartender and places his empty beer bottle onto the bar top, taking the new one that he slides over to him.

"You weren't in class, so I just assumed." I shrug, taking another sip of my drink as I admire the way his black t-shirt hugs his shoulders and arms. He's usually in hoodies in class, so when I catch the sleeve of ink trailing up his right arm, it takes me a few seconds to tear my eyes away from the swirls and hard lines of the black ink etched there. I haven't seen him in a short sleeve up close before, but I could see the outline of it from the TV last night.

"I was meeting with Coach," he explains, taking a step closer to me when a pair of guys step up behind him and motion for the bartender's attention. "How's the article going?"

"Good. Really good. I have it all outlined and ready to go."

"When's our next interview?" He grins, taking another sip of his drink.

"Friday?" I ask, watching as he leans into the bar and nods. "Same time?" I confirm.

He shakes his head. "I can't do the morning this week, we have a team meeting. What about after the game?"

"I have work until ten." I shake my head.

"Perfect. Come over after."

I raise a brow and laugh. "That's a bit late, don't you think?"

"Ten? Not really."

I look down at my hands for a second and then nod. "Okay. Friday at ten."

"Perfect." He takes another long pull of his beer. "I should get back before they think I've bailed on them." He nods to the back of the bar.

"By them do you mean Jackie?" It slips out before I can stop it, and when I look up to see him raise his brows slightly, my cheeks start to burn.

"I don't typically bring my study buddies out to the bar with me, Ryan." He smirks.

"I think you and I have different ideas of what it means to be study buddies," I chide.

"We could become study buddies and find out." He raises his eyebrows suggestively.

"Beck, what's the hold-up?" A guy about the same height as Tristan walks toward us, and when he steps into the better lighting near the bar, I recognize him as one of Tristan's roommates who I played video games with the other day. He's covered in tattoos, two full length sleeves of ink are etched on his arms, and when he looks over at me, I see the recognition hit him instantly as his lips quirk up.

"Hey, Ryan." He nods toward me and then looks back to Tristan with raised brows. "You're up for beer pong."

"Do you want to come hang out?" Beck asks, motioning toward the back of the bar where a ping-pong table is set up, and what appears to be the entire basketball team surrounding it.

"I—no, thanks. I think I'm fine here." I shake my head and sit back on my stool.

He slides off his own stool and takes another sip of his beer, watching me before narrowing his eyes playfully. "You'd rather sit here by yourself and eat stale chips and salsa instead of hanging out with me? I'm a little offended, Ryan."

I'm about to make a joke about how the stale chips still make for better company, but the small voice in the back of my head echoes, much louder than before.

Such a prude.

I look down to the half empty glass of vodka cranberry in my hand for a second before bringing it up to my lips and downing the rest of it. I lick away the errant liquid from my lips as I place the empty glass onto the bar top and slide off of my stool, reveling in the surprised look on his face as he grins down at me. Placing his hand on the small of my back, he leads us through the crowd toward the ping-pong table.

TEN

ABBY

"Do you want to play?"

A loud roar of the surrounding crowd makes me jump, and I realize that the current game just ended as the short guy with the man bun that I saw earlier on the dance floor downs his cup of beer. He holds up his middle finger at the players across the table while they chant along with the rest of the crowd for him to chug.

"I shouldn't. I don't know how to play; I would be really, really bad," I warn, taking a step back so a few people can pass by me.

When James walks up to the table and sets up new cups, pouring beer into each one, Tristan claims the other side.

"Even better, we'll finally have an even match for James," Tristan teases, raising his voice loud enough so the man in question could hear him over the pounding of the music. James doesn't look up from pouring the frothy liquid; he just shakes his head with a smirk.

"I'll play if you do, Abs," Jenny says, stepping up to the table. Her long hair has been pulled back into a ponytail since I saw her last, and her cheeks look rosy as she steps into the light. She must be a few drinks deep to get that kind of glow.

I bite the inside of my cheek and look at her, contemplating how embarrassing this is going to be. I almost step back and decline, but when I look back up to Tristan, he nods his head to the table, motioning for me to come stand next to him.

"Come on, Ryan." He grins. "Live a little."

I raise a brow at him before looking back over at the table. "Alright, fine. How does it work?" I ask, stepping up to our side of the table. He grins and begins to set up our cups, pouring and arranging them into a triangle as he explains the game.

"The objective is simple. Get this little ball into any of their cups.

If we make it, they drink. If they make it, we drink. Usually, we have a *whoever misses it, drinks it* rule, but to make it fair, we'll just split it evenly." Tristan plucks the ball from the table and tosses it into the air a few times, catching it easily.

Across the table James points to the cups and says something to Jenny, who looks like she's genuinely trying to focus, but her eyes keep flicking down to his lips and I can only imagine what she's thinking about. Tristan calls out something I don't understand and releases the ball into the air. As it flies across the table and lands in the cup in the dead center of the triangle, I realize he was calling out the cup he was aiming for—and he made it.

My face pales. Is this the level that he thinks I'm going to be able to play at? If so, he's going to regret partnering up with me.

He grins down at me and extends his hand in a low-five, and I slap it just as James sinks a shot into his own previously called cup.

"I'll take this one," he says, drowning the cup quickly and putting it aside. As he hands me the now wet ball, I shake it a little and a few droplets soak through my lace top. I have a feeling I'm going to smell like beer by the time I get home, but with all of the other smells circulating the bar, beer is the least of my worries.

A small crowd of people have taken an interest in the game, appearing confused as they look between us, and I try not to think about how mismatched Tristan and I must seem to them. I lock my eyes on one of the cups in the middle of the cluster and bite down on the inside of my cheek as I release the ball into the air. I watch as it arches down toward the formation of cups and bounces off the rim of one, it falters for a second before finally falling into another.

It wasn't even close to the one I was aiming for, but I throw my hands up in shocked celebration and turn to Beck to see his brows raised in surprise.

"Damn, Ryan, are you sure you've never played this before?" He elbows my ribs lightly as we both watch Jenny chug the cup of beer, her nose wrinkles in disgust as she hands the empty cup to James.

"I guess you can add beer pong champ to that list of secret talents," I quip, grinning at the amused look on his face.

I try to pay attention to Jenny as she narrows her eyes on our own triangle of cups and releases the ball, but the tingling traveling up my arm as he brushes against me makes it difficult to think of anything other than how warm he is, and how he smells like the most intoxicating mixture of woodsy spiced cologne and beer.

By the end of the third game, I am very drunk. I only planned on playing one game, but James demanded a rematch, and when that one ended in a near tie, Jenny, of all people, demanded another one. She missed the first two shots but was on a scoring streak by the end, which seemed to give her a bit of false confidence because she only made one shot the last game. Not far off from my two shots, but thanks to Tristan, we ended up on top.

To be fair, it was really a game between Tristan and James the entire time. Jenny and I only dragged them down, but it was kind of amazing to watch the shots they were able to make, especially considering how drunk they were. Though they'd made significantly less impressive shots with each cup they drank.

"Woooo!" I throw my hands into the air as Tristan's final shot lands perfectly in the cup, winning us the third game. The buzz of the vodka cranberries and beer courses through my blood, making my movements slow and heavy, and my voice much louder than I mean for it to be. I turn to Tristan, whose cheeks are now a golden, rosy hue. His eyes are slightly glassy, but wide with excitement as I hold out my hands above my head for a double high five, which he slaps with poor accuracy.

"I don't think I could make another shot if I tried; I'm starting to see double," I laugh.

He nods in agreement and steps back, motioning for the next team to take our place. As I take a step away from the table, I have to grab onto his arm when the room suddenly doesn't feel so stable, but after planting my feet firmly on the ground as I try to stop my vision from spinning, I'm able to find my equilibrium again. He grabs my elbow and watches me until my vision focuses and I nod my head with a lazy smile.

"All good," I say, taking a step forward.

He considers me for a moment before nodding toward the bar. "I think we should get you some water."

"Water sounds nice," I agree.

Honestly, anything would be good to help wash away the gross aftertaste of the cheap beer on my tongue. I follow him as he easily parts the crowd, marveling at the fact that he doesn't have to ease his way through like I do. He doesn't have to navigate it like a maze or keep his eyes on the ground to make sure people don't step on his feet, and he doesn't have to worry about someone knocking him over because as he walks through the crowd, everyone sort of parts for him. I don't know whether it's because he's six-five, and easily taller than anyone else around him, or because he's Tristan Beck, USW superstar, but either way I don't care because not having to push and ease my way through people is a nice change.

I grab onto the bar top to steady myself and he peers down at me.

"You okay?" he teases. I faintly smell his cologne again and the scent relaxes me as I nod up at him. His eyes trail down my body, but they flick back up quickly when he realizes he's been caught.

"I'm good." I grin as I look from the dark jeans up to the t-shirt that hugs his shoulders and arms snuggly. He really should wear short sleeves more often. My eyes catch on the trail of ink climbing up his arm and I'm tempted to lean in and examine it more, to see what each tattoo actually is, but his words pull me away before I can.

"Are you checking me out, Ryan?"

I look back up to see him smirking down at me.

"Are you checking *me* out?" I counter lamely.

His smirk deepens and the dimple in his cheek appears. He steps closer and leans down slightly so I can hear him over the music. "When you're dressed like this, it's hard not to."

I swallow hard as I breathe in his cologne, trying to ignore the way it warms me, even more than the alcohol drowning my blood right now. I climb onto the stool next to me, but when my foot slips and I reach out for the bar top, his hand reaches out to steady me. His hand grips my waist, and I can feel the warmth of him through the thin, lacy material. My breathe catches in my throat as I look up at him, and when he pulls his hand away, my gaze dips down to his lips again. His eyes flick down my body again, and I take a deep breath, imagining what his hands would really feel like on my body.

The bartender places two ice waters in front of us, and the sound of the glass sliding across the bar top pulls me from my quickly spiraling thoughts. I turn on my stool, cheeks burning, and take a few slow sips of the water, trying to ignore the voice in my head repeating Jenny's comment from a few nights ago. *Who better to fuck around with than Beck?*

I meet his gaze as I imagine his hands on me again. "I think I need to pee."

He nods and points toward the bathroom, but the crowd of people surrounding the bar blocks my view. "I don't see it."

"Here, follow me." He grabs my hand and helps me off my stool, leading me through the crowd. When we get to the single room bathroom with the ladies sign plastered on the door, I thank him before pushing it open.

It's a tiny room with a toilet and a dirty mirror and I look back at him before closing the door, noting that he's leaning against the opposite wall of the hallway, apparently not trusting that I'll find my way back on my own.

I'm not going to pee; I don't want to *break the seal* as Nia always says, but I do need to wash the sticky aftermath of the beer off of my hands.

I step up to the sink and flick on the faucet, letting the hot water run over my hands. It's soothing—the warm water and the slick feel of the floral hand soap lathering up between my palms. I watch the bubbles rinse down the sink, and when I look back up into the mirror, I try not to laugh at the rosy glow of my cheeks and the undeniable glossiness of my eyes.

I am definitely drunk. Definitely, definitely drunk.

When I turn off the faucet, I consider my reflection. The girl looking back at me looks different. This Abby is drunk. This Abby plays beer pong with basketball players. This Abby goes with the flow and doesn't stay in to study on Friday nights. This Abby flirts with Tristan Beck at the bar while fantasizing about his hands on her body.

The thought sends a wave of heat down my spine. I try to shake the image as I turn to grab a few paper towels out of the dispenser, but the lever doesn't dispense anything when I pull on it. One, two, three cranks and nothing.

"Come on, my hands are wet." It comes out in a slurred grumble as I knock the top of the dispenser with my fist.

"Ryan?" Tristan's muffled voice echoes through the door. He sounds like he's trying not to laugh, as if he can see me standing here glaring at the napkin dispenser. "Everything okay in there?"

"No," I say flatly, letting my wet hands fall limply at my sides, giving up.

"Do you need help?" I can hear him laughing a little, but the idea of having to walk around the bar with wet hands is way worse than admitting defeat, so with one final glare at the dispenser, I unlock the bathroom door. It opens to reveal Tristan standing in the doorway, leaning against the door frame. He chuckles when he takes in the situation, but he doesn't hesitate as he walks straight to the dispenser and pulls on the lever much harder than I did. With a loud popping noise that echoes around the bathroom, the dispenser is in working order again.

"They get stuck sometimes." He shrugs, and I smile at how he drunkenly stumbles over some of his words. He pulls a handful of paper towels from the roll and hands them over. When I take them from him, my fingers graze his, and I look up to find his eyes trained on me.

My gaze flicks down to his lips for a beat too long before looking back up to his eyes. I'm acutely aware of how close his body is to mine, and when the humor pooling in his eyes quickly evaporates into something more intense, he takes a step toward me.

My breath catches in my throat.

"You're drunk, Ryan." His voice is low, nearly a whisper, and the sound makes my skin flame as I watch his eyes flick down my body slowly, indulgently, before finally meeting mine again.

"So?" My voice catches in my throat.

"So, you're only looking at me like that because you're drunk."

"I'm not looking at you in any way." I stumble over my words, but I know he heard me because his lips quirk up into a cocky smirk.

"You're looking at me like you want me to touch you," he counters, taking another step toward me.

"Hmm," I hum absently as I watch his eyes trail down my body again, lingering on my barely-there lingerie top.

"Do you want me to touch you, Ryan?"

I can barely hear anything over the roar of blood rushing in my ears, and I stop breathing when I take a step back and my feet hit the wall behind me.

Do I want him to touch me?

I look up and meet his eyes. They're trained on me, waiting. I can tell he's not going to take another step toward me until I tell him that I want him to, and when my eyes flick down to his hands, my heart nearly careens out of my chest at the thought of how they would feel on me, exploring me—all of me.

"Yes," I say breathlessly, swallowing hard.

He takes a step toward me, close enough that his minty breath hits my cheeks as he lowers his head, hovering inches away from my lips. His eyes are glassy and hooded, but even in his drunken haze, he places both hands on the wall on either side of my head and moves his lips to my ear.

"We're both very drunk," he says it slowly, deliberately, and the feel of his hot breath on my cheek sends a shiver down my spine in the warm bathroom. "So, I don't want to touch you unless you really want me to."

He pulls back to search my face. I want to look into his eyes, but my gaze won't break away from his lips, which are parted and moist—waiting.

"Abby." He groans inwardly, begging me to confirm that I want this, that I'm not too drunk to consent, that he's not crossing any lines.

I don't bother answering him. Instead, I rock up onto my toes and crash my lips onto his, reveling in the instant response from him. He wraps his arms around me and swipes his tongue across my lips.

I open my mouth for him, but he pulls away with a groan, stepping back long enough to lock the door before connecting our lips again. This time his hands grab the back of my thighs, and he hoists me up around his hips, pinning my body against the wall as his beer tinged tongue rolls against mine.

I gasp at the contact when my skirt rides up and bunches around my hips, leaving nothing but my thin, black underwear as a barrier against the rough material of his jeans. He brings up a hand and cups my cheek, tilting my head back a little more so he can explore my mouth. When he rolls his hips, I can't silence the breathy moan that vibrates in the back of my throat as a jolt of electric pleasure shoots through me. His fingers tighten on my thighs at the sound, and he breaks away from the kiss to slowly brush his lips across my cheek. Stopping just under my ear by the end of my jaw, he licks the sensitive skin teasingly before biting down and sucking.

Oh, my God.

"Tristan." My skin is on fire, as if the nerves in my body are on high alert, threatening to fry if his lips delve any lower. He sucks and nips his way down my throat to my chest, and when he gets to the top of my shirt he looks up, eyes clearing for a moment.

I lift my arms above my head, and in an instant my shirt is crumpled in a tiny pool of lace across the room. His eyes widen as they linger on my bare chest and then he dips his head down and my skin explodes in rush of goosebumps as his mouth explores me.

He delves down, capturing a puckered nipple between his teeth as he explores the other with his fingers, tugging it gently as he rolls it between his calloused fingers. The heat pooling between my thighs flares uncomfortably as a desperate moan slips from my lips. I tug at his shirt, and he reaches an arm behind his head to yank it off, dropping it behind him. Grabbing his face, I bring his lips back to mine, desperate to taste him again. I open my mouth for his tongue to slip through, and I revel in the groan that vibrates in the back of his throat as my hands dip down to explore his hard chest, sliding down to trace the hard indents of each muscle on his stomach until I stop at the top of his jeans.

He steps away from the wall, letting my body slide down until my feet are back on the ground again. Dropping to his knees, he hikes my leather skirt up further and loops his thumbs around my underwear. When his gaze darts up to meet mine, I know he's waiting for confirmation.

The sight of him—drunkenly flushed, looking up at me with the kind of hungry gaze that I've fantasized about since meeting him at that formal—sends a wave of goosebumps up my stomach, shaking my shoulders slightly. The pulsing between my thighs intensifies when he licks his lips, and I release a shaky breath as I nod.

He pulls at my underwear, helping me step out of them before he tosses the scrap of fabric behind him. Gripping my hips, his hold tightens as his eyes slowly take me in. When his hand trails down my thigh to my knee, he lifts it up and positions it over his shoulder, pulling me closer. I close my eyes and lean my head against the cold, tiled wall, trying to slow the thoughts racing through my head.

The part of me that was always too nervous to do this with Tyler is screaming at me to abort mission, but the curious part of me, the part that's practically panting just at the sight of Tristan Beck on his knees in front of me, is telling me to just sit back and enjoy this.

And for the first time in my life, I listen.

I bury my fingers in his curls as he bites down on my inner thigh, just inches away from where I want him most, sending shocks of pleasure up my spine as he sucks hard enough to leave a bruise. When he pulls back, he flicks his tongue across the tender skin, but based on the breathy moans slipping through my lips, he knows that I'm desperate for him—for a different kind of touch.

A strangled moan sounds in the back of my throat and his lips quirk in a haughty grin, as if he knows that I'm practically begging, and when he lifts my thigh a little more, exposing me even more to him, his eyes darken.

He lowers his head again, but it's not to my thigh, and when his tongue drags across me in a long, languid motion, I gasp as every nerve in my body nearly short circuits. He pulls away and licks his lips, already glossy from the contact, and when his gaze flicks back up to mine, I try to steady my breathing. His cheek twitches before he dips his head back down, and my hips start to rock in time with his tongue, chasing the rush of pleasure building in my stomach. When my fingers grip his curls harder, silently begging for my pressure as the muscles in my legs and stomach tighten, he chuckles, and the vibration nearly makes my knees give out.

Tightening his hold on me, his tongue moves faster, rougher, and my head falls back against the wall as my legs start to shake. He slips two fingers into me, curling them up and hitting a spot that I didn't even know existed, and when he reconnects his lips to me, my entire body tenses. My breathing is fast and sporadic, and each breath turns into a small moan as he focuses on the swollen bud of nerves, licking hard enough to make my entire body go numb as goosebumps break out, spreading like wildfire across my skin.

His tongue slows into a lazy rhythm, a teasing rhythm, and my mouth pops open in a soft gasp as my hips rock forward, silently pleading with him to keep going. His tongue slows even more, and I don't have to look down to know he's smirking between my thighs.

My entire body is on fire, burning, electrifying, searing every nerve.

"Please," I gasp, moving my hips a little more, desperate for contact. My words aren't my own anymore, and if I wasn't so desperate, I might have the sense to be embarrassed as I beg him, "please, don't stop."

He pulls back a little more, until I can feel his breath on the inside of my thigh.

"Say my name, Abby. I want to feel you come on my tongue while I'm on yours."

My mouth pops open as his words register.

"Say my fucking name."

I know he won't touch me again until I do, so I lean my head back against the cool wall and breathe his name—a plea to touch me, to bring me back to that paradise on his tongue, to never stop. "Please, Tristan."

He grips my thighs tighter, nearly lifting me from the floor as he pulls me closer, and the echoes of my breathy whimpers sound around us as his tongue finds me again, rougher than before. The pressure at the base of my spine builds quickly, and suddenly I can't breathe as I bite down to keep the loud moan that's on the tip of my tongue from echoing past the bathroom door.

It happens all at once—every muscle in my body tenses until the pressure in my stomach explodes in a million little nerves of rolling pleasure, flooding every inch of my body, searing me, white-hot, from the inside out.

I feel myself pulse around his fingers as every part of me seems to throb in time with his expert tongue. I can't seem to hold back the breathy whimpers that slip through my lips, each one a desperate moan of his name, as every nerve in my body comes alive in a mind-numbing aftershock.

Oh, my God.

Oh, my God.

I keep my eyes closed as my lungs heave in air, reveling in the peaceful warmth currently flooding through my muscles. Tristan slowly pulls away, and I'm acutely aware of the fact that he's supporting my weight since my legs are too weak to actually hold myself up.

Looking down at him, still kneeling in front of me, my chest tightens at the sight of his lips, wet and glossy, from me. It sends a shiver down my spine in the warm bathroom air, and suddenly, I want nothing more than for him to shed his own clothes and press me up against the wall.

I want him.

"Fuck, Abby." He groans, and the rough vibration sparks another flame that heats my entire body, like a white-hot electrical shock straight down my spine. Slipping his two glossy fingers into his mouth, he sucks them clean as he stands up and reaches for his back pocket. He brings a condom pack up between his teeth, tearing it easily as I unbutton his pants and tug them down. The large bulge tenting his tight boxers quickens my careening pulse as I reach to pull them off, but before I can tug them down his hips, the knock that echoes through the bathroom makes me jump.

I look over my shoulder, wide-eyed at the door.

"Abby, are you in there?"

It's Nia. My eyes widen as I stare at the locked door, my mind sobering quickly.

"Oh, no."

Tristan steps back, and I tug down my skirt and rush toward the pile of clothes on the floor, pulling my shirt over my head as I look around frantically for my underwear.

"Here." He smirks, handing me the tiny scrap of cloth.

My cheeks are on fire as I shove them into the small pocket in the skirt.

What the hell just happened?

"Abs, are you okay?"

"Yes, Nia, hold on a sec," I call.

Tristan watches me attempt to fix my hair as he buttons his pants back up.

"She can't know we were in here together." I smooth down my skirt, hoping the crinkled fabric won't give me away.

"I'll stand behind the door." He nods, wiping his thumb over his lips slowly as he smirks at me.

I nod, face burning as I turn around and pull open the door. Nia's standing on the other side, and her eyes narrow as she looks down my body. Her brows knit as she takes me in, but I don't give her time to start questioning me before I grab her arm and lead her away from the bathroom.

"What's going on? Why do you look like you just got run over by a truck? And why were you in there for so long? I thought you left or got kidnapped or something," she says, trying to keep up with my pace as I shoulder my way through the crowded bar.

"I don't know, I think I'm coming down with something," I call over my shoulder as I lead us through the crowd toward the door of the bar. Thankfully, I spot Jenny standing at the bar gulping down a glass of water, and I latch onto her arm as we pass by. She looks confused at first but stops resisting when she sees that it's me.

"What's going on? Are we leaving?" she asks, looking between Nia and I before looking over her shoulder, probably to search for James.

"Was it the beer? Did you drink too much?" Nia asks, digging around her purse for her car keys when we finally push through the doors and step out into the frigid night air.

I should be cold. I should be shivering against the mid-winter wind, but my entire body is still on fire as I lead my friends across the parking lot. When we get to Nia's parked car, she unlocks it with the key fob.

"Yeah," I say breathlessly, looking back at the bar before pulling open the passenger side door. "Maybe I did."

ELEVEN

I am fucked.

The inside of my head is pounding against my skull as I walk through the harshly lit hall to class. We had a sunrise weight room workout this morning, and I nearly puked all over the tiled floor of the gym multiple times mid-lift. Luckily, Micah and Luke were perceptive enough to keep Coach distracted when I looked like I was going to blow chunks, so he never actually found out that I was on the verge of death the entire time. It's not the first time we all rallied to keep Coach occupied so someone wouldn't get caught hungover as fuck at practice. And thanks to their dumbass antics, they saved me from being sent out to run on the snow-covered track, which is his usual hangover punishment. But what's worse than the physical torture I just endured in the weight room, is the conversation waiting for me in chemistry with Abby Ryan.

I fucked up. I fucked up big time.

I knew I was making a mistake the second I pulled her panties down her legs and saw the look flashing in her eyes. Abby isn't a one-and-done kind of girl, and I knew that, but it didn't stop me from giving into the damn near primal need I had for her. Her body, those sexy, breathy moans, God, just thinking about it now is making me hard. I shake the thought of how she tasted on my tongue—because that can't happen again.

One and done, that's the rule. It keeps the line from blurring. It keeps it simple. Easy.

Easy, unlike the conversation I'm about to have with the one girl I should have never let myself hookup with. Out of the fifty-sum girls in that bar last night, I ended up going down on the one who I'd be willing to bet has never had casual sex in her entire life. And now, hungover as fuck, I have to tell her that last night's bathroom hookup was just that—a hookup. And, oh, by the way, you can't bail on the article you're writing on me because my dumbass roommates let it slip to Coach, and now he's asked for a copy of it once it's done. Apparently, it's going to look good to scouts. It shows that I'm *"a team player, on and off the court."*

So, I repeat, I'm fucked.

When I walk into the classroom, my eyes lock in on Abby sitting in her usual seat. Her head is bent down as she types on the iPhone in her hands, and when she finally glances up and locks eyes with me, her cheeks flare a dark red as she looks away.

Fuck.

Fuck, fuck, *fuck.*

I can practically still taste her on my tongue when I sit down on the stool next to her, and I try not to focus on the fact that she's wearing those yoga pants I've grown so fond of as I shuffle around my bag for a second, pretending to look for my pen. And then, when I've finally manned up, I turn to look at her.

Act cool. Act normal.

"Good morning." I grin, setting my textbook down on the table.

"Morning," she replies in the same overly casual tone.

Good, we're on the same page then.

"Alright, we've got a pop quiz today." Hannigan stands up and starts walking down the row of tables, dropping a test in front of each student as she goes. "No talking, no books, no cell phones," she warns. "Once you're done, you can bring it up to me and then you're dismissed for the day."

She drops two tests on our table, and I hand Abby one as I flip it open and read through the questions. It's all fundamental shit that we covered in class this week, all stuff that I learned years ago in my early chemistry classes freshman year. I pick up my pencil and start filling in answers.

When I finish with the final question, I look up to see everyone else still bent over their papers, and I glance over to see Abby biting down on her lip as her eyes focus on a question half way through the test.

Standing up, I pull my backpack onto my shoulder and walk to the teacher's desk. She seems disappointed when I hand her the test, but after scanning it, she looks up with an impressed smile. I turn on my heel and walk out of the classroom, dropping onto the bench outside. I guess I'm going to be here until Abby finishes the quiz, which based on her chem knowledge, could take all day.

I pull out my phone and scroll through the USASN app for a few minutes until a steady stream of students starts to filter out of the class.

I look up expectantly every time the door opens, but it takes fifteen more minutes before she finally walks out of the room. She doesn't look back to see me on the bench, so I stand up quickly and jog to catch up to her.

"Abby, wait up," I call.

She looks over her shoulder and smiles at me, stopping in the middle of the hall to let me fall into step with her.

"Can we talk?" I ask, hating how awkward I sound.

She looks up at me, anxiety flashing in her eyes as she nods.

"Over here." I nod toward a small alcove under the stairs.

Her face is pale as she pulls her gray, knit cardigan tighter around her.

"I—um—just wanted to touch base on what happened last night." I cough a few times and clear my throat.

She nods and looks around to make sure we're not being watched.

"Last night was—it was great, but it was just a hookup. Just a one-time thing." She tenses a little as her eyes widen, and I feel like a complete asshole, so I hurry to add something else to soften the blow. "I still want to be friends, but it just can't happen again." I don't mean to add the last part on, that was more of a warning for myself, because looking down at her now, all I can think about is pushing her against the wall right here, wanting to hear her moan my name again—to feel her around me as I push into her.

The hurt flashes across her face before she masks it and then she nods. I'm not a stranger to having this conversation, but it usually doesn't make me feel like such an asshole.

"I don't mean—" I stop, rubbing my hand through my hair. "I just mean—"

"It's okay." She shakes her head, her voice soft. "I get it."

"You do," I breathe, relieved.

"Sure." She looks away, and I have a feeling she's looking for a quick exit.

"We're still on for the article though, right?" My heart starts to race in my chest as the flighty look in her eyes falters while she considers me. This is what I was scared of. If she bails on me, I'm going to have to somehow explain to Coach that I fucked things up. Literally.

She blinks a few times and looks down at the ground, probably trying to decide if the scholarship is worth having to be around me, but when she looks back up, she seems relieved. She probably wasn't expecting me to want to continue with this little project.

"You don't mind?" She sounds surprised, and I readjust my backpack on my shoulder as I shrug.

"Of course not. I'm actually really looking forward to it." That's a lie, I still fucking hate interviews, but now that Coach is involved, I'm locked in, whether I like it or not.

"Okay." Her cheeks are still red as hell, and when she looks over her shoulder toward the entrance, I can tell that she doesn't want to be here with me anymore.

"Are you still coming over tomorrow? After you get off of work?" She nods and tucks her hair behind her ear.

"I have to go to my next class." She backs up into the wall, and when she looks up at me, her cheeks flame again as she sidesteps the barrier to the exit. "I'll see you tomorrow, Beck."

She turns quickly and walks out of the building, straight into the freezing cold air without waiting to pull on her coat hanging over her arm. And as I watch her go, I run a rough hand through my hair, pulling at the ends with an inward groan, praying that I didn't just fuck everything up.

———

"Don't look at me like that," I sigh, sinking onto the barstool at the kitchen island.

James shrugs and looks back to his scrambled eggs, but I can still see the shock on his face. He keeps his eyes on his food before turning back to me, and I can tell by the *what the fuck is wrong with you* look that he's now giving me, that I shouldn't have told him.

"Why *Abby Ryan*? Out of all of the girls there last night?" He shakes his head as if he can't possibly understand, and I groan into my hands as I lean my elbows onto the countertop. "She's a walking advertisement for long-term relationships, T. She's definitely not the kind of girl you just fuck in the bathroom." He snorts as he shakes the salt and pepper shaker over the frying pan he's cooking out of.

"I wasn't planning on it happening like that," I counter lamely as I spin the cap of my water bottle between my fingers, but I can tell by the snort that echoes through the kitchen that he's not buying it.

I wasn't. When I went out last night, I was planning on getting a little buzzed, hanging out with the guys, and then coming home and watching the Knicks game while trying to get caught up on some homework.

Going down on Abby Ryan in the bathroom of O'Malley's definitely wasn't part of that plan.

"And how did she react to the *just a hookup* conversation?" He tops his steaming plate with enough Sriracha to feed a small country and then drops down onto the stool on the other side of the island.

"Fine, I guess." I shrug, watching with a scowl as he scoops up a Sriracha drenched pile of eggs and shovels it into his mouth. "She said she was fine and was cool with finishing the article."

He glances up, freezing mid-chew. "She's still writing the article?"

A few pieces of egg fall back onto his plate, and I flick the cap of my water bottle at him, hitting him on the forehead.

"She's coming tomorrow night to do the second interview." I nod, ignoring his stupid smirk at my choice of words. "And I really don't want it to be awkward."

He considers my comment as he takes another bite. "Abby's a cool girl," he says, shrugging as if that's answer enough for all of my problems. "You said you guys were going to be friends so . . . be friends."

"*Be friends?*" I deadpan, watching him shovel another forkful of eggs into his mouth. "Is that really your grand piece of advice? Be friends."

He nods, as if it's obvious.

"Be friends," I repeat.

"Coming back from a hookup with a friend isn't easy, but it's doable. You just have to work on the friendship and stay away from any situations that are going to end up with you two fucking in the bathroom."

I glance up at him again, but he doesn't seem to be fucking with me. He's serious about this whole *be friends* thing. "How do I work on the friendship?"

"Just do what friends do, T. Don't overthink it." He stands up and drops his fork into the sink with his plate. "It's pretty simple—just don't fuck her." He smirks, and I flip him off as he walks out of the kitchen, leaving me alone with nothing but the residual smell of Sriracha drenched eggs and the same four words repeating over and over in my head.

Just don't fuck her.

I can do that. I think.

TWELVE

I've been sitting at the diner bar top for the past hour rolling the warm, just-out-of-the-dishwasher silverware into neat napkin rolls. It's typically my least favorite thing to do while working, but today I don't mind the tedious work as I desperately try to think of an excuse to text Tristan as to why I can't come over tonight.

I don't want to see him. I don't want to write this article anymore. And I don't want to lock myself into a project where I'll have to be around him more than I already have to be. I'm embarrassed. Mortified, actually.

I was drunk, really, really drunk, but even with the mixture of the vodka cranberries and the cheap beer running through my system, I wasn't drunk enough to not know exactly what I was doing. I felt every kiss, every touch, every breath, every single moment, and now I can't stop thinking about it. About how it felt to be so reckless in the bathroom of a dirty college sports bar, to have my clothes shed and tossed into a pile, to have Tristan focused completely on me, on my body, making me feel the most raw and alive I have ever felt. Of course, as soon as those memories rush through me, I can't help but miss how his fingers felt trailing down my body, touching me in ways that Tyler never even came close to.

With Tyler I was methodical. I took off my own clothes, made sure the lights were always off, and refused to step outside of the tiny box that I created for myself out of pure embarrassment. I didn't want him to see me naked, I didn't want him to touch me for very long, and I sure as hell would have never let his lips anywhere but my own while having sex.

Drunk Abby didn't take a baby step away from her comfort zone, she dove head first without a life vest into the churning black water below. And now, sober Abby has to deal with the consequences. Namely the one where Tristan Beck had to pull me aside and spell out the reality of the situation—you're just a hookup.

A hookup. Something I never would have imagined being or doing a few weeks ago. But I can't lie, when I went into that bathroom, I thought about it, too. I thought about Jenny's comment— about what it would be like to have him touch me, to lock my inner prude into a closet and just explore like every other college girl does. And I did. I knew that Tristan Beck doesn't date. I knew he only hooked up with girls. It's not a secret, rumors of his latest sexcapades spread across campus like wildfire.

He's Tristan Beck, USW's star basketball player, playboy extraordinaire. I knew what I was doing. So, why do I feel like this? Like I want more. Like I already miss something that we never even had.

"So, that guy never texted?"

I look up to see Lacie wiping the bar top a few stools down, her lips pulling down in a frown as she examines me sitting here with the silverware sitting idly in my hands. Pretending that I feel like shit because Dean hasn't texted me—which is just the cherry on top of this pity party sundae—is an easy out, so I take it.

"Yeah, I guess he wasn't really interested." I shrug, pulling off the ends of a napkin and stacking the pieces into a neat pile.

Lacie sighs inwardly and pulls out the seat next to me. "Maybe he lost your number." Her voice is soft, and the tone eases some of my discomfort, even though her excuse is kind of ridiculous. I raise a brow at her, and she grins back sheepishly. "It could happen." She nods her head, but there's no conviction behind her words and we both laugh at the attempt.

"He wasn't even that cute anyway." She smiles at me, eyes widening in the conspiratorial way they always do when she's about to talk shit about a mean customer to make me feel better. "I bet he just pussied out. He probably just realized you're way too cute for him anyway. Didn't want to get hurt." She winks, and I bite the inside of my cheek while grabbing her hand and squeezing.

"You're too good to me, Lace."

She winks again before sliding off the stool and walking around the bar top to grab a new sanitizing spray bottle.

Glancing at the clock, I take a deep breath and start to stack the napkin rolls into their plastic bin. I have three minutes before my shift ends. A notification lights up my phone, and I look down to see Tristan's name on an unopened text. Lacie glances over at me near the register, and I shake my head to her unasked question. It's not Dean. She looks a little disappointed but turns her attention back to cleaning the bar top as I slide open the message.

TRISTAN: *Hey, Ryan. Have you eaten yet?*

I try to stop the flutter in my stomach as I reread the message. Trying to keep it as casual as possible, I type out and then delete my response a few times before landing on the simple message.

ME: *Not yet.*

TRISTAN: *What kind of pizza do you like?*

ME: *I'm not picky.*

TRISTAN: *Ryan, answer the question.*

ME: *I'll just have whatever you're having.*

TRISTAN: *Ryan.*

ME: *Fine. Pineapple.*

TRISTAN: *You're one of those . . .*

I bite down on my lip as I type out my response.

ME: *How did I know you were going to be like this?*

TRISTAN: *Be like what? A normal, rational human being who knows not to put pineapple on pizza?*

ME: *Fine, get me a veggie instead.*

TRISTAN: *VEGGIE? ABBY RYAN, ARE YOU JOKING?*

ME: *I SAID I WOULD EAT WHATEVER.*

TRISTAN: *Pineapple it is. See you soon?*

ME: *I'll be over in fifteen.*

I look up to see Lacie staring at me with a raised brow and a smirk on her face. "That's not Dean, huh?" I hear the bite of accusation in her voice.

"It's not." My face heats up as she places a hand on her hip.

"Then why are you smiling like an idiot at your phone, Abby?"

I feign innocence as I lean over the counter to grab my purse.

"I don't know what you're talking about, Lace," I say, pulling my purse over my shoulder and waving, already making my way through the empty diner toward the door.

"Abby!" she exclaims.

"Have a good weekend, Lace." I smile over my shoulder as I walk through the door, smirking at the sound of the bell echoing as the door closes behind me.

———

I spend the ten-minute drive from the diner to Tristan's giving myself a mental pep talk. *You can do this. You can be just friends. It doesn't have to be awkward.* I end the pep talk with the reality of the situation—*you don't have a choice, you need this article.*

That clears my mind a bit, which is good because when I pull up to the house, the same three cars and motorcycle are parked out front, meaning that all three of Tristan's roommates are home.

The instant flood of embarrassment rushes through my veins again. *Did he tell them?*

I've kept to my story of not feeling well with Nia and Jenny, which has proved to be harder than I imagined because I've never really kept anything from them before. I can't tell them, though, because if I do, it'll shatter the last bit of normalcy I need to stay sane post bathroom incident.

Grad school, Abby, grad school.

I take a deep breath and release it.

So what if they know?

So what?

Turning off my car, I revel in the last bit of circulating heat before grabbing my bag and booking it across the icy yard and up the steps toward the front door. Three knocks later, I look over my shoulder and double check that I remembered to press the lock on my car, and when I turn around again, Tristan is smiling down at me in the open doorway. His black Nike joggers sit low on his hips as his black t-shirt hugs his shoulders nicely.

Ignore the arms. Ignore them.

He steps aside, and I walk into the warm house, my eyes instantly landing on the three familiar faces sitting on the couch.

"Ryan." One them, Micah, I think his name is, grins as he places a long, fully inked arm onto the back of the sofa. His voice draws the attention of the other two, who both look over at me and grin.

"Hey, Abby." James grins.

"Hey." I smile, pulling my bag further up my arm, trying not to focus on how closely Tristan is standing next to me. I can smell his cologne from here, and the scent is intoxicating.

"You work at the diner?" The youngest of them, who I think is named Luke, motions toward the apron still tied around my waist. I nod, tucking my hair behind my ear, trying to seem as casual as I can.

"We're gonna go get drunk at some frat, want to come with?" Luke's voice takes on a distinctly flirty tone, which falls flat halfway through his sentence after his eyes flick to Tristan.

"I think I need a little break from drinking." I laugh, and when my words register, I look over at Tristan, who's rubbing the back of his neck. The muscles in his cheek tense as he tries to hold back a smile.

"Fair enough." Luke shrugs before they all turn back to the video game.

Tristan nods for me to follow him, and I fall into step beside him as we walk across the room toward the hallway leading to his room. When he closes the door behind us, I look around the room again. This time, the dark gray walls seem familiar, but when I drop my bag and take in the messy unmade bed, a flash of a memory sends a shiver down my spine as I imagine how different it would have been if we were here, alone, without any roommates to interrupt us.

"Are you cold?"

Turning to see Tristan watching me from the door, I shake my head, but I don't miss the way his eyes travel down my body as he walks toward the desk to pick up a piece of paper. I bend down and grab the change of clothes I brought with me, eager to get out of my work clothes that have a tendency to smell like burgers and fries after my shifts.

The bathroom door connected to his room is cracked open, and I walk toward it quickly.

"I'm going to change out of my work clothes," I say.

He nods as he shuffles through some of the papers on his desk, and I shut myself into the bathroom, taking advantage of the moment alone to examine the cleanliness as I step out of my jeans. He has a few bottles of cologne sitting next to his deodorant on the countertop next his toothbrush and toothpaste, but other than that, the clean counter is empty. I pull my shirt over my head and fold it before stepping into my yoga pants and slipping into my USW hoodie.

I step back into his bedroom to stop myself from smelling his cologne like a stalker, and when he looks up from his desk, his dark green eyes consider me through thick lashes. That familiar tingling sensation starts to climb up my spine as I cross the room again.

"So . . . I've been thinking," he says, leaning back in his desk chair as I zip my clothes into my bag and climb onto his bed, settling down in the same spot as last time. I take advantage of the fact that it isn't made this time and wrap part of the blanket around me. When I look back up at him, he's bouncing a pen between his fingers.

"Thinking what?"

"Thinking that I don't know much about you." He leans forward in his chair and considers me, like he might find all that he's looking for by searching my face.

I consider his comment for a moment and shake my head. "Sure you do," I argue.

"Knowing that you suck at chem isn't what I'm talking about, Ryan." His lips quirk.

I feign offense and place my hand against my chest but drop it back to my lap quickly when he smirks at my dramatics. "Why do you want to know about me?" I hear the doubt in my voice, and he looks genuine when he shrugs and raises his brows earnestly.

"We're friends, Ryan, or at least, I'd like us to be."

I look down at my hands folded in my lap. Being friends would make this article a lot easier. A truce of sorts, to not let the awkwardness of our drunken hookup make our future interviews unbearably awkward.

"Yeah, I'd like to be friends."

He grins. "Let's make it fair. For every question you ask me, I get to ask you one, too."

"You want to interview *me*?" I laugh, and when he nods seriously, I realize that he's not joking. "You're serious?" I gape.

A knock at his bedroom door makes me jump, and when Tristan calls for them to come in, James pops his head into the room. His eyes immediately land on me, wrapped up in a blanket on the bed.

"We're about to head out to that party, T." He gives Tristan a knowing look that makes my face feel a lot hotter than it was moments ago, and when Tristan nods, James grins before he backs out of the room again. He pauses just before he closes the door and says, "Your pizza was just delivered."

Tristan stands up and drops his phone into his pocket as he walks to the door. When he looks back at me, he grins and nods toward the hallway, waiting for me to follow him out. I slide off the bed after detangling my legs, and when I stop short behind him, he grins down at me as he pulls open the door, motioning for me to go ahead of him.

"First question," he says, falling into step beside me as we walk toward the kitchen. "Why would you ever put pineapple on pizza, Ryan?"

THIRTEEN

ABBY

"Don't be a drama queen," I tease. "Eat it."

He looks at me with mock horror as he brings the pineapple covered pizza slice to his lips, and with the most dramatic groan I've ever heard, he takes a bite. I lean forward on the bed and pull my bottom lip between my teeth as I wait for him to un-scrunch his eyes and swallow the bite. When his emerald eyes finally open, they meet mine, and he considers me for a moment before shrugging nonchalantly.

"Okay, so it's not terrible."

"What was that?" I lean toward him and cup my hand behind my ear, a smug smile growing on my lips.

He rolls his eyes, but his dimple betrays him, followed by the smile he was trying to hold back.

I sit back on the mattress and close the nearly empty box of pineapple pizza. There are a few pieces left, which I'd be willing to bet he's going to eat tomorrow now that he's had a taste of the pineapple heaven.

Wiping my hands clean on a napkin, I glance down at the notebook in front of me. Half of the questions have already been filled out since we did a quick-fire question and answer type interview through dinner. I kept to the easy questions, which he answered pretty well.

I look up as he pops off the top of one of the beers he brought from the kitchen. I opted for a water bottle, which I have capped and resting in my lap, but when his eyes flick up to mine, he raises a brow and extends the bottle in his hand.

The last thing I should be doing right now is drinking with Tristan, but every time I look at him, a flash of our bathroom encounter plays in my mind. So, honestly, I could really use the buzz to relax.

The beer is definitely better than whatever we were drinking at the bar last week, but it's still beer, so I take a few long sips of it and try not to focus on the terrible after taste.

The sound of another bottle cap popping off pulls my attention back to see him taking a long sip from his own beer. His eyes seem to have lost some of the humor, and I can tell the taste of the beer has brought back his own bathroom memories because he's now clearing his throat as he rubs the back of his neck.

This is what I didn't want—the awkward after.

I can't seem to process the fact that the man sitting across from me has not only seen me completely naked, but has touched, and kissed, and explored me in ways that no one else has before. The thought makes my face burn and I look away, allowing my hair to fall from behind my ear, shading my face slightly from his gaze.

He clears his throat, and I glance back over to him. "Why don't we make the rest of this a less formal interview," he offers with a reassuring smile. "We could make it into a sort of game—more laid back and fun."

I raise a brow and smile at his clear attempt to make me feel more comfortable. "What kind of game?"

"It'll be a question game, so you can get the rest of your interview done," he explains, leaning back in his chair and picking up the tennis ball size basketball. He tosses it into the air a few times, catching it easily as he keeps his eyes on me. "You ask a question, and if I don't want to answer, I drink." He holds up his beer bottle and grins. "And the same for you."

I look down at my beer and trail the pad of my thumb down the neck of the glass, drawing a line in the condensation. That does sound less awkward than him just asking me questions.

I look up from the bottle to meet his eyes, and when I nod, he smiles and leans back in his chair.

"Okay, I'll go first." He drums softly on his bottle as he considers me. "How are you so good at video games?"

I laugh at his question and consider bringing the bottle to my lips to keep some air of mystery but decide to save the drinking for questions I actually don't want to answer. "I have two older brothers, Mark and Jeff, who only paid attention to me when they wanted to try out new wrestling moves, use me as their paintball target practice, or needed a third player for their video games." I shrug, grinning at the rush of childhood memories. "I always opted for the third option, so I ended up getting pretty good."

"They used you as target practice?" He seems amused and horrified at the same time.

"Only a few times, and it was mostly to tease me. They purposely missed. I was only shot once in the leg, and when Jeff realized that he actually got me, he carried me all the way back home from the park and helped me ice it." I smile at the memory of Jeff's usually tanned face paling instantly as he ran all the way home with me in his arms.

We were so young then. I was mid-elementary school and still so desperate for my brothers' fleeting attention. "I was sworn to sibling secrecy, and I thought that if I kept the secret, I would finally be welcomed into their little pack, so I kept my mouth shut. It didn't last long, though. When my dad saw the huge purple bruise on my leg the next day, he pried it out of me."

Tristan smirks. "My dad would have killed me if I ever shot Olivia or Melody with a paintball gun."

"Oh, he nearly did. He took us out back and gave me the paintball gun and sixty seconds of unrestricted payback time. I had terrible aim, so my dad made my brothers wear blindfolds and those ankle weights to slow them down. I still only got a few good shots in, but they ended up running into each other, which was hilarious."

"Your dad sounds like a badass." He laughs, and I bite down on my lip as I smile at the memory.

"Yeah, he really was." The familiar pain in my chest pulses, and his eyes widen when he realizes what I mean. When he blinks away the shock and leans forward, all the humor is gone from his face.

"I'm so sorry, Abby. I didn't know . . ."

His eyes are searching my face, but I look down at the left over pizza on the plate in front of me and count the pineapple chunks on the slice—something my grief counselor taught me to keep my mind from spiraling. Counting keeps you grounded, so I count the chunks again before glancing back up at Tristan with a shaky smile.

"It's been a few years," I say before taking a long sip of the beer in my hands.

He nods, not really sure what to say, but sips his own beer.

"My turn," I say, trying to pull the humor back into my voice. I glance down to the list of questions, but as I scan through them, none of them seem even remotely interesting. Glancing back up at Tristan, I bite the inside of my cheek as a million non-article related questions fill my mind. Taking another long sip of my beer, I lick the errant liquid from my lips before landing on a safe question. "What's your dream team to play on?"

He smirks as he leans back into the chair. "On the record, I'd be happy to play on any team, and I'd be honored just be drafted." His response is quick and rehearsed, but when he leans in, his voice is lower, as if he's worried someone might overhear him. "Off the record, I've always dreamed of playing on the Knicks."

"The Knicks?" I practically snort.

He can't be serious; the Knicks have sucked for years.

"My dad's from New York. Even though I grew up here, I was raised a Knicks fan. It would be nice to be able to play on the same team that my dad and grandad watched together when he was a kid, you know?"

I watch his face as his words sink in, and when they do, my lips pull up at the thought of a tiny Tristan watching basketball with his dad, continuing a tradition that his father and grandfather started years ago.

"That's really sweet," I admit. When his eyes meet my own, my stomach tightens, sending a shiver down my spine that spreads across my body. He looks down at the beer in his hands, and I take a deep breath, looking down at the notebook in front of me.

"My turn," he says, breaking the silence. "What was your favorite concert? If you've ever been to one."

I consider my options for a moment, and then, slowly, I raise the beer to my lips and take a sip.

His eyes widen and he leans forward in his chair. "You're drinking for that question?" he asks incredulously.

"It's embarrassing." I shrug.

"Well, now I have to know." He grins.

"I already drank." I smirk, holding up my beer. I drink again for good measure.

"I'll give you a veto on one of my drinks then," he offers.

I sit back to think it over.

"Deal," I agree as a sly smile slips onto my lips. He eyes me warily, as if wondering if he made a mistake making the deal. "I've only been to one concert, so I guess it wins by default. I was sixteen and I went with my friend Sara, who won tickets from a radio station contest," I say, smiling at the memory.

"Which band," he prompts, clearly aware of the fact that I don't want to admit it.

I stare at him for a moment, biting back an embarrassed smile.

"Come on, Ryan, it can't be that bad," he urges, amusement lighting up his eyes.

"Fine. One Direction." I watch him, waiting for the inevitable teasing.

He sits back in his seat with a shrug. "Me, too, actually. Olivia was obsessed with them, and my parents never let her go to concerts alone, so I had to take her."

"*You've* been to a One Direction concert?" I gape.

"I've been *dragged* to two of them, actually," he corrects.

"Let me guess, you're a Harry girl?" I grin, tucking a strand of hair behind my ear.

He doesn't miss a beat. "Zayn, actually."

I blink, staring at him in disbelief before his words fully sink in. I nearly spill my beer as I fall back onto the bed laughing at the thought of Tristan standing in a sea of tween fangirls at one their concerts. When I catch my breath again, I peek up to see him grinning.

"You *would* like Zayn," I tease, rolling my eyes dramatically. "The bad boy of the group."

"You're definitely not into Zayn," he narrows his eyes at me playfully. "He's not your type."

"Not my type?" I laugh at how matter-of-fact he said it. "What's my type then?"

He's quick to answer, as if it's obvious. "You're into the goody-two-shoes, cardigan wearing, have-you-back-by-ten type," he says, grinning when my cheek twitches.

I consider his assessment. I don't have to look up to know he's waiting for my reaction, so I hold my composure for as long as possible before the laugh slips from my lips. I would never admit it to him, but I guess that kind of *is* my type—save for the cardigans. Tyler didn't wear cardigans, but he certainly was a rule follower, and he always made sure I was back home by my curfew at eleven. But I'm not going to tell Tristan that.

"Am I right? Is that your type?" His mouth pulls up into a smug smirk.

"Maybe, maybe not." I shrug as I bring my beer up to my lips to cover my smile.

"Is it still?" His voice is lower, and when I look back up at him, he's watching me curiously.

Am I still attracted to the good boy type? Yeah, of course.

Does the person I've been fantasizing about for the past few weeks fit into that category? Absolutely not.

My eyes coast over his tanned face and curly hair, down to his chest and arms—one of which is coated in ink, trailing from his wrist up and disappearing under the black cloth of his shirt. The swirl of ink is distracting, and I wish I would have paid more attention to detail when he stood in front of me, chest bare, and tattoo completely uncovered. I was distracted, with blinders on and hands eager to explore then, but now, I want to trace the black lines and follow them from start to finish up over his shoulder.

The man sitting in front of me is everything but my type. He's not clean cut, not a rule follower, and certainly not one my mother would ever approve of, which I guess has been more of a prerequisite than anything else in the past.

Tyler's dad was a respected surgeon in town; his sister was in her third year of medical school; and Tyler had just been accepted to Florida's most prestigious private college when we started dating. Introducing him to her was easy, because I knew he would check all of her boxes before even speaking with him. He wore button up shirts and loafers, his hair was always cropped short, and he spent weeks at a time with his family at their vacation home up in Cape Cod.

He was the definition of what my mother would have picked out for me. My mother made sure to mention all of this when I told her that we broke up, as if his father's career choice, and their real estate catalog was enough of a reason for me to stay in a dead relationship.

Looking up at Tristan, I can't pretend that he didn't completely shatter everything I thought I liked. Everything that I thought was good for me.

Before him, I spent years thinking that the routine-like sex in dark rooms with a boy who knew nothing about my body, besides what it could do to make *him* feel pleasure, was enough. But after feeling the way Tristan's fingers felt on my skin, the way my body reacted to him, to his lips, his tongue—I don't think I can ever go back.

I look up to see him watching me.

"I don't know," I admit, but it comes out as more of a whisper when his eyes flick down to my lips. His eyes don't leave my mouth as he puts his beer down on the desk next to him, and my breath catches in my throat as he stands up, taking a step toward the bed. The near empty beer bottle now feels incredibly heavy in my hand as I watch him take a few more steps, eyes locked on mine as he closes the space between us.

He stops at the edge of the bed, leaning over slowly as I tilt my head back to bring my lips closer to his. But just as I feel his hot, spearmint breath just inches from my lips, we both jolt away from each other when the bedroom door opens quickly, crashing against the wall as Luke stumbles in.

"Hey—oh, Abby, you're still here." His voice echoes loudly around us and he smiles widely at me before his eyes slide over to Tristan.

"You're sloshed, McConnell," Tristan groans with an inward sigh, moving away from the bed. "Go to bed."

"I'm not sloshed, just slightly intoxicated," he corrects, although his words are slurring together pretty severely, incriminating him just as much as his swaying is. He grins at Tristan, who has now walked over to him and grabbed his shoulder to make sure the swaying boy doesn't face plant on his bedroom floor. They both tower over me as I slide off the bed.

"Your sister's here, man. I didn't even recognize her. But I guess now I can see it." He grabs Tristan's shoulder and narrows his eyes to steady his vision as he looks at his teammate's face, as if he's trying to piece together the similarities between Tristan and his sister.

"Olivia?" Tristan's brows knot as he looks at Luke, but the freshman nods his head as if it's obvious.

"She was at the party."

A loud crash echoes down the hallway from the living room, and the gasp and bubbly laugher that follows makes Luke grin as he points over his shoulder to the open door. "Told you."

Tristan drops his hand from Luke's shoulder and pushes past him. I follow him quickly, nearly crashing into his body when he stops short at the end of the hall leading into the living room.

"Olivia? What the fuck?"

I step to the side to get a clear view of the living room, and my jaw drops when I see his sister, clad in a little black dress and tall platform heels, on the floor with her heavy eye makeup slightly smeared. Her cheeks are flushed a bright pink and based on the way she's stuck on the ground, trying to grab the back of the couch to help her stand back up, I can tell that she's absolutely smashed.

"Hey, bruv." Her too-loud voice is slurring and her eyes are glassy as she squints up at her brother. Her lips pull back into a sheepish smile as she laughs nervously, but when her eyes slide from his to mine, she beams up at me from the floor.

"*Abbbby.*" She waves a few times and then puts her hand back on the couch when she starts to sway on the floor, like she might fall over even though she's already sitting.

Tristan takes a deep breath and walks over to where she's sitting on the hardwood. He bends down and hooks his hands under her arms, gently lifting her back up to her feet. He keeps his hand on her back to make sure she doesn't fall again, and when she looks up at him, she smiles appreciatively before looking back at me.

"What are you doing here, Abby?" She grins at me as she kicks off her platform heels.

"What are *you* doing here?" he asks her, but she ignores his question as she drops down on the leather couch, plucking the TV remote and an open bag of chips from the side table.

"Do you have Hulu?" she asks, turning the TV on as she sticks her hand into the chip bag.

Tristan stares at his sister incredulously, and when James walks out of the kitchen with a glass of water and a medicine bottle in his hands, his eyes lock on Tristan's.

"What the fuck is going on?" Tristan asks, his hands knotting in his hair in frustration.

"We found her at the party," James explains, handing Olivia the water and pills as she flicks through the lineup of shows. She thanks him before downing the pills easily.

"Abby, come sit and watch TV with me." She pats the seat next to her.

I look up to Tristan to see him pulling his phone from his pocket.

"I tried to call you," James says quietly.

"My phone was on silent," Tristan sighs, scrolling through the notifications on his screen. He shakes his head as Olivia crawls across the couch to grab the blanket laying on the other end. They both look away quickly when her dress rides up, which she fixes clumsily and looks over at me, laughing.

"Do you like *The Bachelor*, Abby?" I don't know if I'm supposed to interact with her or ignore her, so I just nod and look up to meet Tristan's eyes as he sighs heavily.

"Do you mind babysitting her for a little while, just to make sure she doesn't go anywhere? I need to call my mom and let her know where she is and figure out what to do with her tonight," he asks as he pushes his hair off his forehead.

"Yeah, of course," I say softly. I want to reach out and comfort him somehow, but I keep my hand to myself and watch as he smiles weakly. I can practically feel the stress and confusion radiating off of him as he shakes his head.

"She's never done this before. She's still in high school. I think this is the first time she's ever drank. And she was at that frat party alone? If James wouldn't have found her——" He winces, glancing over his shoulder at her.

It could have been bad. Really, *really* bad.

"I'll keep an eye on her." I don't know what else to say, but when he looks back down at me, he smiles and nods before turning on his heel and disappearing into his room. I can just barely hear the distant hum of his voice when I turn back to the couch to see Olivia holding the remote close to her face, squinting to see the buttons.

I settle down next to her on the couch just as she finds whatever she's looking for, and when she presses the button, a show starts to play on the huge flat screen.

"So, this isn't *The Bachelor*, but it's kind of like it," she explains. Her words are slow and she's pointing the remote at the huge screen trying to explain the concept to me. She explains the premise of the show, and when she looks over and smiles up at me, she holds open the blanket for me to scoot closer to her before offering me the half-eaten bag of chips, nearly spilling them in the process.

She gives me a sheepish grin before nuzzling down further into the couch, pointing the remote at the TV to turn up the volume on the reality dating show. It drowns out the soft hum of Tristan's voice echoing indistinctly from the hall, and I nuzzle down next to her as we watch the opening credits.

———

Olivia passed out two minutes in with her head resting on my shoulder and her soft snores reassuring me that she's still breathing. I don't mind, especially because her small body is radiating so much heat under our shared blanket, that it makes up for the barely-there flame licking at the wood in the fireplace.

"Thanks for staying with her, I know it's getting really late." I look up to see Tristan walking toward me with my bag in his hands. His eyes flick to his sister before meeting mine again. I move slowly, making sure not to wake her as I slide off the couch and tuck the blanket securely around her sleeping body.

"What did your mom say?" I whisper, taking my bag from him.

"Just to let her sleep here." He shrugs, falling into step beside me as I walk to the front door.

I'm surprised when he follows me out rather than saying goodnight at the door. I don't look over at him as we walk side by side to my car, but I'm hyperaware of him as he matches my slow pace, keeping my eyes trained on the ground, searching for ice patches.

"I'm sorry we were interrupted again," he sighs as I unlock my car remotely, stopping at the driver's side door. The cold night air is nipping at my cheeks and nose, quickly sending goosebumps down my arms. I look back up at him, and a shock of heat rushes across my skin when he takes a small step toward me.

"It's okay," I say, but my voice is lost in the wind and my hair is whipping around my face in the icy breeze. My heart is beating quickly, fast enough to hear the rushing of blood in my ears, and my cheeks flood with heat when he takes another step closer. I watch breathlessly as he closes the space between us, and when he raises his hand to tuck a wayward strand securely behind my ear, he hesitates as he considers me for a second before his thumb slowly wipes a small flake of snow off my cheek.

I can smell him, the spiced cologne mixed with his beer-tinted spearmint breath. It's intoxicating. His eyes search my face for a long moment before falling to my mouth.

I want to rock up onto my toes to connect our lips, to feel his warm breath heat them, to taste him on my tongue again, but his words echo through my mind.

It was just a hookup. Just a one-time thing.

It can't happen again.

The distinct sound of a text notification echoes through the silent street, and his eyes flick up to meet mine again, sobering quickly from whatever he was thinking about. He clears his throat and blinks a few times as he takes a step toward my car.

"Goodnight, Ryan," he says, opening my car door for me. His voice is flat and his eyes are trained straight over my head.

I hesitate for a moment, confused and wanting, but turn and climb into my car when he keeps his eyes averted from mine. I keep my gaze on the steering wheel as he closes the door behind me softly, and only look up at him when he turns around to jog back up his driveway. He disappears back into the house without a second glance, and I try to keep my breathing even as I wait for my car to heat up.

Just friends. You're just friends. It was just a hookup.

It can't happen again.

I pull out my phone, hoping for a distraction from the thoughts running rampant in my mind. Expecting to see a text from Jenny or Nia, I'm confused by the text from the unknown number.

I have to read it twice before it fully registers.

UNKNOWN: *Hey, Abby. It's Dean, the guy from the diner. Full disclosure, I'm kind of drunk. But this isn't a drunk text. I've been waiting to send this text since the day I got your number, but my roommate said I had to wait the appropriate amount of time, or I'd come off too eager and scare you away. I Googled how long I should wait, and the GQ article said a week, so I waited a week. So, this is my not-too-eager-slightly-drunk-but-not-a-drunk first text.*

I bite down on my lip and look back up at the house. When I finally look back down to my phone, I click out of the text before tossing my phone onto the passenger seat. I try to steady my breathing to keep the tears that are starting to well in my eyes from falling, but the scent of him that's clinging to my hoodie is now circulating around my car in the warm air, like a haunting reminder.

It was just a hookup. It can't happen again.

I repeat his warning over and over as I pull out onto the street.

Just a hookup.

You were just a hookup.

FOURTEEN

TRISTAN

The muffled voices and laughs go silent when I walk into the kitchen. Luke and Olivia are sitting at the island eating cereal while James is stirring cinnamon into his oatmeal on the stove. I'm more than a little shocked that Luke is even awake before noon, but by the look he's giving Olivia, I have an inkling of why. I shoot him a warning glare when I pass by, restraining myself from knocking him in the back of the head as I go.

Dating your friend's sister is against bro code, and it's amplified when you're teammates. He catches my warning look and leans back in his stool, putting enough space between him and Olivia for it to look kosher, all while Olivia types on her phone, completely unaware of the silent interaction.

"Good morning." She smiles up at me when she puts her phone down, but her voice is too perky to match her appearance. Her curls are piled into a messy knot on top of her head and her makeup is smeared around her eyes. Her little dress seems to expose even more skin in the daylight, which just makes my head hurt more. I notice the glassiness in her eyes when she rubs them, smearing her makeup further.

She's definitely hungover and based on the distinct smell of rum permeating from her, I can only imagine how much she actually drank last night.

I offered to let her sleep in my bed, but even drunk as hell, my little sister held onto her stubborn streak and demanded to camp out in the living room.

"How'd you sleep?" I ask, grabbing my own bowl from the cabinet, skirting around James to get a spoon out of the silverware drawer. I had two beers last night, barely enough to give me a buzz, and yet I woke up feeling like absolute shit.

If I'm being real, it probably has more to do with the fact that I almost kissed Abby twice last night rather than the beer I consumed. But I don't really want to think about that right now.

"The couch was fine, this hangover is killer, though." She downs her entire water bottle before slumping down until her forehead is resting against the countertop.

"I bet." I hop onto the counter near the stove and pour milk over my cereal. "I can smell you from here. Did you drink rum last night or bathe in it?"

Olivia doesn't bother lifting her head when she flips me off.

"So, you and Ryan, huh?" Luke says, leaning his elbows onto the counter as his eyes meet mine. He has a shit-eating grin on his face that only grows when James turns around and Olivia's head pops up.

Jesus fucking Christ, I'm actually going to kill this kid.

"She just interviewed me." I shrug and stuff a spoonful of cereal into my mouth, praying that Luke was too drunk to remember what he saw.

"Didn't look like just an interview from what I walked in on." I freeze mid-chew and narrow my eyes at the freshman, my expression blatant—*Tread carefully, kid.*

"What did you walk in on?" James asks wide-eyed, abandoning his oatmeal on the stove to turn around and look at Luke.

"They were about to make out." He grins, pulling at the strings of his hoodie. "And based on the look on her face, she really wanted it. She was giving him *fuck me* eyes."

I don't have to look over at James to know that he's grinning. For someone who was just giving me the *"you can be friends after hooking up"* pep talk, I figured he'd be a little more disappointed in me.

"Oh, my God, are you and Abby together? Like *together*, together?" Olivia squeaks, her eyes wide. I can practically see the wheels in her head turning, and knowing her, she's already planning a summer wedding for us.

"No, we're not together." I shut her down quickly, shoving another spoonful of cereal into my mouth while glaring at Luke.

"Why not? She's so nice, *and* she's super hot—like the naughty schoolgirl kind of hot," she muses, smirking at James who's nodding in agreement as he pours his oatmeal into a bowl.

I fucking know. That's the problem. Every time I'm around her, I seem to be more attracted to her, and last night it was bad enough for me to almost cross that line again—*twice*.

"Plus, she likes *Love Island*, so I like her even more now."

"Why don't you date her then?" I mutter between chews, watching a few pieces of cereal fall back into my bowl.

The groan of approval from Luke is enough for me to send the dish towel next to me flying at his head, which he barely dodges.

"Go get into the shower, Liv. You smell like a walking bar. I can't bring you home smelling like that." Olivia rolls her eyes at me but slides off the stool and walks out of the room without a fight because she knows I'm right. Mom might be cool with her going out with her friends to a college party, but if my dad saw her in that dress, smelling like an entire bottle of liquor spilled on her, he'd have a heart attack.

When the sound of my bedroom door closing echoes through the quiet house, I look over at James, who seems amused as he pushes oatmeal around his bowl. "We didn't kiss," I maintain.

"But you almost did," Luke counters, winking.

"Almost doesn't count, dick wad," I say, flipping him off.

Luke shrugs and dodges another dish towel before sauntering out of the kitchen.

Groaning, I push my fingers through my hair.

"Project *just friends* didn't work out as planned?" James asks, taking up the stool Luke just left.

"It was going well at first." I shrug, trying to think back to how it all went downhill so fucking quick. "We were eating pizza and hanging out, doing her interview questions, and then it just kind of happened—or almost happened. Luke walked in before anything could *actually* happen." I glance up to see him watching me expectantly, and I groan before admitting to the second part. "And then it almost happened again when I walked her out."

"T—" He shakes his head and looks down at his bowl. "You have to be careful, man."

"I know that," I snap, jumping down from the counter. "I'm not doing this on purpose."

"I know you're not. It's different. You're actually into her." He shrugs, taking a big bite of his oatmeal.

I don't say anything as his words sink in.

Actually into her?

I'm not into her. I just like being around her sometimes.

She's witty, and fun, and attractive as hell, and she's relaxing to be around. Everything just kind of slows down when I'm with her, and somehow, I'm not hyper-focused on shooting percentages, or three-point shot records, or what scouts are going to be at the next game.

I look up to see James watching me with smug smile.

Fuck. I guess I am into her.

"I'm not," I lie, shaking my head. "But even if I was, nothing could happen." It's the same thing I've been saying for the past three years, but somehow it doesn't feel the same anymore. "I don't even know where I'm going to be in a few months. I could be here or in fucking Canada for all I know, and she can't move with me. She's going to graduate school, and then we'd be in a long-distance relationship and those never fucking work." My fingers are digging into the back of my neck as I try to release some of the tension there, but it doesn't seem to be working.

"It's not the best situation to start a relationship in," he agrees. "So, you've got to be a hell of a lot better at keeping it under control."

I nod, thinking back to last night, to how close I was to kissing her again.

"She's into you, man. And it's not fair to either of you to pursue something that's never going to happen."

The sound of footsteps approaching silences us both, and Olivia pops her head around the corner and smiles, her wet curls dangling as she eyes us. My hoodie and sweatpants look massive on her small frame, but it's a welcome change from her barely-there dress.

"Are you ready to go? Mom just called and said Mel and the babies are over for brunch."

I nod, putting my empty bowl into the sink. She says goodbye to James and disappears back to the living room where I can hear Luke talking to her. Her laugh echoes through the room, but I'm too distracted by James's words replaying in my mind to care about Luke flirting with my sister.

It's not fair to either of you to pursue something that's never going to happen.

The words sting more than I thought they would, but they're true. Nothing can happen between me and Abby. No matter how much I might want it to.

FIFTEEN

TRISTAN

"Are you still mad at me about last night?"

I glance over at Olivia sitting in the passenger seat of my truck. She's pulled her wet hair into a knot on the top of her head and she looks like she's drowning in my clothes.

"No, Liv, I'm not mad."

"Then why are you in a mood?"

I shrug. "Just tired."

That's not a lie. I didn't sleep much last night, but my apparent mood has more to do with the shitty reality check I had this morning than my lack of sleep.

Being around Abby was easy when I didn't really know her. She's hot, but it's not like I'm not around hot girls all the time. Hooking up with her was easy because I was drunk and I told myself it was just another hookup, just another one-time thing, like every other girl. It wasn't until after the bathroom incident that things changed, and it wasn't until this morning that I realized I wanted her, really wanted her, in more than my usual hookup-only way.

The scent of her vanilla apple spice perfume lingered on my bedsheets last night, which made falling asleep without fantasizing about her impossible. I thought the hot shower would clear my mind, but it only ended up spurring the memory of me pushing her up against the bathroom wall. The memory of how her naked body felt under my tongue was enough to make me hard, but it was her fucking breathy moans that sent me over the edge in my own hand, imagining what it would sound like to make her moan my name again.

"I like her, you know," Olivia chirps, pulling me out of my quickly spiraling thoughts. When I look over, she's watching me with a smug smile.

"Who?"

"Abby." She rolls her eyes. "And I think you do, too."

I turn up the radio to shut her up, but she just talks louder.

"I can tell that she likes you. Why don't you ask her out?"

I'm not about to tell my baby sister about my *only fuck them once* rule so I just shrug.

"I don't need a girlfriend right now, Liv. I need to focus on school and the rest of this season before the draft."

She raises a brow. "That sounds like a bullshit excuse."

It does sound like a bullshit excuse, even to me, but it's the reality of the situation. That, and the fact that even if we did date, I'd be leaving in a few months to join whatever NBA team drafts me, and I doubt it's going to perfectly coincide with whatever graduate school she ends up going to.

Why start something that already has an expiration date on it?

I try to push the thought of Abby to the back of my mind as I pull into the driveway of my parents' house, next to the familiar shiny black Kia with a *baby on board* sticker stuck to the back window.

"Mel's here," Olivia hums as she pushes open her door and drops down onto the cement barefoot, her platform heels dangling from her hands as she runs up the driveway and into the house.

When I close the front door behind me, Olivia's laugh sounds from the kitchen.

"Wait, who brought you to Tristan's?" My older sister's confused voice echoes down the hall as I close in on the kitchen. When I round the corner, she's standing near the sink, bouncing a bundle of white-blonde curls in her arms. Her eyes are locked in on Olivia as she finishes telling her about her first college party experience. Apparently, I'm the only one who thinks she's still too young to be drunkenly stumbling around USW's campus.

"James. He saw me at the party and made me come home with him," Olivia finishes as she extends her hands out to grab Gigi, who's giggling at the ridiculous faces Olivia's making at her.

"Good morning, honey," Mom calls over her shoulder from the stove when she spots me. The sound of popping bacon, and the aroma to match, is enough to make my mouth water. I grab a piece of bacon from the plate next to the stove as I kiss her cheek, narrowly missing her slap on my shoulder when she shoos me away from the food.

"Hey, Mel." I grin, peering over the top of her head as I pull her into a hug, searching the kitchen for my three-year-old niece's long blonde curls. A giggle sounds from the pantry, and I meet Mel's amused eyes. Georgia's favorite game to play is hide and seek, and apparently, we're already in a game.

"Is Garrett here?"

"No, he got called into work this morning." Mel sighs, stepping away to fill up the sippy cup in her hands with apple juice.

I step back to get a good look at Gigi, who's now dancing in Olivia's arms as she sings a nursery rhyme to her. Her eyes crinkle in a laugh when Liv starts to bounce her to the rhythm, and without missing a beat, I easily scoop Gigi out of Olivia's arms. I continue the song, but with a much more ridiculous voice, which earns a louder giggle from the baby in my arms and the toddler in the pantry.

"Give her back," Liv whines, popping onto her tiptoes to make more faces at Gigi.

"She wants to see her favorite uncle," I argue, spinning around to shake her off so I can have the giggling girl's full attention. "Isn't that right, Gi?"

My niece is the spitting image of my older sister, aside from the white-blonde hue of her curls. The same green eyes and olive skin we all share was passed down to her, along with a deep dimple on her right cheek—a characteristic that only Gigi, Liv, and I share, which was passed down to us by my grandmother.

Gigi reaches up and pats my chin, rubbing her soft hand across the stubble curiously. Her little index finger traces the outline of where my stubble meets the smooth skin on my cheek.

A sneeze sounds from the pantry and I turn around, handing Gigi back to Olivia before turning to the pantry. "Has anyone seen Georgia?"

Mom smiles and glances at the pantry. The slots are wide enough to ensure that the little girl is definitely watching me, so I make a show of looking around the kitchen—opening the trash can, peering into the cabinets under the sink, even opening the cookie jar on the counter.

"Colder." A little voice shouts as I open the oven.

"Did you hear that?" I gasp and look around wide-eyed, trying to keep a straight face. I take a big step toward the living room and wait for another clue.

"Colder." She giggles, louder this time.

Turning around, I take a few big steps toward the middle of the kitchen.

"Hotter." Her voice is much quieter now, and I grin.

"I wonder where she could be," I muse, rubbing my chin theatrically. Moving quickly, I pull open the pantry and snatch Georgia, throwing her tiny body over my shoulder and tickling her sides as she screams between laughs.

"Look who I found hiding out in the pantry, Gram," I say, walking to Mom and turning so she can pinch Georgia's cheeks.

Pulling Georgia upright again, I kiss her cheek before setting her back down.

"So back to your drunken night out," Mel says, pulling Olivia's attention away from blowing raspberries on Gigi's stomach. "Why were you even there in the first place? I wasn't allowed to go out to college parties until I was actually *in* college." She raises a brow and looks over at our mom, who seems unaffected as she pulls another strip of bacon out of the frying pan.

"Leave her alone, Mel. It was one night out, and she went with her friends. Plus, just because you weren't allowed to doesn't mean you didn't still go. I heard you sneaking out of your window all of those times."

Mel smirks and shrugs, as if to say, *good point.*

She looks back to Liv. "So, who'd you go with?"

"Leslie and Nicole," Liv says, pouring a glass of orange juice.

"And why didn't you *go home* with Leslie and Nicole?" Mel asks, crossing her arms across her chest.

Liv nods for me to take Gigi from her, so I pull her into my arms and grab her sippy cup from the counter.

"I lost them." Liv shrugs, popping a sliced strawberry into her mouth. Mom's already laid the table with sliced fruit, cinnamon rolls, and a steaming stack of her famous pancakes. My stomach growls at the smell, even after my bowl of cereal from earlier.

"You lost your friends on your first night out? That's like rule number one in the girl code, Liv. You have to make sure you don't lose each other; nights out can be dangerous if you're not paying attention."

Mom nods at that as she walks over to the table and sets down the plate of bacon, which is a silent cue for us to come sit down.

"I know that, but Nicole was meeting up with her boyfriend and Leslie disappeared to go to the bathroom and then texted me five minutes later that she was going home with some frat guy." Mel groans as she grabs Gigi's bib from her diaper bag. "I guess it's lucky that I ran into Luke," Olivia muses with a smile.

"Luke?" I prompt. "I thought you said James was the one who found you?"

Olivia looks up at me, eyes narrowing, as if she's challenging me to make a big deal out of this.

"Well, yeah. James found *us.*"

"Olivia," I warn, my tone a deadly contrast to my bouncy movements and the giggles coming from Gigi.

"Nothing happened. We were just hanging out." Her voice is sharp and defensive. "And so what if it did? You can't tell me who I can and can't be friends with. Luke's a nice guy, and if I want—"

"Luke's not a nice guy, Olivia. And he doesn't have *friends*, he just hooks up and moves on," I warn, sliding Gigi into her highchair.

"Not everyone on your team follows your stupid *no girlfriend* rule, Tristan," she bites back. "Some of them actually want to have more than meaningless sex with random jersey chasers."

The energy in the room stills as her comment hangs in the air. I glance over at my mom, who's trying to look busy with the napkin in front of her, but I catch the distinct look of shocked sadness on her face.

Fuck.

"Did Luke tell you that?" I say through my teeth.

I'm going to fucking kill him.

"No," she says too quickly. I raise an accusatory brow and she narrows her eyes at me.

"Olivia, that's enough." My mother's sharp voice surprises both of us.

"Mom, you can't seriously be on his side. He can't tell me who

I can and can't be friends with," she yells, her eyes widening in disbelief.

"I'm not taking sides, Livy. I just want to have a nice, peaceful breakfast with my children."

The only sound in the entire room is Gigi's small fists banging on the table. Georgia is climbing into her booster chair, and I meet her eyes, relieved that she doesn't understand what's going on.

"I don't think you have room to talk about Tristan when you went out looking like a cheap hooker last night, Liv." Mel smirks playfully, tossing a grape at Olivia.

Olivia's jaw drops as she stares as Mel, but her pissed off expression cracks quickly and suddenly she's laughing.

"I didn't look that cheap," she counters, with absolutely no conviction in her voice.

"More like a discounted high-end hooker," I agree, easily dodging the strawberry she launches at my head.

The sound of my parents' bedroom door closing echoes down the hall, and when Dad rounds the corner and sees all of us sitting at the table, he smiles and starts toward his own chair.

His walk is off, and by the set of his jaw, he's trying to mask it as much as he can, but the small wobble of his left leg is evident. He looks at me, and with a short shake of his head, he dismisses the question I haven't even asked yet.

I glance over to see Mom and Mel making the girls' small sampler plates of the breakfast items, and I lean toward my father, keeping my voice low. "What's wrong with your leg, Dad?"

He doesn't look at me as he pours sugar into his coffee.

"Just tweaked it, it's nothing." He shrugs.

"It doesn't look like just a tweak. What happened?" I counter.

"There was a little accident at the shop."

He's worked at the mechanic shop in town since he moved here from New York. He's had some pretty close calls over the years, but he's never really been injured. I would never say this to him because he's way too proud, but I'm guessing this injury has more to do with his age than anything else. Every time I see him, he looks like he's lost even more weight, like he's withering away right in front of my eyes.

I know the answer, but for some reason, I still ask, "Have you gotten it checked out?"

He snorts and takes a sip of his coffee. "We'll talk about it later," he shuts me down. "Now, pass your old man the pancakes."

———

I know without a shadow of a doubt that my mother's pancakes would be my dish of choice for my last meal on earth, but today, my syrup-soaked pile was left nearly untouched on my plate. The idea of my mother knowing about my one-and-done sex life was bad enough but seeing my father limp around the house made me lose my appetite.

I followed him into his office after breakfast and waited for him to speak, but he stubbornly kept quiet as he settled into the armchair in the corner. His walk became more of a limp with each step, and by the time we were at his office, I had one arm around his waist, supporting his weight as he wobbled to the armchair.

"You should take a break for a while, take some time off."

He lifts his feet onto the ottoman in front of him, wincing when he readjusts the position of his leg.

"I'm fine, Tristan." He shakes his head curtly, and I know he's getting annoyed.

"You're almost sixty, can't you retire?"

He looks uncomfortable as he glances down at the cup of coffee he brought with him from breakfast.

"You don't have a retirement," I surmise, shocked.

His eyes meet mine before flicking over to the closed door. "Keep your voice down," he says quietly.

"Mom doesn't know?"

"Tristan," he warns, but my mind is reeling.

How does he not have a retirement? My father is the most frugal, responsible, calculated man I've ever met. He clips coupons every Sunday, for fuck's sake.

"How?" I ask, genuinely shocked.

He looks like he's considering something, and when his eyes meet mine, he sighs. "I had a retirement, but I invested it into something that I believe in."

I stare at him as his words sink in. Invested it?

"Your high school coach pulled us for a meeting when you were a freshman. He said he'd never seen a talent like you with so much drive. He said if you were to be fully committed, you would make it all the way to the pros." I stare at him. "You stayed out back shooting that ball until midnight most nights; you watched game tape for fun on the weekends; you had a journal to keep track of your shooting percentage. You were in love with that game, you still are," he says.

My chest tightens as the gravity of the situation hits me.

"We couldn't afford to send you to those camps every summer or sign you up for those elite leagues without dipping into our savings. There's a reason most people from your school couldn't go, Tristan. Those camps, some of them were a few grand just to sign up—just to be considered—but I knew how important they were to you. I knew what they meant for your future. Then, you got injured and had to have that surgery. It all added up."

"You used your retirement on me? On my basketball?"

He leans forward in his seat and shrugs.

"Why would you do that? Do you know the percentage of people who *actually* make it to the NBA?" The blood drains from my face. How could he be so careless? So reckless with his entire life's savings? "Barely anyone makes it; less than one percent," I continue. I feel my hands tugging at my hair, but I don't remember putting them there.

"But you did," he says softly.

"Not yet," I snap, shaking my head as I pace the small office.

"Not yet." He nods. "But you will."

I glare at him, dumbfounded. "Are you crazy?"

He grins.

What the actual fuck is going on?

"Tristan, stop pacing, you're making me dizzy."

"*You're* making *me* dizzy," I shoot back lamely. "Why would you risk everything? Why wouldn't you tell me? Your entire future was riding on me, and I didn't even know it." My words are rushed and I have to rake in a breath of air.

"Because of this," he says, motioning toward me. "I didn't want to stress you out."

"Well, I'm pretty fucking stressed now," I say.

He raises a brow and I shake my head, not in the mood to be reprimanded for cursing in front of him.

"What if I don't make it?" I ask, my voice hoarse. The image of my parents losing their house and everything they've ever known flashes in my mind and I want to puke.

"Then we'll figure it out." He shrugs easily.

"*We'll figure it out?*" I repeat incredulously.

I take a step toward the door, unsure of what to do or say. My mind feels numb as I think back to every time I signed up for a league or went away to those elite basketball camps over the summer. How did I not wonder how they'd paid for it—my mechanic father and stay-at-home mother?

I'm antsy and have a sudden urge to go to the practice arena and get some shooting time in, or at least go for a run, something other than stand here and think about how my parents' entire future is riding on me not being a complete failure.

Walking to the door, I pause before pulling it open.

"I was never worried," he says softly, and I glance over my shoulder to see him leaning back into the chair, a wide grin spreading across his face. "I've always known you'd make it."

SIXTEEN

ABBY

"Abigail, are you there? Hello?"

I click the BlueTooth button on my phone and turn up the volume in my car to hear my mother's impatient voice ringing through the speakers. I barely had enough time to get my car turned on and the heat circulating before she called. I really need to stop telling her my work schedule.

"Yes, Mom," I say, clicking my seatbelt into place.

"How was work?" she asks. The shuffling of papers in the background and the clicking of her heels on the hardwood floor of her office echoes through the line.

"It was fine, kind of slow."

I look both ways before slowly pulling out onto the main road toward my apartment. I hate driving during the winter in Washington. The thought of hitting a patch of ice and crashing into a tree to my very painful death always seems to haunt me whenever the temperature drops, especially because I never had to worry about icy roads growing up in Florida.

"How are your classes going?"

"They're going good." I try to sound upbeat, but honestly, today has been terrible, and I just want to get home and hide away in my room for the rest of the weekend, drowning myself in ice cream and terrible reality TV shows.

An uncomfortable heat washes over my body as the memory of Tristan walking me out to my car replays in my mind.

He almost kissed me.

Almost.

"Good as in you're going to have a 4.0 semester? Or good as in you don't really care?"

I bite down on my tongue as her words pull me out of my reverie. "My classes are going well, Mom," I rephrase.

"I'll take that as a no to the 4.0 question."

"I don't know yet. I'm only a few weeks in, and I'm taking some really hard classes." I glance over at the screen on my dash illuminated with her contact name and I'm tempted to press the *end call* button. This is hardly the conversation that I want to be having right now.

"You need to study more if you're struggling, Abigail. Jeff was in a much harder program than you and he had no problem graduating with a 4.0. At some point, you have to stop blaming the classes and start taking responsibility for yourself and your lack of discipline."

My 3.9 GPA will haunt me for the rest of my life.

"I know, Mom. I'll study tonight."

I hear her typing on her phone and I wait for her to come back to the conversation. "I ran into Tyler's father today." If I wasn't driving, I would have rolled my eyes so hard they might have fallen out of my head. "He asked about you. He mentioned that Tyler is still single."

"Hmm," I hum, trying not to take the bait. The *end call* button is looking even better now, but I focus on keeping a safe following distance between myself and the car in front of me, trying to ignore the rush of annoyance that always seems to accompany my phone calls with my mother.

"I told him you were still single as well, and that Tyler should reach out to you again."

"Why would you do that?" I groan.

I want to be surprised, but the fact that my mother meddled in my love life—a love life she knows absolutely nothing about—is far from surprising. Especially because it really has nothing to do with me at all, rather the connection she lost with Tyler's family when we broke up.

"You two were good together. It wasn't fair of you to just dump him like that."

I pull into the parking spot in front of my apartment building and put my car in park. "I didn't like him anymore, Mom. What was I supposed to do?"

She scoffs. "You barely gave him a chance, Abigail."

"We were together for three years. I think that's enough of a chance."

She's quiet for a moment and then her voice falls into a familiar terse tone. "Do *not* be disrespectful to me, Abigail."

Running a hand over my face, I lay my head back against the headrest and sigh inwardly. "I'm sorry."

"I have a conference call now, I have to go," she says.

"Okay."

"Love you."

I bite down on the inside of my cheek. "Love you, too, Mom."

The phone call with my mother was the cherry on top of my already terrible weekend, which is why I stood in the stream of scalding water for longer than I probably should have. The way the heat unfurled my muscles and hazed my mind was too good to give up.

Now, dressed in an oversized USW sweatshirt and polka dotted sleep shorts, I scan the freezer for the cookies and ice cream I bought the other day.

"Rough shift?" Jenny asks when I fall onto the couch across from her. Nia is sprawled out between us with her legs propped up on a stack of pillows, and both of them are holding wine glasses brimming with the dark red liquid. I shrug and pull the top off the container, digging my spoon into the icy goodness. Taking my first bite, I relax into the cushion and revel in the way it melts on my tongue.

Ice cream fixes everything.

"Are you okay, Abs?"

I don't look up to meet Nia's eyes as I consider her question.

Am I okay?

I've been trying to keep myself together since last night, but I can feel the glue starting to come apart. I thought I could do this. I thought I could be spontaneous and fun and shed my prudish skin for once in my life. Which I did, except I didn't just take a step out, I got a running start and catapulted off the freaking ledge into the unknown.

And that's where I'm at right now—the unknown.

I know a few things, though.

First, Tristan doesn't date.

I've known that since before I even spoke to him, and I knew that before I kissed him in the bathroom. It's not like I went into this blindly;

I was well aware of the unspoken rules which became even clearer after he pulled me aside and said them to my face—*just a hookup.*

Second, I don't hookup.

Or, I didn't. Still don't? I don't know anymore because if I'm being completely honest, I know that if we wouldn't have been interrupted in his room last night, I wouldn't have stopped him from going further than kissing, or further than what we've already done. Which is how I know that I've broken the single most important rule of casual hookups. I've started to actually like him.

Like, *like* him, like him.

"Abs?"

Looking up, I realize that Jenny and Nia are watching me.

"I need to tell you guys something," I say, trying to swallow the knot in my throat. Jenny pauses the rerun of *Sex and The City* playing on the TV and they both sit up.

"Did something happen?" Jenny asks, tucking her legs underneath her.

"You could say that." I nod before eating the lump of ice cream from my spoon. I know I can't tell them about Tristan. It's too complicated. I still have to write this article, and I have class with him, not to mention the amount of times I'm sure we'll bump into each other at parties or events now that we actually know each other. I need them to know, just not that it's about him.

Taking a deep breath, I dig my spoon into the ice cream. "I kind of met a guy."

They both gasp dramatically, and I can't help but laugh at the sound.

"Oh, my God, Abby," Jenny squeals, pulling her blanket closer around her as she sits up, careful not to spill her wine.

"Who is it? Do we know him?" Nia asks, putting her wine glass down on the coffee table. She must be serious, if she's putting down her wine.

"You don't know him," I say quickly, trying to think about how I can stay as close to the truth without making it obvious. "He's in my newspaper class. He's helping me with the scholarship article I'm writing about Tristan."

That's a half-lie, which I guess makes it a half-truth, too.

"What's his name?"

I glance around until my eyes land on the paused scene on the TV. Carrie's on and off again beau, Mr. Big, is smiling on the screen.

"For the sake of anonymity, let's just call him Mr. Big." I smirk.

Nia's eyes widen and her devious grin makes me laugh. "Abby Ryan, oh, my God. This is going to be good; I can feel it."

My face is already burning. I've listened to countless hookup stories from Nia, and even a fair few from Jenny, but I've never been one to go into detail about my own sex life. Not that there was much to tell, until now. I need to band aid this, to rip it off quickly and get it over with.

"We hooked up."

There's a moment of silence in the room and then an explosion of squeals.

"When?"

"Where?"

"How far?"

"Was it good?"

"Did you finally get your O?"

"Oh, my God, *Abby*."

I hide my face behind a couch pillow, suddenly wishing I would have just brought this secret to the grave, but when Nia leans forward and snatches the pillow out of my hands, throwing it across the room, I know there's no going back now.

"We need answers, Abigail." She grabs her wine as she falls back onto the couch, and when her eyes meet mine again over her glass, my face burns so hot that I'm pretty sure the skin on my cheeks might actually melt off.

"Okay, well without going into too much detail—"

"What? No. We want the details," Jenny cuts in.

"Every single one." Nia nods. "*Every single one.*"

I take a deep breath as I think back to the night at the bar. "Well, it was the night we went out to O'Malley's."

Nia's eyes widen and her jaw drops. "Was it in the bathroom?"

Oh, my God, was it that obvious?

I nod sheepishly and watch as Nia jumps to her feet, turning to Jenny. "I knew it! I told you she wasn't really sick. I called it." She turns back to me with a smug smile on her face. "Jenny thought you were too innocent; she didn't believe me, but I knew."

"Wait . . . Mr. Big was at the bar that night?" Jenny's brows pull together, as if she's trying to piece it all together.

"Mhm." I hum quickly, trying to stomp out any suspicion that it might have been Tristan. "I ran into him after we played beer pong with James and Tristan."

She seems confused, but thankfully, she was even drunker than I was at that point, so she won't be able to point out any inconsistencies in my lie.

"Tristan and I went to the bar to get water, but he disappeared," I say as casually as I can. "And then Mr. Big saw me and came over."

"Wait, let me get this straight. You, Abigail Ryan, the most innocent, rule loving girl I know, drunkenly hooked up with a guy in the bathroom at O'Malley's?"

I roll my eyes and nod. "Yes, Jenny, miracles do happen."

"Am I being *Punk'd?*" She turns and looks around the room dramatically.

"I knew it," Nia repeats, sitting back in her seat with the smuggest grin I've ever seen. "Did you guys have sex?" She eyes me over the rim of her wine with a raised brow as she takes a long sip.

Does oral sex count as sex?

"Not in the traditional sense," I say slowly, hoping that I won't have to actually say the words out loud. I might have made it this far into the conversation without dying, but if I have to say the words *went down,* I will actually implode of complete and utter embarrassment.

Nia glances at Jenny and then back at me before licking the air in a long languid motion, her brow raising in question.

I nod and shovel another bite of ice cream into my mouth. I keep my eyes on the carton as I dig my spoon in again, and when I finally look up, the grins on both of their faces makes me groan.

"Did you . . .?" Jenny asks as her eyes widen.

Did I have an orgasm? Yes.

"Mhm." I hum and bite down on the inside of my lip to keep from smiling, but when I look up to see my two best friends grinning at me like I told them I just won the lottery, I can't hold it back.

"I feel like a proud mama bear right now," Nia says, wiping a fake tear away. "I need to know this guy's name and address. I have to send him a thank you note with flowers or chocolate or something." She grins as I stick my tongue out at her.

"So have you seen him since?" Jenny asks, too excited to be off-topic.

"A few times." I nod. "He's still helping me out with the article."

"And have you hooked up again?"

"No." I shake my head. "But . . . we almost kissed the last time I saw him."

"So, you guys are like friends with benefits then?" she clarifies.

Is that what we are?

I mean, technically, we've only hooked up once. I don't think you could really categorize us as much more than a one-time hookup if we haven't actually hooked up again, no matter how many times we've *almost* kissed.

"I don't think it's that serious." I shake my head.

"Well, whatever you are, welcome to the amazing world of casual hookups, Abs. No feelings, no strings, no stress." I don't meet her gaze. "You don't have feelings for him . . . right?" she prompts, but by her tone, I can tell that she already knows. "Oh, no, Abby."

"Oh, yes," I say flatly, stabbing my spoon into the ice cream a little too aggressively before popping another spoonful into my mouth.

"Have you told him?" Jenny asks.

"There's no point. He's made his opinion on the situation pretty clear. He doesn't date."

"He sounds like a douchebag," Nia snaps. "But hey, now that you're pseudo-friends with Beck, you should ask him what to do. There's no better person to get advice from on fuck boys than the king fuck boy himself."

I bite the inside of my cheek to keep from laughing, but when I look up at my best friends, I can't hold it in. "He's not that bad." I defend with a shrug. "He's actually kind of sweet."

She waves my comment off, as if I couldn't possibly be telling the truth. "Yeah, I'm sure he's great." I can practically taste her sarcasm. "So great that I would usually suggest that you hook up with Beck to get over Big, since the best way to get *over* someone is to get *under* someone new, but the last thing we need is for you to fall for Tristan Beck." She snorts, falling back into the couch cushion.

I try to keep my laugh as casual as I can as I take another bite. "Yeah." I shake my head, as if the thought alone is hilarious. "That's the last thing I need."

SEVENTEEN

ABBY

I can't tell if the sharp pains in my stomach are period cramps or just a side effect of the anxiety rippling through me as I stare down at the practice test in front of me. I failed. I missed nine out of the twenty questions. I even missed the extra credit questions, which according to Hannigan, should have been easy bonus points.

The fact that I missed nearly half of the questions is bad enough, but to make matters worse, Hannigan wrote commentary on the outer margins of my test. Apparently, she thinks I should consider *hiring a tutor* or *rereading the chapters*. I can tell by the way she worded it that she doesn't actually think I read them in the first place, which just goes to show how little I understand this stupid subject.

I knew I wasn't great at chemistry, but I had no idea I was this bad at it. I want to cry, but I know those tears have more to do with the influx of hormones currently wreaking havoc on my uterus than the semi-rude comments on my paper.

"This is a good indication of how well you're understanding the material so far," Hannigan says to the class as she sits down at her desk. "You can pinpoint the concepts you're not understanding and study them before the first unit exam on Thursday."

I uncap my highlighter—the neon yellow one designated for high priority tasks—and highlight the note I had made about the exam in my planner last week when it was announced.

Tristan coughs a few times, but I keep my eyes trained on my planner. Apart from a sleepy *good morning* from him, we haven't had much of an opportunity to speak once class started. Hannigan jumped straight into our new chapter lecture and then passed back our quizzes, and while I usually enjoy letting Tristan distract me, I'm actually thankful for the distraction from *him* today, because I don't want to have to talk to him.

I don't want to have to acknowledge what happened on Friday, but knowing him, I'm in for another *it can't happen again* talk, which would effectively strip me of all the remaining self-confidence I have.

"Do you want me to help you study for the exam? I'm free after practice tonight."

My gaze flicks to the untouched test in front of him. He doesn't have a single red mark or note scrawled into the margin on his paper asking him if he needs to be recommended a tutor. Instead, Hannigan left him a small note at the top of the test next to the large *A+* that looks a hell of a lot like a smiley face. Of course, even our chemistry professor flirts with him.

I glance back to my own practice test again. If it wasn't covered in enough red ink to look like a pen bled out on it, I probably would have said no. I spent the entirety of yesterday in bed, binge-watching ridiculous dating reality shows while eating nearly an entire pack of Oreos. I decided then, as I closed up the considerably lighter pack of cookies, that I needed to move on from whatever *this* is.

My plan was to keep as much space between us as possible. To keep our conversations centered around the article while only spending time together during class and the few more interviews that I still have planned. It seemed like a great plan, but that was before Hannigan slaughtered my practice test.

"Sure." I nod, trying to ignore the traitorous part of me that's reveling in the idea of spending tonight with him. "That sounds great."

———

"So, let's consider the molecule acetone. It's a polar molecule, and the central carbon is double bonded to an oxygen atom, which has two lone pairs," he explains, pointing to the diagram he drew for me. I nod, trying as hard as humanly possible to soak in all of the information in front of me.

"The oxygen atom has a partial negative charge, and the carbon atom has a partial positive charge, so what do you think will happen if that acetone molecule is placed near another acetone molecule?"

His gaze scans over me, trying to see if I'm actually understanding what he's saying, which I am, for the most part, but *God*, this subject really sucks.

"A dipole-dipole interaction," I say slowly, looking up at him to make sure I'm not completely off base with my answer.

He grins at me and nods.

"The carbon from the second molecule is going to be attracted to the oxygen of the first molecule because opposites attract, so this negatively charged oxygen atom will be attracted to this partially positively charged carbon atom, which creates this dipole-dipole interaction," he says, pointing to the specific molecules in the diagram with his pen.

"Okay, that makes sense." I nod slowly. "It's a lot easier to understand when you break it down like this. I don't understand why Hannigan goes a hundred miles per hour in her lectures. How am I supposed to learn like that?" I sit back on the couch and sigh, noticing the smile he's holding back as his dimple indents slightly on his cheek. As a chemical engineering major, I'm sure that for him, this is like teaching someone the ABC's.

"Aren't you in a freshman chem class, Ryan?" Micah asks with a smirk as he props his long legs up on the coffee table in front of him. He crosses one ankle over the other as he tosses another kernel of popcorn into his mouth. He's lounging on the other side of the couch with the video game controller in his hand. Apparently, watching me struggle to learn basic chemistry is more entertaining than killing people on *Call of Duty*.

"It's not as easy as it sounds," I defend, but I know my argument falls flat when Tristan looks away, hiding the grin on his face.

I was more than a little relieved when he led us to the couch to study rather than his room. If I'm going to successfully get over whatever *this* is, I probably shouldn't be studying with him in his bed. The downside to being in the living room is that his roommates have an uncanny ability to make a ridiculous amount of noise, no matter what they're doing.

Micah was generous enough to plug in a headset to his controller so the insane sounds of gunshots and explosives no longer echoed through the living room, but his constant stream of profanities whenever he would get shot at were not so quiet.

Luke was out here playing video games with Micah for a while until he got a FaceTime call which he ran into his room to take. He looked over at us before disappearing into the hall, and by the quirk of his lips, I have a feeling it wasn't his dad calling to check in like he said it was when he shot up from the couch.

I don't actually think James is home, or if he is, he's been shut away in his room.

"I think we should go over solubility again," Tristan says, shuffling through his papers to find the notes he wrote down for that chapter.

It's been two hours since we started studying and my brain feels like it's melting inside my skull. Not only is this material extremely hard to understand, but there are five chapters of it to go through for the test. I'm about to protest when the front door opens, and a group of guys walk in. All of them are ridiculously tall and seeing them all together looks like some kind of circus group, though I figure they're more likely on the basketball team than some weird traveling carnival.

The guy in the front of the group spots us on the couch first and he nods toward us. His familiar short red hair catches my attention, and it takes me a second to place him as the guy that asked Nia to dance at the bar.

"Hey, T. Didn't realize you had company over." He grins at me in the way people do when they want you to know that they recognize you without actually saying it.

I grin back.

"You would have known if you texted first, Emery," Tristan says, turning back to the stack of papers in his hands, completely unfazed by the towering group of guys now scattering around the room.

Half of them disappear into the kitchen, and it only takes a few seconds before the distinct sound of beer tops hitting the counter sounds. The other half drop down onto the couch, already fully absorbed into the game Micah's playing.

"You still down to play some CTF?" Emery asks, taking a beer from the guy who just walked out of the kitchen with two in his hands.

"Can't, we're studying." He shakes his head, pulling the familiar paper out of the stack titled *isotopes* in his boyish scrawl.

"What's CTF?" I ask, crossing my legs under me as I uncap my water bottle.

"Capture the flag." Emery grins.

"Capture the flag?" I laugh. "I haven't played that since elementary school."

"We play a more badass version. You wanna play?" He winks.

I glance at Tristan, who seems annoyed by the interruption.

"I could use a little study break," I admit.

"They turned CTF into a drinking game." He shakes his head. "I don't think it's the best study break activity."

"Come on, Beck, don't be such a kill joy," he goads, winking at me again.

"Fuck off, Emery," Tristan shoots back quickly, handing me the paper.

The group of guys surrounding Micah all explode off the couch in an eruption of cheers, sending the paper in my hands flying into the air out of surprise. Tristan catches it easily before it can hit the floor while I look to the screen to see that Micah just won the game.

"I don't think I can spend another minute learning about chemistry," I groan, taking the paper from him again. I eye the sheet, realizing quickly that even though we've reviewed this chapter tonight, I've already forgotten most of it.

"Yeah, come on, T." Micah grins, rounding the couch. "You guys have been at it for like two hours. You need a break."

I try to ignore the coughs and laughs of the surrounding boys, but my cheeks still heat a little at the comment.

"Yeah, come on, T." I imitate Micah, and when Tristan turns back to look at me, I'm rewarded with the most amused look as his brows raise. The memory of him asking me to play beer pong flashes in my mind, and I echo his words back to him. "Live a little."

———

"I don't think you understand what you just got yourself into," Tristan says as he holds the door open for me. We're the last two out of the house because he insisted that I layer up with one of his hoodies before going out, *"just in case."*

I didn't understand the concern, seeing as I already had on my own hoodie, but when we step out to see the group of boys all loaded with paintball guns, the odd request suddenly makes more sense. Though the material of his hoodie is thick and falls to my upper thighs, I doubt it's going to do much to protect me from the sting of a paintball gun.

"Oh."

"Don't worry," he says, leaning over to whisper near my ear as we reach the outer circle of the group. "It's just a precaution. I won't let them shoot you."

Emery's standing in the middle of the circle with a small stack of red and blue pullover vests in his hands, which he holds up as he says, "Rules are simple. Face and balls are off-limits. Vests are the targets. If your target is hit, you're out of the game." I glance around to see that everyone already has their vests on. "You can reenter the game once you down two beers. You can carry two with you for instant re-entry, but it'll weigh you down." He nods towards the box of canned beers sitting at the top of the driveway. "The first team to collect the other team's flag and bring it back to their side wins."

After tossing two red vests to Tristan, he shuffles through a duffle bag at his feet and pulls out two more paintball guns.

"No shooting Ryan," Tristan calls loudly. The gravity in his voice surprises me, and when everyone in the group turns to look at him, I follow their gaze to watch his jaw tense as he eyes his teammates. Severity shines his emerald eyes, as if he's daring anyone to challenge him. I look over my shoulder toward the group who are all staring back at him, nodding curtly in a silent agreement. Like soldiers falling into rank, the line of authority is displayed right here in front of my eyes. Tristan is their captain, their leader, on and off the court.

"She's going to have a flag belt on instead." He explains as he hands me the bright yellow flag belt. "She's off limits. No exceptions."

The collective gaze of the group falls on me and I give a sheepish wave. I wasn't expecting to be the exception to the rule, but I'm definitely not going to complain about it. Getting shot with a paintball gun hurts in normal temperatures, I can't even imagine how bad it would hurt in this freezing weather.

"I'm about as athletic as a slug, so I won't be hard to catch anyway." I shrug, clipping the belt around my waist. I'm probably more of a liability for my team with this belt, because if it's going to come down to me outrunning anyone, let alone the guys watching me re-adjust the flag belt, I don't stand a chance. When I look up, I catch Micah grinning from across the group.

"That's the spirit, Ryan."

———

I don't know why I agreed to this.

Capture the flag with paintball guns is already way out of my element, but the fact that it's pitch-black, and our playing field spans the entire street, makes this that much more anxiety-inducing.

Apparently, the entire team lives on this street, divided up into different houses based on their friend groups. In fact, every house in this neighborhood is rented out to USW students, which makes me feel better about the fact that I'm currently hiding behind a huge tree in some random person's front yard. But still, I can barely see two feet in front of me, and the nearest streetlight is at least ten yards away. I could just camp out here, but I'm starting to realize that the longer I stay still, the quicker I'll turn into a human icicle.

I was running behind Tristan when the whistle first sounded to start the game, but I quickly realized the insane difference in our ability to run, and after about ten seconds of sprinting, I was winded enough to find refuge behind this tree to catch my breath.

I really should start working out.

Peeking around the thick trunk, I don't see any movement, but to be fair, I don't see much of anything in this lighting. I can hear my teeth starting to chatter, and a shiver runs up my spine as a gust of wind blows my hair across my face.

"Screw it," I whisper, pulling my paintball gun close to my chest as I sprint into the general direction where I lost Tristan. The rapid clicks of a paintball gun pulls my attention toward the street to see Micah gunning down a blue vested guy. Neither of them seems to see me, so I keep going, stopping behind a huge truck to catch my breath. I glance down to double-check that my flag belt is still intact, but nearly jump out of my skin when a voice sounds behind me.

"Hey, Ryan."

I yelp as the sound of my paintball gun firing echoes through the street. When I look over my shoulder, I spot Tristan immediately, doubled over with shaking shoulders as he tries his hardest to silence his laughs.

"Why would you sneak up on me like that?" I hiss at him, my face burning hot from the fact that he literally just scared a shot out of me. He starts to say something but can't seem to stop laughing long enough to actually get it out.

"Ryan—why is your finger on the trigger?" He kneels down next to me behind the truck, and when his emerald eyes meet mine, his lips pull back into a teasing grin.

"I don't know, to be prepared for when someone sneaks up behind me, maybe?" I shoot back lamely.

"You almost shot your own foot," he points out. "And probably gave away our location in the process." He reaches over and readjusts my hand, so my finger is nowhere near the trigger.

"Whatever," I say, biting down on my lip to keep from laughing. "You almost just gave me a heart attack."

He grins, but when a snap of a twig sounds from behind us, his eyes narrow and he props his gun up, ready to fire as he surveys the surrounding area. "We need to move, follow me," he whispers. "And stay with me this time."

"Well then stop running so fast," I grumble, following him around the side of the car.

Keeping his gun ready to shoot, he starts jogging—at a much slower pace than before—through the shadow of the trees. I keep my eyes trained on the ground, praying that I won't trip over something and face plant into the icy grass.

I don't even realize that he's stopped jogging until my face smacks into his back, and I let out a low groan as I rub my tingling nose. I try not to focus on the fact that I'm breathing much harder than he is as he scans the area.

"That's the flag." He motions around the tree that we're now crouched behind. I hold onto his arm as I lean around him, eyeing the neon green flag sitting on a trash can. Two guys in blue vests are guarding it.

"Okay, here's the plan." He pulls me back out of view, and when I look up at him, his eyes are alive and bright, nearly glowing in the dark shadows. He's speaking so quietly I have to lean in a little more to hear him, and his spearmint breath warms my cheeks. "I'll take both of them out so you can grab the flag. Then we'll make a break for it," he says.

"There has to be more of them around here." I shake my head as I survey the pitch-black area.

"Don't worry, I'll cover you. Plus, they can't shoot you, Ryan," he reminds me, tugging gently on my flag belt.

I look down at the belt around my waist and fiddle with the clasp, making sure it's on as tightly as possible. When I look up again, he's grinning down at me.

"What?" I laugh.

"Nothing." He shakes his head. "You just look hot with a paint-ball gun."

I glance down at the gun, willing my cheeks to listen to me for once in my life and not flare red-hot, but when the familiar warmth floods my face, I look up to see his dimple deepen. His eyes meet mine for a second before he blinks.

He turns away and clears his throat softly. "You ready?"

Stealing another look at the two guards, I blow out a long, resigned breath and nod. "Ready."

It happens before I can even register what's going on. Four loud pops make my heart stop dead in my chest, and seconds later, both of the guys guarding the flag scream as they clutch their chest.

"Fuck." One of them, that I now recognize as Luke, screams out as two bright yellow paint splatters mark his chest. "That really fuck-ing hurt."

Not wasting a second, I start to sprint toward the flag. Just as I manage to grab the green fabric, a grunt sounds behind me, and I pivot to see Tristan swearing as he turns around. Three bright yellow splatters color the back of his red vest.

A flash of blue is sprinting straight toward me, and I bring my gun up frantically, pulling the trigger as quick as I can. With six loud pops, I watch awestruck as the blue vested boy walks into the glow of the streetlights, cursing loudly as he looks down at the paint splattered across his arm. I somehow managed to get him three times in the upper arm and once on the very edge of the target near his shoulder.

"It counts," I gasp, turning to a wide-eyed Tristan.

The original two blue vested guards have disappeared, likely to the beer box to down their two beers to reenter the game, but I know they'll be back soon.

"I have two beers," I say quickly, pulling the two cans from the front pocket of my hoodie before handing them to Tristan. I can't get shot, but if someone pulls my flag off, I also have to drink to get back into the game, and if I somehow make it through this entire thing without drinking at least once, I'll be shocked.

I feel extremely exposed standing in the middle of the road under the streetlamp with the neon green flag in my hand, but I wait as Tristan pops both open and downs them quickly, tossing the empty cans into the trash bin the flag was just sitting on. The guy I just shot is disappearing toward the house for his own beers.

"We're never going to make it over that line." I shake my head.

"Not with that attitude," he says, pulling his gun up to his line of vision, surveying the area.

I want to roll my eyes, but the anxiety is now seeping through my bones. Three of their team members know we have the flag and all of them are currently downing their own beers to reenter the game, all of them with the one mission of stopping us.

I glance down to the flag in my hand.

Of stopping *me*.

"Do you want to hold this?" I ask.

He doesn't even glance at me as he shakes his head.

"You've got this, Ryan."

"I most certainly do not," I counter, tightening my belt.

He doesn't give me much warning before he starts to run toward the shadow of the trees. I can barely see as I follow behind him, but the adrenaline pulsing through my veins is helping me to keep up with his quick pace.

The streetlight in front of their house signals the line between territories, and as we come to a stop at the edge of the tree line, it's about six houses away. All we have to do to win is get this flag over that line, which wouldn't be a big deal if the four blue vested guys we just shot a little bit ago weren't patrolling the street directly across from us, waiting for us to pop out of the shadows.

Our cover is about to run out, and our only path to the finish line is in the reach of the streetlights.

"Fuck, okay," he whispers, turning around to look down at me.

The flag in my hand suddenly feels like a live grenade, but I keep my hold on it as I stare up at him. His eyes lower to my belt before flicking back up to my eyes. "I have an idea. Do you trust me?"

I take a step back, but I nod.

"Just follow my lead," he says, turning back toward the line.

I don't have time to argue because he's already running to the edge of the shadows, and I follow right behind him. At the last second before he steps out into the light, he turns around and swoops down, throwing me over his shoulder before turning back and full-on sprinting toward the line.

The scream catches in my throat when I realize that I'm upside down, and I grasp for the material on the back of his hoodie while making sure to hold onto the flag like my life depends on it. He has a tight hold on my waist but the pressure of his shoulder on my stomach is enough to make me nauseous, so I squeeze my eyes shut.

The guys' screams echo down the street behind us as they catch sight of us, and the sound of footsteps pounding the pavement sends my heart into overdrive.

"Don't shoot," one of their voices carries. "She's off-limits."

The sound of hard footsteps gains behind us, and I open my eyes to see Luke only a few strides away. His brow is set, and his eyes are zeroed in on the flag billowing out behind us as Tristan pushes us forward. Pulling my gun up, I aim it at the freshman whose eyes grow wide as he narrowly dodges the paintball bullet.

Tristan's throaty laugh shakes his body beneath me, and I watch Luke throw his hands up over his head in defeat as he watches us step over the line.

In one quick motion, Tristan has me on my feet again, his hands firmly planted on my hips as I sway for a moment, waiting for the blood to rush back down and my vision to clear. Just as everything stops spinning, I feel the instant loss of heat as he releases me and steps away. The rush of red vests crashes around us in a tangle of hands connecting in high fives and shoulder slaps all around me.

"Holy shit, that was awesome." Micah grins, reaching his tattooed arm out to me for a low five. "You two actually make a pretty good team."

I slap his hand and glance over my shoulder, searching until the familiar emerald eyes catch mine. One of his teammates is pulling him back, dropping an arm around his shoulders to rub their hands through his hair. He manages to escape their embrace, and when he looks up, I catch his flushed cheeks and toothy smile from here.

"Yeah." I laugh, dodging the playful swat toward my butt from Luke as he walks by. "I guess we do."

EIGHTEEN

ABBY

I watch with bated breath as the bowling ball soars towards the pins and hits the target with annoying accuracy.

The boy in a perfectly pressed blue button-up shirt spins on his heel and grins at me, his face illuminated by the reflection of the giant disco ball hanging above the lanes.

"How are you so good at this?" I'm practically pouting as I pass by him to grab my neon pink ball. I've barely knocked down any pins, and my past three turns were all gutter balls. I'm pretty sure he could miss every pin for the rest of the game, and I still wouldn't have a chance of winning.

"You can still put on the bumpers, I won't judge," Dean says.

I don't have to turn around to know he's smiling.

Taking a deep breath, I release it slowly, trying to center myself as I stare down the pins. At this point, I just want to knock *one* down.

"Do you want some pointers?"

I jump a little at his voice and look over my shoulder to see him walking toward me. His cheeks are slightly flushed, and when I nod, he stops right next to me, hesitating for a moment before guiding my bowling ball up so that it's aligned with the center of my chest.

"Make sure to keep your thumb in line with the pins," he says as his hands adjust the ball slightly, so my wrist is angled up and my thumb is in line with my target. "And try to keep it as smooth as you can. You kind of fidget before you release, and it knocks off the trajectory of the ball."

He demonstrates the correct motion for releasing the ball, and I nod along, attempting to look like I'm paying attention to his step-by-step tutorial instead of checking him out.

His blond hair is styled so that his bangs are pushed back off his face, and his high cheekbones, boyish smile, and ocean blue eyes are more charming than I remember from our diner encounter. He steps back and motions for me to go ahead, and his encouraging smile turns into something decidedly more amused as I give him a thumbs up with the hand not currently holding the ridiculously heavy ball.

"Here goes nothing," I sigh, bringing the ball up to my chest the way he instructed. With one swift movement, I bring my hand back and then propel it forward, keeping my thumb directed toward the pins. The ball hits the lane with a thud, and it veers off toward the right and clips the pins at the edge of the formation, knocking down four.

The crash of the ball blends in with the rest of the games in the bowling alley, but I revel in it all the same. It may only be four pins, but it's more than I've managed to get all night, and I'm not about to downplay that victory.

Turning on my heel, I want to launch into the air in a celebratory dance. If I could do that heel-clicking thing without breaking my ankles I would have, but for my own safety, I settle for finger guns pointed at the ceiling as I wiggle my hips.

"That deserves a beer." Dean laughs. "Both the pins *and* the dance." I grin at him and blow on my finger guns before holstering them at my sides. "Any preferences?"

"Whatever they have on tap is fine." I grin, dropping down into the cold plastic seat at the table designated for our lane. He nods before turning and walking toward the concession counter.

The bowling alley is a lot busier than I would have imagined for a Tuesday. Nearly all of the lanes are occupied, and the line for beer and food, which Dean is now at the tail end of, is at least ten people deep.

When I woke up this morning, I definitely wouldn't have guessed that I'd be on a date with Dean Ambrose tonight, but now that I'm here, I'm glad I texted him, even if it was just to keep myself from texting Tristan to ask him why he wasn't in chemistry.

I was more than a little shocked when he'd asked me out by lunch, but Nia's comment kept playing in my head every time I tried to type out an excuse to get out of the date.

The best way to get over someone is to get under someone new.

I'm not planning on getting *under* Dean but spending my night at the bowling alley is already an improvement from last night. I laid in bed and ate an entire sleeve of Oreos while stalking Tristan's

Instagram after I got home from the impromptu paintball game with his teammates.

So it's progress.

Plus, as Nia pointed out when I texted her about the date proposal, I could use a little confidence boost after being friend-zoned. Hookup-zoned? One-time hookup-zoned?

I don't know, but whatever it was, it sucked.

I deserve someone who won't write me off as nothing more than a drunken hookup.

Someone who wants to take me out on a proper date.

Even if it is bowling.

"Hurry, half times almost over."

Three guys in USW Warrior hoodies and baseball caps claim the lane beside ours, directly in my line of sight from the position of my seat. I pull my phone from my pocket so I'm not staring at the group, but the commotion in their lane is a lot more interesting than the Instagram feed I've already looked at a million times today.

The tallest of the three is flicking through the channels on the TV above their lane until a shot of three reporters appears on the screen. He sets the volume high enough that I can hear it easily from my seat before he drops down at the table with his friends.

"—But in this game so far, Tristan Beck has single-handedly carried his team." My head snaps toward the TV fast enough to warrant whiplash.

Even when I'm on a date, I can't escape him.

"He's made twelve three-pointers, has forty-eight points, all while the rest of his team put together has only made thirty-three points. He's kept his team in the ballgame with a level of athleticism I don't think we've seen so far this season."

A slow-motion replay of Tristan juking out his defender before stepping behind the three-point line and releasing the ball plays on the TV. He turns while the ball is still mid-air and starts to run back to get ready to defend the next play.

"He's got the athletics." The other reporter nods, clicking the remote in his hand to rewind the clip. He presses play just before he releases the ball. "And a hell of a lot of style, look at that release, that form, and the swagger on that boy. He doesn't even stop to watch that three go in."

"That's a number one pick if I've ever seen one." The other reporter nods. "And I'm no betting man, but if I were, I'd be putting all my money on seeing Tristan Beck's name announced first in the draft this year."

"He's certainly one to keep our eyes on. The second half of the USW, UCLA game is starting now. From the newsroom at USA Sports Network, this is Greg Bradshaw signing out."

The station logo flashes on the screen before cutting to the tip-off of the second half. Even on the small screen, I recognize Tristan instantly. His crimson and black uniform makes him look even tanner than I remember from last night, and his tattooed arm is in a black compression sleeve that spans from his wrist to the middle of his bicep, revealing only part of the ink that trails up and over his shoulder.

The players find their places around the circle as the referee prepares to toss the ball into the air. I recognize Emery as he shakes out his arms, preparing to go against the other team's center in the tip-off. I spot James, Micah, and Luke on the court, too.

"Here you go, sorry that took so long, that line was so slow." Dean drops down into the seat across from me and my mouth instantly waters as I eye the mass of cheese fries he sets down between us. "Bon appetit." He grins.

"This is amazing," I say, nearly burning my tongue as I swallow the gooey, cheesy goodness. I ignore the tinge on my tongue as I reach for more.

"Everyone always underestimates this place, but it's got the best deal on beer, and the most amazing cheese fries in town," he says, scooping up a handful for himself.

"I drive past here all the time on my way to work, but I've never actually been inside," I muse, glancing around the bowling alley.

It has an arcade attached at the far end, which seems to be even more popular than the actual bowling lanes. In addition to the giant disco ball slowly rotating on the ceiling, there has to be a million twinkling lights in all different colors surrounding it, giving off a twinkling sky impression, just with a rainbow color effect.

"How long have you worked at the diner?" Dean asks, wiping his hands with a napkin.

"Since freshman year. They've been really great about my schedule for classes and keeping me on even though I go home to Florida every summer, spring, and winter break." I pick through the remaining fries, trying to find one with some cheese.

"Florida, huh?" He grins. "I think that makes us rivals."

I raise a brow as I bite into the fry.

"I'm from Georgia. Go Dawgs."

That explains the slight twang to some of his words.

"And to think, this was going so well." I bite down on my lip to keep from smiling as he tilts his head back and laughs.

"Hey, I chose to come to USW, so that has to earn me back some brownie points, right?" I shrug, narrowing my eyes as if I'm really contemplating. "Plus, I taught you that awesome bowling trick, that has to count for something, too."

"That's true." I nod. "I guess I can forgive your terrible taste in football teams."

He holds up his beer at that before taking a sip.

"So, what made you come to USW?" he asks, sitting back in his seat.

"Well, Washington is the farthest state from Florida, so that was really the top-selling point." I laugh.

"Running away from an ex-boyfriend?" he asks with a teasing smile, digging back into the fries.

"More like an overbearing mother." I take a sip from my beer.

"Ah." He sucks in a breath through his teeth. "I feel that. I came here to get away from my dad. Somehow, I didn't think about the fact that even with an entire country separating us, he could still call me."

"Exactly." I laugh, sitting up in my chair. "I could be in Antarctica and my mother would somehow find a way to contact me."

"If it was a normal *hey, how ya doing, son* conversation I wouldn't mind, but I can only sit through so many lectures about me carrying on his legacy as a partner in his firm so many times before I actually go crazy." He shakes his head, and my mouth drops open.

"Your dad's a lawyer?" I ask a little too loudly. His brows raise slightly at my outburst and he nods. "My mom's a lawyer. She has her own firm."

"So you feel my pain then." He laughs, leaning his forearms onto the table.

"Well, kind of, but not really," I admit, taking another sip of my beer. "I have two older brothers who were given the guilt trip about joining the field and continuing her firm. By the time I was old enough to think about college, she had already given up on me since I was so vocal about not wanting to follow that path. And it also helped that my brother, Jeff, decided to go to law school, so she'd already found her replacement."

"You're lucky." He laughs. "My older sister went to cosmetology school, which I think is awesome, but in my father's eyes, it's the equivalent to going to clown college. I was his only hope at that point."

I imagine my mother would have a similar reaction, which is ironic, because for someone who looks down on cosmetology as a career choice, she'd probably have an actual heart attack if she missed her hair appointment every four weeks at her salon.

"So, *are* you?" I ask. "Studying to be a lawyer?"

He looks like it physically pains him, but he nods. "I didn't want to at first, simply because everyone expected me to. I even told my dad I was majoring in philosophy my freshman year just to tick him off, but when I took introduction to law, everything kind of just clicked, you know? I'm good at it, and I'm interested in learning it, which I guess is a pretty good sign that I should pursue it, even if it means having to go to law school after this."

"I'd say so." I smile, drinking the last sip of my beer.

"What about you?"

"Journalism," I say. "I'm applying to grad schools now."

"Any top contenders?"

"NYU is kind of my dream school, but I'm still waiting to hear back."

"Another great location." He smirks.

"Far enough away that she can't stop by." I laugh.

The guys at the table next to us explode onto their feet, and I search the TV above them to see the camera is zoomed in on Tristan. He's smiling, a full teeth-baring, dimple indenting, breath-catching smile.

"USW takes the game with that impressive final shot by Tristan Beck," the reporter says as the instant replay starts.

Luke is dribbling down the court as the rest of the players set up on the arch around the hoop. James and Micah both cut through the center, but Luke keeps the ball as the UCLA defense denies a clean pass for both guys.

Tristan runs through the arch, his defender hot on his heels, before juking and running back to his original position. Luke throws him the ball and he pivots, sets his feet just outside of the three-point line, and releases the ball just as the light on the timer ignites.

The ball sails through the air and finds the net perfectly.

Dean lets out a low whistle. "*Damn*, that guy's good."

I cough to cover my laugh as the irony of the situation hits me. I doubt Dean would be praising the guy if he knew what he did with his date a few weeks ago.

"Let's go find an after-party," one of the guys says as he turns his hat around on his head. "Gotta celebrate that win with or without them."

"Oh, they'll be celebrating," the tallest one says as he pushes back his own chair to stand up. "I'd bet my left nut Beck's gonna get some good UCLA pussy tonight."

I freeze as the words hit me, and when I look up, the group is already out of earshot as they walk toward the exit.

"Well, I should probably get you back since you have class in the morning," Dean says, glancing at his watch. "It's almost ten."

Standing up from my seat, I nod as I pull my coat on and readjust my purse, trying to stop the words from playing on repeat in my head.

Beck's gonna get some good UCLA pussy tonight.

It doesn't matter what he does tonight, I remind myself. He can do whatever he wants. We're not together.

I bite down hard on the inside of my cheek as I follow Dean out of the bowling alley toward his shiny, red Jaguar parked near the front. I pull my coat tighter around myself and try not to imagine all the UCLA girls waiting outside the locker room right now.

Dean cranks the heating, and I immediately feel the warmth surround me as the air circulates around his car, but glancing at my shaking hands sitting in my lap, I know it has nothing to do with the icy wind we just walked through.

NINETEEN

TRISTAN

By the time I get back to the hotel room, it's nearly eleven, which according to Coach, means lights out.

After his usual *If I come by your room and find out you're not there tonight, I'm going to run you so hard in the morning you're going to wish you were dead* speech, he watched us all unload from the bus and file into our rooms—two per person—before finally retiring into his own down the hall.

Win or lose, Coach has a zero-drinking policy for away games. Although, in the entire time I've known him, he's never stayed awake long enough to actually enforce it.

"You sure you don't want to come with us?" James asks as he pulls off his shirt and smooths out the short sleeve button-up he's now dousing in cologne.

Since he wasn't there for the paintball game last night, he's the only one on the team without at least one huge bruise coloring his skin a deep purple or blue. Our targets were on our chest and back, so most of us managed to hide our battle scars from Coach, who would have been so pissed off, he would have sent us out onto the UCLA track to run before the game.

Aaron Penn, one of our freshmen, was the poor unfortunate soul that Abby shot in the arm four times. He managed to hide his four huge bruises with a compression sleeve, but I could tell by the way he was moving in warm-ups that he was hurting. Luckily, he's a second string who barely gets off the bench, so it didn't actually impact the game.

"Yeah, I'm going to stay in and study." I peel off my hoodie and toss it on my bed. The weather in LA is a lot warmer than Pullman and paired with the post-game adrenaline still coursing through my veins, I feel like I'm about to overheat. James doesn't call me out on the lie as he laces up his shoes, but I can tell by the twitch of his cheek that he knows exactly what I'm doing. "Text me if you need help, though. Don't let Micah or Luke get too fucked up; Coach will kill them if they puke on the plane," I say, squeezing the back of my neck to release some of the tension built up from the game as he crosses the room and picks up his wallet, phone, and room key from the dresser near the door.

He nods absently as his fingers tap out a text on the screen. When he finally stops texting, he looks up. "Luke wants to know how big the after party can be on Friday."

"I don't care."

"It's your birthday party," he counters.

"Just tell him to go easy on the invites. I don't want to wake up the next day to a fucked up house," I shrug.

He nods and types the reply. "I never thought I'd see the day you'd ditch post-game beers," he says, slipping his phone into his back pocket.

I shrug again, uncapping my Gatorade to take a sip. "Priorities, man, gotta study."

He nods sarcastically as he pulls open the door and pops his head out into the hall to double check that Coach is still in his room. When he walks out, he starts to close the door, but pops his head back in quickly, his gaze falling to the phone in my hands.

"Tell Abby I said hello." He pulls the door closed with a soft click before I can flip him off.

I've been thinking about calling Abby to help her study tonight since she has a closing shift at the diner tomorrow night—or at least, that's what was written down in her planner.

Scrolling through my contacts, I click on her name.

I hesitate, looking at the time. It's kind of late to randomly call her. She could be studying, or writing an article for the paper, or hanging out with Nia and Jenny, or she could already be asleep. Hovering over her contact for a second longer, I click out and open Instagram. Abby's the kind of girl who barely ever uploads pictures to her actual account, but will update her story throughout the day, which has become quite entertaining for me over the past few weeks.

As expected, her icon appears at the top of my feed, and I click it quickly. A few pictures of a bowling alley, one of cheese fries, and then two more of her holding up a wine glass in front of the camera pop up. The last picture was uploaded fifteen minutes ago.

Scrolling back to her contact, I click the FaceTime button.

I sit back in bed as it begins to ring, running my hands over my hair to make sure it didn't dry in a fucked up way after my shower. When her face appears on the screen, I can't help but grin at the look of utter confusion knotting her brows. Her hair is pulled into a messy knot on top of her head and she's wearing the same hoodie I let her borrow last night for the game of paintball.

I conveniently forgot to ask for it back, the same way she conveniently forgot to give it back before leaving.

"Hey." She looks more shocked than anything as she stares at her phone, and I can tell by the two quick hiccups that rattle her shoulders that she's drunk.

"Are you drunk?" I laugh.

She looks at the wine glass in her hands and brings it up into shot, a demure smile on her lips.

"I may or may not have had a drink or two *or three* when I got home," she says, taking a sip of the pink liquid which has been poured to the very top of her stemless wine glass.

"From bowling?" I tease.

"Yes, from bowling." She grins. "How did you know that?"

"You post about a million times a day on your Instagram story." I laugh.

"You watch my stories?" she blanches.

"Where do you think I get my daily entertainment from, Ryan?" I grin. "One night your baking chocolate chip cookies while watching *The Bachelor*, and the next you're out bowling. You're a wild woman; it's riveting to watch."

She sticks her tongue out at me and then rests her head back against her headboard. Her cheeks are flushed a pretty pink, and she looks like she's swaying slightly as she giggles.

"Hey, I can be wild," she defends.

"I know. I remember." I grin.

She looks up over the camera toward the door, as if to make sure no one can hear us, before looking back down. Her cheeks flush an even prettier hue, and I grin as she brings her wine glass up and takes a long sip before another hiccup shakes her shoulders again.

"I saw your game."

I uncap the Gatorade and down a few gulps, wishing I wouldn't have forgotten to grab a few water bottles before leaving the UCLA arena.

"They said you have a lot of *swag.*" She uses air quotes around the word.

"Are you quoting yourself?" I grin.

"No, I'm not quoting myself. I'm quoting Greg Bradshaw—or whatever his name is—from USASN." She takes another sip of her wine.

"Sounds like something Bradshaw would say." I nod. I've met the guy a few times, and he sounds like a perpetual frat douche when he talks, but he always seems to hype me up in post-game reports, so I don't mind him too much.

"Some guys were watching it at the lane next to us," she says quickly, tapping her finger on the wine glass while her eyes focus on the liquid. "They said they were going to celebrate the win at an after party."

"Sounds like USW—any excuse to get drunk."

She nods slowly and then drowns the rest of her glass, which was almost entirely full. I raise my brow as she looks back at the camera. Her eyes are unsettled as they flick between the empty glass and the camera.

"Why aren't you hanging out with UCLA girls tonight?" Her voice is soft but harsh at the same time, like an accusation she doesn't want the answer to.

Drunk Abby is cute.

Drunk and jealous Abby is something else entirely; something that makes me wish I wasn't hundreds of miles away right now.

"Do you want me to be hanging out with UCLA girls tonight?" I try not to smile, but I can't help it because her face pulls into a scowl and then flattens out quickly as her drunken mind tries to piece together my response.

"No," she squeaks, shaking her head. "No—I mean, I don't care. You can do—" *Hiccup, hiccup.* "—Do whatever you want to do." She shrugs, not at all convincing.

"I am doing what I want to do," I say.

She stares at me for a moment as the words hit her, and then she looks away smiling.

"Okay then." She nods.

"Okay then." I grin.

She leans out of shot, and I can hear the sound of her wine glass being set onto what I assume is her nightstand, and when she comes back into shot, she burrows down further into her sheets. I can't see much of her surroundings, aside from her gray, pleated headboard and the mound of pillows surrounding her head.

"Why are you calling anyway?" She laughs.

"I was going to help you study for the exam, but it seems like that might be a lost cause at the moment since you're drunk."

She purses her lips, contemplating the idea of studying, and then shakes her head. "Definitely too drunk to study."

"That's a shame." I grin.

"Why's that?"

"Now I don't have an excuse to stay on here." I adjust my own pillows and slide further down under the duvet.

"Hmm." She hums, resting her head against a pillow. "I could think of a few things that don't involve studying."

"Are you propositioning me for video sex right now, Abby Ryan?"

"No," she gasps, her eyes widening quickly.

Even her drunk self blushes at the thought.

"I was talking about the *interview*."

"Mhm." I hum.

She ignores me with a roll of her eyes. "I was thinking that it might be nice to get a few quotes from your family for the article," she says quickly. "To add a more personal touch."

I can already feel my mother's excitement at the prospect of being interviewed. "You might just make my mom's entire life by interviewing her." I chuckle, rubbing my hand through my hair.

"Your mom is very sweet." She grins.

"She is." I nod. "She's the best."

Her smile twitches and then fades slightly as she looks away.

"She likes you a lot," I add, hoping to pull her smile back.

She looks back at the camera and her eyes widen with amusement. "Yeah, she told me." She grins. "She messaged me on Facebook earlier."

My head falls back onto the stack of pillows and I groan. "She added you on Facebook?"

"Mhm." She hums. "She sent me the cutest message about how happy she is that I'm writing the article on you."

"Of course she did." I laugh. Sounds like something my mom would do.

Abby's eyes dart up and then the screen goes black as she shoves the phone under her covers. I can barely make out the green and red plaid pattern on her pajama pants in the darkness.

"Are you talking to someone?" Nia's voice is barely audible, but I turn up my phone volume to try to hear what she's saying.

"No." Abby's voice is a little louder, but too quick to properly feign innocence.

"You definitely are," she counters, her voice growing louder. "I heard a guy's voice when I walked by."

"Must have been the TV," Abby says, but I can tell by her tone that she's already told on herself by smiling.

"Is it Mr. Big?" Nia asks. "Oh, my God, is he still on the phone?"

I raise a brow at the nickname.

Mr. Big? I think that's a compliment. Right? I'm definitely going to take that as a compliment.

"Nia, go, I'll talk to you after."

"Are you having phone sex right now?"

"*Nia,*" Abby squeaks, and I hear Nia laugh as the sound of a door closing echoes through her room.

Abby waits a few seconds, probably to make sure Nia isn't going to pop in again, before pulling her phone back up from under the sheets.

"I am so sorry about that," she says in a whisper.

I can't hold back my smirk, so I just decide to go with it. "Mr. Big, huh?"

Her face pales and then flushes quickly. "You heard that?"

Placing my hand behind my head, I nod. "I've had a lot of nicknames, but I've got to say, Mr. Big might be my favorite."

"It's not what you think." Abby shakes her head quickly. "It's from a show."

"Mhm." I grin. "Sure it is, Ryan."

"I'm serious, you can look it up." She laughs. "I wouldn't even know what your—" Her eyes widen, and she clamps her lips closed. Even drunk Abby has a filter, albeit a much more delayed one, but her words linger between us, and I can't help the laugh that practically echoes through my hotel room.

"I just mean, it's not like a descriptive nickname." She bites down on her lip and looks away, mortified.

"Right," I agree, reveling in the sight of her—cheeks flushed, face bare, hair pulled up, while wearing my hoodie. I watch her face with a wicked grin, knowing that my words are about to light her cheeks on fire. "But it could be."

TWENTY

When Tristan invited me to his birthday party, I figured it was going to be a bit different than the usual brunch celebrations Jenny, Nia, and I usually throw for each other. I definitely wasn't expecting to walk up to his house shaking from the bass of the song blasting while overflowing with drunk USW students, though.

I have to pull into the driveway behind his truck, because there isn't a single open spot on the entire street. A few stragglers outside eye me curiously as I cut the engine, and I revel in the last few moments of heat before throwing open my car door and sprinting up the frozen drive.

I don't bother knocking since the music is loud enough to send vibrations through the door, but I hesitate by the entryway for a second as my eyes adjust to the lower lighting. Multicolored Christmas lights are strewn across the ceiling of the living room, paired with a few strobe lights, which effectively sets the rave-like vibe. The crowd pulses rhythmically to the music blaring through the speakers, and their hands create a sea of neon light with their glow stick bracelets.

It's too dark to search for Nia or Jenny from here, so I ease my way through the group of people circled around the kegs near the entryway to get closer to the living room. I nearly shriek when someone grabs my wrist and tugs me back, but when I see Nia's bright eyes staring back at me, I stop resisting, and let her lead me back toward the kitchen.

Jenny's sitting on one of the stools at the island, and she sits up straighter when she spots me, waving a little too enthusiastically to be sober. Nia drops my hand and rounds the island, pulling out a red solo cup from the pack. She has about six glow stick bracelets on her left wrist, which cast a glow on the bottle of Fireball she's currently pouring.

"Come on, babe, you've got to catch up," Nia yells over the music, sliding over the shot she just poured for me.

I take a step closer to Jenny when a guy double my size stumbles past, his eyes not so subtly locking in on my chest as he goes. I tug at the pale pink, silk camisole, but the deep cut of the neckline doesn't offer much coverage. The top of my black lace bra is peaking out, and I feel even more exposed than I originally anticipated when I picked it out of Nia's closet. Paired with the same leather mini skirt from the last time we all went out, I'm giving off major Nia vibes.

"Oh shit, that's strong." I cough into my hand as the liquid sends a shock of heat down my throat. Jenny grabs me a can of Coke from the cooler next to her, and I pop it open and chug a few sips to clear my mouth of the aftertaste.

Nia smacks her lips as she pours me another shot. "Come on, slow poke, you've got to catch up." She grins, sliding me the next shot.

"I've been at work," I remind her, throwing my head back and swallowing as fast as I can. I have a bad habit of letting the liquor sit in my mouth, which only makes the experience worse.

"All the more reason to take another shot." She grins as she slides me another one. I push it away, shaking my head as I down a few more gulps of the Coke, desperately trying to wash away the putrid aftertaste.

"You deserve to let loose, Abs. It's Friday night, you don't have work tomorrow, and plus—" Her words are already a little slurred, but I appreciate the pep talk all the same. "—Who knows how many more opportunities we'll have like this before we graduate." She pouts, and Jenny leans in next to her, mirroring her expression.

"Come on, Abs, get drunk with us," Jenny coaxes.

"I drove here," I counter, shaking my head. That excuse is long gone, though. After taking that second shot, I pretty much solidified the fact that we'll be taking an Uber home tonight. I'll just have to come pick up my car tomorrow.

"We both know you're not driving tonight." She rolls her eyes dramatically. "Plus, look around, Abs. Have you ever seen so much free liquor?"

The kitchen is stocked with more liquor than I've ever seen in my life—there's handles of Captain Morgan, Bacardi, Patron, Jack Daniel's, Jameson, Smirnoff, and even a few bottles of Jaegermeister, and that's just on this side of the kitchen.

I have a feeling that Luke McConnell sponsored tonight's party.

"It would be sacrilegious to *not* capitalize on this moment." Nia nods seriously.

"I guess I can't argue that." I laugh, taking the shot. It burns like hell going down, even with the Coke as a chaser, and a shiver runs down my spine as the liquid immediately warms my body.

"That's my girl." Nia grins, capping the Fireball.

"You deserve it." Jenny nods, leaning onto the island from her perch on the stool. "You've been so stressed this week with that exam."

I have been stressed. The past couple of days have been a blur of stress-eating and hardcore studying for the chemistry exam that—thanks to the all-nighter I pulled Wednesday night—I passed with flying colors. Well, maybe not flying colors, but a ninety-three is fine with me.

So, I guess I do deserve to get a little drunk tonight.

I earned it.

It doesn't take long for the shots to hit, likely because I haven't had time to eat dinner, so my system is running solely on Fireball. After feeling the buzz start to tingle on my skin, I slipped open the pantry and snooped around the shelves, which were stocked almost exclusively with granola bars and protein powder, until I found the bag of pretzels. I've been eating handfuls while Nia and Jenny filled me on what I missed at the game.

I grab another handful before Nia drags us out into the middle of the dance floor, and I pop one into my mouth as I toss my head back and throw my hands into the air, reveling in the tingling sensation that has effectively numbed my entire body. I know that I should be trying to keep my movements aligned with the beat, but at this point, I'm too warm and numb to care.

I spot Luke dancing on the coffee table a few feet away, and I wave, extending a pretzel to him. He plucks it from my fingers gingerly with an excited smile, as if he's never been offered such an amazing gift.

See, he gets it.

He pops the pretzel into his mouth and extends his hand to me, pulling me up onto the coffee table next to him.

"Hey, Ryan." He grins down at me, and I reach up to pat his cheek which is smooth, as if he just shaved it.

"You're so tall," I muse, patting his cheek again. "You're younger than me, but you're so much taller than me." I knit my eyebrows together. "That doesn't seem fair."

His eyes widen slightly at my comment.

"You've had a few drinks, haven't you?"

I pop another pretzel into my mouth and move my hips to beat, beaming down at Nia who's giving me a thumbs up, like a proud mother at her daughter's first dance recital. It's usually Nia who's up on tables dancing, but when I glance around and feel the rush of people's eyes on me, I start to understand the appeal.

"I've had a few shots." I shrug. "But I'm still catching up."

He nods, accepting another pretzel from me, as if me carrying around a handful of pretzels is the most casual thing in the world. His eyes dart down to my chest for a beat too long, and I glance down to see that almost the entire left cup of my lacy bra is exposed.

"*Oops.*" I laugh, pulling it back into place.

When I look back up at him, he's smirking at me.

"You look really good tonight, Ryan," he says, leaning down so I can hear him over the pounding music.

I stifle a laugh at the comment, looking up into his icy blue eyes.

"Are you flirting with me, Luke?"

He grins. "I might be, if you weren't off limits."

"Off limits," I repeat, popping another pretzel in my mouth.

"Unofficially." He shrugs as his eyes flick over my shoulder and a smirk pulls at his lips as he murmurs, "Speak of the devil."

I follow his gaze to see Tristan walking toward us. I can tell by the glassy haze of his eyes that he's already had a few drinks. He's eyeing Luke, who backs away from me, putting enough space between us that I could reach out and still not touch him.

Tristan stops at the edge of the coffee table, and my eyes widen when I realize that I'm looking *down* at him.

"Hi." I grin, resting my pretzel free hand on his shoulder to steady myself.

When his gaze meets mine, the cloudy haze evaporates quickly, and I run my thumb over the stubble on his jaw, focused on how good it feels against my skin. I pull my hand away when the thought of how it would feel between my legs sends a wave of heat through my stomach.

"Hi." He smirks. "I thought you were standing me up on my birthday, Ryan." He laughs, reaching up to grab my waist to steady me as I drop back down to the floor beside him.

"I'm sorry, it was crazy at work." I shake my head, thinking back to the mayhem of it all. "We got slammed because of the game."

He looks like he's about to say something, but Luke drops down next to us and pulls his attention.

"We should play drunk *Jenga* now," he calls over the music. "I'll go get it set up in the kitchen."

"*Jenga?*" I gasp.

"Drunk *Jenga*," Tristan corrects, leading the way toward the kitchen. "Which I'm guessing is going to be a much more entertaining version."

"Hey, I love *Jenga*," I defend, thinking back to the summer nights spent with my dad and brother's playing the game while my mom worked late on whatever case she was defending.

Jenny and Nia are already standing around the island when we round the corner to the kitchen, and it takes me a moment to process the fact that Jenny is nuzzled under James's arm while he's leaning down to whisper in her ear. I glance over to see Tristan looking at the two of them with a drunk smile on his face.

"Finally." I grin. "Looks like your wingman duties actually paid off."

His gaze flicks down to me and he's silent for a long moment before he nods.

"Yeah," he muses softly. "I guess they did."

His gaze lingers on me as I look back up to the group, and I reach up and tuck my hair behind my ear, hoping that he's not staring at pretzel crumbs on my face or something.

"—If you don't want to do the dare on the block, you'll have to take three shots," Luke explains, placing the last block onto the tower on the kitchen island.

"I'm awesome at *Jenga*." I'm practically bouncing on the balls of my feet, and when I look up at him, he seems amused.

"Why does that not surprise me, Ryan?" He laughs, taking a long sip of the drink in his hand.

"Everyone needs a drink to play," Micah calls out, lining up a row of red solo cups on the counter as he flicks the cap off the vodka bottle in his hand. "Who needs one?"

I raise my hand, along with a few others who have congregated around the island. A few of Nia and Jenny's sorority sisters are scattered throughout the group, and the height difference between the girls and the guys—that I now recognize as Tristan's teammates—is comical. Glancing up at Tristan, I realize we must look like that, too, since the top of my head only comes up to the middle of his chest.

"Okay, T goes first since it's his birthday," Luke insists, handing out the drinks that Micah just poured. I take a sip and nearly choke. It's straight vodka with a splash of Sprite.

Tristan steps forward to examine the tower before pulling out a block near the middle. "Down the hatch—finish your drink." He chugs the rest of his cup, and then takes the new drink James passes to him.

Micah steps forward and pulls a block from the stack. His brows raise as he reads it off. "Baby got back—the person with the best ass has to drink." His eyes flash as he looks around the group, and when he settles on one of the blonde sorority girls, he holds his cup up towards her. "Drink up, Barbie."

The girl takes a long sip of her drink, and when she pulls her cup away from her mouth, her lips are perked up in a smug smile as she looks around the group. Her eyes settle on Tristan as she picks her own block.

"Old maid—longest time since sex drinks." Her eyes flick up and she smirks. "Not me. I got it this morning."

Going around the island, everyone rattles off their answers. I'm too shocked by the fact that Tristan hasn't had sex in a few weeks to realize that everyone is staring at me, waiting for me to answer.

"I guess I lose." I laugh, holding up my drink before taking a long sip.

"How long, Ryan?" Micah's grinning at me from across the island. I can feel Tristan's gaze on me.

"Oh, um . . ."

How long has it been?

I guess I've never really given it much thought. I broke up with Tyler when I went back for summer break last year, and we didn't have sex before that conversation, so that means the last time I had sex was . . . last spring break.

Eleven months.

"Almost a year," I say quietly, trying to shrug it off.

I glance up to Tristan and watch his brows raise.

"Damn, Ryan. You should drink twice for that, you've practically re-virginized." Emery snorts from the other side of Nia, and I watch as she elbows him in the stomach.

"That's only if you're not counting oral sex," she defends, her words slurring a bit as she looks at me with an encouraging smile that I know is meant to say, *I've got your back, girl.*

My face floods as the collective gaze of everyone falls on me again, and when I glance up at Tristan, he's hiding his smirk behind the lip of his cup.

"My turn," Jenny says suddenly, trying to pull the attention away from me. She steps up to the tower and pulls a block out from an impressive spot near the bottom. Smirking over her shoulder at James, she reads the block.

"Never have I ever—play one round with the group."

Stepping back beside James, she bites her bottom lip as she thinks. "Never have I ever . . . had sex on campus."

Her eyes are trained on James who hesitates before bringing the cup to his lips. A surprising amount of people around the island also take a drink, and when I look over at Tristan, he has his cup pressed to his lips, too.

Of course.

I raise a brow at him, and he grins, leaning down to whisper in my ear. "You should let me tutor you in the library sometime."

My breath catches in my throat, and I turn back to the group as my mind spirals with flashes of all the different things we could do between the shelves in the library. The feeling of his stubble on my thumb pops back into my mind and I flush again.

The next few turns go by quickly since I'm paying more attention to the man standing next me than the actual game, but I remember the highlights—one of the sorority girls has to send a sexy picture to a random contact in her phone, James has to take off his shirt for the remainder of the game, and Luke takes three shots to get out of doing whatever his block says.

When it's my turn, I relax when my block says to take a shot for each sexual partner I've ever had. I take a single shot and step back in line, silently thanking God that I didn't have to take a sexy picture and send it out like the sorority girl did.

Tristan steps toward the tower again.

"Take a body shot off of the person to your left."

A rush of heat unfurls in my stomach when his gaze meets mine. The light-hearted energy that was buzzing between us seconds before has evaporated and has been replaced with something much heavier.

The sexy photo girl standing directly across from us snorts, and I glance up to her. "You might as well pour those three shots now, Beck," she laughs.

"Shut the fuck up, Karin." Nia snaps.

"What? I'm not trying to be a bitch, I'm just saying." She shrugs, holding up her hands. "But since you're not a quitter, you can do it off of me instead." She smirks at Tristan.

The comment stings and the rush of anger that surges through me manifests in a whirlwind of confidence I didn't know I had. I step up beside him, and before my mind registers what I'm doing, I pull off my shirt, looking Karin dead in the eye as I drop it to the floor at my feet.

I try not to focus on the fact that there are at least twenty people staring at me in my little lace bra. I know if I think about it too long, all of my false bravado will evaporate into thin air. So, I turn to Tristan, who's looking down at me with wide eyes.

"You don't have to do this, Abby. I'll drink the three shots," he offers quickly, moving in front of me to block me from view.

"I know I don't *have* to," I say, leaning around him to smirk at Karin, who now looks like someone just shoved something nasty under her nose. "I *want* to."

"That's my girl." Jenny grins, holding up her cup.

"Yes, Abs. Take it off," Nia cheers, flipping off Karin.

I grin at them before glancing at the kitchen island. There's enough room for me to lay on it, so I turn around and jump, scooting my butt onto the cool surface before laying down, careful not to go near the tower of blocks.

"Well, let's do this right then," Micah says, closing the refrigerator with a salt shaker, a bowl of lime wedges, and a bottle of tequila in his hands.

I wiggle my high-waisted skirt down a little, just enough so that my belly button is exposed as Micah hands the salt to Tristan. His emerald eyes are darker than before as he steps up to the counter, sprinkling a trail of salt up my stomach toward my chest.

"You sure about this?" he asks, handing me the slice of lime.

The surge of adrenaline racing through my veins is as intoxicating as the liquor.

"Happy birthday." I smirk, placing the lime between my teeth.

His eyes flash as his brows raise, and I watch his gaze trail slowly down my body to my belly button, where he tips the bottle and pours the tequila. It pools in a small puddle in the middle of my stomach, and I swallow hard, trying to keep my breathing even to keep the liquid from spilling.

He hands off the bottle, and his bright eyes catch mine before he ducks his head and licks the trail of salt in one torturously slow motion. I close my eyes and revel in the way the feeling of his stubble against my skin sends a shiver up my spine. He sucks the liquor from my belly button, and when I open my eyes, he's hovering above me, his tongue wetting his lips.

My breathing isn't as controlled as before, and my mouth goes dry as his hungry stare locks in on the lime between my teeth. I taste the splash of lime juice when he connects our lips, and the slow, teasing flick of his tongue before he pulls away. I'm still a little dazed when he grabs my hands and helps me down from the counter, making sure that I'm steady before he releases me, and my face starts to burn as the sound of his teammates lewd cheering and whistles echo through the kitchen.

I lock eyes with Karin as Tristan bends down to pick up my shirt for me, and a smug smile spreads across my face as I wipe away the errant lime juice from my lips with a single swipe of my tongue.

TWENTY-ONE

TRISTAN

It's nearly two in the morning, but thanks to the Red Bull I've been chugging as a chaser all night, I'm fucking wired.

My heart is racing in my chest, and my leg is bouncing quickly in tandem, attempting to burn through some of the pent-up energy flooding my veins as I sit on the couch. I know Abby can feel the movement of my leg since she's sitting next to me, but she doesn't turn around to tell me to chill the hell out; instead, she leans back and places her hand on my knee, stilling my manic bouncing. When her eyes meet mine, I see the hint of humor gleaming there, and I relax back into the couch, focusing on how her thumb is now making slow, calming circles on my jean-clad knee.

When her eyes settle back on Jenny beside her, I glance around the room to the rest of the stragglers who stayed behind when everyone else left for the frat that's currently trying to hot-box their entire house. Since we get randomly drug tested for basketball, my entire team is scattered across the living room. Most of them are spread around the TV, all trying to focus on the video game as they scream their slurred advice to Luke, which ultimately ends up getting him killed.

A few of my teammates are trying to shoot their shot with whatever sorority girls are left, and I'm not surprised to see Micah leaning against the wall, talking to two sorority girls who are both running their hands up and down his chest, their eyes locking together in the way that most guys only dream of. I'd be willing to bet my entire bank account that my boy is about to have a threesome, which is all but confirmed when the blonde reaches over and connects her lips with the redhead while her hand skims down Micah's stomach.

I make eye contact with Emery on the other end of the couch with Nia on his lap; he's giving me the universal *nice, a threesome* grin.

I shake my head and snort at the unspoken language we all seem to have, but I guess that's what happens when you spend four hours together nearly every day.

His grin widens when Nia leans in and whispers something in his ear, and when his eyes flick up to her and he nods quickly, I don't have to guess what that's about because she stands up and walks toward us, bending down to eye level with Abby.

"I'm going home with Nate, babe."

Abby glances over Nia's shoulder to my teammate, who's now corralling the rest of the guys by the TV toward the door. I've never actually seen the other end of these conversations, I'm usually the one waiting for the girl to finish talking to her friends, so we can go back to her place and fuck.

"I've gone home with him a few times before, he's not a serial killer or anything. Plus, it's just down the street." She laughs, clearly seeing the hesitation on Abby's face.

"Okay." She nods. "But still keep your location on, and call me if you need anything, okay?"

I stand up and walk toward the entryway where the team has started to congregate, reaching out to slap the hands of each one before they file out of the door, likely on their way back to one of the other houses on the street to keep the party going. I guess that's one of the pros of your entire team living on the same street. That, and the never-ending supply of protein powder.

"Thanks for coming, man," I say to Emery, who pulls me in for a hug and slaps me hard on the back.

"Happy birthday, T." He pulls back and glances over my shoulder to the couch. "Hope you get lucky tonight, brother." He whispers with a wicked grin, stepping back in time to sling an arm around Nia as she walks up.

"Ready?" she asks, smirking up at my teammate.

The door closes a little too hard behind them, and I smirk as Nia pops her head back into the house, her glassy eyes wide as she pats the door. "Sorry about that." She laughs and then closes the door softer this time.

When I turn back, Micah and Luke are setting up the ping pong table in the middle of the living room. I catch sight of Abby lounging on the couch, her red cup pressed to her lips as she tilts her head back and takes a few long sips. Her eyes meet mine over the lip of the cup when I stop at the edge of the couch.

"Where's Jenny?" she asks, searching the empty room.

"Probably half-naked in James's room by now. They snuck back there when everyone was leaving." Micah snorts, tossing an arm around the shoulders of the small blonde next to him. The redhead sidles up to his other side, her finger tracing the waistband of his black jeans.

"What?" Abby squeaks, eyes widening as she glances toward the hallway.

"You can play with us if you want, Ryan," Luke offers, tossing a ping pong ball up into the air. "We can make room for one more."

"No, thanks." She shakes her head and settles back onto the couch where I sit beside her.

She seems content to watch the beer pong game from the couch until Micah sinks the first shot and we realize that it's actually a game of *strip* pong. Her cheeks flood when the blonde girl shimmies out of her shirt, revealing a barely-there bra. I take that as my cue to stand up and extend my hand to her, which she takes without question.

"Let's get out of here before we see something we can't unsee." I chuckle, pulling her into the hall, just in time for her to miss the red-head pulling off her top, revealing her bare chest and pierced nipples underneath. I catch Micah's dumbass grin before I round the corner.

I can only imagine the night he's about to have.

"Are you sure? You don't have to stay up with me if you want to go to bed. I can just wait out there for Jenny on my phone or something," she says, but by the way she's following closely behind me, I know that she'd much rather not witness whatever's about to happen out there.

I glance back to see her eyes widen a little when the distinct sound of a moan echoes through the hall from James's room, and she hurries past me, apparently not interested in whether or not I'm going to take her up on her offer to go to bed. When she pushes open my door, she glances around the room, and her shoulders relax as she steps inside.

"I'm not really tired." I shrug, closing the door behind us.

The sounds of laughter echoing down the hall from the living room are nearly silenced by the door, but I turn on the TV quickly to drown out any overflow noises. While I'm used to falling asleep to the sounds of my roommates fucking, I'm sure Abby isn't.

"What do you want to watch?" I ask, sitting on the edge of the bed as I flick through the options. "I made Luke sign me into all of his accounts, so I have Hulu, Netflix, HBO, Amazon Prime, Disney Plus . . ." I glance over to see her perched on the other side of the bed, pulling the blanket around her shoulders as she kicks off her heels, which fall to the ground with two small thuds on the hardwood.

She looks up at the TV and shrugs, and I can already see the tension in her shoulders is gone as she takes another sip from the red cup in her hands. She's spent more time in here with me than anywhere else in the house, which is obvious by the way she relaxes against the headboard as she takes a deep, relaxed breath.

"I'll watch whatever you want to." She's practically nuzzling into the bed, and I eye her tiny, leather skirt riding up her thighs, which she pulls at, trying to keep it from bunching up.

"Do you want something more comfortable?" I ask, standing up and walking to the dresser. I already have a few options pulled out when I glance over my shoulder to see her looking down at her skirt, running her fingers over the smooth material. She seems reluctant, but by the way she's sitting, her outfit can't be comfortable.

"I don't know, I probably won't be here for that long." Her eyes flick to the sweatpants in my hands, and I turn around again, pulling out a hoodie from the drawer, extending it to her with a smirk.

"It's pretty late, Ryan." I shrug. "There's a good chance Jenny's just going to pass out in James's bed for the night. You might as well stay over, too, since you're too drunk to drive and the Uber prices are going to be insane at this time."

She considers my words as she eyes the black hoodie in my hands, and I can tell by her sigh that I'm just voicing all the things she's already thinking. Her eyes flick up to meet mine, and I smile as I hold up the clothes, which she takes from me with a quiet, "thank you."

She slips into the bathroom, and when the soft click of the door echoes through the room, I pull off my shirt and step out of my jeans. I toss them into the dirty hamper by the bathroom door before pulling on a pair of gray sweats, and I'm still searching through my drawer for a shirt when the sound of the bathroom door opening sounds.

Abby steps out with her clothes and my sweatpants folded neatly in her hands. I catch sight of the black lace of her bra tucked underneath her leather skirt, and I try not to think about the fact that she's practically naked under the hoodie. Her legs are bare, but the hoodie falls halfway down her thighs, and it's almost comical that she's more covered now than when she was in the leather skirt. Somehow, it's a hell of a lot sexier than her actual outfit, but I have a feeling it's because it's *my* clothes that she's wearing.

"They were too big and kept falling down," she explains, placing the sweatpants down on the dresser.

I make an effort to keep my eyes on her face, which is flooding pink again, as her eyes rake down my chest, lingering near my waistband.

She clears her throat and walks past me, placing her clothes in a neat pile by her purse on my desk. When she turns around again, she rakes her hair back and ties a hairband around it.

"I have an extra toothbrush," I say, walking into the bathroom to search through the basket of extra toiletries. When I hand it to her, she takes it with a smile.

"Oh, perfect. I was worried I'd have to use my finger." She laughs, flicking on the faucet and running the fresh bristles under the water.

I try not to smirk at the words, but she catches my failed attempt at maturity and her cheeks flush as she holds her brush out to me. I squeeze a line of paste onto the bristles before loading up my own.

We stand side by side in the mirror as we both scrub our teeth, only she's the kind of person who doesn't get toothpaste suds all over her face, and I look like I'm foaming at the mouth, which makes her laugh so hard she has to turn around to gain her composure before turning around again. I grin at her amused expression, letting the foam drip down my chin to the sink before I wash it all away.

"How do you make brushing your teeth dirty?" She laughs.

"I make a lot of things dirty." I grin.

She tries to ignore me, but a smile pulls at her lips.

We share the mouthwash, and I hand her the face wash, but after two washes, she eventually just uses lotion to get the rest of the stubborn makeup off her lashes. That gives me enough time to wash my own face and take out my contacts before she's done.

As she dries off her face, I feel her eyes on me while my fingers hover above the glasses case in the drawer. When I glance over to her blurry figure, I decide that I'd rather look like a fucking idiot than miss a single moment of her in nothing but my hoodie.

I slip on the black-framed glasses and turn around quickly, walking out of the bathroom before she can get a good look at me. I fucking hate glasses. I've been wearing contacts since I was fourteen, and aside from my roommates and family, no one even knows I have them. She seems to pick up on my discomfort, because she doesn't mention them as she follows me out of the bathroom, flicking off the light as she goes.

"So, what should we watch?" I ask as casually as I can, grabbing the remote on the end of the bed.

She's grinning at me as she settles down on the other side, and when I finally break and glance over at her, my cheeks start to burn like a little bitch. I look away again, clearing my throat as I flick through the options on Netflix, wishing I would have just kept my contacts in. Sleeping in them once wouldn't kill me.

"You look really hot in glasses."

My gaze flicks back to hers, and I raise a brow at the comment.

"I just mean you really pull them off." She flushes, and by the way she sways slightly as she nestles herself into my bedsheets, it's clear she's still a little buzzed. "Like, some people look nerdy in glasses, but you don't. I don't know if it's the tattoos, or the abs, or the arm muscles or something, but you look . . ." She trails off as her eyes coast down my bare chest again. When she looks back up, her eyes dart toward the TV as she shrugs, cheeks burning. "You just look good in glasses."

I never thought I'd be thankful for these fucking things, but I make a mental note to wear them around her more as I try to hide the dumbass grin on my face.

"What are we going to watch?" she asks as she wiggles further down under the duvet, as if she's trying to bury herself.

"You pick, I'm going to get us some water and snacks." I grin, slipping off of the bed.

Her eyes light up. "Do you have chocolate milk?"

"Chocolate milk?" I snort. "I'm sure we have chocolate syrup, so I can you make some."

"Well—" She bites the inside of her cheek as she contemplates the offer. "No offense, but I'm kind of particular about it, like the milk to chocolate ratio and the way it's stirred and everything."

I raise a brow at that. "Would you like to come make your own chocolate milk, princess?"

"That's probably for the best. I'd hate for you to butcher it." She throws the blankets from her body immediately, tugging at the hem of the hoodie so it doesn't ride up as she hops out of the bed. An excited smile pulls at her lips when she crosses the room and stops beside me.

"I didn't realize you could fuck up chocolate milk." I snort, stealing a look at the girl falling into step beside me as I walk into the hall. She's biting down on her lip as we turn the corner into the living room, and I breathe a sigh of relief when the room is dark and empty. Abby follows close behind me, not even trying to stifle her laugh when I nearly trip over a rogue shoe left in the middle of the room.

When we get to the kitchen, the microwave is washing the room in a faint, warm light, just enough for me to catch the pink flush in Abby's cheeks as she pulls open the refrigerator.

I rifle through the pantry, looking on the top shelf for the goodies we usually stash up there. Pulling down a pack of Oreos and a bag of SunChips, I hesitate when the bag of pretzels catches my eye, but I figure she's probably tired of those, so I stick with my original choices.

When I turn around, Abby is bent down so she's eye-level with the glass as she slowly fills the bottom portion with the chocolate syrup. Her eyes are narrowed in concentration as she sets down the syrup and starts to pour the milk. I drop the cookies and chips on the kitchen island, and grab a spoon from the drawer for her, which she takes from me with a smile.

"Just wait until you taste this." She grins, stirring the milk until it turns brown. When she stops stirring, and the liquid settles, she offers it to me. I bring the glass to my lips and take a slow sip, letting the sweet liquid wash over my tongue before I swallow. She looks up at me expectantly, hands intertwined together in front of her.

"That's some damn good chocolate milk." I nod, grinning down at her. She bites down on her lip and takes the cup from me, and the low moan that sounds from her throat when she takes a sip from the cup sends a shiver down my spine.

"You know how you said you were only in chemistry because you needed an elective credit?" she asks, reaching for the pack of Oreos on the island. Her wicked smile is distracting enough, but when her eyes flick up to mine as she puts the cookie between her teeth, I can feel the telltale pulsing in my groin. I raise a brow at the random change of subject, but nod, enjoying the sight.

"Well, I'm glad you picked chemistry instead of interpretive dance or whatever it was." She smirks, biting down on the chocolate cookie as her wide eyes gleam playfully. "Because you saved an entire class from having to witness you dance."

"Oh, is that right?" I laugh, plucking the rest of her cookie out of her hand. She smiles up at me, challenging me with a playful quirk of her brow. "Do you need a refresher on my moves, Ryan?" I toss the cookie into my mouth before stepping back and grabbing her hand, pulling her to me as I spin us around.

Her surprised squeal is lost between us as I lead her in the most ridiculous dance I can think of—full of spins and dips, not bothering to keep a consistent pace or genre of dance. One second, we're slow dancing—my hands on her waist, and hers on my bare shoulders— and then the next, I'm spinning her around the kitchen while her head is thrown back in the cutest laugh that reverberates around the empty room. When she meets my eyes, her rosy cheeks damn near glow in the warm light from the microwave.

"See." I smirk. "I could have taught that damn class."

She tightens her hold on my arms as she steadies herself from the spins, and I grin down at her, reaching to tuck a few strands of hair that fell from her ponytail behind her ear. Her eyes widen a little at the gesture, and I hesitate, my fingers hovering by the shell of her ear.

Her lips part as her eyes drop down to my lips for a long beat, and the air immediately changes around us when they flick back up to my own. I know I should take a step back—hell, ten steps back— but when her hold on my arm tightens a little and she wets her lips, I know I'm a goner.

"We shouldn't," she whispers with a slow, dazed shake of her head, but her eyes flick down to my lips again, and I feel the pull in every muscle in my body. Like gravity, she's pulling me in without even trying.

I take a step toward her, and when she doesn't stop me, I take a few more, leading her back until she bumps into the kitchen island. I tighten my grip on her hips and lift her onto the cool surface, bringing her closer to my eye-line.

I know she's right. I know we shouldn't. I'm breaking my one-and-done rule, but looking in her deep blue eyes, I can't deny that one-and-done was never going to work, not with Abby.

No matter how hard I try, I can't stay away from this girl, not when her skin feels like pure, electrifying energy under my fingertips, and I crave the taste of her whenever she's around.

I bring my hand up to cup her jaw, searching her eyes for any sign of hesitation, but her body is a deep contrast to her whisper. Her chest is rising and falling quickly, and she opens her legs so I can step into the space between them, bringing me close enough to smell her minty breath and the vanilla apple spice of her perfume mixing together in the most intoxicating way.

Her hands trail up my stomach, and when she reaches my shoulders, her eyes break from mine as she watches her fingers follow the outline of the tattoo there. A low groan rumbles in the back of my throat at the touch. The way her soft fingers barely brush my skin is more sensual than anything she's ever done before, and I have to close my eyes to appreciate the way my skin reacts to her—the way energy trails after her fingertips on my skin like static.

I know I should tell her that all of this can't change anything. That I still can't give her what she wants. That I'm so damn close to everything I've ever worked for, and I can't risk changing those priorities now. But I don't have to, because when her finger trails up my cheek and smooths out the tension line between my eyes, just under my glasses, she sits up a little straighter, bringing our lips that much closer.

"I know," is all she says, holding my stare for a long moment before sitting up a little straighter and tilting her chin up, bringing her lips closer to mine. My eyes flick to her lips, and when they part, and that innocent look in her eyes turns molten, the last thread of restraint I was holding onto so desperately snaps. I lean down and connect our lips, and as if my body was drenched in gasoline and her eager lips were the match, I was on fire.

I know I should stop. I should stop us from crossing the dangerous line we've been dancing on since O'Malley's, but her body's so soft under my hands, and she smells like vanilla apples, and she tastes like spearmint toothpaste and chocolate cookies, and honestly, I can't fucking think straight anymore.

Her lips part in a moan, and I take full advantage, sliding my tongue through the seam of her lips where her chocolate-tinted tongue brushes against mine. A low groan vibrates in the back of my throat when she rolls her hips against mine, and I wrap my fingers around her thighs, pulling her body even closer to the edge, needing to close every inch of space between us. When she wraps her legs around my waist, I revel in the way her small body fits perfectly with mine.

She breaks away with a shaky breath, and I examine her face in the dim, warm light. Her eyes are molten and her cheeks rosy, and she considers me for a moment before her lips pull back into a tentative smile as she lifts her hands above her head. It only takes me a second to register the meaning before my hands move to the hem of the hoodie, and I pull it up over her head, dropping it to the ground behind me.

The light blue cotton underwear is the only thing she has on, and I grin at the white polka dots peppering the fabric before letting my eyes settle on her flushed breasts. Her pale pink nipples are puckered, and the rush of goosebumps that floods her stomach and chest shakes her shoulders slightly as I take a second to really take her in—to commit every curve, and line, and freckle to memory. I was too drunk to really appreciate her last time, but I'm not drunk now, not anymore, and when I look back up at her, her cheeks are bright and her deep blue eyes are trained on me.

She doesn't seem embarrassed at my gaze, and she isn't wide-eyed and nervous like she was in O'Malley's. Instead, her eyes are dark and hungry, and the sight makes my dick twitch.

I pull her lips back up to mine, reveling in the feel of her body under my exploring hands. She arches her back, pushing further into my hands when my thumb brushes against her nipple, and I break away from her eager lips long enough to dip my head down and slip the pebbled bud into my mouth. The throaty gasp that slips from her lips as I pull the bud between my teeth and suck sends a shockwave of pleasure straight down my spine.

I kiss, and lick, and nip my way up her chest to the soft column of her neck, and when I brush my lips across her jaw, her lips are eagerly waiting for me. Her hands explore my shoulders and chest, and when they delve lower, taking time to trace each muscle as she goes, she stops at my waistband, tracing the line softly, teasingly. I slip my tongue into her mouth, grinning when I'm rewarded with the sexiest moan I've ever heard. I groan against her lips as her hand slips into my pants, and I swear to God, my skin explodes when her soft fingers curl around me. My groin pulses hot in her hands, and a soft moan escapes her lips when my mouth latches onto the sensitive skin on just below her ear and I start to suck. My exploration of her neck doesn't last long because I'm desperate to taste her chocolate lips again, and when her hand starts to move slowly, pumping me softly, I kiss her deep enough to coax out a breathy, desperate whimper.

My fingers are wrapping around the band of her underwear when the sound of a door closing snaps my eyes open. Looking down, I watch the lust in her eyes extinguish as she looks over her shoulder, and when she releases me and meets my wide eyes, I feel the panicked energy radiating off of her as the sound of footsteps grows louder.

I help her off the counter, and she grabs for the hoodie on the floor by my feet while I adjust myself so it doesn't look like I've pitched a fucking tent in my sweatpants. She pulls on the hoodie and drops down to the floor, kneeling to be hidden behind the kitchen island as James appears in the doorway. He looks a little shocked to see me, so I reach for the chocolate milk on the counter and nod toward him as nonchalantly as I can.

"Hey, T." He nods, rubbing his hand through his completely fucked up hair. It's sex hair on a whole new level, and I feel a streak of pride for my best friend as he pulls two glasses out of the cabinet.

"How's Jenny." I grin, my eyes flicking down to Abby who's kneeling in front of me. Her eyes widen as she tries to listen for James's movements. Honestly, the sight of Abby on her knees in front of me is enough to pull me into a million different fantasies, so I look back up at James who's filling two glasses with water.

"Fucking amazing, man." He smiles. His eyes finally meet mine after he puts the water pitcher back into the refrigerator. "She's—" He shakes his head, and I can tell by the look in his eye that he's still dazed from their time spent tangled between his sheets.

When his eyes clear again, he looks down at the cup of chocolate milk and frowns. "What are you doing up at two forty-five in the morning drinking chocolate milk? You hate milk."

I glance down to see Abby's brows raise and have to keep a straight face as my best friend exposes me.

"Couldn't sleep." I shrug.

He narrows his eyes at me and glances around the room from his spot by the doorway, but when his eyes land back on me, he just shrugs like he doesn't care enough to spend another minute away from the girl in his bed.

"Night, T."

"Night." I nod, watching as he turns to walk out of the kitchen.

"Night, Abby," he calls back, not bothering to look over his shoulder at us as he disappears into the dark living room. I don't have to see him to know that he has a smug ass grin on his face.

Abby's face pales, and even though we've clearly been caught, she still stays kneeling until the sound of his bedroom door clicking closed echoes softly through the quiet house. When she stands up, she tugs the hoodie down as far as it can go, not meeting my eyes. I can practically feel the uncomfortable energy radiating off of her, so I grab her chocolate milk and cookies from the counter and nod for her to follow me back to the room.

I place her chocolate milk on the nightstand on her side of the bed—fuck, on *that* side of the bed—and turn, smiling at her as casually as I can as I reach for the remote.

"So," I say, clicking on the TV. "What are we watching tonight, Ryan?"

She hesitates by the bed, but when I pull the duvet up and slide down into the sheets, making it clear that I have no intention of doing anything physical, she climbs in after me. There's a pillow-sized distance between us, which I make sure to respect when I turn off the lamp, allowing for the light from the TV to be the only thing illuminating the room. She pulls the duvet up to her chin and grins up at me, her eyes sparkling as she plucks the remote out of my hand.

"I'm about to introduce you to the best show you'll ever watch." She smiles up at me, and I let out a breath of relief at the humor now pooling in her eyes.

Clicking through the options, she presses play on a reality dating show that I usually would have vetoed on the spot, but honestly, I don't think I'll be paying much attention to the TV anyway, because even now—at three in the morning, pre-hangover, makeup free, and with the residual flush from our kitchen make-out—Abby Ryan has never looked more beautiful.

TWENTY-TWO

TRISTAN

The sound of my phone vibrating against the nightstand is the first thing that registers when I open my eyes. I have to blink a few times to adjust to the harsh sunlight currently streaming through my bedroom window, and it takes me a few seconds to realize that the soft snores are coming from the girl currently sleeping on my chest. Her fingers are splayed open on my stomach, and I can smell the vanilla apple spice of her hair when I tilt my head down to get a better look at her face.

She looks so relaxed, and I'm tempted to reach out and tuck the hair that's fallen onto her cheek back behind her ear, but I freeze when she starts to move. Her face nuzzles deeper into my chest, and a few nonsense gibberish words escape her lips in a whisper before she settles.

My phone starts to vibrate again, and I grab for it, trying to keep my body as still as possible to not wake her up. When my fingers close around the phone, I flick my gaze back to Abby's still sleeping form before sliding my thumb across the screen, currently illuminated with the ridiculous duck face selfie Liv saved to her contact.

"Hey." My voice is still thick with sleep, even after clearing my throat.

"Are you seriously still sleeping?"

"What do you want, Liv?"

Abby lifts her head and looks up at me. She blinks a few times in a half-asleep way that makes her look like a lost puppy, and I grin down at her as her eyes finally clear of the sleepy haze. Her cheeks heat when her gaze falls to her hand on my stomach.

Sitting up, the sheets pool around her hips, and I spot the pastel blue of her underwear on her hip as she runs her hands through her slightly frizzy bed head.

"To make sure you're still coming to breakfast. The one we

scheduled last week for your birthday. You know, the one Mom and I have been slaving over for the past forty-five minutes?" Liv snaps.

I pull the phone away from my face to look at the time. "Fuck, I forgot to set my alarm." I groan and slide out of bed, grabbing for my glasses.

"Mel, Garrett, and the girls are already here so hurry up."

I don't bother saying goodbye before I end the call and toss my phone back onto the bed.

"Is everything okay?" Abby asks, pulling her hair back into a ponytail. She has a small red mark on her cheek from sleep, but she still looks more attractive than anyone I've ever woken up next to.

"I'm supposed to go to my parents for breakfast," I say, stretching my hands over my head until the three pops from my back sound.

"Oh, okay." She pushes the blankets away from her and slides out of bed, making sure to keep her hands on the hem of the hoodie so it doesn't slide up, as if I didn't pull it off of her last night. I grin at the gesture.

She's reaching for the pile of folded clothes by her purse when the words slip through my lips. "Do you want to come with me?"

She freezes and looks over her shoulder at me, brows raised. "To breakfast?"

Nodding, I grab for a fresh shirt from my dresser and pull it over my head before dropping my sweats and stepping into a pair of jeans. When I button them, I glance back up to see Abby watching me, her cheeks a little pinker than before.

"You could do that family interview you've been talking about." I shrug and pull on the *USW Basketball* hoodie sitting on my dresser. I can tell that I've sparked her interest because she looks down at her skirt for a second before looking back up at me with an excited smile.

"Are you sure they won't mind?"

"Are you kidding? My mom would love it if you came." I snort. "She'll probably be happier to see you than me right now, especially if you're going to interview her."

Abby bites down on her lip as she considers, and when her eyes fall back down to the leather skirt in her hands, she grins. "Well, I do have a change of clothes in my car," she says softly, as if she's trying to convince herself.

"It's settled then." I grin as I step into the bathroom and turn on the faucet. I don't have to look up to know that she's followed me in, and I hold back my smile as I squirt a line of paste onto her toothbrush.

––––––

I have to admit, I never thought I'd see Abby Ryan sitting in the passenger seat of my truck, but when she looks up at me and grins as she surfs through the radio stations, I can't believe I'd never paid much attention to her before.

The morning sunlight filters through the truck windows and the light settles around her like a halo. The strands of lighter blonde in her chestnut hair are illuminated as it spills down her back in loose waves on top of her gray, fleece sweater.

"Get out of here." She laughs, swatting away my hand from trying to take over the stereo controls. "I'm going to pick something good. I promise."

"Good luck with that." I snort. I can't stop myself from grinning when she intertwines her fingers around mine in an attempt to keep me from messing with the radio controls. "This car hasn't heard a good song since my aux outlet broke last year."

"How old is this thing?" She gapes, pressing extra hard on the dial to get it to switch stations.

"Hey, don't hate on Bertha," I defend the old truck, rubbing the steering wheel affectionately. "She's a '94, but she runs well for her age."

Abby snorts. "Mhm, she looks it."

I'm about to defend Bertha when Abby pulls her hand away from mine and gasps so loud that my heart clenches in my chest.

"What?" My eyes search the road for the massive nuclear explosion that must have happened right in front of us to warrant that kind of reaction, but there's nothing that unusual about the slow current of traffic ahead of us.

"This is my karaoke song," she squeaks, turning up the radio loud enough that I can feel the vibrations through the steering wheel. She sways to the beat, or tries to at least, as much as the seatbelt will allow as she sings along to the song. Her eyes are closed as she belts out the lyrics in the most off-tone rendition I've ever heard. It's honestly the most endearing thing I've ever seen, especially because she's singing into the invisible microphone that she's holding up to her mouth.

"But how, do you expect me, to live alone with just me? 'Cause my world re-volves around you, it's so hard for me to breathe."

She opens her eyes, and my chest tightens when I find them brighter than I've ever seen them. She sways in her seat, completely off beat now, and her smile is damn near blinding as she tilts her head back and sings along to the song. Her smile is fucking contagious, and I have to remind myself that I'm driving, which is a real travesty, be-cause tearing my eyes away from her is almost painful.

I merge into the right lane and put on my blinker as we come to a stop at the red light, and when I glance over at her again, I can't help the chuckle that vibrates from my chest. Her eyes grow wide, and she beams at me when she realizes that I'm singing along with her. I have to admit, this song was a banger.

She watches my lips, and when she realizes that I actually know the lyrics, she sticks to only singing her parts. We both sound like dying seals as we try to hit the high notes, but we just take it in stride, not letting it stop us from belting out every single word.

"I walked, I ran, I jumped, I flew right off the ground and float to you, there's no gravity to hold me down for real."

If any of the guys saw me right now, they would never let me live this down, but when I watch Abby try her hardest to hit the high note—her cheeks flushed and eyes bright as she beams at me—I hon-estly don't give a fuck what they would think. I would belt out any song if it would make her smile like this.

I turn up the volume even more as it reaches the best part, letting it blast through the speakers of my shitty old truck as I pull off the main road and into my parents' neighborhood.

"But somehow I'm still alive inside, you took my breath, but I survived, I don't know how but I don't even care."

We sing the end of the song together as I pull up behind Mel's Kia, but even after putting the truck in park, I don't cut the engine yet. When the song finally ends, Abby's face is flushed, and I watch as she reaches to turn down the radio when an insurance advertise-ment starts to play.

"I can't believe you know the lyrics to that song." She laughs, com-pletely out of breath as she sits back in the seat.

"Who doesn't know the lyrics to that song?" I counter, finally cut-ting the engine.

The heat stops blowing from the vents, but it's still warm in the truck. I sit back and watch as she runs her fingers through her hair, smoothing out the ends which melt from a medium brunette to a dark blonde hue that I imagine is from her summers spent in Florida. Her eyes flick to the house, and I feel the change in the air between us as she runs her hand over the front of her jacket and yoga pants, as if they were wrinkled. For being her *"just in case"* clothes that she keeps in her car, they're hardly creased. Also, who the hell keeps just in case clothes in their car?

Abby, that's who.

"Ready?" I ask, pushing open my door.

She nods, pushing open her own door before I even have a chance to open it for her. She fumbles with the strap of her purse when she stops in front of the truck beside me.

"I have to warn you," I say, leading her up the drive, keeping an eye out for ice patches. "My mom makes the world's best pancakes, so after you eat these, pancakes will be ruined for you forever."

Her shoulders relax a little as I step back and let her walk through the open door before me. The smell of buttermilk pancakes hits the second we walk through the doorway, and I smirk down at her, as if the smell alone is enough to prove my point.

She follows close behind as I lead her down the hallway toward the kitchen, and I don't have to look back at her to know that her eyes are glued to the gallery wall of embarrassing pictures. When the sound of her quiet gasp hits me, I know she's spotted the one of me smiling like a four-eyed dweeb, braces on full-display, with acne-spotted skin, for my sixth-grade school picture. The most mortifying thing of all is that I begged my mom to let me bring a basketball with me as a prop, which is forever memorialized in the picture of me holding the ball to my chest like it's some kind of trophy. There are a million things wrong with that damn picture, but no matter how many times I complain about it, Mom refuses to take it down.

I've dealt with the years of teasing from my friends and teammates, but I've never brought a girl over, and now, as Abby bites down on her lip to keep from laughing, I'm beginning to remember why.

"You were so cute," she coos, pulling out her phone and pointing it at the framed picture.

"Oh, no you don't," I say, plucking her phone from her hands.

"What—no, give it back." She grins, trying to jump to steal the phone back. I've got at least a foot on her, and it doesn't take much effort to hold it out of her reach.

"That picture doesn't leave this house," I deadpan. "In fact, we won't talk about this picture ever again after this. It's like it never existed. Deal?" I raise a brow, dangling her phone just out of reach.

"But—" She pulls her brows together, turning back to the picture. "This is pure gold." She glances back at me over her shoulder. "Iconic, really."

I give her a blank stare, and after biting the inside of her cheek, she finally relents. "Okay, fine. I promise not to mention *the picture* ever again." She uses air quotes. "Unless someone else mentions it first, then all bets are off." She grins.

I narrow my eyes at her, clearly not convinced.

She holds out her pinky, all humor gone from her face. "I pinky swear it."

I curl my pinky around hers, chuckling at the way mine dwarfs hers. "Alright." I sigh, handing her back her phone.

"What took you so long—Oh, my God, Abby?" Olivia's voice echoes through the hall, and when I turn around, she's walking toward us. She completely ignores me as she wraps her arms around Abby's shoulders, pulling her into a tight hug.

The sound of a chair being pushed back hastily sounds, and seconds later, Mom appears at the entrance of the kitchen. Her eyes are wide as she takes in the girl currently hugging back my obnoxious sister.

"Oh, Abby. Hi, sweetie. What a wonderful surprise," she chirps as she wipes her hands on the bottom of her apron, hurrying toward us.

She pulls me in for a hug, eyes crinkling in a smile as I bend down to kiss her cheek. Her attention doesn't stay on me long, though, and seconds later she's pulling Abby into a hug.

"I didn't know you were coming along, sweetie," she says, squeezing Abby tightly before releasing her. "Livy, could you go set another place at the table, please?"

She nods toward my sister who disappears into the kitchen.

Abby's cheeks are tinted pink, and her eyes dart up to mine. "I hope it's okay," she says quietly, readjusting the purse on her shoulder.

"Of course, it is." She waves off her concern. "You're always welcome."

Abby's eyes widen a little as she smiles at my mom, and I swear I almost detect a glimmer of sadness in them when my mom reaches down and squeezes her hands before turning around and leading her out of the hallway and into the kitchen.

Everyone is already sitting at the table when Mom releases Abby's hand and motions for her to sit at the empty seat beside mine. Everyone's eyes are trained on Abby as I pull out her chair for her, and when she sits down, she looks over at me as I sit down beside her.

"Abby, this is my sister Melody, her husband Garrett, my dad Amos, and my nieces, Georgia, and Gigi." I motion toward each person as I list them off. "Everyone, this is Abby."

"It's nice to meet you all," Abby smiles, and her cheeks turn a darker hue of pink as everyone considers her. Their expressions range from confused, to excited, to mystified.

"It's nice to meet you, Abby." Melody grins as she wipes the errant syrup from Georgia's mouth.

"I don't mean to be rude but—" Garrett narrows his eyes in mock confusion as he points between us. "—What is someone as gorgeous as you doing with this guy?" He motions to me, and I flip him off with a lazy grin.

———

Abby slowly relaxes as we eat breakfast. At first, she's quiet, and mostly only speaks when someone asks her something, but by the time she finishes her stack of pancakes, she's carrying on conversations without me, only glancing over occasionally.

Most of her time was monopolized by my dad who asked about where she's from, but Abby was more than happy to answer his questions about the small beach town she grew up in.

Mel was more interested in learning about Disney and the best time of year to visit since she wanted to plan a trip for Georgia's birthday this summer. I was tempted to remind her that just because Abby's from Florida, doesn't mean she's a fucking travel guide, but Abby didn't seem to mind giving the best tips for traveling around Florida.

Somehow, the vacation conversation led into them discussing their favorite show. Garrett catches my attention when he rolls his eyes and leans back in his chair, pulling out his phone. I can only imagine how many times he gets stuck in the middle of these conversations whenever he comes to visit with Mel.

"I tried to get Tristan to watch it last night, but I don't think he was actually paying attention." Abby laughs as her eyes flick up to mine.

I raise a brow at the accusation and poke her in the side. "I was paying attention," I lie.

"Name one of the islanders then," she challenges, swatting my hand away as her brows raise to match mine.

I pop a strawberry into my mouth to buy some time, but honestly, I'm fucked because she's right, I wasn't paying attention at all. I was distracted by the fact that by the middle of the episode, she was cuddled up next to me in the same position that we woke up in this morning. So I was a little more interested in watching the way my fingers were tracing random shapes on the exposed skin of her thigh, rather than the constant drama of the show.

"Michael." I shrug, taking a shot in the dark. I briefly remember some dude with a shit-load of tats saying that was his name, but it could have been Marcus or Miles or Martin for all I know. Like I said, I was a little preoccupied.

She looks impressed when she nods, and I look down at her with an *I told you so* grin that I definitely shouldn't be able to give her right now.

"You were hanging out last night?" Olivia asks. Her tone is innocent, but I can tell by her smirk that she's fishing for information, and by the way everyone else is staring at us, I know they're all wondering the same thing. Abby's cheeks flush, and she looks up at me as she takes a sip of her water.

"Mhm." I shrug, hoping they'll move on, but of course, Olivia doesn't.

"And you're together this morning," she observes, her eyes narrowing as her smirk grows. I stare at her blankly before flicking my gaze to my mom, who's wiping her mouth with her napkin. But even her smile is hard to miss.

"Well, she wanted to come interview you all for the article," I say, looking at Abby for confirmation.

"Oh, right." She nods, looking back at my mom. "I'd love to interview you, if you're up for it."

The look of unadulterated excitement beaming from my mom

is like nothing I've ever seen before. She looks wide-eyed from me to Abby, and then back.

"Right now?" she gasps. Her hands move to smooth out her hair currently pulled up into a bun on the top of her head.

"We can do a family picture another day if you'd like. This would just be a voice recorded interview." Abby smiles.

"Yes, of course." She beams at me as she pushes back her chair. "I've been thinking about what I'd want to say in case you ever wanted some background information on Tristan. Let's go into the living room; we can clear this up after."

She waves for us to follow her, and Abby grabs her purse, grinning up at me as she follows my mom's lead by sitting down on the couch. I fall onto the cushion beside her, and Olivia and Melody sit on the other side of her, while Garrett and Dad conveniently disappear into the other room where I can hear the distinct sound of Greg Bradshaw's voice doing the weekly rundown on USASN.

Mom's eyes grow wide as she gasps. "I almost forgot—I've already pulled a few pictures out of storage for the article." She hurries around the corner and through the hall where she disappears into the office and then reemerges with a big stack of pictures in her hands. I groan as she waves them excitedly. "I picked out my favorite ones."

Abby is practically beaming as she eyes the stack, and I lean back into the couch as she hands her the pictures. The very top one is of a toddler me standing naked in the tub with a little rubber ball in my hands and a toothy grin on my face.

For fuck's sake.

I try to ignore the fact that Abby is flipping through the stack as she asks my mom and sisters a series of different questions ranging from *"What is your favorite memory of Tristan as a child?"* to *"When did you realize he might have NBA potential?"*

It helps that my mom is sitting straight up on the couch, her hands folded in her lap demurely, with a big ass smile on her face, like she's being video recorded or something. She's basking in her twenty minutes of stardom, and honestly, the look of excitement in her eyes whenever Abby asks her a question is worth all of the embarrassing pictures that are currently sitting in Abby's lap. For all of the basketball practices and games she's sat through cheering me on, she deserves her moment to shine, even if it's just a few quotes in an article.

When Abby reads off the last question on the list—"*Where do you see Tristan in ten years?*"—my mom hesitates as she eyes me.

"I know he'll be a big NBA star." She smiles. "I don't know much about the NBA, but I know that my son has more passion for that sport than anyone else I've ever met." She looks down at her hands, and when she looks back up, her brows are pulled together slightly, and I notice the worry lines starting to crease. "I just hope that in ten years he'll find balance. I hope he'll be happy in his career, as well as his home life. And I hope I'll have some more grandchildren running around by then." She grins, looking to the two little girls playing in the middle of the living room.

When her eyes flick back up to me, she searches my face before her eyes flick to Abby, a smile growing on her lips.

"That was perfect." Abby smiles, picking up the recorder and clicking it off before she tucks it back into her purse.

I glance down at my phone and stand. "We should probably get going," I say, sliding the phone back into my pocket. "I've got a lot of homework."

"Oh, alright," Mom says, leading us out of the room and through the hallway toward the door. "You should come with Tristan to his granddad's birthday party. I know they'd love to meet you and you'd be able to get a great family picture." She smiles, turning around when she gets to the front door.

Abby's eyes widen a little and she looks over at me.

"You should. My granddad's a real character, you'd love him." I laugh.

"We'd love to have you there," Mom adds. "It's not next Sunday, but the Sunday after, the seventeenth."

"The seventeenth." Abby nods and her eyes dart up to mine quickly, as if to make sure that I'm sincere about my invitation. When I nod, she smiles back at my mom. "I'll be there."

Mom beams and pulls Abby into a hug, and I turn to see Olivia and Mel with the girls behind us. I reach down to grab Georgia, who wraps her arms around my neck and hugs me hard. I can tell by the look in her eye that she's tired, so I don't mess with her too much. Instead of my usual tickle, I place a loud smacking kiss on her cheek, which she smiles at. Putting her back down, I reach out for Gigi, who's waving around the block in her hand. I blow a raspberry kiss on her cheek, which sends a giggle echoing loudly through the room. Glancing over, I lock eyes with Abby, who's grinning at me over my mom's shoulder.

"Happy birthday." Mel smiles, taking Gigi back.

"Thanks, Mel." I pull her into a loose hug, not wanting to squish Gigi.

Olivia opens her arms, and I pull her in.

"Happy birthday, you old fart." She smirks.

I reach out to pinch her arm like I always do, but she swats my hand away and jumps out of reach, sticking out her tongue at me. When I turn around, my mom extends her arms and I walk into them, pulling her to me tightly as I lean down and kiss her cheek. Her voice is so soft I almost miss it, but when I pull back and look down at her, I know I heard her right.

"I like her a lot." She smiles up at me, squeezing my hand.

I glance over at Abby, who's now bent down to say goodbye to Georgia, and I can't help but mirror her smile as she leans into the toddler's open arms.

Yeah, me, too.

TWENTY-THREE

ABBY

I'm honestly not sure what was worse—the hangover, the inquisition I walked into when I got home from breakfast, or the fact that I still can't seem to stop thinking about how good it felt to have my fingers knotted in Tristan's curls while his lips explored me again.

I knew from the moment he hesitated in the kitchen that nothing had changed. I was still just a lust and liquor fueled temptation to him. Except something had changed. I had.

I didn't care about the title, or the meaning of it, or hell, even the consequences, I just knew that I wanted him. And if that tiny sliver of a moment in his barely lit kitchen, slightly drunk, with chocolate-tinted lips at three in the morning was all I was ever going to get, then I wasn't going to pass it up.

But now that it's over and I'm left with the memory of what his fingertips felt like tracing circles on my back as I fell asleep in his arms, I'm realizing the high I felt while his lips crashed down onto my own, comes with a low. A low deep enough to keep me dazed, and wanting, and confused, all while wishing it could happen again, even just one more time.

The daze lasted all weekend, which was mostly spent in the same pajamas I pulled on Saturday afternoon when I got home from breakfast at his parents' house. After being practically criminally interrogated by Jenny and Nia for the details of my sleepover—and the dramatics that came along with them realizing that Tristan is Mr. Big—I spent the rest of the weekend in bed with a bag of Cheetos and my favorite Netflix shows, shamelessly wearing his hoodie just to smell the cologne still clinging to it.

To make a pathetic weekend even worse, while I was smack dab in the middle of throwing myself a pity party, I was slapped in the face with the one thing I didn't realize would hurt the most until it was said out loud—*"James and I are officially dating."*

It was a tough pill to swallow. The words sparked the jealousy that comes along with the harsh realization that there's a big difference between being the girl that's conveniently there when you're drunk and horny, and the girl you actually want to date.

It didn't take long for James to become an almost constant presence in our apartment, and even though I've done a pretty spectacular job of looking happy for them, I've been wallowing silently in the mess I made for myself, because it's getting harder to not think about the what if's.

What if things were different.

What if that was us instead.

What if I wasn't just a hookup.

I'm usually pretty good at shutting down those thoughts before they can spiral out of control, but it's hard when I walk out to see them cuddled up on the living room couch, or when I'm scrambling to find my headphones when their muffled moans echo down the hall in the middle of the night—or the middle of the day, or honestly, any time they venture into her room alone.

Which is why I'm currently sitting in the coffee shop on campus, trying to study with my chemistry textbook and flashcards sprawled out in front of me. I'm ten cards deep when the familiar voice sounds.

"Abby, hey."

I look up to see Dean standing at my table. He pulls off his beanie to reveal the tousled blond locks underneath, and his blue eyes scan the table in front of me before meeting mine, his lips turning up in a smile.

"Hey." I grin, putting down the small stack of cards in my hands.

"It's good to see you." He runs a hand through his hair as his cheeks warm a bit.

"Yeah, you, too." I nod, and my eyes widen when I remember that I never returned the text he sent me Friday night. In my defense, I was already pretty drunk by then. "I am so sorry about not texting you back," I start quickly. "I've been super busy. But I wasn't ignoring you, I promise." I motion toward the table in front of me, thankful that the explosion of flashcards might actually back up my excuse.

I really wasn't trying to ignore him. I just completely forgot that he even texted me in the first place.

"It's okay. I figured you were probably busy." He shrugs, and I can tell by the tilt of his lips that he's trying to seem casual about it, to not make me feel bad, but I still feel like a complete jerk when his eyes meet mine again. "I'm here with a few friends. We're about to play some card games if you want to join us." He nods toward a booth by the front window, and I glance over my shoulder to see the four people all unwrapping themselves from their scarves as they settle into their seats with their coffee.

"Oh." I consider the offer while biting the inside of my cheek.

"You don't have to if you need to study," he says quickly, but the part of me that still feels guilty for not texting him back makes me shake head and start to pack up my flashcards.

"I'd love to, actually." I smile, pushing back my chair as I grab for the steaming mug of hot chocolate on my table.

———

If you would have told me a few months ago that I'd be hanging out with a group of pre-law students—and actually having a good time—I wouldn't have believed you.

I've spent more than my fair share of time with lawyers, law school interns, and pre-law students at my mom's office. From my experience, they're typically not the crowd I'd voluntarily spend my free time with, but after an hour of being around Dean's friends, I have to admit, they're actually kind of great. It kind of pains me inside to admit that because I can already picture my mother's smug smile, as if she's here watching me befriend her people.

"Bullshit, Dean." Viv, the girl with the tight black bun and cute green sweater, grins at the boy sitting to my right. I lean back in my seat as I take another sip of my hot chocolate, trying to hide the amused grin that's currently tugging at my lips. I'm ready to watch the show-down that's about to play out in front of me, which only gets better when Dean's jaw tightens as he looks back at Viv, his eyes narrowed slightly as he considers her.

"Are you sure you want to do that, Viv? That's a big stack of cards to gamble for a pair of twos." He leans forward, pulling his cards flush against his chest to keep them hidden. "You've only got, what, two cards left?"

Viv leans back in the booth, impervious to Dean's mind games.

When her cherry lips pull back into a grin and her perfectly waxed brow props slightly, I have to stifle my laugh as the rest of the group starts to hype her up for her Hail Mary call.

If Dean turns over the two cards on the table and they are in fact a pair of twos, Viv will have to take the entire stack underneath, which is almost certain death for her chances of winning; however, if he turns over the cards and they aren't a pair of twos, he takes the lot. It's a risky move, some might even say it's a sacrificial move, but honestly, after losing three consecutive games to the guy sitting smugly beside me, the five of us seem to have formed an unspoken bond to make sure he doesn't win again.

"I said bullshit, didn't I?" Viv challenges.

I'm really starting to like this girl.

We all watch as Dean reaches for the stack of cards, and his hand hesitates for a moment as his eyes scan the booth. When his lips quirk up, he turns over the cards in his hand as he drops them onto the pile. The group breaks out into hysterics when a four and a seven are revealed, and Viv's grin grows into a full-on smug smile as she fans herself with her cards triumphantly.

"Pick 'em up, Deanie boy," Viv gloats, holding her hand up to me for a high five, which I slap earnestly.

Honestly, seeing Dean finally lose a round is more gratifying than I thought it would be, so when he looks over at me, feigning shocked betrayal as he watches my hand connect with Viv's, I can't help but laugh.

The surrounding tables are all staring at us now that the two boys, Jack and Dillon, are leaning over the table, wrestling past Dean's defense to rub their hands roughly through his hair. When they sit back, the blond locks are left sticking up in every direction, like he just stuck his head out of a window on a highway.

His hands are already trying to pat down the mess, but when he glances at me, I can't help the laugh that escapes my lips as his cheeks redden. His toothy smile flashes before disappearing when he glares at the guys across the booth from us.

"Real mature guys." He shakes his head, but I can tell by the twitch of his cheek that he's failing to hold back a grin as he pulls on his beanie.

"Usually, I'd want a pumpkin muffin or a latte for that kind of win, but since Sam and I have to head out to the mall now, I'll settle for a more vocal prize. How about, *Vivian Nguyen, you are the best Bullshit player in the world*," Viv says, tossing her cards onto the table.

Dean scrunches his face, as if the words are going to physically hurt him to say, but he repeats the words, albeit it much less enthusiastically than Viv. "Vivian Nguyen, you are the best Bullshit player in the world."

"Well, it's not as heartfelt as I would have liked, but I'll take it." She grins, nodding to Jack and Dillon to scoot out of the booth so she can get out.

"Why are you going to the mall?" Jack asks, sidestepping a girl who has three coffees balanced in her hands as she walks past our booth, nearly knocking her over in the process. She sends him a glare, and he looks away quickly with an *oh, shit* look on his face.

"I need new shoes for the gala dinner tomorrow," Viv says, sliding out of the booth. "And I'll probably end up getting a new dress, too, because let's be honest, I have zero self-control."

"So glad I agreed to go with you." Sam rolls her eyes, but she grins at me as she scoots out of the booth. "We're stopping by the Auntie Anne's so I can get a cinnamon pretzel and a cherry slush. If I'm going to be stuck watching you model dresses for the next three hours, I need a cherry slush."

Viv rolls her eyes as she nods, and I grin at the gesture. You know you've got a real best friend when all they require is a slush to sit and watch you try on dresses for three hours. I'm not saying that I've been dragged along for that exact same thing, but I'm also not denying it. Thanks a lot, Nia.

"We should head out, too, I need to study," Dillon says, pulling on his coat. "Frederick's exam is pass-fail, and I'm *not* retaking civil law over summer." He scowls at the thought as a theatric shiver runs down his body. "Could you imagine spending every day with Frederick over the summer? I'd rather die."

"I found a study guide online," Jack says, slapping Dillon on the shoulder before turning back to us and giving that universal *see ya later* head nod. Dillon grins at me and Dean before following his friend out of the coffee shop.

"It was nice meeting you, Abby." Viv grins as she wraps her scarf around her neck. "I'm sure we'll see you around soon."

"It was nice to meet you both." I smile, watching as the girls re-treat toward the door behind Jack and Dillon.

"I should probably get going, too." Dean sighs. "I have a pretty big test on Thursday that I haven't even started studying for." He slides out of the booth, and I pull my bag onto my shoulder before sliding out myself.

"I'm really glad that I ran into you," he says as he opens the cafe door for me to walk out ahead of him. He slides his hands into his pant pockets, and I watch as his breath comes out in small puffs in the cold evening air when he falls into step beside me. His nose and cheeks are already starting to turn pink, which somehow makes his deep blue eyes look even more vibrant.

"Me, too," I admit, pulling my bag up further onto my shoulder. "I'm sorry, again, for not texting you back the other day."

He shakes his head, and I can tell by the brightness in his eyes that he really doesn't hold it against me. "I texted you because I was going to ask you something, but I'm glad you didn't text back because it's probably better for me to ask in person."

His eyes flick over my shoulder and then back nervously as he shifts his weight from one foot to the other. "We have this gala dinner tomorrow night. It's kind of like a networking fundraiser that all of the pre-law students have to go to, and we all get a plus one. So, I was hoping you might want to come with me."

I'm sure I look shocked because he smiles at me, the kind of smile that says, *You can say no, I won't mind,* but also, *Please say yes,* which honestly, is pretty adorable.

"It's a lot more fun than it sounds, I swear." He chuckles as he runs a hand through his hair. "My friends will be there, too. We'll proba-bly ditch the gala and go hang out somewhere else after we get credit for being there. But I figured it would be a lot more fun if you were there with me."

"This is like a formal gala?" I ask, already thinking about the dif-ferent dresses in Nia's closet.

"Yeah. I know it's not the most traditional second date, and you'd probably much rather go to the movies, or mini golfing, or something, but—"

"No—" I interrupt quickly. "This sounds perfect."

His brow raises as he smiles at me, as if he thought he was going to have to do more convincing than that.

"Okay, great." He smiles, a toothy grin that warms me in the cool air. "I can pick you up tomorrow at seven," he offers, already starting to walk backward toward his red Jaguar parked a few spots away.

"Tomorrow at seven." I nod.

When he turns around, I don't waste time getting into my car and cranking up the heat as fast as I can. It takes a few seconds for the air to start circulating, and I fish out my phone from the bottom of my bag while I'm waiting for the heat to start defrosting my fingers and cheeks. There's an Instagram message waiting for me when my screen illuminates.

My finger slides across the screen hastily to open the message when I realize who it's from. He replied to the picture of the hot chocolate that I posted to my story from the coffee shop. The message is short, but I read it over a few times, biting down on my lip to keep from smiling like an idiot at my phone in the middle of the busy coffee shop parking lot.

Looks good, Ryan, but it's no late-night chocolate milk.

TWENTY-FOUR

"Are they still staring?"

I bite back a smile as I look over his shoulder toward his group of friends.

"Mhm," I hum, glancing away quickly so they won't catch me peeking.

"They're not very conspicuous," he mutters, but I catch the twitch of his cheek when his eyes meet mine. When his hot breath hits my cheek, I can faintly smell the liquor he's been sipping on since we got here. It's the same glass I've been sneaking sips from when no one was looking, since I forgot to bring my fake ID with me.

I've always been a year younger than everyone else in my friend group, since the private school I went to in Florida allowed for kindergarten students to start a year earlier than the public schools around us. I was a year behind my friends in everything—getting my period, my permit, my license, and now, not being able to buy a drink legally is just another thing to add to that list.

"I like them," I admit. "They're fun, and relaxed, and not at all what I thought a group of pre-law students would be like." I smile as I run my hand over the smooth material on his shoulder.

Dean is a boyish kind of handsome. He has wispy blond hair, sharp cheekbones, and a barely-there southern accent that has me intrigued by every word, just waiting to see if the little twang will show itself when he's not paying attention to it.

And now, as his hands tighten on my waist and his movements become a little more confident, I try to keep my mind focused on how the twinkling lights hanging from the ceiling are casting a pretty glow on his face, and not the fact that every time I close my eyes, I can't help but picture Tristan here with me instead.

He tightens his hold on me a little more, and I glance away, letting my eyes scan the room. The decorations are completely different from when I was here for the formal. Rather than the slightly cheesy under the stars theme the room was decorated in before, it's now beautifully adorned with white linen accents and hundreds of flickering candles strewn on nearly every open surface around the room.

"You know, I've always hated coming to these things," he says, pulling my attention back to him as his eyes scan the crowd around us. When they land on the older couple dancing closely next to us, he smiles. "But somehow, you've managed to make this one of the best nights I've had in a while." His eyes flick back to mine again and I don't try to hide my smile.

"Even better than our night of bowling, beer, and cheese fries?" I tease, raising a brow.

"The cheese fries were good," he nods, "but I have to say, the highlight of that night for me was your victory dance. How many pins did it take for you to break out into dance? Three?" he teases, tightening his hold on me as the song changes into something a livelier.

"Four," I correct. "I dance at four pins, thank you very much."

"If that's all it takes to get you to pull out the finger guns, I'm going to have to take you again soon."

I glance around and revel at the realization that no one is paying any attention to us. We're not being watched by the couples around us, and I'm not getting weird looks from the rest of the girls in the room, wondering why I'm the one who was chosen to dance. Instead, it's just us. Just Dean and I—and I have to admit, it's a great feeling.

"It's a date." I nod, looking back to him with a playful smile.

He grins, eyes flicking down to my lips. My breath catches in my throat as they linger on my mouth, and I look away quickly, pretending to admire the decorations again. When I look back to him, he smiles at me softly, casually, as if I didn't just ruin the perfect moment for our first kiss. That easy smile eases some of the nervous energy pulsing through me, but when he pulls me a little closer and leads me, albeit a little off beat, to the rhythm of the song, I can't shake the confusion.

I like Dean—he's sweet, and kind, and handsome, and yet, my stomach dropped at the thought of kissing him.

Maybe I'm just not ready. Maybe it takes a little longer for me to be comfortable kissing a boy I barely know. Maybe I'm overthinking this.

My chest tightens as I look up at the twinkling lights strewn above because I know that none of that is true. They're all excuses, fickle white lies I tell myself to avoid the same cold, hard truth I've been avoiding all night—he's not Tristan.

Lifting my hand from his shoulder, I tuck my hair behind my ear, trying to clear my head before I start to spiral down that rabbit hole.

"Are you hungry?" he asks, clearing his throat as he drops his hands from my waist. "For something other than these grossly over-priced finger foods." He eyes the appetizer table with an exaggerated grimace, and I laugh at the genuine look of disgust on his face when he remembers the salmon bite he tried earlier. When he looks back at me, his eyes wrinkle in a smile, one that I know is meant to say, *It's okay, we don't have to talk about it.*

My shoulders relax at the look, grateful that he isn't bitter about the silent rejection—that he's letting me move at my own pace here. I meet his curious gaze and smile, intertwining my arm with his when he holds it out for me.

"Starving." I admit.

———

"You're breathing on me, dude," Dillon snaps, motioning for Jack to scoot closer to the door.

"I can't stop breathing, Dillon, I'll die," Jack snaps back, but he wiggles in his seat, trying to squish closer to the door.

Since this is a five-seat car, and there's now six of us squished in-side of it, the backseat is a little tight; and by a little, I mean that I've never been more claustrophobic in my life. Since Dean drank a lit-tle more than he was planning to at the gala, we had to ride with the rest of his friends. Watching Dillion, a man who I'm almost certain is just as tall as Tristan, if not taller, cram into the back of Viv's Nissan Rogue with three other people, myself included, might be the high-light of my night.

He really should have just taken the front seat, but since Sam won dibs on the way out to the parking lot, he took the loss like a champ and agreed to ride in the back with the rest of us.

I've tried to make myself as small as possible, nearly leaning on Dean to give Dillon more room. As nice as he is, I can tell he doesn't do well with close quarters, which is why Jack is now getting snapped at again for breathing in his personal space.

"If you push me any farther, I'm going to fall out of the car," Jack laments, elbowing Dillon back.

Dillon sighs in defeat and arches his back so he can reach into his back pocket. His knuckles graze my thigh as he reaches back, and he shoots me an *Oh, shit, I swear to God I didn't just try to feel you up* look.

"It's fine." I laugh, leaning even further onto Dean so he can reach his pocket without fear of touching me again. He grins as he pulls out his phone. Dean glances over at me with an amused look since I'm now dangerously close to sitting on his lap.

"Fuck, how did that happen? We were just up." Jack gapes.

I look back at Dillon, who's now scrolling through the phone he's been glued to all night. Jack is leaning over to get a good look at the screen, his eyes widening.

"Don't know," Dillon groans. His thumb scrolls quickly on the screen until he finds the page he's looking for. "Fuck, Beck looks injured."

My eyes snap over to his screen to see the USASN app open with a live stream of the game. He's right. I spot Tristan instantly, trailing behind as everyone else runs toward the other side of the court. He's limping, favoring one leg as he jogs to catch up.

"Of course he would get hurt when we play Duke," Jack snorts, leaning forward to get a better view of the video.

"If it's bad enough to keep him out for the rest of the season, we're fucked. There goes our chance at winning the finals this year," Dillon curses, adjusting the brightness on his phone so he can see the stream better. I don't realize that I'm also leaning over to get a better look until the car comes to a hard stop as the front tires hit the curb.

"Oh, shoot. Sorry about that." Viv laughs, smiling sheepishly into the rearview mirror.

She puts the car in park, and I look out of the window to see that we're at the diner.

Dean has the door open before Viv can turn off the car, and I'm sliding out behind him as I try to process everything I just saw on Dillon's phone.

Tristan is hurt.

He's limping across the court in Duke's arena right now.

There's not much I can do since he's in North Carolina. Hell, even if it was a home game and he was a ten-minute drive away, I wouldn't be able to see him right now. But still, even knowing that, I can't seem to calm the anxiety that's now flooding my veins.

Is it serious?

Will he be out for long?

Is he okay?

"Are you okay?" The question takes a moment to register, but when I look up, Dean's hesitating by entrance of the diner, his brows knitting.

I nod as I walk through the door he's holding open for me, and I attempt my best casual smile as I pass. He considers me for a second but seems to buy it before scooting into the booth behind me. When we're all packed in, we place our orders without even looking at a menu.

Lacie's our server, and when she finally recognizes the boy sitting next to me, she smirks and sends me a *You've got a lot of explaining to do* look before turning to put our orders in.

I don't know if it's because I was stuck snacking on cucumber hummus bites all night since it was the only vegetarian friendly option at the gala, or just because the shake truly was the best they've ever made, but I have never tasted a more delicious chocolate milkshake in my life.

Between dipping my fries into the ice cream goodness, and eating the two—yes, Lacie hooked me up with *two*—cherries, I was in food heaven. Or, I would have been, if I wasn't completely distracted by the fact that somewhere out there, Tristan is hurt. And while it could be nothing, it could also potentially be career-ending, and I have no idea which one it is.

The entire table is mid-debate about which comedy is the best—my vote is for *The Hangover*, while the rest are throwing out options like *22 Jump Street*, *Step Brothers*, *40 Year Old Virgin*, and *Anchorman*—when my phone starts to ring.

"I'm offended that you think *Anchorman* even deserves a spot in the top ten, Dean." Sam scowls, flicking one of her fries at him. "I mean come on, have some taste."

"Like *Step Brothers* was any better?" he defends. "At least mine—"

When I pull my phone from my bag, my heart careens in my chest as the name on my phone sends a shock of adrenaline through my veins. I hold my phone to my chest and look back up to the table, still mid-debate.

"I should probably take this—it's a family thing," I breathe, sliding out of the booth.

Dean looks over at me, brows raised slightly. "Is everything okay?"

"Yeah, everything's fine." I nod, taking a step back. "I'll be back in a second." Turning toward the door, I try to keep my heels from echoing loudly on the tiled floor as I hurry out of the diner.

The frozen night air hits my exposed skin and sends a rush of goosebumps up my arms. With each step I take away from the entrance, the thin satin material of my dress makes me wish I would have remembered to grab my coat. But even with the flood of goosebumps now ravaging my arms and legs, I'm not worried about the icy wind blowing my gown around my ankles; instead, I'm watching anxiously as my finger slides across the screen, accepting the FaceTime call.

It takes a second for the call to load, and I take that time to walk toward Viv's Nissan, letting the rhythmic sound of my heels clicking loudly against the cement calm me slightly. When his face finally pops onto my phone, I release my lip from between my teeth.

"Are you okay? I saw that you were limping, but I couldn't tell how bad it was," I rush, trying to search his face for any sign of pain, but he seems relaxed as he leans against a plain white wall. He has headphones hanging from his ears, and aside from the wall, I can't tell much about his surroundings, other than the low hum of voices around him.

"You—wow, you look amazing, Abby," he says softly. His eyes widen as they trail down the screen, and I can tell he's looking at the gown. "Is that the dress you wore to the formal?"

I glance down at the golden fabric, shocked that after everything that happened to him tonight, this is what he's focused on. When I look back up at the screen, he's grinning at me.

"Focus, Tristan," I chide, trying to bite back my smile as his brows raise in appreciation. "The last thing I saw was you wobbling around the court and I'm kind of freaking out here."

"I'm fine, Ryan." He shrugs easily. "I tweaked my ankle, but the trainer said it's not a big deal. I just need to ice it for the next few days and then I'll be good to play on Friday."

He's fine.

The anxiety that's been weighing me down for the past thirty minutes evaporates as I lean against the hood of Viv's car.

"Now back to the dress." He grins, dimple indenting softly. "Let me see it."

I raise a brow but extend my arm to get a wider shot so he can see at least the top half of the gown. When his eyes flick down the screen, I know exactly what he's staring at, so I bring the phone back to its original position and shake my head at his boyish antics. His grin deepens, so much so that I wish I could poke his dimple, which is now in full effect.

"Is that Ryan?" Luke pops onto the screen and his eyes widen when he sees me. "Damn, Ryan." He grins, blocking the elbow shot Tristan takes. "Why are you so dressed up?"

"Yeah, why are you so dressed up?" Tristan asks, his brows pulling together.

"It was for school—just a fundraiser thing." I shrug, tucking my hair behind my ear as it whips around my face in the wind. I'm hoping they won't press for more information, and when Luke's eyes flick off-screen to whoever is standing behind the camera, he laughs and nods toward them before waving and saying goodbye to me.

When Tristan pulls the phone closer to him, I realize his curls are still wet from his post-game shower.

"So, you were traveling for the game this morning, that's why you weren't in class," I surmise, crossing my left leg over my right as I pull my arms around my chest in a sort of hug. I'm not going to last much longer out here without freezing, so I'm trying to appreciate the moment for as long as I can.

"Yeah, and I was in a meeting with Coach on Monday morning about the combine, so that's why I missed yesterday, too," he says, running his hand through his hair.

"Are you going to be in class tomorrow?" I ask. "We have a lab."

"I wouldn't miss it, Ryan." He smiles, narrowing his eyes at me playfully. "I couldn't possibly leave you alone with the chemicals—too much of a safety hazard."

I roll my eyes, but I bite down on my lip to keep from smiling.

"Why are you outside without a coat on? You look like you're freezing," he asks, brows pulling together.

I do feel like I'm about to turn into a human icicle, but I pretend like I'm not freezing my butt off in the thin material of my gown as I shrug.

"We're about to board now," he sighs as his eyes scan the room he's in, "but I wanted to call before we got on the plane."

I nod, biting down on the inside of my cheek.

Is this our new normal? FaceTime calls after every away game?

I try to hide my smile, but when Micah's voice calling for Tristan echoes through the phone, I know we don't have much time left.

"We're boarding now, T."

"I'm coming, give me a minute." Tristan looks up and nods at him before looking back down at me. I try to mask my disappointment, but by the way his lips pull down, I know he can still see it.

His eyes trail down the screen again, and when they coast back up, he's searching my face. "I have to go," he sighs, leaning his head back against the wall. "I'll see you tomorrow in chem?"

"Yeah." I smile, wishing more than anything that he could stay on for just a little bit longer.

He smiles back, and I hear the sound of a terse older man's voice yelling at him to get his ass on the plane.

"I really have to go now, or Coach is going to kill me." He grins. "But I'm glad I got to see you." His eyes search the screen in front of him, and his dimple deepens as he says, "You really do look beautiful tonight, Abs."

TWENTY-FIVE

TRISTAN

"I would definitely fail this class without you." Abby groans, wrapping her maroon scarf around her neck.

I let the classroom door close behind us as I fall into step beside her, trying not to laugh at the look of utter incredulity on her face. "Who in their right mind would let freshmen handle chemicals like that? That can't be safe."

I try to hold back my smile as I push the building door open and step back so she can walk out first. The early morning air stings my cheeks, and I watch as the breeze whips her hair around her face, sending the vanilla apple spice of her perfume into the air between us. She tucks the strands of loose waves behind her ears and pulls her bag further up her arm as she leads us toward the courtyard.

More eyes are trained on me than usual today, and all of them are locked in on my ankle as I walk by, probably trying to figure out whether or not I'll be out for the Oregon game on Friday. I clench my jaw and try my best to keep from wobbling, but the faint throbbing is starting to hurt again, and I know I won't be able to make it all the way to my class across campus without giving in to a small limp.

I rolled my ankle pretty bad in the game last night. It hurt like a bitch, but once the trainer gave me the thumbs up, my ass was back on the court. We were playing Duke, and I wasn't about to leave my team to play the second best ranked team in the league without me. That, and the fact that Zayn Williams, Duke's star shooting guard and Grade-A asshole, made a show of smirking at me when the trainers were checking out my ankle on the court, as if to say, *Can't keep up, Beck?*

I usually don't let the shit talk get to me, but I've had an unspoken competition with Williams since I was a freshman. He's one of the only players who the analysts predict might be able to knock me out of the top pick for the NBA Draft, and because I'm a proud ass-hole, I couldn't let him win. The fact that I dunked on Williams *twice*, even with my throbbing ankle, was just the cherry on top. That, and the fact that we still managed to win after losing our lead.

My ankle throbs again, and the trainer's advice echoes through my mind—*"Ice and heat, just keep switching and you'll be fine."* I iced it this morning while I was studying for the exam I have tomorrow in my Organic Chemistry class, and now that it's starting to hurt again, I know I should probably get some heat on it.

"I really don't want to go to my next class." Abby frowns, pull-ing my attention away from my ankle as she grabs her planner out of her bag. When she flips it open to today's date, I don't miss the three different streaks of highlighter reminding her of an essay that's due Thursday and that she has work tonight at five. The final thing on her to-do list makes me smile, because only Abby would pencil in a time to call her mother.

"Skip class." I grin as her brows shoot up.

"I can't just skip." She balks.

"Why not?"

My eyes catch on the practice gym on the other side of the court-yard, and when I look back down at Abby, an idea sparks.

"What if I miss something important? How would I take my lec-ture notes?"

"Get them from someone in your class." I shrug, already leading us toward the practice gym. I don't think she's realized we've gone off course from our usual route through the courtyard. Every day I walk her toward the Journalism building before we part ways at the inter-section that brings me right to the Engineering building.

I can tell she's actually contemplating it by the way she's biting down on the inside of her cheek, and when she looks up at me, I give an encouraging nod. "I'm serious, Abs. Skip with me."

Her brows raise and she looks back down at her planner, as if the explosion of multicolored highlighter lines and to-do lists will somehow give her the right answer. When she sighs and flips the book closed, I know I've won.

"Where would we even go?" she asks, sliding her planner back into her bag.

My eyes find the practice building again. "I have an idea, and I promise you're going to like it, you just have to trust me." Her brows lift a little as she slows to a stop. "Do you trust me?" I ask, extending my hand to her.

She considers me for a moment, and a flash of the first time I'd extended my hand to her replays in my mind. She looked mystified, completely and utterly confused in that moment.

Thinking back now, I want to kick myself for not asking her to dance, just to dance. Not because James wanted to get Jenny alone. Not because I was being a good wingman. Not because I was hoping he would do the same for me later when I wanted to get Tori Hansen alone long enough to ask her to go home with me. Looking at the girl standing in front of me now, I can't imagine a world where I don't ask her to step out onto the dance floor with me.

She takes a deep breath, and when her eyes meet mine again, her lips pull back into a soft smile as she nods her head. "Of course, I do."

She places her hand in mine, only this time is so much different than the last, because this time, I don't plan on letting go.

"I don't think I'm allowed to be here."

Her whisper is barely audible above the sound of the weights dropping back into the racks inside the gym. It's true, she's definitely not supposed to be in here since she's not a student athlete, but since it's nine in the morning on a random Wednesday, I doubt anyone is going to bother us where we're going.

A few people are scattered around the weight room, mostly the football crowd, but I spot Micah at one of the squat racks. His headphones are swaying from his ears, and when he looks up from resetting the bar into the rack, he spots me and nods. His eyes scan away and then back quickly when he spots Abby next to me. The bored expression on his face turns into something a lot smugger, and he smirks at me before shaking his head and going back to his workout. Abby seems too distracted by everything else going on in the room to notice the exchange.

"If someone stops us, I can tell them you're on the bowling team or something."

She jabs me lightly with her elbow, but I catch the way her cheek tightens.

Abby follows me past the locker rooms, her eyes trained on the wall of team pictures. She's trying to find the basketball section, and when she finally catches sight of them, I stop so she can rock up onto her tiptoes to find the years she's searching for. The gallery wall has team pictures all the way from 1972, so it takes a moment for her to find the recent ones. To be honest, I've never actually taken the time to look myself.

"You all look so serious," she says with a grin. "Like it's a mug-shot or something."

"We were trying to look intimidating." I laugh. "That was the first year we won the finals, so we were all pretty hyped."

After finding the other pictures, she finally steps back and nods for me to continue, and when I pull open the double doors at the end of the hall, I'm rewarded with the sound of her small gasp.

"I didn't know we had a pool," she says breathlessly, walking ahead of me. The doors click shut behind us, and the sound echoes loudly in the empty room.

"It's heated." I grin.

She looks over her shoulder at me, and I nod as she slips off her shoe and sticks her toe into the water.

"Mmm," she hums. "It feels amazing."

When the sound of my Nike's being kicked off echoes through the empty pool room, she looks back over at me, but it isn't until I pull off my hoodie and shirt that her eyes widen. She hasn't moved, and I know that she's watching my movements as I unbutton my jeans and step out of them, leaving me in my black boxers.

"You're actually going swimming?" She balks, eyes darting toward the door. "What if someone walks in?"

"Swim practice doesn't start until three on Wednesdays." I shrug.

"But someone could still walk in. A coach or janitor or—"

I turn around to face her as I step back toward the edge of the pool, and she trails off as her eyes coast down my body. She bites down on the inside of her cheek, and I watch as they fill with that pretty rosy hue I love so much.

"No one is going to walk in, Abs. We're here, all alone in this big empty room with a heated pool. It would be a shame for it to go to waste," I counter, taking a final step back until my heels hit the edge of the pool. I give her a final smirk before I lean forward and kick off of the pool's edge, flipping back into a tuck mid-air before crashing into the warm water below.

When I resurface, my curls are hanging low on my forehead, and I catch the smile on her lips as she gives one final look toward the door.

I watch from the water as she steps out of her other shoe, and when she strips down, I have to bite back my laugh as she folds her clothes neatly and places them on the bench next to my pile of haphazardly thrown pants and shirt.

She's in a little white bra and panties that hug her ass nicely, and when she bends over to pick up her fallen sock, my dick twitches. I don't have much time to admire the sight before she turns around and raises an amused brow, as if she knows why I have a dumbass grin on my face, and when the amused smirk pulls at her lips, I have a feeling she did it on purpose.

That smirk turns into something much brighter, and with a running start, she cannonballs into the water with a laugh that echoes around the empty room. When she resurfaces, she smiles up at me as she sinks further into the water, and when she disappears entirely below the surface, I watch as she swims the entire length of the pool underwater, coming back up for air in the shallow end.

Our time in the pool was mostly spent filtering through different childhood games, although some of them definitely didn't go as planned. When she demonstrated how to walk on her hands across the length of the shallow end, I thought for sure that it would be easy to recreate, but three-seconds in, I had somehow inhaled enough water to fill my lungs, and I shot back up quickly, coughing as the water poured out of my nose.

When she finally caught her breath from laughing, she swam over to me to make sure I was okay.

"You're not supposed to *drink* the water, babes." She grinned, but when I reached out to pull her to me, she swam away, just out of my reach, with the kind of smile that could lure any man to his death.

I found out quickly that, while Abby Ryan is pretty damn good at everything she does, she has two known weaknesses—chemistry and Marco Polo. Every time I'd get even remotely close to her she'd start laughing, which made finding her easy as hell. I played along, mostly because I liked the sound of her laugh echoing around the room, but every time it ended with me wrapping my arms around her and her refusing to believe that I didn't peek.

Now, I'm facing away from her with my eyes closed, trying to listen for the tiniest noise so I can turn around and catch her before she gets to the other side. This was my favorite pool game to play as a kid, but somehow, it doesn't seem as fun with Abby because she hasn't made a peep since we started. Not a rustle, or a splash, or even a laugh.

A splash finally sounds, and I turn quickly to see that she's still at the starting line, smirking at me.

"Are you going to stay there the entire time?" I tease.

"I've been there and back already, and you didn't notice." She grins, splashing again from her safe place at home base.

I raise a brow at that. "Did you forget to mention that you're part fish?" I laugh, watching as she swims closer to me.

"This is so nice," she murmurs, closing the space between us as her hand floats on top of the water, following the soft ebb and flow. "I used to swim every day at home. Sometimes, I would spend the entire day in our pool during the summers. My dad used to call me his little frog." Her eyes are crinkled in a smile, and when they meet mine, I notice a brightness to them I haven't seen before. "He taught me how to swim when I was three and I've loved water ever since. It's so freeing."

I can stand here in the middle of the pool, so I reach out and grab her waist, pulling her toward me. Her fingers trail up my arms until they finally tighten around my shoulders. She's still kicking a little, but I'm supporting most of her weight now, and she grins at me as she reaches out and traps one of my curls between her fingers. She examines it before running her fingers through the rest of them, and my eyes close briefly as I revel in the feel of her nails raking through my hair. When I open them again, her hands are finding their place back on my shoulders.

"Thank you for bringing me here." Her voice is softer, and her eyes wide and earnest, framed by dark lashes dripping with water droplets. She grins at me as she tilts her head back to dip her hair into the water, and the strands float out around her head like a chestnut crown. "I think I needed this," she admits, staying still in the water.

My gaze travels down her exposed neck, and I watch her chest rise and fall slowly with each breath. When she tilts her head back up again, a few droplets of water race down her face, and I reach up to wipe away the black smudge of makeup under her eye with my thumb. Her eyes find my lips before coasting back up to meet mine again. They're darker than before, and the familiar energy crackles between us as she pulls herself closer to me, pressing her chest against mine.

She brings her hands up to my face, cupping my cheeks as her eyes fix on my lips again, and my pulse picks up as she leans in, slowly bringing her lips closer to mine.

She's going slow on purpose, it's a teasing and maddening pace, but I can't bring myself to look away from her lips as she slowly closes the space between our mouths. She's a breath away, and I can smell the mix of spearmint gum and mocha coffee on her breath when her lips finally graze my own. It's light as air, and if I wasn't hyperaware of her every movement, I might have missed it. But now that I've had a taste, I tighten my hold on her and pull her towards me, needing more than the light brush to satisfy the hunger building inside of me.

She indulges me, opening up for my tongue to sweep inside to taste the chocolate coffee on her tongue. When her fingers thread through my curls along the nape of my neck, I pull her closer, reveling in how fucking good her small, soft body feels pressed against mine. Her legs wrap around my waist, and when my hands find their way up the soft planes of her thighs to her ass, a groan vibrates in the back of my throat when she grinds her hips against me. She does it again, slower, more teasing, with the kind of pressure that sends a jolt of pleasure straight up my spine.

"Abby." It comes out a throaty groan, a warning.

"Tristan," She murmurs back. Her voice is innocent and teasing as her lips pull back into a smile against mine. It's a smug smile, smug enough that I know *she* knows exactly what she's doing.

My grip on her ass tightens, stilling her movements. I can't fuck her. One and done, that's the rule. I can't fuck her. I probably shouldn't be making out with her, either, but I don't really want to think about that. Not right now.

Her tongue brushes against mine, slower than before, less rushed, and her fingers loosen in my curls as they slide down to cup my cheeks softly while she takes her time exploring my mouth.

I match her slower pace, trailing my hands from her ass up to her back, brushing my thumb along the line of her spine until a soft shiver shakes her shoulders in my arms. When a soft, content sigh rumbles in the back of her throat, I grin.

Breaking away from her mouth, I trail my lips across her cheek to the edge of her jaw, just below her ear where I know her sweet spot is. She tilts her head back, exposing her neck to me, and I lick the hot skin before closing my mouth around it and biting. The shiver that runs down her body in the warm water only encourages me, and after sucking harder on the sensitive skin, I delve further down her neck before coming back up to her lips.

Her breathing is much heavier now, and my eyes trail from her swollen lips to the two hardened nipples that are straining against the white cotton bra. Reaching up, she brings my mouth back to hers, letting my tongue brush against hers once more before she pulls back enough to trap my bottom lip between her teeth in a soft bite. I tighten my grip on her, pulling her closer, but before I can connect our lips again, she pulls back.

Her cheeks are rosy and eyes bright as she trails her soft fingers down my temple and cheek, tracing the small indent of my dimple curiously. She considers me for a moment, and I revel in the feel of her in my arms as she leans in and presses a soft, slow kiss to my lips. Her lips hover near mine, and I don't need to open my eyes to know she's smiling.

When she leans back in my arms, her hands leave my face and reach up to the top of my head. She maneuvers her weight quickly, and before I catch onto what she's doing, she has me dunked under the water. When I resurface, she's already got a head start swimming across the pool. Her eyes are bright when she looks over her shoulder at me, and I swear my heart pounds a little harder at the sight.

"Come on, slow poke." She grins, her deep blue eyes a stark contrast to her swollen red lips. "Catch me if you can."

TWENTY-SIX

ABBY

I can feel the fatigue weighing me down as I close my car door behind me.

My hands are on autopilot as I start the engine and crank the heat, but they fall back to my lap as I lean my head against the headrest.

In the nearly four years that I've been working at Over Easy, I have never experienced a more disastrous and stressful shift. It was a shit show, an absolute shit show. Three of our six scheduled waitresses called out sick tonight, but I couldn't even be mad about it since I was the one who answered the phone when Lacie, Nicole, and Maria called. There wasn't a sliver of a doubt that they were really sick, because mid-conversation, Lacie put the phone down to throw up.

I'm a sympathetic puker—a really attractive trait, I know—which means I had to hold my hand over my mouth as the sounds echoed through the receiver. I stayed on the phone long enough to wish her well before hanging up and running into the back where I had to cycle through the three deep breathing exercises I know of to keep from upchucking all over the bar top.

So, it was up to me, Josie, and Kelsie—the newest hire who just finished her final training day last week—to manage the Friday night crowd that always flocks to the diner for the basketball games.

Needless to say, we got wrecked.

I take another minute to catch my breath before clicking my seatbelt into place. I'm turning onto the main road that brings me back to my apartment when the display on the dashboard lights up with my mother's name.

I groan inwardly because I know I can't ignore her call again. It's been four days since I've called her back, and if I try to push it to five, she might actually track me down to kill me.

"Hey, Mom." I try to sound upbeat because the last thing I need is for her to ask how much sleep I'm getting, or whether or not I'm being wise with my time allocation.

"Abigail, why haven't you called me back in four days?"

I take a deep breath and tighten my hold on the steering wheel as I take the left turn toward my apartment complex. The roads are still pretty busy around campus since everyone is leaving the arena now that the game is over.

I try to focus on relaxing my tense muscles as I reply, "I'm sorry, I've been working a little more than usual since some of my coworkers are sick."

"Right, Jeff mentioned that you were extra busy this week. Nana also said you called her yesterday," she says, though it comes out as more of an accusation—*You have time to call your brother and grandmother, but not me?*

Technically, I didn't call Jeff, he called me when I was on my way home from work the other night. It was a little out of character, since most of our communication is reserved for our random back and forth conversations on Snapchat.

"It was on my way to work; I only had ten minutes," I defend, but I know I've already lost the battle, because to her, calling Jeff and Nana, and not her, is like a slap to the face.

"Right. Well, catch me up now, then. Nana mentioned an article you're writing. She said it was for a scholarship?"

I let the question hang between us for a moment. What she's really saying is *Why didn't I know about it? What kind of article is it?* And *how much is the scholarship worth?*

There's a reason I haven't mentioned the article to her, well, multiple reasons, actually, most of which are listed above, but mostly, it's because I don't want to hear the judgment in her voice when I tell her it's for USASN. If my mother knew I was spending my time writing a sports article, she might actually blow a fuse.

You're not seriously wasting your education to become a sports journalist are you, Abigail? I can hear the lecture now, *The joke of the journalism field, you wouldn't really stoop that low.*

"Abigail? Hello?"

"I'm here," I say, trying to think of the most vague way to tell her about the article without setting her off. When I turn into my apartment complex, I pull around the bend, parking in my usual spot up front. Parking isn't too crowded tonight, since most of the student population is still making their way home from the game—or more likely, to a bar to celebrate our win.

"I'd like to hear all about the article. You can tell me about it over dinner when I'm in Pullman."

I nearly choke on my own spit when her words register.

"You're coming *here?*" I know I sound like I'm being strangled, so I clear my throat and try to pull back the last bit of fleeting composure I can muster.

"Yes. If you would have called me back, I would have been able to tell you that. I'm coming to Pullman in three weeks."

"You're coming here. To Pullman." I repeat slowly, to make sure there's no mistake.

Victoria Weisman-Ryan has never stepped foot in Pullman, Washington. Not to drop me off or help me move into my dorm freshman year. Not to visit for my birthday. Not even to be with me when I had appendicitis my sophomore year and Jenny and Nia had to drive me to the ER in the middle of the night where I was taken into surgery.

"Yes, I'll be there on the twenty-fourth—well, I'll be near there. I'll be in Spokane." The sound of her slippers against the hardwood of the house echoes through the phone. "I have a business meeting there the following day, so we'll have to just do dinner."

I glance around, trying to picture my mother here in Washington, but it just seems . . . wrong.

"I'll need you to come to me, of course," she continues. "Since Spokane is an hour-and-a-half away, you'll need to drive up. We can have dinner at my hotel."

I nod, and when I realize that she can't see me, I say, "Okay."

The clicking of her slippers subsides. "I'll see you in three weeks."

"Three weeks." I nod.

A migraine starts to pound in my head, and I know I need to down ibuprofen in the next five minutes or I'm going to suffer all night. The bright headlights of someone pulling into the spot next to me sends a jolt of pain through my skull, and I keep my eyes down to shield them from the light.

"I have to go, Mom," I say, turning off my car. I linger in the warmth for a little bit longer, knowing just how ice-cold the unusually strong winds are tonight.

"Alright, call me tomorrow," she sighs, the annoyance clear in her voice. "And Abigail?"

I grab for my purse on the passenger seat and rummage for the travel-size ibuprofen bottle. I pull it out quickly, thanking my past-self for forgetting to bring my water bottle in with me yesterday. "Yes?"

"Answer when I call you."

She doesn't bother to say goodbye before the click of the disconnection echoes through my phone. When I pull it away from my face and look to the screen, it's back to the picture of Jenny, Nia, and I smiling that I have saved as my lock screen. Their faces beam back at me until the screen goes black, and I drop the phone onto the passenger seat as I down the two headache pills, praying it will miraculously cure my rising stress level. Tossing the closed bottle back into my purse, I lay my head back against the headrest, closing my eyes as I replay the conversation in my mind.

My mother is going to be here in three weeks.

My safe haven is about to be breached by the one person it was meant to keep out, the one person I chose to move across the country to get away from.

I'm now cycling through the same deep breathing exercises from before, because now I'm starting to feel nauseated again, and I know it has nothing to do with the stomach-bug going around.

When the three soft knocks on my window echo in my car, my eyes shoot open. It's dark in the parking lot of my apartment, and it takes a second for my eyes to adjust to the lighting before I recognize the familiar curls, emerald eyes, and soft dimple of the man currently bending down near my driver side window.

My heart hammers in my chest when I open the door, and he takes a step back to lean against his truck. "Are you planning on sleeping in your car tonight, Ryan?"

I climb out but lean back in to grab my purse and the two textbooks I left in here from class yesterday. When I stand back up and hip check my door closed, he's grinning. I have a feeling it has more to do with the fact that he just saw me bent over in tight leggings rather than his lame joke.

"What are you doing here?" I don't mean to sound short, but when I look over at him, he doesn't seem offended.

He reaches out and takes the two books from my arms, and I don't protest, because honestly, I don't know if I would have made it up the steps to the second floor with them weighing me down. I'm running on fumes here, and the phone call with my mom was the cherry on top of my shitty day.

"I'm supposed to be picking you up to meet everyone at O'Malley's." He falls into step beside me, matching my slow pace, which must be like walking in slow motion for him and his long legs. He seems amused as I practically zombie march toward the apartment building. "But I have a feeling we're going to be staying in tonight."

I glance over at him. His smile has melted into something much more bemused as he watches me struggle to climb the stairs, and by the time we get to the top, his hand is on the small of my back, giving me the slightest push to help me up the final three.

I am done with today.

Physically, I don't think I've worked this hard since I tried out for the soccer team freshman year of high school. The try out consisted of running two miles, full field sprints, and agility drills. Needless to say, I didn't even make it to the sprints, and if it wasn't for the fact that we were running on a trail in the middle of the Florida wilderness, I wouldn't have finished the two-mile run, either.

"You okay, Abs?" His voice is soft as he reaches out for the keys I'm fumbling with. I let them slide through my fingers, and he hesitates as his eyes scan the different apartment doors around us. I realize he's waiting for me to point out which apartment I live in, and that's when it hits me that he's never actually been over before. For all of the time we've spent together, it's never once been at my apartment.

"Yeah, just tired from work." I motion toward the first one on the left with the pink floral wreath and the *come in and cozy up* doormat. He slides the key into the lock and stands back as he pushes the door open, waiting for me to lead the way. I've been at work all day, so my eyes scan the apartment, praying that Nia and Jenny didn't leave the place a mess before heading out for the game. Aside from the basket of laundry sitting on the kitchen table, and the mess of papers and textbooks littering the coffee table, it's relatively clean.

I flick on the lights, and when I turn around, Tristan is standing by the door with my textbooks still tucked under his arm. His eyes scan the apartment, and I follow his gaze, taking in the open concept living space. It's a lot smaller than his house, but it's cozy. There are scented candles on almost every open surface, a million decorative pillows on the light gray, L-shaped couch in the living room, and at least ten different vases of decorative flowers placed strategically around the room to give it a homey feel.

"Where do you want these?" he asks, holding up the books.

"Oh, right. In here." I motion for him to follow me through the living room toward the hall, and when I push open my bedroom door and flick on the lamp, I turn to watch him examine my room. He walks past me and places the books on my desk, and his fingers skim over the wooden surface, reaching for the picture I have framed there.

It's a family picture from when I was a kid—my seventh birthday. Jeff and Mark are smiling at the camera while my mom stands behind them, a hand on either of their shoulders. My dad is standing beside her, hugging me securely to his chest while I'm hanging upside down. My arms are dangling above my head and I'm frozen, rosy cheeked and mid-laugh, while he beams at the camera. It's the kind of smile he always had on his face whenever he would drop down onto the floor next to me and color, or play tea-party, or have our cannonball competitions. The same one I would pay any amount of money to see again, even just for a second.

Placing the frame back onto my desk, he turns around. His lips pull down a in a thoughtful frown, but when his eyes meet mine, he perks them up into a soft smile as he takes a deep breath.

"Have you eaten?"

I shake my head.

"Alright, you go take a shower, I'll make dinner, and we'll stay in and watch a movie or something," he says, already moving to the door. "I'll call James and let him know we're not coming out to the bar."

He doesn't give me time to process his words before he's out of my room, and when I finally register what's happening, I stick my head out of the room to catch him before he hits the living room.

"I'm vegetarian," I call after him.

He doesn't stop as he rounds the corner, and his soft chuckle echoes through the empty apartment as the opening and closing of the kitchen cabinets starts to sound.

"I know, Ryan," he calls, and I don't have to see him to know that he's smiling. "Now get your ass into the shower."

———

The hot water worked wonders on my muscles.

I took extra time to massage the body wash into my sore muscles, deep conditioned my hair twice, and while I waited for the hair mask to work its magic, I made sure to shave all pertinent areas . . . you know, just in case.

By the time I'm dressed in my favorite pair of black and white polka dot sleep shorts, Tristan's black *Warriors Basketball* hoodie, and a pair of purple fuzzy socks, the mouthwatering aroma of mac and cheese wafts through the apartment—my absolute weakness.

I pad out to the kitchen, but because my socks are so fuzzy, they silence my footsteps and I'm able to watch Tristan work over the stove without him knowing he has an audience. He has a few pans on the burners, and I realize that the smell of the mac and cheese isn't the only aroma wafting from the kitchen. Leaning against the entryway, I enjoy the sight of him stirring the contents of the pots while his head bobs absently to the music playing softly from the radio Nia always keeps in the kitchen.

It's an older song, one I don't recognize, but I make a note to look it up later and add it to the new playlist I made a few nights ago titled *Tristan.*

When he turns around to grab for the kitchen towel by the sink, he spots me and grins as his eyes take in my pajamas.

"Nice hoodie." His dimple pops in his cheek, and I tuck my wet hair behind my ear as I look down at it.

"Full disclosure, you're probably never going to get it back," I admit, burying my hands into the front pocket.

"That's fine." He grins. "It looks better on you anyway."

His gaze coasts down to my pajama shorts and fluffy socks. My heart starts to beat a little faster when he lingers on the short hem before looking back up to my face. He blinks a few times, and then looks down to the kitchen towel in front of him.

"Dinner's ready." He clears his throat, turning away from me as he opens the cabinet to grab two plates. I bite back a smile at the fact that he's explored the kitchen enough to know where everything is. "You should go pick something for us to watch," he calls over his shoulder, but keeps his eyes on the stove as he starts to load the plates up. He's blocking my view, so I can't tell what else he's made, but whatever it is, it smells delicious.

I scroll through Netflix until I land on one of the shows I've been meaning to start. Nia and Jenny both binge watched it without me when it first came out, and it's been sitting in my to-watch list ever since.

"Okay, be careful it's hot." Tristan hands me the steaming plate and sets his own down on the coffee table as he pulls two water bottles from under his arm. When he drops down onto the couch beside me, I lift up the knit blanket, inviting him to scoot closer. Once we're tucked in, I finally look down to the plate in my hands. Huge mountains of mac and cheese and mashed potatoes are piled onto the plate next to a steaming black bean veggie burger.

"Are you trying to feed an entire village?" I laugh, picking up my fork.

"Didn't know what vegetarians eat." He shrugs, scooping up a forkful of mashed potatoes. "So, I made you a bit of everything."

I look back down at the plate and smile at the thought of him standing in front of the pantry, trying to figure out what to cook.

"So, what are we watching tonight, Ryan? Please, for the love of God, do not make me watch *Love Island*," he pleads between bites of mac and cheese.

I elbow him lightly as I click onto the show. The first scene of *Stranger Things* begins to play, and I pull my legs up to settle deeper into the couch as I take my first bite of food. He's so close that my entire right side leans against him and if I tilted my head the slightest bit, it would be resting against his shoulder.

"I've heard good things about this. Micah wouldn't shut up about it when it came out," he says as we watch someone in a lab get chased down a hallway.

By the time the first episode ends, we're both done with dinner, and he reaches over to grab my plate and set it down on the coffee table before pressing play on the second episode. Only this time, he raises his arm when he leans back into the couch, and I don't hesitate for a second to nuzzle into his side as his arms come down around me.

Halfway through the second episode, my eyes start to flutter shut as his thumb traces slow, rhythmic circles on my bare thigh, and while the soft motion eases any remaining stress from the day, I drift off in his arms for the second time this month.

TWENTY-SEVEN

ABBY

The mid-February air has an unrelenting bite to it as the tail end of a winter storm passes over Pullman. I've managed to stay wrapped up inside for the past couple of days to ride it out, but even with the distraction of writing the scholarship article, I haven't been able to get my mind off the fact that Tristan has been across the country for the past four days.

When he called me Saturday and told me that the head coach of the Houston Rockets had invited him to meet the team and tour the facilities, I squealed so loudly I probably injured his hearing a little. But now that he's been gone for four days, I can't deny that I miss seeing him every day in class.

I feel his absence every day in the smallest ways. The most obvious hits me every morning when I look over to the empty stool next to me in chemistry. But it also comes in waves, like when I'm able to focus for too long on the lecture and realize that I should have been poked, or whispered silly jokes, or passed a note with a cheesy drawing of an atom a few times by now.

I can tell that James misses him, too, because last night when I walked out to the living room to see him lounging on the couch scrolling through his phone, his eyes lit up when he saw me. Although, I have a feeling it was because he could hear Tristan's voice coming from my phone as we FaceTimed.

The look nearly broke my heart, so I handed off my phone to James while I got a drink. I watched the guys delve into detail about Tristan's trip as I poured my glass of water, and it struck me that Tristan was filling him in on details he'd told me days ago.

The thought that I was becoming Tristan's go-to for all of his exciting news sent a thrill through me, and we ended up staying on the phone until I fell asleep again, like we have every night since he's been away. Our nightly FaceTimes turned into good morning texts, which turned into all-day conversations, only pausing for my classes, shifts at the diner, or meetings he was scheduled to take with the coaching staff in Houston.

I feel like a teenager again, constantly hooked to my phone, anxiously waiting for the next text or call. So when I check my phone after I park in the Over Easy parking lot, I sigh inwardly as the blank screen flashes back at me. The last text from him was twenty minutes ago when he said he was about to get a tour of the arena from the head trainer. I type out another message, letting him know that my shift is starting and that I'll FaceTime him after work, and then I push open my car door and step out into the frosty air.

I pull my coat tighter around my chest and keep my head down, but the wind whips my hair around my face, and the instant sting against my cheeks and nose sends a trail of goosebumps down my spine. The sun is setting against a cotton candy sky, and the fleeting sunlight washes the diner in a warm hue as I hurry through the doors, sending the sound of the bell hanging from the entrance ringing through the diner.

I immediately spot my two favorite co-workers huddled by the register, and by the smirk on Lacie's face, I can tell she's been waiting all day for me to get here just so she can grill me about my date with Dean. Since she's been sick the past few days, we haven't actually worked together since she saw me on my date. Based on the mirroring smirk on Josie's face, I have a feeling Lace must have already filled her in on the details.

I brace for the onslaught of questions as I round the bar top, but the inquisition doesn't hit immediately. Instead, Josie extends a small bag to me with an excited smile. "Happy Valentine's Day, Abby. Or, as I like to call it—Galentine's Day."

My jaw drops a little as I take the small gift bag from her, and after I drop my purse, coat, and scarf under the bar top next to theirs, I turn back to the girl smiling expectantly at myself and Lacie.

"You got me a Valentine's Day gift, Jo?"

"I made them in the art class I taught last night at the community center. They're supposed to be for a significant other, but since I don't have a boyfriend, I made them for you and Lace." She smiles at Lacie before looking back to me, waiting for us to open the bags.

I tug softly on the tissue paper and pull out the picture sized canvas. My eyes widen as I take in the painting in front of me. The canvas is filled with the most intricate watercolor flowers, melding together in strokes of pastel pinks, and greens, and purples. The soft brush strokes blend together, creating a lifelike bouquet in the most beautiful painting I've ever seen in real life. The bit of yellow at the very bottom catches my attention, and I smile when I realize that it's Josie's initials painted in her artistic signature—*JG*.

Josie's a freshman art student here at USW, and while she's a few years younger than me, she's easily the most talented person I've ever met. I'm still in awe of her talent every time I'm able to sneak a peek at her sketch book or when she shows me a snapshot of whatever painting she's working on in the art studio on campus.

I instantly picture how amazing this will look framed on my fireplace mantel, and when I look back at Josie, she has her bottom lip pulled between her teeth, waiting for our reactions.

"This is beautiful, Jo. Thank you so much." I hold the picture carefully out of harm's way as I pull her into a hug, and when I release her, I can't help but stare at the painting again. I admire the effortless look of the perfect strokes as I carefully put it back into the bag and place it near my purse.

"Well, now I feel like a bitch for not bringing Galentine's Day presents for you guys." Lacie laughs, pulling Josie into a hug.

"Honestly, I should have at least written you a poem or something." I grin.

The familiar ding of the bell from the kitchen sounds, and Lacie turns on her heel and heads toward the food pick up station in the kitchen. When she rounds the corner again, she has a triple dipper dessert in her hands with three spoons poking out of the ice cream.

"This can be my present." She grins, placing the dessert onto the bar top between us. "Dig in, ladies."

I glance around the nearly empty diner to make sure we're not neglecting any customers. While Over Easy is the place to be on Sundays for our brunch special, or even Fridays when O'Malley's is overcrowded, it's not exactly the number one pick for a romantic Valentine's dinner. Aside from two older couples and a blonde girl who's absently shoveling fries into her mouth as she reads from the anatomy textbook in front of her, the diner is pretty much dead.

"Great idea, Lace." Josie grins, picking up her own spoon. "What better way to forget that I'm single on Valentine's Day than to fall into a sugar coma?"

I follow their lead, scooping a bite of ice cream, brownie, and hot fudge onto my own spoon.

"Hey, I'd rather be single than still be with RJ," Lacie mumbles with a full mouth.

"Come on, Lace, RJ wasn't that bad," I defend, thinking back to the nerdy IT major who was hopelessly in love with her for like a year before she even gave him the time of day.

"He was fine." She shrugs. "And if it wasn't for the fact that he had a severe foot fetish, we might still be together."

Josie nearly chokes, and I rub her back as she coughs. When she finally catches her breath again, she starts laughing. "You're not serious. Please tell me you're not serious." She gapes.

"I'm very serious." Lacie laughs humorlessly as she stabs the brownie. "He couldn't even get hard without rubbing my feet," she whispers, and when Josie and I look at each other wide-eyed, we both lose it.

"Just stay a virgin, Jo. It's not worth possibly falling in love with a foot lover." Lacie sighs, turning around suddenly and disappearing around the corner to the kitchen.

I glance over at Josie to see her cheeks turning a dark shade of red, and she coughs a few more times as her eyes dart around the diner, probably to make sure no one heard Lacie's virgin comment. I don't think Josie meant to tell us about her v-card. It kind of slipped out one night when I had them over to the apartment for a girl's night a few months ago. Nia and Jenny were out at one of their sorority charity events, and I was hosting the first ever Over Easy girls night in.

Josie ended up getting wasted on Amaretto sours—literally sloshed—and after Lacie prodded enough times, she spilled the beans.

When her eyes meet mine, she shakes her head, more amused now that she's confirmed no one's heard Lacie's comment. "Does she have no concept of an inside voice?"

I grin, because no, she doesn't.

Lacie rounds the corner again, and when I catch sight of the fudge bottle in her hand, I can't help the laugh that bubbles out of me. She pours the chocolate gold until there's a pool of it coating the ice cream.

"So, Abs." She points her spoon at me and narrows her eyes. "Spill it."

"Spill what?" I play dumb and dunk my spoon into the fudge.

"The details about your date."

"Date? With who?" I smile innocently.

"Who do you think? Dean." She rolls her eyes, leaning onto the counter as she digs her spoon into the fudge again.

The diner door opens, and my eyes widen when the familiar wisp of blond hair and bright ocean eyes connect with mine. His lips instantly tilt into an easy smile, and it takes me a second to realize he's holding a picnic basket in his arms.

Dean and I have been texting back and forth casually every day since our date, and when he asked if I was available tonight, I felt terrible telling him I had to work.

"Oh, my God." Lacie gapes.

"What?" Josie whispers as her eyes dart between Lacie and I.

I put my spoon down and round the bar top as Lacie whispers. "That's Dean."

His easy smile widens when I reach him. "I know you said you have to work tonight, but I figured the diner might be a little slow since it's not the most romantic place near campus." His eyes scan the dead diner with a satisfied smile. "So, I figured if you can't leave the diner for a date, I'd bring the date to the diner." He holds up the picnic basket.

I'm speechless as I take in the boy in front of me.

His eyes widen a little as he searches my face. "I hope this is okay, if it's too much I can go—"

"No." I shake my head quickly. "This is—" I look down and spot the bouquet of roses peeking out of the basket. "This is amazing, Dean," I say breathlessly.

My heart stumbles over itself in a painful way when he reaches down and hands me the flowers. They smell amazing, and I look up at him with a stupid grin on my face when I realize this is the first time I've ever been given flowers from a guy—aside from my dad, of course.

"Do you think you could take a little break from work, maybe like thirty minutes? I know I shouldn't keep you from your shift for long, but I have some goodies in here." He nods to the basket.

I only have a fifteen-minute break, but I don't even have time to think because Lacie is already leaning over the bar top with the biggest grin I've ever seen.

"That's fine, take all the time you need, lovebirds."

Dean grins and waves at her, and I can't tell if he recognizes her from the other night, or if he just assumes my coworkers are always this nice.

I follow him as he leads us to a booth near the back, and when he unloads the food, wine, and dessert from the basket, I have to bite down on my lip to keep from smiling like an idiot. No one has ever done anything like this for me. The most Tyler ever did was send me a fruit basket for Valentine's Day our first year of dating, but to be fair, he was also an entire country away.

When I settle down into the booth, I scan the table. Chocolate covered strawberries, take out from Vinny's—the Italian restaurant down the street—a bottle of white wine, and my absolute weakness—a whole basket of garlic bread.

"I ordered you baked ziti—no meat." He grins, pushing the container towards me.

I can feel Lacie and Josie's eyes on me as we eat, but every time I glance over, they both duck under the bar top, as if hiding is somehow less incriminating than just turning away.

"I know you've been super busy lately, so I'm glad I was able to see you today," Dean says between sips of the sweet wine he's poured for both of us.

"Me, too." I smile.

"I know we haven't known each other for long, but I feel like we just kind of click, like we understand each other, you know? Maybe it's the shared trauma of growing up with lawyer parents." He grins at me, and I laugh. "Or maybe it's the fact that since we both can't dance, we end up swaying off-beat like rhythmically challenged idiots, or that I'm pretty sure my friends like you more than me already—but whatever it is, I think there's something real here." He considers me for a moment, his eyes searching mine. "And I really hope you feel the same, because I'd like to keep exploring whatever this is between us."

My mouth is drying up because I know he expects me to respond, but honestly, I don't know what to say.

"And I don't want to come off too strong. I know this is still early on, but I haven't felt this way about a girl since—well, for a long time. And I'm not going to ask you to be my girlfriend, or to be exclusive, or anything yet." His lips tilt up into a smile. "But I really do see this going somewhere, and I just want you to know what my intentions are. Are you okay with that?"

I have the sudden urge to cry and squeal at the same time, because Dean is telling me everything I've wanted to hear for the past two months, only it's not coming from the person I want to hear it from, and that realization is like a slap to the face.

I take a long sip of my wine, and when I meet his eyes, I will myself to push aside the voice inside my head screaming at me *He's not who you want! He's not Tristan!* Because while the past few weeks of late-night make outs, steamy pool dates, and falling asleep in his arms have been the best two weeks of my life, I can't forget that it's been under the unspoken agreement that none of it really means anything.

I knew what he was thinking the night of his birthday when we danced in the kitchen, and he looked down at me like he wanted to kiss me. *Nothing has changed. This can't be more than a hookup.* I read the look loud and clear, and I've been okay with it, because it came along with the moments that were too good to pass up. But now that Dean is sitting in front of me, telling me all of the things I've wanted to hear, I can't deny that the second thoughts are starting to creep back in.

My time with Tristan is finite. I can practically see it slipping through my fingers, no matter how hard I try to stop it. But when I look up at Dean, somehow, deep down, I know he would stay. He would stay with me for as long as I allowed him to. And that could mean until graduation, or for the years to come while we built a life together with a perfect white picket fence, 2.5 kids, and the kind of stability I've always craved.

He's everything my mother always wanted for me, and while that thought alone makes me want to push him away, I can't help but wonder if maybe she's right. His final words echo through my mind again as I take a sip of my wine—*I just want you to know what my intentions are, are you okay with that?*

"Yes." It comes out as a sort of whisper, but his smile is blinding, and it warms me as he leans back in the booth with the clear rush of relief spreading across his face.

The ring of the bell catches my attention and I watch as a crowd of drunk guys stumble into the diner. There has to be at least twenty of them, and when I look back to Dean, he's already starting to pack up the leftover food.

"I should probably let you get back to work. I don't want to get you in trouble."

I nod, wiping my mouth with a napkin as I help him load up the basket. I catch sight of Josie seating the group at the high-top on the other side of the diner, and she pulls out her order pad to grab their drink orders. When one of them reaches out to grab her butt, she takes a step back out of his reach and looks up at me with that *save me from these pervs* look that we've all perfected for whenever the drunk douchebags come in. We can usually handle it ourselves, but in case they don't settle down, we have Mickey, one of our burly cooks in the back, throw them out.

Dean seems to sense the need for me to get back, because he stands and pulls the basket back onto his arm. Josie is back behind the bar now, starting to pour their drinks, so I don't feel too bad when I offer to walk him out. I send her a look over my shoulder before I walk out into the freezing air that's meant to say, *I'll be right back, I swear*, which she just grins at.

Dean's red Jaguar is parked next to my car, and the brake lights flash as he clicks the unlock button on his key fob. He drops the basket onto the passenger seat before turning back to me, and the gust of wind pulls at his blond hair. The diner's strobing neon sign casts a blue light onto his face, making his eyes flash an impossibly vibrant sapphire as he takes a step toward me.

"Thank you for tonight," I say, wrapping my arms around my chest, trying to preserve the last bit of heat that I possibly can in this weather.

"Of course," he says, taking another step.

There's not much space between us now, and I tilt my head back slightly, watching the way his breath comes out in tiny puffs of warm air. He's not much taller than me, so the motion only brings our lips closer, which makes his eyes widen slightly. I watch as they slide down to my lips, and I know he's leaving this moment up to me—I could kiss him, or I could say goodnight. There's no pressure, no expectations, and that's why I take the final step forward, closing the space between us.

Our lips connect in a clumsy kiss, and he reaches up, cupping my cheeks in his palms as he steadies us. It's slow and intentional, as if he's thought about this moment for a while. Our lips move together with an even pressure, not too soft, not too hard, but he doesn't slide his tongue across my lips, and I appreciate how slow he's taking this. His lips brush against mine one final time before he pulls away, and when my eyes flutter open, he's smiling down at me.

"Happy Valentine's Day, Abby."

TWENTY-EIGHT

ABBY

The entire arena is standing now, watching anxiously as the timer slowly ticks down, each second bringing us closer to our first possible loss of the season. Jenny clenches my hand in hers so tightly that it's starting to lose feeling. It's a comical difference to Nia, who's more interested in scrolling through her Instagram feed than watching the game. Although, she does glance up occasionally in detached amusement whenever Jenny and I start screaming our heads off at particularly exciting plays.

"Get your head out of your ass and get back on defense, McConnell!" Their coach's bald head has been turning a concerning shade of red since the second half started, and now that we're down by two, I'm starting to worry that the old man is going to give himself a heart attack.

I would hardly say Luke has been slacking out there, but I have a feeling their coach just needs someone to let out his anger on, and turning around every few minutes to yell at Micah while he holds a bloody rag to his nose, doesn't seem to be cutting it for him.

We were up by twelve points in the first half, but by the beginning of the second, the energy on the court had changed drastically. I could tell that the USC players were starting to get pissed off by our defense shutting down every single one of their plays. They hadn't scored in almost three minutes, which in basketball, is an eternity. Micah's defense was on a whole new level tonight, and since he was on Tucker Buchanan all night, USC's top scorer, the team was essentially shut out.

I saw it happen. It was slow at first, the comments in his ear while he defended them, the cheap shot elbows in his ribs when the refs weren't looking, all leading up to the sharp elbow to the face on the way down from a dunk. It was the most poorly executed cheap-shot I've ever seen. It was blatant, to everyone but the refs, apparently, and that's when Micah blew his fuse.

He not only lunged at the guy who caused his nose to pour blood down his face and onto his jersey, but he cursed out the ref who pretended like it wasn't on purpose, which ultimately got him ejected from the game. Tristan had to literally pull him away from the ref, wrapping his arms around his friend and dragging him toward the sidelines.

Sitting in the second row, just behind the home team, I caught his eye as he passed Micah off to their coach. I could tell instantly by the stone set of his jaw that he was just as pissed off as his bloodied teammate, only he knew better than to lose his temper on the court.

Now, we're down by two with thirty-seconds left on the clock, and worst of all, it's not our ball. It's not impossible—nothing is impossible in basketball, as my dad always used to say—but it's also not ideal. Especially since our best defender is now benched for the rest of the game with a possible concussion.

Luke is now defending Tucker Buchanan, who looks a little smug as he dribbles the ball lazily, as if to taunt him to come and get it. Trying to steal the ball at this point is incredibly risky, but when I glance up at the time ticking away, I don't see any other option other than to force him to shoot or pass the ball. Luke's eyes are trained on Tucker, and I can practically see the gears in his head working, trying to figure out the best plan of action as he pressures him farther away from the basket.

Their coach screams at him again, something about getting his head out of his ass, but he ignores him as his eyes flick down to the ball in Tucker's hand. Luke lunges, and although Tucker takes a step back, Luke is too quick and his hands close around the ball as he pushes past Tucker. The arena erupts, and I throw my hands up with the other twenty-thousand fans now screaming our lungs out as Luke single-handedly reignites our hope at the last second.

Tristan, James, and Emery are all sprinting down the court to catch up, but Buchanan is already on Luke with his arms pulled up above his head, blocking any chance of a clean shot. Luke looks up at the shot clock, and when it drops below six seconds, I feel like my heart might actually pound right out of my chest. We are so close, so freaking close to keeping our undefeated title. We just have to make one more three-point shot.

Buchanan is boxing him out, but Luke steps back and brings the ball up, ready to shoot.

"What is he doing? That's going to get blocked!" Jenny screams in horror, bringing her hands up to her mouth.

The collective screams and gasps echoing around the arena seem to mirror her, and I bring my own hands up to my mouth as I watch Luke. There's no way he can make this shot. It's not possible. Tucker Buchanan is a wall of a man, and with his huge arms extended, I don't think anyone would be able to make a shot like that. But it looks like he's going to try anyway.

Luke pulls his arm back and releases the ball, only it doesn't shoot forward toward the basket like we're all anticipating, because he fakes the shot and passes the ball to his left, all while keeping his eyes on the basket for the perfect fake-out.

The ball soars to his left, straight to James who pulls the double-team instantly, leaving Tristan wide open up to catch James's pass. He takes a few steps back, planting his feet well beyond the three-point line, before bringing his arm back and releasing the ball. It rolls off his fingers a half second before the clock hits zero, and the timer blares impossibly loud as the entire crowd watches the ball with bated breath.

The ball soars straight toward the basket, and the desperate hands of the USC defenders all try to knock it off course, but it's just out of reach as it starts its descent. Every single person in the arena is frozen in place as we watch the ball soar toward the basket, and when it finds the net perfectly, the eruption is near deafening.

I turn to Jenny and we both scream as we wrap our arms around each other, jumping up and down in celebration before pulling back to watch the team rush the court. I throw my hands into the air and tilt my head back, watching the confetti rain down on the lower bowl of the arena from the rafters. I'm suddenly surrounded by a sea of crimson and white raining down around me. I flatten out my hands to catch a few fluttering pieces in my palms while the ever-growing cheers and screams of the students around me send a charge of excitement through my body.

When I look away from the explosion of confetti and search the mass of bodies celebrating on the court, my eyes instantly lock with his, like two magnets falling into place. His flushed face breaks into a blinding smile when our eyes connect, and somehow, in a sea of twenty-thousand erupting fans sending enough energy through the arena to feel like static electricity on my skin, it's his smile that spikes the adrenaline in my veins.

———

"The locker room is connected to this back lobby. It's where their families can wait to meet up with them after games," Jenny explains as we round the back corner of the arena. A light flurry has started to fall, and my boots crunch against the snow as I wrap my scarf a little tighter around myself to preserve the last bit of body heat. "Julie gave me her access card since she doesn't usually stick around after the games."

I can tell by the smile on her face that she's trying to seem casual about the fact that James brought her home this past weekend to meet his parents, but it doesn't stop me from teasing her about it because we all know that it's a huge step for them.

The way James looks at her says it all—he's in love. And even though Jenny swears that they haven't said it yet, I know she feels the same. No one would voluntarily listen to James's ten-minute speech on *The Top Five High-Level Optimizations That Can Drive Better Marketing Performance* twenty times in a row to give him constructive criticism before his presentation unless they were in love. I sat through two sittings and nearly fell asleep before making a break for it to study—which was really just an excuse to finish watching *The Office* in my room.

"Julie gave you the pass, huh?" I grin, elbowing her lightly as she scans the key card. She smirks at me as the small light on the scanner turns green and beeps softly. When she pushes open the door and leads us into the small lobby, the rush of warmth surrounds me instantly.

It looks exactly like the lobby in the main entrance of the arena, only much smaller. There are plenty of armchairs and benches lining the walls, flanked by large potted plants that add a much-needed pop of color to the modern whites and grays of the tile floors and walls. A few families wait in the middle of the lobby, but the majority of the people loitering around the far wall of the room are definitely not family. There's a group of at least fifteen girls huddled together, and it only takes a few seconds for me to figure out that the gang of girls who look like they've just come from a night out at the bar in their miniskirts and crop tops are the infamous jersey chasers I've heard so much about. I understand the nickname now; it's pretty clear what these girls are here for, but the name still feels too slut-shamey for me.

I can't deny the instant surge of jealousy that sears through me as my eyes scan over their crowd, though. They're all gorgeous. The kind of gorgeous that makes me feel a little out of place as I scan their group.

The thoughts flash in my mind before I can stop them—how many of them have caught Tristan's eye before? How many of them have gone home with him after games like this? The thoughts make my stomach knot and I have to turn around to keep from falling down that rabbit hole because I don't want to know who he's been with, even if it was before he knew me.

The sound of a door swinging open echoes through the lobby and when my eyes scan down the hallway toward the locker room, I watch as the team pours out. I spot Luke first, leading the pack of freshly showered guys toward the lobby, but he doesn't notice us because his eyes are already locked in on the girls standing behind us as a lazy grin slips over his lips.

When they start to disperse around the lobby toward their families, I catch sight of Tristan nodding as his coach says something to him. His curls are still damp, and he runs a hand through them as his eyes scan the lobby, searching the faces in the crowd until they land on me.

It happens instantaneously—his shoulders relax and the small tension line between his brows disappears as his smile deepens, lighting up his perfectly tanned face.

My body is practically begging to run to him, to wrap my arms around his neck and connect our lips—and if we weren't in front of an audience of strangers, his entire team, and his coach—I might have. But I don't actually know what the rules are for whatever this is, so I just smile back and watch as he turns his attention back to his coach. Once the old man pats him soundly on the back a few times, he turns around and starts back toward the locker room, his clipboard tucked snuggly under his arm.

Tristan's gaze finds me again as he crosses the lobby, cutting through the crowd straight toward me. He has his athletic bag hanging from one shoulder, which he drops to the floor when he reaches me.

"Hey, Ryan." He grins, opening his arms. I don't hesitate to wrap my arms around his neck, and when he envelopes his arms around me tightly, my feet lift off of the ground as he pulls me up with him. He only lets my feet dangle for a few seconds before leaning back over and placing me back onto the ground, but even when my feet find the floor again, he doesn't release his hold on me. Instead, he turns his head and rests his cheek against the top of my head, effectively melting me on the spot.

When he finally loosens his grip on me, I pull back enough to look up to him. His eyes are bright, and his dimple is indented deeply as he reaches up to tuck my fallen hair back behind my ear. My gaze dips down to his mouth and I'm dying to rock up onto my tiptoes and connect our lips, but Jenny's voice begrudgingly pulls my attention away from the thought.

"Let's all go to O'Malley's for drinks." She grins, securely wrapped in James's arms.

"Hell yeah," Luke calls, already halfway toward the door. "First round's on me." The offer has the group of girls following him out of the door.

I can feel Tristan's hand on the small of my back as we follow the group out of the lobby doors. I have a feeling it's because the icy sidewalk below is a death trap for people like me who are working with less than stellar coordination, and he's already preparing to try to save me from busting my butt on my way out. With my eyes focused on searching for ice patches on the concrete below, I don't even see it coming when the explosion of snow rains down on me.

I look up instantly, and when I find the telltale trace of a snowball mark on Tristan's shoulder, the explosion suddenly makes a lot more sense. His eyes search the parking lot, and when he spots Luke bent down, reloading his ammunition, he drops down next to me to start packing his own snowball.

"Oh, my God. No, no, no." One of the blonde girls standing next to Luke makes a break for cover behind the red Jeep closest to her, quickly followed by her friends. Watching them try to navigate the snow-covered parking lot makes me glad that I went with my boots tonight.

Emery's laugh echoes through the parking lot as he runs for cover behind one of the cars to start making his own stash of snowballs. Nia follows close behind him as she brings her hands up to cover her head.

James grabs Jenny's hand and pulls her behind Tristan's truck for cover, but I bend down beside Tristan and start packing my own ammunition. His brows raise playfully when he realizes I haven't taken the coward's way out behind the safety of the cars like my roomies.

"Good luck out there, soldier." He winks, and in an instant, he's back upright with a small stack of snowballs clutched to his chest.

The sound of the impact and Luke's unmistakable groan echoes from across the parking lot when I stand back up with my own small pile of ammo. The snowball flies past my head so fast my hair blows back, and my wide eyes dart toward Luke who's holding up his hands with a *I wasn't aiming for you, I swear* expression. His eyes snap back to Tristan, who pelts another snowball straight at his face.

I have terrible aim, and I have absolutely no shot at dodging a snowball, so with the newfound realization that playing with these guys is going to hurt a hell of a lot more than getting hit by one of Nia's snowballs, I duck behind the Honda Civic closest to me.

I'm considering just waiting out the war, but when Micah jogs by, I'm too tempted. I grab one of the frozen balls and launch it at him as he passes. It misses terribly. It doesn't even break on impact when it falls to the ground and rolls into a mound of snow near the row of bushes by the building. I reload, searching for an easier target. Maybe someone who's not running.

Tristan fires his last snowball at Micah, and it connects perfectly on his shoulder, but he doesn't have time to register the hit to his upper body, because Luke fires a second shot, and it hits him right in the groin. He falls to his knees in a slur of curses ending in, "What the *fuck*, Luke?"

I ditch my spot behind the car and try to keep as silent as possible as I sneak up on Tristan. He's still laughing at Micah, who's now clutching his stomach, and looking decidedly more green than he did a few seconds ago. The snow crunches loudly under my boots, so my surprise attack is foiled as I launch the snowball toward him. The snowball is small and compact, and I watch in horror as it swerves off its intended trajectory toward his chest and makes perfect purchase just above his right eye. The grunt that sounds through the parking lot sends a stab of guilt straight through me, and my lungs freeze in my chest as I drop my remaining snowballs and sprint to him.

"I am so sorry. I wasn't aiming for your face, I swear. I just have terrible aim—" I reach my hands up, placing one on his shoulder to keep him still while I gently run a finger across his brow bone, making sure that my terrible aim didn't accidentally break anything.

To be fair, I wouldn't actually know what a broken brow bone would feel like, but when I add a little more pressure and he doesn't wince or pull back, I'm fairly certain that the damage can't be that bad. It's not bleeding, and apart from the slightly red tint from impact, he looks okay. I still take my time, though, slowly feeling around his brow and even down to his cheek, testing for any sensitive areas.

His face has relaxed from the shock of impact, and now he's watching me fuss over him with an amused grin. I try to keep my focus on my fingers, now brushing lightly across his temple, but it's hard when his eyes are unapologetically focused on my lips.

Our faces are inches apart, and my breathing quickens when his fingers reach up and brush across my cheek, pulling my windswept hair away from my lips. His eyes connect with mine again, and the deep emerald there extinguishes the last bit of resolve to focus on his brow, especially because his hand is now cupping my cheek, warming the chilled skin underneath.

"I missed you, Abs." His thumb caresses my cheek, and my heart tumbles over itself. This is what I've been craving for the past week— his touch, the way my skin warms instantly to him, the way his spearmint breath sends a wave of excitement through my body. I haven't actually felt his lips on mine since the pool, and now that he's so close, I can hardly breathe at the thought.

"I missed you, too." My voice is lost in the commotion around us, but his eyes are trained on my lips, and when his grin widens a little, I know he heard me.

His hands are still cupping my cheeks as he considers me, and I tilt my head back to bring our lips that much closer. There's a noticeable clarity to his eyes tonight, but my train of thought is effectively derailed when he leans down to bring his lips close to mine at a torturously slow pace. He knows it's killing me, because his cheek twitches when an impatient huff leaves my lips, but he doesn't give me the relief just yet as his lips hover over mine.

"Say it." His voice is low, a throaty whisper, close enough that I can taste his spearmint breath on my lips.

I'm desperate for him. To feel his lips on mine, to taste him on my tongue, but even now, as the icy air pulls past us, his words send a wave of heat through my veins, warming me more than anything else ever has.

"I missed you, too, Tristan."

I only get a flash of his satisfied smile before he connects our lips, and like lungs finally breaching the surface after being pulled under for far too long, I can breathe again.

I intertwine my fingers in the curls at the nape of his neck and pull him closer to me, sighing softly against his lips when his hands find their way down to my waist and around my back. He pulls me tight against his chest, and when his tongue slides across my bottom lip, a soft moan slips through my lips as my tongue brushes against his.

His lips are familiar to me now, like a map I've already memorized, and his thumb caresses my cheek once before his hand slides down to my jaw. His lips quirk when his thumb slides across my throat, feeling my careening pulse underneath.

"Get a room!" Luke's voice echoes around the parking lot, and I don't have to open my eyes to know that Tristan's raised his left hand off of my waist to flip him off. It's an empty threat, though, because he's smiling against my lips.

A few cat-call whistles sound around the parking lot from his team-mates, and I revel in the feel of his tongue exploring my mouth for a few seconds longer before he retreats.

I'm breathless and dazed when I finally open my eyes again, but even in my kiss-induced haze, I realize now how suddenly clear everything is. If last night's kiss with Dean taught me anything, it's that I'm full-in, too, only I'm full in with Tristan, and no amount of cute dates, rose bouquets, and promises for the future can change that—even if it is the safer option.

And if this is all I'll ever be able to have—passionate kisses in snowy parking lots, steamy pool dates, and dinners shared together on my couch, then I don't want anything else. I can handle the fallout and the heartbreak when it inevitably comes, because the reality of the situation is that I'm not willing to give up the best thing that I've ever known, no matter how temporary, for the security of something that will never measure up.

Tristan Beck is unlike anyone I have ever met. He's a maddening and intoxicating paradox of a man, pushing me away and pulling me in without even trying. And no matter how hard I try to fight it, I can't deny it anymore, because looking up at him now, as he smiles down at me while the snow flurries catch in his curls, I know that I am completely in love with him.

TWENTY-NINE

TRISTAN

When I pull up to the curb outside of Abby's apartment, she's already halfway down the stairs, her black leather purse swinging from her shoulder as she clutches a professional looking camera to her chest. Her chestnut hair is blowing out behind her in loose waves as she takes the last few stairs at a jog, and when she looks up at my truck, her lips pull back into an excited smile as she crosses the small lawn toward the parking lot.

I lean over and push open the door for her, and when she climbs into the truck, she clicks her seatbelt into place before tucking her hair behind her ear and smiling up at me. I want to lean over and kiss her, but I have a feeling if my lips connect with hers right now, we'll never leave the parking lot.

"I have something for you," she says instantly, pulling me out of my daze. Excitement radiates off of her as I put the truck back into drive and pull out of her apartment complex.

She pulls something out of her purse and holds it to her chest, but I have to keep my eyes trained on the road because for some reason, Sundays are always a lot busier around campus. My mom would actually kill me if I got into a fender bender and missed my granddad's birthday party. Although, her real annoyance would be because Abby didn't make it to the party, because ever since the girl sitting beside me agreed to go, my mom hasn't been able to go an entire phone call without mentioning it to me. Hell, even my grandma called the other day to confirm that I was bringing *"my lady"* with me.

I didn't bother correcting her, because honestly, it was kind of nice to think of her that way.

"You said before that your aux outlet broke and you haven't been able to listen to good music ever since," she says, pulling my attention away from the busy road for a few seconds to catch the bright gleam in her deep blue eyes. Her cheeks are still a little rosy from the cold air outside, so I reach down and turn the heat up. "So, I made you a mixed-tape—or CD, I don't really know if it's still called a mixed-tape when it's in CD form—but you know what I mean." She reaches toward the piece of shit radio on my dash and I catch a glimpse of the top of the CD before she slides it into the player. Her perfect handwriting is shining in glossy pastel pink marker: *Tristan's Mixed Tape*.

She pulls her bottom lip between her teeth, and I watch her inspect the radio controls with a look of complete concentration as she tries to figure out how to get the CD to play.

When I glance back up at the road, I have to hit the brakes a little harder than usual when the yellow light at the intersection flashes red. When she glances up at me, I'm able to play it off like I didn't just almost run the red because I was staring at her, and her eyes focus back on my old as dust stereo with a smirk. Her eyebrows pull together as she presses the play button, but nothing plays through the speakers.

My truck takes a few seconds to load the CD, but when the first few notes of the song starts to play through the speakers, she leans back in her seat and I don't have to look over to know that she's smiling, because I can feel it. Like the heat circulating in the car, I feel the energy change with her toothy grin.

I'm a little too distracted by the way her eyes are now shamelessly coasting down my body to realize I recognize the song playing through the speakers, and when her eyes finally flick back up to mine, she's grinning at me.

"I may have peeked at your music library." She sits back in her seat with a satisfied smile on her lips. "But it's a mix of both of our music, so there's something for each of us on here." She leans over to turn up the volume as the light turns green, and I focus back on the road so I can merge us onto the highway safely.

The playlist jumps from Drake to Travis Scott to Post Malone to Mac Miller to Taylor Swift to One Direction to *Nickelback*, and I'm pretty sure I even heard that Year 3000 song. It's a mess of genres, and yet, somehow, in the most comical way, it flows surprisingly well.

One second we're rapping together—or rather, I'm rapping and Abby's spitting gibberish because she clearly has no clue what the lyrics are—and the next she's belting out the older Taylor Swift songs that have been ingrained into my memory from listening to Olivia blast them constantly.

She nearly loses it when I'm able to sing along to the Jonas Brothers' songs, but I have Mel to thank for that one. And when she unapologetically screams the lyrics to the Nickelback song, I decide to join her, because let's be real here, if Abby Ryan is belting out Nickelback in the passenger seat of your truck, you can't not join in.

Each song is like a mini concert in the cab of my shitty old truck, and I sneak a peek at her whenever I can, while still keeping us coasting on the highway toward my grandparents. My favorite part of this entire ride is learning that Abby is the kind of girl that sings along to every song she hears—whether she knows the lyrics or not. On more than one occasion, she's sung out the wrong lyrics and then shrugged while letting her head fall back against the headrest in a laugh.

So now, as we're halfway through Drake's *Best I Ever Had*, I purposely fuck up some of the lyrics, just to try to conjure up that laugh of hers again.

I have my eyes focused on the road while trying to think of funny fake lyrics, but when I hear the soft click, I glance over to see Abby holding the camera up to her face with the lens pointing straight at me.

I raise a brow and my lips quirk up as I look back at the road. A few more clicks sound and I know I probably have a dumbass grin on my face right now, but I can't help it, because when I glance back at Abby, her bright smile freezes my lungs in my chest.

"One more," she promises, maneuvering around in her seat to scoot closer to me while still keeping her seatbelt on. She rests her head on my shoulder, and I make sure we're clear on the road before looking over, smiling up at the camera as she holds it out. She snaps the selfie of us and turns the camera around to inspect the picture in the display screen.

I have to keep my eyes on the road, so I don't get to peek at the picture, but she just hums happily beside me as she turns off the camera and places it in her lap, keeping her head resting against my shoulder.

She stays here, leaning against me while her index finger traces letters on my jean clad thigh. If I wasn't so dazed by how good it feels to have her so casually close, I might have been able to focus on the words she was writing out on my leg, but what I don't mistake is the shape of the heart that she punctuates her final word with.

When we pull off the highway, she lifts her head and scoots back toward her seat, and I instantly miss the way her vanilla apple spice infused my space. She puts the lens cap back onto the camera and then gently places it into her bag before pulling down the mirror. I can see her messing with her hair from my peripheral.

"You look amazing, Abs." I try to soothe the nervous energy spiking around her.

"I think I might be overdressed," she says as her eyes scan over my black jeans and gray Nike hoodie. She reaches down and smooths out the suede, high waisted skirt. The material stops mid-thigh, but it's met by her black, sheer tights which hug the entire length of her legs, disappearing into the ankle boots on her feet. Her turtleneck is tucked into her skirt, and the maroon scarf hanging loosely around her neck makes her cheeks look even rosier.

She looks more attractive than anyone I've ever seen in a turtleneck. Maybe it's because I've seen what's underneath, or the fact that I have the perfect roadmap of where the sweet spot on her neck is, or maybe, it's simply because Abby looks perfect in anything she wears.

"You're perfect." I shake my head.

Her shoulders relax a little when we pull up, and I hold my hand out behind her as we walk up to the house, keeping an eye out for any ice patches on the concrete drive.

She grins up at me nervously before following me through the front door.

The inside of the house warms me instantly and the smell of pumpkin candles and my grandma's famous chocolate cookies bring me back to the countless days I spent here growing up. The sound of my granddad laughing catches my attention, but I don't even have time to look down at the girl beside me before my mom's head pops around the corner.

"They're here," she calls over her shoulder as she hurries toward us. Her eyes are flicking between myself and Abby as her smile widens, but the girl standing beside me wins out and my mom wraps her arms around her tightly. Her deep blue eyes flick up to meet mine over my mom's shoulder, and I can see her relaxing into the embrace as I grin at her.

"I'm so glad you could make it, honey," she murmurs softly, pulling her tighter to her before finally releasing her. "I've been telling

Grandma and Grandad all about you, they're so excited to finally meet you."

Her eyes sweep over to mine and she pulls me into a hug, but my eyes are still trained on Abby. She's being pulled into the kitchen by Olivia and my grandmother, who's already complimented her on her outfit, and with one final look over her shoulder, she sends me an amused glance before my grandmother sits her down at the kitchen island and starts to load up a plate for her.

———

"I was not crying," I defend, but it's useless because everyone in the room is nodding at Abby, as if to say *Don't listen to him, he's just embarrassed.* Even Garrett is nodding along, and if I wasn't holding his baby in my arms, I might have pelted the teddy bear sitting on the couch next to me straight at his face, because he definitely wasn't at my kindergarten Thanksgiving play to witness me cry on the stage when I realized I forgot my one line.

"Your line was literally *Happy Thanksgiving.* How do you forget those two words?" Olivia snorts. She's lounging on the couch on the other side of the room with a piece of red velvet birthday cake on her plate.

Her comment sparks a smile from Abby sitting next to her, while Georgia cuddles close to her on her lap. She's letting the toddler play beauty salon with her purse of pretend makeup, and when our eyes meet, her smile deepens as the little girl smooths a brush over her cheeks.

"No more smiling," Georgia chides, pulling her fake lipstick out of her purse. "I need to paint your lips now."

Abby tries—and fails miserably—to not smile, because now I'm full-on smirking at her, and she has to look away to not get reprimanded again by the three-year-old on her lap.

"You know, I think I might actually have that tape," Grandma muses from her spot next to me on the couch. I lean back and give her my best brown-nosing smile as a silent plea for her to conveniently forget that the tape even exists.

"Yeah, I think you're right, Mom." Dad grins, standing up from his seat at the kitchen table. He's been reading the Sunday paper while sipping on his coffee since we finished lunch. Mom's eyes light up as she takes another sip from her own coffee.

"Why don't you help me find it, Tristan?" He nods toward the guest room where my grandparents have all of their old pictures and video tapes stored in the closet. I can tell by the way he's looking at me that we're not going to be looking for a stupid old tape, so I stand and gently place Gigi in Olivia's arms before following my dad out into the hall. I catch Abby's eyes as I go and watch as Georgia's small hand gently turns her head back to the front where she runs another brush over her forehead.

My dad leads the way into the guest room, and I brace for bad news, because why else would I get summoned to look for a stupid old tape? He stays silent as he opens the closet, and I hesitate by the door, watching as he bends down and picks up a small box labeled *2000-2004 Grandbabies*.

"We're not actually going to look for that stupid tape, are we?" I blanch, watching him start to sift through the VHS tapes. He doesn't look up at me as he pulls one out of the box and reads the faded writing on the side.

When he finally does look back up at me, he has a smile on his face. "Are you going to tell your old man what's going on, or do I have to wait for an engagement announcement?"

I blink a few times as his words wash over me. "What?"

"I thought it was just your mom being your mom at first." He shakes his head, the smug smile still glued on his face as he returns his attention back to the box of tapes in front of him. "I thought she was making something out of nothing because she liked Abby so much, you know, trying to will it into reality, or whatever they call it." He picks up another tape and reads the writing on the spine before placing it onto the bed and digging back into the box. "But I'm not blind, son, I can see what's going on here."

"It's—" I shake my head. "It's not like that, it's nothing serious." I shrug, but even as the words come out, I know they're not true, not anymore.

He doesn't look up at me, and I know he's pretending to be more interested in reading the spines of the tapes than he really is, because this isn't something we do. We don't talk about girls, or feelings, or being in love.

We just don't.

The knee-jerk response slips out of my mouth before I can stop it.

"Nothing is happening with Abby. We're just hanging out." I cringe at the words, because even though my dad is an old man compared to other dads, he sure as hell knows what I mean by that. "And nothing can happen. Not with the draft coming up."

I say the same thing that I've repeated to myself every single day for the past month, but when my dad's eyes finally lift from the tape in his hands, I know he hears how weak my resolve is.

"You're going to let the draft keep you from being with Abby?" He doesn't say it like an accusation, but it still feels like one.

"It's too complicated." I shrug, rubbing my hand over the back of my neck.

"What's complicated about it, son? I'm not following."

Part of me wants to bail—to make a break for it and go back to the living room, to hang out with everyone, to act like everything's fine—but when I glance back up and see my dad considering me with a frown, I know I can't run from this anymore.

"I can't start something that already has an expiration date on it." It comes out in a whisper.

"What?" He sets down the tapes and my heart clenches in my chest. This sure as hell is not how I thought I was going to spend my granddad's birthday.

"I don't know where I'm going to be after the draft. I could be any-where. In any state. In any city. And I have no say." He nods but stays silent. "And she's going to grad school somewhere. And I can't ask her to leave that and come with me. I can't do that. So then we'll be stuck in two different cities across the country, and I'll be in too deep by then, and I can't—" I look away from my dad to the floor in front of me.

"I get it." His voice is lowered to meet mine, and I don't have to glance up to know that he sat down on the bed. He takes a deep breath, and the sound somehow soothes me, at least a little. "I get that you don't want to open yourself up to that, and I'm not saying you're wrong, I just think—" He shakes his head, and I catch the motion in the corner of my eye. "I'm just saying there are some things in life that are worth the risk. I would hate for you to wake up ten years from now—surrounded by all of your accomplishments, all the fame and glory you've always wanted—and wonder what could have happened if you would have just taken a chance on her."

I look up from the floor to see him watching me.

"Life's one big game of high-risk, high-reward, son. And I know it's not my place to say, but—" He smiles, pointing toward the wall behind me. "Tristan, I really think the girl sitting out there right now is worth the risk."

He looks back down to the tape in his hands and sighs before he stands and collects the rest of the tapes. He places them back into the box before packing it back in the closet where he found it. When he turns around, his eyes meet mine, and I can feel the sincerity there, the real faith that he trusts my instincts—that being with Abby isn't a mistake.

He pats my back on the way out and I catch a glimpse of the single tape he has clutched in his other hand before he leaves me alone in the room to stare at my reflection in the mirror hanging over the dresser.

Life's one big game of high-risk, high-reward.

His words repeat in my mind as I step out of the room, and when I stop by the hallway entrance, I lean against the wall as I look out into the living room.

Everyone's sitting around the TV as the old tape plays, and I instantly spot five-year-old me on stage, but my attention doesn't linger on the screen for long because my gaze is pulled toward my girl, now cuddling Gigi to her chest as the little girl plays with the block in her hands. She's smiling at the baby as she gently tucks a stray curl behind her ear, and when her finger trails down her cheek and pokes the baby's little dimple, my chest tightens.

My dad's right, it is high-risk, high-reward, and when she glances over her shoulder, scanning the room until her eyes meet mine, I know she's worth the risk.

THIRTY

The sky above is a dark wall of deep gray and black as far as I can see, and the low warning rumbles of thunder vibrate through the truck as we speed down the empty highway.

I've been trying not to smile like an idiot for the past twenty minutes as I look through the adorable family pictures I was able to take before we left. I'd taken at least twenty different shots of them standing together in front of the fireplace when his grandma requested that I use the timer to get into a picture with them. I was about to object, because it didn't seem right to barge in on their family photo, but as soon as she asked, his mom insisted, claiming that it would only be right to have a picture of us all together.

It only took me a few seconds to figure out how to configure the settings for the timer, and then I was corralled into the middle of the group, right between Mrs. Beck and Olivia. I ended up standing right in front of Tristan, who I looked up to see smiling down at me as the first shutter of the camera sounded. I turned my attention back to the lens and beamed at the camera to take a proper picture, but as I look back now at the camera roll, my heart tumbles over itself as I watch the moment play out on the small display.

The first picture shows me looking up at Tristan as he smiles down at me while everyone else smiles at the camera. The second shows me looking back down at the camera with a beaming smile, although Tristan's smile is noticeably different than before—it's a softer smile, a warmer one, and his eyes aren't looking up at the camera, instead, they're still trained down on me. His eyes stay on me through the third and fourth picture, and it's not until the fifth that his eyes are looking up at the camera again, though his warm smile remains on his face for that one, and the sight sends a shiver down my spine.

Looking down at the display, I already know that I'm going to print the picture out and frame it, even if I have to keep it hidden under my pillow. The fact that I have a picture of Tristan smiling down at me is enough for me to actually melt on the spot, and when I smile up at the man next to me, who's humming along to the song playing softly in the background, he just glances over with a lazy grin, as if this moment—us driving home right before the huge storm hits—is somehow the most peaceful thing in the world to him.

I place the camera into my bag and settle back into the seat when I see the sign for Pullman. We're only five minutes away from his house, and if we're lucky, we'll beat the storm before the downpour starts. It's nearly four, and the sun should be setting soon, but the wall of black clouds doesn't allow for the fleeting sunlight to peek through.

The small town I've grown so fond of passes by as we drive past campus. The usually busy streets and sidewalks are nearly empty since everyone has already escaped inside, and as he turns onto the main road past the university, the first flash of lightning illuminates the black sky. A loud clap of thunder follows almost instantly, and then as if on cue, sheets of fat raindrops start to fall heavily against the truck.

Tristan flicks on his blinker and his windshield wipers as he pulls into the turn lane toward the entrance of his neighborhood. He drives us along the curved roadway, trees lining each side, as if the neighborhood is nestled in the middle of a forest, and I admire the way the wind is now pushing and pulling the leaves of the trees in a sort of dance.

My heart clenches painfully in my chest when the truck dips suddenly and a loud boom sounds.

"Oh, shit. That was the tire." He pulls off to the side of the road, and I grab the seat to steady myself as the off-kilter ride of the front tire jostles the truck. "I'm going to check it out," he says, cutting the engine before pushing open his door and hopping out quickly. He runs around the front of the truck toward the front passenger tire, and when he leans down, he shakes his head. He's already drenched with his hoodie clinging to him as his curls fall into his eyes.

He mutters a silent *"fuck"* outside the window, and I have to hold back my smile when he jogs back to the driver's side and hops back in.

"Okay," he says, closing the door behind him. "The front tire is popped, and I could put on the spare, but Luke has my car jack." He shakes his head to get his curls out of his eyes as he grabs his phone from the seat next to him. Scrolling through his contacts, he presses on Luke's name, but groans when the voicemail connects instantly.

"I think his dad's in town; they're probably out at dinner," he sighs.

"We're not far from your house," I shrug, pulling my purse over my head to wear cross-body.

"You want to run for it?" he asks, the shock clear in his voice.

"It's that or let you freeze here," I point out, noticing the goose-bumps climbing up his neck. "How far is it to your house?"

"About a two-minute jog," he runs his hand through his curls to sweep them out of his eyes.

"Okay then," I nod, zipping my purse closed to make sure the camera's safe from the downpour. I don't give him a chance to argue before pushing open my door and hopping out of the truck. The rain is coming down harder than I thought, and I barely have enough time to round the front of the truck before I'm fully soaked. My tights cling to my legs in the most uncomfortable way, but there's no going back now, so I start running.

I last about thirty seconds before I need a breather, and I bend over to put my hands on my knees. My heart pounds in my chest as I heave air into my lungs.

"You have to stand up straight, hands over your head to open your lungs. Otherwise, you won't get enough air," Tristan instructs. He doesn't look annoyed when he stops next to me, but by his steady breathing, I know that he's not even winded yet. I stand up straight and bring my hands over my head, reveling in the instant relief of a full breath of air.

The rain pelts down on us relentlessly, and I feel terrible that he's stuck here with me while I try to pull air into my lungs, but when he grins down at me, it's genuine, even if it means nearly freezing to death out here.

"We're almost there," he smiles, nodding toward the street sign two houses away. "That's the turn to my street."

I nod and readjust my purse before running again. As much as my is body screaming at me to stop running, the voice inside my head yelling to get out of the freezing-cold rain is much, much louder. Goosebumps cover every inch of my skin, and my breath forms small clouds in front of my face as I go. The only thing that keeps me from falling to the ground and just accepting defeat while I die as a human icicle is the sight of his house.

"You sound really winded." His voice pulls my attention away from the house in the distance, and I don't know whether to be more offended by his comment, the fact that he sounds like he's not even running when he talks, or the amused smirk pulling at his lips.

"I warned you before," I wheeze. "I'm as athletic as a slug."

"Do you want me to carry you the rest of the way?" he asks. I know he's being genuine, he would probably piggy-back me the rest of the way if I wanted, but it's a matter of pride now, so I wave him off as I push through the very real feeling of me possibly dying.

When we get to his driveway, I don't slow down until I'm under the cover of his porch, and that's when it hits me full force. I'm shivering so hard my teeth are starting to chatter, and he doesn't hesitate to push open the door and lead me through the living room where Micah's sprawled out on the couch with a paperback in his hand and a pen absently placed between his teeth.

His eyes scan up from the book and widen at the sight of us, drenched and shivering as we run through the living room. Tristan pushes open his bedroom door and leads me straight to the bathroom, cranking the shower on before turning around to pull out a handful of towels from the linen closet.

"You need to get out of those clothes or you're going to get sick," he says, stepping back toward the door. He hesitates for a moment as he takes me in, shivering by the now steaming shower with my hands clutched around my chest, dripping rain droplets onto his bathroom floor.

The steam from the shower paired with the heat from the house has already helped to defrost me a little, but the cold is bone-deep now, and somehow, I don't know if I'll ever feel warm again. When he turns, I watch him walk out of the now steaming bathroom to leave me to shower.

"Tristan, wait!" I call.

He hesitates by the door, but when he looks over his shoulder at me, heat starts to course through my frozen body. He watches as I tug my turtleneck over my head, and I drop it onto the floor beside me in a mess of wet cotton. Goosebumps ravage my stomach and chest, but when he turns back around and takes a step closer, another wave of heat courses through my veins, warming me from the inside out.

"Abby." His voice is throaty as his eyes slowly explore my body before meeting mine again.

I try to kick off my ankle boots, but nearly trip in the process, and have to steady myself on the counter. He takes a few steps toward me, hesitant and cautious, before kneeling down and taking my boot in his hand. He eases it off gently before tossing it aside, motioning for me to lift my other foot for him.

The sight of him kneeling in front of me sends a shiver down my spine that has absolutely nothing to do with the freezing rain. When he tosses the other boot aside, he looks up at me, and my breathing quickens as he watches me through thick lashes.

I reach up to unclasp my skirt, and his eyes don't leave mine as the drenched material slowly slides down my legs into a pile around my feet, leaving me in my black tights and underwear. I don't even remember what bra and underwear I picked out this morning, but by the look on his face, he seems to appreciate them. I reach to pull down the tights, but his hands come up to grasp mine, stopping me.

"Are you sure?" His eyes are clear and searching as he looks up at me, and my heart lurches in my chest at the sight.

Am I sure? I have never been more sure of anything in my life, because if this is the only time I'll ever get to be with Tristan, to really be with him, I don't want to pass it up.

"Yes." My voice is stronger than I thought it would be and the certainty in it rings clear.

He doesn't seem to need any more confirmation than that because his fingers grab for the material of the tights and he pulls it down quickly, freeing my legs from the uncomfortable damp material as I step out. He rises back up to his feet and pulls off his hoodie and shirt in one quick motion, dropping the wet cloth to the ground before stepping forward and connecting our lips.

His kiss is urgent, and hungry, and searching, and it sends a shock of heat through my body, straight down my spine to the heat already burning between my legs. I wrap my arms around his shoulders as he leads me back until I'm flush against the wall next to the shower. I don't even realize that my body is still shivering until his hands find the bare skin on my rib cage, warming my frozen body with his touch.

He breaks away from the kiss long enough to search my face before he tugs open the shower curtain, and my stomach flutters as he reaches for the button on his pants.

"Wait," I say quickly.

His eyes dart up to mine and he freezes.

"I want to do this part," I admit, watching as my shaking fingers slip the button from its hold. I feel his eyes on me as I slowly trail his zipper down, and when I look back up at him, his eyes are darker.

I tug his jeans down until they fall to his ankles where he steps out of them, leaving him in his black boxer briefs which strain against the outline in the front.

He moves quickly, and the shocked laugh that slips through my lips echoes through the bathroom as he reaches down and lifts me up by my thighs. I wrap my legs around his waist and smile down at him as he steps into the shower, closing the curtain behind us.

The water is a decadent warmth against my skin, but all I can focus on is how his lips are connected to the spot right under my ear that sends electric shocks through my body. He props my back against the wall of the shower, which has thankfully warmed from the steam as he slips a hand back and unclasps my bra.

The white cotton bra slips down my arms, and he pulls back from my neck to watch the warm water stream down my exposed breasts before his lips delve lower to explore the newly exposed skin. My head rolls back the second his teeth graze my nipple, and my arms tighten around his shoulders as I bite down on the inside of my cheek to keep quiet. I'm hypersensitive to his every movement, and when he wraps his lips around my nipple and flicks his tongue in a slow, teasing rhythm, my hips rock involuntarily, grinding against him as a desperate gasp falls from my lips.

He takes his time exploring my chest with his mouth, nipping, and sucking, and using that tongue in ways I didn't know existed, and when he knots his hands in my hair, he tugs gently, trailing his lips up my neck to the sensitive spot just below my ear. When he bites down and sucks harder than before, my eyes widen and then flutter closed in pure ecstasy.

His grip tightens on my thighs as he grinds against me, and when he adds pressure to the suction on my neck, the pressure building in my stomach flares white-hot. Every breath turns into a moan, but even knowing that Micah's home, I can't stop the noises from slipping through my lips. He bites down onto my neck roughly one final time before dragging his tongue against my feverish skin and pulling back. When his eyes find the spot his lips were just connected to, a flash of satisfaction spikes in the emerald there before they connect back with mine, considering me with a molten stare.

He steps back from the wall, placing me back onto my feet, and when he kneels down in front of me again, my lungs freeze in my chest as his thumbs wrap around my underwear. His gaze flicks back up to mine, and I nod instantly, watching as he pulls them down my legs.

He positions my leg over his shoulder, and I try to steady my breathing as I lean my head against the wall. He's slow and teasing as he sucks, and nips, and licks the skin on my inner thigh, wrapping his arms around my thighs to steady my already weak legs.

A breathy, impatient moan slips through my lips when he licks the inside of my thigh in one long, torturous motion. The shocks it sends directly to the swollen bud between my legs is enough to make me knot my fingers in his curls and bring his mouth to where I want it most. He laughs at my lack of patience, and the sound makes my stomach tighten as I bite down on the inside of my cheek, wanting nothing more than for him to connect his lips to me.

He tightens his arms around my thighs and pulls me closer, and I swear to God, my vision goes black when his tongue drags across me in a slow, deliberate motion. My breathing is quick and irregular as I focus on how unreal his tongue feels against the pulsing, swollen bud of nerves, and the pressure building in my stomach makes my legs weak. When he starts to flick his tongue harder, my hips grind against him desperately.

I'm on the edge, reveling in the intense flood of pleasure, and when he slips a finger into me and hits a spot deep inside, every muscle in my body tightens before releasing. The first tidal wave of sweet bliss racks through my body, and I can't seem to quiet the loud, breathy moans that echo through the bathroom, but to be completely honest, I can't even remember why I'd want to at this point. He slows his tongue as the aftershocks pulse through me, and the soft brushes slowly bring me down.

When I look down at him, his lips are glossy, and he grins up at me as his tongue slides across his bottom lip. The sight alone nearly makes my legs give out, and when he stands, he reaches behind me to turn off the water as he reconnects our lips. His mouth doesn't leave mine as he pulls open the curtain and hooks his arms under my legs again, and I'm barely aware of anything other than the fact that his tongue is caressing mine in the most delicious way as he carries me out of the bathroom.

When he leans over and my back connects with the soft cotton of his sheets, I look around. My eyes dart to his door first, and when I notice that it's closed, I look back to see him hovering above me. His eyes are dark, and his wet curls are dripping water down his neck to his shoulders and down his chest. The sight alone is enough to make my hips rock up to him, and he reaches down to cup my cheek in his hand as he connects our lips again.

He kisses me long enough for me to lose my breath before finally pulling away and standing back up from the bed. When he opens the drawer on his nightstand, the heat pulsing between my legs flares as I watch him slip his drenched boxers down his legs. I've touched him before and seen enough of his erection in his boxers to have an idea of what to expect but seeing him now is completely different. I've only ever seen one penis in my life, and it was connected to Tyler who was barely 5'10. Tristan is a much bigger person in general, so it shouldn't surprise me that he's bigger in every aspect, but honestly, the sight is still a little jarring. He looks back up at me, and when our eyes meet again, they're clear and searching.

"Are you sure this is okay?" His voice is throaty, and the sound alone makes my skin tingle.

I nod quickly and watch as he crawls back onto the bed, hovering over me again. He hands me the condom with a grin, and I tear it open with shaky hands. I've never done this part. Tyler always took care of it, but there's something incredibly intimate about rolling the condom onto Tristan. His head falls onto my shoulder with a tortured groan and his hips lurch forward slightly as my fingers push the latex over him. Brushing a single kiss onto my shoulder, he looks down at the condom and pinches the front, creating a pocket in the front of it.

I lean back into the comforter, and when he looks back at me, I grab his face and bring his lips to mine, desperate for the feel of his tongue on mine again as my heart pounds painfully in my chest. He gives me exactly what I want, and a shiver races down my spine as he leans on to his elbow, freeing his hand to explore my body again.

I'm nervous, and excited, and impatient, and I can tell by the slow pace of his fingers on my skin that he's taking this slower than he usually would, as if he can tell that my heart is nearly racing out of my chest.

His fingers start on my cheek and trail down my neck where he traces my collarbones and then dips around my breast where the pad of his thumb skims over the smooth skin to my ribs. The feel of his calloused hands makes my hips rock against him, and his erection presses heavily against my stomach as he continues his slow descent. His lips never leave mine, and he brushes his tongue against mine, slowly, teasingly as he grabs onto my hip tightly. A throaty groan sounds in the back of his throat, and when his fingers finally delve lower to find the pulsing between my legs, I push up into his hand, desperate for relief. His thumb grazes over the swollen bud, brushing torturously slow circles that send a flood of pleasure through my veins as he moves his hips, lining us up perfectly.

He's pushed up against me softly, tentatively, as if he knows that I might need a minute to catch up to him, and his lips leave mine and trail down my neck to my shoulders, peppering soft, warm kisses as he goes. When he pulls back to look at me, I reach up and brush his curls out of his eyes, and he captures my hand in his own, bringing my fingers to his lips to press a soft kiss onto the tip of each one. When his teeth graze roughly across my palm, a shocked gasp slips from between my lips, and the white-hot heat pulsing between my legs flares.

"Tristan, please." I'm practically panting, and the sound pulls a smug smirk onto his lips, enough to gently dent the dimple in his cheek.

When he brings his lips back down to mine, they're searing, and searching, and claiming, and the gasp that slips through my lips is lost on his when his hands grip my hips tightly and he thrusts forward, eliciting the most divine feeling of him filling me. It's the most intoxicating sensation, and my body ignites in a flood of heat when he pulls out and thrusts again, hard enough to coax a shocked moan from my lips.

When he tightens his grip on my hips to keep me in place underneath him, I can barely focus on anything other than the overwhelming sensation of him. He's everywhere, all around me, inside of me, gripping my hips, breathing out the most intoxicating soft groans into my ear, brushing soft kisses across my throat, sending a shiver down my spine at the feel of his stubble grazing across my neck.

The sounds slipping from my lips aren't even mine anymore as the rhythmic rocking of our bodies pulls me somewhere else entirely. I've never felt anything like this before. It's like every experience I've ever had leading up to this point has been erased. Every touch, every clumsy kiss, every single moment shared in dark rooms with Tyler—it's all gone, because it doesn't even fall into the same stratosphere as this.

"You feel—fuck, Abby, you feel so good."

His hands grip the back of my thighs, and he lifts my hips from the bed, changing the angle as he quickens his movements. My eyes shoot open as the new position sends a rush of goosebumps across my body. He grins down at me, and I reach up to caress his cheek, mesmerized by the intense pleasure shining in his eyes. When his grip tightens on my thighs, his hips move faster, and I thread my fingers through the soft curls at the nape of his neck, pulling him down to connect our lips again.

His tongue slides into my mouth, and I taste the spearmint on his breath mixed with the faintest taste of red velvet from the cake we ate earlier. It coats my tongue until it's all I can think about, and when he groans into the kiss, the now-familiar pressure between my thighs builds dangerously, tightening every muscle in my body until my back is arched and I'm clinging to him desperately. His tongue brushes against mine softly, tenderly, and it's an intoxicating contrast to the fast, rough strokes of his hips. He lifts my leg higher up on his waist, and when he hits a spot deep inside of me, my shocked moan is silenced on his lips as my fingers dig into his back. Every muscle in my body tenses tightly when he hits that same spot again, and then everything outside of the man I'm clinging so desperately to falls away as my veins flood with the kind of mind-numbing pleasure that I've only known right here with him.

He rubs my thighs as the orgasm rocks through me, and when his movements become quicker and more desperate, I know he's on the edge, too. He gives one final thrust of his hips, and when his breathy groan echoes between us, I reach up and run my fingers through his still-damp curls, grazing my lips across the feverish skin on his neck.

He sinks down onto me, holding his weight on his elbows to keep from crushing me, but I wrap my arms around his neck and pull him closer, wanting to ingrain this moment into my memory. He finally pulls back after a minute, and the sated warmth in his eyes is possibly the most beautiful thing I've ever seen. Grinning down at me, he sweeps a wayward strand of hair away from my face before brushing his thumb across my cheek and connecting our lips again.

I'm not sure how long we've been here like this, tangled up together, listening to the rain tap softly against his window while we explored each other slowly, innocently, contently, but when he finally pulls away, he looks dazed and sated and warm.

I watch as he climbs off the bed and walks back into the bathroom where he pulls off the condom and drops it into the trash. He switches on the shower, and when he turns around, he leans against the door frame as he considers me, cheeks burning, and still breathless from our time spent tangled up together.

"Want to join me?" he asks, nodding back to the shower.

I slide off the bed, wrapped in his bedsheet as I pad over to him, and when he opens his arms for me, I revel in the feel of them wrapping around me tightly. His thumb brushes along my jaw, tilting my head back to connect our lips in a kiss that steals the air from my lungs and sets fire to my skin. When his tongue brushes against mine lazily, I rock up onto my tiptoes and wrap my arms around his shoulders, letting the sheet fall around my feet as my body molds against the hard lines of his. His lips pull back into a smile as he slowly leads us back to the shower, and when he pulls me into the warm spray with him and cups my cheek to kiss me deeper, I know this is exactly where I'm supposed to be.

THIRTY-ONE

TRISTAN

I can't stop smiling like a fucking idiot.

Not when Micah and Luke busted my balls for *"that truly award-winning performance"* when I walked out to get Abby a glass of water. Not when Luke came along to help me change my blown tire and wouldn't shut the fuck up about how he'll *"never be able to see Ryan the same way again."* And definitely not now, as Abby pulls open the passenger side door of my truck that's currently idling in front of her apartment building.

She's practically drowning in my hoodie and the smallest pair of sweats I could find, but even though she tied them as tightly as she could, they're still dangerously close to falling down her legs if she doesn't keep a hand secured on the waistband.

Reaching over to help her into my truck, she grins up at me as she tucks the black tote bag and her backpack onto the seat beside us.

"Okay, all set," she chirps, pulling her seat belt into place.

She's already messing with the stereo controls to get the CD to play, and I don't bother trying to hide the ridiculous grin on my face, because when I look over at the girl sitting in my passenger seat—with her hair pulled up into a messy knot and the residual glow from our time spent locked in my room—she's wearing the same damn smile on her perfectly swollen lips.

The last few minutes of sunlight are finally poking through the passing storm clouds, and the golden light catches her silhouette, illuminating around her like a halo. She's fucking glowing, radiating the warmest energy I've ever felt as she leans back in her seat, eyes closed softly, head tilted back against the headrest, humming along to the song playing through my shitty old speakers. She turns up the volume as I pull back onto the main road, and an undeniable warmth spreads through my chest. Like a flame, she's warming my entire body just by sitting here beside me.

I try to focus on the traffic congesting the streets around campus to keep me from stealing glances at her, but every time we hit a red light, I find myself focusing on how her voice sounds singing along to the songs she put together just for me—for us.

I reach out and capture her hand in mine, resting our intertwined fingers on my leg. I don't need to look over to know she's looking at me, but when I finally break and glance over, her surprised smile deepens as our eyes meet. She scoots a little closer, resting her head on my shoulder like she did when we were on our way to my grandparents' house.

When I asked her to stay the night with me, it didn't take much convincing. I think it helped that I was midway through lathering her up with my body wash and pressing soft kisses to the new bruise blooming on her neck. Her argument about not having her clothes, or books, or laptop all fell to the wayside when my lips trailed slowly across her jaw to connect with hers. When a content sigh rumbled in the back of her throat as my tongue slid through her eager lips, I knew I'd already won.

The sun is setting by the time we finally pull into my driveway, and the loss of the warm light drops the temperature even more. I reach over and grab her tote and backpack before she can and toss them both over one shoulder, holding a hand over her back as she walks up the icy drive. Her steps are careful to avoid any ice patches, and when she pushes open the front door, the instant warmth inside welcomes us.

Micah and Luke are still lounging on the couch, only now there's a mess of empty beer bottles littering the coffee table and a few bags of chips laying open beside them. When they look over toward us, both of their gazes linger on Abby. I can tell they're both dying to make some smart-ass comment about her sleeping over or coming back for seconds, but they both keep their mouths shut when they catch my warning glare.

"Hey, guys." She smiles, completely unaware of the death glare I'm sending them.

They both grin at her as she tucks a fallen strand of hair behind her ear and crosses her arms across her chest. She's trying to be as casual as possible but standing here in my clothes is kind of a dead giveaway of what we just did. I mean, if we're being honest, they knew what was happening anyway. Abby wasn't exactly using her inside voice, but I'm sure as hell not going to tell her that; she'd never come back.

"Hey, Ryan," they say, smirking at each other before looking back to the TV. Her cheeks warm a little, and I know she's worrying about whether or not we've been caught.

"Your pizza just got here," Micah says, eyes still fixed on the TV.

"Pizza?" Her brows pull together, and I grin at her, already retreating to the kitchen to grab the two boxes sitting on the counter.

"I was going to steal a piece, but Jesus fuck, you two have terrible taste." He snorts. "Who the fuck orders two pineapple pizzas?"

I round the corner just in time to see the smug smile pull across her lips as her wide eyes meet mine.

———

I don't know how she convinced me to put on *Love Island* over *Stranger Things*, but here we are, three episodes deep while lounging on my bed. And fuck, I'm actually kind of invested at this point.

"Oh, my God, no, no, no." She gasps, bringing her hands up to her mouth as one of the girls reenters the villa. I have to admit, this part is pretty shitty. The chick's partner just tried to dump her for someone else without her knowing, and to make matters worse, she just admitted to being in love with him. So, yeah, that's a pretty solid reaction to the shit playing out on screen.

"That's what Olivia meant when she said he was a dick," she mumbles, as if all the dots suddenly connected in her head from an earlier conversation.

The preview for the next episode plays, and I glance over to see her eyes glued to the screen. Until Abby, I'd never met anyone who could rival my little sister's love for ridiculous reality TV shows.

Rolling off the bed, I grab our abandoned pizza boxes on my desk before walking out to the kitchen. The house is silent, apart from the low hum of the TV echoing from my room. Micah and Luke are probably getting shit-faced at O'Malley's right now, and I'd be willing to bet my entire bank account—not that there's much in it—that James is crashing at Jenny's again.

I drop the two empty pizza boxes on the kitchen counter and pull out the chocolate syrup and milk from the refrigerator. Trying to recreate the exact measurements she used the first time she made it, I lean down to get a better look at the amount of chocolate syrup in the cup. When I finally decide that it's as close as I'm going to get, I pour in the milk and take my time stirring until the brown liquid looks just right.

Grabbing the pack of Oreos, two water bottles, and the chocolate milk off the counter, I balance everything in my arms as I make my way back to my room.

The credits are still rolling on the TV when I push open the door, but my eyes only linger on the screen for a second before I spot Abby pulling her plaid sleep shorts up her legs. Her purple, polka dotted underwear are lacy and pretty damn transparent, and the sight stops me in my tracks. I watch them slowly disappear underneath the fabric of her shorts, and when I look back up to meet her eyes, she's peering over her shoulder at me. Her lips pull up into a playful grin that spikes my heart rate, and I close the door behind me with my foot. When her eyes slide from my dumbass grin to the glass in my hands, her lips pop open slightly.

"Is that chocolate milk?"

I nod, appreciating the way my hoodie slips back down her thighs, covering her shorts to make her legs look bare.

"I don't think I've ever been more turned on," she teases, sitting down on the edge of the mattress.

I hand her the glass and watch as she brings the drink to her lips, moaning as she takes her first sip. I appreciate the show she puts on when her eyes roll back dramatically and she starts to fan herself, and when her eyes finally meet mine again, I don't miss the humor pooling in them as she takes another long sip.

"I never thought I'd be jealous of chocolate milk," I admit, dropping the Oreos onto the mattress beside her.

"You can have some if you want." She grins up at me, extending the glass.

"Oh, I definitely want some." I nod, taking the glass from her. But instead of bringing it up to my lips, I place it down on her nightstand and step between her legs, cupping her face in my hands as I lean down to bring my mouth to hers.

The instant taste of chocolate syrup coats my lips, and I mimic her dramatic moan from before, reveling in the feel of her lips pulling back into a smile against mine. I pull back just enough to catch the amused look on her face as she bites down on the inside of her cheek to hold back her laugh.

"Yeah." I grin. "That's pretty damn good."

She grins up at me before her eyes flick down to my mouth again, and I lean down, connecting our lips in a slow, leisurely kiss.

Her hands brush up my arms until they're laced in my hair, and when she opens her mouth for my tongue to slip through, I wrap my arms around the back of her thighs and pull her up to me, moving us further up the mattress. Her legs lock around my hips as I settle over her, and she pulls me closer as my tongue explores her mouth, brushing against hers slowly as the softest moan sounds in the back of her throat.

It feels like a dream, being so close to her.

She tastes like chocolate, and even after using my body wash and shampoo, she still somehow has the faintest scent of apples and vanilla, as if it's just a part of her. I run my hand up the outside of her thigh, appreciating the way her soft, smooth skin feels against my calloused fingertips. I can feel the smallest rock of her hips when my tongue brushes against hers, and her fingers tighten in my hair to pull me closer, deepening the kiss.

When I finally pull away, she's breathless and her cheeks are flushed with that rosy glow I love so much. I reach my hand up and sweep my thumb across her jaw, grinning at the instant shiver that the touch evokes.

I'm starting to learn how her body reacts to me—where to kiss to pull a breathy moan from her lips, where to caress to make her hips rock up, where to trail my fingers to make her even breaths turn into desperate pants. She's looking up at me, watching my face as I brush my thumb gently over the bruise growing on her neck. I haven't given anyone a hickey in years, since high school, probably. Maybe even before that. I never wanted to leave a mark on any of the girls I fucked, because it was temporary, over and done and forgotten by the time I pulled my pants back up. But the sight of the light purple and blue bruise on Abby's neck sends a wave of satisfaction through my veins—it's a mark; a claim; a promise; a desperate hope that she won't leave.

"Stay with me," I say, brushing my thumb over the bruise again.

She smiles up at me, her brows pulling together in amused confusion as she runs a light finger over my brow, tracing the bone there.

"I am." She laughs. "I didn't wear my PJ's just for fun." She glances down to her pajamas, and I lean down, running the tip of my nose from her cheek to the hickey and down to her collarbone, just barely exposed from the hoodie. I place a soft kiss there and pull back to look into her eyes.

"I don't just mean tonight," I say.

Her brows raise, and her pulse quickens in the dip of her throat as her fingers freeze in my curls.

"Stay with me, Abby."

"I—I—what?" Her voice is so soft that I might have missed it if my eyes weren't trained on her lips.

"I'm sorry it took me this long to realize what I want," I say, reaching up to cup her cheek. "I'm a fucking idiot."

Her lips part slightly, but by her blank expression, she's not processing my words.

"I want this. I want everything that comes with it—the label, the corny dates, meeting your family, remembering anniversaries, bringing you flowers, making you chocolate milk before bed, being Facebook official. . .if that's even still a thing." I smirk down at her. "I don't really know what else, I've never had a girlfriend before, but whatever this is—I want it." Her mouth falls open wider as she begins to understand what I'm saying. "I guess what I'm trying to say is that I want you, Abby. I want every part of you. Tonight, tomorrow, every single day. I've wanted you since you put your hand in mine at that ridiculous formal, it just took me a little while to figure it out."

She's silent as she searches my face, and then her eyes start to water. I pull back, chest tightening as I think back to which part of my dumbass speech could have hurt her feelings, but she doesn't give me time to ask before she crashes her lips onto my own. Her tongue brushes against mine, and when her hand presses softly against my shoulder, I roll back, letting her straddle my hips. She breaks the kiss, the residual taste of chocolate syrup still on my lips as she pulls her hoodie off, leaving her in her plaid pajama shorts.

A wave of goosebumps races up the bare expanse of her chest, hardening her nipples and flushing the skin on her cheeks. I want to follow the small bumps, exploring every inch of skin they touch until they disappear on the smooth column of her neck. Her skin has the faintest golden tan, as if it'll never fully go back to its original shade after being out in the Florida sun for so many years. When my thumb caresses the spot on her hip bone where her tan line starts, another shiver runs up her spine. She tugs at the bottom of my shirt, and I help her pull it off, tossing it somewhere over my head before I meet her eyes again. I know I need to get the words out before this goes too far and I can't think straight, so I shake the nerves and just go for it.

"At the risk of sounding cringey as fuck because I don't really know how to do this." I mirror the soft smile now spreading across her face. "Will you be my girlfriend, Abby Ryan?"

She considers me as my hands settle on her waist, and when the words leave her perfectly swollen lips, I swear to God my heart freezes in my chest.

"I'm yours, Tristan Beck."

THIRTY-TWO

I woke up this morning to the feel of Tristan's stubble grazing across my skin as he brushed slow, soft kisses all the way up my spine. His lips trailed across my shoulder and up my neck, and when I rolled onto my back to pull him closer, his lips lingered on the tender bruise on my neck until they finally connected with mine. I could tell by his damp curls and the fresh smell of his body wash that he had just gotten back from his early morning workout.

I could have spent the entire morning like that, lazily exploring his mouth while his hands trailed down my naked body. They stopped only to hook under my knees and pull my legs around him as he hovered above me, grinding his hips into me in a torturously slow, teasing motion. I was practically panting by the time his fingers grazed across my hip bone, and I was fully expecting this to lead to him shedding his clothes and us cutting class to stay in bed like we did Monday *and* Wednesday morning, but when I tried to tug his sweatpants down, he chuckled and pressed a final kiss to my shoulder before retreating.

The past three days have been a blissful blur, and I'm honestly still waiting to wake up and realize that all of this was some incredibly vivid dream.

On Monday night, after he got out of practice, Tristan showed up at my apartment with a bouquet of roses, a box of chocolates, and a freaking corsage for our dinner date. It was simultaneously the most adorable and hilarious thing to watch him slip the flower onto my wrist with such concentration. When he finally had it secured, he stepped back to get a better look as I modeled it for him by posing with my hand on my hip.

Since I skipped prom, both junior and senior year, I haven't ever worn a corsage, so I can't deny that it felt kind of amazing to have it on my wrist, even if it was a bit over the top for a dinner at Vinny's. His dimple indented every time his eyes found the flower as we ate, so I happily obliged when he requested that I keep it on after we got back to my apartment and he helped me out of my dress, leaving me in nothing but the flower bracelet as his lips explored my already tingling body.

On Tuesday, I was fresh out of the shower from my shift at the diner when he called. I had just pulled on the hoodie he left for me and a pair of polka dotted pajama pants when his face flashed on my phone. I was fully prepared to just hang out like we usually do on our FaceTimes, but he instantly started to explain that we were going to be pressing play on the same movie at the same time so we could watch it together while on FaceTime. As if that wasn't already the cutest thing in the world, his dimple was the deepest I've ever seen when he told me to go check the pantry where he had secretly stocked the same popcorn, Hershey Kisses, and sour straws that he had brought to Arizona with him, because, *"If we eat the same snacks it's like we're really together."*

It was the cheesiest and most adorable thing he's ever done. I could hear Micah and Luke giving him shit the entire time he was explaining it, and when he mentioned the snacks, their howls of laughter echoed through my phone until Tristan finally kicked them out of the hotel room and told them to go find a park bench to sleep on.

As if eating sour straws on FaceTime while watching a movie with my boyfriend wasn't enough to make me the literal happiest girl on USW's campus, I'm also still riding the high from the number of orgasms I've experienced in the past four days.

I feel like I've been enlightened, like Tristan opened my eyes to what sex actually is. And now, I wouldn't just say that my sex life with Tyler was vanilla—as Nia described it—but instead, low-fat, vegan, sugar-free, you-probably-can't-even-categorize-this-as-ice-cream ice cream.

In just the four days that we've been together, somehow my entire world seems to have shifted to fit him perfectly into my life. I crave hearing his voice, the way my body needs his touch, and whenever we're alone for too long, the tender, sweet kisses that he always presses to my neck, and cheeks, and lips, always seem to lead to me trying to undress him, because honestly, there's just something so irresistible about the way his fingers feel on the most innocent parts of me that makes me wish they were somewhere else entirely.

Now, the feel of his thumb rubbing small circles onto the small of my back has lulled me into a sleepy daze, and when his lips brush against the top of my head, I blink up at him to see him looking down at me with a lazy smile. He tightens his hold on me, and I reach up and poke his dimple, which only makes it indent further as his grin deepens.

I was a little shocked when he pulled into this field, but once he helped me climb into the bed of his truck—which I'm pretty sure he filled with every pillow and blanket in his entire house—I realized pretty quickly that the reason he drove us twenty minutes south of Pullman was to get far enough away from the city lights to actually see the stars.

The drive alone was enough to put a smile on my face, because any time we're in his truck for longer than five minutes, I always end up scooting close to him and resting my head against his arm, writing out hidden messages with my finger on his thigh for him to guess. He used to never guess right, but I'm starting to suspect that he was guessing wrong on purpose the entire time just to make me laugh, because now, he's starting to get suspiciously good at it.

"My parents used to take us out here when I was a kid." His voice is throaty, and I can feel his chest vibrate against my cheek before I glance up to see him looking up at the stars. He rests his head back against the truck and his cheek twitches into an absent smile. "I used to think the stars were all different planets, and that the light was coming from their houses and car headlights, shining all the way across the galaxy." His eyes flick down to mine, and I smile up at him as he intertwines our fingers in his lap. "Olivia and I used to sit here and come up with a story for each one. What life would be like up there."

My gaze coasts away from his face toward the night sky, and I can practically see a little Tristan out here in this field with his family, coming up with the different stories for each star.

"What's the story for that one?" I grin, pointing at the brightest dot in the sky.

His eyes follow where my finger is pointing, and he grins. I know he can't possibly remember the stories, at least not for each specific star, but he plays along anyway, making up a story for each one that I point out. After the fourth one, I can tell he's running out of ideas, and when I notice the faint twinkling light of a plane flying way up beyond the barely there layer of clouds, the words leave my mouth before I realize what I'm saying.

"Look—a shooting star. Make a wish," I whisper, squeezing his hand as I point to it. The memory of my dad resurfaces instantly, and my chest clenches in the painful way it always does whenever I think about him for too long. My lungs freeze as the old memory, dusty and forgotten, resurfaces from some distant part of my mind I didn't realize I could still access.

The small beach town I grew up in was too close to the city to allow for any real stars; so instead, my dad would always point out airplanes at night. Whenever we would catch one flying overhead, we would wish on it, like a shooting star in the sky.

I never questioned it because it just seemed so normal, so ordinary, like looking both ways before crossing the street, or washing your hands before dinner—we wished on planes in the night sky.

It wasn't until I got a little older that I realized how lucky I was to have a dad who made such magical moments seem so normal, so much a part of everyday life that I didn't even notice them as they were happening. I haven't wished on a passing plane in years, I haven't even thought of it since I was a kid, but somehow, the distant sound of the plane engine flying overhead pulls me back to being a little girl, standing on the beach behind our house with my hand held securely in his. Even behind closed lids, my eyes burn as they start to water, and my lungs freeze in my chest when his words echo through my mind—*Make a wish, Sweet Pea.*

I bite down hard on the inside of my cheek to try to keep from crying, because breaking down in the middle of this perfect date is not okay, but when the first choked sob escapes my lips, I know I'm too far gone to stop it.

Tristan jolts up next to me like he's been electrocuted, and his hands find my shoulders instantly, rubbing calming circles up and down my arm.

"What happened? Abby, what's wrong?" His voice is panicked, and the anxiety radiating off of him is palpable as his hands reach up and cup my face, wiping away the tears that are now streaming down my cheeks with his thumbs.

When I finally open my eyes, my vision is completely blurred by the constant stream of tears, but I can see enough of him to know that his eyes are wide. He's searching me, my face, my body, as if he's looking for some kind of physical wound.

"Abby," he pleads. "Please, Abs. Talk to me."

His wide eyes are desperate as he searches my face, and my chest only tightens when I realize that he looks like he might actually have a panic attack if I don't tell him what's wrong with me. I try to pull myself together so I can explain why I'm having a level-ten break down right in front of him. Quick, desperate breaths rake through my lips as soon as I try to speak, as if I wasn't breathing this entire time, and when the fresh air makes me feel a little less light-headed, I realize that maybe I wasn't.

"My dad." It's all I can get out before the pressure in my chest feels like it's about to explode and I can't hold back the sobs anymore.

The worry in his eyes eases when he realizes I'm not having a heart attack, and he just nods as he pulls me into a hug, letting me bury my face into his chest as the sobs rock through my body. I haven't cried like this in months, and I haven't cried like this in front of someone else in years. Probably not since I finished grief counseling my senior year of high school.

"I'm so sorry," he says softly against my hair while his hands rub my back. "I didn't realize—I didn't know this would be hard for you. I would have never—" But he doesn't finish because I can tell that he still has no idea what set me off.

I was fine two seconds ago; I was teasing him about his different star planets, and joking about an airplane being a shooting star, and now I'm crumbling into myself as the sobs rock through me.

His hands rub soothing circles on my back as I tighten my hold on the front of his hoodie, and the slow circles seem to be helping to ease the waves of sobs from spilling through my lips.

I'm crying—I mean, God, I am really crying right now—the loud, snotty, mascara-down-my-cheeks, puffy-eyed, I-can't-breath kind of crying. But even now, as another wave of sobs shakes through my body, I know they aren't sad tears. I mean, yeah, they are, but they aren't at the same time. They're *shocked* tears. They're *I miss you* tears. They're *I can't believe I let myself bury that memory for so long* tears. They're *I'm so glad I remembered that* tears.

The pressure in my chest starts to ease as he continues to rub my back, and I can finally breathe without gasping. My heart is pounding, and I have to take a few deep breaths to release some of the pressure building in my head.

"I'm happy." I try to say, but it comes out as a strangled croak.

His lips quirk slightly as he reaches up to wipe my cheeks, and when he pulls his thumbs away, they're coated in my black mascara.

"I'm no expert at emotions, baby, but this doesn't seem like a happy kind of moment."

Baby. The word makes me smile a little as I sit back and use the sleeve of my hoodie to wipe away the makeup under my eyes.

"I know I probably look crazy," I say, but it comes out in a sort of laugh, and once the first giggle slips through my lips, I can't stop, because I know I look crazy, and yet somehow, even after witnessing that entire mess, he's still rubbing my back and looking at me with that amused smile that only hints at the dimple in his cheek.

He rubs my back until my breathing has gone back to normal, and when he hands me the water bottle that he has next to him, I take a few long sips. That's when the situation fully hits me. I just had a full-on meltdown in front of him, sobbing and heaving—the entire water works show.

My cheeks burn as I hand the water bottle back to him, and now all I want is to evaporate into the chilly night breeze and pretend like this never happened. I can't believe I just broke down like that. I can't believe I just ugly cried in front of him. I can't believe I just ruined this entire date.

"Can you tell me about him?" he asks softly, as if he's trying to make sure he doesn't overstep any boundaries.

I look up from my hands knotted in my lap, willing my white-hot blood not to sear the skin on my cheeks. He's watching me carefully, but his eyes are a bright green, earnest and genuine, and I could actually start crying again because I know, I know that he truly wants to hear about my dad.

"Really?" I ask, sitting up and wiping the sleeve of my hoodie under my eyes one final time as I breathe in to clear my stuffy nose.

"Only if you want to." He smiles, repositioning himself so I can scoot next to him again. He lifts his arm and motions for me to cuddle up with him. My skin is still burning from the residual embarrassment that keeps coursing through my veins, but even now, while I'm completely mortified and still wishing I could just evaporate into thin air, I can't pass up the opportunity to cuddle up to him.

"What do you want to know about him?" I ask as I nuzzle my face into his chest, ignoring the fact that the entire front of his hoodie is damp from my tears. The tension in my shoulders relaxes as his arms wrap around me tightly.

"Anything." He smiles. "Tell me your favorite memories of him."

I pull back a little to look at him, and when his bright eyes meet mine, the rest of my anxiety eases away in the cool breeze as he reaches up and catches a strand of hair between his fingers, tucking it behind my ear. His soft smile warms me in the cool night air as much as his embrace does, and I take a deep breath as I try to think about all of my favorite memories.

"That could take a while." I laugh, leaning over to rub my nose against his cheek softly. It's warm and the feel of his stubble makes me grin. I press a whisper of a kiss to his cheek before pulling back and nuzzling back into his chest.

"I have all night, Abs." He smiles into my hair, pulling me closer.

"Okay." I bite down on my lip, trying to think about where to start as his thumb traces soft circles on my legging clad thigh. "I guess I should start with the most important thing." I grin, catching the string of his hoodie between my fingers. "He was the best dad in the entire world."

He grins and nods, urging me to tell him more as he presses a kiss to the top of my head. I rest my cheek against his chest and tell him about the first memory that pops into my head.

I don't know how long we stayed out in the middle of that field, but I told him everything, every memory that I could still access.

I told him about the time he checked me out of school early so we could go explore the new aquarium by the pier when I was in second grade. I told him about how he used to make me chocolate chip waffles every Sunday. I told him about how we used to watch the same movies over and over until we could quote them to each other, even though it drove my mother crazy. I told him about how he used to leave little notes in my lunchbox for me to find. I told him about how I almost crashed us into an ice cream truck when he was teaching me how to drive. I told him about how he wore one of those joke handshake shocker things when my Homecoming date came over to get me freshman year.

And I told him about my favorite memory of all—the memory I can't believe I could have ever forgotten—how we used to walk hand in hand down the beach, our eyes glued to the dark expanse of black sky, always searching for our shooting stars.

THIRTY-THREE

TRISTAN

I woke up this morning to the feel of Abby's cold nose nuzzling into the crook of my neck. She kissed her way up to my cheek, and then traced every line and curve of the ink etched into my shoulder down to my wrist with a feather-light touch. It was somehow the most relaxing thing I've ever experienced and paired with her fingers dragging gently through my hair, I was dangerously close to drooling all over her pillowcase. When I finally opened my eyes, she smiled up at me with an innocent, *Oh, you're awake, what a surprise* look, as if she wasn't purposely trying to get me up.

That smile turned into something much sexier when she climbed into my lap, straddling my hips while she grazed her lips over my collarbone. I knew exactly what she was doing, and when she pulled back to look at me again, the playful gleam in her eye had me wide awake. My fingers were already looping in the waistband of her pajama pants, but her hands came up to stop me before she wiggled off of me, rolling off the bed and stopping by the door. Her brows were quirked, and a smirk was pulling at her perfect lips, as if to say *Come on, sleepy head, let's go.*

I didn't hesitate for a second. I was out of bed and pulling my sweats up my legs before I could ask where we were going, but to be honest, it didn't even matter where she was leading me, because I know I'd follow Abby Ryan anywhere.

———

I know I should be listening to James right now, but even though he's sprawled out on the couch next to me, absently listening to Greg Bradshaw list off this week's highlights, I can't take my eyes off of Abby. She's wearing yoga pants, which I think she's quickly realizing are my favorite item of clothing, because she smirked at me over her shoulder when she slid them up her legs earlier, wiggling her ass as the blue cotton underwear on her hips finally disappeared under the black leggings.

If we wouldn't have just had sex in the shower, I probably would have been tempted to pull the leggings back down, but since I keep forgetting to buy a box of condoms to leave at her house, we've somehow already managed to have unprotected sex twice. Actually, three times, if the two times in the shower count as separate times, which, I guess they do. We probably shouldn't go for a fourth before she gets on birth control.

"—He said it wouldn't impact his game, but he still seemed really pissed off. I could see him doing something stupid to get back at him on the court."

Glancing back over to James, I blink a few times, trying to get that memory of the shower sex that Abby and I just had out of my head. He's staring at me with a cocked brow, and I know I've been caught, but I try to save face anyway. I wasn't paying attention to the details, but I still got the gist—Luke has something against one of the University of Central Washington players.

"What's the kids name?" I ask, glancing back up at the sports reporter still reading off stats on the TV mounted over their fireplace.

"Grayson Wilder," James sighs, pulling my attention instantly.

"Wilder?" I gape.

Grayson Wilder is the freshman shooting guard on UCW's roster. From the pissed off ramblings I've heard from Luke all season, I've gathered that they played on rival high school teams. I have a feeling he doesn't like him because out of every college freshman in the country, Wilder is the only one who could give Luke a run for his money. Wilder is Luke's own personal Zayn Williams. I get the deep sense of competition, but there's a difference between heated competition on the court, and bad blood, which Luke seems to have with this Wilder kid.

"What's his problem with Wilder?"

"No one knows; he just keeps saying that he's an—"

"Excuse me, can I have everyone's attention, please?" Nia's voice sounds from the hallway, and we both look over from the couch to see her walking past us, straight to the kitchen where both of her roommates are still cooking breakfast.

Both of them stop talking and look up expectantly at their

roommate as she leans against the entryway with a wicked grin. Nia's gaze skims from the girls over to us and then back again.

"Just a PSA—don't forget that I share a wall with the hall bathroom. So who ever had sex in the shower this morning—*twice*—my group project partners heard the entire thing while we were on our call."

Abby's face pales instantly and then flames bright red as she looks down to the cutting board in front of her.

"Hey, at least they don't know which one of us it was, they just know it was one of her roommates," Jenny offers, but it's useless, because if they heard anything at all, it was her moaning my name.

"And while I'm happy you started your day with multiple orgasms—truly, I really am, in fact, I still need to send you a box of chocolates for giving Abby her first one at O'Malley's—I don't think my marketing research group wants to hear it." She looks over at me and smirks before turning back to Abby. "Actually, no, scratch that. The creepy kid, Charles, who I'm pretty sure I caught watching porn in class the other day, looked pretty dazed the entire time. He made up some excuse about needing to feed his fish before signing off early, so I think he might have appreciated it a little *too* much."

I don't hear the rest of Nia's comment because my mind can't seem to stop replaying the same three words over, and over, and over—*her first one.*

Abby isn't looking at me. In fact, she's looking everywhere else but at me. When she turns around and starts messing with the plates laid on the kitchen counter, I know what Nia said is true. I gave her her first orgasm in the bathroom at O'Malley's.

I probably have a dumbass grin on my face, which I try to hide by scratching my chin, but when Abby rounds the corner with two plates in her hands, I know she sees it the second she stops in front of me. I reach out and take my plate from her, and when she scoots over to sit on the cushion next to me, I grab her hips and pull her down onto my lap instead.

She doesn't try to wiggle away like I'm expecting, instead, she scoots back so her butt is on the cushion next to me, and her legs are in my lap. She takes a bite of her avocado toast, and I look down to see that her eyes are already glued to the screen, but I can tell she's not paying any attention to the feature documentary currently playing on

USASN, because her cheeks brighten at my stare. When I lean over to brush my lips gently against the shell of her ear, she shivers before the words even leave my lips.

"Your first one, huh?"

She takes another bite of her avocado toast, but she's trying not to smile, and when her eyes meet mine, I reach over and cup her cheek, tilting her face up to connect our lips. She tastes like avocados and orange juice, and when her soft, content sigh vibrates in the back of her throat as she opens her mouth to let my tongue slide inside, I can't help the smug smile that pulls at my lips, because there's something fucking amazing about knowing that even though I wasn't her first, I was her best.

———

The first time I stepped into the USW arena was on my ninth birthday. I didn't know it at the time, but my dad had saved for months to buy us those two tickets—lower bowl, half-court, so close to the action I swear I could see the sweat dripping off the players' faces. I stuffed myself with hotdogs and drank so much Coke I was practically vibrating in my seat. It was such a close game that I screamed until my throat was raw and I was out of breath, but it was worth it to cheer on the players I had only ever seen as small dots on my TV screen.

I passed out in the car on the way home and woke up groggy from my sugar crash to my dad carrying me into the house. It was the best day of my life. Or it was, up until I stepped back into the arena ten years later with a USW jersey on my back.

It was a true full-circle moment, standing out on the court looking at my parents in the stands. And now, four years later, with only a few games left in my senior season, the energy in the arena ignites when twenty-thousand screaming fans erupt around me as I fake out my defender, stepping back behind the three-point line before releasing the ball.

We're up by one with thirty-seconds left in the second half. UCW is playing better than they have all season, and I know it's because Grayson Wilder and Luke have made it personal from the second they both stepped out onto the court.

Coach caught on pretty quick to the shit-talk and volatile energy flaring between the two, so he put Micah—our best defenseman—on

Wilder to keep Luke from doing something stupid that could get him ejected from the game. But even with a new defender, Wilder has still managed to sink some pretty fucking impressive shots, making sure to rub every single one in Luke's face with smug-ass grins that were clearly meant to say, *Fuck you, McConnell.*

Wilder has the ball now, and we barely have time to get down the court before he shoots, well beyond the three-point line, in the most showboaty shot I've seen in a while. It's a dumbass shot. If he were on our team, Coach would be chewing his ass out right now because there's absolutely no need to be that far out and reckless, aside from wanting to show off. But when the ball finds the net perfectly, he turns around with a smirk and starts jogging back on defense.

Now, we're down by two, and when I glance up to the clock, the adrenaline in my veins spikes as the timer slips under ten seconds. We have one shot. We need a three or we lose our undefeated title, and I can tell by the pissed off look on Luke's face that he might actually explode if we lost it to Grayson Wilder.

Micah's already dribbling down the court, looking around for an open lane right before he passes to James, who passes to Luke—who looks like he wants nothing more than to shoot as a final *fuck you* to the kid defending me—but since his own defender has him boxed out, he doesn't have a clear shot.

I catch the look in his eye when he throws me the ball, and I nod at him before looking Wilder dead in the face. He's flushed and panting, as if he's never played so hard in his life. We're the top ranked team in the league and they've kept us on our toes this entire time, which is impressive enough, not even counting the fact that their senior point guard is out with a torn ACL. But there's a reason why we're number one, so when I step back behind the three, shooting the ball just as the final buzzer sounds, I watch as he turns, wide-eyed and desperate, to follow the ball as it sinks perfectly into the net.

The entire arena explodes, sending a shockwave of adrenaline into my veins as I scan the stadium, searching for the section I know Abby's in.

"Hey, good game, Beck." The unfamiliar voice pulls my attention back to the court and I'm a little surprised to see Wilder standing in front of me. His hand is extended, and I take it, pulling him into a hug so he can hear me over the deafening roar of the crowd.

"Good work out there, Wilder. Keep it up and you'll be a real force next year." I pat him on the shoulder a few times, and when he pulls away, he has a bright smile on his face.

"I know Luke and I don't get along, but I just wanted to let you know that I've always looked up to you, and it was awesome to play on the same court tonight. I can't wait to watch you in the big leagues next year." He glances over my shoulder, and I already know he's searching for Luke. "I guess I should probably go find McConnell and congratulate him," he says it with a sort of scowl as he walks away, but I don't have time to watch Luke and Wilder have a pissing contest because my eyes are already searching the stadium again.

The second I spot Abby in the crowd, she has her arms wrapped around Jenny, hugging as they jump up and down. When she finally pulls away from her friend, she looks back at the court, and when our eyes lock, she beams at me, waving like a kid at a parade. I grin at her as I jump up and grab the guardrail, pulling myself up into the stands. Coach is screaming at me to get my ass back down onto the court, but I ignore him as I hop the rail.

The second my feet hit the cement, random hands are reaching out to slap me on the back, or trying to take selfies as I walk by, but my eyes are trained on the girl in the second row. Her eyes are wide, but her lips pull up into a smile as she watches me push through the exploding crowd to get to her.

I can still hear Coach threatening to beat my ass if I don't get back down to the court, but to be completely honest, I don't give a fuck. I push past the last person in the row of seats and snake my arms around her waist, lifting her feet off the ground as I pull her against my chest. Her loud squeal pulls a smile to my lips, and I know I'm definitely getting her all sweaty, but she still wraps her arms around my shoulders and pulls me close, relaxing into me.

She doesn't seem to mind the sweat when I put her back down, because she tilts her head back to smile at me as she brushes a fallen curl out of my eyes. When I cup her cheeks and look into the deep blue eyes that could damn near drown me, her warm smile nearly stops my racing heart, and I know, in this moment I know that I love her. I guess if I was honest with myself, I've known for a while, but

I can't push it down or ignore it anymore, because I've fallen. Fuck, I've really fallen.

I don't even realize that the entire section of fans are watching us, but when I lean down to connect our lips, the crowd around us explodes. I slide my tongue across her lips, reveling in the way her lips pull back in a smile against mine, because she knows exactly what I'm doing. I'm claiming her. I'm announcing to the entire school—hell, to the entire world—that she is mine. That Abby Ryan is my girl. And when she knots her fingers in my hair and pulls me closer, I know that she's claiming me, too.

THIRTY-FOUR

ABBY

I've already finished three glasses of water and the entire loaf of complimentary bread since the hostess sat me down at this table ten minutes ago. I'm anxiously eating just for something to do to keep my mind off of the fact that my mom is here, in Washington, moments away from sitting across from me for an entire dinner.

I'm buttering another slice of bread when I spot her white-blonde hair. She's in a perfectly tailored black pantsuit, and the sound of her heels clicking against the marble floor rings out like warning bells.

I stand up, smoothing out any creases in the skirt of my white dress, and when she stops in front of me, her eyes survey me as she reaches out and wraps her arms around my shoulders. She's never been a hugger—I can count the number of times she's actually hugged me in the past four years on my hand—but I'm guessing that her first visit to Washington is enough of a momentous occasion to warrant one. That, or she's well aware that we're being watched by the surrounding tables, and she has to keep up appearances.

I wrap my arms around her, and the familiar Chanel perfume surrounds me, but she's already pulling away and sitting down before I can really appreciate the way it makes me feel like a kid again.

"How was your flight?" I ask, pulling my napkin back into my lap as I sit.

She's already flipping through the wine menu, and her eyes don't look up when she says, "Terrible. It was delayed, turbulent, and there was a crying child sitting next to me. I wasn't able to get much work done." Her eyes finally flick up as I nod, trying to seem sympathetic. "I have a meeting tomorrow morning with Roger Mangarelli to discuss buying his firm," she says, flagging the waiter down with a flourish of her perfectly manicured hand. He spots her quickly, and she puts in her drink order before looking back at me. "He moved up here after he retired and has been running it remotely for the past few months, but I have a feeling he's going to be inclined to take my offer. I've already acquired quite a few of his clients since he left." She smirks, leaning back in her chair.

I nod encouragingly, because if I can keep her talking about herself, then that's less time that I have to talk about me.

"How's work?" I ask, reaching for another piece of bread to butter.

"It's great. We hired on a few new interns." The way she says it pulls my attention back to her, and when her smirk deepens, I already know something is about to piss me off. "I've been meaning to tell you—well, I figured you would find out when you come back for spring break in a few weeks—Tyler is now interning at the firm."

Of course, he is.

"Tyler's an accounting student, why would he be interning at a law firm?" I don't try to hide my annoyance because this is absolutely ridiculous. And she definitely wasn't going to tell me. She was going to wait for me to come home and stop by her firm for lunch or bring her something that she *"accidentally"* forgot at home, just to have me run into him.

"Law firms require accountants." She shrugs, smiling up at the waiter handing her the wine glass. He glances over at me before leaving, probably trying to see if I want some kind of alcohol. I'm sure I look like I could use it, but I don't even want to know what my mother would do if I pulled out my fake ID in front of her.

"Okay." I shrug, making a mental note not to randomly stop by my mom's office when I'm back home.

"He wanted me to tell you that he said hello." She's watching me over her wine glass, but I look down to the untouched bread on my plate and wait for it in *three, two, one.* "Ignoring his texts is rude, Abigail."

There it is.

"I've just been busy." And I don't really want to talk to him.

"Well, you should at least text him back and tell him that you're going to be down for spring break. Maybe you two could go out for lunch, or coffee, or dinner. You know, to reconnect."

That's a no—a hard no—but I just shrug and nod because I'm picking my battles here and I'd rather wait to get lectured about this when she's not sitting here in front of me.

"But enough about that. How have you been doing? I know about your *good* grades." That's a stab at my 3.9. "And your hectic work schedule. But how's everything else? How are the graduate school prospects?"

My throat dries out at the question, and I take a long, drawn-out sip of my water, trying to waste even a few seconds of time.

Luckily, the waiter comes by before I'm able to respond, and I'm saved for the next minute while he collects our orders. They've been the same since I was a kid—salmon for her, and some variation of pasta for me. I went for the three-cheese mushroom ravioli, but when I handed my menu to the waiter, I was tempted to reach out for his hand and hold him here, because she can't possibly lecture me with a stranger here to witness it. But instead, I watch him walk away, like my last life vest floating off with the current.

"So." She raises her brows, and I swallow hard. This is it. This is what I've been dreading since she told me she was coming to Washington.

"They're good." I nod, and then mentally slap myself for using the stupid word she hates so much. "I mean—it's going well, I've heard back from a few schools." There, that's a safe landing, I think.

"Just a few? It's nearly March, Abigail. You should have heard back from nearly everywhere by now, aside from the ones who are waitlisting you."

"Right—I meant that I've heard back from almost everywhere." I amend. My hands are smoothing out my dress under the table to get rid of the excess sweat now permeating from my palms.

"And what's the verdict?"

"Georgetown, Stanford, Berkeley." I try to think of the other acceptance letters sitting in my desk drawer right now, but I'm kind of blanking because I know she doesn't care about any of those schools, she's asking about one in specific.

"Columbia?" Her brow raises only slightly.

"I haven't heard back from them yet," I lie. "But I'm sure I'll get the letter any day now."

"I'm sure they're not sending out acceptance letters this late, and if they are, it's because you were waitlisted, and I'm honestly not sure which is worse." Her laugh is humorless, and the comment stings, because she's right.

Not about Columbia—I've known for weeks that I wasn't accepted there—but about NYU. Why would they wait so long to send an acceptance letter? They wouldn't.

"You know, if you would have joined student government like I told you to, you probably would have gotten in." She leans back in her chair and blots her perfectly painted lips.

It physically pains me to not roll my eyes, but I somehow manage to keep my attitude to a minimum as I nod. I looked into student government my freshman year after she lectured me about extracurriculars for an hour on my first day of classes. I quickly realized that the entire organization was pretty much run by the political science majors, which makes sense, but it also meant that my chances of making it into a spot were slim to none. That, and the fact that I really, really didn't want to be in student government.

So, with the newfound realization that I was truly a country away from her, I never stopped by the office to turn in my application to run. It was the most liberating feeling to drop the application straight into the trash, and I even went out with Jenny and Nia to an ABC party that night to celebrate. The memory of Nia wrapping me in layers of pink streamers flashes in my mind, and I realize that the ABC party on the first night of freshman year was actually the first time I ever saw Tristan. He was hard to miss. You can't exactly look like him and fly under the radar, especially not while only wearing a bit of caution tape wrapped around his hips.

"What do I always say, Abigail?" Her words pull me out of my daze, but I know exactly what she's asking because she's asked this exact question a million times. *What do I always say, Abigail?* is her favorite segue into a lecture.

"You reap what you sow," I mumble, grabbing for my water.

"You reap what you sow," she repeats. "And since you decided to take the easy way out and not apply yourself during your undergraduate, you're going to have to deal with those consequences in graduate school."

"I'm a section editor on the university newspaper," I remind her. "And I have a job, and I volunteered at the animal shelter three times a week last semester."

I kind of got sucked into the last one. I was walking through campus to get to the newspaper room when I saw a pen of puppies in the courtyard. I couldn't just walk past that, I'm not heartless, but in order for me to play with them, I had to speak to the shelter coordinator who had me signed up to volunteer before she could finish telling me about the entire litter of puppies who had to be euthanized that morning because of a lack of resources. Needless to say, I cried for the rest of the day, but I ended up loving my time volunteering at the shelter.

"How many journalism students do you think are on their university's newspaper? How many have jobs? And I'd hardly say playing with dogs all day is real humanitarian work. Don't tell me you really thought you were going above and beyond. You were taking it easy, and we both know it. And for what? To graduate with a 3.8 and a few volunteer hours?"

I have to bite the inside of my cheek to keep from screaming *3.9, I have a fucking 3.9*, but the tears now burning my eyes are enough of a distraction because I refuse cry in front of her.

"I didn't come here to fight with you, Abigail."

My brows raise on their own account, but I bite my tongue to keep from saying something to set her off. The waiter comes out with our food before she can say anything else, and I keep my eyes down so he can't see that I'm on the verge of a breakdown as I pull apart the last slice of bread and shove a piece into my mouth. He sets my ravioli in front of me and leaves quickly, apparently picking up on the tense energy.

"Why don't you tell me about that article you're writing for the scholarship Nana mentioned?"

"There's not much to tell. I wrote an article for a scholarship and now I'm waiting to hear back." I shrug and pick up my fork, pushing my ravioli around, hoping that my appetite might come back.

"Don't be a smart-ass."

My eyes flick up and connect with her icy blue stare. She considers me for a second before bringing her wine glass back up to her lips, as if daring me to keep pushing her.

This is the fine line we've walked my entire life. She pushes and pushes and pushes, and when I finally start to snap back, she dares me to keep going, to see what will happen. I've never actually been brave enough to do it.

"It's a feature article." I sigh, and when her lips quirk up, I suddenly feel like I'm nine again, getting in trouble for whatever it is that she decided to be mad about that day.

"Okay." She nods. "About who?"

I sink down in my chair a bit and spear my fork through a ravioli a little too aggressively. When I look up, she's watching me expectantly. I could have finessed my way around all of the other questions, but this is direct, and there's no way to get around it.

"A basketball player." When her brows pull together, I sigh. "The article is for USASN. That's who's offering the scholarship." I can already see the disapproval in the set of her lips. "I don't have to use the scholarship money towards a sports journalism degree, I can put it toward any kind of journalism, I just have to write a sports-related article for the scholarship," I explain quickly. When her brows relax and she sits back in her chair, I know I've just avoided a very unpleasant conversation.

"Well, that should be easy then. I can't imagine you're going to have much competition if you're going against sports journalism students." She smirks at me, daring me to disagree, but I don't take the bait.

"So, you're writing a feature article on an athlete." She shakes her head, as if she couldn't possibly wrap her mind around the idea of anyone wanting to read a feature on an athlete. It's a bit dramatic, even for her, because our TV was turned onto USASN most nights, and she definitely knows how big sports journalism is.

"Yes."

"So, who's this basketball player that you're writing about?"

"Just a guy I go to school with." I'm avoiding specifics here because I like the fact that my two worlds are completely separate. She can't try to control that part of my life if she doesn't even know it exists. "He's actually really good; there's a lot of media coverage on him since he's going to the NBA, so I'm hoping that'll help my article and my chances of winning the scholarship."

"Tell me about him." She places her wine glass down on the table to start eating, and when I tell her about him—without giving away too many identifying details—she just nods, as if she's genuinely interested in hearing about the star basketball player from my school. I make sure to hit all of the main points that I wrote in my article because I feel like I have to prove to her that I know what I'm doing. That I know how to write a good feature article. That it wasn't a mistake to major in journalism like she always told me it would be.

"It sounds like a riveting read." She puts her fork down and picks up her wine glass again. I can't tell if she's being sarcastic, so I nod and pick up my own fork, just to have something to do with my hands. The ravioli doesn't look very appetizing, but I ate so much bread before she got here that I'm too full to eat anyway.

"How did you meet him?"

"Oh—well, he's kind of a friend of a friend," I say as nonchalantly as possible, glancing up to see that she's sitting back in her chair now with her wine glass pressed against her lips.

She nods and runs her index finger down the stem of her glass. "When did you meet him?"

"January," I say, thinking back to the formal.

"And how long have you been sleeping with him?"

My breath catches in my throat the second I register her words and I start coughing. It takes a full minute of loud, eye-watering, people-turning-around-to-stare-at-me coughs for me to clear my windpipe, and when I look back at my mom, she's frowning at me.

"I—what?" I reach for my water and practically drown the entire thing to soothe my now raw throat.

"How long have you been sleeping with him?" She repeats herself in a slow, condescending tone, as if I was too stupid to understand her the first time.

"I'm—why would you—I'm not—"

"Don't insult me, Abigail. I'm not an idiot."

I'm about to protest again, to try to slap a huge detour sign on this conversation and steer it toward something less painful—like my obvious shortcomings as a daughter, or all of the reasons why I'm not as good as my brothers, you know, all of the conversation topics that she loves most. But her icy blue stare holds me in place and I can't seem to speak.

"Are you really going to make me ask a third time?"

"Not long." My voice is barely a whisper, but she heard me loud and clear because her lips are pulling into a scowl.

She closes her eyes for a long moment before opening them again, and when her icy stare meets mine, I sink into my chair a little bit. "You know the most disappointing thing about all of this isn't even that you're sleeping with him, it's that you don't understand why you shouldn't be. And maybe that's my fault. Maybe I sheltered you too much. Maybe I wasn't hard enough on you. Maybe I should have thrown you into the deep end and made you learn how to swim instead of coddling you so much."

I'm mortified that I just admitted to having sex with Tristan to my mother, especially since we've never actually spoken about sex, aside from the *you need to wait until marriage* rule that she laid down for me when I turned fifteen. But more than anything, I'm confused, because I don't think her anger has anything to do with the fact that I'm not a virgin. It seems like she's more upset about *who* I'm sleeping with.

"You don't even know him." It comes out as a whisper, and I don't know if she even heard me.

"I thought I raised you better than this. I thought I raised an intelligent woman. But it seems to me there's still a foolish, immature little girl sitting in front of me."

The words hit me like a slap to the face.

"I'm foolish for having a relationship? For caring about something other than my career for two seconds of my life?"

It's a low blow, one that I thought would slide past that metal exterior she always has up, but she doesn't even seem affected as she shakes her head.

"It's not about having a relationship. You can have a relationship and still be successful, that's not my point. You're foolish for sleeping with the subject of your article, Abigail," she snaps.

"What does that have to do with anything? It's just an article for a scholarship. You're blowing this way out of proportion." I shake my head, trying desperately to understand where this is coming from.

"You don't even see it. Your head is so far up in the clouds you have no sense of reality, do you? No idea of what life is really like." She considers me before putting her wine glass down on the table and leaning forward, making sure I don't miss a single word. "You have no idea what it's like to be a woman in a male-dominated field. You have no idea what it's like to go to work every day and have to work twice as hard as any man there just to be seen. To gain the kind of respect the men around you get handed from the beginning. But you will, because journalism and law are one and the same, Abigail. They are both fields dominated by men who will only view you as a pretty-faced airhead until you demand to be seen differently and earn their respect. And if you come in with an already tarnished reputation, you might as well just quit now." She sits back and her eyes flick around the room, making sure that we're not pulling the attention of those around us.

I'm trying to process her words, I really am, but everything has slowed down around me, and I can't seem to compute what's going on. I know what she's saying is true, though. I've heard countless stories from the women at my mother's firm who left their last job because their bosses treated them differently than their male coworkers. Hell, even Nia experienced it over the summer when she had an internship at a PR firm. She was given a stack of paperwork and a tiny cubicle while the male interns were brought into closed-door meetings to pitch ideas. It happens. It's real. But what does that have to do with Tristan?

"Reputation in the professional world is everything, and a good reputation once lost is lost forever. The worst thing you could possibly do is make a reputation for yourself as a journalist who sleeps with the people she's writing about."

"We're not just sleeping together, Mom. He's my boyfriend. We're together, we're—"

When she shakes her head in one curt jerk, my words catch in my throat.

"It doesn't matter. The only thing they're going to see is that you crossed that line. That you took a professional situation and turned it inappropriate. Whether it works out in the long run or not doesn't matter."

"So then I won't ever bring up the article. I'll keep it out of my portfolio, I'll—" Only I can't. Even if it was sent straight to the trash at USASN, I already submitted it to the school paper. The paper that was sent out to print this afternoon. Any time someone searches my name, that article will come up. It will be tied to me forever.

"I know it's not ideal, I'm sure you really like this boy, but you have to think about—"

"I love him." It's barely a whisper, because that's all I can seem to muster.

She considers me, brows raising in surprise, before taking a deep breath. "I'm not trying to be cruel, Abigail." She sighs as she sits back in her chair. "I want the best for you. I have always and will always want the best for you. I just need you to open your eyes and look around— look at how the women in your field are treated, look at how women who crossed that line are treated. Look at the facts. But please, don't just rely on the future you see through your rose-colored glasses."

My hands shake in my lap as her words wash over me.

A good reputation once lost is lost forever.

"Don't ruin your career before it even has the chance to begin, Abigail. Not for a man. Not for anyone. You didn't work this hard your entire life to let it be taken from you now. Or at least, I hope I raised a strong enough woman to know that she deserves better than that."

I know she's still talking, still lecturing me about being better than this, but I can't hear anything other than the distant echoes of her voice as I try to piece everything together. To think of something, anything, that could fix this. My eyes burn as I try to blink back the tears, and since I don't want to cry in front of her, I look down to my hands in my lap. I try, I really, really try, but when her words echo through my mind again, the first few tears fall onto my hands.

I want to ignore it, to deny it, to brush everything off and will my-self to believe that she's wrong, that she couldn't possibly be right, but as much as I want to ignore her warnings, I know that she is.

Her chair scrapes softly against the floor as she stands, and I glance up, watching as she reaches into her purse. She pulls out a small stack of cash and places it onto the table before stepping back and pulling on her coat.

"I should head up. I need to prepare for my meeting tomorrow."

She hesitates as she fixes the collar of her coat, and for a second, for one infinitesimal moment, I almost think that she's going to come to hug me. That she's going to wrap her arms around me and hold me. But instead, she sighs heavily and turns on her heel, walking straight toward the door without a second glance.

I'm not really sure how I manage to walk through the restaurant and out of the lobby while holding my composure, but the second I close my car door behind me, I break. I shatter into a million pieces as her words replay over, and over, and over in my head.

Don't ruin your career before it even has the chance to begin, Abigail.

Not for a man.

Not for anyone.

THIRTY-FIVE

It's almost ten, and even though I should be studying for my organic chem test tomorrow, I let Luke and Micah convince me to join their NBA2K tournament. We're three games deep, and somehow, I've won every one so far. I have no fucking clue how, especially since I haven't actually played in a while, but since I've beat Luke nearly every game, and his puffed up ego can't seem to wrap his head around that, he's been bitching the entire time. Apparently, it's only because he *"gave me the good controller"*—the one that hasn't been brutally disfigured from him and Micah slamming it down like assholes every time they lose a game—which, to be fair, is probably true. But regardless of how it's happening, it's really pissing him off.

"What the fuck?" He stands up from the couch as my player steals the ball from his, as if standing is somehow going to give him an advantage. "This game is fucking glitching! Did you see that shit?"

I honestly have no clue how this is happening. Luke should be beating my ass right now since this is all he and Micah seem to do when they're not in class, practice, or getting fucked up at a party. He's usually impossible to beat. I'm more shocked than he is that I'm actually winning.

"Right in his fucking mouth." I laugh, watching the replay of my player dunking a nasty one in his player's face. Micah leans over and slaps my outstretched hand, and we both watch as Luke stares in disbelief at the screen. It's pretty clear from that play that his controller was glitching, but when I glance back at Micah's damn near giddy smile, I know we're in agreement that we're not going to admit it.

"That's—no, fuck that—no. This is fucking bullshit." He flings his controller down into the couch and we all watch as it bounces high off the cushion and hits the floor with an incriminating crack. I glare at him as he rubs his hands through his hair roughly, because that's now the third controller he's broken.

"Whatever. I'll buy a new fucking controller," he snaps.

"Don't blame the controller, bro. You just fucking suck," Micah calls, tossing another chip into his mouth. Luke flips him off before disappearing into the kitchen, where the sound of a beer top popping off and hitting the counter echoes through the living room.

Micah grins at me, the kind of smile reserved for rare, fleeting moments like this when Luke McConnell finally isn't the one rubbing his 2K wins in our faces.

"I want a rematch." He calls out as he rounds the corner into the living room. I toss the controller to Micah and get up, stretching my arms above my head to get those three cracks from between my shoulders. My legs still fucking burn from the three miles coach made me run during our morning workout yesterday for my stadium jumping.

It was still worth it.

"I'm tapping out for the night, boys. Abby should be here soon." I glance down at my phone, hoping to see something from her, but aside from the usual stream of texts in our team group chat, there's nothing new from the one person I actually want to talk to right now. I was supposed to get a FaceTime from her two hours ago after she got out of dinner with her mom, but instead I got a text—*I can't talk, but I'll see you soon.*

I have a feeling dinner didn't go well, so I already raided the pantry for some candy, threw my hoodie in the dryer to keep it warm, and have *Love Island* waiting for us on the TV in my room. I was expecting it, though. Most people don't look like they're about to death march straight into war before they have dinner with their mom, but that's exactly what Abby looked like—like she was preparing herself for the worst.

Before she left for dinner, she was dressed like she was going for a job interview, and paced the house like she'd explode if she wasn't constantly moving. I could tell it was just nerves, because when I pulled her down into my lap and buried my face into her neck, pulling her close, she finally relaxed, even if it was just for those five minutes.

I can't imagine being that anxious to see my family, especially not my mom, but I guess that explains why she's always so excited to come with me whenever I have to stop by my parents' house, even just for a few minutes.

Luke makes a whipping sound as I walk into the kitchen, but I ignore their laughs because I know they don't get it. Hell, I didn't get it until a few weeks ago. I was so focused on my one and done mindset that I didn't even know what I was missing. But after a week of being with Abby, I can't imagine going back to that—to before.

I have someone to text all day, which I honestly thought would be annoying, but every time I look at my phone and see a text from her, I smile like a fucking idiot, because I know it's either going to be a corny joke she just thought of, a meme she saw online, or her saying how much she misses me after only being away from me for a few hours. It's also pretty game-changing to have someone there when shit goes wrong. I never thought it would feel so good to have someone to call up and complain about my organic chem professor, or Coach when he's in an extra pissed off mood, but she just lets me rant until I'm not even mad anymore and then she says some cheesy inspirational quote that makes me laugh. Somehow, I always end up at her apartment by the end of the phone call, knocking on her front door and grinning down at her as she answers with her phone still pressed to her ear. And the sex—God, the sex. The sex is fucking incredible. I mean I could go on and on about it, but when I think about my favorite parts of Abby, the sex doesn't even make the top three—hell, the top ten—because every other part of her is that fucking amazing.

I grab two water bottles from the refrigerator, and when the three soft knocks from the front door sound, Luke makes another whipping sound. I flip him off as I walk past, and when I pull open the door, it takes me a second to register Abby's puffy face and swollen eyes.

"What's wrong?" I take a step toward her and reach out for her hand, but she brings it up to her mouth and shakes her head as the tears well. They start to spill over as her shoulders shake in a silent cry.

Her eyes flick to my two roommates on the couch, and when I glance over at them, they're both looking away at nothing in particular, but they're suspiciously quiet as they try to listen in.

"Can we go to your room?" The raspy croak of her voice makes me wince, because it's the voice of someone who's been crying for a while.

I nod, stepping back to let her inside. When I follow her through the living room, both Micah and Luke turn to the black screen of the

TV, pretending like they don't know what's going on. Abby doesn't look over at them, she just walks through the living room toward the hall, and when she pushes open my bedroom door, her shoulders fall when she notices *Love Island* on the TV and the pack of candy on her nightstand.

"Abs," I say softly, tossing the two water bottles onto the bed before reaching for her, but she takes a step back from me and pulls her arms across her chest in a sort of hug. That's when I realize she's still crying so hard that her entire body is shaking.

"Abby, please." I take another step toward her, but she shakes her head and takes a step back, and I swear to God, my chest feels like it's going to break open.

"I—I can't hug you, because if I hug you, all of the resolve I've managed to find in the past two hours that I've been driving will dissolve and I—I just can't, I just—" Her voice breaks into a soft sob and she closes her eyes as she takes a deep breath. When she opens her eyes again, she nods slowly, as if she's mentally giving herself a pep talk. Her eyes are focused on the USW logo printed on the front of my hoodie when she speaks again.

"I just realized how careless I've been, how *stupid* I've been, and I'm so sorry that I didn't realize this before . . . before we got this far." Her voice cracks again, and when another sob slips through her lips, she brings her hands up to cover her face.

I shake my head, dumbfounded as I push my glasses further up the bridge of my nose. The knot in my throat is growing, but when I take a hesitant step forward, she pulls her hands away from her face, and I know she doesn't want me to touch her. The realization is like a slap to the fucking face, because from the day that I met her, she's never looked at me like that.

"Is this about the condoms? Because I know it was stupid, but I went to the store today, and we could get that Plan B pill if you're worried—"

"It's not about that." She shakes her head, bringing her hand up to wipe her nose on the sleeve of her coat. Her mascara has already started to run, and the sight pulls me back to the other night in the field.

"We can't be together anymore, Tristan."

The words stab straight through my chest, and I don't know how long it's been since I've been able to inhale air, but I'm starting to feel light-headed. She doesn't even give me a chance to try to answer, though, because she's already going again, speaking so quickly I can hardly keep up.

"I need to focus on myself and my career, and I can't be with someone who I wrote an article on. It's unprofessional. It's disreputable. It makes me look like I sleep with everyone I interview. And I can't have that kind of a reputation going into grad school, I've worked too hard to get to this point and—"

"We're not just *sleeping together*, Abby. You're my *girlfriend*," I interrupt, but she just keeps going, like I didn't say anything at all.

"I need to be realistic about this. I mean, you're going to get drafted in a few months, and you're going to get a ton of media attention, and they're going to dig, really, really dig into your life, because that's what they always do. And there will be no hiding this—" She motions between us. "—And if I'm being honest, I don't want to have to hide my relationship. I want to be able to get married, and have babies, and not worry about whether or not people will put the pieces together, and have my whole career fall apart because of one stupid fucking article."

I've never actually heard her curse before, and it catches me a little off guard, but she doesn't miss a beat. "—But I can't go my whole life waiting for the other shoe to drop, Tristan. I can't wonder when it'll get out, or what people will think of me when it does."

My brows pull together because I'm confused as fuck. *Marriage? Babies? Articles?* I can't keep up. But I can't even try to unpack all of that, because I can't focus past the fact that she's saying all of this because she's leaving me.

She's leaving.

"You're leaving me because of the article." My voice breaks, and I bite down so hard on the inside of my cheek I can taste blood, but it's that or cry, and that's not going to fucking happen.

She's silent for a long time, and I realize it's because she's crying again. She turns away from me, and when the strangled cry echoes through my room, I swear my chest cracks wide open. When she finally turns around again, she wipes her tears from her face.

Fuck. Even now, right in the middle of Abby fucking dumping me, all I want to do is reach out and pull her to me, to wrap my arms around her and hold her until she stops crying.

"I'm so sorry," she croaks while taking in a shaky breath. "But it's better now than in a few months when we're in too deep, right?"

I'm surprised when a harsh laugh bubbles out of my chest, and her eyes widen as she looks up at me.

"It's a little late for that don't you think, Abs?" My voice is hoarse, and she winces at my words.

I don't think I could be any deeper than I am now. I'm in deep, as deep as you can be, too fucking deep, and I don't know if I'll ever find my way out.

"I'm so sorry."

I'm sorry. The famous last words.

I'm paralyzed as she walks past me, and when my bedroom door closes, the knife in my chest turns until every part of me feels like it's on fire. Like I'm burning from the inside out.

I pull open my bedroom door, stopping at the end of the hall to see Micah and Luke staring at me wide-eyed on the couch. And I know, I know that they just heard it all because they're both on their feet already, moving quickly as if the wound tearing open my chest is somehow visible.

Micah runs into the kitchen, reappearing with a bottle of rum. His voice is clipped as he uncaps the bottle and passes it to me. "Tell James to get home now. We're getting shit faced tonight."

Luke pulls his phone out, but I don't bother trying to catch what he's saying to James because all I can seem to hear are her words echoing over, and over, and over in my head.

We can't be together.

We can't be together.

We can't be together.

I'm sorry.

I take the bottle from Micah, bring it to my lips, and fucking chug.

THIRTY-SIX
PART A

TRISTAN

She never came back.

I don't know what I was expecting when I watched her walk out of my bedroom, but falling asleep drunk as fuck, staring at my black phone screen wasn't it. I was practically seeing double, and even though my blood was drowning in enough whiskey to make my world spin, there was one thing that was clear as fucking day—she was gone.

She's been gone for a while. Or, at least it feels like it, but that might just be because I've been distracting myself enough to not have to think about specifics anymore. I don't want to think about how long it's been since she looked up at me like she didn't even want me to touch her. I don't want to think about how many times I've picked up my phone and almost called her. I don't want to think about the amount of times I damn near spiraled and drove to her apartment. I don't want to think about the fact that even though it's been five days since she walked away, the echo of her is still here, feeding me that dangerous bit of hope that maybe she's not really gone, that maybe she'll come back.

I held onto that hope on the first day when Micah and Luke took me out to a bar in Creekview, a run-down town twenty minutes south of Pullman. It was a shit hole, but they had cheap beer and whiskey strong enough to make me forget why I was even sitting there in the first place. Luke bought me enough liquor to drown myself in, and by the time we walked out of the pub, I was stumbling so hard he and Micah had to practically carry me back to the Uber. Which, thinking back now, was pretty fucking impressive since they both went drink for drink with me. We were all sloshed, damn near numb to the world when Luke called shotgun and Micah dropped down into the backseat beside me. Micah's not one to talk about feelings, which is why, even drunk off my ass, I was surprised when he gave a slurred speech in the back of the Uber about how much he looks up to me. He rambled on about how someday he wants to be as good of a man as me; about how I'm more family to him than I'll ever know; about how he knows things will work out for me, even if they're pretty fucked up right now.

He shook his head with a short laugh, as if he couldn't believe he was actually giving me a pep talk. When he ran a rough hand through his hair, I knew that for him, it was his way of trying to help me, to be there for me in his own way, in the only way he really could. It didn't last long, though, because even drunk as fuck, Micah doesn't keep his walls down for long, no matter who you are. I'm pretty sure I blacked out after that, because the last thing I remember from that night was Luke laughing his ass off about how soft Micah was getting, and Micah knocking him in the back of the head.

I held onto the hope that maybe she was struggling as much as I was on the second day. We had an away game, and as I sat in the airport terminal, hungover and numb, I scrolled through her Instagram for two hours. I'd scrolled so many times I'd practically memorized the captions to each picture, and when I got back down to the very first one—the one of her and her dad—I scrolled back up, desperately hoping that she'd finally post something to her story. To give me some idea of how she's doing.

She never did.

I managed to push it all down by tip off, to focus some of that built up anger and frustration into my game, but a few hours later, I was four beers deep, trying to drink enough to forget my own fucking name while the rest of them were celebrating. I was pretty fucking successful, and by the time I stumbled back into the room, I was pulling out my phone as I kicked off my shoes.

The resolve to give her space shattered with that last drink at the bar, but before I could press call on her contact, James snatched my phone out my hands and shook his head.

"No, T. You can't, you said you wouldn't."

I did say that. I was five whiskeys deep at O'Malley's the night she left when I gave a shitty pep talk to myself about not breaking; about giving her space; about letting her process this; about giving her time to realize that she still wanted me, that she wanted to come back. It ended with James nodding along sympathetically as he downed his own drink in solidarity, and when I shook off the feeling of the liquor burning my throat, I promised myself that I wasn't going to do something stupid—like call her in the middle of the night and beg her to come back to me.

But that was the first night—the night I was still selfishly holding onto the hope that *she'd* break before I could—and two days later, things had changed. Namely, the realization that this wasn't some kind of fucked up nightmare was finally starting to set in. Waking up without her small body cuddled up against me, or smelling the vanilla apple spice of her whenever I'd nuzzle my face in her neck or she'd climb onto my lap, or the sound of her gasps, and laughs, and squeals, and moans—all of it, I fucking missed all of it, and suddenly, the idea of calling her and trying to talk her out of this was the only thing that made sense.

"Give me my phone, J." I held out my hand, watching him expectantly. He considered me for a long moment before taking a step back and shaking his head.

"Sleep on it, man. If you still want to call her in the morning then go for it, but you're drunk and it's late, it's almost three in the morning, and—"

I reached for the phone, nearly snatching it from his hand, but my drunken movements were slower, heavier, and when he juked my hand and tossed it across the room to Micah, I turned and glared at him.

"Give me my phone."

"He's right, T. Ryan's probably asleep anyway. You should just wait until—"

I walked toward him, but his eyes widened when he realized I wasn't fucking around and he tossed the phone across the bed to Luke, who looked down at it wide-eyed, as if Micah just tossed him a live grenade.

I didn't say anything as I walked toward him, and when he took a step back, and then another, and then another, I watched his drunken mind slowly process his options here. He could give me the phone, or I could take it from him.

I was a step away when his eyes flashed in panic and he looked over his shoulder, dropping my phone into the glass of water on the nightstand.

I never got to call her, but then again, she never called me, either.

The third day was a blur of miles on the track—mostly because Coach could tell I was hungover as fuck, and also because somehow, out there on the icy asphalt, things finally didn't feel so fucking heavy. I don't know how long I ran, but by the end, I was throwing up in the trash can on the sidelines. I skipped the bar that night, opting to stay in and crash in bed early, trying desperately not to think about how fucking empty the bed felt without her in it.

The fourth day felt better, at first.

I finally manned up and called my mom back. I'd been avoiding her calls since it happened, not wanting to have to explain why she'd probably never see Abby again. I couldn't avoid it forever, though, which is why I went over before practice. The house was quiet when I walked in, aside from the soft hum of the TV in the living room. I dropped my gym bag down on the floor by the door and walked through the hall, stopping dead when the new frame caught my eye as I passed. It was right in the middle of the wall, shiny and new, and when I stopped in front of it and leaned down to get a better look, my heart stopped in my chest.

She was there, right in front of me, beaming at me—deep blue eyes crinkled in a smile, cheeks slightly flushed. She looked radiant, even frozen in time. I stood there for a while, taking in the picture that somehow blended so perfectly with the rest, as if it was meant to be there, and when my throat tightened as I took a step back, the footsteps from the kitchen pulled me away from her.

"Hi, honey. I didn't know you were coming by." Mom beamed at me as she pulled me down in a tight hug, and when she pulled back, her eyes scanned the room behind me. "Is Abby here, too?"

"No." I cleared my throat and shook my head.

"Oh, you'll have to give her this for me then." She hurried past me, grabbing for the familiar maroon scarf hanging from the coat rack near the door. "She left it at granddad's party."

It hit me all at once—the vanilla apple spice, the soft material spilling over my fingers, the flash of her wearing it, smiling up at me in the passenger seat of my truck.

I'd held it in pretty good since I watched her walk away. I'd pushed it down and numbed myself with enough liquor to make me forget my own name, but when I looked down and met my mom's searching gaze, I knew she knew.

"She's not coming back?"

I looked away and coughed, focusing on pushing down the knot in my throat, but when her soft murmur of my name registered as she pulled me in to a tight hug, I couldn't seem to stop it from fucking wrecking me. All of it. The memory of her—wrapped up in my bed sheets, the taste of her cookie tongue, her warm laugh echoing around us, the feel of her smooth thigh under my thumb as I drew shapes on the exposed skin, her soft snores when she'd fall asleep on my chest, her nightly chocolate milks, her six million different highlighters left around my room after she'd study—of *her*.

I tried to hold it in, I really fucking did, but when my mom's whispered words registered, I broke.

"I'm going to miss her, too, honey."

I cried like a bitch. I cried like I was five again, finding refuge in my mom's lap, and yet somehow, breaking down in my mom's small embrace as she held me close was the first time since Abby left that I didn't feel so fucking alone.

Alone. I guess that's something that I'm going to have to get used to.

THIRTY-SIX

PART B

ABBY

It's been five days.

Five days of randomly bursting into tears throughout the day. Five days of not being able to sleep until Jenny or Nia inevitably crawl into bed with me when they hear me crying in the middle of the night. Five days of not being able to actually hold down anything that I try to eat. But more than anything, it's been five days of wondering if I just made the biggest mistake of my life.

The first day was the worst, but I guess that's how it always goes. I skipped all of my classes, sat on the floor of my shower, and cried until I felt like I was drowning—like I physically couldn't rake in enough air into my lungs. It wasn't until Nia knocked on the door and pulled me out of the ice-cold stream that I realized I was having a panic attack, and it wasn't until she wrapped me up in a towel and held me in a tight hug that I realized my body was shaking so hard my teeth were starting to chatter.

The second day was a little better. I had a shift at the diner, and honestly, it was a nice distraction. Or, it was, until Nancy turned all of the TVs in the diner to the away game broadcasting on USASN. I tried, I really, really tried to not watch it, to not pay attention to the reporters' commentary, but the second Tristan ran onto the court, I couldn't look away.

I stood in the middle of the diner, wide-eyed and unable to breathe as the camera panned across the court to show him warming up. It wasn't until the entire tray of plates slipped from my hands and shattered on the floor at my feet that I finally looked away from the TV.

I think Nancy could tell something was wrong because she sent me home early to get some rest. Only, I didn't sleep, I didn't even change out of my sweater and jeans before I crawled into bed and watched the entire game on my phone, not paying attention to anything else but the man in the crimson jersey and curls running across the court.

I stayed up until four in the morning staring at my phone, hoping that he might call, that he might break and need to hear my voice. Because I knew, in that moment I knew, if he called me and told me he wanted me, I wouldn't be able to say no.

I spent most of the third day drunk. Hammered, actually.

I climbed onto the kitchen counter and raided the alcohol cabinet above the refrigerator. I sat on the kitchen floor while I drank the co-conut rum and ate the rest of the Hershey Kisses that Tristan bought me for our FaceTime movie date. It didn't take long before the com-bination wreaked havoc on my empty stomach, and I spent the rest of the afternoon—and most of the evening—sitting on my bathroom floor throwing up.

When Jenny got home from school, she found me asleep on the bathroom floor clutching his hoodie, which wouldn't have been that embarrassing if it was just her that found me, but it wasn't. James also got to witness that shining moment of glory, too.

I was still too drunk at that moment to care, so much so that I couldn't actually stand on my own. James had to carry me into my room, where Jenny pulled my shirt over my head and helped me into one that didn't have vomit on it. I guess I'm not as skilled as I thought at drunk vomiting, but I did manage to keep his hoodie clean, so I guess even hammered in the middle of the day, I had my priorities straight.

I don't remember much from that day, other than patting James on his cheek affectionately while he carried me through the hall. Apparently, I made him pinky promise not to tell. I passed out before I could tell him who, but I think we all knew who I was talking about.

Thursday was the first day I made it to classes again. I showed up to chemistry fifteen minutes late, just so I could peek into the win-dow and abort mission if he was there. He wasn't. In fact, I found out pretty quickly from the kid at the table next to ours that he hasn't been in class all week either.

I guess it was a little relieving, but also incredibly disappointing, because if I was being honest with myself, all I really wanted was to see him again. And not as a tiny dot on my phone screen.

I made it through all five classes without breaking down, which was a pretty big win for me, so I went to the cafe on campus to reward myself with a coffee. That's where I saw him. Only it wasn't the person I wanted to see; it was the person I'd been unintentionally ignoring for the past week—Dean.

I knew I owed him an explanation, because after he texted me Sunday morning, apologizing for not being in touch for the past week since he was in Georgia for his sister's wedding, I never texted him back. He didn't seem angry with me, so I couldn't exactly say no to him when he asked to sit down and talk. I just nodded and followed him to the same booth that we sat in the last time we were there.

I spoke first, because the last thing I wanted to do was draw this out, but I didn't know where to start. A lot had happened since I'd seen him last. I'd had a boyfriend. Broken up with said boyfriend. And now I'm drowning in the after of it all.

I kept it simple and said that I didn't think we should see each other anymore. That I was emotionally unavailable. That I was still getting over my ex. That I wasn't interested in pursuing anything. I wanted to be as clear as possible, even if it was a little harsh.

He seemed shocked, which I guess makes sense because the last time we saw each other, we had kissed. We had sat in the booth of Over Easy and ate dinner together. But so much has changed since then.

I was fully expecting him to get up and walk away, but when he just nodded and said "*okay,*" I didn't really know what to say. *Okay*? It was his next words that really shocked me, though. "I understand, Abby, it's alright. I just hope we can still be friends. I've really enjoyed hanging out with you, and I know my friends would kill me if you stopped coming around."

I was too shocked to answer right away, so he reassured me that it would be as friends, just friends, and that he had no expectation of anything romantic to come from it. That he just enjoyed my friendship and didn't want to lose it.

I have to admit, I felt incredibly guilty that I didn't tell him sooner, that I left him in the dark for so long because I was scared of hurting his feelings. When the words left my lips, it took a second for me to realize that it was me who said them. But I didn't regret them, because I was genuinely interested in staying friends with him.

"Why don't you guys come to Jenny's birthday party tomorrow?"

I could tell he definitely wasn't expecting that response, probably because he hasn't seen Jenny since the puke incident with Nia, but it's more of a party-party than a birthday party, and she *did* tell me to invite whoever I wanted to. Plus, it's at O'Malley's, so it's definitely not a private party.

He just smiled and said he'd check with the gang and let me know. He ended up paying for my coffee before getting his to go, leaving me standing there feeling like not everything in my life was crashing down around me.

Now, it's day five, and while I've managed to make it the entire day without crying, I'm still not sure if I'm ready to see Tristan.

"I don't think he's even going to be in there." Nia shakes her head, linking her arm in mine. I've been standing outside of O'Malley's for the past five minutes trying to build up the courage to walk through the doors, but every time I try, I chicken out.

When she pulled up with Emery, she hopped out of his car and hurried over to me, wrapping her arms around me because she could tell by the tears welling in my eyes that I was on the verge of another breakdown. It didn't help when Emery gave me a quick nod, a cold nod, a *We're not cool anymore, Ryan* nod before walking into the bar. Nia glared at him, but I just shook my head, because I know I deserve it. If the tables were turned, I'd do the same.

"If he's in there, we'll take a few birthday shots with Jenny and then dip. No talking to him, no looking at him, and absolutely no fucking him in the bathroom, no matter how good he looks. Deal?"

A smirk pulls at my lips and my chest tightens painfully when I realize how foreign it feels to me now, how out of place. Her smile falters when our eyes meet, and when mine start to well, she steps forward and wraps her arms around me, squeezing me tightly as I try to blink away the tears threatening to fall.

"I know this is hard, but you're doing the right thing, Abs. You're doing what's best for you. If this was him, if his career was on the line, he would do the same."

I nod and squeeze her tighter to me, reveling in the flood of memories her perfume conjures. It hits me all at once, all of our memories from the past four years. All the nights we spent on the couch watching murder documentaries and eating take out. All the parties she pulled Jenny and I out to. All the times she sat in the library with me, way past the time she was done studying, just so I wouldn't be there alone.

If I wouldn't have met Nia and Jenny, my entire life would be different right now, and that alone is reason enough to walk through those doors and celebrate Jenny's birthday with her.

"I love you, Abs," she says, pulling away and grabbing my hand. "Just remember, the code word is pineapple. You say that, and I'll get us out of there real quick."

I grin, nodding at her as she beams at me, and when she pulls open the door of the bar, I follow my best friend inside.

————

My plan of action was to stay sober—to hang out with Jenny and leave before I could get too overwhelmed. I even have a new episode of *Love Island* and a frozen pineapple pizza waiting for me at home. Except, things haven't gone to plan, because I am now *very* drunk. James bought Jenny twenty-two shots for her twenty-second birthday, which is pretty cute, but also kind of ridiculous. How is anyone supposed to finish twenty-two shots?

She didn't even try, instead, she pulled James, Nia, and I up to the bar with her and divvied them between us. Nia and I were both responsible for five, and James and the birthday girl took the two extras. I was going to try to get out of it, but when Jenny gave me her signature pout and begged me to get drunk with her—*"It's my birthday, Abs!"*—I couldn't say no.

So, here I am, five shots deep, sitting at the bar trying to figure out whether it's the alcohol, the free chips and salsa, or the fact that Tristan is across the room playing beer pong that's making me feel nauseous.

I've been trying not to look at him, but ever since Nia left me to go pee, I haven't had someone to distract me so I've already managed to look six times. Six times. It's been like thirty seconds.

I stuff another chip into my mouth and bite down on it a little too hard while staring at the rows of liquor bottles on display behind the bar. I know he's been watching me. We keep locking eyes, and every time his eyes widen a little, as if in question, wondering if it's okay to come up to me. But each time, I look away, because I don't know what I'm supposed to do. I've never had to deal with being around an ex-boyfriend. My last ex lives across the country, so I never had to worry about running into him at a bar before.

When my text tone sounds, I dig it out of my purse and look to the entrance to see Dean, Viv, Sam, Jack, and Dillion all walking through.

I wave at them, but I don't think they see me, so I jump down from my stool—taking a second to steady myself, because I almost face planted on the way down—and ease my way through the crowd. My boot-clad feet get stepped on twice as I edge through the mass of people, and I nearly trip and face plant—again—over a rogue shoe on the ground, but I somehow manage to break away from the sea of people unharmed to greet my favorite group of law students.

"Hey, lawyer friends." I grin and wave. My hand feels incredibly heavy and slow from the tequila, and I can already hear how slurred my words sound, but it just seems to amuse them because they all smile at me.

"Drunk Abby is so cute," Viv says, pulling me into a hug. "Thanks for inviting us. We've never been to this bar; I hear it's where all of the jocks hang out."

Her eyes are already searching the bar behind me with a mischievous smile. Sam pulls me into a hug and grins when I wobble as she releases me.

"I need a few of whatever you've had." Her hands latch onto my shoulders to steady me, and I honestly don't have any excuse besides just being incredibly drunk because I'm not even wearing heels. I'm in a sweater, jeans, and ankle boots.

Dean grins as he steps closer to clear the walkway to the door for a group of drunken sorority girls to pass by us.

"Already sloshed and it's only nine. You make me proud, Abby." Dillion holds out his hand, and I slap it with terrible aim, almost missing enough to slap him in the face.

"Holy shit, that's Luke McConnell," he balks, looking straight over my head. I glance over my shoulder to see Luke leaning against the bar. He's a whole head taller than everyone else around him, and he's talking to the bartender while his arm rests casually on the shoulder of a blonde girl I don't recognize.

"Do you think he'd take a selfie with me, or is that weird?" he asks, already taking out his phone.

"Dude, be cool," Dean chides.

"Why have we never come to this bar before?" he muses as his eyes scan the rest of the bar, widening every time he catches sight of one of Tristan's teammates. Jack is straining his neck to see over the crowd too, and when Dillon's gasp sounds, I nearly jump from the way he reaches out and grabs Jack's arm.

"That's Tristan fucking Beck."

I never thought I'd hear Dillion squeal, but there it is.

"What, where? Where? I don't see him?" Jack cranes his neck, and when his eyes land on the back section of the bar near the beer pong, his eyes widen. "Oh, my God, he's looking over here."

My stomach tightens and I tuck my hair behind my ear.

"Act cool," Dillon says, looking away toward the wall next to him. "Do you think he'd sign an autograph for me?" he asks, still looking at the wall, as if that's somehow more natural than just talking to us.

"An autograph? Really, Dil?" Sam snorts, crossing her arms across her chest.

Dillion turns to look at her with raised brows, as if he can't believe she *wouldn't* want an autograph. "Do you realize how good he is, Sam? He's projected to be the first draft pick . . . he's the leading scorer in the entire league . . . he's probably going to win MVP this year . . . he's going to . . ."

"Okay, okay, I get it." She snorts, holding up her hand to stop him. "Go get your autograph before your head explodes."

"You're laughing now, but when you see the resale value on it in two years, I'll be the one laughing my rich ass to the bank."

"I think you need a drink," she decides, linking her arm in his and leading him toward the bar. Jack and Viv follow close behind them, and I turn to follow when Dean's voice pulls my attention.

"I'd love to say hello to Jenny. We all chipped in for a present. It's just a gift card to the cafe on campus because we didn't know what she would want." Dean smiles, sliding his hands into his pockets.

"Oh." I blink a few times when I register that he's asking me to introduce him again since he hasn't seen her in so long. "Right, sure." I nod, looking over my shoulder to try to find her white-blonde top knot over the crowd. When I finally catch sight of her standing with James near the lounge, I nod for Dean to follow me.

Passing by the bar, I catch sight of Dillion's excited smile as he holds up the camera to get Luke into the shot. Luke seems unfazed by it, like he's used to people coming up and asking for pictures, and when his lips pull back into a casual grin, I can tell that even though he'd never admit it, he secretly likes the attention. I'm sure it doesn't hurt to have the girls around him see him taking pictures with fans. That must be a real aphrodisiac for some of them.

I lead us through the crowd, taking a little longer than I probably should because the tequila has my head spinning now. Dean doesn't seem to mind our slow pace though, and when I glance over my shoulder to make sure I haven't lost him, he smiles down at me. When we finally make it to the edge of the crowd, I spot Jenny with her head tilted back in a laugh as James whispers something in her ear. Another group of people cut me off, and I wait for them to pass before hurrying forward, but it's only after I round the corner toward the lounge area, that I notice they aren't alone. Nia and Tristan are standing beside them, and when his emerald eyes catch mine, my heart clenches painfully in my chest.

We've been avoiding each other this entire time. Or really, I've been avoiding him. When I saw him walk in a few minutes after Nia and I did, our eyes connected across the room instantly. I slid off my stool and made a break for the bathroom, where I did three rounds of deep breathing exercises, cried a little, gave myself a pep talk in the mirror, reminded myself that I'm doing this for my future self, cried a little more, and then pulled myself together and walked out. I cycled through each stage pretty quickly. All in all, I was probably in there for ten minutes, but it worked, because I stepped out with the intention of not letting myself run into him. I've obviously done a great job.

"Hey, Abs," Jenny squeals, wrapping her arms around me and pulling me into a clumsy hug, as if she didn't just see me twenty minutes ago by the bar. I let her squeeze the breath out of me for a few seconds before she lets me go and beams at me.

I glance down at her hands to see she has a nearly empty liquor glass. She definitely didn't stop at the six shots, and I can tell by the way she's smiling at me that she's gone—like outer space, on another planet, see you in another galaxy kind of gone. I glance over at Nia, and she nods as if to say, *Oh yeah, she's a level ten right now*. Level ten for Jenny means one thing: affectionate babbling.

"I've missed you, Abby Bear, where have you been? You look so pretty tonight. Doesn't she look pretty, guys? You're so beautiful. You're my best friend—and Nia, too—" She looks over her shoulder and reaches out a hand for Nia to grab, as if she doesn't want her to feel left out. "I just love you guys so much. I'm so glad you came out tonight, Abs. I know you've been having a rough week. But I won't tell anyone that you cried while looking at your favorite dog accounts on Instagram yesterday. I promise that will be our little secret." She closes her lips and tosses the key over her shoulder.

"Okay, that's enough of that," Nia interjects, tugging Jenny closer to her and wrapping her arms around her in a hug while sending me a *I can't believe she just exposed you like that* look. My eyes flick to Tristan, who's rubbing the back of his neck, and I'm shocked to see that he looks like he's trying to hold back a smile.

My legs buckle, and I know it's because they're dying to run to him. To wrap my arms around his neck and hold him. To tell him how sorry I am. That I'm wrong. That I don't care about the consequences. That I want him no matter what. But even drunk and wanting, I know that I can't do that, because I'm not wrong, I just want to be.

When the sound of a throat clearing echoes beside me, I glance over to see Dean. My eyes widen and I smile sheepishly up at him because I completely forgot he was even here.

"Oh, right, I'm so sorry. Dean, you remember Jenny and Nia." I point to them, and he nods with a smile, and then my eyes flick to the rest of the group and I hesitate.

Tristan's smile is gone. It's been replaced with a scowl as he stares at Dean, as if he just realized that he wasn't a random stranger standing near us. I feel his energy change instantly, and my anxiety flares because I've never actually seen him look so pissed off.

"This is James, Jenny's boyfriend. And this is Tristan, my—" I hesitate and falter for a second, and when the words tumble out, my cheeks burn, because I didn't mean to say them like that. "—My Tristan."

Tristan's eyes flick back to me, and they soften instantly as he considers me. I swear my face is on fire now, but I decide to power through and act like that didn't just happen, because otherwise I might die of embarrassment.

I glance over to see Dean's eyes widen as the recognition sets in, but I don't think he was paying enough attention to catch my slip up.

"Hey, it's nice to meet you, man. I'm a big fan. Well, I'm not really a basketball fan, but I've seen a few games and you've got a really impressive shot. I mean that buzzer-beater against—who was it? UCLA? That was really impressive."

Tristan's eyes are back on Dean, and my lungs freeze in my chest at the way his jaw clenches as his eyes flick to the space between us, as if to say, *You're standing too fucking close.*

Dean glances down at me, but when he looks back up at Tristan, he shifts uncomfortably as he takes a small step away from me.

"So, Dean, it's been a while," Nia says loudly, drawing his attention. "How have you been?"

Her eyes flick to me and I know what she's thinking—*This is bad, abort mission, jump ship, get the hell out of here.* But what exactly am I supposed to do?

I know that Dean is answering Nia, but I honestly don't hear anything he's saying because I'm glancing over my shoulder, trying to think of a way to get us out of this silent testosterone battle before it escalates. When I look back at Dean, his jaw tightens as Tristan interrupts him mid-sentence.

"Hey, Drake, why don't you go get a drink?" He nods to the bar, but the way he says it sends a chill down my spine, because it's not a suggestion. "You're looking a little thirsty."

Dean's brows raise, and he stares at Tristan as if he can't believe he just spoke to him like that. I can't believe he just spoke to him like that, and according to James's shocked expression, he can't either. Dean glances down at me before looking back at Tristan, and when his brows pull up, my stomach tightens because that's a light bulb moment—he knows. When I look back at Tristan, he's staring at Dean pointedly, waiting for him to walk away.

"It's Dean," he corrects, but his eyes only meet Tristan's for a few seconds before he looks back over at me. "I guess I could use a drink. Abby, what do you want?"

I blink a few times before I realize he's asked me a question. "Oh, no, it's okay." I shake my head.

"I don't mind." He shrugs, smiling down at me in a sweet way that I know is meant to piss off Tristan. "I'll already be over there, might as well."

"Vodka cranberry," I say quickly, hoping that he'll just walk away and the ridiculous amount of tension that's building to dangerous levels right now will ease.

"Alright, I'll be back." He sighs.

"Take your time, Darwin."

I glare at Tristan, but he's not looking at me, he's smirking at the boy turning toward the bar. Dean glances over his shoulder, contemplating whether or not he should correct him again, but he just turns around without a word and pushes through the crowd. I don't even have time to turn back to the group before his words hit me.

"Can we talk, Abby?"

My chest tightens when I look up to see him watching me. He's already taking a step back, and my throat tightens a little because I know I probably shouldn't be alone with him right now, but I can't even think straight with the liquor coursing through me and the bone-deep longing I have just to be next to him. To touch him. To hold him. To kiss him. To feel his arms around me again.

Nia blatantly says the word pineapple while fake coughing, but I just shake my head as I walk past her. He places his hand on the small of my back as he leads me toward the back of the bar. The crowd parts, as it always does for him, and I try not to focus on how the skin on my back is now tingling where his hand is.

I don't even realize where he's leading me until he opens the door of the women's bathroom, but I don't hesitate as I walk in, because honestly, I'm drunk enough at this point to kick the level headed part of me straight back into that closet and throw away the key.

The sound of the lock clicking into place echoes heavily around us, and I glance around the bathroom, trying to ignore how the atmosphere in the small room is already changing, like the energy around me is finally finding its equilibrium again. Like everything is finally settling into place just by being near him. Like I can breathe again.

He takes a step toward me, and I drop my gaze to the floor when the flare of heat ignites in my stomach at the first inhale of his cologne. My entire body is begging me to take a step toward him, and like two magnets just barely grazing each other's magnetic field, I feel the pull.

"Five days." His voice is hoarse, and when I look up, I see the hard set of his jaw and the desperate look in his eyes. "That's all it took you? Five days to start dating someone new?"

It hits me hard, like a slap to the face, but mostly because of the agonized look on his face. "I'm not dating him." I shake my head.

A harsh, humorless laugh slips through his lips. "Right."

"I'm not. We're just friends. We're here with a group of people."

"Maybe you should tell Dorian that."

"It's Dean—and I have."

"Well, tell him again."

"Tristan."

He looks down at me and I swear my heart stops beating. He's so close, a step away. I could reach out and pull him to me. I could grab his face and connect our lips. I could melt into him and never look back.

"You're not dating him?" he confirms, his jaw still tense.

"No." I shake my head softly.

"Are you—are you sleeping with him?" His voice cracks and the desperate sound freezes my heart in my chest.

"No. No, of course not."

He nods, and his shoulders relax as the tension in his body releases all at once. When his gaze meets mine again, my eyes start to burn, and I know I'm not going to be able to push it down anymore. His brows raise, and he takes a step toward me, slowly, hesitantly, as if he's waiting for me to stop him. But I don't have that kind of restraint anymore, I'm honestly shocked I had it in the first place, and part of me wishes that I wouldn't have had it at all. That I would have let him pull me into a hug and talk me out of this. Out of everything.

"Don't cry, Abs." His voice is soft, and the second his words register, I lose it. He pulls me close, and when his arms tighten around me, every muscle in my body relaxes as the first sob slips through my lips. I wrap my arms around him, clinging onto him like a life vest in the middle of this ocean I've been drowning in for the past five days.

He rubs soft, soothing circles across my back as I bury my face into his hoodie and inhale him, and like the drug he is, he sends a warmth through my body, a high I've only ever gotten right here in his arms.

"Do you hate me?" It echoes through the tiny bathroom in a choked whimper.

"Hate you?" He tenses, and I tilt my head back to meet his searching gaze. His brows are pulled together, as if it's the most ludicrous question. "I could never hate you, Abby." He seems so sure, so certain, and that breaks my heart all over again.

"I hurt you," I argue, biting down hard on the inside of my cheek to stop another sob from escaping my lips.

"Yeah." He nods, looking over my head as his throat bobs with a hard swallow. "Yeah, you did, but it would never make me hate you, Abs."

"You're too nice to me," I whisper, but I look back down and nuzzle into his chest because this could be the last time he ever holds me like this and I don't want to waste a second of it.

"You're my girl," he says it so casually, so matter of factly, that my heart stops in my chest. "Even when you're not my girl, you're my girl."

A new wave of tears spring in my eyes and he reaches down to cup my cheeks, tilting my chin back to look up at him as he searches my face. His eyes linger on my lips and the part of me that knows I should take a step back and walk away is screaming at me; but I don't listen, because I need this, like I need air in my lungs and blood in my veins. I need him.

"I knew what I was doing when I asked you to be my girlfriend. I knew it was a risk. But I don't regret it for a second, none of it, because even if that's all we're ever going to have, it would have still been worth it." My chest tightens as the tears start to spill again, quick and unrelenting, a current of all the heartbreak from the past five days.

His eyes drift to my lips again before meeting my gaze, and I'm desperate to feel them on mine, to lose myself in him, but he doesn't bring his lips down to mine. Instead, he tucks my hair behind my ear and brushes his thumb softly across my cheek. "If I know one thing for sure, it's that life is one big game of high-risk, high-reward, Abs. And call me crazy, or stupid, or fucking insane, but when it comes to us, I don't think I've lost yet."

THIRTY-SEVEN

It's been two weeks.

Two weeks since O'Malley's. Two weeks since Abby broke down in my arms. Two weeks since I told her I wasn't giving up on us. Two weeks since things started to go back to normal—or at least, a new normal. Our new normal.

We're still broken up, which fucking sucks, but it is what it is. I can't change it. I won't pressure her to do something that could potentially hurt her. So, we're here, in a sort of limbo where we find ways to do things that we used to do under the pretense of it being casual, or for school, or as just friends—like FaceTiming.

We've FaceTimed every night for the past two weeks. If anyone asks—which they don't because they know exactly what we're doing—we could say that we're studying, that I'm simply helping her learn the new chapter before the pop quiz. But every night she pulls out her chem notes and absently reads through a few lines before her eyes flick up to the screen and she grins, as if to say, *Okay, I think we're safe now.*

Then we slide into our old normal—or as close to our old normal as we can without crossing any lines. She tells me about work, and school, and how she's getting nervous about NYU, and the bangs she's contemplating getting, and the weird noise her car's been making; and I just sit there, grinning like a fucking idiot, because *she's here.* She's right here in front of me, talking about nothing and everything at the same time, and I know it's not nearly what I want, but it's all I'm able to have right now, and that's okay, too.

I tell her about my days, too. About the family picture my mom printed and hung on the gallery wall, about how hard Coach is running us now that we're days away from the semi-final game, about the organic chem TA that I swear has it out for me, about the house fire

Micah almost set the other night trying to make popcorn on the stove, and how the Raptors, Knicks, Suns, Spurs, and Celtics have all contacted Coach about setting up meetings to talk about the draft.

Her excited squeal was loud enough for Micah to come running out of his room, wide-eyed and searching. When he spotted my phone propped up next to me as I ate a bowl of cereal at the kitchen island, he sighed and walked back into his room. He tried to seem annoyed by the interruption, but I caught the twitch of his cheek before he turned.

He's wearing the same shadowed smile now as he pushes a beer across the hightop toward me. I take it, sipping the cheap beer while keeping my eye on the door.

I would have never agreed to purposely ride out a snowstorm in a sports bar surrounded by a bunch of drunk idiots, but since James told me that Abby agreed to go, I wasn't exactly going to pass up an opportunity to be locked in with her for a few hours.

O'Malley's usually closes whenever a big storm passes through since the roads get closed down, but since it's St. Patrick's Day, they decided to stay open and host a *snowed-in* party.

I wasn't surprised when Luke and Micah decided to go, because getting snowed-in at a bar is something those assholes live for, but I was a little shocked when James said he was tagging along. I guess Emery convinced Nia to go, who convinced Jenny, who convinced James, and all I needed to hear to get my ass here, was that Abby was also coming.

The bar's packed, and since their special for the holiday is dollar beers, everyone's already drunk.

"Is she on her way? The roads are closing any minute," Jenny asks, looking over her shoulder toward the door. "She said she was coming when I talked to her a few hours ago."

Nia reaches into her pocket and pulls out her phone. She presses call on Abby's contact before propping it between her cheek and her shoulder as she reaches for the basket of chips in the middle of the table.

"Hey, babe. Are you almost here?"

I trace the lip of my beer bottle, attempting to look like I'm not eavesdropping, but when she gasps, my gaze darts up to see her eyes widen. My lungs freeze in my chest when I catch the unmistakable echo of a sob.

"Abby, what's wrong?"

I can't hear shit, not with the music fucking blasting and the loud palaver ringing around us, but when another choked sob echoes through the line, Nia cups her hand around the phone, trying to block it out as she attempts to soothe her. She tries to calm her down enough to speak, but it doesn't seem to be working.

The stool scratches loudly against the floor as I stand, pulling everyone's attention as I reach for the keys in my pocket.

"I've got it," I say to Nia, already stepping away from the table.

"The roads are closed, T." James calls after me.

Fuck. He's right. It's past five.

I don't look back as I push through the door and step into the storm; it's a blur of white snow caught in currents of ice-cold wind. My cheeks burn as the frozen air whips around me, already seeping into my clothes as I take another step into the parking lot.

The sound of Abby's sob echoes through my mind again, and I tug the top of my hoodie up, pulling the strings taut to tighten it around me, trying to keep as much heat in as I can. With one final look back at the bar, I start running.

———

My lungs burn from the frozen air as I take the stairs by two, but I don't stop running until my fist connects on her apartment door. My pulse is careening in my chest, sending a wave of adrenaline through my blood. I have no idea how far that was, but whatever the distance, it has to be a new record for me. I guess getting sent out to the track for showing up to practice hungover so many times actually paid off.

I wait a few more seconds before knocking again. When the door finally opens to a dark apartment, it takes my eyes a second to adjust to lighting before Abby's tear-stained face comes into focus. Her arms are wrapped around herself, and she blinks up at me with puffy, swollen eyes.

"Abs." My voice catches in my throat.

I take a step toward her and gauge her reaction, but when she doesn't step away, I pull her into my arms. Part of me is expecting her to step away, to put space between us and tell me that she doesn't want to cross that line, but when she wraps her arms around me, her entire body slumps into me as a sob slips through her lips.

She doesn't seem to mind that my clothes are soaked from the snow, and I hold her tightly as I lead us further into the apartment, kicking the door shut softly. It takes me a few seconds of fumbling in the dark to find the light switch, and when it turns on, Abby buries her face in my chest, muffling a sob that shakes her shoulders.

I tighten my hold on her, well aware that there's nothing I can do to stop the sobs slipping from her lips now. They're frantic and intense, rocking her entire body as she tries to rake in air. I've seen her cry—I've seen her really, really cry—but I've never seen her like this before. Not this bad.

I have no idea how long we've been standing here, but I don't loosen my grip on her until she turns her face away from my hoodie, nuzzling her cheek into my chest as her sobs finally ease and her breathing slows.

I don't release her, and when she relaxes into me, I know that it's helping. Somehow, standing here with me is helping. I rest my cheek against the top of her head, appreciating the feel of her in my arms again. When she finally speaks, her voice is throaty and worn, and I know instantly that she's been crying for a very long time.

"I'm sorry I didn't make it to the bar. I really wanted to, I just—I couldn't handle it."

She tilts her head up, meeting my gaze.

"What's going on, Abs?"

She takes a deep breath and opens her mouth, but closes it again, as if she doesn't know what to say, as if she doesn't know how to say it.

"Can I show you something?"

My brows raise, but I nod. With a deep, shaky breath, she leads me through the dark hall to her room. I hesitate by the door when she picks up her phone from the floor. The screen is cracked to shit, and I don't remember it looking like that when I saw her the other day in class, but she unlocks it as she drops down onto her bed.

She glances up at me standing in the doorway and pats the spot next to her. I drop down beside her, watching her face as she clicks onto the voice recordings she has saved. She bites down on her lip, fighting back another sob, and when she presses play on the recording saved from this date five years ago, my heart clenches painfully in my chest, because I think I know what's happening.

The voice that echoes through the phone is older, smooth, and I know who it is instantly.

"Hey, Sweet Pea, I just got your message. I'm on my way now. I know you said you have a stomachache, but what do you think about a quick ice cream stop? I'm thinking a triple-fudge sundae might be just the thing. You know ice cream always

fixes everything. Plus, it's St. Paddy's Day, we have to celebrate, right? I'll see you soon, honey. Love you."

My heart sinks into my stomach as her body starts to shake again, and when I wrap my arms around her, she melts into me, as if she can't physically hold herself up any longer.

"He was coming to get me from a sleepover because I had a stomachache. I had cramps, freaking period cramps. I called him to come get me instead of taking medicine and just sucking it up."

Her fingers latch onto the front of my hoodie, like I'm going to disappear if she doesn't hold me here.

"I was being ridiculous. They were just cramps. I was fine. I didn't have to call him. I just—I just wanted to come home. I didn't know—I would have never called him if I knew." Her voice breaks, and I swear to God, my heart shatters. "I fell asleep and missed his call. When I saw his voicemail, it was two hours later. He never made it to get me—They found his car rolled over in a ditch. A hit and run. A drunk driver."

Fuck.

I don't know what to say.

What am I supposed to say?

"I'm so sorry, Abby." I tighten my hold on her, resting my cheek on the top of her head. Her body relaxes into mine as I rub slow circles on her back, trying to measure the unsteady rhythm of her breathing under my palms.

When she pulls away to look up at me, I wipe a tear from her sallow cheek. She leans into the touch, and I hold her there, watching the tension ease from between her brows as I brush my thumb across her cheek again. It's a dumbass move. I know I shouldn't be doing this. Holding her while she's upset is one thing, but this, this is something else. Like the dumbass I am, I make another slow, gentle pass over her cheek with my thumb, only this time, a shiver shakes her shoulders at the touch. She tilts her head back, bringing her lips closer to mine, and when her tear-filled eyes flick down to my mouth, my heart pounds painfully in my chest.

This is crossing a line. It has to be.

"Can we—I know we shouldn't, I just—Can we just forget everything." It comes out in a croak, a desperate plea. "Just for a few hours, just while we're here."

My throat is damn near closed as her words echo through my mind.

Forget everything? What does that mean?

"Please." Her voice cracks, and it tears my heart open. "I need to forget, just for a few hours. I need to forget how messed up everything is. I just—I need you." Her eyes flick down to my lips again and she sits up straighter, pulling herself close enough to me that I can feel her warm cookie-tinted breath on my lips.

We shouldn't. It's taken us this long to get back to normal—to our new normal—and I don't want to mess that up.

"*Please*, Tristan."

She leans closer, eyes trained on my mouth, and when her deep blue gaze flicks back up to mine, I can't think straight anymore.

Fuck it.

I pull her lips to mine, and I swear to God, my heart stops at the touch. It short circuits, and it's like every fantasy I've had for the past three weeks come to life, only better, because this Abby is real. Her kisses are urgent, and desperate, and searing as she knots her fingers in my hair and pulls me closer to her, moaning softly against my mouth when I grab her hips and pull her onto my lap. I know she needs this more than anything right now, and a selfish part of me revels in the fact that she needs *me* when she's at her worst. That I'm the one she needs to lose herself in when everything else is crashing down around her— that I'm the one she looks for in the middle of the chaos.

I slide my tongue into her mouth, like a puzzle piece falling into place, and when she grinds herself against my hard-on, already pushing into my zipper, the throaty groan that echoes in the back of my throat makes her shiver in my lap. Every nerve in my body is on high alert as she grinds herself into me again, molding her soft, warm body to mine, like she can't stand for there to be any space between us. I want to feel her skin, and hear her breathy moans, and watch her eyes roll back as she comes undone underneath me over, and over, and over again. But when I bring my hand up to her cheek and brush my tongue against hers, I know I need to tread carefully here. I know she needs a distraction, but I don't want her to regret this. So with all the resolve left in my body, I break the kiss and pull back to see her eyes soften nervously as her brows pull together, as if she's scared that I'm going to bail, as if she's nervous that I don't want her.

I want her. Fuck, want to be inside of her more than anything, but I need to make sure she's really okay with this.

"Abs." I search her flushed face, and when her swollen eyes meet mine, my chest tightens painfully, because I can see, I can actually *see* how fucking broken she is right now. "Are you sure you want to do this? We don't have to—We could watch a movie, or I could make you dinner, or we—"

"I don't want dinner." Her words are clipped and desperate, and when she cups my cheeks and brushes her thumb across the line of my jaw, I'm mesmerized by her. Just by being here, just by being so close, she has me dazed and wanting, and when she licks her lips, I suddenly can't remember why I shouldn't bury myself in her right now. "I want *you*. I want to feel something other than this—I just—I want you to make me feel good. I want you to make my body feel good. I want you to make—I want you to—I want you to fuck me, Tristan."

Fuck me. She's never said that before, but when I meet her gaze, I know she means it. She wants me to fuck her so she can forget. She wants a distraction from all of the shit in her life. I can't do much for her right now. I can't bring back her dad; I can't change what her mom said to her at that dinner; I can't make this fucked up situation go away, but what I can do is make her feel good, so that's what I'm going to do.

Gripping her thighs, I hold her to me as I stand, laying her down on the bed before her shocked gasp can echo around the quiet room. By the time I break the kiss to reach back and tug my hoodie and shirt off, her cheeks are already pooling with that rosy hue I love so much.

It's surreal, being here with her again, but I try not to think about how many times I've fantasized about this over the past two weeks as I lean back down and pull her hoodie over her head, leaving her in nothing but her plaid pajama pants. I hesitate, considering her. She's bright-eyed and flushed, and I can't help the way my chest tightens when I notice the pain that's been pooling in her eyes for the past three weeks slowly easing away. This is helping her—us, here, alone—and if this is all I can do to help her not feel so broken right now, I'm going to fucking do it right.

I pull her lips back to mine, trying not to think about how fucking bad I wish this was happening because she wanted *me* and just not as a distraction, but I shake those thoughts when she unbuttons my pants and tugs them down my legs with an impatient huff. I smile against her lips, because I know this is her favorite part—undressing me.

Her lips pull back into a smile when my thumbs loop in her waistband,

and when she lifts her hips for me, I pull her shorts down her legs, tossing them behind me before reconnecting our lips. Her hands explore my chest and stomach as I explore her mouth with my tongue, grinding my hips into her. When her hand slides down to the waistband of my boxers, I pull away from her eager lips to find her molten eyes staring up at me.

I need to forget, just for a few hours.

I need to forget.

Slipping down between her thighs, I push aside the tiny strip of blue cotton and drag my tongue across her, tasting her, reveling in the sweet warmth of her. She's wet, really fucking wet, and she's already coating my lips as my tongue parts her. I take my time licking my way up to her clit, slow and soft, with just enough pressure to make her head fall back as a tortured moan slips through her lips. She writhes under me, her hips lifting up from the mattress, searching for my tongue, silently begging for more. Gripping her thighs, I pull her legs open wider, and when I look up at her, panting and molten-eyed, with the kind of flush I only get to see when I'm here, between her thighs, I'm desperate to be inside of her.

Bringing my tongue back to her clit, I slip a finger inside of her and rub her g-spot, moving in a perfect echo of my tongue. I smirk against her when her entire body tenses and her back arches off the bed, and when I suck on the bud of nerves, she's coming on my tongue with the sexiest moans I've ever heard. They're breathy and desperate, echoing around the room as I slow my tongue to bring her down softly.

Her chest is rising and falling quickly but starts to slow now as she relaxes into the mattress, limp and sated. I turn my head, brushing the tip of my nose across her inner thigh to place a single, soft kiss there. Pulling back a little, I grin at the glossy stamp left from my mouth, and when I glance up at her, she's propping herself up on her elbows, watching me with rosy cheeks and dark eyes.

Wiping my thumb across my wet mouth, I brush the remnants of her slowly up her stomach. Her back arches and hips twitch, but her eyes don't leave mine. My thumb paints a glossy path, around her belly button, between her full, flushed breasts, all the way up until I'm leaning over her, my mouth hovering just above hers. I can taste her cookie tinted breath on my lips, and it almost tastes as good as she does on my tongue. Bringing my hand up to cup her cheek, her eyes widen and a soft inhale of a moan echoes around us as I slide my thumb across her lips.

My eyes fix on her lips as I lean down, hovering just close enough to brush my lips against hers as I say, "You taste so fucking good."

Slipping my tongue into her mouth, I'm rewarded with a breathy whimper as she greedily sucks on my tongue, tasting herself while my hand slips between her thighs again. Her hips rock up, grinding against my palm while my thumb rubs circles on her clit. Her hands slip down my stomach, and when her fingers find my waistband, she tugs my boxers down my hips impatiently.

I want to make this last, to take my time with her, but I'm fucking desperate for her and every moan, and whimper, and gasp makes my dick twitch in her hand. Sitting back on my knees, I slide her underwear down her legs, tossing the cotton fabric onto the floor. I hesitate when I realize that I don't have a fucking condom. It's not the first time I've fucked her raw, but I run a rough hand through my hair as I say, "Fuck, Abby, I don't have a—I didn't bring a condom."

She shakes her head quickly, and the last thread of control snaps when she practically pants, "It's okay, it's fine."

Grabbing her hips, I flip her over onto her knees, grinning at her sharp gasp as she grabs the headboard to steady herself. I grip her ass as I slide into her, reveling in the sweet moan that she tries to quiet as her head falls back. She feels so fucking good, so much better than the fantasizes I've been clinging to for the past three weeks. Her hand is pressed against the headboard, holding her in place, and with each stroke, deep and hard, her moans echo around us, drowning out the sound of the snow pelting the window.

Reaching down, I find a quick rhythm of my thumb on her clit, reveling in the sight of her grip on the headboard tightening as a salacious melody of whimpers echoes around us in the moonlit room. When her legs start to tense, I pull my hand away, smirking at the breathless, indignant groan that slips from her lips.

"Not yet, baby."

I need this to last a little longer, and if she comes now, I know I'll be right behind her. Tightening my grip on her ass, I try not to think about how fucking tight she feels, but that doesn't last long, because when she arches her back, I clench my jaw to hold back the groan as the added pressure sends a shock of pleasure up my spine. When turns her head, I catch the smug smile on her lips.

My thumb is still wet from her, and I'm tempted to suck it clean just to taste her again, but when she arches her back a little more, I clench my jaw as I bring it to the base of her spine, slowly trailing it up her back. Her soft inhale only encourages me, and when I lean down to her soft, fragrant skin, I drag my tongue up the wet trail of her spine. Reaching her ear, I brush my lips back down the column of her neck before grazing my teeth across the soft plane of her shoulder.

She feels so good, so fucking good, and I have to focus all my attention on not blowing this too soon because I've been desperate to be inside of her for three fucking weeks and now that it's happening, I want to savor every second.

But as good as this feels, this isn't how I want to come, not now, not when this could be the last time. I pull back, sliding out of her, and when she looks over her shoulder, she rolls onto her back, wrapping her legs around me to pull me closer. She brushes her fingers through my curls, gasping against my lips as I slide back into her. Her moans, soft and breathy, match the unhurried pace of my hips, moving in deep, lazy strokes as I fuck her slowly.

I've had a lot of sex in my life, but I've never made love, not until now—not until Abby.

She reaches up and traces my lips with her finger, slowly, intricately, as if she's committing the shape to memory, and I can't seem to tear my gaze away from her eyes, which already look so much brighter than they did moments before. When she finally drops her hand from my lips, I reach up and push her hair back behind her shoulder before brushing my thumb against the sweet spot on her neck. A shiver runs down her spine at the touch, but I can't seem to look away from the skin, because it's completely healed from the hickey I gave her last month.

She watches me for a moment before she tilts her head, exposing the skin to me, and when my eyes flick back to hers, my heart rate spikes, because I know what she wants. I don't hesitate to connect my lips to the skin there, and my tongue tastes her with slow, languid lick. My hips speed up, and when a raspy moan slips through her lips, I smile against her neck before biting down and starting to suck.

I take my time, reveling in the way her body is molded to mine, moving with me, perfectly in sync. Her lips brush against the shell of my ear, and when I nudge my hips forward, harder than before, those sweet, breathy moans fill my ear.

Pulling away, my eyes lock in on the already budding bruise, and I brush my thumb against it slowly, trying not to think about the fact that my place in her life will fade faster than this mark on her skin.

I think she can sense my spiraling thoughts, because her finger pokes my cheek, right where my dimple is, trying to pull me back. When I meet her eyes again, she smiles up at me. It's a real a smile, and seeing it for the first time in three weeks is like looking straight into the fucking sun—it warms me, wholly, completely, from the inside out.

I could stay like this and bask in her warmth all fucking day, but she grins at me as she guides my lips to hers again, and when she bites down on my bottom lip, I'm back.

The base of my spine tingles and I know I'm close. Tragically close. But I can tell by the way her moans are coming out short and fast that she is too, so I reach down and pull her thighs tighter around my hips as I quicken my thrusts, making sure to rotate them in the way that I know she likes. Digging her fingers into my back, she tightens and pulses around me as her head falls back, moaning my name over and over, like a desperate, breathy plea. The sound sends me over the edge, fragmenting my mind into a million pieces as pleasure ripples down my spine and courses through my muscles.

The familiar sated daze clouds my mind, and when she reaches up and caresses my cheek, I intertwine my fingers with hers, holding it there.

Stay. Stay with me, please.

She smiles up at me, her cheeks radiating that perfect rosy hue that I love so much—the glow that I only get to see right after we have sex. I lean down and brush my lips against the feverish skin, reveling in the feel of her fingers running through my hair gently before she trails her fingertips up and down my back.

I brush my lips across her jaw and down her neck, pressing a gentle kiss to the bruise now growing there. When she pulls me close, I nuzzle my face in her neck, inhaling the intoxicating vanilla apple spice of her.

I want to stay like this forever, wrapped up with Abby while the snowstorm raging outside keeps the rest of the world away; because in this moment I know, this is heaven, this is home.

THIRTY-EIGHT

ABBY

I never thought I'd wake up in Tristan's arms again, but that's exactly where I am when I open my eyes. My mind is still hazy from sleep, but even so, I know immediately that I shouldn't be here. I shouldn't be naked, wrapped up in the bed sheets we were tangled in last night. I shouldn't be cuddled up to him, and I definitely shouldn't be listening to his heart pound surely in his chest, attempting to lull the spiraling thoughts threatening to pull me under.

I know if I close my eyes, I could convince myself, if only for a few more hours, that this is reality. That waking up with Tristan in my bed is somehow still a possibility for us. But even as I try desperately to stay here, in this half-asleep, nothing-in-the world-is-wrong daze, I know I'm lying to myself. Tristan and I aren't together, and tomorrow morning he'll be back in his bed, and I'll be here, alone.

My chest tightens at the thought, and when I look up, I can see the outline of him—his face, his nose, his cheeks, his eyelashes, his curls splayed out on the pillow underneath his head. He's illuminated by the moonlight washing the room in a barely-there, pre-dawn light, and he looks so serene, so complete, so different from how he's looked since we've broken up. He's had a seemingly permanent tension line between his eyes, and he's always so tense, so uneasy, like he's waiting for something else to happen—to hurt him.

I know I shouldn't wake him up, but I can't help myself from tracing the curve of his cheek and the hard line of his jaw. The stubble feels amazing against the soft pad of my finger, and I want to lean over and feel it against my tongue—to taste him, to mark him the way he did me, to commit every moment of it to my memory—because I know this is the last time I'll be here like this with him.

I trail my finger from his jaw, down his neck, across his collarbone, and over his broad shoulder where the expanse of black ink trails down his arm, stopping at his wrist. I've traced the tattoo a few times, it's all swirls and hard lines and abstract designs. It seems like such a part of him, like it was meant to be there. I trace the line down the swell of his bicep, and I can't imagine what he would look like without the artwork permanently pressed into his deep olive skin.

I'm so focused on tracing the lines that I don't even realize he's awake, that he's watching me. He brushes his thumb against the sensitive spot on my neck where I know there's a dark hickey blooming. Closing my eyes, I revel in the touch, smiling at the thought of how the dark bruise must look—like a tattoo pressed into my skin by his rough mouth and warm tongue. His thumb brushes over the bruise again, and when I look up to him, he's considering me, as if he's trying to focus wholly on this moment, too.

I should apologize for waking him up, but I can't seem to find the words, because his eyes have mine locked in place. When he slides his hand up to cup my cheek, my pulse quickens in my throat.

Could this be it for him?

The morning after. The sober-minded regret.

Does he regret this?

His brows pull together as if he can read my mind, and then his gaze falls to my lips, and then to my neck, and then finally, to my bare chest, where a rush of goosebumps has spotted my skin.

This is it. This is the last time we will ever be here like this.

The last time his calloused hands will ever trail down my neck and trace my collarbone. The last time I'll feel his thumb brush ever so lightly across the side of my breast as he makes his slow descent to where he traces the tan line on my hip.

His eyes linger on his thumb tracing the line of tanned skin, and when they slowly make their way back up my body, I can tell that he's trying to commit this moment to memory. That he knows, too. This is the last time.

My chest is rising and falling quickly by the time his gaze meets mine again, and the pressure is already building in my stomach from the lightest, most innocent of touches. He knows my body better than anyone, than even me, and when his thumb brushes over the small freckle near my belly button, a shiver shakes my shoulders.

"I love this freckle." He runs his thumb over it again. I watch his fingers trail down my stomach, lower and lower, and when he scoots down and pulls the sheets off of me completely, my breath catches in my throat.

His eyes flick up to mine and he reaches for my leg, pulling it up as his lips brush against my ankle. "And this one," he muses against my skin. I tear my eyes from him long enough to see that there's a freckle on my ankle I never realized I had.

He leans forward slightly and trails his lips up my calf, stopping at my knee where he gently pushes his nose against me, opening my legs wider so he can press his lips to the freckle on the inside of my knee. "And this one."

His eyes flick up to mine, and that's when I realize that I'm breathless, propped up on my elbows, watching him slowly brush his lips against my knee again. His molten eyes slowly coast down my body before he continues up my leg.

My hips start to move as the pressure between my legs flares uncomfortably. I need him to touch me, to give me relief, but he just keeps his lips on my inner thigh as he slowly moves upward, nudging my legs open wider. I know where he's going next, and my mind nearly explodes with anticipation as my hips rock again. When his lips stop at the freckle on the top of my inner thigh, I'm desperate for him.

"But this one." His voice has lost all traces of sleep, it's heavy and throaty now, and the sound alone sends a shiver down my spine. "This one is my favorite." He brushes his lips against the freckle ever so softly, lighter than air, and then he rubs his cheek against it. My eyes fly open; the feel of his stubble against the incredibly sensitive skin is like an electric shock of pleasure through my body.

"Oh."

His lips quirk as he looks up at me through dark lashes, and then he lowers his head again, but this time, it's not to my thigh. His breath hits me first, making my head fall back as my stomach knots and unknots, desperate for the touch. His tongue finds the swollen bud of nerves and a desperate, breathy noise slips from my lips as the first shocks of pleasure shoot up my spine.

He wraps his arms around my thighs, and I know he's about to pull me down the bed to get a better position, but he doesn't have the chance, because the three soft knocks on the door make us both jump.

He looks over his shoulder and then back at me, eyes wide as he finds the alarm clock on my nightstand.

"Oh, fuck."

Three more knocks sound before James's muffled voice echoes through the door, "We've got to go, T. We're going to be late."

Tristan rolls off the bed and stumbles around until he finds his boxers. He pulls them up his legs quickly, and as he pulls on his pants, I lean over and grab his hoodie, which somehow almost got knocked under my bed.

He's tugging on his shirt when he looks at me, and I hold out his hoodie to him while biting down on the inside of my cheek, because I don't want to cry. I don't want to ruin this, but when he takes the hoodie from me, I know that he knows it, too. This is it.

Three more knocks sound and Tristan's shoulders tense.

"I'm coming, J. Give me a minute, fuck."

James mutters something about running on a track for being late, but my eyes don't leave Tristan's as he steps towards me. "I'll see you in chem?"

I nod, trying to smile, but I think he can tell that I'm struggling because he leans down and cups my face, caressing my cheek once with his thumb. "We'll figure this out. Somehow, someway, you and I will figure this out. I refuse to believe there's a world where you and I don't find each other in the end, Abs."

I don't say anything, not because I don't want to, but because his words have frozen my lungs in my chest. He presses his lips to mine, and I tilt my head back, opening my mouth for his tongue to slide through to mine. His kiss is slow, and deliberate, and all-encompassing, and when he finally pulls away, his dark emerald eyes meet mine for a moment, and I know that he means it. That he has faith that somehow, someway, we'll be together.

He tilts my head back and connects our lips again in a soft kiss, and then he walks out of my door, leaving me to wonder if maybe he's right. Maybe we could be together. Maybe I was wrong.

———

I'd already convinced myself that everything was going to work by the time I got to chemistry. That Tristan and I were going to be okay. That I was going to go to grad school, and get a job, and no one would care that I was with the man I wrote an article on. People meet their partners at work all the time. It's not that big of a deal.

Tristan sent me a text a few minutes before chemistry started to let me know that he got pulled into a last-minute Skype meeting with the head coach of the Orlando Magic, so he wouldn't be able to make it to class. So, instead of paying attention like I should have been, I started drafting my speech to my mother.

I had bullet points, arguments, and three different plans laid out based on her projected reactions. I was ready to launch into an argument about how *times have changed since you started your career, Mom. Women are respected more now. We don't have to deal with the same issues that you did when you started law. Journalism is different. It's more forgiving. I'll be able to explain myself. I'll be fine. My career will be fine. Everything will be fine.*

But I didn't get to make that phone call, because when I sat down in my Writing for Publication class next to Hanna, one of the girls in my graduating class, she looked so mad I could practically feel her anger radiating off of her like radioactive waves.

"Are you okay?"

She glanced over at me, as if just realizing that I was there, and then she broke. "Have you heard about Danielle Young? I'm fucking pissed," she snapped. "I'm so livid, I don't even know what to do. How could they do that to her? She's been there for *twelve years*. She was the lead female host. She worked her ass off and was one of the most respected journalists at the network. Resigned my ass, they gave her an ultimatum—resign or be fired. It's bullshit. Do you know how many of those hosts have slept with their sources? There's an entire exposé site on Greg Bradshaw. He fucks around more than anyone—and he's married! And did you see his tweet? That guy is a fucking douche, I swear to God. I—"

"Han—" I hold out my hand to stop her because I am not following in the slightest. "I don't know what you're talking about."

Her eyes widen as she pulls out her phone, clicking a few times before handing it to me. It takes a second for me to process the article headline, but when I do, my heart sinks deep into my stomach.

Danielle Young, USASN reporter, and co-host of USASN's Daily Sports Report, resigned after information on her relationship with Chad Wickham was leaked early yesterday morning. Young recently wrote a profile on Wickham highlighting his highly anticipated return to the NFL after his season-ending knee injury last year. The article has since been pulled from USASN's online publication.

"She was fired for it," Hanna says. "But it gets worse, way, way worse." She grabs the phone and opens Twitter, and when she hands it back to me, Danielle Young's name is typed into the search bar. She's trending, and when I scroll through, I instantly recognize the name on the top tweet: Greg Bradshaw, the USASN reporter.

@GregBradshawUSASN: It should be common knowledge, but in light of the recent scandal, all female journalists should take a few hours every night to repeat this little piece of career saving advice—do not sleep with your source.

Oh, my God.

"Keep reading, it just gets worse the further down you go."

@BrettFieldsUSASN: We can't trust female reporters who sleep with their sources. We all know the power a man holds over a woman once he spends the night in her bed. That will always get in the way of the truth.

"Did you get to the one about getting nasty? I hope that guy gets hit by a bus."

I scan the tweets until I find the one she's talking about, and when I read it, my skin flushes white-hot with anger.

@KyleWilksUSASN: Danielle Young was just doing her job. Good reporters know that sometimes they have to get nasty for access. I'm sure this wasn't the first time.

Oh, my God.

There are three trending tags related to Danielle Young right now.

#sleepingwiththesource

#gottagetthatbyline

#nastyforaccess

"She was sleeping with the man she wrote her article on and she got fired," I clarify as I scroll through the tweets. I'm praying that I'll read something else, that some other reason will pop up, but as I read through, it's clear—she's being crucified for her romantic relationship with her source.

"Yeah, they were dating. It ended and somehow it got leaked that she was seeing him. She resigned, and now this shit is blowing up, and I've already read three articles about how *'often women reporters are secretly successful because they use their sex appeal,'* and how we *'can't get good interviews without using sex as leverage,'* and how we *'are never going to be taken seriously as professionals until this stops happening,'* it's insane." She crosses her arms across her chest and leans back in her chair with an exasperated look on her face.

"And yet no one cares when the male reporters have their relationships leaked. It's not sensationalized; it's not smeared across the media and internet for entertainment. It's buried. It's glossed over. It's *just a part of the industry,*' apparently. Greg Bradshaw isn't allowed to interview the Women's Olympic swimming team anymore because he was so inappropriate with them that they cut access. Does that get covered? No. He has a different reporter stand in for him, and he moves on without issue because he's a big name and the network doesn't want to lose him."

"That's so—" I don't even know how to finish that sentence.

That's so what?

Fucked up? Unfair? Sexist?

Yeah, all of the above.

"Poor Danielle," I breathe, tapping on her Twitter account. She hasn't tweeted since yesterday afternoon. Before the news broke, I'm guessing. The last tweet is of her smiling with a WNBA player for an interview. The blonde-haired journalist looks so happy in the picture. She's beaming at the camera as she holds her mic with the USASN logo—like it's a trophy. Something to be proud of. Something that she earned. Not anymore, apparently. Now it's being ripped from her hands.

My chest tightens as it all starts to sink in.

This happened today. A few hours ago. Danielle Young, a respected lead host journalist was fired for her relationship with her source.

I stand up and hand Hanna her phone back.

"I need to go," I mumble, pushing my seat back under my desk as the uneasy rumble in my stomach starts to make me nauseous.

"Abby?" she calls, but I don't look back.

I hold my hand up to my mouth as I run through the hall, pushing past the crowd of curious onlookers as I shove the door of the English studies building open. I want to make it to my car, to not throw up in front of all of these people, but I don't have much of a choice, because the second that my fingers wrap around the freezing cold metal of the trash can, I lean over and watch my stomach empty in a mess of bile as Danielle Young's smiling face flashes in my mind again.

Like an omen.

Like a warning.

THIRTY-NINE

TRISTAN

"What the fuck is going on out there? This is embarrassing. Is this your first little league game, ladies?" Coach slaps his clipboard against the locker, sending a loud crash echoing through the silent visitor's locker room.

The only sound left is the heavy breathing of my teammates, and I look away from Coach who's starting to turn an angry shade of red. My eyes find the floor, watching the sweat from my face drop down to the tile as I sit with my elbows on my thighs. Adrenaline is still coursing through my veins, making my knee bounce in place, and all I can really think about is how badly I want to fuck up Ty Marcus, and how grateful I am that Micah and James got to me before I could actually do any real damage.

Luke's own bouncing leg is shaking the bench beside me. I don't have to look up to know he's wearing the same scowl that I am because I can feel his pissed off energy building on top of my own. We've both been antsy all day, and I could feel his anxiety building the entire car ride up here.

I usually wouldn't have minded the forty-minute ride to the University of Central Washington, especially since it's always exhilarating to sit in the passenger seat of Luke's expensive ass sports car while he fucking sends it on the highway. But no matter how fast he pushed it, I couldn't stop thinking about Abby.

She texted me last night saying she felt sick and needed to skip our FaceTime call, which isn't a big deal, but when she showed up to chem this morning looking pale and shaky, I knew something was wrong.

I couldn't ask her about it, though, because the second she sat down, Hannigan started to pass out a quiz. I finished it in a few minutes and sat there watching her struggle through the fifteen questions.

She kept second-guessing herself. Filling in an answer and then erasing. Filling in a new answer and then erasing. I wanted to just take her
damn eraser away because for the most part, she was getting it right
on the first try. I couldn't sit there and watch her erase her entire test
for the third time or I was going to go crazy, so I dropped off my quiz
with Hannigan and waited in the hall for her.

It took her twenty more minutes to finally walk out, and when I
slipped my phone back into my pocket and fell into step beside her,
she didn't look up at me.

"How do you think you did?"

Her eyes were still fixed on her bag as she rifled through it. "I have
no idea. It made sense, and then my mind kind of fogged up and I felt
like I was forgetting a step, but I couldn't remember what it was, so, I
don't know." She gave up searching her bag and readjusted it on her
shoulder as she led us toward the door.

"Wait," I said, stopping in the middle of the walkway. A few people looked up at me curiously as they passed by, but Abby didn't meet
my eyes as she stood next to me. Instead, she absently searched the
passing crowd around us, and that's when I realized that she was trying to avoid me. "Can we talk for a minute? I mean, you look—I know
you said you didn't feel good, I just want to make sure you're okay."

The muscles in my neck tensed the second her deep blue eyes
flicked up to mine, because I recognized that look. It was the same
look she had when she walked into my house crying. The same look
that's burned into my mind like a fucking brand.

Fuck.

She didn't say anything, and when she nodded and led us toward
the small alcove under the stairs to get out of the way of the busy
hall, I tried not to think about the fact that this was really happening
again. After everything, after all of it, she was leaving me again. By
the time she turned around to look at me, a painful knot had already
formed in my throat.

"Do you know who Danielle Young is?"

What?

"The USASN reporter?"

"Yes." She looked down to the phone in her hands and pulled up
a screenshot. When she handed it to me, I was still too distracted by
how fucked up her phone screen was to actually focus on what she

was showing me. I'm pretty sure she threw it against the wall the other day when she was listening to her dad's voicemail before I got there. When I finally focused past the shattered screen, the article title hit me like a slap to the face.

Fuck.

"She was fired for sleeping with her source. Or, she resigned, I guess, but we both know it was that or be fired. Actually, according to the leak, they were dating, not just sleeping together. It was an NFL player that she wrote a profile on. It's our exact situation, only she's a well-established journalist, and I'm a college student who's only ever been published in my school's paper, Tristan. If they fire her without question, imagine what they would do to me. I don't stand a chance."

Fuck. Fuck. Fuck.

I didn't even know what to do other than stare dumbfounded at her because what could I do? What could I say? The evidence for all of the anxiety and doubt that her mother planted into her head was right there in front of us. Like a cosmic *told you so.*

"Scroll to the next screenshot," she instructed, and when I did, my stomach dropped as I read the tweets she had saved.

There were a few smaller USASN reporters that I recognized, and then there was Greg Bradshaw. I had to read it over three times before it fully clicked in my head, before I was able to fully comprehend that this wasn't some kind of bad joke. He's always been a douchebag, but I had no fucking clue it was this bad. I had no idea he was this much of a condescending prick. As if his tweet wasn't bad enough, the hashtags trending with her name were like the icing on the entire fucked-up cake.

#sleepingwiththesource
#gottagetthatbyline
#nastyforaccess

I couldn't even think about Danielle Young, all I kept imagining was Abby being the one mentioned in these tweets. Abby's name being smeared for entertainment. Abby's career being publicly destroyed.

"I—I don't know what else I can do. I mean, even though I won't be in sports journalism, I'll still have this hanging over my head. I'll still be in danger, because the rules are the same no matter what you're writing about. I'm a reporter and you are my source and I took a professional situation and turned it inappropriate." Her voice was weak, trained, as if she'd run through this conversation in her head a million times already. Which, knowing Abby, she probably had. When her eyes flicked up to mine, they were wide and pleading, like she was desperate for me to understand. "There's a chance that—this could mean I'd be giving up my career."

The air froze in my lungs, but even if I could have spoken, I wouldn't have known what to say. She's right. The evidence is clear. The reality is—it's me or her career.

Part of me wanted to ask her to choose me. To just forget grad school and come along with me to wherever the fuck I end up being drafted. To sit beside me on a plane while we fly to new cities, and sleep in new hotel rooms with me every night for my games. To go out and explore during the day and then sit front row in the arena at night and watch me play. To not worry about a career, because I'll make enough for both of us. I'll support her. I'll support us. We'll have more money than we could ever want if my contract is what it's projected to be. The last first pick signed a twenty-million-dollar contract for the first two years—twenty-million for two years of work. I could support us for the rest of our lives, and we won't have to worry about money, or careers, or assholes judging her for wanting to be with me.

But I couldn't say that, because we both know she wouldn't want that. She would never be happy with a life like that. She's too ambitious, she's too independent, and that's one of the reasons why I'm in love with her.

When I looked down at her again, she was trying to hold back tears as she took her phone back from me, because she knew, and I knew, there was nowhere to go from here. We were at a dead end, unless she's willing to give up her career, and as much as I'd love to hear her say those words, I don't think I could actually let her go through with it. Not for me.

"I get it," I said, but it barely came out as a whisper, and I had to clear my throat.

She wrapped her arms around herself, and I knew she was trying not to cry. I took a step back, because I needed to get out of there before I broke the fuck down. Because I knew, that was really it, that was the end of us.

"You're going to be an amazing reporter, Abs."

Her eyes widened slightly, and I wanted to reach out—to kiss her one last time, to brush my thumb over the hickey that she had covered on her neck, to hold her, to pull her to me, to bury my face in her neck and feel her arms wrap around me again, but I couldn't. That wasn't my place anymore. That wasn't what she wanted anymore. So instead, I stuffed my hands into my pockets as I turned around and walked out of the building, straight into the ice-cold rain.

"McConnell, I swear to God, if you don't stop trying to pick a fight with Wilder, I'll run you so fucking hard your feet will bleed. I don't care what the hell your issue is with him. I don't care if he fucked your girlfriend. I don't care if he ran over your childhood dog. I don't care what the fuck he did—when you're on that court, your focus is winning. Do you understand me?" Coach's voice pulls me back, and I catch Luke's jaw tense, as if he wants to say something, but he just nods. That's when Coach's eyes flick to me.

"And I don't even want to know what the fuck is wrong with you right now, Beck." He slams his fist against the locker, but I don't raise my eyes from the floor, because I'm really not in the fucking mood to be screamed at right now and I don't want to snap on him. "Six turn-overs? You've barely made a shot all night, and God damn it, you're just as bad as this asshole." He nods curtly to Luke. "Picking fights on the court, are you fucking insane?"

"He was taunting me," I say through clenched teeth.

The senior, Ty Marcus, who's been defending me all night has been shit talking me since we stepped out onto the court. I'm not new to shit talk, it happens every game. I usually don't listen to it, but when Marcus started talking about Abby, it was like someone was twisting a broken arm.

It started with lame little taunts like, *"Where's your pretty little girlfriend tonight, Beck? Are you going to jump into the stadium again tonight like the pussy-whipped little bitch you are?"* But then he started pushing it, and no amount of elbows to his ribs, or threats to beat his ass if he didn't shut the fuck up were working.

"I can't blame you, Beck, she's fucking hot. I've been thinking about her a lot lately. That ass. That mouth. I bet she's good with that fucking mouth. Maybe I should find out. I bet she's going to sound so fucking sexy moaning my name while she forgets you even exist—Oh, Ty, right there, Ty."

That's when I fucking lost it. I lunged at him, and if Micah wasn't right there to grab me and literally pull me off the court while I was still trying to get to the son of a bitch, I probably would have fucked Marcus up past recognition. Because it was like he was stabbing an open wound—the one thing I haven't been able to stop fucking thinking about since I walked away from Abby. She's going to move on and find someone new. She's going to get married, and have kids, and be happy. And even then, I'll still be here, thinking about her, wishing that somehow it could have worked, wondering what it might have been like if things were different.

FORTY

I've been running a lot lately.

Running mile after mile on the track as punishment for showing up hungover as fuck to practice every day. Running to keep my mind on something, anything other than the memory of Abby leaving me again. And running from the terrifying reality that she won't ever come back, no matter how much I want her to, because she can't.

"Okay, listen up."

I don't look away from the inside of my locker as Coach's voice echoes through our locker room. His pissed off level has finally eased back down from *might have a heart attack any second* to his normal *kind of pissed, but easily set off* level. He's adjusting his tie for the hundredth time since he walked into the locker room an hour ago, and I feel the anxiety radiating off of him from across the room.

"This is a big one tonight. This is what we've been working for the entire season. Every sunrise weight room workout, every practice that ran late, every sprint, every mile on the track, every minute that you've put toward this sport was to get you to this point. I have confidence that we'll be able to keep our undefeated title, but you need to be the ones who believe it. You need to be the ones wholly focused. You need to not let those assholes get into your heads again like UCW did. Otherwise, you can kiss Vegas and the final goodbye. This is a mental game as much as it is a physical one and you need to be prepared."

Luke tenses beside me, but his petty rivalry with Grayson Wilder isn't what Coach is talking about. He's talking about me almost getting into a fist fight and beating the shit out of Ty Marcus for talking about Abby. He's talking about me losing my cool on the court for the first time since I've played for him. He's talking about me needing to get my head back on straight because this is the biggest game of the year, aside from the final, and I can't fuck it up for us.

There's more media coverage on this game than any other we've had this season. News reporters from every major sports network are already lined up in the lobby waiting for the pre-game interviews to start. This is a huge game for me, and Coach's eyes are boring into my back, like he's trying to make sure I know it.

I know it, how could I not?

Every muscle in my body has been painfully tense since I woke up this morning, and while it's easy to say that it's because of the game tonight, I know that it's not. It's because I wake up every morning still expecting to see Abby in bed next to me, cuddled up in my arms while her soft snores ease me back to sleep, just to enjoy the moment for a little bit longer. But she wasn't there this morning, she hasn't been there for a while, and that's been weighing down on me more than any game ever could.

And even though I know I should be trying to relax and focus, I can't seem to stop thinking about her—about whether or not she'll be at the game, if she's just as fucking broken as I am, if she's already called up Damon for a date to help her move on, if she's already forgetting about me.

Luke's elbow knocks me hard in the ribs, and I look up to see Coach staring at me. His mouth pulls down into a deep frown as he narrows his eyes.

"What? Sorry." I sit up, clearing my throat.

He narrows his eyes even more, as if to say, *You better get your head straight. If you lose this game because you're not focused, I will kick your ass.*

"Our team interview is about to start," he repeats. "Everyone needs to be suited up and ready to walk out in twenty minutes."

"Okay." I nod, already standing up to pull off my shirt. Coach gives me one last look before turning back around and closing his office door. The second the click echoes through the silent locker room, everyone breaks into normal locker room antics, but I don't have to look down to know Luke's watching me anxiously.

"What?" I snap, pulling on my dress shirt.

The press interviews before the game have a strict dress code, suit and tie, as if interviews couldn't get any worse.

"You're good, right? This whole Ryan thing isn't going to fuck you up tonight?"

I don't look at him as I button up the shirt, because honestly, I don't know. "I'll be fine." I shrug, pulling on my dress pants.

"I—I know Micah and I have just been pouring liquor down your throat for the past few days, but you can talk to me, too, if you need to. I can be there for you, you know, like you were for me. Fuck, we can even go up to the rooftop again. I'll get a twelve pack and—"

I shake my head curtly, cutting him off. "I'm good, Luke. I'll be fine."

Brody, my old captain, brought me up to the rooftop of O'Malley's my sophomore year. I was drunk and spiraling. It was the first time I'd bombed in a game. Everything about my game was off that night, so much so that Coach pulled me and benched me for most of the second half. Watching the USASN reporters fucking shred me for it after didn't help. I ended up getting drunk as fuck with Micah—who somehow drank even more as a freshman than he does now—and when Brody pulled me away from the bar top where I was doing body shots off the two jersey chasers I went home with that night, I didn't argue as he led me through the back door into the alley. I watched, confused as fuck, as he looked up, searching the building. It wasn't until he jumped up and grabbed the bottom rung of the fire escape ladder that it clicked in my head.

We sat up on the rooftop for a while, and somehow, being up there, I didn't feel like I was drowning in it all anymore. The voices of the reporters weren't so loud and watching the headlights of each car slowly pass by reminded me of being a kid, sitting in that field in Creekview with my family, looking up at the stars again. He knew I needed that—an escape, a hideaway, somewhere where turnovers, and shooting percentages, and assists didn't fucking matter.

I took Luke up to the rooftop last Christmas Eve, and it wasn't until we got up there, buzzed and cold as fuck, that I realized I was following in Brody's footsteps. That I was now the captain offering refuge to the person who needed it most. He looked out at the small town he'd only known for a few months like it was home. Like watching the cars pass slowly, and the drunk college students stumble down the snow-covered sidewalks, slurring out butchered renditions of Christmas carols as they went, was exactly what he needed. We sat there for a while, silently watching the glow of the Christmas lights shine off the fresh snowfall below, and then he looked down at his hands and broke down.

As much as I'd like to ditch this interview and watch the sunset on the bar rooftop right now, drowning my sorrows in cheap beer, I can't. And even if I could walk away from all of this, I wouldn't want to talk about it. I can't talk about it. Not with Luke, not with Micah, not with James.

The one time I even tried to talk about it, I ended up breaking the fuck down in my mom's arms. So, I've been holding it in. I've drowned myself in enough whiskey to fuck up my liver, but even being black out drunk isn't the sweet relief it used to be, because now, even when I'm fucked up enough to not even know who the fuck I am, I still know *her*, and I still know that she left. I don't need that to happen again right before interviews, and definitely not before our semi-final game.

Luke just sighs and starts to pull off his own clothes to change, and I try to not think about his comment as I finish pulling on my dress pants and shoes. When I reach for my tie, my eye catches on my phone and my chest tightens when the Instagram notification lights up my screen. I grab for it so quickly the few guys around me all turn to look, but it's not Abby, it's just another random message.

I sit down on the bench and click on the app, refreshing it quickly. Her picture doesn't show up on the top of the newly updated list, but I click on her profile just in case. It hasn't been updated since Monday morning, and it's making me even antsier to not know what she's doing.

Other than the week we weren't talking when she broke up with me the first time, she hasn't gone a single day without posting something—a picture of her avocado toast, a snap of a random dog she saw on campus, a selfie with her and Jenny or Nia, a picture of her TV with *Love Island* on. Something, she always posts something, and I've been waiting for it. Like a fiend desperate for their next hit, I've been waiting for some snapshot into her life since I walked away from her Tuesday. But it hasn't come yet.

I just want to fucking see her. To see what she's doing. To see if she's okay. To see if she's hurting. I just want to feel like I'm with her, even for a moment, to pretend like this shit isn't real. I need to know if she's in bed watching TV, or studying, or watching a movie with Jenny, or making dinner. Anything, I just need something, some part of her to fill this empty space in my life where she used to be.

I scroll through the pictures of her smiling at the camera, of her on a beach back home, of her toes in the sand while she reads a book, of her and Nia and Jenny smiling while they hold up mimosas at brunch, of her smiling while wearing a volunteer shirt as she cradles up a puppy in her arms, its nose pressed against her as its tongue laps against her cheek.

I've looked at each one of these pictures a million times by now, but somehow, they still seem to cut just as deep as they did the first time I spent thirty minutes scrolling through until I reached the first picture she ever posted. It's a picture of her and her dad smiling while feeding manatees at a spring. She looks a lot younger in the picture, maybe sixteen, and I can tell by the date that it must have been taken a few months before he passed.

"T, you almost ready?" I glance up to see James grimacing as he tightens his tie around his neck. If anyone hates interviews as much as I do, it's James.

"Yeah." I sigh, glancing down to Abby's Instagram feed one more time before locking my phone and tossing it back into my locker. The familiar nervous energy that always seems to build before interviews hits me full force. For some reason, it doesn't faze me to know that our games are broadcasted to hundreds of thousands of people, but when I have to sit in front of a hundred cameras and answer questions, I can't shake the anxiety. It shouldn't feel any different, but it does.

"Alright, let's head out. We have fifteen minutes of media interviews, and then twenty minutes to come back here, change, and get onto the court for warm-ups," Coach calls, walking past us toward the door. Making sure my tie is secured correctly before sliding on my jacket, I follow James into the hall toward the lobby where the media location has been set up.

A long stage stands at the far end of the lobby, and rows of at least thirty reporters sit in front of it with their cameras set up behind them. They all turn to watch us file up the two stairs onto the stage and sit down at the long table facing them. There's a single microphone set up on the far right side of the chairs, and one by one a reporter will stand up and walk to it to ask us a question.

There's a water bottle, a name tag, and a list of the reporters placed in front of each of us. I reach for the bottle, just to have something to do with my hands.

"Are we ready, Coach Kennley?" One of the media coordinators with a huge headset is shuffling around the stage, moving around empty seats, double-checking name tags, and keeping track of the time before we go live.

Coach nods with a grunt, and I have to hold back a smile, because as much as he tries to come off as this big hard ass, he's terrified of public speaking and these kinds of interviews always kill him.

"Alright, we're live, first up," the guy calls to the reporters. "Name, network, and a quick question. No follow-ups. Make sure to address the player specifically. No team questions." He steps to the side and the first reporter steps up to the microphone.

He asks Coach about line-up choices, expectations, and a few other things that I don't listen to as I relax into my seat while I take a drink from my water. Two more reporters cycle through, only their questions are directed at me. They're easy to answer because they're mostly about projected obstacles for the game and our strategy to stay focused. Micah gets a question about his defense tactics. Luke gets a few about his first semi-final game. And then a younger-looking reporter steps up.

"Andrew Campbell, USW newspaper." I glance up at the guy standing by the microphone and examine him. USW newspaper, that means he's Abby's classmate. He must have seen her recently, more recently than I have at least, and part of me wants to ask him how she is, if she seems okay, but I just bite my tongue and listen to his question. "This question is for Tristan Beck. You were down by six with a minute thirty left in your game Tuesday against UCW, but you managed to gain the lead and pull out the win in the end. How do you prepare for those kinds of situations?"

Easy.

"We run a ton of late-game situations in practice. It's one of our main focuses, so that preparation really helps in those high-intensity moments."

He nods and the next reporter steps up to the mic.

"Lucas Haverty, Pullman Times. Beck, you're projected to be the top pick in the draft; does that projection add any extra stress going into this game?"

"I try to not look at projections. I like to be grounded in the moment and try to play my best, regardless. But yes, it definitely adds a little extra stress to know that so many people are watching me with those expectations." I lean back in my chair and pop open the water bottle again. There's a small intermission between questions as the next round of reporters step up, and when the familiar arrogant smile flashes behind the microphone, I tighten my grip of my water bottle.

"Greg Bradshaw, USASN. Hey, Beck, good to see you, man. What was going through your head when you lunged at Ty Marcus in the game on Tuesday? That's the first time we've ever seen you lose your cool on the court and it looked like he struck a pretty personal cord there."

I'm frozen in place. I don't actually know what he asked me because I can't process anything other than the fact that the blond fucker is standing in front of me so nonchalantly. His lazy smile and relaxed stance with his hands in his pockets only piss me off more, because he has an air of complete indifference to him. As if he doesn't give a fuck about everything that just happened to his coworker. As if he doesn't seem bothered about how fucked up the entire situation is. But of course, he doesn't. I shouldn't be surprised. No one would tweet out that bullshit about female reporters if they weren't a complete jackass.

I can't even look at him without the anger building in my chest, and when he raises a brow expectantly, I glance down the table. My teammates tense as they stare at Bradshaw. I told them all of the shit that he did, all about Danielle Young, all about how it's impacted Abby, and when Micah narrows his eyes at Bradshaw, like he might throw his water bottle at him, I know I'm not the only one struggling to stay professional here.

I look down to my water bottle and uncap it, bringing it to my lips to buy more time as I think over whether or not I should say something, whether or not I want to do this—to take such a public stance. But honestly, I know there's no other option. I have a platform right here. I have every major sports network broadcasting me live right now, and I can't imagine a better way to use this exposure than for this. For Abby.

She deserves better than to work in a field where assholes like Greg Bradshaw can say and do whatever they please and not be held accountable. She deserves to have a shot at her dream career and to be taken seriously. And if people like Bradshaw continue to think and act like they have been, she'll never have that chance, even without me holding her back.

I glance up at him again, and when his eyes meet mine, my glare turns glacial.

"Greg Bradshaw." I lean into the microphone to make sure my

words are clear, that there's no confusion, that he hears every single word that I'm about to say. "I am disgusted by your recent tweet about Danielle Young and all female reporters. I will no longer be taking questions from you, or your network, until Ms. Young receives a public apology for her mistreatment by not only you and your colleagues, but the network as a whole."

His eyes widen at my words, and for a second, everyone is quiet as they process what I've just said. And then, the entire room explodes in flashes and clicks of cameras, pointing from me to Bradshaw. His smirk has fallen into a shallow grimace, and I push back my chair and stand up, but before I walk off the stage, I reach down and pull the microphone from its stand, bringing it up to my mouth for one final statement.

"When you learn to respect your female coworkers, let me know. Until then, you should take your own advice, Bradshaw, and spend a few hours every night repeating, *I will stop being a sexist asshole.* Maybe then it'll actually happen."

I toss the microphone onto the table, and the room of reporters explodes as I walk off the stage. I don't stop when Coach calls my name from his seat at the table. I don't stop when the reporters jump from their seats and swarm me with their microphones. I don't stop when I pass by Bradshaw who still looks shell shocked and pissed. And I don't stop to watch the aftermath unfold as I reach the safety of the locker room, because I hear it echo out from the speakers in the lobby.

One by one, each of my teammates leans into their microphone and says, "I stand with Danielle Young," before standing up and walking off of the stage behind me.

It happens all at once, the weight that I've been carrying all day eases off of me as they all run into the locker room behind me, slapping me on the shoulder as their cheers echo loudly through the room. But I can't enjoy the moment until Coach's muffled voice echoes through the speakers in the lobby. He must still be at the table, and I'm guessing he's pretty pissed for having to clean up the colossal mess I just made for him, but when his words finally register, I smile, because I know that he agrees. That he knows we did the right thing.

"Bradshaw, you better get your network executives on the phone, because if you just lost USASN access to Tristan Beck right before the final and the draft, I wouldn't want to be you when you walk into work on Monday."

FORTY-ONE

ABBY

The first notification that rings out isn't a big deal, and most of the people in the audience around me don't look over; but the second, third, and fourth that hit consecutively all earn me death glares from the surrounding students trying to hear Marina St. Clair speaking on stage. Reaching into my bag, I silence my phone and whisper my apology to the girl next to me who looks like she might actually strangle me.

Marina St. Clair is a USW alumnus who graduated with her Master's in journalism from Columbia two years ago. She was invited back to speak about her experiences in graduate school, her four different internships, and her first two years working at a prestigious political publication.

I've been excited about this Q&A since I found out about it a few weeks ago because Marina took the exact path that I'm trying to pave for myself—graduate school, internships, and finally, a steady job working at a publication that, according to her, allows her to write the kind of articles she's actually passionate about.

"I'm sure there's quite a few audience members who are anxious to head over to the stadium to catch the last half of the semi-final game—*go Warriors!*" She smiles at the different cheers that echo through the small crowd. "I won't keep you for much longer. How about one final question?"

The girl next to me raises her hand, and when Marina nods toward her with a smile, she asks about internships—more specifically, how Marina managed to land *four* of them. By the time Marina's done answering, I have half a page worth of notes written out and a newfound anxiety blooming in my chest. Apparently, the resume of internships is just as important, if not more, than the graduate degree itself, and based on Marina's timeline, I'm already behind.

"Alright, I think we'll close out questions there." Paige, our sitting editor-in-chief, who's been moderating this Q&A, thanks Marina for taking time out of her busy schedule to come back to visit us.

Most of the crowd is already filing through the exit of the small auditorium to run across campus to the arena. Glancing over at the clock on the back wall, my chest tightens when I catch the time. It's nearly eight, which means they're probably about to break for half time. Part of me wants to follow the crowd out, but when I look back at Marina speaking to Paige just off stage, I know that this is probably the only chance I'll have to speak to someone who actually has experience in the industry before it's too late.

Edging through the crowd, I slip past the few people loitering near the refreshment table, nearly getting knocked into by a few guys on their way out. By the time I make it to the front of the auditorium, my stomach is a tight, twisting knot and I have to remind myself why I'm doing this—I need a second opinion. I need to know if there's a way. I need to know if there's hope.

Paige's gaze flicks over to me mid-conversation as I walk up, and when she smiles and waves me forward, I look over to Marina who's smiling at me as I stop beside Paige.

"Marina, this is Abby Ryan, she's one of the best and brightest on the paper." Paige beams at me.

"Abby Ryan," Marina muses. "You wrote that feature article on the basketball player." I'm a little shocked that Marina actually read through our latest issue, and even more shocked that she remembered my name on the byline. "I have to admit, I'm not usually one to read sports features, but you did an amazing job with it. There was so much presence in that article; I was captivated the entire time."

"Thank you." I grin, looking from her to Paige and back. "It was my first sports feature, so I'm glad I didn't completely bomb it."

"You killed it, Abs. Seriously." Paige laughs. "It's been this issue's most clicked article by far. Had I known sports features would get that kind of attention, I would've written one myself."

Glancing down at the watch on her wrist, her eyes widen slightly. "I have to go, but please, feel free to stick around for as long as you'd like. Abby, I'll see you in class Monday, and Marina, thank you again for your partnership. It really does mean the world to us." She pulls

Marina into a quick hug before turning and hurrying out of the nearly empty auditorium.

Marina looks over her shoulder toward the door, but before she can excuse herself, I take a step closer.

"Marina, could I—could I speak to you for a second? About your experiences in the field."

Her brows pull up a little, and I know she can sense my anxiety, but she nods and smiles, as if to say, *You don't have to be nervous.* I do, though. I do have to be nervous. Because this is my last thread of hope.

"I wrote an article—" I want to try to keep the situation as vague as possible, to not incriminate myself too much. "And the lines kind of blurred between myself and my subject. I know that especially now, with everything that happened with Danielle Young, it's incredibly taboo, and I just—" I hesitate, because I don't really know what I'm asking here. "I spoke with my mother about it and she warned me away from continuing the relationship, about how detrimental it could be to my career and reputation . . ."

She nods in understanding and I keep going, because if I'm going to do this, I might as well really do it. "And I know that she's right, especially with everything that just happened, but I just—I'm just wondering if maybe you know something different. If maybe, with your experience in the field, you might know something that could be helpful to the . . . situation."

She considers me for a long moment and then looks down to the cup of water in her hands. "Your mom isn't wrong, Abby. You can clearly see that with what just happened to Danielle Young. Women in our industry—in most industries—are held to a different standard, especially when it comes to sex and expectations in the workplace. I knew a few people in grad school who worked as interns at USASN under Bradshaw; it was widely known that he influenced the women around him with sex. He would offer promotions in exchange for favors, he would sleep with sources that he used in his articles, and he's had more than one run-in with women refusing to work with him because of his behavior. So, yeah, unfortunately, your mom isn't wrong." Her voice is soft, but it still hits me like a slap to the face, because that was it. My last, dwindling thread of hope was just cut. "But that doesn't mean that she's right, either."

My eyes flick back up to hers.

"If you were my daughter, I would probably tell you the same thing your mom did. She's trying to protect you. But you have a choice, you always have a choice, and in this situation, you have two options. The first: keep your head down, don't make any waves, write your articles, and work through your career while silently dealing with the double standards and the gross injustices that we as women have to deal with in the workplace. Or option two: recognize that there's an injustice and do something to change it."

Do something to change it.

The words send a rush of adrenaline through me because I've never considered that I actually *could* do something to change it. Not realistically.

"It's not going to be easy. You're going to open yourself up to a lot of criticism and you could see your career literally implode right in front of your eyes. The road less traveled is rarely successful, but that doesn't mean it's not worth taking. And if you are successful, you'll be changing the lives of every woman who steps into our field after you. So, I guess I don't really have a good answer for you, Abby, because it depends on what you're willing to go up against and what you're comfortable with sacrificing."

The adrenaline is still coursing through me because I've already made up my mind before she's finished speaking. I made up my mind the second I realized that I could change it, or try to, at least. That I don't have to be a silent observer of this injustice. That I can take a stand.

"I'm sure that probably wasn't the answer you were looking for but—"

"No—" I interrupt quickly. I can't hide my smile as I say, "It was the perfect answer, actually."

I think she can tell that I've made up my mind, because she smiles at me as she rifles through her bag on her shoulder. When she pulls her hand out, she's holding a small business card.

"I have to head out, but I have a good feeling about you, Abby." She hands me the card. "Please, feel free to reach out if you have any questions or need anything at all."

I nod, eyes trained on her business card in my hand. She starts to turn to the door at the back of the auditorium but hesitates for a moment.

"And Abby?" I glance back to her. "If this is about who I think it is, I'd say he's worth it." She smirks at me before turning around again and pushing through the back doors. The loud click of the doors sliding back into their lock is like a shock through my body, pulling me out of my daze, and when I pull out my phone, I'm shocked to see that I have forty-three notifications—all from Nia and Jenny.

I have to scroll to the top because the bottom messages aren't making any sense. The very first message is a link to a video, and when I click on it, my heart clenches in my chest as I read the description. *Tristan Beck and the entire USW basketball team walk out of a pre-game interview in solidarity with USASN's former lead reporter, Danielle Young.*

I click on the video as fast as I can, and my heart pounds painfully in my chest as I listen to Tristan's speech shaming Greg Bradshaw. He tosses the microphone down onto the table and then walks off the stage straight back into the locker room with the most pissed off expression I've ever seen on his face. Then, Micah leans into the microphone and says, *"I stand with Danielle Young,"* before walking off of the stage behind his captain. Every single one of his teammates follows his lead, until they all disappear into the locker room behind Tristan, leaving his coach alone at the table. He looks shocked, and then a wide, proud smile spreads across his face as he leans forward and delivers the last blow to Bradshaw.

Oh, my God.

I don't have time to read all the messages in the group chat, but I catch the final one from Nia—*if you don't marry him, I will.*

I bite down on my lip to hold back my smile, and I'm already pushing through the front doors of the auditorium, walking straight out into the rain before my mind registers what I'm doing. The droplets of ice-cold rain are soaking through my jeans and knit sweater already, but I tighten my grip on my bag, stuff my phone into my pocket, and start running.

The arena isn't too far from the auditorium, but it's still a three-minute jog, and since I already can't run, and I'm weighed down by my backpack, I'm embarrassingly out of breath and soaked beyond recognition by the time I reach the back lobby of the arena. I try to pull open the door, but it's locked, and that's when I remember that Jenny had a scan card to get in last time.

The same media set up from the video is still constructed in the back lobby, but most of the reporters must be in the stadium now, because aside from a few people with headsets, no one's here. A gust of frozen wind whips my hair across my face, and an intense shiver racks my drenched body as I knock hard on the glass of the door. I must look pathetic enough to let in because one of the guys wearing a headset opens the door for me. I have a feeling he's going to tell me this is a restricted access entrance and to go around, but I don't give him the chance because the second he opens the door, I push past him and sprint toward the hall. He calls after me, but I don't stop as I round the corner.

I've never actually been in this hall before, but I've seen where they usually come out of, so I search the different doors for what looks like the entrance to a locker room. When the sign reading *Team and Coaching Staff Only* catches my eye, I don't let myself stop to think about how wildly inappropriate this entire thing is as I crash through the door and stop short instantly. Tristan's entire team is in a half-circle surrounding their coach who's stopped yelling at Luke about shooting percentages and is now looking over his shoulder at me incredulously.

Almost everyone is staring at me, shocked, and I'm sure I'm a sight to see. Not only should I not be in their locker room right now, but I'm panting hard because I just sprinted across campus, and I'm drenched, dripping a puddle on the floor as my jeans and sweater cling to me while the ice-cold water sends shivers down my body.

I spot Tristan instantly. He's sitting on the bench with his elbows on his thighs and his head down. His eyes don't leave the floor at my intrusion, and I don't need to look at his game stats to know he's been messing up on the court, I can tell by the tense set of his shoulders.

"Ryan?" Micah's confused voice echoes through the room, but I don't look away from Tristan, and when his head snaps up, my chest tightens as his wide eyes meet mine.

"I'm so sorry." I say breathlessly. When my eyes flick up to his coach, I hurry, because I can tell by the way his eyes are flaring that I'm about to get kicked out of this locker room any second. "I was wrong, I was—well, I was right, but I was also wrong. And I—" I probably should have thought about what I was going to say before barging in here with an audience, but I didn't, so I just start to ramble. "I'm sorry it took me this long to realize. I was a fucking idiot."

His lips quirk up when he realizes that I'm quoting him. "And I know it won't be easy, but nothing worth having ever is, right? And even if my career implodes, I know that it'll be okay because this is so much bigger than just you and me. It's about change, it's about first steps, and movements, and starting conversations. It's about every other professional woman in the world who just wants to be treated with the same respect. Who's just in love and—"

His eyes widen, and I realize what I just said—*in love*. I said that out loud. But I don't have time to think about how I feel about that because his Coach is turning toward me and I know I'm about to get booted out of here, so I just keep rambling, because I have a point and I need to get to it.

"And someone once told me that life is one big game of high-risk, high-reward. And even if I lose, even if I ruin my entire career before it even begins, the reward still far outweighs the risk, because more than anything, I am in love with you Tristan Beck. I am wholly, and completely, and incontrovertibly in love with you, and—" The tell-tale sting of tears is starting to prick my eyes, but I don't want to cry in front of his entire team, so I take a deep breath and focus back on him. "And I want to stay. If you—if you still want me—I want to stay."

He stands up and walks toward me, unhurried, as if we're the only two people in here, and the air catches in my lungs when he stops in front of me, blocking me from view from the rest of his teammates.

"You're sure?" His voice is throaty, and I can tell by the desperation in his eyes that he's not letting my words sink in yet, not until he knows that I really mean them.

"I'm sure." I promise.

The harsh set to his shoulders gives out instantly and the uncertainty in his eyes evaporates—it's there one second and then gone the next, and when he reaches up and cups my face in his hands, my lungs unfreeze in my chest for the first time in what feels like years.

"Say it again." He smiles. It's a toothy grin that indents his dimple deeply, and my chest releases every bit of tension at the sight. His eyes search my face, and finally linger on my lips, as if he wants to read them as I say the words. I know exactly what he wants me to repeat, and I wrap my arms around him as I say them.

"I'm in love with you, Tristan Beck."

The tension in his body releases as he pulls my lips to his, and I can't stop myself from smiling when the whoops and cheers from his teammates echo loudly through the room. He ignores it all as he wraps his arms around my waist and pulls me tightly against him. I knot my fingers in his curls and pull him closer, and when his tongue slips into my mouth, a shiver runs down my spine that has absolutely nothing to do with the ice-cold clothes clinging to me right now, because this is it, this is what I've desperately wanted since the night I broke up with him.

Tristan Beck is everything I will always want, he is everything I will always need, and right here—with his lips pressed against mine, and hands clinging to me like I might disappear if he doesn't hold me tightly enough—this is everything. Everything, and so much more, because this is home.

FORTY-TWO

By the time I pull my truck into the driveway, we're thirty minutes late.

Abby's still attempting to smooth down her hair in the passenger mirror, but there's not much her fingers can do to detangle the mess of chestnut knots. Between it drying in frizzy waves from her run in the rain, and my exploring fingers, it's long past the point of saving.

She furrows her brows softly as she works her fingers through a particularly rough section, and with an inward sigh, she finally gives up and pulls her hair up into a ponytail. She considers herself for a second longer in the mirror, wiping any remaining smears of her mascara from the rain, and when her eyes finally flick over to mine, her lips quirk up to match my smile.

"You can't smile like that when we walk in, they'll definitely know."

She closes the mirror and leans back in her seat as she bites down on her lip to try to compose her own smile into something less incriminating. But honestly, my dumbass grin walking through that door isn't the only thing that's going to give away the fact that we just pulled over on a private road so we could shed our clothes. The rosy hue of her cheeks that always appears every time she orgasms radiates like a fucking lighthouse. That, and the fact that we're about to walk in thirty minutes late.

They're going to know what we did regardless, but the smile I can't seem to shake is just the final piece of evidence for anyone who might have any doubts. It won't look too suspicious to my teammates though, because ever since Abby barged into the locker room, I haven't been able to wipe the ridiculous grin off my face.

I could have stood there and held her to me while I explored her mouth all night, but when the cheers echoing through the locker room turned into catcalls, and then finally somehow morphed into Luke and

Micah standing up on the benches and holding invisible microphones to their mouths as they started to commentate like they were watching the beginning of a live porno, that's when Coach put an end to it. "Does this look like a fucking Lifetime movie to you, Beck? Get your ass back over here." His tone faltered and then lightened when his eyes flicked down to Abby, who was looking up at him wide-eyed. And I swear to God, for the first time in four years, I saw Coach attempt to pull a comforting smile onto his face. It looked misplaced, like he shouldn't be able to even move his facial muscles in that way, but when he spoke again, his tone matched the softer exterior and I nearly died of shock.

"I appreciate your plight, young lady, and I have a feeling your speech is going to help Beck stop playing like such an idiot in the second half, but I'm going to have to ask for my captain back. I still have to ream into him for the four turnovers he had in the first half." He sent me a warning glare before looking back to Abby with a much softer look.

Her cheeks were bright as she nodded quickly, and with a wave to the rest of the team and a rushed apology to Coach, she slipped back out of the locker room. Teasing comments erupted from my teammates, but I didn't register any of it, because all I could think about were the three words she whispered in my ear before she disappeared back into the hall.

"*I love you.*"

I had to shake the shock, though, because as soon as I sat back down on the bench, Coach launched straight back into his half-time speech as if nothing had even happened. I think he could see the difference in me since Abby left, because when we followed the rest of the team out of the locker room, he slapped me hard on the shoulder and gave me a look that I know was meant to say, *I better not have let that girl in here for that chick flick shit for nothing. You better be on your A-Game now.*

I just smirked at him, because we both knew that him allowing Abby to stand there and say her piece was an act of desperation on his part. He would have never allowed that had I not fucked up royally in the first half. My mind was still clouded, and every time I looked up into the stands toward the section that I knew Jenny and Nia were sitting, it was like another slap to the face when I saw the empty seat next to Jenny.

I tried to shake it off, to get my head straight, but no matter how hard I tried, I couldn't seem to find my footing. I was losing the ball and missing shots that I should have been able to sink in my sleep, and when Coach finally pulled me out of the game to get my head out of my ass, I knew I needed to figure my shit out. I was midway through a mental pep talk when Abby barged into the room, and I was so focused on going over every single mistake I made in the first half, I didn't even register what was happening until I heard someone say her name.

My heart clenched painfully in my chest when I looked up to see her standing there. She was shivering, drenched, and panting like she had just run a fucking marathon, and honestly, she had never looked more beautiful.

The second our lips connected, the tension left my body, and when I stepped back onto the court, the energy changed. My focus slipped back into place, and I could feel the exact moment the adrenaline flooded through my veins when I spotted her in the crowd.

She must have had another set of clothes in her car because she was in a USW sweater and yoga pants, and most impressive of all, she was dry. She beamed at me as she waved, and when the whistle blew to start the second half, I was finally able to slip back into my normal game-time mindset.

My head was clear, and the energy flowing through me surged when James passed me the ball on the breakaway. We gained back our lead in the first fifteen seconds, and with Luke feeding off of my energy, together we managed to pull into a high double-digit lead, holding onto it until the end. Admittedly, we were getting a little cocky toward the end. Luke sunk a half-court shot with the cleanest release I've ever seen. It was a shot even Coach seemed in awe of. His half smile didn't last long, though, because when Micah taunted the guard who'd been shit talking him all night into following him deep into the paint, he had an arrogant grin on his face as he surged forward, knocking the guard on his ass as he slammed the ball into the basket in what had to be the most impressive dunk he's had all season.

The entire arena exploded at the play, and we couldn't hear Coach's screams over the excited roar of the crowd, but his face was turning a deep red that's usually reserved for when we get our asses chewed out. Micah's smug ass grin as he stepped over the player on the floor only set Coach off even more, because it came with a personal foul for unsportsmanlike conduct.

Micah just shrugged as he walked to the bench, but honestly, we were all on a high, because we knew early in the second half that we had just secured our spot in the final. In the last few seconds, when I pulled the double and passed to Luke, who dunked right as the final buzzer sounded, the entire arena exploded around us.

I took a second to take it all in as my eyes scanned the arena, knowing that was it. That was the last time I would ever play in that arena. The last time I'd ever see the sea of crimson and white cheering me on. It was the last time I'd ever think back to the nine-year-old me sitting in the stands, dreaming of the day that I'd be standing right there on the court. It was a bittersweet moment.

Abby reaches up to poke my dimple, and when I look down at her, she's smiling up at me softly, as if she knows what I'm thinking about. I reach over and intertwine our fingers, tugging her softly until she leans over and rests her head against my shoulder. Her perfume is circulating around the truck with the heating, only it's mixed with the scent of the body wash that I keep in my locker and the faint smell of rain. I close my eyes and lean my head back against the headrest as she traces three words on my thigh. I know what she's writing before she's finished, and when she punctuates it with a heart, I peer down to find her looking up at me.

"I love you, too, Abs."

Her smile is blinding, as if it wasn't the tenth time I've said it to her since she jumped into my arms after the game. She said it first, but I've said it more, and now that I've started, I don't think I'll ever be able to stop.

She leans up and connects our lips. It's soft at first, just a slight brush before her lips hover over mine for a few painfully short seconds. I can smell the mix of chocolate coffee and spearmint gum on her breath, and when she connects our lips again, it's different—deeper, more exploratory. The sound of her seat belt releasing echoes at the same time as she parts her lips for my tongue to slip into her mouth, and my heart pounds in my chest because this is exactly what happened before we ended up on the side of the road.

I brush my tongue against hers and revel in the way she moans softly as she knots her fingers in my hair. The sound of my own seatbelt unclicking echoes through the truck and I reach for her hips, wanting to pull her on top of me, but she pulls back and grins at me before I can reach her. She hooks her bag onto her shoulder and slides out of the truck quickly, winking at me as she closes the door behind her.

I cut the engine and grab my gym bag, tossing it onto my shoulder as I follow her up the drive. I have to inconspicuously adjust myself on the way, but when she glances over at me and pauses so I can catch up to her, she doesn't seem to notice.

"You're going to give us away," she teases. I know she's talking about the grin on my face and not that I've managed to conceal the hard-on I have right now, but she melts into my side as I wrap my arm around her.

To be fair, my toothy grin isn't just because she unbuckled her seatbelt and slid over to connect her hungry lips with my neck while I was driving us off campus, it's also because the girl nuzzling closer to me as we step onto the porch is no longer a *maybe someday* or an *if only things were different*—she's a reality. She's my reality. And now that I have her back, I'm never taking that for granted again. So, if I look like a dumbass who can't stop smiling because he just won the lottery, it's because I did.

"This is me now, baby, take it or leave it," I shrug, knowing that no matter how hard I try, I don't think I'll be able to wipe this dumbass grin off of my face. At least not for a while.

"Hmm." She hums loudly and taps her finger against her lips, as if she's actually thinking about it. I pinch her ass at the gesture. She laughs as she hurries out of my reach toward the front door, and when she grins at me over her shoulder, a warmth spreads through me, because this is real. This isn't some fantasy or fucked up dream that's going to wreck me when I wake up. This is real. Abby Ryan is really standing on my front porch with a beaming smile and the residual glow of the orgasm I just gave her.

I was a little shocked when her kisses on my neck turned into soft bites, which turned into her lips trailing upward, and when her tongue licked across my jaw, I was already parking us on the dark private road that I've never actually seen anyone use before.

It was quick, and desperate, and urgent, and because my shitty old truck doesn't give much room for exploration, I had her on her back on the passenger seat as she fumbled with the button on my dress pants while I pulled off her tight leggings.

I tried my best to find a position and angle that would work in the limited space. I had the emergency brake cutting painfully into one knee, and the seat belt into the other, but the second the first breathy moan slipped through her lips as I entered her, I couldn't think of anything other than conjuring out more, of making her head fall back and her eyes glaze over the way they always do when she's close.

Her foot knocked against the radio controls as she wrapped her legs around me, which resulted in the song that was just barely a hum previously to play out loudly around us. I wouldn't have minded if it were any other song on that damn mixed tape she'd made me, but when *Rockstar* by Nickelback blasted through the speakers, I could feel her body shaking under me as she started laughing.

Her bright eyes were crinkled and her rosy cheeks taut with the huge smile on her face, but her laughter went as quick as it came as I reached down and slipped my hands under her ass, squeezing before I lifted her hips, searching for the angle that I know drives her crazy.

Her laughs turned into shocked moans, which led to that familiar glorious sight of her head falling back and her eyes glazing over. The soft whimpers that slipped through her lips as she tightened her legs around me were all I needed to hear to know that she was getting close. Hell, I was right behind her. She felt so fucking good, and even though I didn't have much room to maneuver, her fingers dug into my back as her shallow moans started to match my quick, rough pace. I had her coming before the song was over. She tightened and pulsed around me, moaning my new favorite words over, and over, and over again as she came, *"I love you."*

I've never done hard drugs, but fuck, if that's not the closest I've ever come to a real high, then I don't know what is.

She pushes open my front door and hurries in to get out of the frigid air, and I follow close behind, immediately spotting most of my team lounging on the couch. They have beer bottles in their hands and whichever random girl caught their eye for the night under their arms. Emery and Luke are leaning forward on the couch, their drinks and the surrounding girls forgotten while they slam their thumbs angrily against the buttons on the controllers in their hands. I don't need to know who's who on the screen, because when one of the players gets killed by a headshot, Luke slams the controller down onto the couch next to him and lets loose a string of curses that's honestly impressive, even to me.

"I'm done with this fucking game. It's broken, or rigged, or their cheating or some shit. No one should be able to get a headshot like that from that far away, it's fucking bullshit." He tosses the controller to Penn sitting next to him and stalks toward the kitchen. When his eyes flick to Abby and I slipping out of our shoes and dropping our bags by the door, he smirks, his headshot already forgotten.

"Well, well, well, look who decided to finally show up," he greets with a lazy grin, holding out a fist bump for Abby, which she happily punches with her own small fist.

"We got caught in traffic," she says quickly, but by the way his grin widens when his eyes flick back up to mine, I know he doesn't buy that for a second.

"Sure you did, Ryan." He nods, leading us into the kitchen.

Abby spots Nia and Jenny by the kitchen island, and by the way Jenny pulls her into a long hug, I can tell that she's already drunk. Nia pulls her in next, eyes flicking up to mine over Abby's shoulder as she whispers something in her ear. When her cheeks flare instantly, I know she's been called out.

"Looks like someone already celebrated." Micah grins across the kitchen. He's got that crooked smile, the one that means he's completely fucking sloshed, and based on the girl licking her way up the side of his neck, I already know the kind of night he's about to have. I flip him off with a lazy grin, but thankfully, no one else adds on to his comment.

Luke's already uncapping the bottle of Captain Morgan, and when he slides a shot across the counter for me, I don't hesitate to down it. One shot turned into three, which turned into a celebratory keg stand, which turned into us playing two rounds of beer pong with the MVP teams—Luke and Micah vs James and I—which ultimately resulted in me being a little drunker than I anticipated.

Abby grins at me from her perch on the kitchen island. She's been talking to Jenny, Nia, and another girl who looks vaguely familiar, but I'm too drunk to identify at this point.

Tossing Emery the ping pong ball, I officially tap out. James is way off his game tonight, and I'm not going down with this ship because he can't make a fucking shot. Somehow, Luke and Micah seem to get better at this game the more they drink, and I'm honestly not sure if I should be impressed or concerned about that.

Sidestepping a few drunk sorority girls on my way to the kitchen, I catch Abby's smile over the lip of her cup when I walk in. I'd be willing to bet it's the same rum and Coke she made when we first got here, because aside from the fleeting bit of the rosy hue from our time in the truck, she doesn't have a drunken flush. Knowing this is my time to sneak us out of here, I make a beeline for the pantry and find the pack of Oreos on the top shelf.

"Wait, Steffy actually called it." Jenny laughs, swaying slightly in place. "At the formal, do you remember, Abs? When I stole you away, she said Tristan should be your fuck buddy."

Abby's brows raise quickly as she looks back at the girl.

"Oh, my God." She brings her hand to her mouth. "You did say that."

"No one ever trusts my matchmaking skills, but I know what I'm talking about." The girl slurs happily, and that's when I place her— Steffy Soranto. I know she's hooked up with a few guys on the team, but aside from seeing her at the sorority events we always get invited to, I don't really know her.

"Which means I have to be invited to the wedding." She grins. "Promise me, Abby. Promise me you'll invite me to the wedding."

Abby laughs uncomfortably and nods, and when her eyes find mine, I try not to bust out laughing at the *save me* look she sends me.

"Want another?"

I glance over to Luke and Micah who are leaning against the counter pouring another round of shots. I shake my head at Luke and watch him shrug before handing the shot over to Micah who drains the cup easily. He's got that, *I'm really fucked up right now, but I'm loving it* smile on his face while the random blonde holding onto him conspicuously grabs him over his jeans. When his eyes flick down to hers in interest, her lips perk up, as if it's the first time he's paid attention to her all night.

It's insane to me that I used to actually look forward to these after parties. That I used to be the one in the corner, drunk as fuck, while some random girl felt me up through my jeans before I bent her over in the bathroom and then moved onto my next conquest. It seems like a lifetime ago, and now that I've had a taste of what life with Abby is like—and worse, what it's like without her—I can't imagine ever seriously being satisfied with that life again.

I open the refrigerator and grab two water bottles, but before I can whisper in Abby's ear for us to make a subtle getaway to my room, Nia's comment rings loudly through the kitchen.

"Well, this is as good a time as any. I have a surprise for you two." She grabs Abby and Jenny's hands, and Abby's brows raise excitedly. "You two have been the best roommates for the past four years and I wanted to do something for you to thank you for always being there for me. For taking care of me when I came home way too drunk all of those times." She looks at Abby, who smiles back at her. "For always cooking for me since I'm a walking fire hazard, for always throwing my clothes into the washer because you know I'm terrible at adulting by myself, for being my shoulders to cry on, for being the best Netflix marathon buddies, and for always, *always* having my back."

"Are you proposing to us or . . ." Jenny smirks at her.

"No, but when you see this, you'll be proposing to me." She grins, sliding her thumb across her phone screen before handing it to Jenny. Abby leans over to read the screen, and when she looks back to Nia, her eyes widen as her mouth drops open.

"You did not." She gasps.

"Holy shit," Jenny breathes. "You bought us—"

"We're going to Vegas, bitches!" Nia screams, throwing her hands into the air.

Vegas? They're coming to the finals?

"Wait, really?" James walks over and examines the phone. When he looks up, he grins at me. "They're on our flight, too."

"You're coming to our game then, right?" he asks Nia, but all I can think about is the fact that Abby is going to be in Vegas with me in a few days. If I wasn't wearing a dumbass grin before, I sure as hell am now.

"I guess we could squeeze your game into our jam packed girls week." She grins.

"Wait, this is real?" Abby asks, still shocked.

"Really real." Nia grins. "It's the perfect way to spend our very last spring break. We leave on Monday, the game is on Tuesday, and we'll be back on Thursday, because I know you like to have enough time before the break is over to get organized for classes." Nia smiles at Abby, and I swear to God, in this moment, I watch my girlfriend fall in love with her best friend.

"We're going to Vegas," she squeals. "We're coming to Vegas with you!" She looks over her shoulder and beams at me before sliding off the countertop and pulling Nia into a tight hug.

"Well, I figured since both of your boyfriends and my *situationship* are going to be playing, we might as well go watch." She grins, taking her phone back from Jenny, whose eyes are starting to water.

"You booked these tickets before we were even back together," Abby muses, looking over her shoulder at me again.

"Well that was kind of the idea for the whole trip." Nia bites back a sly smile as she looks between us. "I was planning on getting you two drunk and locking you in a hotel room until you figured it out somehow. I figured if you had enough break up sex it'd eventually turn into make-up sex. That's like the law of attraction or whatever."

"I don't think that's how that works." James grins.

I can't help the mirroring grin on my face, because honestly, being Abby's best friend, she's a damn good person to have in my corner rooting for this relationship to work.

"The Powerpuff Girls are coming to Vegas?" Luke feigns annoyance, but when Abby smirks at him over her shoulder, his grin reluctantly breaks through.

"I feel like I should be offended by that, but it's actually kind of accurate." Nia snorts.

"Nia you're literally Buttercup, you even have the hair for it, and Abby's too cute not to be Bubbles." Jenny beams between them, and when she reaches up to wrap her arm around Nia's shoulders, she sways off balance and nearly topples over. Nia catches her before she can actually hit the floor, wrapping her arms around her to steady her. Jenny seems completely unfazed as she takes a casual sip of her beer and says, "How have we never thought of this before? That would have been an awesome Halloween costume."

"Okay, let's put the drink down now, babe," Nia says, plucking Jenny's drink out of her hand and placing it down on the counter. "You're at like a ten right now and I need you to come down to like an eight, at most, because I can't babysit you tonight, I'm going home with Nate."

Jenny blinks at her. "That sounds like something a quitter would say, Nia," she says picking her drink back up. "And I'm not a quitter."

Nia raises her brow and gives James a look that says, *I'm tapping out, she's all yours,* which he seems to agree to, because he wraps his arms around Jenny and pulls her back, burying his face in her neck.

"So are you going to give us another one of your award-winning half-time speeches at the finals, Ryan?" Micah calls, but when she doesn't take the bait, he turns to me. "I don't know what was better, though, the speech, or the dumbass smile on T's face after."

"We really should've taken a picture of him for Dorothy. It'd go so well on their gallery wall at home. It could've gone right next to his sixth-grade picture." Luke grins.

I glare at him, because they know damn well that we have an unspoken agreement to never mention that godforsaken picture, but when I look back at Abby, she's practically beaming.

"I love that picture," she coos, bringing her hand up to her heart. "It's my favorite one on the entire wall."

"What picture?" Jenny grins, wobbling slightly. James's arms tighten around her waist, steadying her, but even with his head hidden in her white-blonde hair, his traitorous smile is damning.

I can already see where this is going, and knowing Luke and Micah, I wouldn't be surprised if the assholes had a picture of it stashed on their phone, just waiting for a moment like this to pull it out. I flip off Luke for bringing up the damn picture in the first place and swoop down quickly to hook my shoulder under Abby when she's not paying attention. Her shocked gasp echoes through the kitchen as her fingers cling to the back of my hoodie, and I wrap my arm securely around her waist as I start toward the hall.

"Night, everyone." I call over my shoulder with a lazy nod, holding back my grin when Abby slowly releases her death grip on the back of my hoodie just to slap my ass.

"Wait, what picture?" Nia laughs, desperately trying to get the information before I turn the corner toward my room.

"It's the cutest picture I've ever seen. It's legendary. It's iconic. It should be on billboards and the cover of magazines. But I'm sworn to secrecy." Abby calls back. I don't have to see her face to know that she's fucking beaming at the thought of that picture. When I graze my teeth across the side of her slightly exposed waist, I can't hold back my smug ass smile when her breathy gasp echoes softly around us. I'm still pretty drunk, riding out my post-game adrenaline rush, and now, all I can think about is spending the rest of the night in bed conjuring out more of those little noises I've missed so much.

I turn the corner before she can say anything else, and when we finally get into the safety of my room, I knock the door shut with my foot and deposit her back onto her feet.

She smiles up at me, and when she falls back onto my bed, nuzzling into the unmade sheets, I try not to think about the weeks I spent wrapped up in those blankets, wishing more than anything that they'd start to smell like her again.

But now she's here, conspicuously eyeing the pack of cookies in my hand, and when I toss her the pack of Oreos and her water bottle, she looks up at me like I've just handed her a million dollars. Drunk or sober, it doesn't matter, I know the way to my girl's heart, and it starts with chocolate cookies.

I grab the remote, turning on the ridiculous reality dating show I would never actually admit to liking, and when I look back over, Abby's propping herself up on an elbow, taking a slow, suggestive bite of the cookie in her hand. When her eyes flick up to mine, her lips pull back into a mischievous smile, and my dick twitches in response.

"You know," she muses softly. "I really like these cookies."

I raise a brow, tracking every movement as she leans forward and slides off the bed.

"And I really, *really* like *Love Island*."

She takes another small bite of the cookie, stopping in front of me with a look of faux-innocence, as if she's not purposely trying—and succeeding—to turn me on with a fucking cookie.

"And I really, really, *really* like that sixth-grade picture." Her grin deepens as she looks up at me and traces the line of my jaw while slowly popping up on her toes to bring her lips closer to mine.

"But even more than any of that, I really, really, really, *really* like *you*." She grins mischievously as she presses her lips to mine, and I groan inwardly at the touch. I cup her cheek to pull her closer to me, because she tastes like cookies and a little bit of rum, and the feel of her soft body melting into mine is unlike anything else. Reaching down, I grab the back of her thighs and pull her up, walking her back to my bed where I lay her down gently.

Her fingers knot in my curls, and my lips delve down to her neck where they pull into a smile against her feverish skin just under her ear as I say, "I love you too, Abs."

I don't have to pull back to know she's smiling, and when I nudge her jaw gently with my nose, she turns her head a little more to give me better access to her neck. I take my time licking and kissing and sucking my way up the column of her throat, inches away from her sweet spot just under her ear when her soft gasp echoes between us.

I pull back quickly, confused as she reaches up to the stack of pillows near my headboard, but when she pulls the piece of fabric from under it, my lungs freeze in my chest.

Fuck.

Fuck.

Her thumb brushes across the soft fabric as she considers it.

"You kept it."

Her voice is so soft I nearly miss it, but I clear my throat and nod. I'm debating whether I should tell her that I've kept it under my pillow so my sheets would still smell like her, that I took it with me to every away game, that I started to panic when I realized that after a while, it started to smell more like me than it did her, that somehow, *that* felt like losing her all over again. But when she looks up, I know she knows. She knows all of it.

"You kept it." She repeats, eyes wide and glossy.

"It's all I had left."

I guess I always knew that, but fuck if it doesn't hurt to admit out loud.

"I had your hoodie." She says softly. "I wore it all the time. I slept with it every night. I barely took it off. And after, when we agreed to be friends. And after that, even—after I told you that we couldn't—" My chest tightens at that. At the memory of her looking up at me while any semblance of a future shared together shattered right in front of our eyes. "Even after that, I couldn't let it go. I couldn't let *you* go. I held onto that hoodie like it was my lifeline to you. Like somehow, as long as I had it, I'd have something—a piece of you, at least—to hold onto, even if I couldn't have you. I could turn off the lights and close my eyes and breathe it in and pretend you were there. I could forget for a little while that I lost you." She brings the scarf up to her nose, breathing it in slowly, and when her shoulders fall and the first current of tears trail down her cheeks, I lean down and nuzzle my face into her neck, pulling her close.

"It stopped smelling like you. I lost you. It stopped smelling like you and I couldn't—" Her voice is so small, so broken, that it fucking wrecks me all over again.

"I know." I murmur against the warmth of her neck, holding her tighter. "But you never lost me, Abs. Never. You could have said good-bye to me a million times. You could have moved across the country and forgotten all about me. You could have walked away forever, and I still would have been right here waiting for you."

I would. I would have spent years holding onto whatever tiny details of her life that James and Jenny could give me. Desperately holding onto the nights spent as casual acquaintances, as friends of friends. I would have been grateful for whatever piece of her I was given, whatever moments of her life I was lucky enough to be around for. I would have watched her move on through pictures on a phone screen, knowing that in another life, if I was lucky enough, I would have been the one taking them.

FORTY-THREE

ABBY

I've had a wild and riveting first day of spring break so far.

I've been ignoring my mother's phone calls all morning, and when my phone vibrates against the hardwood floor next to me, I reach for the remote to increase the volume on the TV. I was supposed to fly to Florida this morning, but I know she had a heads up that I wasn't coming because when I canceled the ticket it sent a cancellation confirmation email to both of us. She's been calling me nonstop ever since.

I sent a text letting her know that I was fine and that I was going to stay in Pullman for the break to catch up on schoolwork, but I know she saw right through that excuse because she didn't even bother texting back. Instead, she just calls every few hours, hoping that I'll pick up so she can lecture me about *"sticking to plans that I've made"* and how *"last minute cancellations impact everyone around me, not just myself."* And while that alone would have been enough of a reason to avoid her calls, I'm sure she's also going to dig for information about Tristan.

The last time we spoke, I told her we were broken up, because at the time we were, but now that we're back together, I'm not going to lie to her about it. If my conversation with Marina St. Clair taught me anything, it's that my mother has a lot of great advice and she really does just want to protect me; but in the end, this is my life, it's my choice, and it's my opinion that matters more than anything else.

I could spend my entire life trying to please my mother and still never get the validation I'm searching for, because she'll never give it to me. So, it may have taken me almost twenty-one years to figure it out, but now I know that I need to value and trust my own decisions enough to be confident in my choices. And if she supports me, then that's great, but if not, that's okay, too. I support me, and that's enough.

But for the sake of not ruining my entire spring break, I'm going to avoid that conversation until after we get back from our trip.

The soft knock on my bedroom door pulls me away from typing on my laptop, and when I look over, Tristan's smiling down at me from the doorway. He seems amused that I'm sitting on my floor with an explosion of papers surrounding me, but I just smile up at him as he runs a hand through his damp curls. I'm a little too distracted by how good his crimson *Warriors Basketball* hoodie and black Nike joggers look on him, that I don't notice the bag in his hand until he drops down onto my bed, sprawling his long legs out across the mattress.

His gaze flicks down to the box of cereal I've been grazing on all morning, too busy to actually go out and make myself a proper breakfast, and I nudge it out of sight with my elbow as I bite back a laugh.

I woke up at four AM this morning, curled up in bed beside him, listening to the soft rainfall pattering against the window. But no matter how hard I tried to fall back asleep, to enjoy the last hour with him in bed before he had to get up for his morning workout, I couldn't, because Marina St. Clair's words have been echoing through my head ever since I heard her say them.

Recognize that there's an injustice, and do something to change it.

Over, and over, and over again—while I'm in class, when I'm in the shower, while I'm lying in bed, wrapped in Tristan's arms, watching the moonlight slowly cross my wooden floor like a hand on a clock. It's a constant reminder that when I made my choice to walk headfirst into this, it was with intention. It was with purpose. I didn't do this for *Tristan*. I did this for *me*. I did this for Danielle Young. I did this for every woman I've met at my mother's law firm, hardened and scarred by the men in their industry. I did this for the women I'll never get to meet, for the women that have already come and gone, for the women that started this fight long before I even knew it existed. And for them—for us—I want to do something impactful, something worthwhile. Even if it's only a raindrop in a whirlpool, it's a step in the right direction. It's what I did this for—to write, about things that matter, about things that need to be said, and heard, and understood. To make my voice heard, even if I'm screaming into a void.

That surge of purpose had me wide awake, pulling open my laptop and typing out a rough outline of everything I wanted to include in my article. Ideas, both big and small, some easily executed and others that

I likely wouldn't have access to, not as a random journalism student, at least. But I wrote it all, and by the time Tristan's alarm went off and he started to stir beside me, I had my entire article outline completed. An entire page filled with bullet points, quote ideas, and the different directions I could take it, depending on how big of a spot Paige, my editor-in-chief, would be willing to give me for this article.

I tried to explain it all to him as he rolled out of my bed and pulled his joggers on, but my words were rushed and clipped, and nothing was really making sense because I was too excited to take a second to organize my thoughts in any real coherent manner. I was rambling about exposés and quotes from interns, completely out of breath by the time he stepped up to the bed beside me, and had I any air left in my lungs, it would have frozen right there in my chest when his smile gleamed in the moonlight. It was sleepy, endearing, and toothy, but more than anything, it was proud. He was proud of me.

He's wearing that same smile now as I close my laptop and smile up at him, pointedly eyeing the bag beside him. He gives me a knowing smirk as he digs into the bag and pulls out a pair of red and white fluffy socks. They're exactly like my purple fluffy socks that I love so much, only these have little Dalmatians and fire hydrants on them.

"I saw them and thought of you." He smiles softly, hinting at the dimple in his cheek. "It's like that Dalmatian you follow on Instagram."

"Ziggy." I nod, grinning like an idiot as he tosses them to me. I run my fingers over the soft material, and when I look back up at him, I might actually cry because gift-giving is one of my love languages and this two-dollar pair of socks means more to me than I can actually express to him.

"Right, Ziggy." He grins. "But that's not the best part." When he pulls out a pack of sour straws, my eyes widen. He tosses them to me, and I open the pack, biting down into the blue raspberry candy with a dramatic moan that makes his amused smile widen. He turns to open the top drawer of my nightstand, dropping a box of condoms in before closing it softly. When his eyes flick back to mine, I'm smirking at him with a raised brow.

"Had to restock." He laughs.

I nod and take another bite of my sour straw.

He relaxes back into my bed, eyes trained on the movie playing on my TV, and he kicks off his shoes as he folds his arms behind his head. I pull on my new socks, wiggling my toes inside the fluffy fabric with a ridiculous grin on my face.

"Dalmatians have never looked better." He laughs, raising his brows curiously when his gaze flicks to my laptop. "How's the article coming along?"

"I have the first few hundred words done so far, but for——" I glance over at the alarm clock on my nightstand, "——three hours of work, I'm pretty happy with it. I'm still waiting for Paige to email back about whether or not she has a spot for me in this month's issue since we go to print in three days. She's going to kill me for a last-minute submission, but . . ." I glance at my laptop and grin like an idiot when I look back at Tristan. "This just feels *right*. It's the last issue of the school year, and if I'm going to be remembered for anything—if this is the last thing that I write before I get blacklisted or see my career destroyed—I want it to be this. I want it to matter."

Tristan's eyes soften as he considers me, and when he opens his arms and nods me forward, I don't hesitate to get up and climb onto the bed beside him. His arms wrap around me tightly, lips brushing across my temple in a gentle kiss.

"You're going to be remembered for a lot of amazing things, Abby Ryan, and I promise you, this is not the end—it's the beginning. And I'm going to be here with you every step of the way, every moment, every article, every stupid tweet that Bradshaw or his dickhead cohorts send out. No matter what." I relax into him as his thumb brushes softly against my cheek. His heart is beating slowly as I nuzzle my face into his chest, and when his arms tighten around me, I know that no matter what happens, knowing that my days begin and end right here, I'll be okay. "And just a fair warning." I don't have to look up to know that he's smiling. "My mom is definitely going to laminate every article you ever write. And knowing her, she'll have it framed and put on the wall. So, just prepare for that."

I bite down on the inside of my cheek at the thought, and when he squeezes me tighter, I nuzzle my cheek into his warm chest and match his toothy grin.

"Thank you," I say, watching his finger trace random shapes on the bare skin of my thigh, just under the line of my polka dotted pajama shorts.

"For what?" He murmurs softly, eyes already fixed back on the TV.

I watch his fingers sway softly against my skin.

"For everything. For all of it. For what you said to Greg Bradshaw. For being here for me, always, even when we weren't together. For never holding it against me. For forgiving me for hurting you." His finger stops its lazy rotation on my thigh, and I look up, searching his face as I will myself not to cry at the thought of everything he's done for me. "For never letting go of me, even when the world was burning down around us. For never giving up. For believing, even when I didn't, that this could work. For never doubting that this was worth it."

My voice breaks on that, but before I can look away, he grabs my chin and tilts my head back to look up at him. The first tear falls, and then another, and soon I'm watching him search my face through a flood of every emotion that I haven't let myself feel until now. I lost him. I walked away. I let go, but he never did.

"You came back." His voice is low, a whisper of a breath as he leans in. "Thank you for that." Slowly, softly, he brushes his lips against mine. It's a gentle kiss, so sweet that it makes my chest hurt, but when he pulls away, I reach up and pull him back to me. Only this time it isn't gentle, or sweet, or tender; my kisses are hurried, desperate, hungry— starved for him. And like a match catching fire, he's burning with me.

His hands grip my thighs, lifting me up into his lap, and I pull back enough to grab the hem of his hoodie and tug it up and over his head. I pull his shirt off after, but before I can reconnect our lips, he pulls me closer to brush his lips across my neck. The hickey he gave me during the snowstorm is all but gone now, and when his lips connect to the sensitive skin just below my ear, a shiver runs down my body.

He's taking his time, slowing my rushed pace as his fingers trail up my stomach, lifting my hoodie as they go. I'm not wearing a bra, and I can feel the ache in my breasts as his hands slowly make their way up. His lips are still connected to my neck, only he's not sucking to create a new bruise. Instead, he's pressing soft kisses down the column of my throat, grazing his teeth lightly enough to not do any damage. He's teasing me, and when my hips rock when he adds a little more pressure to his bite, he knows he has me right where he wants me.

His calloused thumb brushes against my perked nipple and the sharp inhale of air makes him smile against my neck.

"Tristan." It's practically a whimper.

That seems to snap what's left of his self-control, because he rolls us over, hands already reaching for my waistband. But before I can lift my hips for him, the ear shattering scream that sounds from the living room freezes my lungs in my chest. I'm already up and pulling open my bedroom door when Nia appears at the entryway of the hall. Jenny pulls open her own door, wrapped up in nothing but her bed sheet while James fixes his pants on his hips. Both are wide-eyed and searching as they look down the hall.

"Oh, my God. Oh, my God, *Abby!*" I hurry forward, fully anticipating a serial killer standing in the living room, but when I scan the room, it's empty, aside from Nia staring at me wide-eyed, holding up an envelope. "It's from NYU."

I freeze as my gaze zeros in on the small white envelope in her hands.

The *small* envelope.

"Oh," I say, breathless.

Tristan's hand rests on my back, gently guiding me forward. She holds it out to me, and I can see my hands reach out and take it from her, but somehow, my hands and my mind don't feel connected right now.

I'm numb, my entire body is numb, and my lungs feel impossibly heavy in my chest as I stare at the envelope. It's addressed to me—to *Ms. Abigail Rose Ryan.* The entire apartment is silent, and I know they're waiting for me to open it, but I don't know if I can.

A small envelope isn't always an automatic no, but let's be real, it usually is. I turn it over and slide my finger slowly, tearing it open. Tristan takes a step closer to me as I pull out the paper, only I don't unfold it right away. Instead, I look up to my two best friends standing in front of me. I applied to NYU for undergraduate, but didn't get in. I always liked to subscribe to the *what's meant to be, will be* mentality, so I didn't let it get me down too much, especially since my time here at USW has been so amazing. But when I think about graduate school, when I think about my future and the career I want to have, it all starts with NYU.

Nia has already committed to joining her dad at the PR firm he owns in Manhattan after graduation, and Jenny just got her acceptance letter to the small nursing school in the city a few days ago. Our dreams of moving out to the city together are completely dependent on what's inside of this letter.

"Abby, come on, I'm dying here," Jenny whines as she bounces up and down, clinging to the sheet wrapped around her.

I nod, turning it over as I unfold it. My eyes take a second to focus, but when they do, I nearly drop the paper as I bring my hand to my mouth and reread the first line over, and over, and over again.

Dear. Ms. Ryan,

It is with great pleasure that I offer you admission to New York University.

"I got in." It comes out as a whisper, and when I look up, Nia and Jenny hesitate until I repeat myself, only much louder this time. "I got in!"

The eruption of screams in the apartment is ear-shattering, the perfect soundtrack to our teary-eyed, uncoordinated, tangled mess of a three-way hug. We're a jumbled mess of jumping limbs, too excited to stand still, and when we all pull away from the hug, we beam at each other before pulling together again and squealing, because *we did it*. The plan we've had since we were freshmen is actually coming true. We're going to move to New York together. We're going to go to school, and start our careers, and live together in the middle of the city that never sleeps. We're going to be New Yorkers.

When they finally release me, I turn to see Tristan grinning down at me. He opens his arms, and I jump up, wrapping my legs around his waist as I bury my face in the crook of his neck. Holding on tight to the letter in my hand, I try to process it all.

I got into NYU.

I got in.

"Congratulations, baby," he whispers into my ear, just loud enough for me to hear over Nia and Jenny's excited voices. They're already planning our move, talking about apartment hunting, and what stores we'll need to go to first when we get there. And that's when it hits me. I'm going to be in New York with Jenny and Nia next year, but I have no idea where Tristan's going to be.

I draw back from him, my heart sinking deep into my stomach. He brings his hand up and caresses my cheek, as if he knows exactly what I'm thinking, but brushes his lips against mine softly as he sets me back down on my feet. When he finally pulls back to look down at me, the same anxiety is mirrored in his eyes—the realization that there's still so much that we don't know yet, that we can't predict, that we can't control.

"It'll work out, Abs." He nods, tucking my hair behind my ear. "Let's not think about it right now, okay?"

My gaze flicks down to his chest and then to the paper in my hands.

"Did someone say celebratory shots?" Nia calls, five shot glasses balanced in her hands.

"Shots at nine in the morning." James nods, grabbing his from Nia's outstretched hand. "Why doesn't that surprise me?"

"*Celebratory* shots," Nia amends. "And if you don't want yours, I'll take it for you." She reaches out to steal it back, but he grins, holding his shot glass out of reach.

"Hey, I didn't say that."

I laugh at that, taking mine from Nia, and when I look back up at Tristan, he leans down.

"Let's celebrate this now and worry about that later," he murmurs, clinking his glass against mine before tilting his head back and drowning the shot.

I want to do that. I want to celebrate this. I want to celebrate what this means for my future. But even after I down my own shot and look up to see him smiling down at me, I can't shake the feeling that my future at NYU might be the one thing that compromises my future with him.

FORTY-FOUR

ABBY

I have twenty-four hours before we go to print.

I've written a few last-minute articles before, usually because an underclassman would drop the ball, and as a section editor, I'd have to rush to fill the open slot. But this is completely different. This isn't a random fluff piece; this is arguably the most important article I've ever written.

It's also the best article I've ever written.

The sincerest.

The most powerful.

It poured out of me the second I sat down at this table, nestled in the back on the sixth floor of the library where no one ever really wanders to. I've been surrounded by bookshelves brimming with the greatest works of the past few centuries as I typed away on my laptop; fueled by the fear, the anger, and most importantly, the determination to write something that matters. To throw my voice out into the world and hope that it's heard, even if it's only a few USW students who are listening.

Paige, my amazing editor-in-chief, was more than a little shocked when I emailed her asking if she had any space left for a last-minute article. I was fully prepared for her to turn me down since we're hours away from sending to print, but she didn't. She gave me ten hours to send over the article, and looking at the clock now, I have three left.

My article is done. Well, nearly.

I'm still waiting to hear back from one of the women I emailed early this morning. I was able to dig through LinkedIn and find a few female interns who were working at USASN around the time Marina St. Clair was in grad school. When she was here for the Q&A, she mentioned that she'd heard about Greg Bradshaw's infamous reputation for trading opportunities and promotions to his female interns for sexual favors, which means, if there was an intern working at USASN at that time, they'd probably know about it.

I managed to find two women, thanks to my sleuthing skills, both of whom I sent emails to ask if they'd be willing to give a quote for my article. One woman, Rei Torres, replied a few hours later, but aside from agreeing that she'd also heard accusations that USASN was known for letting wildly inappropriate incidents slide, she didn't have anything specific she could offer. Except for one thing—a name. Brenda Morgan.

She explained that Brenda was on set the day Bradshaw lost access to the Olympic Women's swimming team. She's one of the only people who actually knows what happened that day. I knew the moment I read the email that it was a long shot, but three mocha coffees deep, I was practically vibrating in my seat as I typed out the email to her, because if I had a quote from her, it would change everything. I would have a statement from an eyewitness, someone who saw firsthand the kind of things Greg Bradshaw has been accused of by so many women. If I had a quote from Brenda Morgan, I wouldn't just be writing an article, I'd be writing an exposé.

But even without Brenda's account of that day, my article is still strong. Everything I need to back up my claims was broadcasted on Twitter and live television a few days ago. The Danielle Young situation is evidence enough of USASN's misogynistic culture; and those tweets, those hashtags, they're just proof of the incredibly flawed values perpetuated by the company and those who are in positions of power within it.

This article might never be taken seriously. It might be skimmed over before being tossed into one of the trash cans scattered across campus. It might only live on in the USW newspaper archive, kept, but easily forgotten. Or it could be the first touch of the black stain threatening to sully my career. It could be what defines me as the woman who doesn't keep her head down; the woman who clears away the self-righteous smoke disguising those who revel in witch hunting, exposing those who set fire to others just to watch them burn.

My cheek twitches at the thought. Maybe that wouldn't be such a bad thing.

I've been playing with fire for so long, it's turned into a friend, licking at my feet, always reminding me how of quickly everything can go up in flames. And if I am going to go up in flames, it might as well be for something like this—something worthwhile.

The sound of a throat clearing startles me, tearing me away from rereading the article for the fourth time since I finished it.

"Excuse me, miss, have you seen my girlfriend?"

Tristan's leaning against the bookshelf closest to my desk, his curls still damp from his post-practice shower. When he grins down at me, the knot of lingering anxiety that's been tightening my chest since I sat down to write the article this morning eases slightly.

"She's five-five, usually has a trail of Oreo crumbs following her, looks sexy as fuck in yoga pants . . ." he smirks, eyes flicking down to my legging clad legs poking out from under the table.

"I don't know, I'm actually waiting for my boyfriend to come get me," I shrug, matching his aloof tone as I lean back in my seat with an amused smile.

"Boyfriend?" His brow raises, as if in challenge. "Damn, I was kind of hoping that you were single. I was going to shoot my shot."

His toothy smile flashes as he extends his hand to me, and when he pulls me up out of my seat, I wrap my arms around his shoulders and knot my fingers in the curls at the nape of his neck, bringing his lips down to mine. It's slow at first, innocent even, until I rock up onto my tiptoes and open my mouth. His tongue brushes against mine as his hands settle on my waist, guiding me back until the back of my thighs bump the desk I've been camped out at all day.

I've waited all day for this, and now that it's happening, I'm going to take my time reveling in it. His arms tighten around me as I pull him closer, not ready to lose the feel of him against me, and when his lips break from mine, they trail across my cheek and down my neck to the spot I have covered with three coats of concealer.

"If you keep kissing me like that, we're never going to make it to O'Malley's," he warns, knotting his fingers in my hair and tugging gently to expose more of my neck. He presses warm kisses across my throat, lingering where my pulse races just under my jaw. When he smiles against the flushed skin, I know he can feel it.

"Maybe we could be a little late," I offer breathlessly.

"We hit traffic?" His voice is throaty as he runs his thumb across my jaw.

WRITE ME OFF | 369

"Had to help an old lady cross the street." I nod, tightening my hold on his shoulders when his tongue drags up my neck. A whisper of a moan slips through my lips when his teeth graze across the skin just under my ear, and my thighs clench as the heat pulsing between them flares.

His lips trail up until they're brushing against the shell of my ear as he says, "I'm going to bend you over this desk, and as much as I love those sexy noises you make when I fuck you, you're going to have to stay quiet. Can you stay quiet, baby?"

My eyes widen at his words, but when I look around, heart racing at the thought of someone overhearing him, I gauge the risk factor here.

The Woodbridge-Poole Library has eight floors, and the sixth floor is almost always deserted. Rows and rows of bookshelves are adorned with every classic piece of literature you could think of, only they've been left untouched ever since the library started to offer free ebook versions a few years ago.

I scan the sixth floor—the bare desks, the shelves perfectly tended to, the thin layer of dust on the keyboards lining the wall; aside from my laptop and mess of papers spread out on the table, everything else is untouched, as if it hasn't been disturbed in a very long time. The occasional rustle of paper or cough that echoes from the lower levels is the only sign that anyone else is even in the building.

"Someone could walk in," I say, but my voice is soft, and even as the words leave my lips, the adrenaline floods my veins.

"That's part of the fun," he argues, his eyes flicking down my body. When he looks back up, his lips pull into a haughty smirk as he whispers, "Come on, Ryan, live a little."

When I look back up at him, his eyes are darkening, curiously waiting to see if I'll take the bait. I nod, quick and nervous, catching his devilish grin as he lifts me onto the table, his hands already eagerly slipping under my sweater.

His hands are quick and methodical, as if he knows we don't have much time, even if we are in the most isolated part of the library. He's already breaking away from my lips so he can pull my leggings down my thighs, my pink cotton panties close behind, and I match his hurried pace, tugging his joggers down his hips. His hands slip back under my sweater, and his fingers have my bra unclasped so fast I feel like I should be offended, but I don't have time to waste thinking about how he's so good at taking off women's underwear, because he tears the condom wrapper and slides it on quickly before grabbing my hips and twisting me around, bending me over the desk.

I've been desperate for this since this morning, and when he slides into me, my entire body comes alive at the feel of him filling me. He pulls back before thrusting his hips again, harder than before in a fast rhythm, hitting a spot deep inside that already has my legs weak. And even though I'm biting down on the inside of my cheek hard enough to hurt, a breathy moan slips out, echoing softly around us. He stills, and the loss of friction is torturous. I grind my hips, trying to bring some of it back, but it's not nearly the same.

My eyes widen when his hand reaches up and covers my mouth, gripping me hard enough my make my jaw ache, but when he starts to move his hips again, my eyes roll back and I'm thankful for the barrier, stifling the noises that I'm powerless to silence myself.

He keeps his hand over my mouth but slips his other under my sweater and up my stomach until he's palming my breast. His hands are calloused and rough, sending a rush of goosebumps up my chest at the feel of them just barely grazing my nipple. It's a whisper of a touch, a teasing caress, and I bite down on his hand, silently begging for him to touch me. His grip on my jaw tightens, and when his calloused fingers pinch my nipple, tugging teasingly as he thrusts into me harder, a rush of white-hot heat surges through my veins, sending goosebumps across my skin and weakening my knees.

I don't think I'll ever get used to this—to sex feeling this good; to being with someone who knows my body well enough to make me feel so alive; to craving him all the time, constantly, no matter what I'm doing.

The sound of a door closing echoes though the library, but from the distant echo of the lock slipping back into place, I can tell that it's not on this floor. I look over my shoulder toward the tiny opening of the hallway, praying no one rounds that corner. The library is silent, apart from the small noises that we can't silence, and when his hand guides my head back to look up at him, all thoughts of security guards or wandering students fade away at his throaty voice.

"Come back to me, baby." His eyes are dark and his cheeks flushed as he leans down, pressing a trail of wet, warm kisses down my neck.

Somehow, the thought of being caught, of someone seeing us like this, sends an excited thrill through me, and when he hits a spot deep inside of me, the tension building in my stomach explodes up my spine in a mind numbing flood of pleasure.

My back arches as I dig my fingers into his arm, but even his firm grip over my mouth can't completely silence the throaty moans. His movements quicken before one final, desperate thrust, and when his head falls onto my shoulder as he groans softly against my throat, I revel in the aftershocks of pleasure still coursing through my veins as he rides out his own high.

The sound of the entrance door opening echoes through the library, and every muscle in my body tenses because that one was definitely on this floor. By the time the voice echoes through the library, Tristan's handing me each piece of my clothing, standing in front of me to block me from view as he pulls the condom off and tugs his pants back up his legs.

I struggle with clipping my bra since my sweater is still on, but give up after a few seconds, opting to just slip my arms through it and pull it off completely instead. I'm shoving my bra, papers, and laptop into my purse as he takes my hand and pulls me toward the exit, dropping the condom in the trash on the way. When we turn the corner, a short, burly guard standing by the door has an unamused frown as he takes us in.

When his eyes flick down to my chest, I'm convinced he can see my heart careening there. Tristan blocks me slightly as he leads us toward the door, nodding to the guard.

"The library closed ten minutes ago; I could fine you both for staying in after hours," he crosses his arms, and when his eyes slide from Tristan's flushed cheeks to mine, I have a feeling he knows exactly what we were doing.

"Lost track of time, sorry, man," Tristan says, not breaking his stride as he pulls us past the guard. I'd be willing to bet he would have stopped us if it was anyone else, but he can't be much taller than I am, and when he glowers up at Tristan, his tough demeanor falters.

"Well . . . don't let it happen again," he calls after us, his voice echoing through the silent library. When I look over my shoulder as Tristan pulls me onto the elevator, an electric thrill shoots through my veins as the doors close behind us.

"So," he says, pulling my attention back to see him running a hand through his tousled curls. His cheeks are still flushed, and when his eyes flash and his lips pull up into a playful smirk, my cheeks flame at the realization of what we just did. "Can I get your number? You know, before my girlfriend comes back."

My heart is still dangerously close to beating out of my chest as the elevator rings out its first ding, bringing us down each level at an impossibly slow crawl, and I pull my lip between my teeth as I take a step back and lean against the elevator wall, reveling in the adrenaline rush still coursing through my veins.

"I don't know . . . I don't think my boyfriend would be very happy about that."

His laugh reverberates around us as he nods, shrugging casually, as if to say, *fair enough.*

The notification that rings out softly from my purse pulls my attention, and when I realize that it's the notification for my *email,* I gasp so loudly I'm pretty sure the guard from two stories up might have heard it.

I dig through my bag, pulling out my phone quickly, not bothering to look at the flood of notifications from Jenny and Nia, likely blowing up the group chat wondering why it's taking me and Tristan so long to get to O'Malley's. When I click open the email, I have to read it a few times before it fully registers, because there's no way I'm reading this right.

It's a reply from Brenda Morgan.

It's a quote. *She gave me a quote.*

FORTY-FIVE
PART I

ABBY

We've been in Vegas for less than an hour and I'm already drunk.

When Nia said we were going hard for our senior year spring break, I didn't exactly know what she meant, but when she poured us five shots of vodka each, I quickly realized that she had absolutely no intention of us being sober for the remainder of the day.

I downed the first four shots fine, but I messed up on the fifth and couldn't seem to swallow no matter how hard I tried. I ended up almost spitting out the shot until I caught Nia's eye and she gave me the *If you spit that out, I will literally kill you and bring you back to life to take two more shots* look that she always gives me whenever it happens. The liquor burned like hell when it finally went down, and I chugged an entire juice box after since it was the only non-alcoholic thing I could find in our room. The warmth spread through me almost instantly as I fell onto the single king-sized bed.

I'm pretty sure half of Pullman was on our plane here. When we boarded, I was planning on sitting with the rest of the students in the front of the plane, but when Tristan took my suitcase and loaded it into the overhead bin next to his in the back with the rest of his teammates, I didn't argue. James looked over at his coach, who was staring at us with an apathetic scowl, and when James turned back, he took Jenny's suitcase and did the same.

We were barely settled into our seats when their coach ambled forward and booted James and Jenny to the row behind us, though. He made Luke sit next to Tristan and I instead, mumbling something about needing to separate him from Micah *"for the safety of this entire aircraft."* All he had to do was point to the seat beside me and Luke dropped into it without argument. I think it had something to do with the near feral gleam in his eye that clearly said, *Fucking try me, McConnell, I'm not in the mood.*

I sat between Tristan and Luke for the entire flight—which would have been fine if I could have just melted into Tristan's arms and read my book while he napped—but I could tell by Luke's constant attempts at conversation that, while he'd never admit it, he's a nervous flyer. We talked about the most random things, and I'd be willing to bet that he spent his entire night watching *The Hangover,* because I've never in my life heard someone slip so many movie quotes into a single conversation with such ease. Every time he managed to do it, his lips quirked up, as if he was waiting for me to realize, and whenever I did, I always laughed, because as ridiculous and immature as it is, *The Hangover* is my favorite comedy, too.

When we landed and shuttled to the hotel, it was apparent that their coach had no intention of letting them relax until after the game tomorrow. Tristan barely had time to press a quick kiss to my lips before getting yelled at to get in line so his coach could give out room assignments.

Nia had pulled Jenny and I into the elevators before I could catch Tristan's room number, but it doesn't actually matter, because according to the itinerary that Nia made for us, the entirety of today is a dedicated girls' day—meaning no boyfriends or *situationships* allowed.

So now I'm here, sprawled out on the king-size bed with a ridiculous drunken grin on my face. I watch Jenny dance around the room as her music blasts loudly through the speaker, and when she jumps onto the bed next to me, she extends her hand to me.

"Come on, Abby Bear, dance with me. We're celebrating."

"Celebrating what?" I laugh, watching her sway her hips to the music as she wiggles her brows, trying to lure me into her drunken dance party.

"Everything—spring break, Vegas, *your article*, all of it. We're celebrating all of it."

Her smile is blinding, although I know it's not just because of the liquor coursing through her right now, it's because she's just as excited about my article as I am. I wasn't exactly conspicuous when Tristan and I walked into the bar the other night after we left the library, only it wasn't about the sex we just had, it was about the quote I'd just secured from Brenda Morgan. I practically ran across the bar, wide-eyed and panting as I flashed my phone in front of their faces. Tristan wasn't far behind, beaming at me the entire time I explained *why* the quote was so important. He'd been a trouper. He sat in the O'Malley's parking lot for twenty minutes with me while I added the quote into my article, and after proof-reading it out loud twice, I finally pressed the submit button.

I checked the university's newspaper website every thirty minutes after sending it to Paige, just waiting for the new issue to drop, and when it finally did the following day, we spent the entire morning at brunch, celebrating with bottomless mimosas and more waffles than I'm willing to admit. But Jenny's right—we're in Vegas, it's spring break, and after submitting that article, I deserve to celebrate. *We* deserve to celebrate.

Grinning up at her, I take her hand, letting her pull me up to join her impromptu concert. We're halfway through screaming out the lyrics to the heartbreak song that doesn't even remotely apply to either of us when three loud knocks echo through the room. I jump off the bed and turn down the music a little on my way to the door, already preparing myself for the noise complaint, but instead of an annoyed hotel worker, four familiar faces grin down at me when I pull open the door.

"I see you've started without us." Luke raises a brow, walking past me straight to the open bottle of Grey Goose on the table. Micah follows him in, flashing a lazy grin as he passes.

James makes a beeline for Jenny, who's already started jumping on the bed again, and that's when my gaze focuses on Tristan, still leaning against the doorway with an amused grin pulling at his lips.

"New man on the Vikings, huh? Should I be worried?"

I raise a brow, as if genuinely contemplating it, but break into a grin when he reaches out to grab me. His arms wrap around me, pulling me against his warm, hard chest as he guides us further into the room enough for the door to close behind us. Leaning down, he presses a soft kiss to my lips. It's innocent enough to not draw attention, but when he pulls away, I sigh at the loss of contact.

"I thought you guys were going to be in practice all day," I muse, wrapping my arms around his waist as I nuzzle into his chest again.

"We've got to be down in the lobby in five, we just wanted to come see your room before we go." His hands cup my cheeks, tilting my head back to reconnect our lips. This kiss isn't as innocent as the last, and I'm breathless when we break apart at the sound of Nia's voice.

"Excuse me." She claps her hands impatiently before planting them on her hips as one perfectly sculpted brow cocks. James and Jenny are laying in a tangled mess of limbs behind her, and Luke and Micah are bent down, raiding our mini fridge. They both pocket a few travel-sized bottles of vodka before standing up, giving Nia their full attention.

"If you have a penis, I'm going to need you to exit the room immediately," she says, pointing toward the door. "This is a girls-only room until the stroke of midnight. We have a strict schedule to stick to for our girls' day."

Jenny places a loud kiss on James's cheek and then smacks his butt, nodding for him to untangle his legs from hers and roll off the bed. He pulls a look of mock betrayal onto his face as he looks between her and Nia, as if offended that she sided with Nia's *no boys* rule. Tristan's arms tighten around my waist at her words, and he buries his face in my neck as he brushes a soft kiss against my throat, silently begging me to let him stay for a little longer.

"You heard the woman, get out of here." Jenny grins, slapping James's butt again when he lingers by the bed.

"Wait, what about tonight?" he asks. His eyes flick up to Nia, who's now crossing her arms with a raised brow, and he starts walking toward the door with his hands up, as if to say, *I'm going, I'm going.* "Are we switching rooms or . . ." he trails off, pausing by Tristan who's still holding onto me tightly, as if his grip on me might save him from getting booted out, too.

"I'll text you." She grins.

"We're in 2503," he says, digging into his pocket before dropping a room key onto the desk. His cheek twitches as he looks back at Jenny, and with one last look up at Nia, he grins, giving a salute of defeat before turning and walking out into the hall. She has a satisfied smile on her lips as she watches him go.

Luke and Micah both grin down at me on their way out, and I catch the travel-size bottles of liquor inconspicuously tucked in their pockets as they go. When I look back up at Nia, her gaze falls to Tristan from her perch on the bed, and he groans into my neck.

"Out, Beck." She points to the door. "She's mine for the next ten hours."

He gives a loud, defeated sigh before placing a kiss on my shoulder and retreating toward the door. I have to hold back a smile as I follow him out, because even though Nia is the shortest one in the room, she's clearly the most intimidating. I hold open the door as he walks out, catching his amused grin when he turns around.

"I'll see you later?" he asks. I know he's really asking if I'm going to sneak up to his room later, or have him sneak down here, or some variation where we all have our own privacy somehow, but that's going to be a little hard to organize since the boys are likely two to a room, and we're all sharing one king-sized bed here. Unless one couple opts to sleep somewhere else, that's not likely to work out.

"I'll text you." I grin, echoing Jenny's words, but we both know that it's a *probably not.*

He presses a kiss to my cheek as he pulls me in. "Be safe, Abs. Don't let Nia get you into too much trouble tonight."

"I'll try, but I can't make any promises. I'm a wild woman, remember?" I grin.

"That you are." He nods, grabbing my chin. His kiss is soft at first, and then his tongue is slipping into my mouth, and I'm knotting my hands in his hair as he walks me back, pressing me against the wall. I forget where we are until the impatient whine of his teammates waiting by the elevator echoes down the hall. When he finally pulls away, he grins down at me, tucking a fallen strand of hair behind my ear before stepping back and following his teammates onto the waiting elevator.

As the door clicks shut behind me, I catch Jenny pulling on her tiny black bikini while Nia fumbles in her suitcase, trying to find the matching top to the red bottoms she has on. When she looks up from the explosion of clothes on the bed, she grins.

"Now that the penises are gone . . ." She stands back up, her red bikini top swaying in her hands as she secures the little sunhat on her black bob. "Let the games begin, ladies."

FORTY-FIVE

PART II

I'm hungry, drunk, and down a hundred dollars by the time we walk back into the hotel lobby. I definitely wasn't planning on spending that much, but when Jenny pulled us into the tiny lingerie boutique a few blocks away, all the level-minded reserve I had slipped right through my drunken fingers. The rows of colorful lace sets were mesmerizing, displayed in long aisles organized by color. My drunken mind was amazed by it, reaching out to feel the soft fabrics against my finger-tips as I held my cup in my other hand, sipping down my *third* tequila mixed drink like it was a juice box.

I walked through the store like it was a rainbow waiting to be ex-plored, admiring the pretty sets as I waited for Nia and Jenny to pick out their favorite pieces; but when I got to the far end of the store where the kaleidoscope of colors faded into white lace, I was entranced. It was the bridal section. Somehow, the little white pieces were more al-luring to me than anything else I'd seen. They were beautiful—elegant, even, sliding like silk through my exploring fingers.

I'll be the first to admit that my collection of bras and panties ar-en't the most seductive. Aside from the one black lace bra that I own, all the rest are basic Target bras. I have a handful of lacy panties—a gift from Nia for my last birthday—but other than those, my under-wear drawer is filled with dull, bikini-style, cotton underwear. I never really gave it much thought and based on the way Tristan's eyes al-ways seem to darken whenever he sees me in them, I don't think he has any complaints about my ten-dollar, value-pack panties. But as I explored the row of white, lacy lingerie sets, I couldn't stop imagin-ing what he would think if he saw me in something like that instead. What his hands would feel like, exploring the barely-there lace wrapped around my hips and chest, lightly veiling, rather than concealing anything underneath.

The thought alone was enough for me to pick up the small, white, lace set and bring it to the checkout counter, barely blinking at the price flashing on the screen as I swiped my debit card. I don't know if that was because of the tequila still coursing through my veins, or the rush of adrenaline that surged through me at the thought of Tristan between my thighs, desperate to pull the scrap of lace down my legs. That same fantasy flashes through my mind again as we cross the lobby, sending a spark of heat across my skin, prickling as it goes, as if each nerve in my body is catching fire.

"Should we go back out to the pool?" Jenny leads us into the elevator, her own much fuller bag of lingerie swinging from her hands as she presses the button to our floor. My shoulders and nose are slightly sunburnt from the three hours we spent out there before we left for the shops, but the poolside margaritas were too good to leave, and with the balmy, desert sun beaming down on us, we were finally able to forget about the cold, seemingly infinite winter we left behind in Pullman. Our little college town does get warm—blistering hot, even—but it's late to arrive and early to exchange for the crisp autumn air that always sweeps in.

Growing up in Florida, I'm used to experiencing a different kind of heat every summer. It's a tropical heat, the kind that warms you from the inside out and goldens your skin while you nestle into the sun-dried sand, falling asleep to the sound of waves crashing on the shore. This heat, dry and parched, isn't nearly as nice as that, but it's better than the frigid wind that's been pulling past Pullman, bringing the ice-cold rainstorms along with it.

"I'm hungry." Nia shakes her head, running a hand through her short black bob. Her bangs fall back into place when she shakes her head a little, grinning at me as I slump back against the elevator.

"I'm starving." I agree, leaning my head against the cool surface. I gaze up at my reflection in the mirrored ceiling, turning my head slightly to get a better look at the rosy hue of my shoulders. It's a minor sunburn, one that doesn't hurt yet, and paired with the small matching patch on my nose, I feel like I'm back home again.

"Let's just order room service then." Jenny nods, stepping out of the elevator when the doors open on our floor. I fall into step beside her, fishing my phone out of my back pocket. Tristan's been in practice and workouts all day, and aside from the few texts he was able to send during their breaks asking how our girls' day was going, I haven't heard much from him.

James on the other hand made quite the impression when he sent Jenny a video of him working out. The entire thing was clearly filmed by Luke, laughing in the background, as he narrated James curling a bar with more weight on it than I probably have in my entire body. The video alone was impressive, but paired with Luke's commentary, it was hard not to join in on the laughs echoing in the background as he turned the video into the introduction of a cheesy porno, giving us a full background story on the lonely gym coach, just waiting for his next personal training session to start.

Turning the camera around, Luke winked. "That's you, Jen. Hope you brought some of those nice little spandex shorts you always wear. You know how I love those."

When a rag flew into shot, catching on Luke's shoulder, he grinned, looking back at the camera. "J doesn't seem to be into that idea, maybe you could just wear them for me then." The camera dropped to the floor, and from the reflection in the mirror, we watched James sprint after Luke, dodging and bobbing through the huge weight room, nearly crashing into their coach who walked into the room.

Luke opted to dive to the side to miss wrecking the old man, and he tumbled to the ground, groaning loudly as their coach stared down at him, unsurprised, as if this kind of thing happens regularly at home, too. The old man simply shook his head as he stepped over the freshman on the ground, walking into the gym to check out the rest of his team. The camera caught the coughs and laughs echoing through the gym from the rest of the team, and my eyes caught on Tristan, laughing along with his teammates, dropping his own weighted bar back into the rack as he lifted his shirt to wipe away the sweat matting his curls to his forehead. My eyes caught on the sweat dripping down his stomach, finding its path down the maze of flexed muscles to his waistband.

Needless to say, after watching that video for a second time, Jenny was the first one to shoot up from her lounge chair by the pool, eager to go shopping. I'm starting to think the lingerie shop was her plan from the start.

"Abs?" I glance up to see Nia staring at me expectantly as Jenny slides her keycard into the door and pushes it open, leading us inside. "Are you cool with just staying in and ordering room service for dinner?"

"Yeah, of course." I nod, dropping my bag down at the foot of the bed beside my open suitcase. I will never not be okay with staying in. That's my first choice, always.

"What do you guys want?" she muses, flipping through the room service booklet. She kicks off her shoes, dropping down onto the bed, reading off the list of food. I kick off my own shoes and drop down on the edge of the king size bed, but I'm only half listening to her read off the menu as I click open the text from Tristan.

Just got out of practice. We're going out for a team dinner. How's girls' night going?

I bite down on the corner of my mouth, trying to keep from smiling at his thinly veiled question. What he's really asking is *How much longer until I can sneak down to steal you away?*

My eyes dart over to Nia, rolled onto her stomach, kicking her legs up behind her as she reads off the menu, giving her commentary on what sounds good. Jenny's nodding along, absently listening to the list of food as she sits on the floor near her suitcase, rifling through it.

I type out my response, taking a little longer than usual because I'm too drunk to spell anything correctly on the first try.

I don't think I've ever had this much tequila in my life.

I grin, sending a skull emoji to punctuate—a perfect representation of my poor liver.

The little text bubble pops up as he types.

You're tequila drunk, huh? Think I can sneak you out? I'm gonna need a taste of that.

I bite back my smile, typing back.

The pool bar is closed, babes. You'll have to wait until tomorrow for a tequila sunrise.

The message pops up quickly, and my skin flames, sending a rush of heat down my stomach to where it pools between my thighs.

I wasn't talking about the drink.

"Okay, what do you want, Abs?"

My eyes dart up, connecting with Nia's. Her brow raises, waiting for my food order.

"That avocado sandwich, no bacon." I say, picking the only thing

I can remember her listing off. She nods, rolling off the bed to pick up the phone on the nightstand. When she smiles at us over her shoulder as she adds two bottles of wine to the order, I smile back, trying to ignore the pang of guilt in my stomach. She planned this entire trip. Booked the hotel, the flights, and the only thing she asked for in return is one solitary girls' day. One single day of no boyfriends, no hookups, no boys. Just us—like it always used to be.

Looking back down to my phone, I type out a quick reply, biting back my smile.

There's a no penis rule on girls' night, remember?

The bubbles pop up and then disappear before popping up again quickly.

Okay, what about tongues? I'm pretty fucking good with my tongue.

The heat between my legs pulses, matching the quick pace of my heart as it quickens in my throat. He knows that, though. He knows exactly what he's doing. But unlike him, I actually follow the rules of girls' night.

Tristan.

I know he can hear my intended tone, because I can practically hear the smile in his.

Abby.

"Okay." Nia puts the phone back on the receiver, rolling off the bed with an excited smile. Kneeling down next to her suitcase, she digs through her mess of clothes, all of which are spilling out of her bag, falling on the floor around her feet. When she finds what she's looking for, she sits back on her heels, holding up a small brown paper bag, her bright smile flashing as she wiggles her brows.

"I brought some bath bombs and face masks. Who's down for a spa night?"

———

"Five hundred." Jenny decides, grinning at me over the lip of her wine glass. A few strands of her white-blonde hair have fallen from her top knot, sticking to the pastel green face mask on her skin. She tries to smooth them back up into her bun as she takes another long sip of the white wine in her glass.

Nia shakes her head, her eyes flicking down to meet mine as she grins, smoothing the brush over my forehead with the heavy, mint-scented mask. The bubbles floating around us in the bathtub are sticking to her skin, and when she stands up, reaching over to place the bowl of leftover face mask on the bathroom counter, the glitter from the three bath bombs she threw in before we stepped in clings to her brown skin, casting a shimmering glow on the white tiled walls around us in the dim bathroom light.

Sitting back down in the water, she grabs her own wine glass before looking at Jenny.

"You're not serious," she counters, raising a brow. "Five hundred? That's insane."

Jenny's lips quirk, running her hand through the glittering bubbles floating around her. When her eyes flick up to mine, she nods toward me. "What about you, Abs? What's your number?"

"A lot more than five hundred," I admit, trying not to think about it. "A lot more."

"You guys are ridiculous." Nia snorts, reaching out to refill her wine glass.

We're already on the second bottle. Clearly.

"He's like seventy, Nia. Five hundred is as low as I'll go."

"A sexy seventy," Nia corrects, raising a finger in the air. "That's a lot different than a gross seventy. Plus, I'm kind of into the whole stern, older man, *I've been bad and I need to be punished* thing. And with how angry he always is, you know he'd be into that."

My nose wrinkles, trying to erase the image of Coach Kennley in a bedroom setting.

"So, what's your answer then?" Jenny prods. "How much would it take?"

Nia bites the inside of her cheek, genuinely considering it. "I don't know. I mean there's a lot of factors to consider . . . Does he have that clipboard? Is he going to make me run laps first? Do I get to keep that shiny whistle after?"

Jenny's eyes widen, looking at me for backup, but when the whistle comment finally registers, I lose it. My laughs echoing around the bathroom are cut short when my elbow slips on the edge of the tub, and I nearly drop my wine glass into the water. I catch it before it can disappear into the depths of the bubbles below, spilling nearly half the contents on me in the process. The sweet white wine soaks into my bathing suit top, trails of it racing down my neck and shoulders into the bubbles.

Looking up, I catch Nia's devilish grin as she grabs the wine bottle and refills my glass.

"Jesus, Nia." Jenny grins, holding out her own glass for more wine. "Why do I feel like you've thought about this before?"

Nia sits back again, abandoning her own glass to sip the remaining wine straight from the bottle. Nia's always been the most sexually adventurous out of the three of us, but this seems a little extreme, even for her.

"Listen, if I don't find a man on that fucking team who's going to actually commit, I'm going to be a perpetual jersey chaser. So, yeah, Kennley could get it."

"A freshman would definitely commit," I offer, grinning when her nose wrinkles.

"Seniors only." Nia shakes her head.

"And senior citizens, apparently." Jenny snorts.

Nia's cheek twitches as she reaches back and grabs a few fries from her plate on the edge of the tub.

"Speaking of committing . . ." Jenny grabs a chicken tender from her own plate beside her, eyeing Nia before taking a bite of it. "What exactly is going on with you and Emery? Are you guys still just hooking up or is it turning into something else?"

Nia takes another bite of the fry in her hand, looking down at the bubbles bobbing in front of her as she shrugs. "I don't really know."

Jenny's eyes dart to mine, and I stay quiet, watching Nia rest her head back on the edge of the tub, looking up at the ceiling.

"We go out all the time, and whenever we do there's always an unspoken agreement that we're going to go home together. Like it's just known. And it's been working out fine like that for a while, you know? He takes me back to his place and we spend hours locked in his room. The sex is good, and when we're alone it feels . . . normal. Like everything is fine. But the second we walk out, and he sees his roommates, or we're in public, he gets distant. He's there, touching me, and pulling me into his lap, but he's not really there . . . not like when we're alone."

So the physical connection is there, it's the emotional one that's missing.

"Have you talked to him about it?" Jenny asks softly.

"And say what?" Nia shrugs, keeping her head back and eyes on the ceiling. "*Hey, I know we agreed to be friends with benefits but I'm starting to fall for you?*" She looks defeated as she says it, but I take a bite of the sandwich on my plate and nod, because, yeah, that's exactly what she should say.

"Yes," Jenny and I say at the same time, and when our eyes meet, we grin.

"No." Nia shakes her head.

"Why not? I mean if you're fine with what you have now then there's no need to say anything, but if you want more, you owe it to yourself to have that conversation with him, babe." Jenny's voice is soft, encouraging as she tries to get Nia to look at her, nudging her with her foot under the water. Nia doesn't lift her head, but her eyes flick down from the ceiling to meet Jenny's. "And honestly, what's the worst that could happen? He says no? He says he doesn't feel the same? Then we go out, get drunk, and forget all about it."

She lifts her head, biting down on the inside of her cheek as she considers us.

"If I tell him I want more, and he doesn't, it would ruin everything."

"It would." Jenny nods, a sympathetic smile tugging at her lips. "But what's worse? Staying silent and falling for someone who will never give you more, or moving on before you let yourself fall too far? Nathan Emery was not the first man you fell for, and he won't be the last, Nia. But it's up to you to decide how long you want to keep yourself in a situation that you're unsure of. If you want more, you owe it to yourself to tell him. To see if it's something he wants, too."

She's silent as she considers that, and when she exhales slowly, she nods.

"You're right." She groans. "I know you're right. He's either going to say he wants more, too, and we'll be together officially, or he'll say he doesn't and we'll stop sleeping together; which is probably for the best, if he's not into me."

"It's worth a conversation." I nod, smiling at her when she sits up, her shoulders a little less tense.

"I'm going to do it tonight." She nods, downing the wine in her glass like it's water.

"To our girl, Nia, for being the badass bitch we know she is." Jenny lifts her glass.

"A queen," I add, raising my own glass.

"An icon." Jenny grins.

"A legend." I laugh.

Nia stands up in the tub, the bubbles clinging to her toned legs as they slide back down into the water. She downs the rest of her wine, her eyes flickering with her trademark energy as she says, "Well, ladies, I guess it's time to either get fucked, or get fucked up."

I stand up, too, watching the glitter from the bath bombs freckle my legs and stomach as I step out and grab a towel. When Jenny steps out beside me, I catch the excited smile she's trying to bite back, because we both know girls' night is officially over.

———

Twenty minutes later, I'm slipping into the white lingerie set.

I run my fingers along the line on my hip where the soft material clings to me, and when I look up into the mirror, my lungs freeze as I admire the lace. It's silky and smooth against my fingertips, and even in the dim lighting of the bathroom, it's almost completely translucent. Standing here with the scraps of lace wrapped around me, I turn slightly, admiring the way the material narrows on my butt, giving a cheeky effect. Not a thong—not quite, but close.

He's never seen me in anything like this. Not even close. And when I run a hand up my stomach to the fabric thinly veiling my nipples, a rush of warmth floods through me.

I've felt confident in my underwear before, in fact, the more and more I take off my clothes in front of Tristan, the more confident I feel, because there's no faking the desire in his eyes when he sees me slip off my clothes, but this is different. This is more than confidence. I feel sexy. I feel powerful.

Wrapping myself in the knee-length, white hotel robe hanging on the back of the door, I walk out of the bathroom, spotting Jenny nestled in bed. She's in a black, silk pajama set, but the red strap of her new lingerie set is visible where her top hangs over her shoulder, too big for her small frame. When she looks up at me, she smirks.

"Operation *Lock Nathan Emery Down* is officially in action. She just left." She sits up, crossing her legs under her. "And James just texted that he's on his way up. He was down in the lobby with the team when I texted him, so if you leave now, you might be able to beat Tristan to his room."

Her eyes flash, mirroring my excited smile as I slip on my sandals and grab the room key James left earlier. Leaving my phone, I give Jenny a hurried wave before pulling open the door and slipping out.

For being fully covered by the robe, I still feel incredibly exposed, but luckily, I only pass by one person on the way up to Tristan's floor. It's silent as I find his room, but when I slide the keycard into the reader, I hurry in at the sound of the elevator bell ringing out in the hall.

There are two beds in the room, both slightly wrinkled from being laid on already. Walking toward the one with Tristan's hoodie tossed onto it, I pull the string of my robe, trying to ignore the knots in my stomach as it falls to the floor at my feet at the foot of his bed.

His room is much colder than ours and a wave of goosebumps races up my stomach as I kick off my sandals and climb onto the white comforter, the soft material caressing my thighs as I pull myself further up the mattress. It's still made with all of the corners tucked in tightly, which doesn't allow me to wrap myself up in them, but honestly, it's probably better that way, because if I'm going for it, I should really go for it.

I lay back on my elbows, hoping to make my chest look bigger, but when the sound of the keycard sliding through the reader rings through the silent room, the air catches in my lungs.

His footsteps echo through the small hallway, but they freeze when his eyes meet mine. His gaze coasts down my body, lingering on my chest, before flicking back up to mine. The shocked expression on his face is already transforming into something much darker, hungrier, but it all disappears when two more footsteps sound behind him.

My eyes widen, and I scramble for a pillow to cover up with as he turns around and blocks the room, gruffly ordering whoever is behind him to leave.

"No, come on. I'm tired. I just want to go to bed." Luke whines.

"Go sleep in the hall," Tristan snaps.

"What the fuck? *You* go sleep in the hall."

"If you take another step into this room, I swear to God I'll knock you the fuck out."

When his threat echoes through the room, the air catches in my throat. This was not supposed to start a fight between my boyfriend and his teammates.

"The fuck's wrong with you, T?" Micah's voice sounds next.

"I can go . . . if you need me to," I say loudly.

Silence.

And then a loud laugh.

"Is Ryan naked right now? Is that what you just walked in on?" I bite down on the inside of my cheek, trying not to laugh, because Micah actually sounds proud.

Tristan looks over his shoulder, his eyes trailing down to the small pillow covering my lingerie before turning back with a grin. "Even better."

He starts to push them out again, only this time, they don't argue.

"Bye, Ryan." They both call in unison, their laughs echoing out in the hall.

Tristan reappears, his cheeks flushed and eyes dark as he crosses the room, stopping at the edge of the bed, eyeing the pillow pointedly. I bite back a laugh as I toss it to him.

His brows shoot up, his eyes trained on me as I lean back on my elbows again. His throat bobs with a hard swallow as his eyes survey my body, slowly, not wanting to miss anything. The lace cupping my breasts is sheer enough to see through to my nipples, hard and sensitive against the lace brushing them as I pull my shoulders back a little more. He takes another step forward, his eyes finally leaving my chest to coast down my stomach, still flecked with golden glitter, until his gaze lingers on the miniature bow on the front of my panties.

His jaw tenses when I climb off the bed, making a point to show off the back of the panties as I step off the mattress.

"Do you like it?" I ask innocently, slowly running my fingers over the lace of the bra, down my stomach, to the edge of the lace underwear. He tracks the slow movement of my hand, taking a step closer when my fingers brush along the line of my underwear, my fingers slipping under the lace fabric as I go.

"Yes—fuck, yes." He clears his throat, his eyes dipping back down to my body as I walk toward him, and when I notice his pulse picking up in the dip of his throat, I can't hold back my smug smile.

I did that. I made his heart race, and I haven't even touched him yet.

He steps toward me, knotting his fingers in my hair as he crashes his lips down onto my own. They're hungry and desperate, and when he pulls me closer, I can feel him pressing into my stomach through his jeans.

I guide my hands up his arms, locking around his shoulders to hold him close as his tongue slips into my mouth. A low rumble sounds in the back of his throat. It's an approving sound, and I smile against his lips because I know he can taste the sweet white wine I was drinking in the bathtub. His lips break from my own, brushing warm kisses across my jaw and down the column of my throat. That alone would have sent a shiver down up my spine, but when his calloused thumb caresses my nipple through the lace, a shaky moan slips through my lips.

Guiding me back a few steps, his other hand unknots from my hair and slides down my stomach, slipping into my underwear. My eyes flutter shut at the touch; a shaky breath catches in my throat when his fingers find the wet heat pulsing between my thighs. He groans against my throat as he slides a finger inside me, and when his calloused thumb brushes against my clit, my fingers dig into his arm.

When the voice in my head starts to scream at me not to get off track, I bite down on my lip, reluctantly grabbing his hand. He freezes, searching my face as he pulls his hand out of my underwear. As much as I want his hands all over me, I know I don't have much time, because if I don't stop him now, he's going to carry me back to the bed and I won't have the self-control to stop him from undressing me and slipping between my legs. But there's something I've been wanting to do, and if I don't do it now, I don't know if I ever will.

I don't waste any time as I tug the hem of his shirt up and over his head, dropping it to the floor as I take him in. I don't think I'll ever get over how amazing he looks without a shirt. His perfectly sculpted shoulders and arms, his defined stomach and chest, all tensing under my touch as I run a hand down his stomach. He looks like he was carved out of stone.

I pry my eyes away from his abs and unbutton his jeans, and when I tug his pants and boxers down, I don't reach back up to connect our lips like I usually would. Instead, I lower myself onto my knees and peer up at him.

I've never done this before.

Tyler always asked for it, but I always refused, too grossed out by the idea of it. But with Tristan . . . with Tristan, it's different. The way he treats my body, like he's worshiping it, like he's lucky to just be with me, it changed the way I viewed sex in general, and now that I'm here kneeling in front of him, I want to make him feel as good as he always makes me feel.

He raises his brows, cupping my cheek in question. It's a sweet gesture, one that I know is meant to say, *You don't have to do this if you don't want to.* But I do want to. I want to reciprocate. I want this to be equal.

In the past few days, I've read more articles on oral sex than I can count, and I try to think back to them now as I consider his erection. It's long and imposing, already slick at the tip with pre-cum.

Licking my lips, I glance up at him before leaning forward licking the small drop, tasting him curiously before leaning in more and slipping him into my mouth. His skin is soft and smooth against my tongue, and the instant groan that slips through his lips sends a wave of heat straight through me, pooling between my thighs. I draw more of him into my mouth and suck gently, massaging the bottom of his shaft with my tongue, and when another groan echoes through the room, I make a note to keep doing that.

He's too big to fit entirely in my mouth, and even though I read a few articles on how to deep throat, I'm too nervous to try. I stick to what I can handle and wrap my hand around the base of him, pumping in time with the movement of my mouth and tongue.

I suck a little harder, rolling my tongue along the line of his head, and when his breathing picks up, his head falls back, knotting his fingers tightly in my hair. A deep sense of satisfaction washes over me when I look up to see him clench his jaw as his chest rises and falls in an uneven tempo. The sight sends a heat wave across my skin, scorching my nerves as it goes.

I take my time exploring him, curiously testing how much of him I can actually take in, and when his hold in my hair tightens, I pull back just enough to suck on the tip of him, reveling in the desperate moan that slips through his lips.

"Abby, fuck." His voice is clipped and horse, a throaty plea. I glance up, watching the muscles in his stomach and thighs tense. Knowing that I don't have much time left, I take in more of him, massaging him with my tongue until his entire body tenses all at once.

I pull away in time for him to coat my fingers, and I sit back, mesmerized as I watch him. His cheeks are flushed, lips parted as his breaths come in short, heavy pants, and his eyes are dark pools of emerald, sated and spent. When he looks down at me, a shiver runs up my spine as I catch the molten haze—the telltale sign of the immediate release of endorphins.

He looks relaxed, a little sleepy, and incredibly sexy.

I love knowing that I just did that to him. That I knew his body well enough to get him there. That I'm the only one who's going to make him feel that way now.

Holding onto my forearms, he helps me back up before grabbing the towel hanging on the back of the desk chair. His touch is gentle as he wipes my hands clean, and when he tosses the towel back toward the bathroom, I look up to see him watching me through thick lashes. I'm breathless as he steps toward me, cupping my face between his hands and tilting my head back to bring his lips down to mine. His tongue slips through my eager lips as his hands trail down my body to hook under my thighs, and when he lifts me up around his waist, I wrap my legs around him as he carries me back to the bed. When he leans over and lays me down on the soft mattress, he finally breaks away from my lips to grin down at me.

"Fuck, that was—fucking amazing."

I try not to let that inflate my ego too much, but I can't help it, because I can tell by the glint in his eye that he really means it. He really liked that. I didn't completely bomb my first time.

"I might have read some articles." I shrug nonchalantly, but when his brows lift, I can't help my amused smile.

"As in . . . that was your first one?" he asks, wide-eyed.

I nod, running my fingers through his curls. His eyes flick back to my mouth, and he has a smug grin on his face as he brushes his thumb gently across my lips.

"That makes me way happier than it should," he says roughly. "I know I shouldn't care, but I . . ." He shakes his head. "I like that a lot. That I'm the only one you've ever had in your mouth like that."

His words set fire to my skin, and when his eyes flick down to my chest, I know he's appreciating the lingerie again.

"We're going to keep this on." His eyes flick up to mine with a smirk. "For now."

I tighten my hold in his curls as he licks my perked nipple through the lace and my back arches when his teeth graze against it, tugging it lightly. "But these." He hooks his thumbs through my panties, sitting back as he pulls them off. "These we don't need."

He tosses them over his shoulder, pulling me down the bed, positioning himself between my thighs. I prop myself up on my elbows, watching him brush his lips across my stomach, over my hip bone, down to the inside of my thigh.

Something as simple as this, as his lips and tongue dragging across my inner thigh sends my heart careening in my chest. It's pounding wildly in my chest, so loud I can hear the roar of my blood in my ears. My eyes widen and a tortured gasp falls from my lips when he bites down hard on my inner thigh. He sucks hard, rough, biting down as he adds more pressure. My head falls back as the familiar sensation sends shockwaves of pleasure through my body, tightening the muscles in my stomach as my hips start to move restlessly. He's giving me a hickey, only this one I won't have to worry about covering up.

He pulls back to examine the bruise, and before I can look back up, his tongue is dragging across me, stopping to brush softly across the swollen bud. A shocked moan slips through my lips and my toes curl as he pulls my thighs open when I try to clench them together.

He pulls me even closer to him as he starts to massage the swollen bud with his tongue, and my eyes roll back when the jolts of pleasure shoot up my spine, radiating through my entire body. My back arches off the bed as breathy moans slip from my lips. I'm vaguely aware that he's probably surrounded on all sides by his teammates, but I can't seem to care enough to silence my moans.

He licks his way down, nipping and tugging on me as he goes. Tightening his grip on my thighs, he lifts them up toward my chest, sliding his tongue deep inside me. My eyes fly open at the feel of him, warm and slick, devouring me. I dig my fingers into the sheets, shaking from the shocks of pleasure shooting through my body.

I'm so close, so, so, so close to that all-encompassing rush of pleasure that I've only ever experienced with him, and when he licks his way back up to my clit and slips two fingers into me, curving them up, my eyes squeeze shut as the first wave of pleasure hits. The currents of pleasure wash over me, numbing my body and stealing the breath from my lungs, and when he slows his tongue, bringing me down softly, the final aftershocks relax my muscles until I'm lulled into a sweet, peaceful oblivion.

The drawer of the nightstand creaks open, followed by the tearing of a condom wrapper, but I'm too heavy and warm to move, so I close my eyes and bask in the way my entire body feels like it's floating on water. When the mattress dips as he climbs back on, his nose gently nudges my cheek. I turn my head, wrapping my arms around him as he smiles into my neck, pressing soft kisses across my throat.

"I love you," I say breathlessly, finally able to open my eyes.

He pulls back, considering me with warm eyes and the most beautiful smile, wide enough to dent his dimple deeply.

"You love me because I just gave you one of the best orgasms of your life, or because you *love me* love me?" he teases, reaching up to smooth my hair away from my face.

I turn my head to playfully nip at his palm, and when I look back up at him, he's still smiling at me.

"Both." I determine honestly. "Definitely both."

He brushes my cheek with his thumb and tilts my chin up to bring me closer. His tongue slips through my eager lips, caressing mine as his hand squeezes my thigh, slowly moving up to my hip where his thumb traces its way up my stomach. The heat pulsing between my legs flares again, desperate for his touch. Desperate for him. I lift my leg, hooking it around him, pulling him closer. He smiles against my lips when I rock my hips up, searching for him. Grabbing my other leg, he tugs it up around his waist, lining us up perfectly, but the ear shattering echo of a whistle blowing loudly in the hall stops both of us.

"Fuck," he shoots up, tugging the comforter roughly to untuck it from the bed. He covers me with it just as the door slams open and a set of heavy footsteps ring through the room. He's still wearing the condom as he grabs a pillow and holds it in front of himself, standing up at the end of the bed like a soldier waiting at attention.

His Coach stops at the hall entrance, his jaw tense as he surveys the room. He doesn't seem even remotely shocked to see me wrapped up in these sheets, and he seems even less shocked to see his player standing naked at the foot of the bed.

"Coach." Tristan dips his head in a casual greeting.

The rest of his team is peering in through the open door, a mixture of amused and worried faces silently waiting for their coach to explode.

"Beck, what the fuck is going on here?"

I pull the blanket tighter around me when their gazes all flick over to me. Tristan must have caught sight of his teammates peeking into the room, too, because he narrows his eyes at them in warning.

"I think you can tell what was going on, Coach," he says, taking a small step to the left to block me from view of his teammates.

"Get your pants on and send your girlfriend back to her room," he snaps, his face settling into a deep scowl. "The most important game of your entire career is in less than twenty-four hours and this is how you're spending your time? You should be sleeping, or going over plays, or watching game-tape. And sending McConnell and Costa to sleep in another room? I walked in and they were sleeping on the floor, sharing a towel as a blanket. I don't know what image will be harder for me to shake—those assholes cuddling together for warmth or you standing here, with nothing but a fucking pillow."

I bite down on my lip, because that's not exactly true, he also has a condom on.

"Ms. Ryan, why do you always seem to pop up in places you shouldn't be?" he asks when his eyes finally flick to me on the bed.

My face burns as I pull the blanket tighter around me.

"I'm sorry," I say, but it comes out as a whisper and I don't know if he even heard it.

He grunts, turning on his heel. "You have sixty seconds to get dressed and get back to your room," he calls over his shoulder before the door slams closed behind him.

I push the blanket off and hurry to pull my robe on, fumbling to tie it securely.

Tristan pulls on a pair of sweatpants, tossing the condom into the trash before turning around.

"Well, that could have gone worse, I guess." He shrugs, running a hand through his hair, trying to smooth it down from where my exploring hands messed it up.

My eyes widen as I look up at him.

"Are you crazy?" I whisper, looking back down at the floor, searching for my underwear. He threw them over his shoulder when he took them off, but I don't see them anywhere.

Three loud bangs sound on the door, and I reluctantly abandon my search, hurrying toward the door. Tristan might not be scared of his coach, but I certainly am.

"Wait up, Abs." He laughs as he grabs my hand, tugging me back to him. Cupping my cheeks, he brings his lips to mine. He kisses me slowly, lazily, and I slowly relax into his embrace when his thumb brushes across my jaw and his tongue slides into my mouth. I almost forget why I'm leaving, until the door opens again and we break apart, looking over to see his coach staring at us, incredulous.

"Goodnight, Ms. Ryan." His jaw tightens, but he's not looking at me as I hurry past. Instead, he keeps his narrowed stare on Tristan. I rush through the door, past the group of his teammates, all watching me with amused grins, and when I catch sight of Nia at the end of the hall waiting for me, I bite down on my lip to keep from laughing. She must have been booted out by their coach, too. She holds her hand out for me, linking her arm in mine when I reach her.

The echo of their coach's scream is clear, even at the very end of the hall. "Are you two serious? You can't keep it in your pants for twenty-four fucking hours?"

Nia and I rush down the hall toward the elevator while we listen to Tristan and Emery get reamed out, and when the elevator doors open, we're nearly mowed down by James who's holding his clothes in his hands and a sheet around his waist. His eyes are wide and terrified as he sprints past us without a word.

Nia and I slam our fingers on the button to our floor as we try our hardest to hold in our laughter, and the doors start to close as their coach's scream nearly rattles the walls around us when he catches sight of James clinging to the sheet around his naked body.

FORTY-SIX

TRISTAN

Worth it. That's all I'm going to say about it.

Coach reamed into me and Emery pretty hard after he kicked Abby out. We probably would've gotten away with just a very pissed off lecture if James wouldn't have run into the room and stepped on the fucking sheet he had wrapped around his hips, effectively pulling it down and flashing the entire team. We've all seen each other naked a million times in the locker room, but this was different, and he knew it because he grabbed for it quickly. But the damage was already done, and that's when Coach blew his fucking fuse.

He set a mandatory pre-dawn workout for us even though we were supposed to have the morning off, and because he really knows how to torture us, we spent nearly two hours cycling through sprinting drills and ab workouts.

I could feel the death glares of all of the underclassmen as Coach blew his whistle and called for us to get back onto the line for another round of keep-ups, but they couldn't be too mad, because they know damn well we've all done some pretty stupid shit to get laid.

That seemed to be the general consensus of the team when we walked back into the lobby after practice, because Luke turned to me, James, and Emery with a wicked grin as he screamed across the lobby that he *"hoped the pussy was worth it."* I just grinned and flipped him off, because like I said before, it was.

He shook his head as he walked through the doors toward the two huge SUVs waiting for him and the rest of the underclassmen. We got a long lecture on the way back from the practice arena about keeping our heads clear today—which meant no drinking or getting into shit we know we shouldn't. He was staring at Micah and Luke the entire time, but they were just nodding along with dumbass grins on their faces, because they knew damn well that no matter what he said, their asses were going to be at the strip club.

I declined when they invited me along, because I've got my girl waiting for me out by the pool. That elicited a round of ball-busting and more whipping noises, since they couldn't seem to wrap their heads around the fact that I'd rather hang out with my girlfriend than get a lap-dance by a stripper.

I took the elevator up with James, who was already talking about meeting up with Jenny for brunch, and I was honestly annoyed that Luke and Micah weren't around to hear it, because if I got shit for going to the pool with Abby, he would have gotten eaten alive for going to fucking brunch. After changing into my swim trunks, I gave James a curt goodbye nod and made my way down to the pool.

Now that I'm walking out, I spot her instantly. She has Georgia in her arms as she bounces softly in the water, and my niece's giggles are echoing loudly around the pool area. When the toddler spots me, she screams my name as she waves excitedly.

Abby turns around quickly and smiles at me, and after handing off Georgia to Olivia, she swims to the edge to see me.

"Come on in, honey, we're teaching Georgia how to swim," my mom calls from her blue float. She has a margarita in her hand and the biggest sun hat I've ever seen on her head. She's in full vacation mode, and I can tell by her laugh that she's not on her first margarita. My dad's lounging on the pool chair behind me, and he tilts his hat up to nod at me as he grins. He lets his hat fall back over his face, relaxing back into the chair, and I swear I hear a snore seconds later.

I turn back to my girl who's watching me from the edge of the pool. Her eyes are bright, and she doesn't have any makeup on, so I can see the flush of her cheeks easily as I pull my shirt over my head and kick off my shoes.

"Hi, baby." I grin, taking a few steps back to get a running start. Her eyes widen as I jump over her, flipping forward before the impact of the water shocks me; it's a lot colder than I was anticipating. When I pop back up, I reach out my hand for her, gently tugging her to me. She smiles up at me as she wraps her arms around my neck, running her fingers through my curls, pushing them out of my eyes.

"Good morning," she hums, placing a soft kiss onto my cheek. I'm sure I still look flushed from the torture Coach just put us through, and when her fingers brush softly from my temple to my jaw, I know she can tell.

"I'm so sorry about last night. I wasn't even thinking about the possibility of room checks. I didn't mean to get you in trouble, and I feel bad about Luke and Micah sleeping on the floor, and I never wanted to upset your coach—" Her brows pull together, cheeks warming. "I think I should find Luke and Micah and apologize and—"

I can't hold back my grin as she babbles. Her brows knit together as she hurries on about how she didn't mean to interfere or distract me, but I can't seem to actually pay attention to what she's saying because she's so fucking cute when she rambles. Before she can launch into the unnecessary apologies that I know are about to come, I cup her cheek and bring her mouth up to mine, effectively shutting her up.

Her lips pull into a smile against mine, and when I slip my tongue into her mouth, all worries of last night seem to ease away as she relaxes into me. A content sigh sounds in her throat as her hand caresses my jaw, and she wraps her legs around my hips, pulling me closer. If my entire family wasn't behind us right now, I would have definitely carried her out of the pool and gone back upstairs to pick up where we left off last night.

"There are children present." Mel's teasing comment catches her attention, and she pulls away from the kiss quickly, eyes widening and cheeks burning when she remembers where we are.

"Leave them be, Mel." Mom splashes her with her free hand as she brings her margarita up to her lips with a conspiratorial smile. "Maybe I'll finally get another grandbaby, since you're not going to give me anymore."

"I gave you two, that's where I draw the line." Mel splashes her back and Abby releases her hold on me to swim back to where the rest of my family is lounging in the middle of the pool.

Most people staying here this weekend are here for the game tonight, so it makes sense that they'd recognize me, but I can't shake the feeling of being watched as I follow Abby back toward my family. Looking around, most people turn their heads away quickly, although a few pool-goers have their phones pointing at me, shamelessly recording.

"Hey, big man." Garrett grins, slapping my outstretched hand. He has Gigi cradled to his chest, her small body melted into his as she somehow sleeps in the midst of the commotion around her.

"I saw Williams on the strip last night when we were walking back from dinner," he says quietly, as if we're being listened to. Which, I guess we might be, with everyone watching us. I take a step closer to him and fix Gigi's little hat as he continues quietly. "He looked focused man, like he's already got his head straight. I've been watching the predictions all week—he's moving up. His stats have been soaring lately. He's not going down without a fight."

I nod, keeping quiet. I already knew about his stats. I've been trying to stay off USASN because I don't want to psych myself out, but it's hard when my entire career has led up to this final game. It's not an all or nothing game. It just might be the deciding factor between the first and second pick in the draft. But apparently, according to the predictions, Zayn's stats are growing at a higher rate than mine, so even if he loses tonight, some are still predicting that he might still secure that top pick.

I don't care about being the first to beat Zayn anymore. The rivalry we had seems trivial in comparison to my other problems now. My main concern is that the Knicks are predicted to have the first pick in the draft, and I need to make sure I secure it, because if not, there goes any shot of Abby and I being in the same city.

I think she's finally forgotten about it, at least for now, because she doesn't seem to have that same tension in her body that she's had since she opened her acceptance letter to NYU. But we can't avoid it forever; come June, I'm going to get drafted, and we could end up on different sides of the country. Hell, the Raptors and the Rockets both had a terrible season last year so they're projected to be in the top three, which means I could end up in Texas or fucking Canada, and there's nothing I can do about it.

I glance over my shoulder, catching her grinning at Georgia who's sitting on Mom's lap on the float. Georgia leans over and rubs her cheek, and Abby's eyes widen at the little gesture before her eyes flick to mine and she gives me the most beautiful, toothy smile.

"You've got this, man," Garrett says, pulling my attention back. "Just put on a show tonight. Make sure the scouts know who's really worth that top pick."

I nod and try to smile at him, but I feel the pressure pressing down on me now because this game could possibly be the determining factor of more than just my career. It could determine my entire relationship.

It could determine whether or not I fall asleep next to my girl every night. It could determine whether or not long-distance might be the thing that breaks us apart.

———

We had it. We had it in the fucking bag.

Zayn was off his game the entire first half. He was missing his normal shots and even had a few sloppy turnovers because he was letting his mess-ups get to his head. I tried not to let the lead make me comfortable, but to everyone around us, it was clear—we were going to win by a landslide. I could tell by the energy in the huge arena that everyone could see where this was going. The part of the stands that were crimson and white were exuding enough energy to raise the hair on the back of my neck, and the blue sections were doing their best to keep up the morale, but honestly, they saw the writing on the wall, and it wasn't pretty.

USW was going to blow out Duke in the finals for the third year in a row.

Or, we were, until Luke fell to the ground clutching his knee.

He was screaming out so many f-bombs I was shocked the ref didn't flag him for it. He was nearly in tears as the medics ran to him, and I watched, frozen in place as my right-hand man was examined on the court. I didn't see what happened, but once I heard one of the medics say *hyperextended*, I knew shit was bad.

Now, he's being helped off the court, half-carried as he limps past the bench toward the locker rooms. I glance over to see Coach staring wide-eyed at Luke, and when he brings his hand up to rub his bald head, I know that the anxiety growing in my chest is for good reason. Even Coach knows it—we're fucked.

Luke is responsible for nearly half our points every game, and so far this game, he's managed to put down thirty-five of the seventy-three points. He's a sharpshooter; he's reliable, amazing under pressure, and most importantly, he's one of the only people that I trust to make a shot if I give him the ball with a less than ideal shooting position. And now, he's limping into the locker room to get checked out by the trainers.

Half the arena is booing him as he goes, while the other half is quiet, processing the desolate realization that Luke being out changes things. It changes everything.

Luke might be a freshman, but he's a huge part of our offense, and now that he's likely out for the rest of the half, my heart slams painfully in my chest, spiking at the realization that I don't know if I can hold this lead on my own.

Duke has been making a steady come back since the start of the second half, a slow but consistent climb. We're up by six and we've only got three minutes left, but in basketball, anything could happen in three minutes. That's more than enough time for them to pull a comeback and even secure a nice lead.

I glance over to see Zayn trying to keep a casual look on his face. It's an asshole move to smile when someone gets hurt, and as much as we don't like each other, I know the guy's not an asshole. But I can't blame him for trying to hide that he's happy about it. Luke blowing out his knee is the opening they need to come back and beat us, and when our eyes lock on the court, he nods, as if to say, *Alright, Beck, it's just me and you now.*

I shake out my arms and nod to Owens, the sophomore who's now taking Luke's place. He's not as reliable of a shooter, but he's fast, and he's a hell of a defender. If we can just put enough pressure on them to keep them from scoring too much, I think I can add enough to our lead to bring this home.

When the whistle blows again, I lock my focus back into place and try not to think about how bad this could be for us. Micah blocks a shot and passes it to James for a breakaway, which brings us up by two, but Zayn pulls back for a quick three and sinks it perfectly in the next play. We go back and forth like this for two and a half minutes. Quick points, desperate shots, stressed defense, easy mistakes made in the heat of the moment on both sides.

There's a lot at stake and it's getting to everyone's head.

Coach is yelling something at us, but I can't make it out as my eyes lock in on the ball in Zayn's hand. He steps back, a cavalier smile on his face as he dribbles the ball lazily, as if he doesn't have a care in the world, as if he knows he's going to win.

They've managed to bring up the score, only trailing by three.

One shot and they'll be tied.

I don't have to look at the clock to know we're running out of time—fifteen seconds at most, and the energy in the arena heightens with each second that passes. The crowd is starting to get restless, standing in their seats, screaming at me to secure this. Their anxious energy is radiating around the arena as their screams grow louder, counting down the clock together.

"*Fifteen.*"

"*Fourteen.*"

"*Thirteen.*"

My heart careens in my chest as I try to pressure him back, the roar of the blood in my ears almost drowning out the countdown from the crowd, but he takes a step back and releases the ball before I can block. Turning, I watch the ball sink into the net, and the air in my lungs catches painfully as half the crowd erupts in ear shattering cheers, because now we're tied.

"*Six.*"

"*Five.*"

The anxiety radiating from the crowd is fucking suffocating, but it's intoxicating, too. The rush, the stakes, the collective inability to breathe. Every single person in the arena is holding their breath now, either hoping that we can somehow sink a shot to win or praying that we choke. Even the crowd's countdown has died away, too invested to even scream out as they watch us start to turn and sprint toward our basket.

Glancing up to the clock, my heart drops.

Three seconds, we have three seconds to make a shot, or we go into overtime.

Coach is screaming, his voice a distant echo in my head. It's the same command, over, and over, and over again—*Get Beck the fucking ball.*

Micah pushes through his double team, trying to knock the ball off course, but he manages to get me a clean pass. I can only take three steps before the clock clicks down to *one,* bringing me to the other team's free throw line. It's nearly a full-court shot; there's no fucking way, but I don't have much of a choice, so I plant my feet and launch the fucking ball, watching it roll off my fingers as the buzzer blares out.

Time has only slowed down a few times in my life, and each time I've been on the court, watching the ball soar toward the basket, desperately praying that it'll find the net somehow. The anxiety rippling through the crowd silences the arena as everyone's cheers catch in their throat, and I stand frozen in place as all twenty thousand of us track the ball's trajectory.

It rotates in midair as it makes its way to the net, and a few Duke players are already grinning at each other as they prepare for overtime, but my lungs catch in my chest when the ball starts to descend in the perfect angle. I watch awestruck as the ball sinks into the net perfectly and the crowd around me explodes into ear-shattering screams.

The energy of the crowd pulses through the arena as the crimson confetti falls from the rafters, and when I look up to the Jumbotron, my face is broadcasted as I shake my head in disbelief, reveling in the moment. This is the last time I'll ever see myself in a USW jersey, and when I smile up at the screen, the decibel of the crowd somehow increases.

I look back down in time to brace for the ambush of white jerseys pulling me into hugs while their screams meld into the crowd's. I don't have time to process it before Micah and Emery are propping me up onto their shoulders, and I grin at my teammates below as Coach yells at them to put me down. I don't think they heard him, but he slaps Micah with his clipboard pretty hard which makes him drop me back down onto my feet.

"God damn, don't be such a buzzkill, Coach. We just won!"

Coach ignores him as he slaps me on the shoulder, and I swear I'm hallucinating when he smiles at me. A genuine, happy, *I'm not pissed in the slightest* kind of smile. It's the kind of smile that says, *I'm proud of you son. I'm proud to be your coach. I'm proud of what you've accomplished in these past four years.* I don't know what to say, and I'm sure he'd be uncomfortable with me saying something heartfelt anyway, so I just smile back at him as the team explodes around us.

Shaking hands with Zayn and the rest of the Duke players goes by in a daze, and I don't really remember what I even said in most of my post-game interviews. They made it easy for us this time by having the reporters line up on the way to the locker room. I stop to talk to a few of them, and when I see the young, blonde reporter smiling at me with the USASN microphone, I smile back at her.

USASN released a long-winded formal apology to Danielle Young the other day. They even had Greg Bradshaw and his colleagues who spoke about Danielle on Twitter sign the apology. I'm sure he didn't really mean it, but it's a start, I guess. I was happy to find out that they even offered Danielle her job back, and I was even happier to find out that she had already accepted a new one at another sports station.

The reporter in front of me looks like she's fresh out of college, and I can tell by the flush of her cheeks that she's flustered, as if she doesn't know if I'm going to blow her off. But when I nod to her, she smiles at me, and the rush of relief in her eyes is clear as she speaks into the mic. I answer a few questions before saying that I have to get back to the locker room to check on Luke, and she grins at me, thanking me for my time. She looks a lot like Abby, only with lighter hair and brown eyes, and I seriously hope that whenever Abby is out on her first assignment, someone is nice enough to her to give her an interview.

Micah finishes up his interview at the same time, falling into step beside me as we enter the locker room. Both of our eyes search the room for Luke, and when we spot him sitting on the bench, a flood of relief washes over both of us. He's sitting next to his locker with a big ass grin on his face and an ice pack taped to his knee.

"That was sick, T," he calls over the rest of the voices. "You fucking sent that shot. Hail Mary-ed that shit." He seems a lot better than before, but when I nod to his knee, his smile falters. "I'm going to be out for a few months. Probably until next season starts. Maybe a little longer." He sighs. "But I can walk on it, and they're going to write me some pain pills for the next two weeks until I start physical therapy."

Coach clears his throat, pacing uncomfortably at the front of the room. When he nods for us all to quiet down, I know he's about to give his famous end-of-the-season speech. It's his usual goodbye speech since the season is done and we don't have practice or workouts anymore. The underclassmen won't start back up until the fall, but for us seniors, this is really the end.

I honestly didn't think it would hit me this hard, but I look away when he starts to talk about how far we've all come, and I have to bite down on the inside of my cheek to keep from crying, because this team has been my family since I stepped into the USW arena when I was a freshman. And now it's over. My time here is done. I'll never wear these colors or play on that court ever again. I knew it was coming, but fuck, it hurts.

I catch James rubbing his eyes on his jacket, and I smile to myself because I know he's thinking the same thing. When I finally look back up, Coach is smiling at us all.

"I've never been more proud to be a coach than I have this season. You've all surprised me in ways that I didn't know were even possible.

You made a real difference in Danielle Young's life. You stood up for something that you believed in, and you did it together as a team." His eyes scan over us, but they linger on me. "I know that you're all going to leave this team and create amazing lives for yourselves. You're going to take what you've learned on that court and use it in your life. You're going to care for those around you like they're your teammates. You're going to work hard until the last possible second. You're going to value truth and perseverance. You're going to understand the importance of teamwork and communication. But most of all, you're going to go out into the world and be great men. And for that, I am proud."

His lips press into a firm line, holding back the tears he refuses to let fall. Clearing his throat, he looks over all of us, managing to pull back his usual stern grimace.

"We're here for two more days, and now that the game is over, I'm planning on viewing this as a vacation. So if you see me out by the pool drinking a fruity drink, keep your dumbass comments to yourself." He narrows his eyes at us, but his cheek twitches. "And I'm not going to babysit you anymore. You don't have a curfew. You don't have strict room assignments. But please, for the love of God, if you call me in the middle of the night to bail you out of jail while we're here, just know that I will neuter you and keep your balls on my desk. Are we clear?"

We all nod our heads, the dumbass grins on our faces clear as he surveys us.

"Alright then, you're all dismissed. I'll see you in the lobby at nine sharp on Thursday morning for the shuttle back to the airport. If you're late, you're staying here. I'm not missing my flight because you slept through your alarm." He nods gruffly. "I'm going to take Mary out for a nice dinner now. Do me a favor—don't embarrass me tonight. I know it's hard for you since it comes so naturally, but refrain from acting like fucking idiots until we get back home." With one final look, he turns and walks out of the locker room.

The room is silent as we wait, making sure he's really gone, and when Micah climbs up on the bench by his locker, he pulls his jersey off, tossing it down on the floor as he calls out, "Hit the showers, assholes. Tonight, we're getting fucked up."

The locker room explodes in chaos as everyone pulls off their jerseys, tossing their shit into their lockers as they walk toward the showers.

The excited voices echoing through the room are hard to decipher, all melding together, shouting out ideas of how we're going to celebrate.

The frenzy sends a rush of excitement through me as I walk toward the showers, and as I turn on the water, I can't hold back my smile as the hot water eases the tight muscles in my shoulders, because it's over. Everything we've worked for this season is done, it's accomplished, we won the fucking war, and now, it's time to celebrate.

Luke turns on the water in the shower next to mine, peeling off his clothes as he steps into the spray of scalding water. Shaking his head to flick his hair out of his eyes, he drops his head back, and in true Luke fashion, screams out a fucking *Hangover* quote.

"Hey, fuckers, you ready to let the dogs out?"

FORTY-SEVEN

PART I

ABBY

"Chug it, Abs," Nia smirks, tilting the bottle up with her finger. I squeeze my eyes shut, trying to ignore the burning in my throat as I chug the vodka.

We're playing catch up since there was so much traffic on the way back from the game, and since we're still only mid-way through getting ready, we've resorted to multitasking. AKA—chugging vodka while getting ready. We were smart about it, though. We made sure to do our makeup *before* touching the liquor.

The drink prices in Vegas are astronomical, so to prevent us from not being able to pay rent when we get back home, we're all trying to get as drunk as we can before we leave so the drinks we do buy help to maintain the drunkenness, not achieve it.

Nia finishes the final touches on my hair, and I admire it in the mirror as I pass her the bottle. I went for my usual loose waves, but somehow, they always look so much better whenever Nia does them. She achieves a level of volume I can never seem to recreate. They look tousled and effortless—a little bit like sex hair, but not in a bad way—and I grin at her in the mirror as she tilts her head back and chugs.

Jenny pulls open the bathroom door, stepping out in a short leopard print dress. The dark material is a gorgeous contrast to her white-blonde hair, falling around her in pretty curls as she leans over and slips on her heels.

"But can you shake your ass in it?" Nia teases, raising a playful brow as she takes another long sip from the bottle.

"Always." Jenny bends over and shakes her butt, arching her back as her head falls back in a laugh. Her dress rides up dangerously high, but stays just below her butt, which for Jenny, means it passes the *can*

I go out in this? test. Her smile is blinding as she crosses the room and takes the bottle from Nia, wrinkling her nose as she chugs as much of the liquor as possible. Out of all three of us, Jenny's the lightweight, and by the way she's swaying in place, I can tell she's already drunk.

I get up so she can take my place, taking the bottle from her as she falls into the chair. Most of her curls held perfectly from earlier, but when she pinpoints a few that lost their bounce, Nia grabs the curling iron and gets to work.

My body is warm and numb and feels lighter than before as I sift through Nia's suitcase, looking for something a little outside of my comfort zone. When my fingers graze a leather mini skirt, I pull it out, brushing my fingers over the smooth fabric.

"You should wear that with the new crop top I got yesterday." Nia nods toward the bag of lingerie sitting on the couch. "It's a less transparent lace, you should be fine to wear it out."

I sift through the bag, finding the black top she's talking about quickly in a sea of red and pink lingerie. It's lacy, but it has a lot more coverage than I was expecting, and when I hold it up to myself, I smile at the thought of Tristan seeing me in this.

Lingerie two nights in a row, I might actually give him a heart attack.

Looking over my shoulder, I catch Nia's eyes in the mirror.

"Are you sure this is okay?"

"What's mine is yours, babe." She grins at me in the mirror, grabbing the hair spray to set Jenny's hair.

Stripping out of my clothes, I pull on the outfit, smiling at the sight of the bruise on my inner thigh. I had to cover it up with concealer when Tristan's mom invited me to meet them at the pool this morning, but most of the makeup washed off by the time I got out. I'm pretty sure Olivia saw the dark purple bruise before I could wrap myself in a towel because she smirked at me, raising a brow as if to say, *I saw that, you nasties.*

Stepping up to the mirror, I smooth my hands over the lace, adjusting the hem. It's a crop top, but paired with the high waisted skirt, only a few inches of my stomach are actually exposed. I can see the outline of my nipples through the lace, but only in certain light, and to be honest, it sends a thrill through me to think of Tristan seeing me in this, of him watching me all night—like a sailor and a siren.

"Okay, you're done, babe," Nia says, turning off the curling iron. "We should get going. I told Nate we'd be up in five and that was like fifteen minutes ago."

Nia never actually had *the talk* with Emery last night. Apparently, their coach barged in right as she was bringing it up, and by the way she's chugging the rest of the liquor, I know she's planning on finishing that conversation tonight.

I don't think she's going to have much trouble with that, though, because out of all of us, she looks the best by far. She's in a short, black slip dress that hugs her so tightly it almost looks painted on. That, paired with the platform heels, her sleek black bob, and cherry lips, she's a walking bombshell.

Slipping into a pair of heels, I find my phone under a mess of clothes and follow them out of the room. I have three missed calls from my mom, a text from her saying that I need to call her back ASAP, a text from Mark saying that Mom is pissed, and three snaps from Jeff, who must be on vacation with his girlfriend Lessa based on the background in all of his pictures.

I send back a few ring emojis and a million hearts because I'm trying to hint as obviously as I can that he needs to propose, and when I slip my phone into my black wristlet and look up, we're already at the elevator.

On the way from the elevator to the boys' room, Jenny trips three times, and now that we're rounding the corner to their hall, I have my arm wrapped around her waist, trying to help her walk in a straight line. I'm not much help, though, because it's the drunk leading the drunk here.

"We haven't even left the hotel yet and you two are already a mess." Nia watches us trudge along behind her, attempting to look as sober as we can as we pass a small family in the hall. I keep my hold on Jenny, knowing that if I let go, she's bound to take a spill and prove Nia's point.

"I'm not even drunk." I lie, laughing as I pull Jenny along with me towards Tristan's room. "Like barely tipsy."

"Barely tipsy." Jenny agrees, laughing along with me.

Nia smirks at us, letting us pass by her to knock on the door. Jenny and I both knock, grinning up at Luke when he pulls open the door.

His eyes widen when he sees Jenny's dress, and I already know what's coming as we walk past him into the room.

"Ma'am in the leopard dress, you have an amazing rack."

She doesn't pay attention to his joke as she hurries forward and throws her arms around James's neck, so I hold out my hand for a high five.

He smirks at me as he slaps my hand.

"How are you feeling?" I ask, looking down to his knee. It seems to be wrapped up under his black jeans and based on the close up the Jumbotron got of him when he was down on the court, clutching it while screaming, I can only imagine how bad it hurt.

"Hurts like a bitch."

"Are you sure you should be going out with us tonight? Maybe you should stay in and relax or just—"

"I'm going to stop you right there, Bubbles. There's no fucking way I'm staying in tonight. We're in Vegas. I've been preparing my whole life for this shit."

I know I should probably argue, but I'm a little too drunk to reason with someone who's even drunker than I am about why he shouldn't be running around the strip tonight, so I just sigh.

"Fine, but be careful, I don't think I could carry you home."

His lips pull back into a drunk grin as he brings his beer bottle to his mouth.

"You're already thinking about taking me home, Ryan?"

I raise a brow, watching his lazy grin turn into something much wider as his drunken laugh echoes around us. "Wait—don't tell T I said that."

I grin, glancing around the room filled with their teammates, but I don't see him anywhere. When I turn back around, Luke's being pulled away to do shots with a few girls I don't recognize. My vision blurs for a second, and I have a feeling that last shot just hit me, so I sit down on the edge of Tristan's bed and look around, trying to spot him in the crowd of his teammates crammed in the small hotel room.

I spot Micah sitting on the couch, his arm draped along the back as he grabs for what looks like a cigarette tucked behind his ear. Pulling out a lighter from his pocket, he lights it, taking a long drag of it, and I realize quickly that it's not a cigarette. When he exhales the smoke, he leans forward, resting his elbows on his knees as he turns toward the blonde sitting beside him. His eyes dip down to her chest and his lips pull back into a lazy grin as her eyes widen, as if she's shocked that he's paying attention to her.

When the mattress dips beside me, I look up to find a pair of glossy hazel eyes considering me. It takes me a few seconds to place him as the freshman I shot in the paintball game.

"Hey, you're Aaron, right?" I ask, tucking a wayward strand behind my ear.

His throat bobs hard as his eyes dip down to my chest, and when they flick back up to mine, he nods.

"I'm Abby."

"Ryan. Yeah, I know." His lips pull up into a grin.

"I'm sorry I shot you," I laugh, but when his eyes linger on my chest again, I try turning my body away from him as casually as I can, realizing that the lighting in here is probably enough to expose me more than I'm comfortable with in this lacy top.

"It's okay." He grins, leaning forward. "It was a lucky shot anyway."

I lean back from him, scooting over to put a little more space between us when I realize that he's definitely trying to flirt with me right now.

"It wasn't lucky. I shot you on purpose." I say flatly.

"Sure you did, Ryan." He winks at me, and I almost stand up and walk away when he starts to lean in again, but his gaze flicks over my shoulder and his smile falters as he leans back quickly.

"You macking on my girl, Penn?"

Tristan's voice sounds from behind me, and the relief floods through me when I look over and smile up at him. Aaron shakes his head quickly and disappears across the room as Tristan falls onto the mattress beside me. His eyes coast down my body slowly, and I bite down on the inside of my cheek when they linger on my chest and exposed thighs.

When his eyes finally flick back up to mine, his dimple is deeply indented and there's a flush to his cheeks—the kind I usually only get to see after he's worked out or right before he's about to pull off my underwear.

"You look—" He shakes his head, his eyes widening a little as they linger on my chest again. "Really fucking good, Abby." He reaches up, brushing his thumb against my collarbone. When a shiver runs down my spine at the touch, his lips pull into a deeper grin.

"We could stay here . . ." His dark eyes catch mine, freezing the air in my lungs, but before he can convince me further, Luke's voice echoes through the room.

"Who's ready to get fucked up?" He looks over to Micah who has his tongue in some girl's mouth. Breaking away from the kiss, Micah glances over at his best friend who's cupping his hands around his mouth as he screams out, "I'm ready to let the dogs out, let's fucking get it."

The drunken cheers of his teammates echo through the room as he turns toward the door, and Micah doesn't even glance down at the girl he was just kissing before he turns and follows his best friend out of the room.

Tristan stands and offers me his hand, and I stare at it for a moment as the rest of his teammates filter out of the room behind Micah and Luke. My heartbeat picks up in my chest as a flash of the first time he held out his hand to me replays in my mind. So much has changed since the night of that formal, and when I look up at him, his face softens, as if he's thinking about it, too.

The palaver around us piques as the team filters out of the room, but all of it fades away when he brings his hand up to my cheek.

"I'm glad you said yes." His thumb brushes gently across my cheek, and my mouth suddenly feels incredibly dry. When he tilts my head back to bring our lips closer, the air catches in my lungs, as if it were the first time he's ever done this. His smile deepens as he considers me and then he slowly pulls my lips to his.

It's a soft brush, a barely-there kiss, but it sends goosebumps down my arms, and I groan impatiently when he pulls away, because I'm not nearly satisfied with just that. I wrap my arms around his neck and pull him back down to me, opening my mouth for his tongue to slip through as a soft groan vibrates in the back of his throat. He smiles into the kiss as his tongue brushes teasingly against mine, and when Nia's voice rings around the room, I groan inwardly.

"Come on love birds, let's go."

I want to shoo her away, to stay behind and enjoy our night here in the hotel room alone, and when Tristan breaks the kiss and grins down at me, I know he knows exactly what I'm thinking. I'm tempted when his eyes flick down to my lips again, but when I look over to see Nia staring at me expectantly as she corrals James and Jenny into the hall, I know I can't ditch them. She grins back at me before turning around and walking out of the room, leaving it open for us to follow behind her.

I stand with a sigh, reveling in the feel of Tristan's hands tightening around my waist to steady me as we go. The elevator doors open as he leans down, inconspicuously sliding his hand under my skirt to caress the bruise between my thighs as his throaty whisper sends a shiver down my spine.

"When we get back, I want you to take off everything but the heels."

———

I've lost count of the shots Nia and Jenny have handed me since we've walked into this bar, but since I swear I can actually *see* the music bouncing around the room, I should probably take a breather. I look over my shoulder to Tristan. He got pulled to the back of the bar to take pictures with a group of people who flew all the way here from New York for the game, and as soon as people realized he was taking pictures, a line started to form around the back wall. It's kind of surreal to see, but I can tell by the huge smile on his face when he signs the back of a little boy's USW jersey, that this is everything he's always dreamed of. I have a feeling he's going to be busy taking pictures with the growing line of fans, so I turn back around and scan the wall lined with TVs. They're all turned to different sports networks, and nearly all of them have Tristan's face flashing across them as different replays of the game play on the screen.

I spot Nia and Jenny playing corn hole on the other side of the bar with James and Emery, and when I turn back from watching Tristan's face flashing on the TV behind the bar, I notice that Micah is sitting on the stool beside me. His brows are pulled together a little as he scrolls through his phone, but when he looks up and notices me staring, he raises a brow.

"What?"

"What?" I repeat with a smile.

"You're staring at me."

"I'm not staring. I'm people watching." I correct with a grin as I bring my drink up to my mouth. I try to find my straw with my lips without looking down, but I just end up fumbling like an idiot until I finally look down and bring the straw to my mouth.

He's laughing at me when I look back up, but I'm far too drunk to be embarrassed, so I just smile at him.

"So, why don't you have a girlfriend?" I ask, and when a few people look over curiously, I realize how loudly I just asked that.

"What?" He laughs, his brows pulling together.

"You're hot, *really* hot, and you have that whole bad boy, dark cloud look going on with the double sleeve tattoos and the motorcycle," I ramble. "But I saw you reading the other day in the living room—like an actual paperback book—which is shocking enough on it's own, but even more shocking, it was a classic."

"Are you trying to hit on me, Abby?" He smirks. "Because T is one of my best friends, and while I understand the appeal of coming over to the dark side for a night, I couldn't do that to—"

"I'm not flirting." I laugh, because I'm not, I'm just nosy. "I just want to know why you don't have a girlfriend. I mean you have to be tired of hooking up with random girls all the time. Don't you ever want something more?"

His amused smirk falters before he looks away from me, and my cheeks flush because I realize that I'm asking him some really personal questions right now. And while I like Micah, I don't really know him that well. Not well enough to pry into his life, at least.

"I think it's probably for the best that I stick with how things are now," he says as he rubs his thumb down the neck of his beer bottle. I'm honestly surprised he even answered at all.

"Why?" My voice is much softer now, nervous that I'm overstepping.

He glances back at me, and my cheeks flare nervously as he considers me. His blue eyes are so dark they're nearly a blackish gray, framed by the kind of lashes I'd kill to have. He's attractive—hell, everyone in Tristan's house is attractive—but Micah has a sort of lost soul, broken spirit, *I'm going to break your heart and you're going to like it* look to him that would definitely be appealing if I wasn't with Tristan.

"I haven't met anyone that's made me want something more and I don't want to waste my time trying for something that's not really there. I think I'll know it when I see it—if I ever see it—but until then,

I'm pretty content with just drowning myself in cheap whiskey and women."

I nod and look down at my drink before looking back up quickly. "And the book thing?" I ask. "Do you really read?"

His brows pull together, and that amused smirk slips across his lips again as he brings his beer back up to his mouth.

"Of course I read, Ryan. I'm an English Lit major."

I nearly choke on my drink when I process that. That's the last thing I expected, but the reporter on the huge TV behind the bar catches my attention when he says Tristan's name.

"Tristan Beck and Zayn Williams are both once in a generation players and it's insane to me that we get to see them enter the NBA at the same time. They've played against each other since they entered the college league together four years ago and we've seen that rivalry grow every single year. Tristan Beck managed to put USW on the map, and we can't discount that when we compare them. Williams walked into a dynasty; Beck built his. Not to say that Willams isn't an amazing player, but let's give credit where credit is due. Game changing players like Luke McConnell and Micah Costa were drawn to USW because they knew they'd be playing with Beck. He was a selling point for the underclassmen who signed on and that changed everything for USW. It's now a top contender for incoming freshmen, and even now as Beck graduates, they still have phenomenal talent like Luke McConnell who will continue that legacy."

The other reporter nods and the picture on the screen behind them changes from a close-up picture of Tristan and Zayn to a video clip of Tristan's game-winning shot. It was nearly a full court shot, and it was astonishing to witness in person. The entire arena exploded around us when the ball went in. Even the Duke fans couldn't deny that it was an amazing shot.

"But even winning the finals doesn't guarantee Beck the first pick in the draft. When you compare his stats to Zayn, you can see that they're nearly neck and neck. Tristan's true talent lies in his offense. He's an incredible player and it's truly mesmerizing to watch him when he's on a hot streak. He has an insane intuition when it comes to last-minute decision making on the court. He's amazing under pressure and he's reliable. If we're down by three with ten seconds left on the clock, I want the ball in his hands because I know he'll get the job done. Zayn has a lot of those same qualities. He might not be at the same offensive level as Beck, but he's a fighter on the court and he's rarely unsuccessful. And more than that, he's a better defenseman than Beck, there's no arguing that. So, at the end of the day, you have two damn near equally impressive players. It's like choosing between two supercharged sports cars. They're both going to be amazing; it just depends which one you like better."

The other reporter nods.

"They're pretty equally matched, but if I'm honest, I think Zayn is going to secure that first pick. He has the offensive talent, but he also has the defensive skills the Knicks really need right now. I think it would be a mistake for them to choose Beck in that regard. You have to look at the player as a whole and identify your needs. Beck isn't going to be able to give the same kind of defensive pressure that Williams will, and looking at New York's line up, we can see that they clearly need that extra help there."

"That's true." The first reporter nods. "If I were New York, I'd probably lean toward Williams as well."

"But I'm sure Beck won't be too upset. If New York secures that first pick, the second will likely be Toronto or Phoenix. Either would be a great team to play for."

I blink up at the TV as the words sink in. Toronto or Phoenix.

My chest tightens painfully, and I slip off of my stool without saying goodbye to Micah. I try to ease my way through the crowd, but I get knocked into three different times by the time I spot Jenny sitting alone.

There's an open seat next to her, which I slide into, and when she glances over at me, I just melt into her wordlessly. She wraps her arms around me, and I can tell that she's confused, but she just lets me slump against her as I try to keep myself from spiraling.

It's just a prediction. Nothing is final.

I try to repeat that to myself a few times, but even drunk me knows that I'm lying to myself. What those reporters said makes sense. If the Knicks get the first draft pick and need help on defense, then it makes sense that they wouldn't draft him. Which means that Tristan could end up in either Phoenix or Canada and there's nothing that either of us can do to change that.

FORTY-SEVEN

PART II

ABBY

I stay here, cuddled up to Jenny in the middle of this busy bar as I try to concentrate on anything other than where Tristan might end up in a few months. I don't know if it's because she's also incredibly drunk, or just because she can tell that I need this, but she doesn't ask me what's going on as she holds me to her, rubbing my back in gentle circles. It isn't until her arms stiffen around me that I pull back, and when her eyes widen as her lips pop open, I follow her gaze over my shoulder to the other side of the bar.

It takes me a few seconds to figure out what she's looking at, but when I catch sight of Nia and Emery, my heart sinks deep into my chest. I don't need to be over there to know what's happening, it's clear on her face. The color from her usually rosy cheeks quickly pales, and while he's still talking, I can tell by her distant, glossy gaze that she's not really paying attention, not anymore. She's trying not to cry, biting the inside of her cheek as she nods. When she finally turns around, she straightens her shoulders and walks through the crowd, stone faced and distant until her eyes flick up to meet ours. That's when she cracks. That's when the current of tears finally breaks the surface and floods down her cheeks.

"Oh no, babe. Come here." Jenny murmurs as she slides off her stool, wrapping her arms around her. I slide off my own stool to rub her back, and when her muffled sob echoes softly around us, my chest tightens.

"He said he didn't want anything more—that I wasn't exactly *girlfriend material*." She pulls back, wiping away the trail of tears as inconspicuously as possible. Her black mascara has somehow stayed in place, and when her wide, brown eyes meet mine, I can't stop the rush of white-hot anger that sears through me.

"Not girlfriend material? Who does he think he is?" I snap. "He was lucky that you even gave him the time of day, Nia. That you even let him breathe in your vicinity. That you graced him with your presence. Not girlfriend material?" I'm genuinely in shock as I stare at her, because if anyone in this entire building—in this entire city, state, country, *universe*—is girlfriend material, it's my best friend. "What a—what a stupid—he's such a—" I'm at a loss for words, rambling, trying to grasp for something to describe how utterly insane this entire thing is.

Not girlfriend material?

"He's a fucking ." Jenny supplies, grabbing Nia's hand.

"A complete fucking douchebag." I agree quickly. "A total dick head."

Nia's lips perk a little as she looks between us.

"He is kind of a dick." She nods, wiping her nose.

"Which is pretty brave for a guy with that hairline." Jenny crosses her arms across her chest. "You'd think he'd tread carefully."

Nia's eyes widen at that, and I bite down on my lip to keep from laughing until her own shocked laugh echoes between us. It bubbles out of her, and when her lips pull up into a smile, my chest releases slightly, because it reaches her eyes.

"You really went there." Nia laughs.

"And I'll stay there." Jenny shrugs, sipping her drink. "Fuck Nathan Emery and his shit hairline. He's an ugly fuck boy with frat boy confidence; we don't need that energy in our lives."

I look over my shoulder, searching the crowd until I spot Emery. He's talking to James and Tristan on the other side of the bar, and when they look up at us with *oh shit* expressions, my eyes narrow.

The flash of anger sears through me as I glare at him. Turning on my heel, I reach for the lime wedge in the discarded drink on the bar top. I don't even have time to think about what I'm doing before I launch the lime wedge across the bar as hard as I can, aiming straight at Nathan Emery's face. It falls short, landing a few chairs away from where he's standing, but he knows that it was meant to hit him, and that's enough for me. Tristan's smirking at me next to Emery, but I ignore him as I flip Emery off for good measure before turning back to Nia.

Her eyes are wide, still brimming with tears, but they're already lighter than before as an amused smile pulls at her lips.

"Did you seriously just throw a lime at him?"

"He's lucky it was just a lime." And that I have terrible aim, but I keep that to myself.

She breaks into another wave of laughter, likely because she knows exactly what I was thinking. My own lips pull back at the sound, but I can still see a few tears streaming down her cheeks, and the sight breaks my heart.

Nia isn't a crier. For as many times as she's consoled me and Jenny over the years, I've only seen her cry a few times. Seeing it now makes me want to turn around and throw one of these steel stools at Emery's face.

"He deserved it." I maintain, reaching out to squeeze her hand. "You know what? Screw Emery. You don't need him. We're going to enjoy our spring break without him. Honestly, he was holding us back anyway. This is a girls trip, remember?" I reach up to wipe the smeared mascara from the corner of her eye.

Her brows pull together as she considers that, and when she looks over my shoulder toward the guys, her shoulders pull back. "You're right. Screw him. I *am* girlfriend material and if he can't see that, he doesn't deserve me anyway."

"Hell yes you are." I nod.

"His loss," Jenny says, holding up her drink.

Nia nods again, only this time her eyes aren't brimming with tears, and when she smiles, there's something final about it, like she knows that Nathan Emery isn't worth her tears. I know that Nia Valtera is too good for someone like Nathan Emery, and when she stands up straight and wipes away the last bit of smeared mascara from under her eyes, I know that she knows it, too.

———

Nia's on her second drink post-Emery and her eyes are already noticeably brighter as she casually scans the crowd around us, likely looking for someone to distract herself with tonight. I'm scanning the crowd, too, desperately searching for someone hot enough to erase any memory of the asshole that just broke her heart, but my search falls to the wayside when familiar arms wrap around my waist. I lean into him, smiling when he leans down and whispers against my neck.

"Hey there, Slugger." I look up to see him grinning down at me. "Micah wants to go to the casino down the street." His dimple indents, and I'm lost in a daze as I take in the slight drunken flush of his cheeks and the glossy effect of his emerald eyes.

"Okay." I nod as I take a long sip from my glass, not wanting to waste a drop of the ridiculously overpriced liquor. When his eyes meet mine, some of the anxiety that's been blooming in my chest since I watched the USASN sports report starts to ease a bit.

His hand travels down my back, sending a wave of goosebumps across my chest when his fingers brush the bare skin on my waist. He lowers his head to my neck again to press a warm kiss just under my ear, and when his lips linger there, my eyes flutter closed as his thumb brushes against my hip bone.

I'm sure we're being watched right now, but I can't seem to bring myself to actually care because the stubble on his jaw is grazing across the side of my throat, and suddenly, I can't breathe. My grip on his arm tightens when his lips brush across my ear, and it takes me a second to realize that Nia's sliding off her stool, mumbling about how she's not drunk enough for *"all of this"* before taking Jenny's hand and following the rest of the team out of the bar.

Before they make it outside, Jenny bends her knees and Nia jumps onto her back, hugging her shoulders tightly as James walks behind them with his hands out, as if he's already preparing for his very intoxicated girlfriend to wipe out on the concrete. Knowing Jenny, that's a pretty good call.

Tristan smiles down at me as he helps me off my stool, and when we step out of the bar behind his team, his arm slides across my shoulders, pulling me in tight to keep me warm against the cool night breeze. I feel him watching me as we follow his team down the sidewalk, but I try my hardest to not look upset, because tonight is his night. It's the biggest night of his career so far, and I don't want to ruin it for him with worries of *what-if's* and *maybe's* and *what-could-have-been's*

The walk to the casino took longer than it really should have because Luke got side tracked by a guy selling lightsabers on the corner of the street. He bought twelve of them and handed them out like candy to his teammates who then proceeded to get into a full on drunken, theatrical lightsaber battle—sound effects included.

When the cops driving past flashed their lights and told them to chill the hell out, Luke sardonically saluted them before ordering his teammates to give their toys to the small group of children who'd been watching them wide-eyed the entire time. The look on their faces were priceless when the giant men handed them their lightsabers, and as we walked into the casino, I looked back to see the little kids recreating the giant battle they had just witnessed.

"What was up their asses? Having a giant lightsaber fight in public isn't illegal," Luke feigns an annoyed snort, but his giant smile gives away his impending joke. "It's just frowned upon—like masturbating on an airplane."

Bingo.

"I think it had more to do with the fact that you were screaming *"you gonna fuck on me"* while beating Penn with the lightsaber." James laughs.

Double bingo.

I look over to Penn, who's scowling while he rubs the back of his head, and I can't stop myself from bursting out into another wave of laughter, because that was honestly the best part of the whole thing. Luke somehow managed to impersonate Leslie Chow's voice perfectly as he attacked Aaron Penn. And somehow, even with an injured knee, he still won.

"You guys suck," Penn mutters, trying—and failing—to shrug off Luke's embrace as he offers to buy him some chips to gamble with. He takes a second to consider the offer before nodding and following Luke into the casino.

Jenny, Nia, and I stayed by the bar in the lobby while the boys played in the casino. Mostly because I have no money to gamble, Jenny's too drunk to play anyway, and Nia just wants to get blackout drunk—which is understandable, since she has to be around the guy that just told her she's not girlfriend material for the rest of the night. The rest of the trip, actually.

Tristan had somehow won fifty dollars on one of the slot machines, and after he came out with a giant grin to show us his new bag of quarters—yes, my twenty-two-year-old boyfriend requested his winnings in quarters so that he could play in the arcade—he and James spent the entire rest of the time playing games.

James cycled through all of the different games in the arcade while Tristan stuck to the claw machine in the corner the entire time. He would go through cycles of being really quiet as he concentrated, to being really pissed off and frustrated every now and then, which I could see because he'd run his fingers through his hair anxiously as he walked away from the machine. But every time, his eyes would always lock with mine, and I'd smile at him, which always made his shoulders un-tense, and then he'd turn around and put more quarters into the machine to try again.

I was tempted to go over and see what he was trying to get, but I couldn't leave Nia. Since we sat down at the mini bar in the lobby, she's managed to down three drinks, and while I know I should stop her, I can't bring myself to cut her off. If Tristan had just dumped me, I know I'd be drowning myself in eighteen-dollar fruity drinks, too.

She's waving down the bartender to order another drink, but Luke's voice cuts across the lobby, and we all turn around to see him walking out with a pissed off scowl.

"Screw this casino. If I wanted to get fucked that hard, I'd go to the strip club down the street."

"It's not the casino's fault you suck, Lukey," I call across the lobby. When his eyes find us at the bar, his lips quirk up.

"You look hungry, Bubbles." He calls back. "Let's go get a burger."

"I don't eat meat," I call back, but regret it immediately when I realize how that could be twisted.

"She did last night," Nia calls over her shoulder while shooting finger guns over her head. She's incredibly drunk right now so I can't be too mad at her, but when the entire team starts to howl and woop as Tristan walks out of the arcade, I want to evaporate into thin air.

He has a ridiculous grin on his face that I suspect has more to do with the memory of what we did in his hotel room last night than whatever he just won in the arcade. When he finally reaches me at the bar, I will my face to cool front the heat now pooling in my cheeks, but it's useless, because when he helps me off my stool, a new rush of warmth floods my body at the feel of his hand wrapping securely around me.

He keeps a steady arm around me as we follow our friends to the restaurant a few blocks down, and I try not to think about the fact that we're being watched by nearly all the passersby on the street. Their eyes widen when they spot Luke and Micah near the front of our group, and then, as if realizing that he's probably nearby, they always frantically search the crowd until they lock in on Tristan.

Most pass by without stopping, only giving quick waves or shouting out their celebratory cheers, but when we get to the restaurant, a group of older guys stops him for a few pictures. He pulls open the door for me, grinning down at me in a silent promise to make this quick, and I hurry in to catch up with Jenny and Nia. The sound of burgers sizzling on a grill is nearly drowned out by the drunken karaoke echoing through the restaurant. I spot Micah and Emery pushing together a bunch of tables near the stage, and an excited thrill runs through me, because I know that Jenny, Nia, and I will definitely be up there at some point tonight.

I sit down beside Jenny who's already brainstorming song ideas with Nia as I flick open the menu. There's usually only one option for me at burger joints and I find it immediately at the bottom of the menu. I don't mind veggie burgers, but it really just depends on the place. Some restaurants have amazing recipes, while others just taste like they put a freezer-burned patty into the microwave and nuked it for a few minutes. I have faith that this place won't do me wrong, though.

When the waitress comes around to collect our drink orders, Jenny flicks her menu closed and asks, "How does the karaoke work?"

"It's first come first serve. We have a sign-up sheet in the back. Should I add your name to the list?"

"Yes, definitely." She beams.

"The wait time's about forty minutes, is that alright?" she asks as she writes each of our drink orders down.

"That's perfect." I grin.

———

I don't know what's more shocking—the fact that this restaurant has the best veggie burger I've ever tasted, or that midway through our meal, Micah bet Luke a hundred dollars that he couldn't get fifteen girls phone numbers in fifteen minutes, and he actually did it.

At this point, I don't know if I should be impressed with Luke's skill or appalled by how easily swayed the girls around us were, but he managed to get five of the numbers from the same table. I have no clue what he said to make that happen, but when he turned back to our table with the smuggest grin I've ever seen, I had a feeling it shocked even him.

Luke's attractive—an effortless, magnetizing, mesmerizing kind of attractive. He has golden tanned skin, eyes the shade of the sea after it rains, and messy, tousled blond waves. He's cocky, and playful, and confident, and always has this energy around him, this look that says—*I know I'm hot, you know I'm hot, let's just skip to the good part.* And even though he's young, he doesn't have a babyface. Instead, he's muscular, and tall, with a smile that I'm pretty sure he spent years and years in braces to achieve. But even with all of that, I'm still shocked that he managed to get fifteen phone numbers in fifteen minutes.

No, actually, he finished with four minutes to spare.

"Don't let it get to your head, Luke." I grin at him down the table. "Everyone within a twenty-mile radius is incredibly drunk right now. It's not a fair game."

"Don't pretend like you wouldn't have given me your number, Bubbles." He winks back. "We both know I'd show you a good time."

Tristan leans forward with raised brows. "You want to repeat that?"

Leaning back in his chair, he flashes a nonchalant smile to his captain. "Assuming she was single, of course."

"Mm, that's what I thought." Tristan nods, narrowing his eyes at Luke for a second longer, but when he leans back in his chair and looks down at me, his amused smile breaks through.

"Next up we'd like to welcome to the stage Tristan and Abby." The announcer's voice echoes distantly in my mind until his words register, and then my eyes snap to the stage behind us before looking back at Tristan.

"What?" I breathe.

Tristan's already pushing his chair back, and when he extends his hand to me, the heat rushing straight up my neck nearly sears my cheeks. His teammates are already howling with laughter, but he seems completely immune to their teasing comments as he smiles down at me with a toothy grin. That's when it hits me—he signed us up before coming to the table, that's why it took him so long.

I mirror his excited smile as he pulls me up and leads me up to the stage. And even though I'm still very drunk, I can't seem to keep my knees from shaking as I pull the microphone off the stand and look out to the dimly lit restaurant.

I've never done karaoke in a place like this. In fact, the first and last time I ever actually sung karaoke was at my sixteenth birthday party. My friends and I spent the late August night on the expanse of beach behind my house singing out all our favorite songs. But aside from us, and my elderly neighbors who sat out on their back balcony and gave us encouraging waves and smiles, no one was around to witness it.

I was fully planning on taking a few more shots before coming up here with Jenny and Nia, but when the warm orange spotlights click on, illuminating us on stage, I know it's too late for that.

"What are we singing?" I whisper, holding the microphone away from my mouth.

"What else would we sing, Abs?" His smile is nearly as bright as the lights shining down on us as the first few notes of *No Air* start to play out loudly through the speakers.

I don't have time to think before the first lines of lyrics pop up on the screen, so I bring the microphone up to my mouth and start to sing. My voice is a smooth, steady contrast to my shaking hand, and looking out to the crowd, I spot Jenny and Nia's excited smiles instantly. They're standing on their chairs dancing to the beat while they scream out their very loud, drunken cheers. I can't help but mirror their smiles as they scream out the lyrics along with me, and when I finally look away from them, I'm shocked to see the rest of his team standing up with their hands above their heads, waving their arms like they're at an actual concert. They're definitely being sarcastic assholes, but they're supportive sarcastic assholes, and I love them all for it.

That respite of nerves is short lived, because the second my eyes scan the rest of the crowd, my stomach knots at the sea of cameras flashing. It has nothing to do with me and everything to do with the fact that I'm up here with Tristan, but it doesn't change the fact that this is definitely going to end up on the internet.

I know he can sense my anxiety when he reaches out and takes my hand, pulling my gaze from the crowd. He smiles down at me as he sings, brushing his thumb in a calming circle across the center of my palm. The tension slowly evaporates from my body at the sight of him next to me, so at ease, so confident, even with a crowd of strangers watching us. He pulls me closer, leaning down to brush the tip of his nose across my cheek and place a kiss just under my ear, and when he pulls back, I'm in a daze. His grin deepens when he brings the microphone back up to his mouth to sing, because he knows it.

He knows that even now, even after everything, he still has this effect on me.

A warmth runs through me that I know has less to do with the alcohol and more to do with Tristan, and it relaxes me enough to forget about the phones recording me and just enjoy the moment, because this truly is a moment that I never want to forget.

I don't have to look down at the monitor to read off the lyrics, so I keep my gaze on Tristan as I let loose and sway happily to the music. The speakers are so loud up here I can feel the vibrations through the soles of my heels, and the feel of the music sends an excited shock through me as the beat starts to build, leading us closer and closer to the big notes in the song. I'm not drunk enough to think I'm going to sound good, but even so, I'm going to go for it—and I know that *that* confidence is definitely a side effect of the alcohol.

He grins down at me when I don't completely butcher the first few high notes, and the thrill that runs through me spurs a new wave of confidence. I start to dance as I sing, swaying my hips and rocking my shoulders to the beat as I tilt my head back to really finish the song strong, because if you're going to sing *No Air* for karaoke, you can't half-ass it.

The final notes are coming up, and I look up to Tristan who's watching me with the kind of unreserved, toothy smile that makes my heart beat faster in my chest. He reaches out for my hand as the beat starts to slow for the much calmer ending, and after we both sing the last few lyrics together, the music eases away, replaced by the loud cheers and whistles from the crowd below.

A shocked laugh bubbles out of me as I smile up at him, because even as drunk as I am, I can't believe I actually just did that. His toothy grin widens as he takes a step closer to me, and when he cups my cheeks and brings his lips down to mine, I can't hold back my smile when the crowd below explodes around us.

FORTY-SEVEN

PART III

ABBY

I honestly thought that singing karaoke on stage twice would be the most adventurous thing that I'd do tonight, but when Nia spotted the bright neon lights of the strip club down the street, I knew things were about to get a whole lot crazier.

I didn't even have a chance to try to steer her toward something else, because the second the words left her mouth, Luke threw an arm around her shoulders and they both drunkenly led our group across the street toward the club.

I caught Jenny's smirk as she pulled James along behind her. He was doing a great job of convincing Jen that he didn't care if they went in or not, but when he looked over his shoulder at Tristan with the most excited smile I've ever seen, I couldn't hold back my laugh.

When I follow Jenny inside, the change in energy is palpable.

The building is dimly light, apart from the huge catwalk-like stage in the middle of the room, decorated with poles every few yards. The spotlights above the stage are flashing a kaleidoscope of colors, perfectly timed with the rhythm of the song playing loudly through the speakers. The air catches in my throat at the site of the three girls on stage, swinging seductively on the poles. Some of them are in lacy underwear, similar to what I wore last night for Tristan, while others don't have tops on at all.

The guys jog down the aisle of tables, dropping down into the seats in the front row, and when I hesitate by the door, Tristan squeezes my hand. I know he's about to tell me that we can leave if I want. That we can walk around the strip or go back to the restaurant and wait for everyone to be done here, but when I catch the smile on Nia's face from across the room near the bar, I know I can't leave her.

She looks over her shoulder, and when her searching eyes find mine, she smiles at me and points to the front row, as if to say, *save me a seat!*

I nod, giving an encouraging smile, one that I hope shows how proud of her I am for how well she's doing tonight. If I were her, I'd also be incredibly drunk, but *I'd* be back at the hotel racking up our room service bill while ugly crying into an entire carton of ice cream.

But that's not Nia.

Nia doesn't process heartbreak like the rest of us mere mortals.

James wraps his arm around Jenny as he leads us down the aisle towards the rest of their teammates, and when he leans down to whisper something in her ear, she tilts her head back, smiling up at him as she slips her hand into his back pocket.

The guys have already claimed most of the front row seats, but we fall into the open seats near the end of the stage. Jenny sends James to sit on the other side of Tristan so Nia can sit next to her, and when he drops down between Tristan and Luke, the freshman's excited commentary echoes down the row as three new dancers enter the stage.

"I love strip clubs." Nia beams as she rounds the corner with a stack of cash and an entire bottle of tequila. "You're gonna love it, Abs. It's so empowering to see those women get on stage and take control. To literally have an entire room of men drooling over them." She laughs as she drops into the seat on the other side of Jenny. "And it's a great way to learn new moves. Just pay attention to what they're doing so you can recreate it later." She winks at me before tilting the bottle back, taking a few long pulls of the tequila.

When Tristan clears his throat on the other side of me, I look over to see him grinning, as if to say, *Yeah, you can try out whatever you want on me later, I'm definitely not opposed to that.*

I raise a playful brow and lean over to press a kiss to his lips. If you would have told me that I'd be kissing Tristan Beck—my *boyfriend*—in a strip club in Vegas at the beginning of this year, I wouldn't have believed you. But when he reaches up to cup my cheek and deepens the kiss, I can't imagine being anywhere else than right here.

I think I've had a little more to drink than I probably should have. But that's okay with me, because by the fifth song, I'm three tequila shots deep and now fully understand what Nia meant. Strip clubs are amazing.

Amazing.

We've been hyping up the girls as they dance on stage, cheering them on while drunkenly swaying to the beat in our seats. Each new dancer that takes the stage always starts near the middle, right in front of the guys, but midway through the song they always inevitably end at the end of the stage, dancing for us. I like to think it's because they appreciate our drunken cheers, but also because other than Luke, Nia's the only one with money to spare.

When one of the busty, blonde dancers dips down so I can tuck a few bills into the garter on her thigh, I smile over my shoulder at Tristan. He's relaxed in his seat, smirking at me over the lip of his beer bottle, as if he's perfectly content just watching me enjoy myself.

He reaches over and rests his hand on my back, brushing his thumb across the hem of the lacy material of my shirt. I sit up a little straighter at the touch, watching his eyes dip down to follow the path of his fingers across my back. A shiver shakes my shoulders when his calloused thumb finds the dip of my spine and slowly follows it up, just under the hem of my top.

When his eyes flick back up to mine, they're darker than before, and suddenly all I can think about is how every nerve in my body is hyperaware of the painfully slow movement of his thumb as it brushes across the back of my ribs and down the curve of my waist.

I sigh inwardly, leaning back into his touch, desperate for more.

When his thumb slowly brushes back up the side of my ribs, I take a deep breath, clenching my thighs together at the heat now pulsing between my legs. His thumb makes a teasing pass up my ribs, just barely grazing the side of my breast.

I need him to touch me.

To really touch me.

A soft, frustrated groan vibrates in the back of my throat when he makes another pass up my ribs, just barely grazing my breast. His brow cocks at the noise, and if I wasn't drunk as hell and desperate for him, I might have been embarrassed by it. He brings his beer up to his mouth again, casually taking a sip before sliding his tongue across his lips. When my mouth pops open at the sight, his lips pull up into a haughty grin. One that makes me clench my thighs a little tighter.

I want to lean over and kiss him, to ask him to take me back to the hotel, to call it a night and spend the rest of the night in bed, but before I can, Nia's excited gasp pulls my attention.

She's waving over a dancer walking down the aisle toward us, and when she requests three dances, one for each of us, Tristan's slow, teasing fingers freeze on my back.

"Merry Christmas, ladies." She smirks, falling back into her chair.

Three dancers walk down the aisle, and when a gorgeous brunette in pretty, pink lingerie stops in front of me, I smile up at her nervously. Tristan's hand slides off my back, and I lean back in my seat as she takes a step closer to me.

I don't have to look over to know that his teammates have left their seats to get a better view of our dances, and when Luke groans loudly as she bends down in front of me, her lips only inches from mine, I can't help but smile.

"What's your name?" I can smell the sweet bubblegum on her breath, and when she smiles, my eyes flick down to her lips.

I glance over to see Tristan staring at me with flushed cheeks, and when she reaches up and gently turns my head back to her, a flood of heat flashes in his eyes. A pulse of heat washes over me at the thought of this turning him on, so when my eyes meet hers again, I smile up at her.

"Abby."

"Abby, that's such a pretty name. I'm Layla."

Her brown eyes are smoked out by black liner and shadow, and when she smiles down at me, I can't help but smile back. This girl is really, *really* good at her job. All she's doing is leaning over and talking to me, but I can already feel the energy spiking from the entire basketball team who are slowly getting closer to get a better view of us.

There are signs all over the room that say *no touching*, but Layla reaches out and grabs my hand as she turns around. She holds our interlocked hands over her head as she sits on my lap and starts to grind her butt against me to the beat of The Pussycat Dolls, *Buttons* blasting through the speakers on stage.

My mouth drops open a little as I watch her hips move in a way I've never seen before, and when she bends over and puts her hands on the floor to raise her butt up as she shakes it, I glance over to see the boys all staring with slack jaws and wide eyes.

Layla flips her hair over her shoulder, and when her eyes flick to

Tristan, she smirks. She reaches back and grabs my hand to place on her hip as she starts to grind against my lap while she guides my other hand down the side of her thigh.

Turning around again, she climbs onto the chair, straddling my hips as she grinds on me while pushing her chest closer to my face. I bite down on my lip to keep from laughing, because I can hear Luke's horny commentary loud and clear, and when Layla brings her lips down to my ear, her bubblegum breath warms my cheek.

"Is he your boyfriend? The hottie with the curls?" she asks over the music, grinding on my lap.

When she pulls back, I nod, and her smirk deepens.

"I can tell." She laughs as she brings my hands up to her stomach, and when she leans over to whisper in my ear again, I can feel her legs moving as she shakes her butt—more for the benefit of the spectators than anything else. "He hasn't taken his eyes off you this entire time."

When she pulls away again, she has a bright smile on her face. Her eyes flick between us and then she asks, "Do you want me to teach you?"

I stare up at her as her words sink in, and I know it's the tequila taking control because I can't believe that I actually say yes.

She holds out her hand for me, which I take as she helps me out of the chair, and when she takes my place, she beckons me forward with a single finger.

"Holy—*fuck*." Luke's groan pulls my attention. When I look over, the entire team is watching me, wide-eyed. My eyes flick down to Tristan in the seat beside Layla, and I can tell that he's having a hard time swallowing, which makes me feel a little more confident as I step up to her.

I glance over to see Jenny's dancer shaking her butt in her face, and Nia's dancer is somehow upside down while Nia throws dollar bills into the air around her.

Layla places her hands on my hips and pulls me closer, slipping her leg between mine until I'm standing as close to her as I can without climbing onto the seat with her.

"You start with your hips," she instructs, slowly guiding my hips in a circular motion, similar to how she was dancing before. She uses the full motion of her hips, making it a very drawn out and exaggerated movement. Nodding, she smiles up at me and then trails her hands down the back of my thighs until she grabs just above my knees.

"Now keep up those movements with your hips while you slowly bend your knees, lowering yourself until you're grinding against my leg."

I glance over at Tristan, whose brows are rising as he watches my body move to the music while I slowly lower myself onto her leg. She nods encouragingly at me as she brings her hands above her head while she moves her stomach and chest to the music.

"Don't forget to use your hands," she says, running her hands up her neck as she tilts her head back until her hands are lost in her hair in an effortlessly sexy way.

I mirror her movements, tilting my head back while trailing my hands up my body slowly, until I reach my neck where they disappear into my hair. She guides my hips back up so I'm standing again as she smiles up at me.

"Now bend over."

The throaty groan that sounds from beside us isn't from Luke this time, and when I look over at Tristan, his eyes are dark and molten. I'm mesmerized by him until Layla's hand closes around mine and tugs me down gently so I'm bending down over her.

"Arch your back," she instructs.

I do.

"Pull your shoulders back a little."

I do.

"Now you can move your hips again, sway to the music."

I do.

Layla beams up at me, and for only knowing her for like three minutes, I feel like this has somehow bonded us, because I beam back at her. The last few notes of the song play out, and I take a step back, extending my hand to help her back up.

I only catch sight of Tristan for a second before I reach down and hand her the entire stack of money that Nia gave me to tip the dancers with. When her brows raise, I don't have time to explain the huge tip, because I'm already following Tristan through the crowd toward the doors, ignoring the catcalls and cheers of his teammates when he leads me out of the room and into the lobby without a second glance.

Our hotel is only a ten-minute walk away, but when he steps up to the curb and hails a cab, I can tell by the way he pulls open the door and stands back for me to slide in first that he's just as affected as I am, just as eager.

He connects our lips the second the cab pulls away from the curb, and suddenly, all I can think about is the feel of his desperate, impatient lips against mine and the sound of the near constant city traffic passing us by outside. The back seat of the cab is dark, a stark contrast to the brightly lit street we're driving down, and when his grip on my thigh tightens as I open my mouth for his tongue, I lose myself in the veiled privacy of the small cab. My hands, now steady and eager from the tequila, are set on exploring him.

When I brush my thumb against the side of his neck, his pulse careens just under my fingertips as he pulls me even closer to him. His kisses are rough and quick—commanding every nerve in my body to come alive when he grabs my jaw and kisses me deeper. The groan that vibrates in the back of his throat when I knot my fingers in his curls sends a wave of heat down my spine.

An impatient groan slips through my lips when he breaks the kiss, but when he brushes his thumb across the line of my jaw and turns my head, giving him access to my neck, I swallow hard as the hot pulse between my thighs intensifies. I cross my legs and readjust my position on the seat, hoping to ease the need there, but it only intensifies when he smiles into my neck, his chuckle a soft, torturous vibration against my skin.

Tightening my hold on his curls, I tug impatiently, pulling him closer to me. His hand slides up my thigh, under my skirt to grab my butt as his teeth latch onto the skin just under my ear, pulling a gasp from my lips that echoes through the cab when he bites down and starts to suck.

My eyes flutter closed as the warm pleasure courses through me, but they fly wide open when I remember where we are. My gaze darts to the cabbie, politely ignoring us as he drums his thumbs against the steering wheel to the beat of the song playing from the radio. His casual indifference relaxes me a little, and while I know I should scoot over until we get to the hotel, I can't seem to bring myself to unknot my fingers from his hair or give up the feel of his lips on my neck. Maybe it's the tequila, but I can't deny that the idea of someone watching us like this turns me on even more.

Tristan's hand slides back down my thigh slowly, and my breathing catches in my throat when his teeth graze across the bruise now blooming on my neck. I bite down on the inside of my cheek to silence my moan as his thumb caresses the inside of my leg. It's an innocent gesture, but paired with the way he's kissing my neck, it sends another wave of heat down my spine.

When the cab finally comes to a stop, Tristan breaks away from me. Digging into his back pocket, he hands the cabbie a few folded bills before sliding out and extending his hand to me. My entire body is on fire as we walk into the lobby. There's not many people loitering around since it's well past two in the morning, but the few that clearly recognize Tristan as we pass by don't approach us. I'm a little surprised that we manage to make it clear across the lobby without an interruption, but when I press the call button and look up at him, I can see why. His jaw is clenched, and cheeks flushed, and the dark look in his eye, the one that sends a shiver down my spine, clearly means he has absolutely no intention of being interrupted right now. It's a hard mask, an intimidating one, and when his eyes flick down to mine, they darken as they dip down to my chest in the bright lobby lights above.

The heat pulsing between my legs flares, and when the soft bell of the elevator rings out around us, I hurry in, slamming my finger against the button for his floor.

Twenty-five.

Just twenty-five floors.

The doors start to close, and while I'm eagerly expecting to feel his lips on mine as the elevator starts its ascent, my breath catches in my throat when he drops to his knees. His hands are sliding up my thighs quickly, not wasting a second, and when he stops at the hem of my skirt, he looks up at me with raised brows.

I nod quickly, eyes flying up to check the empty elevator around us as his hand slides down my leg and lifts it up, positioning it over his shoulder.

This is such a bad idea. We could stop at any floor. We'd be caught in a second. We'd get kicked out of the hotel. We'd—

His thumb brushes across my underwear, circling the swollen bud of nerves. The feel of the lace against my clit is enough to make my legs shake, and when he adds more pressure with each circle, my hips rock forward as a shocked moan slips from my lips. That seems to snap whatever restraint he has left, because he hooks the lacy material with his thumb and pulls it aside, exposing me completely.

I grab the handrail behind me to keep steady, and before I can remember all the reasons why we *shouldn't* be doing this right now, he parts me in one long, tortuous lick. My hands tighten on the rail as my head falls back against the wall, looking up at the mirrored ceiling with wide eyes and flushed cheeks. I can see him perfectly in the reflection, the movement of his jaw as his tongue slides in and out of me, licking his way up to my clit. When he starts to suck, my lungs freeze in my chest.

The soft beep that rings out every time we pass a floor pulls my attention, and my heart clenches in my chest as I watch the number slowly rise.

Eighteen.

His tongue finds a quick pace, sending a wave of goosebumps across my entire body.

Nineteen.

I can't bite back the moans that slip out as his tongue builds me up, and up, and up, sucking and licking and grazing his teeth across my clit, nearly making my legs give out.

Twenty.

He tightens his grip on my thighs, holding me up when my legs start to shake too much to control.

Twenty-one.

"Please, *please* don't stop." I gasp, rocking my hips toward him, begging for more pressure. When I take a hand off the rail to knot it in his hair, tugging roughly, he pulls back to look up at me with a wicked grin before ducking his head back down and setting my entire body on fire.

Twenty-two.

I'm so, so close. Close enough that I can't breathe as my entire body tenses in anticipation.

Twenty-three.

"Alright, baby," he murmurs against me. "Come for me. Come on my tongue."

His rough, throaty voice alone could have sent me over, but when he slides a finger inside and curves it up, matching the fast flicks of his tongue, every nerve in my body explodes.

I slump back against the wall, barely hearing the *ding* of the elevator, signaling our arrival to the floor. My entire body is warm and numb, pulsing with stated heat, too weak to move yet. Standing up, he fixes my skirt before wrapping his arm around my waist, helping to hold me up as the elevator doors open and he leads us out.

With each step, my heels ring out around us in the quiet hall. It's a fast tempo, an excited one—a perfect echo of my racing heart. I lean into him, my legs still too weak to walk on my own, and when we stop in front of his door, a new rush of excitement floods through me. The beep of the card reader echoes loudly as he pushes open the door, and when he steps back and holds it open for me, the anticipation blooming in my stomach flares.

The room is dark, only slightly illuminated by the soft moonlight and a barely-there shimmer of flashing neon lights from the strip below. When the door closes behind us, he takes a step forward, but I take a step back, keeping the small distance between us. His brow raises, and when I perk mine in challenge as I take another step back, closer to the bed, his cheek twitches.

I hold his stare as I reach down and grab the hem of my lacy top. His eyes flick down, tracking every movement before meeting mine again. When I toss the lace to the floor at his feet, his throat bobs in a hard swallow. Reaching back to pull off his own, a shiver runs up my spine that shakes my shoulders. I will never get used to him. To the deep olive skin, the strong arms, the smooth, sculpted muscles on his shoulders and chest and stomach. To the way they all tighten when he takes another step toward me, into the soft glow of the red neon lights shining from the strip below.

I want to keep this little game going, to see who can last the longest without breaking, but when his eyes dip down to my perked nipples and aching breasts, desperate for his touch, we both break. Grabbing my thighs, he pulls me up, connecting our lips as he walks us back to the bed. The tequila in my system is heightening every sensation—the feel of his calloused fingers on my thighs, his tongue slipping through my eager lips, and the pulsing ache building between my legs again.

I need him. I've needed him since before we left. And now that we're finally alone, I have no intention of waiting anymore. He leans forward, dropping me onto the mattress softly before he straightens back up and unbuttons his pants. I barely even have time to wiggle out of my skirt before I hear the tearing of the condom, and after I slide my underwear off, tossing it across the room, I'm naked with nothing but my heels on.

His eyes are still dark, and the sight of his tense jaw sends a wave of goosebumps across my chest because I've never seen him like this. He hooks his hands under my knees and tugs me to the edge of the bed, and when his lips connect with mine again, they're desperate, urgent, claiming—like he needs me to know that I'm his and he's mine.

I wrap my legs around him to pull him to me and the pressure between my legs only intensifies when his tongue slides through my lips. My entire body is pulsing in time with my heart, and I have to turn my head to break the kiss, breathless and panting. He smiles at that, leaning down to drag his tongue up my neck. When he grips my hips, I don't have time to register what's happening before he flips me over onto my belly and pulls me back, bending me over the bed. My toes curl in my heels as he fills me, and he finds a fast, unrelenting rhythm that pulls desperate, breathy whimpers from my lips as he holds my hips in place.

I close my eyes and revel in the shocks of pleasure shooting up my spine, spreading through my body like wildfire. He loosens his grip on my hip and the air freezes in my lungs when he slides his hand around and rubs his thumb in slow circles on my clit. His hips thrust harder, faster than before, and I have to tighten my hold on the mattress to not fall over. I'm right there, on the edge of pleasure and pain, and it feels so good it almost hurts. My legs start to shake, and I grab his arm, digging my nails into the hot skin as I roll my head back. The moans slipping from my lips become more desperate with each thrust and swipe of his thumb, but I want to feel more, I want to feel his lips on me again.

Reaching back, I pull my hair over my shoulder, tilting my head to expose my neck. I almost regret it the second he pulls his hand away, leaving the swollen bud between my legs tender and aching, but when he slowly brushes that wet, glossy thumb down my throat, a breathless gasp slips escapes me.

His hand finds my hip again, and when he tightens his hold on me as he slows his thrusts into a lazy rhythm, my stomach tightens when his hot tongue follows the wet trail up the column of my neck. A shiver shakes my shoulders when his teeth graze the sensitive skin just under my ear, and when he bites down roughly and starts to suck, a shock of painful pleasure shoots up my spine as my throaty moan echoes around us.

I dig my fingers into the sheets when he thrusts harder, sending me over the edge as the first wave of pure bliss floods my veins. When my legs start to wobble, he wraps his arm around my waist, pulling me to him as his hips flex forward, faster, more desperate than before. I can feel his muscles tense as he holds me closer, and then he slows, reveling in his own release as he buries his face in my neck.

I turn around in his hold when he pulls out, wrapping my arms around him as he presses a soft kiss to the new bruise forming on my neck. I smile when he peppers kisses up my cheek, on my nose, across my forehead, over my chin, everywhere but my lips, which I'm now trying desperately to bring to his. He playfully dodges my mouth and lands his lips on every part of my face and neck and chest but the one place that I really want them. My laughs quickly turn into impatient huffs, and when he grins down at me, I pout—a full-on, dramatic, fat-lipped pout—and he finally, mercifully, takes pity on me, bringing his lips down to mine.

His lips are gentle and slow, tender against mine, but when I eagerly open my mouth for his tongue to slide through, he smiles against my lips before tickling my sides, pulling a breathless gasp from my lips as I try to grab his hands.

When he finally pulls back, he grins down at me before climbing off the bed and sauntering into the bathroom. The sink turns on as I scan the room. It's still a mess of cups and empty beer bottles from when everyone was in here earlier, and I sit up to unbuckle my heels, dropping them down onto the floor at the foot on the bed.

The sound of my phone vibrating against the floor catches my attention, and I wrap the loose bed sheet around my body before slipping off the bed and picking up my wristlet from the floor. Unzipping it, I bite down on the inside of my cheek as the contact flashes on my phone. If it was anyone else, I don't think I would have answered right now.

"Hey, Nia."

Sitting back on the edge of the bed, I pull the sheet tighter around me in the cold room.

"Hey, you little slut, are you guys done yet?"

Tristan walks out of the bathroom with a lazy grin on his face, and when my eyes coast down his naked body, I'm tempted to say no.

"Depends," I answer honestly, because if she needs me, I'll be there.

"Come down and meet us by the pool. We're hanging out for a bit before we go up to bed."

Micah and Luke are arguing in the background, and when Luke screams an impressive slew of profanities before a loud splash sounds, I grin, because I don't need to be there to know that Micah just threw him into the water.

"Okay, we'll be right down," I say, watching Tristan's brows raise.

I hang up and smile sheepishly at him, because I can tell by the sleepy, sated look in his eyes that he just wants to climb into bed and cuddle. But we're in Vegas, and it's spring break, and they just won the championship game, so we really should go finish the night out with our friends.

I ditched my heels in the room since they were starting to hurt my feet, so to save me from walking barefoot across the hotel, Tristan's piggybacking me down to the pool area. We both slipped back into our clothes from earlier to make it as inconspicuous as possible, but thinking about it now, that seems kind of pointless. They definitely know what we were just doing.

I'm still a little buzzed, but for the most part, the tequila induced haze has worn off. I press a kiss to his neck as he pushes open the door leading out to the pool, and when we step out, I can already see our friends splashing around in the pool.

When Micah spots us walking up, he raises an inked hand out of the water and rubs it through his hair roughly a few times, smoothing the hair away from his eyes as he calls out, "If you fucked on my bed, I swear to fucking God."

My cheeks warm, but Tristan feigns a guilty grin and shrugs. "Sorry, man."

When he kicks off his shoes and tightens his hold on my legs, I cling to his shoulders as he gets a running start and launches us into the pool. The water is so much colder than it was earlier, and when I detangle my legs from him, kicking to the surface, the cool night air blowing past sends a shiver down my spine before I can even catch my breath.

When Tristan reaches out for me, I take his hand, wrapping my arms around his shoulders so I don't have to tread water. We're in the middle of the pool, but even here, he can easily stand. He grins down at me as he reaches up and wipes his thumb under my eye, pulling a black, mascara covered finger away. I probably look like a drowned raccoon right now, but I'm too tired to really care. His dimple deepens as he shakes his head to get the hair out of his eyes, and when his arms tighten around me, I ignore the sarcastic groans of his teammates as he brings his lips down to mine.

"It's fucking nauseating being around you two." Luke splashes us as he swims past.

Tristan doesn't break the kiss as he lifts his hand from my waist, and I can't hold back my smile as I lift my own, flipping him off together while his tongue slips into my mouth.

When his tongue brushes against mine, the cold water lapping around us suddenly feels much warmer, and the air catches in my throat at the feel of his calloused fingers trailing up my back, slipping just under the hem of my lace top. He smiles against my lips when a soft, barely-there moan vibrates in the back of my throat.

"The fuck is this?"

Tristan breaks away from me, glancing over to Luke who's holding up what looks like a small clear container, the kind that usually comes out of toy vending machines. Tristan's hurried answer piques my attention.

"It's mine." His voice is clipped and tense.

When Luke brings the container up higher to peer inside, his eyes widen.

"Sorry," He clears his throat, tossing the small container to Tristan, who catches it easily and reaches back to stash it back in his pocket.

"Wait." I laugh, trying to grab his hand under the water. "What is it?"

"Nothing." He shakes his head, glaring at Luke who smiles awkwardly back.

"Oh, come on, what is it?" I laugh as he pulls his hand out of the water, holding it over his head to keep the container out of my reach. I look up at his hand, too far from my reach to bother, and when I sigh heavily and look back down, he's watching me, searching my face. When his eyes soften, he lowers his hand back down.

"I was planning on doing this somewhere else—somewhere more romantic than the hotel pool." He searches my face, and my heart nearly stops in my chest at the serious look in his eyes. "I saw you watching the report in the bar earlier, the one about my projected pick, and I know it's been stressing you out lately. Ever since you got your acceptance letter to NYU, you've been worrying about it—about where I'm going to end up." He reaches up, tucking my hair behind my ear, and I watch him, frozen in place as he looks back down and pops the top of the container off. I know everyone's watching us right now, but the new flush of my cheeks has nothing to do with their curious gazes, rather the rose gold ring shimmering in the pale moonlight.

When I saw this in that claw machine at the casino, I knew I had to win it for you, because I'm still broke as fuck until I sign my contract in June and I don't have the kind of money to buy you the ring that you deserve. And I know it's not an engagement ring, I know that it's still too soon for that, but it's—I don't know, I guess it's a promise ring. Something physical to have with you when I'm not there." His eyes flick up to mine, searching my face as he continues.

I don't know where I'm going to be drafted, Abby. I don't know what city I'll be in, or how long I'll be there, or how often I'll get to see you between games and practices. But what I do know is that I'm not going to let it break us. I'll do whatever it takes to make it work. I'll buy a place in New York and fly out to see you every time I have a day off. I'll get on an eight-hour red-eye just to see you for thirty minutes if that's all I have time for. I'll do whatever it takes to make sure that you know, no matter how many miles away we are, I will always be here. I will always want you." He takes the ring out of the container, and when he reaches for my hand, my cheeks flame when I realize that I'm crying.

He slips the rose gold band onto my ring finger, and I stare down at it, reveling in the feel of the cold metal against my skin. A ring—*a promise.*

When I look back up at him, he's searching my face, and I blink away the tears welling in my eyes as I smile up at him. His thumb trails down the line of my jaw, tilting my head back to bring my lips closer to his, and his emerald eyes catch mine as he grins down at me.

"I will always be in love with you, Abby Ryan, and nothing in the world will ever change that."

FORTY-EIGHT

TRISTAN

I never thought I'd wake up with two girls in my bed ever again, but when I turn over and wrap my arm around Abby's waist, pulling her closer to me, I catch sight of another small body beside hers and freeze instantly. It takes a few seconds for the sleepy haze to pass before I recognize that it's Nia's sleeping body cuddled up next to Abby, and a few more seconds of me desperately racking my hungover as fuck brain to confirm that I didn't actually have a threesome with my girlfriend and her best friend last night.

Nia came back with us to crash in our room when Jenny and James called dibs on the girls' room. She was still pretty wasted by that point, so after Abby brought her into the bathroom and helped her change into some of my dry clothes, she passed out cold the second her head hit the pillow.

She really could have taken the other bed with Micah since Luke never ended up coming back to the room, but I think Abby wanted to keep her close by because she tucked her into our bed securely, making sure she had the travel sized bottle of ibuprofen and a cold water bottle on the nightstand beside her, before she followed me back into the bathroom to get ready for bed.

I caught Micah's smirk when I closed the door behind us, and I could tell by his cocked brow that he was fully expecting us to fuck in the bathroom. As appealing as that idea was, I was convinced that no matter how drunk my girlfriend was, she would never knowingly let anyone hear us. The shower incident scared her enough, and if I'm going to bury myself in her, I don't want her to hold back for the sake of the people on the other side of the door. I want to hear her labored pants and sexy gasps and the way her shaky voice desperately moans my name over, and over, and over when she gets close. It's one of my favorite parts of being with Abby—hearing her come undone, knowing that I'm the one coaxing those sexy sounds from her lips.

Her smile deepened when she turned to the faucet, and after brushing our teeth together, I got the perfect view of her ass as she bent over to spit out the suds from her mouth. The room around us warmed with her drunk laughter when she finally caught sight of the toothpaste goatee I had perfectly crafted with the suds on my chin. She turned around, considering me for a moment as she brushed my curls away from my forehead, and after wiping away the errant suds with her thumb, she pulled my lips down to hers.

The soft, sweet kiss turned into something else entirely when my tongue slid across her lips. I was fully expecting her to turn me down, knowing that we had a very thin wall separating us from Nia and Micah, but when she eagerly opened her mouth for my tongue to slip through, I couldn't hold back my grin. I ducked down, lifting her onto the bathroom counter as I greedily took advantage of the last few moments of privacy that we were going to have for a while.

Her body was searching for my touch as my hands traveled down to her hips and under her shirt, trailing my fingers slowly up her stomach. I could feel the first rock of her hips as an impatient groan slipped through her lips, irritated with my slow, teasing pace. I swiped my thumb teasingly across the smooth, sensitive skin under her perked nipples, and she bit down hard on my lip with a desperate moan, making me smile so fucking hard I had to pull away to look at her.

Her cheeks were flushed and eyes molten, and when her gaze flicked to the door behind me to make sure it was locked, she was pulling my shirt off before I could even process the fact that she was about to let me fuck her in the bathroom.

I pulled my too-big boxers down her legs and kneeled down, looking up from between her perfect thighs to see her watching me with flushed cheeks and dark eyes. I had her coming on my tongue quicker than usual, and by the time I stood back up and buried myself deep inside her, she seemed to have lost any motivation to keep quiet as her throaty moans echoed around us. Hiking her thighs up higher to change the angle, I couldn't hold back my smug ass grin when those moans turned damn near desperate. I could tell she was close when her arms started to weaken around my shoulders, and I held her close as she came around me, squeezing me tight as hell as I slowed down, enjoying every second of her sweet warmth. That alone nearly had me coming with her, but it wasn't until her hot tongue slid up the column of my neck to my ear where she whispered those three words over, and over, and over, like a sated prayer, that I found my own release.

I barely had time to help her off the counter before Micah's impatient knocks echoed loudly off the door. That seemed to sober her up from the high I just gave her, and her cheeks flared as she stepped back into her pajamas. I pulled my pants back up my legs, and when she opened the door and slipped past him, I caught the quirk of his lips when he looked down at her. I knew damn well he heard everything, and when his gaze flicked up to me as I followed Abby out, we both nodded with dumbass grins.

When she climbed onto our bed, she re-tucked Nia's sleeping body into the blanket gently, making sure to not wake her. Her cheeks were still flushed with that pretty rosy hue when she looked back up at me, and when she rubbed the open spot next to her with the sweetest smile I've ever seen, I climbed in beside her. She molded her body to mine easily, and with her head resting on my chest, her soft snores lulled me to sleep as I traced the outline of the ring on her finger.

Now, with the morning sun pouring through the open curtains and the sound of the air conditioning roaring dully from the unit under the window, I'm the only one awake. Micah's sprawled out on his stomach in the middle of his bed with his white sheets pooled around his hips, as if he got hot in the middle of the night and tried to kick them off. His untouched back is almost a shocking contrast against the dark swirls and lines of black ink trailing down both of his arms and torso. When I met him his freshman year, he had half a sleeve, and now that he's nearing the end of his junior year, he's the most tatted one on the team by far.

I'm pretty fucking surprised that out of everyone, he's the one who didn't bring someone home last night. But then again, I'm pretty sure I saw him walking out the bathroom in the strip club with some random girl he met at the bar and based on the way she was trying to adjust her dress, I'm guessing he already got his fix for the night.

I glance back down to Abby, brushing my lips against the purple bruise on her neck as I pull her closer to me. It's not too long before her small body starts to stir sleepily in my arms, and I try to hold back my smile when she nuzzles deeper into my chest as a soft, painful groan slips through her lips. She has to be incredibly hungover. Even after chugging two water bottles before bed last night like a champ, it doesn't even come close to the amount of liquor she downed while we were out.

I was pretty drunk last night, but I was on top of my water intake between drinks. After four years of hardcore partying and daily sunrise workouts, I've mastered the perfect water to liquor ratio—unlike my stubborn girlfriend who waved me off every time I tried to remind her to drink a glass of water instead of downing more tequila like it was a fucking juice pack. I know I shouldn't be smiling at her expense, but it's a pretty hilarious *I told you so* as she sighs pitifully into my chest.

Nia starts to stir, and when she lifts her head from the pillow, her short black hair is a mess of flyaways. She narrows her eyes into small slits in an attempt to keep out the harsh sunlight before she buries her face back into her pillow.

"I think I'm dead." Her voice is muffled and cracked, and the sound pulls Abby's face from my chest.

"Me, too." She nods, leaving my arms to crawl over Nia, grabbing for the medicine bottle on the nightstand. Popping open the bottle, she hands them out to each of us. I down mine quickly, opening the bottle of water on my own nightstand, and when I hand it off to her, she winces as she takes her own sip before handing off the bottle to Nia.

I lay back, grinning up at Abby as I open my arms for her, and when she nuzzles her face into my chest again, I rub her back softly. The exaggerated gagging noise from Nia pulls both of our attention, and when we glance over, her nose is wrinkled as she slips out of bed and mumbles, "I'm too hungover for this lovey dovey shit."

The click of the bathroom door echoes through the room, and my gaze drops back down to Abby. Her finger is sliding down the center of my stomach, slowly tracing the muscles there, and when they trace their way back up, I pull her closer to me.

I would have been happy to stay here for the rest of the day—just us, in bed, cuddling while we flip through the three hundred different channels on the hotel TV—but that plan went to shit the second my phone started to ring.

Micah turned over, grumbling half-asleep about *vacations* and *sleeping in* and *turning off the fucking phone* before pulling a pillow over his head. Abby sat up when she caught sight of who was calling, and I grinned as she took one of the six pillows on our bed and launched it at Micah's sleeping body.

He didn't move, aside from lifting his hand and lazily flipping her off as his muffled voice sounded from under the pillow. "That was weak, Ryan, even for you."

She just smiles as she turns back to me, and when I click the green button on the call, I can already hear the chaos that always seems to surround my family. Gigi's cries are echoing loudly through the phone, but fade as someone seems to carry her away.

"Hey, Mom."

"Good morning, honey. How'd you sleep?"

"Great, you?" I ask, stretching my arms above my head until the three pops sound from between my shoulders.

"Amazing, your dad and I went out for dinner last night at that Italian restaurant, the one by the—Georgia, baby, no don't do that, that's dirty. Go wash your hands, please. Remember to count as you wash—sorry, honey, what was I saying? Oh, right, we went to dinner at that Italian place and it was phenomenal. You should take Abby there." When Abby's lips pull into a smile, I know she can hear my mother's voice.

"I'll look it up," I promise, reaching over to tickle her when she nods with a playful smile, as if to say, *You better.*

My fingers connect with the ticklish spot on her waist, and she laughs loudly, which results in two things simultaneously—Micah sitting up and launching a pillow at us, which connects with my shoulder surprisingly hard for someone who's half asleep, and my mom's excited gasp.

"Oh, Abby's there, too? You should come down to breakfast with us at nine, we're going to the restaurant connected to the lobby."

Abby's eyes flick to the alarm clock, and by the excited smile pulling at her lips, I know I'm not going to be able to get out of this. She nods quickly as she rolls off the bed, already pulling her hair out of her bun, and when she walks into the bathroom that Nia just walked out of, the door shuts softly as the shower turns on.

I hold back a groan as I watch my plans of not leaving the bed all day vanish right in front of my eyes.

"Yeah." I sigh. "We'll be there."

We spotted my family immediately when we walked into the restaurant connected to the hotel lobby, and somehow, in the thirty minutes that we've been here, I've managed to down three plates of pancakes. Abby's been stealing bites from my plate, and when she reaches over and steals another piece, she grins up at me as she slips the fork into her mouth, pulling it out slow enough to remind me of when she had something much different between those perfect lips. I know she did it on purpose, because when I clear my throat and sit up straighter to inconspicuously adjust myself, her lips pull back into a smug smile.

I look around, hoping to distract myself from spiraling into thoughts of Abby on her knees again. My dad's mid-conversation with Garrett about coming over when we get home so they can change the oil in Mel's Kia, and Mel's trying to take a picture of Gigi and Georgia, who she has in matching outfits as they eat their breakfast. When I turn back to Abby, she's nodding along with a bright smile as my mom babbles happily between bites of her own pancakes.

"I can't believe they won. I mean, I adore them, but I didn't think they *really* had a chance of winning, you know?" I'm almost a little offended, until I realize that she's not talking about my game, she's talking about the season finale of *Dancing with the Stars*. It premiered last night right after the game, which I know, even though she'd never actually admit it, was the real highlight of her night. I know Abby doesn't watch it, but she beams back anyway, as if she's just excited to be talking to my mom at all.

"It made a perfect night even better," Mom smiles at me as she piles a small scoopful of fruit salad onto my plate. "But the new season should be even better. I hear that they have an NBA player on. A retired one." Her eyes are shining bright, and when she beams at me, I shake my head at the clear suggestion.

"I'm not going on *Dancing with the Stars*, Mom."

I shut that down quickly, but when I glance over at Abby next to me, she's smiling as she pulls the grape off her fork with her teeth.

Oh, no.

"But you'd look so cute," she teases. "And you're already such a great dancer."

"I *am* a great dancer," I agree, stealing a strawberry off her plate.

"I'm great at a lot of things, don't you think?" Her cheeks warm as she swats my fork away, but she grins at me when I pop it into my mouth.

"Imagine Grandma and Grandad watching you dance on TV, Tristan. They'd love it. You should at least consider it," Mom continues, unrelenting. I can already imagine the smirk on my grandad's face. He'd never let me live it down. I'm about to shoot down the idea, *again*, when her eyes widen, and she looks at Abby. "We could have *DWTS* nights, Abby. You could come over when it airs. I'm sure Livy would want to watch, too." She beams at my girlfriend, who's now staring at her like she might actually cry.

"That would be amazing." She nods, blinking a few times to inconspicuously push back the tears now threatening to pool in her eyes. When she looks up at me, my heart clenches in my chest, because I know that my mom inviting her to watch a TV show together means more to her than my mom even knows. Even being here, being around my family, makes her so happy. She hasn't said much about hers, aside from the night we laid in the field, and she told me about her dad, but I can tell by the way her eyes light up at the smallest moments of affection or tenderness from my mom, that she must not experience those with her own. The way her shoulders always tense slightly when my mom pulls her in for hugs, or how even this, an invitation for a night on the couch watching TV, means so much more to her.

Reaching under the table, I thread my fingers through hers, squeezing gently.

She can have it. Nights with my mom, Sunday afternoons listening to my dad ramble about the football game on the TV, getting dragged out back to hit around the volleyball with Liv, babysitting the girls. All of it. I want her to have all of it.

"It doesn't have to be *DWTS*," Mom muses as she pulls a waffle onto her plate. "You should come over for *Love Island*. Livy and I watch it every night when it's on. I mean, you don't have to come every night if you're busy, of course, but if you're free, we'd love to have you—"

"Yes," she says quickly, her eyes wide and smile blinding. "I'd love to."

"Perfect. It'll be a girls' night then." Mom smiles at her before her eyes scan to the empty seat beside me. "Is Olivia not coming?" she asks, brows pulling together.

I glance over at the seat and shrug. How would I know?

"Well, was she awake when you two left?"

Abby looks up at me, and when I meet her gaze, her eyes widen a little.

"I don't know, I haven't seen her this morning," I say carefully because I'm starting to realize where this is going.

Mom's head snaps up. "Olivia didn't sleep in your room last night?"

"No." Abby shakes her head.

I can feel the anxiety now radiating off of her as she looks between us, face paling.

"She texted me—she said—what did she say? Oh, let me look." Pulling out her phone from her purse, she squints at the screen since she doesn't have her glasses on.

"*I'm staying in Tristan's room tonight. I'll be back in the morning.*" She reads out, frowning as her brows pull together. "She spelled tonight wrong. Was she drinking last night?" Her eyes flick back up to us, and I shake my head quickly.

"I didn't see Olivia at all last night. We were out on the strip most of the night and when we got back it was just the team hanging out. I didn't run into her once."

"I'm calling her." She stands up quickly and walks toward the side of the patio where it's less noisy, but the second she moves from view, I catch sight of something through the window to the hotel lobby. It happens so quickly that I almost miss it, but the anger floods my veins like an electric shock when I realize what I'm seeing.

The doors of the elevator open and Olivia hurries out, only her hand is caught by another and she's pulled back. Her head falls back in a laugh as she turns and wraps her arms around his neck, popping up on her toes to bring her lips up to his. I know who it is the second his arms wrap around her waist and pull her close, and when her head falls back and he nuzzles his face into her neck, white-hot anger flares in my chest.

The nauseating scratching of the iron chair against the floor echoes as I stand. I don't even realize that I'm moving until I'm pulling open the door of the restaurant, barely catching the sound of Abby's confused voice calling after me. The small crowd loitering around the lobby moves out of my way, and when he finally pulls away from her neck, his eyes catch on mine as I stalk toward them with what has to be the most pissed off expression I've ever worn.

His lazy grin falls away as he releases his hold on my little sister.

"What the fuck is going on?" I demand, stopping in front of them. Olivia turns quickly, eyes widening.

"Leave it alone, Tristan," she snaps, but she takes a step away from him, as if she can sense the unbridled anger radiating off of me. That's probably for the best, because all I can seem to picture is how Luke McConnell and my little sister just spent the night together.

"My *baby* sister? What the *fuck* is wrong with you?" I shove him hard toward the elevator.

"Tristan." Abby's voice echoes behind me, and I can hear her footsteps running across the lobby after me, but I can't seem to think about anything other than the way Luke's eyes widen as his gaze flicks between mine and Olivia's, as if he's suddenly realizing how badly he fucked up.

"I'm not a baby, Tristan. I'm eighteen. I can do what I want."

"Did you?" I snarl, grabbing the front of his shirt and hauling him closer to me. It's the same one he was wearing last night in the pool, only now it's dry, crinkled as fuck, but dry.

He didn't come back to the room last night, which means he just bought his own, and based on the way my little sister is looking up at him right now, I know exactly why he felt the need to have his own room.

He shoves me off, ripping his shirt out of my grip. "Calm the fuck down, T."

"How is this any of your business?" Olivia snaps.

"*Did you?*" I repeat through clenched teeth, taking a step closer.

He holds my gaze, jaw tightening, but stays silent.

"I told you to stay away from her. From the fucking start, I told you not to touch her."

"I get it, you're pissed, but this wasn't just last night. We've been . . ." He looks over my shoulder, considering her. "We've been hanging out for a while and I—"

"Hanging out?" My words are clipped, laced with anger. "Your version of *hanging out* and hers are a hell of a lot different. And you knew that, didn't you?"

He freezes, meeting my gaze.

"That's what I thought." I snort. "Fuck you, McConnell."

"It's not like that. It's different now—I was going to talk to you. Today. I was going to fucking talk to you today."

"No, you weren't." I shake my head, a humorless laugh slipping through my lips. "You weren't going to tell me, just like you were never going to tell her."

His jaw flexes, but his eyes flick over to hers and I can see the desperate hope in his eyes, praying to fucking God she doesn't figure out what I'm talking about.

"Does she know," I goad, taking a step forward, pushing him back a step.

"Shut the fuck up." His voice is low, just loud enough for me to hear, but when Olivia looks between us, her brows creasing, I know she heard.

"Tell me what?" She steps closer, eyes fixed on Luke. "Tell me what, Luke?"

He glares at me before looking down at her, eyes softening as he hesitates.

"He's been fucking jersey chasers." I say, watching his jaw tighten. "He fucked one in the kitchen the night before we came here. But he never told you that, did he?"

She freezes, her eyes slowly lifting up to Luke's.

"The night before—" she shakes her head, face paling.

"Liv, it's—I didn't know—"

"Before or after you were with me?" She breathes, so quiet I almost miss it.

He stays quiet, and her brows pull together, nearly screaming as she asks again.

"Before or after, Luke?"

Running a rough hand through his hair, he whispers, "After."

She steps back, eyes wide as if he just slapped her.

"Liv," he pleads, taking a step to follow her, but when she takes another step back from him, her eyes wide and glossy, I grab the collar of his shirt and haul him back, forcing him away from her. Knocking my hand away, he turns to me, his eyes feral as he steps toward me.

"Fuck, is this really what you want, T?" He snaps, shoving me back. "You want to hear about how I fucked your sister? How many times I had her coming on my—"

The impact of my fist against his jaw sends a searing pain up my arm, but it's muted when his own fist connects with my cheek. A blistering pain shoots through my skull, and before I can resister what I'm doing, I'm launching myself at him, tackling him onto the titled floor, slamming my fist into his face. His grunts echo through the lobby, melding with the screams of the small crowd watching us. Trying to throw me off, he slams his fist into my stomach, knocking the air out of my lungs before he rears back again to connect with my jaw. I'm about to knock him the fuck out, but I'm hauled back, pulled onto my feet as two inked arms wrap around me, locking my arms at my sides. I lunge forward, trying to break out of the hold, but he tightens his grip on me, nearly knocking the air out of my lungs again.

"The fuck is wrong with you two?" Micah shouts, hauling me back a few more steps.

Luke glares at me from the floor, swiping the blood from his nose.

"Never again," I snap, spitting the blood pooling in my mouth onto the floor at his feet. "You're never going to touch her again."

Standing up, he's silent for a long moment as he holds my stare, clearly understanding the threat there. Fucking my baby sister behind my back was bad enough, doing it again, that'd be it. He'd be done.

Teammates or not—*brothers or not*—he'd be dead to me.

Bringing his hand up to his jaw, he considers me for a long moment before swallowing hard and nodding wordlessly. A silent agreement that we understand each other. That he's not going to touch my little sister ever again. That he's not even going to be in the same fucking room as her, and then maybe, *maybe* I won't fucking kill him.

"Luke." She takes a step toward him, but he shakes his head as he clenches and unclenches his jaw, probably to test that I didn't break it. I wouldn't be surprised if I did; my knuckles are sore, and I can already feel them starting to bruise.

"I'm sorry." His eyes are fixed on mine, but I know that he isn't talking to me, and when his shoulders tense as they flick down to Olivia, she realizes it, too.

"What?" She freezes, her hands falling limp at her sides.

"We can't, Liv. I fucked up. I fucked all of this up. I knew I shouldn't—I knew, but I—I wanted you for so long, and then everything at the park happened, and the night in the car, and I was so drunk and you were there, and I just—I knew I shouldn't have, but I fucked up and I—you were—"

Soft hands find mine, and I glance down to see Abby looking up at me wide-eyed before looking down to my hand. She rubs her thumb over each knuckle, as if to check to make sure it's okay, that I'm not hurt, and when she's convinced that I haven't broken my hand, she interlocks our fingers and rests her head against my arm as her gaze falls back to Olivia. I follow her gaze to see my sister's shoulders sink slowly as Luke's words register.

"A mistake. I was a mistake," she whispers, taking a step back. Luke's shoulders tense, but when his eyes flick back up to mine, I know that he's going to stick to our agreement. That he understands how badly he fucked up. That he knows you don't cross that line—not with your teammates. Not with your roommates. Not with your brothers.

When his eyes find hers again, they soften as he considers her.

"I'm sorry, Liv."

FORTY-NINE

ABBY

I've been stress eating all day.

Or emotional eating. Or hormonal eating. I don't really know, it's probably a mix of all of them, to be honest; but either way, I've already eaten nearly an entire pack of Oreos and finished off the sour straws that Tristan got for me before we left for Vegas—all before sunset.

My inhalation of cookies isn't that out of character for me, even on a good day, but the fact that I woke up with my period only intensified my sugar cravings, and it was further amplified by the anxiety that's been blooming in my chest since I opened my mail this morning.

Most of it was junk mail that I tossed into the trash without opening, but the letter at the very bottom of the pile was addressed to me in a similar style envelope that I opened last week, only this one was much larger. It was from NYU, which I could clearly see by the school crest inked boldly into the top corner of the envelope and on each piece of paper inside. It wasn't anything out of the ordinary, just typical admissions paperwork, and I almost didn't see the letter at the very end of the stack of papers before I slipped them back into the envelope to fill out later. But when I caught the header titled *financial aid,* I pulled it out and read through it quickly.

I had to read the letter three times just to make sure I wasn't misunderstanding it, but after my third read-through, my chest tightened painfully because I wasn't misreading it. NYU wasn't offering me any financial aid. None. Not a single penny.

Every other school that I received an acceptance letter from had sent an offer for at least *some* financial aid. A few offered enough to cover part of my tuition each semester, others offered me a student housing grant so I wouldn't have to worry about living expenses, and one—albeit my last resort school that I applied to in Florida—offered me a full-ride scholarship.

NYU was the only one that didn't at least offer me enough to cover my textbooks, and after reading the letter four more times with the desperate hope that it would somehow change right in front of my eyes, I slumped down into the barstool at the counter.

As I was folding up the financial aid letters and sliding them back into the envelope, another, much smaller, envelope with my name printed across the front caught my eye. I froze in place when I registered the USASN logo on the left corner.

The article.

The *scholarship.*

I bit down on the inside of my cheek as I tore open the envelope, pulling out the letter before I could psych myself out. It took me a second to register what I was reading before my breath slipped through my lips.

Ms. Ryan,

Thank you for your submission to USASN's scholarship contest. Your article made it through to the final two and was the top contender in the eyes of most here; however, we regret to inform you that after further research, you have been disqualified from the scholarship contest.

While we do champion all of our journalists here at USASN to speak out and stand for what they believe in, we as a company value both moral steadfastness and truth over everything else. After reading your most recent article published in your student newspaper, we are unable to move forward with you as a candidate as the clear sensationalized falsities against USASN is a direct violation of our company guidelines.

Two tiny paragraphs, and yet, it felt like a slap to the face. Not only was I disqualified from the scholarship money, but they were calling me a liar.

The sound of the letter tearing in half sent a surge of vengeful adrenaline into my veins, and through the current of hot, angry tears, I stood and tore it again, and again, and again, until all that was left was a pile of resentful confetti in my palms. They weren't just calling me a liar, they were calling Brenda Morgan a liar, they were calling Rei Torres a liar. The anger that pulsed through me heated my skin, but out of all the emotions, all the anger and frustration and helplessness, there was one emotion that was glaringly absent—shock. I wasn't shocked, not even a little bit. Not by their response, not by their petty dismissal of my potential scholarship, not by their refusal to even listen to the accounts of Rei and Brenda in that article. They are choosing to stand behind Greg Bradshaw, to defend his name and his position at their company without even looking into the claims made against him.

But what else can I do? I wrote an article. I published it. I screamed out into the void, hoping someone would hear me. And they did, they did hear me, they just chose not to listen.

That same frustration flared again when I dropped the crumpled pieces of the letter into the trash and stalked toward the pantry, nearly climbing the shelves to get to the brand-new pack of Oreos.

I've been eating my way through that pack all day, and now that I'm lying in bed, wrapped up in my blankets while watching a classic early 2000s chick flick on TV, I'm nearing the end of the final row of cookies. I'm still angry about USASN, and terrified about not having any financial aid for NYU, but somehow the cookies have helped. The cookies and Tristan. I FaceTimed him as soon as I got back to my room, and for the next hour he helped talk me down from the proverbial ledge I was standing on. Even from Toronto, he was helping me pick up the pieces.

He was barely in Pullman long enough to unpack and repack his suitcase before flying out to Canada to meet with the head coach and join the team for practice every night. Apparently, these trips are normal for potential draftees. They're like a practice run—to see how well they fit in and if they have good chemistry on the court. Based on the pure excitement that he's radiated since landing in Toronto, I have a feeling he's fitting in perfectly there.

I know Canada isn't exactly ideal for us, but I can't bring myself to be anything but happy for him. Because even though it would add a lot of stress to our relationship to be apart, I know that we'll make it work. The ring on my finger is just another reminder of that—of the fact that Tristan is just as invested in this relationship as I am, that he loves me just as much as I love him. And if I have to fly out to see him a few times a week, or whenever my schedule at school will allow, well then that's what I'm going to do.

When my phone starts to ring, I glance around the mess of sheets, patting around the mattress until I find it buried under my duvet. I'm fully expecting to see Tristan's name flashing on the screen, but when my mother's name pops up instead, I freeze.

I've been back in Pullman for four days and each day I've called her at least three times, hoping to catch her before her lunch meetings, or on her way home from the office, or before bed; but each time, I've been sent directly to voicemail. I figured out that she was actively ignoring me when I called her office and her secretary, Matthew, slipped up and told me she was between meetings. He transferred my call immediately, only for me to be rerouted back where he awkwardly mumbled something about her being out of the office at the moment.

I'm being ignored, the same way I ignored her while I was in Vegas, and I feel incredibly guilty because I realize now how terrible it feels.

Sitting up in bed, I fumble around desperately to find the remote to mute the TV. I finally find it under the blankets near my feet, and right as I silence John Tucker being berated for scaling the hotel to get into Kate's room, I slide my finger across the screen hastily before bringing it up to my ear.

"Hey, Mom!" I sound a little too excited to be answering a phone call from my mom, but after being ignored for almost a week, I miss her. But she doesn't yell, not yet, at least. Instead, she's silent, long enough for me to pull my phone away from my ear to make sure she didn't actually hang up.

"Well look who finally answered." Her tone is cold and flat, but I deserve it.

"I'm sorry about that—about not answering." I sit up a little more and bring my free hand up to smooth out my hair, as if she can somehow see it through the phone.

"You canceled your flight home to see me, and then instead of giving me the courtesy of calling and telling me, you instead let me find out from a cancelation email and an *I'm not going to make it back to Florida* text?"

I bite down on the inside of my cheek and sink back into my sheets because I know that this is just the beginning, and I might as well get comfortable. I grab another Oreo and bite into it as she launches into her lecture. It's a weird feeling, because as much as I hate being on the receiving end of these lectures, I can't deny that it's nice to hear her voice again.

"—All the while ignoring all of my attempts to communicate with you. I called you. I texted you. I emailed you. All with no response. I called your brother in an absolute fit; what was I supposed to think? You've never done anything like this before. And then I find out from Jeff that you went to Las Vegas? You flew to another state and didn't even let me know? And your picture is all over the internet, Abigail. Mark sent me a link to an article, and I saw the video of you and that boy singing on stage. I thought we talked about this. You were done with him. You broke up. And now your picture is plastered all over these sports publications. Luckily, you can't actually see your face, but anyone with half a brain would be able to figure out it's you with just a small investigation. This is exactly what I didn't want to happen. This is what I warned you about. But do you listen to me? No. Do you ever?"

The picture. Somehow, out of all the people recording us singing that night, only one video got out. And luckily, the quality of it was terrible. Someone managed to get a pretty good screenshot out of it, though. My head was turned toward him, and you couldn't see much of my face since my hair was in the way, but if you know me, you'd know it was me. No one has managed to identify me publicly yet, or more likely, they're just not that interested in putting in the work to identify me, which is fine by me.

The picture surfaced the day we got back to Pullman, and it's been floating around the different sports channels as the reporters talk about the finals. Apparently, they all think it's hilarious that Tristan went all *High School Musical* to celebrate his win. And the fact that the video pans to show the entire team on their feet clapping and singing along, makes it that much better. My personal favorite part is when Luke and Micah join Jenny and Nia on the stools and scream out the lyrics like the drunk idiots that they were. I somehow didn't notice they were doing that when I was actually singing, but I love that it's been recorded so I can watch it over and over again.

I sent it to Luke with a few heart emojis the day it came out, because ever since the fight, I know he's been spiraling. Not that he'd admit it.

He and Tristan haven't spoken since Micah pulled Tristan away, which made for an awkward rest of the trip, and an even more awkward plane ride since their coach made them sit next to each other. I think he was hoping it would spark a conversation, or more likely an apology, but all it really did was keep the most talkative person on the team quiet for the entire plane ride.

They've both been acting like they don't care, like they're perfectly content with pretending like the other doesn't exist, but I know it's all a front. I was hoping that video would cheer him up, but his reply of three blue hearts seemed a bit lackluster, and when I texted him back that everything was going to be okay and that it would all go back to normal soon, he just sent back a simple *thanks, Bubbles.*

The video got a lot of attention for the first two days that it was out, but like all viral videos, it's been all but forgotten at this point.

"I'm sorry."

I don't really know what else to say.

"You're sorry? For what? For ignoring me for a week? For canceling our plans to spend the break together so you could go get drunk and party with your boyfriend—who you told me you broke up with, by the way—in Las Vegas? For me finding out that you lied about staying in Pullman? Yes, I'm sure you're really sorry, Abigail."

"Really, Mom. I am sorry, for all of it, I never meant to hurt your—"

"I don't have time to talk about this. I have a dinner meeting with Craig and his new partner at his firm tonight. I just called to let you know that I also canceled my flight."

My brows pull together as I try to figure out what she's saying.

"Your flight?"

"My flight up to Pullman in three weeks." She says it so casually that it takes me a moment to realize what she means. "I will not be coming up for your graduation anymore, Abigail."

It takes a second for her words to register, and then my lungs collapse in my chest.

"What?" My voice sounds strangled, even to my own ears.

"I will not be attending your graduation. I don't know if Jeff and Mark are going to come, you will need to speak to them about that. And Nana—well, Nana probably will not be going, either. Not if I don't go. She needs assistance flying and I don't feel comfortable with her going without me."

"You're not coming," I say slowly, trying my hardest to wrap my head around this. "You're not coming to my college graduation."

"No, unfortunately I won't be able to make it." I can hear the clicking of her heels against the hardwood in her office and I don't need to see her to know that she's smirking. "It doesn't feel good when someone cancels plans, does it?"

The fact that she's reveling in this, that hurting me back is giving her some sort of satisfaction, just plunges the knife further into my chest. Because she knows how much this is hurting me. She knows how important this day is to me. She knows that I won't have anyone else there. Just her. Just my brothers. Just Nana.

"Please don't do this." It comes out in a choked plea. She doesn't say anything for a long moment, and aside from the click of her heels, the silence fills the void between us like a reminder of the past two weeks that we haven't spoken.

"I didn't do this, Abigail. You did this to yourself. Maybe you should consider that. Maybe you should consider that your actions have consequences."

"I'm sorry. I—" I don't even know what I'm trying to say, but the panic starts to set in as the image of me walking across the stage with no one there to see it starts to set in. I've already been pushing down the thought of my dad not being there, but now, to think that my mother, my brothers, my *Nana* won't be there either? That's too much.

"Please." My voice breaks, and I bite down painfully on my lip to keep from crying. "Please, Mom. Please, don't do this."

She sighs, as if this conversation is starting to annoy her, and when she speaks again, she sounds bored. "I have to go, I need to look over some files before dinner."

The sound of her heels clicking against the hardwood is silenced and I know she's now sitting at her desk because I can hear the sound of thumb tacks rattling in a jar as she opens the top drawer. She stays quiet, and the silence between us is deafening.

"You know, you should really view this as a learning experience, Abigail. Maybe then you'll actually answer when I call."

The call disconnects, but I can't bring myself to pull the phone away from my ear. I'm frozen in place, trying desperately to find some way to process this. To wrap my mind around the fact that I'll be walking across the stage in three weeks and my family won't be here to see it. Not my father. Not my mother. Not my Nana. And who knows about my brothers.

FIFTY

I've flown more in the past two weeks than I have in my entire life.

I barely had enough time to repack my bags from Vegas before flying out to Toronto, and when I finally got back to Pullman, I had three days at home before Coach called me into his office to not only chew my ass out for punching Luke—whose entire left side of his jaw was still tainted a dark purple and blue, a much more noticeable bruise than the one on my own cheek—but also to let me know that the head coach of the Knicks had called and scheduled for me to come out for a few days to meet the coaching staff and join them for practice.

I felt like I was seconds away from waking up the entire time I was there, because walking through the doors of Madison Square Garden was like reliving every dream I've ever had since I was a kid. It was like being transported back to sitting on the couch next to my dad watching the Knicks play on our shitty old TV. I've envisioned that moment since the day I decided I wanted to be in the NBA. When everyone else wanted to be a fireman, or a doctor, or an astronaut, I wanted to be an NBA player. And now, I'm just two months away from the draft.

New York was a lot like Toronto in the fact that I fit into their team almost instantly. I've watched every single game they've played this season, so I've already studied their offense and defense, giving me an upper hand when we would run plays. They definitely don't have the best defense, which only made my shots look that much more impressive, and I could see the head coach and trainer talking behind their clipboards after I managed to sink one of the most impressive shots I've made all season.

I tried to play it off like it wasn't a big deal, but fuck, it felt good to see that shot go in. I was double-teamed, pushed well past the three, and only had two seconds left on the shot clock. My passing lanes were cut off on either side, and I didn't have much of a choice, but it worked out because I managed to juke out one of my defenders, step back and shoot the ball. We all watched it soar toward the net, and when it fell in without even kissing the rim, I could feel the shocked glances from some of the players around me before their hands came down hard on my back with a mixture of comments like *"nice shot, man"* and *"fuck, that was pretty."*

It was surreal to play with some of the guys I've idolized for so long, and while I was out on the court with them, I could feel it—the energy, the excitement, the possibilities. Playing here wouldn't just mean that I'd get to wear the jersey I've dreamed about since I was a kid, it would mean that I'd get to move here with Abby. That I'd get to come home every night to see her doing homework on the couch, or making dinner, or reading in the bathtub, or more likely, hanging out with Jenny and Nia while getting wine drunk on a random Tuesday. It means I wouldn't have to be away from her. And somehow, in the span of the four months of knowing her, that's more alluring to me than anything else.

But I've done all that I can. I played my best in practice, I made my interest in the team clear in my last meeting with the head coach, and now that I'm standing at baggage claim searching for my suitcase, I know that it's just a waiting game from here. They're going to compare us. They're going to see who fits in better with the team, who's more coachable, who had the best chemistry, and since my time with both teams went so well, I have no fucking clue who's going to pick me.

So, now I guess I just keep my head down, stay in the gym, keep practicing, and in two months on draft night, I'll finally have some answers. I'll finally know where I'm going to spend the next few years of my life.

When I catch sight of my gym bag on the baggage carousel, I grab it and pull my cap down further to try to look as inconspicuous as possible, because ever since the final, I've been stopped for pictures and autographs a lot more often than I was before. I have a feeling it's because now I'm not just a college athlete, I'm two months away from being an NBA player. But I don't have a lot of time here, my flight to Pullman leaves in six hours and if this goes to plan, I'll be back here and sitting at my gate with plenty of time to spare. But if it doesn't, then I might be stuck spending the night in some cheap motel some-where near the Orlando airport.

I spot my Uber when I walk out to the pick-up lane, and the heat and humidity hit me like a truck. It's muggy as fuck, and I almost feel like I'm breathing underwater, but my lungs adjust to the humidity by the time I pull open the door and slide into the car.

I managed to take a picture of Abby's driver's license the other day before I left for New York without her noticing, and I'm praying that her home address is still the same, because that's the address I put in for the Uber.

She thinks I'm going out with some of the guys from the team to-night to celebrate before heading to the airport, which should give me enough time to do what I need to do before she FaceTimes or texts. I wasn't going to do this. I was just going to mind my own business and help Abby through this shitty situation in the best way that I could. I was going to be there to support her, to be a shoulder to cry on, to let her know that she has so many people here in Pullman who love her. But when I woke up at three AM the night before I left for New York to an empty bed and the soft cries echoing from my bathroom, I knew Abby deserved better than that. She deserved to have her piece of shit mother at her graduation if that's what she really wanted, even if her mother didn't deserve to be there.

So, now I'm here, in Orlando. I don't actually know what I'm going to say to her. I've never met her, and aside from the quick Google search, I don't know much about her, other than the fact that she's a big name lawyer and a terrible mother.

The forty-minute drive goes by incredibly fast, because I'm dread-ing the moment the car actually stops in front of a house and I have to get out. I'm not scared of confrontation, I don't have any issue telling her how terrible of a mother she is, but I know that I can't do that. I have to be respectful, no matter how hard it's going to be, because whether I like it or not, this is the mother of the girl I plan to spend—well, spend forever with—and I have to keep that in mind. At least until Abby decides on her own that she doesn't want a relationship with her.

The huge oak trees lining the paved road are a clear sign that we're getting close to an expensive neighborhood. I can see glimpses of the ocean as we drive, and when we follow a car into a gated neighbor-hood, I catch sight of the sandy trail that leads right to the beach. The

waves are crashing down onto the shore and the cotton candy sky behind it is actually helping to calm me as the car turns onto the street
I recognize from Abby's license.

We slow to a stop, and I finally bring myself to look up at the
house. It's huge. Probably four times bigger than my parents' home.
It matches the houses around it perfectly, with the impressive stone-
work on the front, the paved driveway, and the landscaping that looks
like it could be in some kind of design magazine.

There are a few cars parked in the driveway, and my mouth feels
incredibly dry, because I never considered the fact that her mom might
not be here alone. That would definitely make this conversation a hell
of a lot more awkward.

I look back over to the driver and thank her before sliding out of
the car, pulling my gym bag up my shoulder as I walk up the drive.

The double front door is huge to accommodate the high ceiling,
and I hesitate for a minute as I stare at the black matte paint. I can't
bitch out now, I flew all the way here. The memory of Abby's tear-
streaked face when she finally opened the bathroom door to let me in
the other night flashes in my mind, and I hear the three loud knocks
before I even realize that I've lifted my fist.

The sound of heavy footsteps approaches, and I know damn well
they don't belong to the small blonde woman I saw in my Google
search. When a guy a few inches shorter than me opens the door, I
realize he can't be much older than me—three, four years maybe. I
catch the similarities of his deep blue eyes and chestnut hair that he
has cropped short, and when his eyes widen and his jaw opens slightly,
as if he can't believe what he's seeing, I know that this is definitely
one of her brothers. He's in a pair of expensive dress pants and shiny
black shoes, but his white button-up has been unbuttoned a little and
his sleeves rolled up.

"Who is it, Jeff?"

A sharp voice sounds from behind him, and when I look over his
shoulder, I see her. She's rounding the corner into the large entrance
hall, her perfectly straightened, shoulder-length, white-blonde hair
bobbing with each step. She has on a perfectly pressed pantsuit, and
the click of her heels against the tile rings louder with each step that
she takes toward us. Her eyes narrow as she approaches, and it's obvious she knows exactly who I am by the deep frown creasing her lips.

"Tristan Beck." Her brother says before I can, and I look back down to see that he's grinning. "Holy shit. It's nice to meet you, man."

He extends his hand, and I take it as some of the anxiety eases a bit. At least not everyone in this house instantly hates me.

"What are you doing here?" Her voice is cold and sharp, but I don't get a chance to answer because Jeff leans around me, trying to look out at the yard.

"Is Abby here, too?"

"No, she's still in Pullman," I say, bringing my hand up to the back of my neck to rub the tense muscle. Her mother's stare is fucking intense, and it's unrelenting as she puts her hands on her hips and narrows her eyes on me. She's still a few feet away, but even with the space between us, her presence is suffocating.

There's not much of a resemblance between Abby and her mother. Abby's soft and gentle and radiates the warmest energy I've ever felt. She has a smile that can literally stop my heart in my chest, and her eyes are the deepest blue, like the warm ocean waves I can hear crashing down onto the shore just behind this house.

Abby is warmth and light, and her mother's icy stare is the absence of all of that.

"Abby's here?" An excited voice echoes from around the corner, and I can hear the sound of a chair being pushed back before soft footsteps grow closer. Her mom turns around and tries to call out that Abby isn't actually here, but the short, older woman with a full head of white hair wobbles around the corner with wide, searching eyes.

"Nana, she's not here, it's just her boyfriend." Jeff shakes his head. Her mom is already walking toward her Nana, wrapping her arm around the older woman's frail shoulders to help turn her back around, but her wide eyes are searching mine as a warm smile slips across her wrinkled face.

"Her *boyfriend*." Her eyes light up even more, and the sight alone warms me, even under her mother's icy glare, because I can see where Abby got her deep blue eyes from.

"Yes, but he was just leaving." Her mother says in a tone so final that I hesitate for a second, wondering if it's even worth trying to argue.

"Nonsense, Victoria." Her Nana shakes her hold from her shoulders and ambles toward me. Her walk is off, and by the wobble of her movements, she must have a bad hip, but she doesn't give any impression that she's in pain as she beams up at me while reaching out her hands.

I take them, expecting a handshake, but she pulls me closer and wraps her arms around my waist in a hug. She's short. Shorter than Abby, and her white hair just barely grazes the bottom of my chest bone. I catch her brother's smirk as he looks at his mother, and I wrap my arms around the frail, older woman to hug her back gently, nervous that I might break her.

When she pulls away, her eyes wrinkle in a smile. "It's so nice to finally meet you, Tristan. Abby has told me so much about you." She squeezes my hand, and her eyes slowly flick down to my arms before gravitating back up. "She never mentioned how handsome you are, though. I can see why she seems so smitten with you."

"It's nice to meet you, Mrs—"

"Oh, no, no. Call me Nana, please." She cuts me off quickly, beaming up at me.

"Nana." I smile down at her, watching her eyes light up as she claps her hands together and turns around.

She's already wobbling back toward the room she came from when she calls over her shoulder, "Come on in, Tristan, we were just sitting down for dinner. Victoria, let's set another place for our guest, shall we?"

Her small hand clutches Abby's mom's and those ice blue eyes widen in disbelief as the older woman pulls her along with her, leaving no room for argument.

"You can leave your bag there." Jeff nods toward the delicate wicker bench near the door. "Don't mind my mom, she's—well, I'm sure Abby's told you all about her. She's not the easiest person to get along with, but she'll warm up to you. Eventually." His eyes flick over my shoulder, considering that. "Maybe. Most likely. I'm Jeff, by the way, Abby's brother." He extends his hand to me after I put my bag down gently on the bench, and I shake it.

"Tristan." I meet his eyes, holding his curious stare, and smile.

"Tristan Beck." He nods with a growing grin. "Trust me, I know who you are. I've been watching you play since your freshman year. When my mom said Abby was dating an athlete, I thought she meant someone on the chess or bowling team or something—you know, someone more Abby-ish. I sure as hell wasn't expecting to her to be dating

Tristan fucking Beck." His words come out quickly, a flood of emphatic disbelief, and my smile widens when his mother's irritated voice echoes around the corner, calling both of us to the table.

———

I decided pretty quickly that coming right out and telling Abby's mom what a bitch she is wasn't exactly the best plan of action. Especially not when I caught sight of Abby's other brother, who introduced himself to me as Mark, and Jeff's girlfriend, Lessa, sitting at the table awkwardly, as if they weren't interested in getting sucked into the drama.

Abby's mom glared at me for most of the dinner, which was surprisingly really fucking good. I've never had steak melt in my mouth like butter before, and her Nana was happy to let me know that it was an old family recipe that she's perfected—and that if I want the recipe, I'll have to marry into the family to get it. She said it with a wink, the kind of wink that said, *I'd be more than happy to see that happen*, but I caught the glare that Abby's mom sent her before she took a long sip of her wine.

Her brothers lasted less than five minutes before breaking their casual facade, and when they both leaned in, eyes wide and cheeks flushed from the beers Jeff brought out for us, I answered all of their burning questions. They asked about my meetings with Toronto and New York, and how I liked the teams, about which one I think I'll get picked by, and after leaning back in my chair and telling them about the past week of my life, they were trading predictions back and forth about where I'll end up.

They had the same look in their eyes as the people who stop me on the side of the street for a picture. That slightly nervous and mostly excited look. The kind I'm sure I had on my face when my dad took me to my first game at USW as a kid.

By the time we had finished dinner, I'd already agreed to get Jeff and Mark season tickets to whichever team I got drafted to and promised her Nana that I'd come back down to Florida with Abby this summer to see her again.

It was the perfect introduction to the graduation conversation, but the second I sat up a little straighter in my chair, her mother's eyes flashed in cold warning. She brought her wine glass to her lips and gave the smallest shake of her head, one that I knew was meant to say, *Not here, not in front of Nana.*

I hesitated for a moment but took a sip of my beer and nodded. It's probably for the best that Nana doesn't hear what I have to say to her daughter, anyway.

"I should probably get going, I have a flight to catch back to Pullman in a few hours," I say, wiping my mouth.

Her Nana's lips pull down into a frown, but she nods as she pushes back her own chair. I shake her brothers' hands and return the small wave Lessa gives me before following her mother and Nana toward the front door.

"You're going to come back down this summer with Abby, right?" she asks, stopping next to me at the door.

"I will." I nod with a smile. "I promise."

"Oh, we're going to have a blast." She beams, wrapping her arms around me again in a soft hug. "Give my Abby a hug for me." Stepping back, she considers me for a long moment before a soft smile lifts her lips. "My Elliott would have really liked you, you know," she murmurs. "He loved his little girl more than anything in the world, and I'm sure he's happy to look down and see her with someone like you."

It takes me a second to realize that she's talking about Abby's dad, and that's when it hits me that she's *his* mother. I should have picked up on that before, because this woman exudes a similar energy as Abby does, so different from her mother's, but now that I see it, I can't believe that it wasn't immediately obvious to me.

"Thank you," I say softly.

"I'll see you again soon." She smiles and squeezes my hands before turning around and wobbling back toward the dining room, only stopping for a second to call over her shoulder, "And would you please tell my granddaughter to send me a picture next time? Had I known you looked like that, I would have paid a little more attention." She smirks over her shoulder, disappearing around the corner.

"She's getting old . . . and senile." Her mother's voice is sharp, humorless. She's standing by the door, hand resting on the knob, as if waiting for me to leave. "Let's speak outside."

I nod and grab my bag, following her out of the house. Her heels click against the paved driveway, each step heightening the unease unfurling in my chest. I pull out my phone and order my Uber as I walk behind her down the driveway, and by the time she turns around at the end of the drive, I'm slipping my phone back into my pants pocket.

"You flew here to speak with me about graduation, I presume." She still has her wine glass in her hand, and she crosses her arms across her chest as she looks up at me, eyes narrowing. For being the same height as Abby, and having the same small frame, she somehow has a much bigger presence.

"I think you should rethink your decision. She told me that you're upset about Vegas, and I get it, trust me, I do. I get that you're upset with her for canceling her trip, but this is uncalled for. What you're doing isn't teaching her a lesson, it's just cruel."

Her scowl deepens. "Do not tell me how to parent my daughter."

"I'm not telling you how to parent. I'm telling you how to not be a piece of shit person."

The words slip out of my mouth before I can stop them, and her eyes widen as her perfectly painted lips pop open. Her ice-cold composure was broken for a second, but it's back in place seconds later.

"This does not concern you. You've known my daughter for a matter of, what? A few months? And you think—"

"What does concern me is knowing that what you're doing is hurting Abby. And if you can honestly look me in the face and tell me that you don't care that you broke your daughter's heart, then I'll turn around and leave right now. But I don't believe that. Because no matter how cold and cruel you are, I know you're not stupid. You and I both know that Abby loves you more than you deserve. You and I both know that while she is one of the most kind and forgiving people in the world, even she is going to run out of forgiveness for you. Because if you push her far enough and she breaks, she will be okay. I will make sure of that. I will give her everything that I can to make up for the shit that you've done to her. She will find a new mother in mine. She will find a new family with me. But you? You'll be alone, here in this huge house, with nothing but the haunting reminder that your daughter is lost to you, and it will be all your fault."

The scowl on her lips falters into something else, something more real, and when she blinks, her chest rises and falls quicker than before as her eyes drop to the wine glass in her hands. When her eyes rise up to mine again, they're clearer, shining with the realization that I'm correct, that Abby will eventually break under all of the bullshit her mom puts on her.

When she takes a deep breath, I'm shocked by her words.

"I'll be there," she says, almost reluctantly, as if she doesn't want to admit that I'm right. "But it's because I want to be there for my daughter, not because of your bullshit ultimatum. She might be blind to it now, but she won't always be. Unfortunately for her, by the time she does recognize that being with you wasn't worth it, it'll be too late. Which is exactly why I will never like you."

The headlights of my Uber flash down the street, and when it slows to stop at the end of the drive, I look back down to see her scowling at me again.

"Trust me, Victoria, we're on the same page," I say with a sickly sweet grin, stepping back toward the car now waiting at the end of the drive. "Because if it were up to me, you'd never step foot in Pullman again.

FIFTY-ONE

The past week has been one big coffee induced blur.

We're two days away from the last day of the semester, three days away from formal, five days away from graduation, and then my time here in Pullman will officially be over.

We have the apartment through the rest of the month, but I promised my Nana I'd come home early to spend time with her before I fly up to New York for my summer classes. So, really, I only have two more weeks here with everyone.

It's all happening so quickly. I feel like I barely have time to breathe, let alone complete everything on my final to-do list of the semester. But even when I do complete something on my list, there's always an odd sense of dread as I cross it off, because each time I do, I know that I'm that much closer to leaving behind the life that I've built for myself here.

It's bittersweet, and I'm trapped in a constant paradox of crying every time I think about leaving Pullman behind and experiencing the inevitable rush of excitement when I remember that I won't just be going home to Florida when I leave, I'll be going to New York— to NYU.

It feels surreal to think that the one dream I've worked toward for the past four years is actually about to come true, but that dream quickly twists into a nasty nightmare when I remember that I still have a few more days of finals left, and I won't actually be free of it until finals week is over. I've drowned myself in so much coffee this week that I'm practically vibrating in my seat at all times. But I can't stop, because even though I've managed to write four ten-page papers, take three final exams, stay late every day to help edit the last newspaper issue of the semester, and keep up with my shifts at the diner, I still have one final exam to worry about.

And even though I've been staying at his house most nights, Tristan and I haven't fallen asleep together in almost a week. He's been sticking with his on-season schedule—waking up for sunrise workouts and training every night with his coach—and since I close at the diner most nights, I don't have much of a choice but to stay up until three in the morning to study. Which means the amount of time Tristan and I actually get to spend together, is slim to none.

Luckily, while Tristan usually ends up passing out by midnight thanks to his own intense schedule, Micah seems to be on the same messed up sleep schedule as I am, so we've made an unspoken agreement to suffer together.

It happens every night—Tristan falls asleep on the couch next to me with his head resting on my leg and his arms wrapped around my waist, and an hour or two later, my hushed laughs from watching Micah practically throw his book across the room, eventually wake him up. It doesn't take him long to drop a soft kiss onto my cheek and retreat, half-asleep and groggy, into his room.

If we'd just focus on our papers, we'd be able to go to bed a little earlier, but Micah and I aren't exactly the most focused pair. We usually end up being productive for a few hours—while simultaneously complaining to each other about how much we hate writing said papers—until one of us breaks into the pantry. Okay, that part is usually me. But regardless, after giving Micah my best *I'll share my snacks if you get them down for me* smile—which he always pretends to be annoyed with, even though I catch the smirk on his face when he pulls down the Oreos for me every night—the cookies are always the beginning of the end of our productivity.

I might be the one to distract us with food, but Micah's the one who always turns on the TV. We've managed to binge a whole season of *Game of Thrones* in the early hours of the night while avoiding our essays, and while the show is excellent study break material, by the time we finish watching both episodes—because you can't just watch one with this show—I'm too tired to continue writing. That's when I pull myself up from my cookie-induced coma, say goodnight to my study buddy, and make my way to bed.

I always feel his arms reaching for me as I crawl into bed beside him, and every night without fail, his lips trail across my shoulder and nuzzle into the crook of my neck as he pulls me close to him. No matter how tired I am, the instant flood of adrenaline spikes my blood when he sleepily presses warm kisses up my neck, knowing that those kisses are always followed by the feel of his calloused fingertips gently nudging at the collar of my shirt so he can explore the sensitive skin on my shoulder.

I melt into him instantly, because our moments at three in the morning, all alone in the darkness of his bedroom, are the only times we have to be together without the worries of the world crashing down around us. I don't have to think about my final papers, or the chemistry exam that I'm truly terrified to take in two days, or where he's going to end up being drafted, because all of those worries fade away into the darkness surrounding us when his teeth graze lightly across the sensitive skin under my ear and his hands travel slowly down my waist.

His thumb caresses over the side of my rib cage, and down my side, lingering on the extra sensitive skin on my hip before he makes his way down to the fabric of my underwear. I can always feel him smiling into my neck whenever the first breathy moan slips through my lips, because he knows what his touch does to me, even now, even after I've had him so many times.

Our times spent together late at night aren't rushed, or hurried, or desperate. Instead, they're slow, and exploratory, and teasing, and when he finally slips his hand into my underwear and connects our lips, my body reacts to him immediately, writhing in pleasure as his fingers work me up, and up, and up until I'm panting hard and biting down painfully on the inside of my cheek to keep from calling out his name too loudly in the quiet house.

I have to admit, most of my reserve to be quiet is spent by the time he slips his boxers down his hips, and when he rolls over and pulls me onto him, my head falls back with a quiet gasp as the instant rush of pleasure shoots up my spine from the feeling of being perfectly and completely filled by him.

My hips move in slow, teasing motions at first, reveling in the sight of his eyes rolling back as the moonlight peeking through his window just barely illuminates him under me. But when a tortured moan slips from his lips and he desperately pleads for me to move quicker, I finally break, giving in to the quick movements that he's guiding me into with his hands on my hips.

The noises that slip from my lips aren't as quiet as they probably should be, but when he gently tugs me down and connects our lips as the all-encompassing flood of pleasure rushes my body, his kisses muffle most of my noises. When I finally regain a semblance of control back from the mind-numbing sensation pulsing through my body, I take his bottom lip between my teeth and bite down before sliding my tongue into his mouth, moving my hips in the same circular motion that Layla taught me. Like clockwork, his body tenses underneath me as he finds his own release.

But now that we only have two days before the semester ends, I decided that everyone needs to step away from studying—even for an hour or two—and just relax and hang out before our time here at USW is over.

Nia, Jenny, and I already have our apartment picked out for when we move to New York, and after Jenny sat us both down, with a very nervous James sitting next to her, she asked if we'd mind if James moved in with us in New York. It's always been just us three, but honestly, the idea of James joining our little roommate group just seemed . . . right.

I was there when Tristan sat him down the other day and asked him to officially be his agent when he signs his contract, which for a sports business major is just about the most exciting thing that could possibly happen. But when you also consider the fact that Tristan let him know his salary upfront, I nearly choked on my sip of water when he said the number out loud. I've never even considered making that kind of money. Never even dreamed of it. And I guess that's when the reality of Tristan's contract really hit me. In a month, he's going to sign a contract that's predicted to be just over twenty million dollars. Twenty million. No matter which team drafts him.

I try not to think about it too much, because the thought makes me a little uncomfortable. That kind of money changes things. It's the kind of money that I'll never be able to match, no matter how good of a job I get. It's the kind of money that means we will never be equal contributors to our life together, and for some reason, that thought makes me a hell of a lot more anxious than I thought it would.

"What's wrong, Abs?"

His arms snake around my waist as he steps up behind me, and when he rests his chin on my shoulder and watches me squeeze the last bit of lime juice into my homemade guacamole, my body relaxes into his embrace. His cologne is enough to make me want to nuzzle my face into his chest and just stay there all night, but we have a game night to get to, and I plan on winning at least once.

"Hmm?" He turns his head so his lips are pressed against my neck, and I realize that I never answered him.

"Just a little tired," I say quickly. Tired, yes, but the cloud that's been hanging over my head all day isn't because of my lack of sleep, it's because it's finally hitting me that nights like tonight are slipping through my fingers. That I really am leaving soon. We all are.

I grab a tortilla chip from the bowl next to me on the kitchen counter and scoop up a generous portion of the dip, holding it up to him. He leans down and closes his mouth around the chip, making sure to get the tip of my finger in his mouth as he does. When his tongue flicks around it, I pull it out quickly with a shocked laugh. I know exactly what he's trying to do, and no matter how tempting it is, we can't just disappear into my room for the rest of the night, especially since *I'm* the one who invited all of our friends over for this game night.

I slip out of his grip and smirk at him as I grab the bowl of guac with one hand and the chips with the other, and when I round the kitchen island and walk toward the living room, his hand cups my butt and squeezes as he walks next to me.

"Alright, who's ready to watch me win?" I grin, putting the last snack option down onto the coffee table before falling back onto the couch beside Tristan. He holds open the gray, knit blanket for us to share, tucking me in around him before reaching for his beer on the coffee table.

"Speak for yourself, Bubbles," Luke snorts, sitting up a little while trying not to jostle his leg too much. I wasn't sure if he'd come tonight, since he and Tristan still haven't spoken since getting back from Vegas, but when I opened the door and he grinned down at me, a six pack of beer and some pretzels in his arms, I knew that was his peace offering.

He sat the six pack down on the kitchen counter next to Tristan and instead of turning and walking away, he held out his hand. Tristan seemed a little shocked as he looked down at it, and when he looked back up, Luke just nodded.

"I shouldn't have. I knew I shouldn't have, and I did, and I'm sorry about that."

Tristan stared at him for a long moment, long enough for me to look over my shoulder and search for Micah and James in the living room, hoping they'd be able to get over quick enough if fists were thrown again, but when I looked back over, Tristan grabbed his hand and shook it.

"And you'll never touch her again," he said, more of a command than anything else. A condition to this offer of peace.

Luke's jaw tightened, and then, slowly, almost reluctantly, he nodded. "I won't touch her."

The look of understanding solidified on his face as he nodded again in agreement; if he has any intention of keeping his friendship with Tristan, Olivia Beck is off limits. Tristan grinned at that before grabbing a beer and herding him toward the couch. The look of relief, of all the worry and anxiety that's been building in him since his fight with Tristan, evaporated as his captain threw a pillow at his face and told him to keep his knee elevated.

He's been going to physical therapy all week for his knee, and I can tell that it's really taking a toll on him because he winces every time his leg is even slightly jostled.

"What should we play first?" Jenny asks, sliding onto James's lap so Nia can sit down next to them.

"What about bullshit?" Micah offers with a grin as he brings his beer up to his lips. He's leaning against the mantle since we don't have a ton of room left on the couch, and even though Luke's offered three different times to move his leg so Micah can sit down, he just shook his head each time and told Luke to watch his knee.

"I haven't played that in forever." Nia nods, already reaching for the deck of cards.

The suggestion spurs the memory of when I played with Dean and his friends in the coffee shop, and a sinking feeling pulls at my chest because I haven't been very good about keeping in contact with him or his friends since I saw them in the bar last. Viv and Sam will reply to my Instagram stories sometimes with hearts, but that's really all the contact that we've had. I make a mental note to text them tomorrow to see how they're doing before reaching over and picking up the Coke can Tristan brought out for me.

"Okay." Luke grins, fanning out his cards in his hands. "Let's do this."

———

Micah won the first round of bullshit, I won the second, and now that we're halfway through our first game of *Monopoly*, Tristan's ridiculous amount of hotels have already bankrupted everyone aside from me and James. He's somehow managed to get an entire corner of the board, and after he loaded them up with hotels, we aptly dubbed that corner *death row*.

He has the smuggest grin on his face when James hands over all of his money and sits back into the couch with a genuinely annoyed look on his face.

"You're so annoying to play this with, ever since we were kids you've done this shit," he mumbles, crossing his arms.

"I've been a good businessman my whole life, what can I say?" He grins at his best friend as he counts the money he just gave to him. When everyone's eyes settle on me, I lean forward and grab the dice.

I'm the last one alive, and if I don't roll a high number, there's a good chance I'll die a quick death on death row, too. Tristan leans forward beside me, and I don't have to look over my shoulder to know he's smirking at me.

"Come on, baby, you've got this," he says softly, brushing my hair back behind my shoulder as he brings his lips to my cheek. "You know you want to land on Illinois Ave."

I don't, actually. That would mean certain death for me, but I can't seem to focus on anything other than his minty breath on my cheek. I bite back a smile as I lean back to look at him smirking at me. If there's one thing I've learned tonight, it's that Tristan Beck is extremely competitive when he plays board games. His smirk deepens as he runs his finger across my jaw slowly, sending a wave of goosebumps down my arms.

"Roll a five, baby."

"That's coercion, T. You can't convince her to throw the game with foreplay," Luke calls, launching a pillow at Tristan who catches it easily and tosses it onto the couch behind him, never taking his eyes off of me.

"I can if it works." He argues, tilting my chin up to bring our lips that much closer. When my gaze flicks to his mouth and my breathing quickens, his smirk deepens even further.

I lean forward, enough to brush my mouth against his as lightly as I can, and when his spearmint breath coats my lips and he starts to lean into the kiss, I sit back and grin up at him. I try to play it off like I'm completely unaffected, which is not true at all, but in the world of mind games, you can't show any signs of weakness—especially not in *Monopoly*.

"Sorry, *baby*." I run my finger along the stubble on his jaw. "But I'm not going down that easy."

His brows raise as his playful grin widens.

I'm probably going to lose. There's like a one percent chance that I make it through his side of the board alive, but still, I'm not going down without a fight.

I roll the dice in my hands—and even make a show of blowing on them for good luck—before releasing them onto the board. I lean forward and watch them tumble until they finally settle, and it takes me a second to realize what I'm seeing.

What are the freaking chances?

When Tristan shoots up onto his feet, he tips his head back and chugs the rest of his beer, and I can't help but laugh, because he truly is the most competitive board game player I've ever met.

"That's fucking bullshit." Micah laughs. "How the fuck did it land on a five."

"Because even the universe respects my rightful claim to the *Monopoly* throne," Tristan says as he puts his empty beer bottle back onto the table and holds out his hand for me.

James and Jenny are making a show of yawning loudly, and when she stands up and he follows, I'm not shocked to see him smirk down at her as she calls out to the rest of us that they're both going to bed.

They disappear into the hall quickly, but it's Luke's snort that pulls my attention. He's still on the couch, but he's trying to stretch out his leg slowly, preparing to stand on it.

"I'm out of here. There was clear collusion going on in that last play." His eyes flick up to mine, and I grin down at him as I reach out and help him up, careful to not bump his bad knee.

"Did you paint this?"

Looking over my shoulder, Micah's bending over to get a better look at the framed watercolor painting on my mantle. The one Josie painted for me for Valentine's Day.

"No, my friend Jo painted it for me."

He considers it for a long moment before standing back up and glancing over at me. "It's actually pretty dope," he says, bringing his beer up to his lips. "He must be pretty good. He ever draw for tats?"

"Oh, no Jo is—"

But I don't get to finish explaining, because I catch the mischievous look in Tristan's eyes just before he swoops down and tosses me over his shoulder.

"Well, this has been fun," he calls, already walking toward the hall to my bedroom. When I catch sight of the stash of cookies in his hand, I can't hold back my smile. "But if you'll excuse me, I'd like to go claim my prize now."

FIFTY-TWO

I never thought I'd actually enjoy myself at one of these sorority formals.

I've been to more of these than I can count, since our old captain, Brody, had a girlfriend in the sorority. He made us all tag along so he wouldn't be alone while he waited for her event management duties to be over. Since the events were always dry, we were stuck pretending to socialize until the big after parties. That's what we were really there for—the seemingly unlimited reserve of liquor that the frats always supplied at their ragers after.

That's actually the first time I saw Abby.

It was the first night of freshman year. We had come straight from practice, and since it was an ABC party, Coach looked like he wanted to smack us all as Nas and Lief, the two sophomore troublemakers, who honestly could have given Luke and Micah a run for their money, wrapped us in either caution tape or athletic tape.

I opted for the caution tape, which was probably a good choice since Lief ripped off an impressive amount of leg hair taking off the athletic tape later that night. A fact that I only knew because, while I was busy in bed with a sorority girl, he was screaming bloody murder as her sister tried to undress him.

The ironic thing is, if it were up to me, that girl in my bed would've been Abby. I saw her pouring a drink in the kitchen, wrapped up in neon pink streamers that covered her a little less than I think she knew, and when I downed my beer and started to step around the table, Lief grabbed my arm and dragged me over to do a keg stand.

I was being hazed—all the freshmen were, based on how much they poured down our throats that night—and when they finally put me back down, she was gone.

We were so close to colliding that night, so close to all of this slid-ing into place—to nights spent in bed with her; to waking up with her cuddled up beside me; to seeing my future shining back at me in those deep blue eyes.

Looking up now, I can't hold back my dumbass grin because those same ocean eyes are flashing under the strobing lights as she dances with her two best friends. She's pulling out the robot, bending over slightly at the waist and letting her arm hang and dangle as Nia and Jenny mirror her movements while their laughs melt into the melody of the song they're dancing to.

Their choice of dance is a hilarious contrast to the sultry move-ments around them, but I can't seem to take my eyes off of Abby. She ditches her robot moves to throw her hands above her head and shake her hips—off beat, of course—to the music while her smile lights up the space surrounding her. When she tilts her head back in a laugh, her long chestnut waves cascade down her exposed back in the form-fit-ting, floor-length, silk, backless dress.

I've only been speechless a few times in my life, and now that I think about it, most of them have been because of Abby. I was speech-less when she pulled off her shirt in my bathroom the first time we had sex, when she broke down in my arms out in the field before she told me about her dad, when she barged into the locker room and told me that she loved me, and again tonight, when she pulled open the door of her apartment. She stood there, blinking up at me as she feigned innocence while her tight dress pulled me down into the dirtiest parts of my mind.

She didn't opt for a semi-conservative dress like she did last time, and I could tell by the smirk on her face when she looked at me over her shoulder as she did a little turn to show it off, that she knew exactly what I was thinking about. That she picked this dress on purpose. That she bought this dress specifically so I could take it off of her. And if we weren't already running late, I would have happily picked her up, thrown her over my shoulder, and spent the rest of the night worship-ing that thin pink material and the body it's clinging so suggestively to.

But I could tell by the way she bent over in front of me to pre-tend to check the clasp on her heel that she was planning on teasing me for a bit first. And now, as she looks over at me from the middle of the dance floor and brings her hands up to knot in her hair while slowing her hips into a seductive sway, she knows it's working. It's really fucking working.

I have to look away from her, because if I keep watching the way she's dancing on Jenny, I'm going to have to readjust myself in the middle of this formal.

"Sup, brethren."

I glance up to watch Luke drop down into the empty seat beside Micah with an amused grin as his eyes fix on the girls on the dance floor.

"They can't pull out the robot one second and then start a girl on girl porno the next, they're giving my dick whiplash."

"You sure it's not from the girl you just fucked in the bathroom?" Micah counters with a wicked grin, already bringing his fists up to knock away the rogue jab Luke throws at his ribs.

He disappeared into the bathroom with a short brunette with curls about twenty minutes ago, and by the way she's adjusting the top of her dress as she whispers to her friends across the room, it's not hard to put two and two together. She kind of looks like Olivia, with her long brown curls and tanned skin, but hell, if he needs to fuck doppelgängers to keep his hands off of my little sister, then by all means, have at it.

"I was helping her fix her dress." He feigns offense, as if he can't believe we would ever suspect him of fucking a girl in the bathroom at a formal. He has a bit of her lipstick on the corner of his mouth, and since he's shamelessly attempting to smooth out his navy tie and retuck the bunched up material of his dress shirt poking out of his waistband, we can all guess what just went down in that bathroom— or rather, who just went down.

"Yeah, sure, and I was just fixing Abby's dress yesterday when you banged on my bedroom door like a fucking ax murderer." I deadpan, thinking back to when I showed Abby a new position with both of her legs up on my shoulders. She liked it, *really* liked it, and apparently everyone in the house could tell—including Luke's poor grandma. "She kicked me in the chest so hard I had the wind knocked out of me."

"I was FaceTiming my Gran, you asshole. She's never going to look at me the same again. She probably thought I was some kind of psychopath watching a porno while talking to her about her corgi's vet visit and how my grandpa is trying to reduce the amount of sodium in his diet. And don't get me wrong, I'm usually a big fan of Ryan's

moans lulling me to sleep every night, it's great spank bank material."
He winks at me as I chuck a rolled-up napkin at him. "But I don't want
to scar my grandma from calling me ever again."

"Don't worry, bro, your Gran doesn't mind." Micah shrugs and
his cheek twitches slightly. "She was telling me how much it turned
her on last night when I had her bent over."

My jaw drops and I look over to see James silently laughing next to
me as Luke lunges for him. Micah dodges him easily and somehow has
the freshman's arm pulled taut behind his back and his head trapped
in a headlock. Luke's face is starting to turn a concerning shade of
red as he struggles to get out of the hold, but Micah looks calm, serene even, as his gaze flicks up to us and he smiles. He looks so casual,
like he's reading the Sunday paper, and when Luke slaps his arm in
defeat, he finally lets him go.

"How the fuck do you do that?"

"Survival of the fittest, young grasshopper. If they can't land a hit,
they can't knock you out."

I'm assuming that's a mentality gained from growing up with
brothers, which I'm pretty sure Micah has three or four of. I think his
family lives nearby, because I've heard him mumble something about
going to see his mom occasionally, but I don't think they're close since
he stayed home for Thanksgiving by himself. I would have invited him
over to spend it with my family if I knew, but when I got home later
that day, his bike was fully packed with snow, completely untouched.

I didn't mention it because I could tell he was uncomfortable by the
way he just nodded at me as I walked into the house and then looked
back to the football game on the TV. I hesitated by the entryway for
a second, trying to figure out the best way to be there for him without making him uncomfortable, so I just went to the kitchen, pulled a
fork from the drawer, and then dropped down onto the couch beside
him and handed over the Tupperware of leftovers my mom forced
me to take home.

He shook his head at first, but I told him it would just go to waste
if he didn't eat it, because I couldn't eat another bite of turkey without
puking. Which was true, but more than anything, I didn't want him to
not eat a proper Thanksgiving dinner. Especially if he spent the entire
day here on the couch watching football by himself.

I could see the small smile on his face when he took the Tupperware, and then we sat there together for the next hour, getting drunk on the seasonal flavored beers that James bought, screaming at the TV for every fucked up call, and breaking into the bag of cookies my mom sent me home with to share with the guys.

When he finally got up to drop the empty Tupperware into the sink and get us another round of beers, I caught the smile on his lips as he fell back down onto the couch—the one that I knew was meant to say, *Thanks, man, for everything.*

Needless to say, he spent Christmas with my family.

"How long do we have to stay at this thing?" Luke groans, leaning back in his chair.

"Yeah, I'm fucking hungry, and I'm way too sober for all of . . . *this*." Micah gestures around the room with a grimace.

I'm honestly shocked that he came with us tonight since he's been adamant about avoiding these events since he got his first invite freshman year. Hell, so was I, but I didn't have much of a choice because on top of Brody practically throwing my suit at me and corralling me out of the door, James has secretly had a thing for Jenny since he saw her at freshman orientation, and when he found out she was in the sorority that invited the entire basketball team to come, he was there before the girl could even hand him the tickets. I'm supposed to bring that little piece of information to the grave, though. He told her—and told me to pretend—that he's only been into her since last year, but we both know the truth. James Parsons has been in love with Jenny McPherson for years, and I'm planning on dropping that little truth bomb during my best man speech.

But every formal and lame sorority event that he dragged me to was worth it, because if he wouldn't have needed a wingman, I wouldn't be here tonight with Abby.

"We're going to the after party at Jenny's sorority, but I'm down to stop by Over Easy for a burger first," Luke says, already pulling out his phone and drumming his thumbs quickly on the screen. When my phone dings in my pocket, I know that he just texted our team's group chat.

I could go for a burger, and I know they have a few vegetarian options that Abby likes, so I'm sure she'd be down.

"Think Bubbles could get us a discount? I already know I'm going to get stuck paying for this bill."

"You're the one that always offers to pay," James counters.

"That's because acts of kindness are one of my love languages, you asshole." Luke grins, referring to the quiz Abby was reading in a magazine the other day. She convinced him to take it while they were hanging out on the couch watching TV, and he's been pulling that little tidbit of information out of his back pocket every time he does the smallest thing for any of us.

"Great, well you're really going to love me tonight. I'm thinking a burger, some nachos, meatloaf, chili cheese fries, and that peach pie. You know how much I love that peach pie." Micah grins, slapping him hard on the back.

"Jesus, if you're going to fuck my wallet that hard, you better at least put out."

"I *always* put out." Micah nods. "Just ask your gran."

The music slows down into a soft strumming song, and when I look back up to the girls, they're all holding hands as they dance, taking turns twirling each other around while their dresses flow out around their legs. When Abby twirls Nia with a beaming smile, an idea sparks, and I look back to Micah who's scrolling through his phone.

"Micah, go ask Nia to dance."

His eyes flick up from his phone, and he considers me for a moment, trying to figure out if I'm fucking with him. When he realizes I'm being serious, his gaze coasts over to the girls dancing behind him.

"Come on," I urge, nodding toward the dance floor. "I need a wingman."

He looks like he's going to argue for a second, but with a resigned sigh, he slips his phone into his pocket and stands up.

"You owe me," he calls over his shoulder as he heads toward the girls.

He nearly gets wrecked by a drunken girl who topples into him as he goes, but he stops and steadies her before continuing on. The girls all look up at him at the same time, eyes widening and lips pulling up into smiles when he extends his hand to Nia. She takes his hand with an amused smile, and when he pulls her aside to an open spot and places his hands high on her waist, she looks over her shoulder and gives a knowing smirk to me and James who are already on our feet.

"Cool, just leave me here alone, thanks." Luke's voice is nearly lost in the music, but we both ignore him as we walk away from the table.

I'm already halfway through the crowded dance floor when I catch sight of her standing still in the middle of the moving bodies, and when her red lips pull back into a bright smile as her deep blue eyes lock with mine, my heart beats a little faster.

Her silk dress is reflecting the soft strobe lights above, giving off a warm glow, and the sight is breathtaking because it looks like she's actually radiating a soft light. When I finally stop in front of her, I smile down at her as I extend my hand.

"I was hoping I might be able to steal you away for a dance."

Her eyes widen, and I know she realizes that I'm being corny as fuck because I'm quoting myself from the last time we were in this hall for a formal—the first time I ever asked her to dance with me.

She places her hand in mine and her smile is blinding as I pull her close to me, bringing my nose down to breathe in the vanilla apple spice of her shampoo. Her dress is the softest material I've ever felt, and I caress my thumb across the small of her back, just to feel the way it slips so easily under my touch. Her hands slide up my arms, finding their place on my shoulders, and when she tilts her head back to look up at me, she smiles and brushes a fallen curl off my forehead back into place.

"So, Micah's on wingman duty tonight?" She perks a brow and her lips twitch.

"I passed the torch." I nod.

"Maybe it's a good luck torch," she muses. "Maybe he'll be next up to find someone."

I glance over to Micah, who's nodding at whatever Nia is saying, but by the way their hands are placed on the most innocent parts of each other, it's clear that neither of them are interested in crossing that line.

"Maybe, but probably not tonight," I admit. "We're about to head out to the diner, so unless his girl works there, I'd say his time is running out."

She smiles a little at the thought, but then shakes her head, as if to say, *Yeah, I don't think he's going to have much luck there, either.*

Well, there *is* Josie. She's so cute, and sweet, and talented, but I—I don't know. I don't know if they'd click." She looks over her shoulder at my teammate, and when he catches us both looking, he gives us a *What the fuck are you staring at* look, which we both laugh at.

"She's like his exact opposite. He's all hard lines, and black ink, and storm clouds and Josie is literal sunshine. She wears a ribbon in her hair, she almost always has some kind of bright colored paint dried onto her hands, she always slips into Spanglish whenever she's excited, and she has a presence that just kind of—I don't know—lights you up." She glances back at Micah for a moment, and before he can catch her, she looks back up at me with a shrug. "If they weren't complete opposites, and I wasn't absolutely sure he'd break her heart . . ." She shakes her head.

He'll find someone," I say, pulling away from her a little to twirl her under my arm. Her dress flares out around her legs along with her hair, and when she turns back to me and grins, I lock my arm around her and tilt her back into a dip.

A breathy laugh slips through her lips as she relaxes in my arms, letting her head tip back. When I pull her back up and catch the flush of her cheeks and toothy grin in the twinkling lights above, I'm struck by the memory of us in my kitchen, dancing in the dim microwave light in the middle of the night.

So much has changed since then, and when she grabs my tie and tugs me down gently to bring me in for a kiss, I cup her cheek, reveling in the feel of her lips pressing against mine. I've kissed her hundreds of times by now, but yet the energy that seems to flow over my skin every time she parts her lips to let me in is still there, just like the first time.

Her fingers knot in my hair as she sighs into the kiss, and when she moans as I caress the soft line of her jaw, I know that she's just as affected as I am. That she's been waiting all night for this, too. That she'd be more than happy to ditch everyone and find some solitude together between my bedsheets.

I can already feel the heat tingling down my spine, which means I need to put an end to this before we end up fucking in the bathroom tonight, too. When I pull away from her, she huffs impatiently, and I can tell by the flush blooming across her cheeks that she wouldn't be opposed to the bathroom idea. But as I bend down to whisper in her ear, her head turns and an excited voice speaks before I can.

"Abby, oh, my God! I didn't think we'd see you here."

I look up to see a short girl beaming at Abby. She's in a glittering lilac dress and her jet-black hair is pulled up into a polished bun on the top of her head. I vaguely remember seeing her from somewhere, but I can't place it as Abby drops her hands from my shoulders and pulls her into a hug. When she pulls away, she's beaming at the girl.

"Tristan, this is my friend, Viv. Viv, this is my boyfriend, Tristan." She motions between us, and the girl gives me a smile with a wave.

"Viv, you look amazing."

She smiles as she looks down at her dress, smoothing it out before looking at Abby's with a grin.

"You have to tell me where you get your dresses. First, that gorgeous gold one and now this." She looks like she wants to reach out to feel the silk, but since there's no good place to touch her without awkwardly feeling her up, she bites down on her lip and keeps her hands to herself.

"My friend Nia actually gifted it to me as a graduation present. She gets them from this designer out of New York. Her name is Este something—"

Viv's eyes widen before flicking back down to the dress with a dropped jaw. "Este Montague?"

"Yes, that's the one." Abby grins, smoothing her hands over her dress.

"Those dresses are like a thousand dollars." She gapes. Her hand twitches, as if she really wants to feel the silk now.

Abby tenses next to me as her jaw drops a little. Her eyes scan down to the dress, and she looks a little paler than before, probably because she can't believe that her best friend would spend that kind of money on her.

"Oh, babe, over here!" Viv waves her hand above her head, and when Draco appears from the crowd, my hand tightens around Abby's instinctively. It takes me a second to process that, and then I make myself relax, because this isn't a pissing contest anymore. Abby is with me. There's no more competition. He's not a threat.

The tension in my muscles eases even more when he drops a quick kiss on the girl's cheek and smiles at us. His eyes flick up and away from mine quickly, as if he's not sure if I'm going to be a raging asshole again. The tinge of guilt hits me hard, because I shouldn't have been that big of a dick to him. I wasn't in the best state of mind. Hell, let's be real, I was fucking broken, and from all the context clues I was picking up, I genuinely thought he was the one who was going to replace me. To make Abby forget about me. But it doesn't change the fact that

I was an asshole, so I extend my hand and give him a self-deprecating smile, the kind that says, *I know I was a massive douchebag, and I'm sorry.*

"Dean, it's nice to see you again."

He looks a little surprised that I actually said his name, but even in his shocked state, he shakes my hand and smiles up at me.

"You, too. I'm glad to see it all worked out." He nods to Abby whose cheeks are a little red, as if she was already preparing for this interaction to go south, but her shoulders relax when she sees our hands shake.

"So, I hope it's not weird—I told him it wouldn't be, you know, since you're with Beck now." The girl looks up at Dean and smiles as he wraps his arms around her shoulders. "Dean and I are kind of dating now."

Abby looks a little shocked, and then she breaks into a huge smile.

"That's amazing. You two are perfect for each other, I don't know how I didn't see it before."

"Yeah." She grins up at Dean and wraps her arm around his waist. "We're going to the frat house if you guys want to come along. I think Dillion and Jack might actually have a heart attack if you came to one of their frat's parties."

Abby looks up at me, and I'm about to tell her that we already promised to go to the diner with the team, but she looks back at Viv and shakes her head before I can. "We already have plans, but I'd love to meet up before I leave for Florida. I'll be here for two more weeks. Maybe we could go to the coffee shop? I'll even bring Tristan along so Dillion and Jack can bat their eyes at him the entire time."

Dean's already searching the crowd around us, and when he nods and waves to someone, I glance over to see a tall dude and a much shorter one standing by the refreshment table. Both of them are staring at me with slack jaws while a blonde elbows the shorter one in the ribs to get his attention.

"Sounds like a date." Viv grins. "We better get back to the guys and Sam, but I'll text you to set that up. Fair warning, Dill and Jack are probably going to faint." Her eyes flick up to mine and she grins. "Just prepare yourself, I'm sure Dillion's going to bring a million different things for you to sign."

"Looking forward to it." I grin back, flexing my hand for added effect. "I'll make sure I'm warmed up."

She pulls Abby in for another hug, and I shake Dean's outstretched hand one more time before they both turn and head toward their friends.

"Oh, my God." Abby's eyes widen and she grabs my hand, tugging the sleeve of my suit jacket back to expose my watch. "Oh no, no, no. Shit, we have to go."

Grabbing my hand, she pulls me through the crowd. When we get back to the front entrance, she's nodding at Jenny and Nia, who both have huge grins on their faces. Nia tosses Abby her phone, which she was holding in her purse, and when she waves goodbye to them, Luke and Micah's brows pinch together.

"I thought we were going to the diner together?" Luke calls. "Bubbles, you were supposed to get me a discount!"

"Find Josie, she's working tonight. Tell her you're with me and she'll give you one!" She calls over her shoulder, already pulling me along behind her.

I wrap my arm around her waist and tug her out of the way of a guy holding two cups of punch, saving her from getting trampled. When she looks back up at me, she grins sheepishly before pushing open the doors and leading us out of Carson Hall. Her hair blows back as a gust of chilly night air sweeps through the courtyard, and I slip out of my suit jacket and lay it over her shoulders, earning a smile from her as her heels click against the pavement, punctuating each one of her hurried steps.

"Are you going to tell me where you're taking me, or should I guess?"

"It's a surprise." She stops, reaching up to gently loosen my tie before sliding it off and unknotting it into a smooth ribbon.

It's a black tie, the same one that I wear for all of my interviews, and when her fingers glide across the soft material, she smiles up at me. She cups my cheek and when she rocks up on her tiptoes, I lean down to meet her in the middle, connecting our lips in a kiss that sends another wave of heat straight down my spine. When she finally pulls away, I catch her toothy grin before she slowly places the material over my eyes, tying it snuggly into a blindfold.

"Can you see anything?"

I try to open my eyes, but aside from the tip of my shoes, I can't see shit.

"Nope."

"Good." I can hear the smile in her voice and the scraping of her shoes on the cement as she turns and looks around.

"We're really close, I promise."

Taking my hand, she leads me down the sidewalk. The sound of the muffled music from the hall is barely a whisper as we walk further into campus, and now, the only sound I can really hear is the clicking of her heels against the cement, blending together with my own much heavier footsteps.

It's nearly ten, but campus is even more deserted than it usually is this late at night since classes are over and most people aren't planning on stepping foot back here until classes start again for the summer term. But for us, this is the last time we'll ever be here—as students, at least. I tighten my hold on her hands and she squeezes back.

"We're almost there," she says, pulling me closer so she can wrap her arm around my waist to guide me down each of the three steps slowly. The stairs are a pretty big hint to our location—we're either by the student union or the arena. They're both an equal distance from Carson Hall, but since it's dark as fuck out, and I can only see my shoes every few steps when we approach a lamp post, I have no real sense of direction right now.

"You're not planning on killing me, right? Because I told my mom that we'd be over for dinner tomorrow night, and I'd really like to have her lasagna one more time before I die."

She pokes me in the side.

"If you don't stop asking questions, I might. Here—step down, one more—perfect. Okay, do you have your wallet?"

My lips quirk because now I know exactly where we are. I reach into my back pocket and pull out my wallet, handing it over to her.

"I haven't signed my contract yet, Ryan, so if you're planning on killing me for my money and dropping my dead body into the ocean, you're about a month premature."

"I'd never dump you in the ocean, babes. Dead bodies don't sink unless you puncture the lungs. That's how amateurs get caught. I'd bury you in the desert. No one's ever found in the desert."

I grin, blindly reaching for her, and when my hands cup around the curve of her ass, I squeeze just as the soft beep of the card reader sounds. The AC rushes out when she pulls open the door and the familiar smell of the arena lobby hits me full force.

"And I have to marry you first, silly. Otherwise, I won't get a penny of your money."

I can practically see her biting her lip as she tries to keep a straight face. When she pulls me in and slips my wallet into my back pocket, I bend down, grazing my nose against her cheek and down her neck before biting down on her shoulder.

She squirms under me, and when her hands find my chest and skim down my stomach, I smile against the smooth skin of her shoulder. Reaching up, I move to pull off the blindfold, because I'd be willing to bet her cheeks are rosy and she has that look in her eye, the one that she always has right before she lets me pull her underwear off, but she catches my hand.

"Not yet." She pulls it back down. "One more minute."

She threads her fingers in mine and pulls me through the lobby toward the arena. I want to tell her that the arena is locked down whenever it's not being used for games, but I keep quiet, because I don't want to ruin this for her—whatever this is.

I can tell by the way her footsteps quicken that she's excited, and when we come to a stop, I can just barely make out the USW Warriors logo on the floor outside of the entrance. It doesn't strain against the deadbolt lock like I'm expecting, instead it opens, and the smell of the court cleaner hits me as she pulls me in. My brows pull together when I smell something else, something that smells suspiciously like pineapple pizza.

Her heels are even louder against the court floor, and when she finally stops and turns to me, her fingers start to pull gently at the blindfold until my tie falls away. I have to blink a few times to adjust to the harsh arena lighting, but when I do, she's smiling up at me, her bottom lip between her teeth as if she's waiting nervously for my reaction.

I look up from her to see a mountain of pillows and blankets piled on the other side of the court. Two small lanterns cast a warm light on the blankets, and I catch the two pizza boxes stacked near a cooler with my favorite beer buried in the ice. When she walks toward the mass of blankets and turns back to me with a blinding smile as she looks up at the Jumbotron, I follow her gaze.

Oh, fuck.

The DVD menu for the new Marvel movie is playing on the screen.

"I know you've been wanting to see it, so I pulled a few strings." She grins, pulling me toward the nest of familiar blankets from her apartment. I kick off my shoes and drop down onto the pile of blankets, expecting to feel the hard surface of the court, but the pillows stacked underneath gives enough padding to create a sort of mattress.

"How did you pull this off?" I laugh, a little shell-shocked as I glance up to the huge screen above us before looking back down to see her beaming at me. She starts to bend down to unbuckle her heels, but I reach out and pull her foot onto my lap slowly, unclasping it for her instead.

"I may have sweet-talked Dwight in the tech room." She smiles sheepishly. "And promised him free dessert at the diner for the next year. Which I'll have to let Josie know about since I won't be here," she muses, as if just remembering that she'll be in New York. When she looks back down at me, she places her bare foot back onto the floor and places her other foot into my lap for me to unbuckle. "He agreed to play it on here for us. He should be pressing play on it in exactly two minutes and then he said he'd head out for a few hours to give us a little privacy before coming back and locking up."

My eyes flick up at that, and I can't hold back the dumbass grin on my face, because even though I've never admitted it, having sex on this court has always been a fantasy of mine.

I can tell by the mischievous glint in her eyes that she knows exactly what I'm thinking, and when the lights all cut out, leaving us in a barely-there glow from the lanterns, the sound of the intro music starts to blast through the speakers and we both look up to see the screen playing the first scene of the movie. I scoot back, making enough room for both of us, and she lowers herself down next to me, pulling her dress up to her thighs to free her legs.

We settle back and watch the movie, breaking open the pizza boxes and beer, and by the time we're halfway through the movie, she's already eaten her way through half of the pack of Oreos she had tucked away behind the cooler. I can't pretend to be interested in the movie anymore, because the girl lying next to me smells like apples and vanilla, and the way her fingers are running through my curls is sending goosebumps down my back. All I really want to do is taste her lips, which I already know are going to be the sweetest mixture of beer and Oreos.

When I turn to look at her, she's already smiling up at me as she places a cookie between her teeth. She takes a small bite of it, and when I tuck her hair behind her ear and run my finger across her jaw, she shivers.

"I love you." I whisper, leaning closer to her until I can practically taste her minty chocolate breath on my tongue. When she smiles, a real, tooth-bearing, eye-wrinkling smile beneath me, my heart stops in my chest, because fuck, I really do love her. More than anything.

She traces my mouth with a thoughtful expression, like she genuinely wants to memorize the dips and curves, and when her eyes flick back up to mine, she smiles before cupping my cheeks and pulling my lips to hers. I was right—she tastes like beer, and pineapple, and chocolate, and I'm already desperate to drown myself in her, but when she pulls back and grins up at me, I don't hesitate to fall back into the pillows when she pushes lightly on my shoulder.

She climbs on top of me, straddling my hips, and my heart hammers in my chest when she leans down and grazes her lips across my cheek, stopping at the shell of my ear. And I swear to God, in this moment, I fall in love with her all over again when I finally register her words. "You love me because I'm about to give you one of the best orgasms of your life, or because you *love me* love me?"

She pulls back enough to smirk down at me, to see if I caught the fact that she's quoting me, but when she reaches up and brushes her thumb across my bottom lip—probably to swipe away her lipstick which is already a little smeared on her perfectly swollen lips—it hits me. Like a fucking semi speeding down the highway, it hits me—this is it for me.

Abby Ryan is it for me.

She waits for me to say it, slowly slipping the straps of her dress down her arms until the silk is pooling at her hips, exposing her bare chest underneath, and I swallow hard as I take in the sight of her, rosy-cheeked, slightly buzzed, and fucking glowing in the dim, warm light of the lanterns.

"Both." I nod, already reaching up to cup her cheek to bring her lips down to mine. "Definitely both."

FIFTY-THREE

ABBY

"Wait, wait, wait—let me get this straight." Lacie sits back in the booth and holds up her hand to stop me mid-sentence. "You guys spent your spring break in Vegas, had hot post-lap-dance sex, and then he gave you a *promise ring* in a pool?" Her eyes are wide and incredulous, as if she honestly doesn't believe me. "We're talking about the same guy, right? Tristan Beck, six-five, curly hair, dimples—or, as I like to call him, *the face that dropped a thousand panties?*"

"Yes." My nose wrinkles at the name, because while I am painfully aware of Tristan's well known sexual history, I don't like to think about it. I don't hold it against him, we didn't even know each other then, but still, it makes me nauseous to think about him doing the things that we do with anyone else. Of him seeing someone the way he sees me. Of him touching them the way he touches me.

I blink a few times to shake those thoughts before I start to spiral, and when I look up, Lacie's smiling sheepishly at me. I manage to give a, *It's fine, let's just not talk about this ever again* smile, and she nods quickly before reaching for another napkin and silverware set to start rolling.

I follow her lead, plucking a warm, just-out-of-the-dish-washer fork, spoon, and knife from the basket before rolling it into a napkin. I've rolled at least a hundred of these in the past forty minutes, and while I usually love my shifts with Lacie and Josie, I can't deny that I'm incredibly thankful that my shift is over in five minutes. Working at the diner is great most of the time, because we're usually so packed that time flies by, but on rare occasions like tonight when the diner is absolutely dead, we're stuck doing tedious busywork like cleaning off menus, spot cleaning booths of scuffs, and rolling extra napkin rolls.

But fortunately, I get to slide out of this booth in five minutes, grab the to-go food already waiting for me on the bar-top, and go home where Nia and Jenny have already set up girls' night for us in the living room.

Face masks, fuzzy blankets, pajamas, wine, two different kinds of chocolate cookies, three new serial killer documentaries that were just uploaded on Netflix, and best of all—the deliciously greasy diner food that I'm bringing home.

It's going to be amazing, and if I'm honest, it's much needed, because ever since Tristan got home from New York—*and* Florida—I've been attached to him like a moth to a flame.

I would have probably been extra clingy anyway since he was gone for so long and I missed him, but after finding out that he flew to Florida just to talk my mom into coming to my graduation, it's like the gravitational pull I always feel when I'm around him was thrown into hyper-drive.

He's only been back in Pullman for three days, and yet, in that time we've spent more time in bed exploring each other than the past two weeks combined. I missed him, of course, but my newfound addiction to my boyfriend stems from something much deeper, something rooted in the fact that I somehow fell even more in love with him when my Nana told me all about their dinner together.

I knew the dinner couldn't possibly have been what changed my mother's mind, I know her well enough to know exactly how that dinner probably went, but neither one of them have given me much detail about what happened other than my mother telling me how I *"need to wake up and leave him before he ruins my life"* and Tristan telling me that they had a *"much-needed conversation about the reality of the situation."*

I was tempted to push the conversation to find out exactly what was said, but I thought better of it, because maybe it's for the best that I don't know what he said to her. Especially because I got what I wanted. My family will be at my graduation. My mother, my Nana, my brothers, even Lessa. And I know that even though he can't be there, my dad will be watching, too.

"Well, I have officially never felt more single in my life, so thanks for that, Abs." Josie's laugh pulls my attention away from the napkin roll in front of me, and when I glance up, she's smiling at me as she leans back into the booth, her own stack of napkin rolls sitting beside mine in the middle of the table. "I guess I should probably just accept my fate now, right? I'm going to die a lonely, old, virgin. Why put off the inevitable? I should just go adopt my six cats now."

"You're not going to die a lonely, old, virgin, Jo." Lacie and I say together.

Lacie's eyes flick up to mine, and I grin at her as I slap her outstretched hand in a high five.

Josie doesn't look convinced.

"You're still a freshman, Josie. You're practically still a baby." I shrug, tossing a bunched up napkin at her to get her attention. "You're going to find an amazing guy, I promise."

Her lips twitch as she looks up at me. "You don't happen to know anyone, do you?"

I consider my catalog of single guy friends, who, let's be real, are mostly limited to Tristan's teammates. I skim through the list in my head quickly before giving her a sheepish smile, because the list pretty much boils down to Luke, Penn, and Micah, and as much as I love them, I wouldn't trust any one of them to not break Josie's heart.

Her lips deepen in an, *I told you, I'm going to die alone* smirk and I nudge her shoe gently with mine under the table.

"Oh, wait, here we go. My psychic senses are tingling, Jo." Lacie winks at me before closing her eyes, rubbing her temples for dramatic flair. "Yeah, I can already see him now—he's kind of hipster-looking, he definitely has a man bun, super clean-cut, in fact he's probably a youth pastor or librarian or something. He drives a Prius, wears Tom's, spends his weekends looking up new vegan recipes, likes to take long strolls through farmers markets, exclusively wears cardigans, and gives off major *I'm rich, but I don't like to talk about it because it's my daddy's money* vibes."

Josie's eyes widen as she watches Lacie, and I can't hold in my laugh, because she looks like she actually wants to throw the spoon in her hand at Lacie.

"Don't put that out into the universe, Lacie!" She tosses the crumpled up napkin at Lacie. Her brown eyes flick over to mine and she shakes her head in mock horror—or real horror. I'd be horrified, too, if that was my future.

"I'm manifesting a man for you, Jo." Lacie grins, tossing the napkin back at her.

"Was that your interpretation of my perfect man? Because if so,

I am offended. I don't know if I'm more offended by the man bun or the Tom's." She laughs, knocking Lacie in the ribs with her elbow.

"Man bun," I supply quickly. "Definitely the man bun."

Josie points at me with the spoon, as if to say, *Thank you for backing me up here.*

Lacie puts up her hands and shrugs. "I'm just telling you what I saw."

"Well unsee it, please." Josie laughs, her brown eyes crinkling in an amused smile as she looks between us. "Because if that's all I have to look forward to, I'd rather stay a virgin."

I glance at the clock hanging just below the neon *Over Easy* sign behind the register and shoot up from the booth. I've officially been off of the clock for two minutes. The groans from Lacie and Josie echo behind me when they realize that my time with them is officially up.

Suffering at work isn't nearly as bad when you're not alone, but I can't stay and hang out, I have a serial killer marathon waiting for me at home.

I round the bar, grabbing my purse and the steaming bag of food before calling out my thanks and goodbyes to the cooks in the back. They all give their usual noncommittal grunts, which I've learned over the four years that I've worked here to mean they're all probably watching Netflix on their phones while pretending to look busy in case one of the owners walks in. It sounds rude, but really, it's their way of saying, *Bye Abby, have a great night, drive safe, we love working with you,* just not in so many words.

Lacie and Jo are both turned around in the booth, and I catch the dramatic pouts on their lips as I push open the door and grin at them.

"Love you guys, don't have too much fun here without me." I call over my shoulder, rubbing in my freedom just a little bit more as I walk out into the empty parking lot.

The air is much warmer than it has been lately, and the fact that I'm not immediately reaching to pull on my coat is enough to make me smile as the breeze rustles through the trees surrounding the parking lot.

I unlock my car and gently place the food into the passenger seat before sliding into the driver's side. I have the car turned on, the air on low, and my go-to playlist—the same playlist I made for Tristan for his car—playing before I sit back in my seat and scroll through my notifications.

I have a few texts from Tristan, mostly telling me how the boys are also having a boys' night tonight after Luke gets back from physical therapy. He sent me a few pizza and beer emojis, which I, of course, had to reply to with four eggplant emojis.

I scrolled through the roommate group chat, replying to anything I missed, until I clicked out and opened the last notification—a text from Jeff.

Unsurprisingly, it's a meme. More specifically, a sports meme. I read through each picture with scrunched brows because I don't understand the joke, but we both know that it's not meant for me, it's for Tristan. He's been sending me memes to forward to Tristan since he got back to Pullman, which is honestly kind of adorable, because that's the Ryan sibling way of showing love.

I'm about to send a screenshot of the meme to Tristan when my phone lights up with a call. I hesitate as I stare at the unsaved number. I usually wouldn't answer, but the call is labeled as a New York number, and the only connection that I have to New York is NYU.

Connecting my phone to my car's BlueTooth, I accept the call as I click my seatbelt and pull out of the parking space.

"Hello." I sound embarrassingly nervous for no reason, and even though I know she can't see me, I bring my hands up and smooth out my hair. This is exactly why I'd much rather get an email. At least with those I can type and delete and retype my responses a hundred different times without looking like an idiot.

"Hello, good afternoon. I'm calling to speak with Abigail Ryan."

"This is she."

I can already feel my heart starting to race in my chest as I try to figure out what this call might be about. For some reason, the words *Sorry, Ms. Ryan, your acceptance to NYU was a mistake* keep running through my head like a broken record. They wouldn't really rescind my acceptance, would they?

USASN did.

USASN labelled me a liar, a sensationalizer, a falsifier.

Is that what this is about? Did *USASN* reach out to them?

"Ms. Ryan, my name is Angelica Ferris, I'm the head of the professional development team here at The Metropolitan Post. How are you tonight?"

The Metropolitan Post.

Oh, my God.

My hands tighten on the wheel as I try to keep calm, but my heart's pounding so hard in my chest I can barely breathe.

"I'm well, how are you?"

"I'm great, thank you. Well, I'm sure you must be very busy with finals coming up, so I won't take up too much of your time. I'm calling to let you know that out of the three hundred applicants for the internship contest, I'm happy to say your article was by far the most captivating read. It was incredibly well received here at The Metropolitan Post. We've been looking for something with this much moxie and heart for a long time, for a writer with such a strong sense of self and the determination to stand for what they believe in. I was so moved, especially by that last line, the one about being a raindrop in a whirlpool of change in the industry."

I hesitate, brows pulling together as I desperately try to figure out what's happening. I never submitted my article to them. I had no idea they even had an internship contest; it certainly wasn't on any of the sites I've been looking on.

Angelica doesn't miss a beat, though. "Of course, I knew it was going to be something special when Marina hand delivered it to my desk. She seemed so excited, so sure that you and your article were exactly what we were looking for. I should have known she'd be right."

Marina—*as in Marina St. Clair*? She's the only Marina I know, but why would she have submitted my article? How did she even *read* my article? I knew she read the feature I wrote on Tristan, but my USASN exposé?

"Marina St. Clair submitted my article for an internship?" I confirm, pulling into the turn lane of my apartment. The click of my blinker echoes softly through the car as I try to process this, squinting at the harsh light of the nearly setting sun.

"She didn't tell you?" Angelica muses.

"I had no idea."

I had no idea Marina St. Clair read that article. I had no idea Marina St. Clair even remembered me at all. We had one conversation, and even though she gave me her business card, I've been too chicken to actually reach out to her.

"Well, then I guess I should probably explain the internship." She laughs, and the casual sound relaxes me a little as I turn into my complex. "The Metropolitan Post is a political publication here in New York. We're choosing three applicants for our fall term internship. It's a paid internship, of course, and you'd be working with the entire team of journalists while you're here. It's not a coffee-run, stuck-in-the-closet-filing-paperwork kind of internship; it's incredibly hands on. Out of the three interns, one will be chosen to publish with us at the end of the term, and of course, that intern will be awarded the scholarship that goes along with it. That scholarship is conditional to in-state tuition; as long as you're attending school in New York, we will pay for your full first year of tuition."

Scholarship.

Scholarship.

The weight that's been crushing me since I opened the financial aid letter suddenly doesn't feel so heavy, and as I pull into a parking space, I have to bite down on the inside of my cheek to keep from crying.

"Thank you so much." It comes out a little choked, and I clear my throat softly to cover up the fact that I'm dangerously close to sobbing. Happy sobbing, of course.

"So, is that a yes then?" I can hear the smile in her voice, and it's infectious, because suddenly I'm smiling as I wipe away the rogue tear racing down my cheek.

"Yes, yes." I nod quickly. "Thank you, again. This is—this really means so much to even be considered."

Marina said it during her Q+A, internships are the hardest part of grad school. They're what make or break you. They determine your future just as much as the degree itself. I've been so wrapped up in worrying about how I'm going to pay for grad school, I haven't even had the chance to start worrying about internships yet.

"We all thoroughly enjoyed reading your work, Ms. Ryan. It was so refreshing to see such confidence and resoluteness in an article written by an undergraduate. Usually, we don't see that until a journalist is well into their career. It comes with time, and if this is where you're starting, I can't wait to see what your future holds."

"Thank you." It's all I can seem to say. "Thank you so much."

"Now for the less exciting part." Her fingers typing away on her keyboard echo through the phone, and the sound relaxes me a little as I lean back in my seat. "We need to confirm some information. It makes sense now that your application wasn't fully filled out if Marina was the one to submit it. Do you have time now to answer some questions?"

"Sure." I pull out my phone and text the group chat that I'll be up in a few minutes, because knowing Nia, she's already impatiently checking the pantry for a pre-dinner snack.

"Marina mentioned that you were starting grad school, but she didn't specify which one. If you're not in New York, we do offer remote internships, you just wouldn't be eligible for the in-state tuition scholarship."

"NYU." I say quickly.

It's always been NYU, but now that I'm saying it out loud, it feels so real.

"That's perfect, NYU is really close to our main office; you'd be able to walk over after classes. Do you have a preference for which journalist you'd like to work under? You'll be working with the entire team, but this will be your main point of contact, your mentor through the process."

I don't have time to even think about the question before I say, "Marina. Marina St. Clair, please."

I wouldn't even be having this conversation if it wasn't for Marina.

"I had a feeling you'd say that." I can hear her smile as she types on the other end. "Alright, well I've got you confirmed in our system. We're going to be sending out an onboarding email with the required paperwork shortly. If you could just send us back the filled-out information by Monday morning so we can get it processed, I would greatly appreciate it," she says. "Your first day will be August 3rd, does that work for you, Ms. Ryan?"

"Yes." I smile, trying to wrap my head around the fact that this is really happening. "That's perfect."

FIFTY-FOUR

ABBY

I'm not sure what was more surreal—seeing my family sat at the same dinner table as Tristan's, or watching them interact as if they've known each other for much longer than the two hours that my family has been here in Pullman.

Aside from the fact that my mother has refused to even look at Tristan since she walked into the restaurant, I'd say the dinner has gone extremely well so far. I'm not sure if the easy flow of conversation was simply because of how well everyone got along, or if it had more to do with the three bottles of wine that my mother ordered for the table as soon as she sat down; but I don't mind either way, because seeing my Nana and Tristan's mom fawn over us while holding hands and drunkenly giggling is possibly the cutest thing I've ever seen.

I could tell the conversation was making my mother uneasy, though. Her eyes were distant, trained on the far wall as she sipped on her wine, as if she was thinking back to something, and when she blinked and looked at me, her eyes were clear as she took a deep breath and downed the rest of the glass.

I considered her for a moment, trying to figure out where her heightened discomfort could have been coming from. I know she doesn't like Tristan, but even she is polite enough to be civil and cordial towards him and his family for one dinner. The stiff set of her shoulders and fine line of her lips wasn't just because she was roped into coming to this dinner, it was something else, something deeper. I just couldn't figure out what.

The shrewd set of her eyes as she watched the rest of the table and picked at her salmon only intensified when Nana, three glasses deep in the sweet white wine, told Tristan how handsome and gentleman-like he was, *the perfect husband*, her eyes darted to mine, a clumsy wink punctuating her very clear hint. My gaze flicked over to my mom, watching the inconspicuous eye roll that I'm sure I was the only one privy to, but she didn't seem to get genuinely uncomfortable until Mrs. Beck reached her hands out to me, pulling my attention back to tell me how much she agreed, and that in her mind, I was already her daughter.

She was most definitely drunk when she said it, but by the genuine smile and tears brimming in her warm eyes, I knew that she meant it. I nearly cried at the comment, but I managed to bite down on the inside of my cheek hard enough to push back the emotion, because while *she* is completely toasted, I'm stone cold sober, and crying in the middle of this restaurant in front of both of my families is something my brothers would never let me live down.

I caught the shocked look on my mother's face when I leaned back in my seat, but it was gone as quick as it came, and after sitting quietly through the rest of the dinner and dessert, I caught her watching Mrs. Beck. She seemed like she was trying to gauge her, to figure out if she really meant it—if she really thought of me as part of her family already.

I might have been the only one paying attention to her enough to see past the indifferent, cool exterior she's so perfectly crafted since I was a child. She managed to pull a soft, demure smile on her lips as she ate a few bites of cheesecake, masking the unease that I could feel radiating off of her. I wanted to say something to calm her, to make her feel better, to pull her attention away from whatever it was that was weighing down on her so heavily, but I was at a loss for words. I was terrified of saying something wrong, of pushing her away even further, especially the day before my graduation. So instead, I sat back in my seat and tried to focus on the way the rest of my family melded so perfectly with his.

Jeff and Mark were vying for Tristan's attention the entire time. I knew they were both fans of basketball, but I wasn't expecting my older brothers—infamous for their complete lack of interest in anything related to my life—to be so eager to get to know my boyfriend. Especially since the most interaction they ever had with Tyler would have been described as hazing, at best. I think they felt the need to put up the boundaries my dad would have if he were still here, and so the first night Tyler ever came over, they pushed him down onto the couch and interrogated him for forty minutes about his *intentions* with me. That then lead into a lecture about what was and wasn't appropriate to do with me, which ultimately lead to them spending a mortifying amount of time drilling into his head that if his penis came anywhere near me, they'd cut it off and shove it down his throat. When Tyler and I *did* start having sex, it was never at my house, which was probably for the best.

But looking at them here, wide-eyed and rosy-cheeked, sipping their beers while basking in my boyfriend's attention, I have a feeling they'd happily pimp me out to him for even a few more minutes of his time.

He was enjoying their attention, though, happily listening to them rattle off every embarrassing story of my childhood that they could remember. He was leaning back, his arm draped around the back of my chair while he brought his beer up to his lips, grinning at the punch line of every story, trying not to laugh. He found the one about me getting nailed in the face with a basketball when I was seven especially funny, and when he looked over at me after I elbowed him in the ribs for laughing for so long, he leaned in, his beer-tinted breath warming my cheek as he said, "I'm sorry, baby, I really am, it's just—I can picture it so well."

Needless to say, I ignored my brothers' walk down memory lane' for the rest of the dinner, and instead, listened to Lessa tell Mel and Olivia about the different trips she's taken around the world for her travel blog.

Now, she's detailing her latest trip to Greece, and I lean in, grabbing the last garlic knot to take a bite. The waiter stops at the table, refilling my ice water before placing the bill down next to my mother, as if she already discretely discussed with him the payment arrangement. My mother always pays, regardless of who we go to dinner with. I used to think she just enjoyed treating those she was around, like it was her version of connecting with them, of showing her appreciation for the time spent together since she's practically allergic to any kind of affectionate emotion. But now, I'm starting to wonder if it has more to do with control than kindness.

Slipping a few crisp bills into the receipt book, she stands up, pulling everyone's attention as she slips her white coat back on, fixing the lapels with a bored look at my brothers. It's a clear sign, one that all of us have learned to read since we were kids—*It's time to go. Now.*

"This has been a lovely dinner, but we should get back to the hotel; it's getting late."

Tristan reaches back for his wallet, and for the first time all night, my mother finally looks at him. She considers him as he eyes the bill book, but when he looks back up, ready to insist on paying, she shakes her head. It's a curt nod, an inarguable one, and he hesitates for a second before dropping his hand and nodding, leaning back in his seat.

I honestly don't think he could have afforded to pay the bill, since my mother insisted on eating at the most expensive restaurant in Pullman.

"This was so lovely, Victoria. We should do it again if you're ever back in Pullman," Mrs. Beck beams at my mother, her cheeks vibrant from the wine in her glass. She's been going glass for glass with my Nana, who's now happily relaxed into her own seat, her shoulders twitching every few seconds with hiccups.

"Oh, you'll have to come see us in Florida." Nana muses, beaming at Mrs. Beck.

Olivia leans forward, her eyes brightening at the offer.

I smile at the idea, trying to imagine Tristan's family in Florida, in my home.

Looking back up, my mom simply nods, a silent promise that I'm sure she has no intention of keeping. The table all stands, extending their hands, exchanging *It was so nice to meet you*'s and promises to see each other at graduation tomorrow.

I feel my mother's stare on my back as I pull Lessa into a hug, promising her that we'll spend time together when I come back to Florida this summer before leaving for New York. Tuning around, I grab my purse and take a step back, anxiety blooming in my chest as she steps up beside me.

We both watch everyone say their goodbyes, pulled into last minute conversations and excited predictions for tomorrow. Jeff and Mark are stretching out their hands to Tristan, pulling him in for a hug as they grin up at him, throwing around the idea of going out on Mark's boat whenever Tristan's back in Florida.

My breath is frozen in my lungs, waiting for her to say whatever it is she's been waiting to say since I sensed her unease halfway through dinner. But to my surprise, she doesn't say anything as steps closer to me and clears her throat, a silent demand for my attention. Turning to her, she considers me for a long moment before sighing and nodding softly.

"I have something for you. I wasn't sure what I should do for your graduation gift. I—I wanted it to be something meaningful, something more than a signed check in a card."

Stepping back, she pulls a pink gift bag from under the table, hidden away beneath the white tablecloth. I didn't notice her bring it in, and when she hands it to me, my brows raise curiously, looking down into the perfectly placed white tissue paper, hiding whatever she has tucked inside.

Taking it, I pull at the tissue paper, blinking down at the binder in the bag before pulling it out and examining it. It's a smooth material, the same pastel pink as the gift bag, embossed with golden writing in the center of the cover—*Abigail Rose*.

It's a photo album.

I flip it open, smiling at my dad's face beaming at camera as he holds me, a toddler covered in white sand and sunscreen, in his arms.

"I wanted you to be able to take it with you to New York, to have something that might remind you of home." Her eyes flick up to mine, softening slightly. "Something that might make you want to come back to visit."

I look back down, flipping through the memories of my brothers, of my dad, and even a few lost memories of my mom, holding me close as we smiled up at the camera. I was so small then, tucked in her lap and wrapped in her arms, holding onto her like she'd disappear if I let go.

My chest tightens when the sharp realization hits that she did, she did disappear. This Mom did, at least—the one who looked so young, so soft and sweet as she nuzzled me to her. The one who's warmth I could almost feel, radiating through the picture.

I close the album, placing it back into the bag.

The goodbyes are starting to quiet down around us, and I can see Mrs. Beck watching us curiously from the corner of my eye. I wonder how odd it must seem to her, to see a mother and daughter act so awkward with each other, so uncomfortable, especially to a woman who's so close to her own children.

Looking up from the gift bag, my mom's eyes drop from mine to her hands, messing absently with the small strap of her purse on her shoulder. She seems like she wants to say something, but when she stays silent, a lump forms in my throat at the reminder that this nearly didn't happen. If it wasn't for Tristan, she'd still be in Florida right now, and the thought of how different tonight would have been freezes the air in my lungs, my eyes burning with the tears threatening to spring there.

"Thank you," I say, my voice so soft it's nearly lost in the voices echoing through the restaurant. But I know she heard me, because she looks up with a searching gaze as I say, "For being here. For flying up." It comes out a little choked, and I tuck my hair behind my ears, avoiding eye contact as I clear my throat, because we don't do this well—being vulnerable, I mean.

I'm almost expecting her to say something rude, something about only being here so Nana could see me graduate, but when I glance back up to see her lips tighten into a whisper of a smile, my shoulders relax a little.

Her gaze is pulled over my shoulder as Tristan steps up behind me, his hand finding the small of my back. Her chest rises in a deep breath, but when she exhales slowly, she simply nods to him. Her stare sharpens, and I look up to see his jaw tightening as he nods back, the same hard, unimpressed expression mirrored on his face. Somehow, it seems like an entire conversation, and yet, the silence is suffocating. When his thumb caresses a soothing circle on my back, I take a breath.

Her stare eases when it focuses back on me.

"I'm . . ." She looks back down at her purse, her brows furrowing as she hesitates, as if she is trying to find the right words. A seed of anxiety blooms in my chest as the silence builds between us, but when she looks back up, her words are rushed, and unsure, and foreign to me, as if they feel wrong coming out of her mouth. "I'm proud of you, Abigail."

I don't really remember the rest of the goodbyes with my family—the hugs and smiles and soft Nana embraces, the attempted noogies by my brothers, the promises to meet up for a celebratory lunch after graduation tomorrow. I don't even really remember walking out of the restaurant, other than feeling Tristan's hand on my back, softly leading me to his truck.

I replayed her words over, and over, and over in my head, trying as hard as I could to take a mental snapshot of that moment for safe keeping; trying to remember the way her voice sounded as she said it.

I wanted to remember how it made my chest feel lighter than it has in years, how it sent a wave of intense emotion through me that I only managed to keep under control until I closed the door of Tristan's truck and broke down in the passenger seat.

He let me cry without saying anything, and when he pulled me to him, holding me tightly, I could feel all the walls that I built up, brick by broken brick over the past twenty years, crash down.

I finally heard the one thing that I've been so desperately pining after for years, and while I'm not naive enough to think she'll ever say it again, I needed to feel it, wholly and completely, in that moment, in my safe place. And that's what Tristan is for me. Inside his arms, while the playlist I made for him hums softly in the background and the smell of his cologne starts to circulate around the truck, I'm in my safe place.

FIFTY-FIVE

I was able to sit still through the first six speeches given by the faculty and staff without letting my mind wander. I was even able to keep my attention on the stage for the valedictorian speech, the three choir performances by the graduating seniors, and the guest speaker—who I vaguely recognized as one of the big business moguls who attended USW in the early 2000s—but now that the dean of students is standing behind the podium reminiscing about his own graduation with a wistful look on his wrinkled face, I can't seem to keep my attention on the ceremony.

Instead, I'm looking down at my leg, restlessly bouncing underneath me, trying not to give in to the emotion that's been brewing since last night; trying not to think about how soon, in a matter of days, I'll be taking a flight out of Pullman, away from everything I've built here in this small college town.

I knew it was coming—the heartbreak, the inevitable homesickness—and it hit me full force while I celebrated in O'Malley's with my best friends last night. After our family dinner ended, Tristan and I promised to meet everyone at the bar, but when we showed up rosy-cheeked and a little disheveled, I could tell that everyone knew we didn't really hit traffic in the sleepy, post-term college town. But aside from an exaggerated wink from Luke and a knowing smirk from Nia, no one called us out for stopping off in the parking lot behind the closed down supermarket to make the most of one of our last nights together.

I felt the first real twinge of heartbreak when I drunkenly high-fived Micah after we won a round of beer pong against Nia and Luke. His gray eyes were crinkled in a smile as he threw his arm around my shoulders and held up his beer in celebration, and I realized that in the few short months that I've known him, he was finally starting to let me through the boarded up walls that, to my knowledge, only his roommates have been able to push past.

He grinned down at me, and while the music was blaring and the loud conversations and laughter from the crowded bar around us nearly drowned it out, I know I heard him correctly because I could read his lips in the dimly lit bar.

"Gonna miss you when you're gone, Ryan." He grinned down at me, his lazy smile a little wider thanks to the alcohol drowning his blood. *"It was kind of nice having a girl around all the time. You and Jenny made the house feel a little less—I don't know, lonely, I guess. It was nice."*

My heart broke a little more when Jenny dragged me over to the bar and pulled her stool as close to mine as she could so we could reminisce as we downed the three shots she ordered for us. She was definitely coming close to *level-ten-Jenny,* which was pretty apparent by her drunken babble, but I didn't mind in the slightest as she rattled on about her favorite memories of us through the years.

Meeting for the first time in our freshman dorm.

Blasting our favorite playlists while we cleaned the apartment— which always turned into an hour-long concert of us dancing around and singing way louder than our neighbors probably appreciated.

Her and Nia pulling me out to our first college party on the first day of freshman year—the same *Anything But Clothes* party that I saw Tristan at for the first time. Thinking back, I was instantly distracted by the memory of him with neon caution tape wrapped around his hips, leaving the rest of his perfectly sculpted body on display.

I remember that moment so vividly—pouring my rum and coke a little slower than necessary just to get a few extra seconds to admire him standing across the kitchen with the rest of his team.

But when Jenny's glistening eyes caught my attention, I tried to push the thought of how good he looked that night to the back of my mind and focused on my best friend, who was dangerously close to breaking down as she pulled me into a hug, nearly toppling us off of the stools as she swayed back slightly.

I held onto her tightly and let the rosy smell of her perfume pull me back into those memories, wanting to laugh at myself as I felt my own eyes start to water. I owe so much to her and Nia, and when I pulled her closer and told her how much I love her, she tightened her hold on me, and I knew she knew exactly how much she means to me.

As if that wasn't enough, my heart broke a little more when Luke dropped down onto the couch beside me, resting his arm on the back of the couch as he smiled down at me, offering some of the chips he brought over from the bar. I accepted them happily, too buzzed at that point to get up and grab some of my own. His smile grew when I pulled out the bag of chocolate cookies that I packed in my purse for when I inevitably got a sweet tooth craving—which has only escalated since I started the pill a few weeks ago. And so we sat, side by side, sharing our snacks and taking pictures with ridiculous filters for my Instagram stories.

That's the moment our group chat was born.

Luke pulled out his phone, a chocolate cookie stashed between his perfect teeth as he added each of us to the chat—Micah, Tristan, James, Jenny, Nia, and me.

"The wolf pack has grown by three." He smirked, sending a single eggplant emoji to the group.

I could have cried again. I could have wrapped my arms around Luke and held him to me while I appreciated how much I loved my little family, *my wolf pack*, here in Pullman, but I didn't have the chance, because when the sound of Tristan clearing his throat softly pulled my attention, I looked over my shoulder to see him smiling down at me with his hand extended.

And that's when I felt my heart really break. It shattered in my chest when he pulled me out onto the dance floor with a giant grin on his tanned face as he wrapped his arms around my waist and rested his chin on the top of my head. He led us in a slow dance, completely offbeat to the fast-paced song blasting through the speakers around us, and when I closed my eyes and tried to memorize the way his arms felt holding me to him, and how I just fit against his chest, like a puzzle piece sliding into place, I knew that was a moment I wanted to live in forever.

I guess that's when it hit me—Pullman was my home for the past four years, but as of a few months ago, that all changed. Because when I looked up to see him smiling down at me, his dimple indented deeply as he stepped back and lifted his arm to spin me under it, I knew that Pullman wasn't my home anymore. He pulled me back into his arms, only this time his hand came up to cup my cheek, tilting my head back to look up at him, and when he smiled down at me before bringing his lips down to my own, I knew—*he* was my home.

When the orchestra starts to play on stage, I look up, pulled out of the spiraling memories from last night. That's probably a good thing, because when I reach up to inconspicuously dab away the tears slowly springing in my eyes, threatening to ruin my eye makeup, I catch sight of my family in their seats. My face flames at the sign my Nana is holding up over her head proudly, reading the huge crimson words painted onto the white poster board—*Proudest Nana in the world*.

Sitting beside her, my mother looks decidedly less excited about the sign, but she seems too distracted trying to figure out how to work the camera in her hand to tell Nana to calm down.

Jeff and Mark, who I suspect were the culprits behind the sign idea in the first place, look entirely too happy about the situation, likely because I'm sure they can see me turning a dark shade of red from their seats. When they flash big grins and sarcastic thumbs up, I know that's their way of teasingly saying, *Proudest brothers in the world*.

Lessa is the only one who's trying to help me out, and thankfully, she's able to distract Nana, pulling out her phone to show her something, effectively pulling her attention and allowing for her to drop the sign. When I catch Tristan's amused smile as he looks over his shoulder at me from the front row, I know that he saw it, too.

His head turns back quickly at the sound of heavy footsteps walking across the stage, and when I follow his gaze, Coach Kennley is walking to the podium. His bald head is reflecting comically in the spotlight hanging above him, and he shakes the dean's hand quickly before taking his place behind the podium. He blinks out at the crowd, considering us all for a long moment before pulling out notecards from the pocket inside his suit.

Leaning into the mic, he smiles, but even from here, I can see his face pale as he looks out to the packed stadium. "Don't worry, this is the last speech you'll have to suffer through before the graduates walk. Although, thanks to my terrible public speaking skills, it will undoubtedly be the most torturous."

A low rumble of laughter echoes around the arena, and he seems to relax a little at the sound. That small moment of comfort all but evaporates when a loud roar of cheers sounds, turning the heads of every graduate to see the entire basketball team standing in the front row of the stands. They're waving around red and white streamers, signs for each graduating senior, ridiculous looking pompoms, and if I'm not mistaken, I'm pretty sure I spot Luke holding a vuvuzela blow horn.

Their coach motions for them to sit down, and they obediently oblige, but not before Micah cups his hands around his mouth and yells for his coach to, *"take it off"* which elicits a rumble of laughter from the floor of graduates. His coach simply shoots him a withering look before fixing his tie and leaning back into the microphone, his face even paler than before. Every time I've been around Coach Kennely he's had such a solid, stern presence; it's a little unnerving to see him so . . . nervous.

"I have been fortunate enough to coach here at the University of Southern Washington for the past thirty years. They have been some of the best years of my life, both personally and professionally, and I owe a thank you to each and every one of my players for that." He smiles, gaze flicking through the sea of black graduation gowns, searching for each of his three graduating seniors.

"I like to view each practice as an opportunity to teach these young men. Not just about shooting positions, or defensive intelligence, or how to set up the perfect pick and roll—I like to teach these men about life. About what it means to be a good man in this world, about what it means to be a good person in this world. But what I've come to find over the past few years is that I've stopped teaching as much, and I've started learning." He pauses, spotting James a few rows over from me. He nods to him, smiling softly before continuing.

"I've watched these freshmen, who come to me as boys, turn into men by the time they leave. I've watched them grow and learn from the world around them, a world that has changed so drastically since I was a player on this court. They're learning, and adapting, and stepping up in ways that I never even dreamed of. These men perform in an arena where they are not accustomed to being heard—but rather seen. These men are athletes. They are warriors. They speak through action—through scoring points and defending their basket. They speak through fighting for their team's undefeated title and the reputation of this school. But as of late, they have proven me prouder than I could have ever imagined, because they are stepping outside of what is expected and encouraged of athletes. They are taking stands and making choices and using their position of influence in this world for the benefit of those around them. And that stride toward change was led by one player in specific—Tristan Beck."

My heart stops in my chest as I sit up straighter, trying to see over the crowd, but everyone else around me is also craning their head to see Tristan, so all I can see are the bobbing caps and swaying tassels.

"Tristan Beck came to this school when we were at our worst. We had the worst record in our division's history. We hadn't won a game in God knows how long. I had to stop keeping track to keep up morale in the locker room. And while he had the option to play at any school in the country, he chose here. He chose us. And because of that, we have built a dynasty together. A dynasty that will become his legacy when he leaves here. And after speaking with his fellow teammates, the dean of students, and the entire training and coaching staff that have had the pleasure of working with him for the past four years, there has been a unanimous decision to gift Mr. Beck with the highest honor an athlete can be given."

He steps back, motioning toward a stagehand below. When a black cloth is pulled down from the rafters, my breath catches in my throat at the white USW jersey hanging above.

Tristan's jersey number—3—and his last name are inked boldly across the back.

"In honor of his contributions to his team, and to this school, The University of Southern Washington has decided to retire Tristan Beck's jersey."

I'm crying. I'm crying hot, fat, mascara ruining tears as I join the rest of the arena's deafening cheers. The entire floor of graduates stands, turning toward him while cheering—thanking him, one last time, for bringing so much pride to our school. For reigniting a school spirit that had been extinguished for so long. For creating something that we'll all be proud to watch grow long after we all leave here.

His cheeks are flushed and he shakes the hands of the few graduates who have actually left their seats to go see him, and when I look up in the crowd, I can't hold back my laugh as his teammates scream their heads off, waving around their banners and streamers. Luke stands up on his seat, brings the horn to his lips, and blows hard enough to create a noise so loud my ears actually start to ring.

I catch sight of Tristan's family sitting a single row behind his team, and when his mom leans into his dad's shoulder as he wraps his arm around her, trying to wipe away his own tears with the tissue in his hands, a new wave of tears spring in my eyes.

"Alright, alright." His coach leans into the microphone, motioning for everyone to settle down, but it takes a few moments for the stubborn crowd to silence their cheers, because this is the last time that they'll ever be able to cheer for him—as a USW student, at least.

He looks up at the stadium, eyes wide, as if he's realizing this is the last time he'll ever experience this, and when he smiles and waves up at the crowd, silently thanking them for their support for the past four years, their answering screams send a rush of goosebumps down my arms.

When the cheers finally die down enough for his voice to be heard again, Coach Kennely leans into the microphone and thanks everyone for supporting the team. And with a smile that looks shaky, even from here, he descends the stairs and walks right up to Tristan, who stands and wraps his arms around his coach.

If I wasn't crying before, I am now, and when the girl sitting next to me offers me a tissue that she pulled from the pocket of her gown, I take it quickly. By the time I look back up, his coach is taking his seat, and the dean of students stands while the first few rows of students are led backstage.

He says a quick closing statement about being extraordinarily excited to see what we all accomplish, and then the first graduate's name is called, and we all watch as she leads the first line of graduates out onto the stage. They shake the hands of the six faculty members standing in a row, look out to the crowd and smile, and then walk off the stage as official USW graduates.

Tristan is the first of us to walk, and as predicted, when his name is announced the entire arena claps, though it's nearly drowned out by the sound of Luke's horn. He smiles wide at the dean as he shakes his hand and then makes his way across the stage, waving to Georgia who's sitting on Garrett's shoulders, waving her hands frantically over her head to try to get his attention.

Since we're going in order of our programs, both Jenny and Nia walk before me, and I swear I nearly burst my vocal cords screaming for them as they cross the stage. When our little section of journalism majors is ushered to the back, my heart hammers painfully in my chest as I follow them up the back steps.

Don't trip. Don't freeze. Shake with your right hand. Don't forget to smile.
I rattle off the different reminders just in case, and when the person standing with a clipboard asks for my name, I stare at her dumbfounded as I wrack my brain. It takes a few seconds for me to register her question before I tell her, and I shake out my trembling hands as the person ahead of me walks out onto the stage.

Ushering me to the edge of the curtain, she smiles, as if she can feel my anxiety.

"Wait for your name, then walk."

I nod.

I don't even have time to take a full breath before my name echoes out through the speakers.

"Abigail Ryan."

I start to walk, but the explosion of noise startles me, and I look out to the crowd to see Tristan smiling up at me as he claps from his seat near the front. Jenny and Nia's high pitched screams are clear and I catch their hands waving in the air excitedly, but they're overpowered by the deafening sound of that ridiculous horn that Luke is blowing into full force as the entire basketball team screams out while waving around their streamers and pompoms.

I briefly catch Tristan's family standing and cheering, and then my eyes land a few rows back to my Nana, who is all but jumping up and down while waving her sign around. Thankfully, I make it to the dean without tripping, and I accept my diploma while shaking his hand— with the correct hand, thank God—and thank him before moving on to the next three faculty members, who all have their hands outstretched for me to shake.

It happens so quickly. One second, I'm smiling and shaking hands, and the next I'm walking down the steps and being ushered back toward my seat with the rest of the journalism majors. I can't seem to take my eyes off of the paper in my hands, the one that cost more money than I'm willing to think about at the moment, and I can't hold back the huge smile pulling at my lips, because *I did it.*

I'm a college graduate.

I stare, dazed and in disbelief at the diploma for the rest of the ceremony, and then, after the dean shakes the last graduate's hand and steps back up to the podium, he directs us all to stand.

I place my diploma down on my seat and stand with the rest of the students. My adrenaline spikes when I catch Jenny leaning around the person next to her, just to be in my eye line, and when she gives me a *Holy fucking shit this is really happening* look, I beam at her. The crowd has already started cheering, and the energy building around the room is coaxing more adrenaline into my veins, enough to make my heart race in my chest.

"Now, it is my great pleasure to ask this year's graduating class to please turn your tassels from the right to the left."

His comment is lost in the all-encompassing explosion of cheers from the surrounding crowd, and I look up to my family as I lift the tassel on my cap and move it to the other side. My Nana is in absolute shambles, wiping her tears with a tissue while still trying to hold onto her sign with one hand. Jeff and Mark have their hands cupped around their mouths as they cheer, but it's my mother's smile that captures my attention. She's holding the camera up, snapping pictures, but I can clearly see the white glint of her teeth as she smiles widely behind it.

The graduates around me all count down, and the universal chant grabs my attention.

"*Three, two, one!*"

I catch on to what they're doing, and I fling my cap into the air alongside everyone else, just in time to watch the sea of black caps collide with the bright red and white confetti now fluttering down from the rafters. I can't take my eyes off the falling confetti, because paired with the cheers I feel vibrating through the arena, sending a shiver down my spine, this is a moment that I want to live in for a little bit longer.

I watch the confetti snow down around me, reaching out to let a few land in my outstretched hand, and when I look back down, I catch the familiar emerald eyes watching me.

Most of the graduates are already moving around the arena, but I'm frozen in place, watching the confetti fall around Tristan as he takes a step closer to me.

He has both of our caps in his hands and a few of the red confetti pieces stuck in his curls, like actual snow flurries, and when he smiles down at me as he brushes a wayward piece of confetti off of my cheek, I turn my head slightly, leaning into his touch.

His eyes shine in the lights above, and I'm mesmerized when they wrinkle slightly as his smile widens, deepening his dimple enough to make me want to reach up and poke it. My heart pounds hard in my chest again, only this time it has nothing to do with the worries of graduation, or my Nana's embarrassing sign, or the thought of face-planting on the stage. This time, it's because I'm intoxicated by the man standing in front of me.

When he cups my cheek and grins down at me, as if he can read my thoughts, my breath catches in my throat. He leans down and connects our lips, slow and soft at first, but when I taste his spearmint breath on my lips, I sigh happily against his lips as I open mine, desperate to taste him on my tongue. He smiles into the kiss, and when he drops the caps in his hand onto the floor at our feet and snakes his arms around my waist, every part of me relaxes into his embrace.

His tongue slips into my mouth, and suddenly, in a room full of thousands, it's just us.

I'm in awe of him, I'm high on him, and when he pulls back just enough for his lips to brush mine as he whispers, "I love you," I can actually feel the exact moment that he sets my soul on fire.

"I love you more." I smile up at him, already rocking up onto my tiptoes, wanting nothing more than to bring my lips closer to his, to close the space between us again and get lost in him.

Pulling me closer, he shakes his head, leaning down to whisper, "Not a chance, baby. Not a fucking chance."

His smile deepens, and I know that no matter what happens, no matter what life throws at us, we're going to be okay, because he's right—life is one big game of high-risk, high-reward, and looking up at him now, I know without a shadow of a doubt, that he's worth the risk.

EPILOGUE

ONE MONTH LATER

TRISTAN

This feels like a dream.

I've watched the NBA draft every year since I was a kid. It was my favorite day of the year, not just because my dad would waive my bedtime so we could see it all play out live on our shitty old TV, but because it was the one day my mom would turn a blind eye to the piles of chips, ice cream, cookies, and candy my dad would lay out for us on the coffee table.

I'd stuff my face with popcorn while we'd down our beers—mine of the non-alcoholic root variety—and watch as each player was drafted to a team. It was exciting, but admittedly, I was more excited about the fact that I was hanging out with my dad after my bedtime.

When I got older, I learned to appreciate it a little more. My root beer turned into actual beer, and I understood the gravity of the situation as each name was called out. The players on the screen were living my dream. They were experiencing the one thing that I was working my ass off to achieve. And now that I'm sitting here, surrounded by an arena full of basketball fanatics, I can feel their energy piquing as the producers with headsets and clipboards run around the arena floor, directing cameramen to kneel near specific tables as they yell into their headsets about sticking to the schedule.

I've glanced down at my watch every thirty seconds for the past fifteen minutes. The draft goes live in less than five minutes, and based on how the cameraman kneeling a few feet away from our table is adjusting the lens and giving a thumbs up to one of the producers behind me, I know that my face is about to be broadcasted all over national television.

I pull the sleeve of my suit jacket back to check my watch again, but before I can read the time, Abby's hand brushes over mine, interlocking our fingers. She pulls my hand into her lap, and the cool caress of her silk dress against my fingers as she leans her head against my shoulder is enough to pull my attention away from the cameras, and stages, and excited fans still finding their seats in the surrounding arena. When she brings my hand up to her lips and presses a soft kiss to my palm, the tension that's been building since we sat down starts to ease.

"Everything's fine. Everything's going to be okay," I say, more to myself than to her, but she looks up and her smile deepens at my words.

"Everything's going to be okay." She repeats softly, just loud enough for me to hear. "No matter what."

No matter what.

The Raptors have the first pick, but to be completely honest, I don't think they're going to draft me. According to Greg Bradshaw's latest report, Zayn's meeting with the head coach went so well, they almost extended an official offer. By the huge smile on his face as he leans back in his chair to talk to his mom, it's clear that he feels it, too—he's going to be the number one pick. He's going to Toronto.

Zayn and I have had this unspoken competition since I met him freshman year. We've always been so closely matched it was impossible to not give into the rivalry, especially since the media would constantly pit us against each other. But if taking second place means that I get to live with my girl in New York, then fuck it, I'll happily take the L this time.

I pull her close, resting my chin on the top of her head. The smell of her vanilla apple spice calms me further as I try to pay attention to my mom gush over how surreal this feels—how she remembers me playing in my very first basketball game as a toddler—but the sound of that godforsaken horn turns all of our attention toward the stadium seating.

I spot Luke in the first row instantly. He flashes a wide grin, leaning back in his seat as he throws his arm around Coach's shoulders, giving him a look that's clearly meant to say, *I told you the horn would work.*

My entire team is sitting front row. I knew they were coming, thanks to the picture Micah sent me this morning of them all crowded together, flipping off the camera as they boarded their flight, but it's still surreal to see them all here.

The infamous chime echoes loudly through the arena as the lights drop, leaving the stadium in near darkness, apart from the candlelight flickering on the tables of potential draftees and the spotlights settling on the stage. The commissioner makes his way across the stage toward the podium, and when he stops and considers the crowd with a satisfied smile, my heart hammers painfully in my chest.

The crowd's wild cheers send a current of energy around the dark room, building the kind of adrenaline in my veins that I've only ever experienced on the court, and a wave of goosebumps rushes over my arms and down my back as the chime echoes through the speakers again, signaling the start of the draft. Luke's horn blares in an ear shattering rumble around the stadium, and when it's cut off sharply, I don't have to look over to know that Coach must have knocked it out of his hands.

It's palpable—the excitement, the anxiety, the fear—and when I look around the arena floor at all of my fellow draftees, I know this is a moment I'll never forget.

"Welcome to this year's NBA draft." The commissioner's voice reverberates loudly through the arena but is still somehow nearly drowned out by the screams and cheers of the crowd.

This is it.

This is what I've worked my entire life for.

Every grueling practice. Every sunrise weight room workout. Every lap on the track. Every sprint on the court. Every injury. Every weekend I spent playing in tournaments and elite leagues just to be seen by scouts. Every hour spent alone in the practice gym working on my shot long after everyone else went home for the night. This is what I've worked for—and now it's finally here.

This is the start of my career.

Abby's hands squeeze mine, and I want to look over to see her smiling up at me, but I'm frozen in place as I watch the commissioner lean forward into the microphone and wave his hand to signal for the crowd to quiet down.

"With the first pick in this year's NBA draft, the Toronto Raptors select Tristan Beck from the University of Southern Washington."

The crowd in the stadium explodes around me, but even though I know I've just heard that right, I can't fucking think straight. I can't process anything because my entire body feels numb and detached as I push back my chair and wrap my mom in a tight hug. When she finally releases me, I pull my dad into a hug, then my sisters, and then I turn back to see Abby standing behind them, tears streaming down her face as she watches Olivia finally step out of my embrace.

Toronto Raptors.

Toronto.

She's crying, but when I step toward her and she tilts her head back to look up at me with the brightest smile I've ever seen, I can tell that they aren't sad tears—they're excited tears, happy tears, proud tears.

I know I don't have a lot of time, so I cup her face and lean down to brush my lips against hers. It's a quick kiss, but it's exactly what I need to ground myself again, to not feel so numb to the entire situation, and when I pull away and look down at her, she beams up at me.

"No matter what," I say, taking a step back toward the stage where I have to go shake the commissioner's hand, but I don't turn around until her smile deepens, and it's damn near blinding as she repeats my words.

"No matter what."

ACKNOWLEDGMENTS

Thank you to the readers who have supported me from the start. Thank you for loving these characters as much as I do. Thank you for being so patient and kind with me and my ever-changing publishing schedule. Thank you for making my dreams come true. I hope you know my characters will always be here, waiting with open arms to hold you close whenever you need them.

Thank you to my friends who had to listen to me ramble about these characters for months before I plucked up the courage to actually write them. And thank you for listening now, when I randomly call or text in the middle of the day or at two in the morning, desperate to tell you the new scenes or chapter ideas that just popped into my head.

Thank you to Miaya for always reminding me of why I started. Sometimes it's hard to see the light at the end of the tunnel, but it's not so bad sitting in the dark when I'm with you.

Thank you to Jen for helping me edit this monster of a manuscript. You are so kind and I'm so thankful we were able to work together on this project.

Thank you to Stacey for formatting. Thank you to Wendy for giving me the tips of the trade before I was even in the door. Thank you Klay Thompson for being so attractive I daydreamed about dating an NBA player. Thank you to Taylor Swift for writing the kind of music that inspires entire novels. Thank you to the little girl who never gave up on her dream, even when it felt impossible.

And finally, thank you to Justin, for running through the rain with me.

To stay updated, follow me on Instagram for the latest updates!

www.instagram.com/brandydavisauthor

Printed in Great Britain
by Amazon

66501820R00314